THEY SHALL NOT PASS

by Bruce Palmer

THEY SHALL NOT PASS

HECATOMB

HORSESHOE BEND

MANY ARE THE HEARTS

FLESH AND BLOOD

BLIND MAN'S MARK

They Shall Not Pass BY BRUCE PALMER

 *A Novel of the Spanish Civil War*

Doubleday & Company, Inc., Garden City, New York, 1971

All characters, with the exception
of well-known historical personages,
are fictitious, and any resemblance
to actual persons living or dead is
coincidental.

Grateful acknowledgment is given to the following for permission to reprint their material.

From *The Abraham Lincoln Brigade* by Arthur H. Landis. Reprinted by permission of the author and Citadel Press, Inc.

From "Why I Write" in *Such, Such Were The Joys* by George Orwell, copyright 1945, 1952, 1953 by Sonia Brownell Orwell. Reprinted by permission of Harcourt Brace Jovanovich, Inc., Miss Sonia Brownell and Secker & Warburg.

From *The Gypsy Ballads of García Lorca*, translated by Rolfe Humphries, copyright 1953 by Indiana University Press. Reprinted by permission of the publisher.

From *The Last Great Cause* by Stanley Weintraub, copyright © 1968 by Stanley Weintraub. Published in New York by Weybright & Talley, Inc. Reprinted by permission of David McKay Company, Inc.

Dedicated to the memory
of
Robert A. Fox

Contents

Contents

THEY SHALL NOT PASS

REGIONS AND PROVINCES OF SPAIN

PROLOGUE

The Enemies of the Republic

The Republic of Spain was born in April 1931, upon the resignation of one man, General Miguel Primo de Rivera, military dictator for seven years, followed by the abdication of another man, Alfonso XIII, king for twenty-nine years. Spanish opinion held Alfonso guilty of tolerating Primo de Rivera in violation of the constitution and then for accepting the general's impulsive resignation. Supporters of a republic won clear victories in the national elections of that month in the cities and larger towns. Monarchist delegates dominated all the rural districts and managed to gain, by fair means or other, a majority in the nation. But to the king, the trend was clear. He no longer enjoyed the devotion and support of the entire Spanish people. Rather than lead his supporters, he abandoned them and left for exile in Paris. Although there was no bloodshed in April, the Republic of Spain had enemies from the moment of its birth.

Cardinal Segura, Archbishop of Toledo and Primate of the Spanish Roman Catholic Church, eulogized the self-exiled king, warned his followers of the threatened destruction of the institutionalized church and traditional Christian ideals and discreetly recommended violence and self-sacrifice as weapons of defense. A street squabble in Madrid exploded into riot. A Jesuit church was burned and arson flared in the southern province of Andalusia. Individual officers of the Spanish Army, having sworn allegiance to the Republic they served, organized the first of their conspiracies.

More than one million Anarchists, dominated by a secret and militant internal group, opposed both formal government and institutionalized religion, since both, they were persuaded, were founded on the moral evil of uncontrollable authority. They envisioned a simpler, purer Spain formed of local self-governing bodies voluntarily united into a new nation through the ideals of their prophet, Bakunin. Their power lay in numbers. Their weapons were the violent strike and acts of terror. They were dreamers who converted by "propaganda of the deed," sincere believers in their right to wreck the Church and the State in order to usher in a new, perfect world. True to their faith, they boycotted the new elections in June. When the voters returned sixty members of Right-wing parties to the Cortes, the national parliament, and 477 members representing the liberal Center and Socialist Left, the Anarchists called for general strikes across Spain. In Seville, thirty were killed, two hundred wounded as government troops fired field cannons in the streets. The new Republic, in its first test, answered violence with bloodshed.

The liberals dominating the government wrote a constitution expressing their views alone: equalitarian, anti-aristocratic, and anticlerical. State payments of salaries to local priests were to cease by 1933; all religious orders were to be supervised by the state, the Jesuits to follow Alfonso into exile. Religious education was to cease, civil divorce was instituted and the Church was disestablished. Five members of the Republican Cabinet were members of Masonic lodges, secret societies introduced into Spain in the eighteenth century.

A half-hearted attempt was made to reform the traditional system of absentee landowners, tenant farming, and conscious exploitation of the landless *braceros* of the agricultural south. Since the new constitution recognized the provinces of the nation as having some rights to self-government, first the Catalonians, then the Basques sought autonomy. Industrial Barcelona, Spain's biggest seaport, became the capital of the Republic of Catalonia, federated to Spain. Since the Middle Ages, the leaders of the pious Basques had gathered beneath the ancient oak tree in the town of Guernica to exchange vows of loyalty and respect with the Spanish monarchs, "For God and our old laws." Now they sought to disengage themselves from the anticlerical Republic. Three of the four Basque provinces voted for autonomy on the Catalonian model. The province of Navarre, homeland of the Carlists, voted to remain integrated with a Republic its landowners and aristocrats despised.

The Carlists justified their growing conspiracies in the name of traditional Spain—Dios, Patria y Rey—God, Country and King. The first crude plot in 1932 extended their influence into Castile and south to Andalusia, but led only to scattered shooting in Madrid and the arrest and deportation of 150 army officers and aristocrats to colonial outposts in Spanish Africa. The next year, the Anarchists struck in the province of Cádiz. The Republican Minister of the Interior attempted to legalize the execution of prisoners. Forces of the Right and the Left joined to denounce the brutal repression as a national disgrace.

In order for the people to approve or reject the flood of new laws implementing the constitution of 1931, new elections were held. The government retained only 99 seats in the 1933 vote while the Center coalition gained 167 and the Right, now dominated by the Catholic Party, won 207 seats. The Spanish Socialists broke their alliance with the bourgeoisie in order to capture the working classes from the Anarchists.

Before 1933, Fascism had Spanish admirers of both the German and Italian models, for Berlin was the citadel of anti-Bolshevism and Rome was the capital of the Church as well as of Mussolini's Blackshirts. Catholicism, it was argued, was part of the Iberian racial inheritance. The loud-spoken young men of good family and high ideals found the Fascist solution flattering and compelling. Their leader was José Antonio Primo de Rivera, the handsome, talented and charming son of the now dead but well-remembered dictator. In 1933, José Antonio founded Falange Española, the Spanish Phalanx, and the walls of Spain began to wear its symbol—the yoke and arrows.

The Spanish Communist Party, numerically insignificant and divided into quarreling factions of Stalinists and Trotskyites, lent its meager strength to short-lived alliances with the Anarchists, but kept themselves from the contamination of parliamentary co-operation and ideological compromise. The Communists alone had direct linkage, through agents of the Comintern, to a major foreign power—the Soviet Union.

The new government slowed or halted earlier reforms in agriculture and education and failed to implement restrictions upon the Church. Amnesty granted to political prisoners returned the Carlist conspirators and disloyal army officers to Spanish soil. Old plotters were set free to combine with new conspirators of increased idealism or fanaticism on both the Right and Left. The Catholic Party grew in influence as the Anarchists swelled in numbers. Combining with the Socialist trade union, which had smuggled arms into the province of Asturias, the Anarchists proclaimed a general strike. The leaders of the Catholic Party were denounced on the Left as pro-Fascists, as three members were invited to cabinet posts in a reshuffled government. Catalonia threatened to secede from the Republic entirely. Street-fighting in Madrid was snuffed with the arrest of Socialist leaders. All of Spain looked north to Asturias.

The rising of October 1934 in the mountains and mines of that province was unique in a political unity forged through joint workers' committees. In response to what they saw as a bid for power by the Catholics and Fascists, the factory hands and miners mobilized a working-class army of 30,000 men, Anarchists, Socialists and Communists combined in a Spanish Soviet beneath the red banner. The weak government garrisons were overrun or scattered, churches and convents burned, the bishop's palace and the University of Oviedo wrecked. Members of the Civil Guards and the police were killed when they surrendered. Rebellion on the Left threatened all of Spain.

The government called on two generals, Goded and Franco, and agreed to their recommendation that elements of the Army of Africa, the Spanish Foreign Legion and Moorish regulars, be used for the liberation of Asturias. Mercenaries and Moors would keep the illusion that Spaniards were not yet killing Spaniards. The Republic invaded itself.

ASTURIAS—1934

The lamp on his helmet dimmed. The shapes of the opened crates flickered before his eyes. He heard Jaime and Simple grunt as they heaved the last box. The floor of the elevator shivered as it hit, then dipped as Jaime and Simple climbed on. He could not see their faces clearly now. They panted like dogs.

"Let's go."

Jaime dragged the mesh door shut and tripped the brake. They began to float up the greasy cables, lifted through the darkness.

"Paco?"

"What?"

He shook his head slightly. It was his father's helmet, and Tomás had a big head. The helmet slid, and the flickering lamplight just touched Jaime's face. It was cold in the mine shaft. Steam gushed out of Jaime's mouth as he talked.

"That last heavy one was just dynamite, Paco. No more hand bombs."

"I know it."

"And no more cartridges for the rifles."

"I know it."

"Then why did we come down?"

"Because he said to, my father. Tomás said bring up the crates."

"Empty."

"Shut up. Don't you think I wanted to go down there with the others?"

"You wanted to walk under a white flag?"

"Listen. I want to live under a red one. But anything my father does, I can do."

The light flared up for an instant, then died. Simple laughed softly in the darkness. Paco felt the blood burn in his face. His hands clenched, and his heart jolted. He wanted to kick them both, even if they were his cousins. He opened his fists. It was so dark. It was the helmet lamp going out that Simple had laughed at, that was all.

Paco groped to the nearest crate and sat down. It was so cold and black in the mine, as black and cold as death.

The box he sat on and could feel but could not see now had painted letters on the sides: JIBOUTI. That was someplace in Africa. The crates had been smuggled in from Portugal by Comrade Medina. From the ship *Turquesa*. They had been filled with hand grenades, the Mills bombs. Others had been filled with cartridges, one hundred and sixty-five in each paper pack. Thousands of cartridges, cool and slick with oil. How many there had seemed when they handed them out, the first days of the rising! The smaller crates were from the barracks of the Guardias Civiles and Asaltos in the town. Crates of shells for the mountain guns, the cannons Tomás and the others had captured.

The Guardias Civiles had surrendered first. Why, no one knew. They were shot at once. Then the Assault Guards had surrendered. They had dragged the cannons up to the slag heaps near the abandoned mine shafts. Then Tomás and the others had raised the hoist, swinging the elevator cage out. The Asaltos knew then what the people were going to do to them. They stood there, every breath blowing white in the twilight. The Asaltos had their hands tied with the harness. Everyone fell on them, kicking and punching, and dragged them over to the open shaft. Then they began to scream and pray and bite. The miners took turns, one holding the shoulders, the other the legs. They threw the Asaltos down the mine shaft. One by one.

Now gray light flowed around them. Paco could see the cables pour down through the roof, shudder like snakes in the guide-rings, then down through the holes in the elevator floor. Now he could hear the whine and groan of the pulley and the chatter of the brake. He squinted against the light that spilled down on them. His breath blew like smoke. He squatted and touched the crate. JIBOUTI. Some place in Africa. Empty crates. All empty.

The Moors came from Africa. Not from Jibouti, from Tetuán. The Legionarios were from Africa, too. The Moors were black, but the men of the Foreign Legion were white. He and Jaime had found a dead one behind the washing shed after the first ambush. On the tunic was a unit emblem, a skull, a death's head.

The warning bell jangled, and the elevator slowed, jolting as the brake jaws clamped on the lifting cable. Now Paco could hear the voices of the waiting miners, a gobble of sounds that echoed around him. The light now was strong, bright, cold, and pure. His lids fluttered, and he scrubbed the tears from his face. They would think that he was crying over the empty ammunition crates. The iron gangway slammed. Somebody began shouting.

"Here they are! See? One, two, three, four, and six and . . ."

Paco pushed Simple aside and dragged open the mesh gate. He stepped out, jostled by the waiting men. He wanted to hit them and so shoved his fists into his pockets. He butted through the crowd. He saw Fernando, his uncle and Jaime's father. They had come back then from talking with the colonel who commanded the Legionarios and the Moors.

"*Tío*, 'Nando. How did it go?"

Fernando shook his head slightly. The effort made him sway. How many days and nights had he been fighting? Paco looked back at the elevator cage. Maybe thirty men clawed and shoved at the gate. The hopeful ones, the ones that have to see to believe and even then don't believe and start to blame the leaders and talk about swindles and stolen money. One of them was still counting the boxes in a shrill, weary voice.

"Ten and two is twelve and . . ."

Paco slipped between the men and struck down the counter's hand.

"Empty, stupid! Every mother of them is empty!"

"Empty?"

Paco grabbed the man by the shoulder of his sheepskin and flung him forward into the elevator. Simple dodged aside and stood moaning and pointing his finger from crate to crate.

"Yes, empty. Look inside and see. When you get done, shit in one and send it to the colonel!"

Everyone was quiet. Paco walked slowly out of the building. Jaime followed him. The sun was bright. Outside there were more miners, standing or squatting, waiting. Waiting for nothing. One of the captured mountain guns stood behind a slag heap. The crew sprawled on the slag, smoking and waiting. For nothing.

Paco pulled the cold mountain air into his chest. His hands stopped trembling. The air of the mountains seemed to steady him, all the way through. He found his uncle.

"I shouldn't have done that, 'Nando."

His uncle turned around. His face was clenched with weariness like a fist. His eyes were bright red, and he swayed like a drunkard.

They looked down into the valley where the river, black with coal dust, black and cold the river poured down to the *pueblo* far below. Something felt wrong. It was quiet, that was it.

Fernando tilted his head very carefully, until his chin-stubble rasped on his sheepskin. Paco looked. On the staff in front of the company building where U.H.P. headquarters was, a flag rippled in the breeze. A white flag—a flag made from the sheet pulled from the bed after some of the men had done with the foreman's wife.

Where was the *bandera roja,* the red flag?

"We've surrendered?"

Fernando raised his head and let it drop, just like a mule, spent after a double shift. Jaime began to cry. Fernando swung his fist and hit him, just enough to make him stop.

"Don't be a woman, *hijo.* There's a truce. Tomás spoke with the colonel. Colonel Bravo. A Castilian, no less. Oh sure. *Gran caballero. Jefe de moros* . . . a chief of Moors. There has been no shooting now for two hours. Look."

Paco saw the glitter of bayonets beyond the entrance to the shipping docks and over at the pit head of Three Shaft. Two groups of soldiers there. But none at U.H.P. headquarters.

"What's up?"

Paco stared around, stunned. It was over? All they had fought for? The government of the Republic had beaten them? It couldn't be. But it was.

"Listen, 'Nando. What are they going to do?"

His uncle dropped his heavy arm on Jaime's shoulder and straightened himself for the effort of talking.

"Tomás called to Portugal on the telephone. Comrade Medina. Then he tried for Durrutti in Barcelona. But the Legionarios cut the wires."

"The soldiers . . ."

Fernando tried to imitate the Castilian officer.

"Colonel Bravo, mounter of sheep and goats, lover of his right hand, has given us his word as an officer and a gentleman that the Moorish Regulares and the troops of the Foreign Legion will be withdrawn from all areas presently occupied in the province of Asturias."

"To do what, start the shooting in Oviedo again?"

Fernando laughed without making any noise. He turned away.

"There's no one left to shoot in Oviedo."

Paco waited until his uncle and cousin were out of sight behind the slag heaps. Then he walked to the office building. There were many men there, some still with their useless rifles and U.H.P. arm bands. They stood in groups, sharing their tobacco and talking softly, not yet blaming anybody. But they broke off to look at Paco as he walked by them, and no one spoke.

When he reached the steps of the building, the door flew open and a shower of papers spilled around him, like dirty leaves torn from the trees.

"Burn these papers! Light a fire, comrades!"

Only one man in all the mines shouted like that. Paco grinned and ducked as another basketful of papers splattered over him. He saw the letters made by the big rubber stamp his father had made especially in

Madrid. U.H.P. U.H.P. Big red letters. Tap, tap on the ink pad and slam on the paper and there you had it. The thing was done and officially so. U.H.P. Unión de Hermanos Proletarios.

"Burn it, all of it, before those bastards come down here!"

A truck passed. In the back were some buckets, two Moors, and Padre Ortega, the village priest, the young one. Paco looked at the Moors —scrawny, dark men with baggy pants and soiled capes snugged around their shoulders and dirty turbans. That was what came from Tetuán.

Paco snucked in the back of his throat and spat at the Moors and the priest.

He pulled open the door and went into the office to see his father, Tomás.

The truck stopped. The two Moors sitting on the tailgate did not move. Padre Ortega stepped between them and clutched his case to his chest. He jumped, his robe fluttering. He jolted on the hard earth and stumbled forward, off balance. He straightened and took three deep breaths before he turned around. What seemed to him to be a platoon of soldiers filled the entrance of the elevator house. Over the doorway was painted the number 3 and beneath it, in crude lettering: AQUÍ DUERMEN LOS ENEMIGOS DE LA PATRIA. Some distance, twenty paces or more, from the building, a larger group of Moors squatted on the ground. One of them was "sleeping," too, face down and twisted, halfway between the two groups of men. The priest hesitated, then walked to the entrance of the mine shaft. He tried to form a prayer as he walked, but the feeling that he was watched drove the words from his mind.

"You sent for me?"

One of the Legionarios turned, a wine bottle held up to his mouth. He drank greedily, his throat jerking, staring at the priest around his fist. He lowered the bottle, belched and scrubbed his mouth with his hand. He grinned, showing dark, broken teeth through a ragged, dirty beard.

"Eh, you took your time, priest. We've got a dying Christian here!"

They had all been drinking, the priest saw. Bottles looted from Sánchez's *taberna*. Some of the Legionarios stared at him, grinning. Others ignored him and passed bottles back and forth. There was no pleasure in their drinking; they were merely getting drunk. There seemed to be no officer with them.

"Who is in command here?"

"Him."

The soldier pointed with the bottle. Padre Ortega saw a man, sprawled on his back, inside the doorway. His tunic had been cut open and a crude pad of dirty cloth, already sodden with blood, tied with twine over the wound in his side. His arms and legs were flung out, as though he had been held down by his comrades.

"That's the sergeant."

The priest walked over and fumbled open his case. The soldiers moved aside enough to let him pass, then closed in again. He could smell the wine as they breathed. He took out the vial of oil and a bit of cotton, then knelt and looked at the wounded man.

He was big, nearly two meters tall, heavy legs and a torso like an animal. The ribs bulked like barrel staves, showing beneath the pale dirty skin. Under a swarm of matted hair, the word SWEET had been tattooed over the left nipple, SOUR over the right. The pale, scarred skin lifted and fell.

"What happened?"

The priest could feel the soldiers gather closer around him. He stared down at the wounded man. The face, under the beard, was burned almost black by the African sun. The hands, curled like paws, were dark as gloves. Ortega took out the box containing the Host.

"The blacks wouldn't bring them up."

"The bodies, you mean?"

"Right. They're queer, the moros, see?"

The Legionarios were amused by something. The priest could hear them butt each other and snuffle with drunken laughter.

"Queer?"

"Ah, they don't like them when they're busted up. A dead one's got to be all in one hunk or they won't touch him, see?"

"And so there was a fight and a Moor is dead and this one stabbed in the belly."

"What eyes, priest! Madre, he sees everything, this priest!"

Padre Ortega leaned over the wounded sergeant and shut his mind to the circle of bodies that stood over him, breathing on him. He began. The heavy, naked chest rose and fell. Ortega averted his eyes from the tattooed words.

When he touched the oil-soaked cotton to the man's closed lids, the lashes twitched and opened. Ortega drew back his hand. The wounded man stared up at him. His eyes were a pale, glittering green, clear and malicious. He did not blink, but stared like a cat, fully conscious. Ortega half heard a rumble of laughter as he touched the bit of cotton to the dry, bristled lips.

The man surged up, flailing his arms and roaring. His rib cage squashed down on the bandage, and the blood ran as from a sponge.

"Oh, Jesús, Jesús! I'm alive again!"

The priest scrambled away from him, his knees ripping his robe. He turned clumsily, shielding the Host, as a fist clubbed his shoulder.

"I was a dead one, but now I've come back, you shits!"

The soldiers around Ortega howled with laughter and pounded each other. He clawed at their boots and belts, trying to rise, but they stumbled back away from him. A paw seized his shoulder and drew him up. He swayed, sputtering incoherently. The sergeant flung him away and danced in a drunken circle, shouting in some wild tongue. Laughter beat against the priest's ears. He stood stupefied, feeling the seep of rage into his chest, watching the sergeant stagger out through the doorway, pawing at the holster slung on his hip. He tugged out a pistol and fired at the Moors, bellowing obscenities. He stumbled to the body, shouted something, and kicked the dead Moor.

The dark faces beneath the turbans were slack with dread. The Regulares scrambled to their feet and came to attention. The rear ranks gibbered and darted like dark, skinny fowl, away, whirled, bumped together and back into formation while the Legionarios around Ortega brayed with laughter and flung empty bottles at them. The sergeant whirled, his ripped tunic spreading like a skirt. Blood dribbled down on his trousers and boots.

"Open the lift gate! They're going down!"

Metal clashed somewhere in the dim building. The Legionarios swarmed aside to form a gauntlet. The sergeant swung off to the right, double-timing, waving the heavy revolver and shouting. Suddenly, the Moors broke and poured, shrieking and gesturing, into the gauntlet. The Legionarios cursed and kicked them and jabbed with fists and bottles. Ortega saw dark, twisted faces, white, frightened eyes and snapping jaws. He pressed back, driving his heels into the plank floor, until he broke free. Shaking, he slumped beside his case.

The gauntlet closed, crushing some of the Moors on, into the building, pressing the frantic bodies into the elevator, sealing the others back at the doorway. The floor shivered. Fists beat against flesh. Men screamed and cursed.

"Let it go!"

The machinery rattled, stopped and chattered again. The cage dropped. The cable drum whirled. A wild, wowing moan floated up the shaft.

"Hey!"

Winy breath gushed against Ortega's face. The sergeant towered over him. The priest's eyes were level with the Legionario's matted chest. Beneath the fur, like flat little worms, the letters read SWEET and SOUR.

"See? I told you shits it would work. Now get those piss-pants away from the door and let this thing in skirts out of here!"

Padre Ortega picked up his case, stepped back a pace, and looked up at the sergeant. He saw the pale sheen of the eyes and a broken nose, a scar slick as leather across the brow and twisting the right brow, quirking the flesh.

"Your name and rank, soldier? I will report this to your commander!"

"Ohhh, you will, eh? Go ahead, nun-fucker! You didn't think I really wanted you, did you? We don't need your kind here. Get out!"

Ortega dodged the hand that clutched at him. The soldiers did not move. He pushed between them, setting his feet down with care. They tried to trip him. He broke away into the open air. The Moors were back, squatting on the ground, cowed and silent. The priest walked to their dead comrade. He knelt and began to pray. It wasn't permitted. He prayed. The dead man was a non-believer, a son of Islam. Ortega prayed.

When he opened his eyes and rose, the Moors were staring at him. He felt suddenly cheap, ashamed, a fool in the eyes of everyone.

"What did you go and do that for, you bead-biter?"

The priest began walking toward the truck. He heard the heavy thud of boots behind him.

"You ruined it, you little shit!"

Ortega was nearly to the truck. He wanted to run. The sergeant caught him and dragged him around. The priest forced himself to look up into the scarred, bearded, sunburned face.

"Your name, Sergeant?"

The green eyes gleamed. Ortega could hear the slow *pit-pit* of blood dropping on the sergeant's boot. He flinched back as the soldier's arm surged up and the ripped tunic fluttered. A pistol wavered in front of the priest's face.

"You believe in death, don't you?"

Ortega moved for the truck.

"In *death!* Don't you?"

"And in life, you poor . . ."

Ortega watched. The thick, strong fingers, furred and broken-nailed, rammed the cylinder out, caught the bullets and thrust one back. The revolver jerked, the cylinder snapped in place and whirled, zizzing, and stopped. The sergeant placed the muzzle against his head. The front sight vanished into his thick, dusty hair. He pulled the trigger. The firing-pin snapped.

"Here, priest."

Ortega stepped to the side and bumped against the fender of the truck. The sergeant shifted, a slow, sauntering step, and slouched, his bulk blocking the door to the cab. He held the revolver in his thumb and forefinger, the butt out to the priest.

"Take it, believer. Not afraid, eh? No, not afraid. Here, then."

The sight of him sickened Ortega. He stepped warily around him, moved to the rear of the truck, and stood there trembling. The two Moors sat looking at nothing. Ortega jerked his head.

"Get out. *Fuera!*"

The Moors slipped down and drifted away up the slope. Ortega heaved himself up on the tailgate, stumbled erect, and beat his case on the top of the cab. He felt contaminated.

"Hey, you."

"Tell Colonel Bravo it was Tiger. Got that? Tiger. That's me."

A third Moor tottered over and set down his bucket. He joined the first two. All of them scooped up dirt and began to wash their hands, chanting softly.

The truck groaned past a bonfire of burning papers, turned through the gate, and rolled down the road to the village on the floor of the valley where the black river flowed cold.

His mother straightened when he walked through the door. She set her hands on her hips. The wooden spoon dribbled, and she wiped it absently on a bit of sacking.

"So."

"What are you cooking?"

"*Judías blancas.*"

"With sausage?"

"*Qué va*, sausage . . . Where is he?"

"He's not coming home. He sent me. What's that funny smell?"

Paco sat at the table. He felt very sleepy. Something in the fireplace flared and died to soft, flimsy ash. He sniffed. The white beans smelled good. He yawned.

"We're all marching into town."

"Are we?"

"The men."

"The men. Then there will be three. Him, 'Nando and Carlos. A parade. The rest will watch."

Paco knew she was crying. He was too exhausted to go to her. He stared dully at the fire. It was odd, all ash and no heat.

His mother cried for what seemed a long time. She brought a wooden bowl of beans to the table and a spoon. He began eating. The spoon felt very heavy.

"*Hay vino?*"

"*Sí.* They took everything from Sánchez."

"They are drunk at the mine. The Legionarios."

He drank from the cup. It was good wine. He looked at her.

"They were not the only ones who took from Sánchez."

"A small skin, only. Five liters."

Paco shrugged. Sánchez had been shot the second day. His mother reached out and touched him on the arm.

"The priest was here with your papers."

"Ortega? What papers?"

"From the parish register. From the school. Yesterday and today, this morning. He walked from door to door, house to house. Giving away the papers. Saying that because of the wood and charcoal running out, we should cook with these. If we wanted. I looked. Everything. Papers saying when you were born and baptized. All the papers from the school."

"Father Ortega?"

"That's what priests do in the Socialist Revolution. They give away papers about children."

Paco ignored her and finished his beans. He pushed the plate to her and she went and refilled it. He drank some wine. He felt better. He watched his mother.

She was fat, the only women of a miner who was fat. She still wore her hair in a single long braid like a girl. She wore black always. Her mother and father had died and she had buried three babies, all girls. He, Paco, was the only child.

He had seen her only four times since the rising. Before, she sang all day long and laughed a good deal. Now she looked as though she had been beaten with a whip. She sat, looking at the earthen floor, her fingers locked together on her knees.

"I would sleep."

"Not here, Paco."

"Why not? It's over. We're surrendering. They will go away, the Moors. I'll get your bucket back. I'll bring you the flag . . . the sheet, you know. You want the sheet, don't you?"

"You are crazy. This whole thing has made you crazy. First Tomás, now you. Even the priest."

"That was because we didn't shoot him, that's all. Now he tries to lick our hands."

"Go away from here, Paco. Now. The priest says . . ."

"My father . . ."

"Your father. How many times has he pounded the table with his craziness about the revolution being over when the last king is strangled in the guts of the last priest? Eh? All that Russian nonsense. I burned all those books, too. Bakunin. Marx. May I never see them again."

"But . . ."

"Get out, I say! Get Jaime and Simple. I have a bag of food and a skin of wine. Paco, go away before they catch you! *Hijo mío*, I stole for you. Never, even as a girl, did I steal! Get out!"

He glared at her. He walked to the fireplace and took the long knife from its place.

"Here is my food."

"Paco? Paquito . . ."

He closed the door. She threw something, and it hit the door. He grinned and slipped the knife inside his sheepskin, into the sheath under his left armpit. It lay flat against his side there. He turned down the hill, jumped over the gutter and walked to the corner. The windows in the low stone houses were all shuttered. He turned the corner and saw the truck.

Before he could get out his knife, they had him. One of them, a big man, held a revolver against the back of his head, grinding the muzzle into his skull. Hands slapped his sides and up his legs. They shoved him to a ladder. He climbed up into a truck. They pushed him forward, in with the others. He heard Simple moaning. The truck started, bucked forward and rolled down the road toward the village. Paco lowered his hands and looked around. He saw the sons of the miners . . . José Zurrabán, Curro Alvarez and his kid brother, Rubio Sánchez, Big Ears, and Little García. They had all helped in the fighting. Now they stood with frightened faces as the truck rocked down the road. Curro's kid brother was only eleven years old. There were two Legionarios in the truck. One of them, a big, bearded sergeant with green eyes kept poking a cocked revolver at Curro's brother.

Padre Ortega climbed the stone stairs, holding his case and a packet of letters and newspapers handed to him by the *sereno*. For fifteen days of shouting, turmoil, dynamitings, parades, proclamations, and blood-letting the U.H.P. militia army had sealed the province of Asturias off from the rest of Spain.

Now it was all over. The newspapers and letters proved it—more than the empty rifles and the white flags.

He stubbed out his cigarette and turned the letters over. He longed to rip them open, to feast on them. Just the sight of them caused him to forget that for every hour for two weeks he had lived expecting to be arrested and shot.

A bill from the stonemason for the repair of the steps. A schedule of local meetings sponsored by CEDA. Ortega jutted his lower lip. The very name offended him: Confederación Española de Derechos Autóno-mos. Why did Right-wing Catholic parties always choose such pompous titles? He tossed the schedule aside unread. There would be no meetings of the CEDA in Asturias for a long time. He had presided over the graves of most of the active members.

Three personal letters. The first was the hysterical plea from the old woman who claimed to have visions of the Virgin on the third Saturday of every month. What she wanted was very simple, really. She wanted to meet with the Holy Father in the Vatican and be canonized as a saint. Another anonymous note from the provincial capital, denouncing him again. Ortega glanced at the sheet. It was typed, this time on expensive paper:

You should wear dynamite fuse instead of a collar . . . Red scum . . . blasphemies . . . may you choke on the wine at Mass . . . if the Bishop wasn't senile you'd be . . .

The third letter was from the Bishop. Ortega began reading at the bottom of the first sheet.

While I seemed to have misplaced my copy of the *Syllabus of Errors,* I believe I can recall the essence. The third error, my son, goes thus:

"Human reason without any reference whatsoever to God, is the sole arbiter of truth and falsehood and of good and evil; it is a law unto itself, and suffices, by its natural force to secure the welfare of men and nations."

I am sure that is close to the original. It will do, at any rate.

You must believe me when I say that I write to you not because I have received a certain kind of letter . . . many of them, in fact. No, I am an old man and used to receiving that sort of brainless diatribe from self-styled guardians of the altar. It is your last letter to me . . . and, of course, the upheaval in the province. The radio last week said 50,000 miners in arms against the government. Do you wonder that the Republic sent in the troops? Can anyone wonder?

I believe that your prediction of this insurrection was based on much more than casual observation of the members of your parish. You said that they hate the Church because they hate the friends of the Church. But they must know that you are their friend. Do they hate you?

Ortega nodded sadly and rolled another cigarette. How could the Bishop understand? He was too good. He would interpret what had happened at the mine with the dead Moor and the soldiers as simple madness.

The priest smoothed the sheets and read on.

You state that the Church has done nothing to rebuke or correct those who exploit the poor. If we grant, lamenting, that this is so, has the Republic done more? Did your miners rise against the Church or the government in Madrid? But you say, my son, that it is *reasonable* that the Asturians turn to force. Here, clearly, you must admit to error. Is not force the antithesis of reason? Your analogy to Our Lord driving the money-changers from the temple is, I fear, false, too. It is error to believe that reason "is a law unto itself."

You see my old fingers shake so that I blot these pages. I do not know whether or not this Larra and his gang of Socialist-Communist-Anarchist cut-throats have killed you or not. Am I scribbling words to a dead man, a dead priest? If you are alive, now you know what this Larra has long called "the propaganda of the deed." You say you tried to befriend him, but he reviled you. Beware of pride, my son. It is likely that he did not understand you, because he cannot. Do you know that the Minister . . . you know who I mean . . . has almost certain proof that it was Larra and his two brothers who set fire to the Jesuit church in Madrid three years ago? Is sacrilege an act of reason? And it is by their acts that men are known, is it not?

I am deeply worried, I confess, by your involvement in . . .

Ortega sighed and set the pages down. The Bishop went on and on, nearly a dozen pages covered with his peculiar, slanting scrawl. It was cruel and pointless to write to the Bishop. The old man loved Spain nearly as much as he loved the Church. Now with the monarchy gone, the new Republic had shown itself anticlerical.

The Bishop was afraid. Afraid for the Church, afraid for Spain.

Ortega stood up and walked to the window that overlooked the Plaza Mayor. And what do I fear? I am afraid. Only I am afraid for the people. And I am afraid for myself . . . afraid that I will die in some pointless fashion, some stupid accident, a mistake, a ricocheting bullet fired at someone else. That is what I dread. That I will die not a martyr, but a fool.

I must write to him, just a few lines and say that I am well and all is quiet once again.

The clock in the tower struck the hour of four. As the priest stood at the window, smoking, he saw the first men appear. They drifted in small groups out of the side streets and leaned against the walls of the buildings or slipped like cats into the cafés and bars. A metal shutter rattled. A group of dynamiters, each man with a loop of yellow fuse around his neck, marched in a ragged column. The big square began to fill with people, all of them men.

His sleeve brushed the Bishop's letter to the floor. He picked up the scattered sheets and glanced at the last page.

I have given more than serious thought to all this, my son. I have asked for divine guidance. It has become clear to me that the living Church . . . the people . . . need you. I feel now that you must leave your present parish and carry your undeniable talents elsewhere. The Church needs fighters, too. You must explain to me how it was that you were able to thwart

the government's edict that would have closed your school. That
was courageous, in the Christian sense.
    In Morocco and the other colonies . . .

    Ortega dropped the letter on his desk. There it was. His punishment.
Stop what you are doing, stop thinking what you have thought. We are
forced to send you to Africa. But that will not be necessary, my Bishop,
for the government of the Republic of Spain has sent Africa to us. I
have looked at its faces and seen its eyes.
    The priest left his room, hurried down the stairs and out into the
street. He plucked at his skirts and muttered as his knees butted against
the ripped cloth. The October afternoon was cool and long-shadowed
and the clouds had already drifted between the mountain tops, spilling
like soft seas against the granite peaks of Asturias.
    At every corner stood a squad of Moors or Legionarios with fixed
bayonets. Ortega glanced down into narrow side streets. The barricades
had been abandoned by the U.H.P. militia. Soldiers were gathering
the stacked rifles. Truck motors echoed, the cough and snarl of animals,
off the gray stone houses and cobbled streets.
    The Plaza Mayor was filled with men, all facing the Guardias Civiles'
headquarters and barracks building on the south side of the square. The
priest stared glumly at the bullet-pocked façade and the starred windows.
The red banner had been removed from the second-floor balcony. Voices
murmured around him, a low, bitter rumble of voices in the local dialect.
He looked at face after face. Gray, lined brows and rutted cheeks; weary,
saddened eyes; cigarettes pasted to dry lips; faces with coal dust pressed
into every pore by years of toil in the mine shafts; throats tugged ropy by
too much work and not enough food; a mob of faces bled of hope.
    Then Tomás Larra walked out on the balcony. He was alone. He wore
a white shirt, white as snow, and loose yellow trousers. The priest saw him
drag his hand across his brow, raking his thick hair. Then the hand
clenched in the salute of the fist, the elbow crooked. Around Ortega the
clenched fists were raised in answer, without a sound. Larra began to speak,
his voice beating down on them from the splintered balcony, a hoarse,
powerful voice that echoed off the buildings and sank onto the mass of
upturned faces.
    "Comrades, miners, and red soldiers! This afternoon I come before you,
convinced that we have done our best and now can do no more. I
come to speak of the sad thing that has happened to us. Our glorious
insurrection in the name of all the people has fallen."
    A brute murmur rose from thousands of throats. The clenched fists
wavered and fell like sickled wheat. Larra gripped the railing and leaned
forward. He waited until a truck motor snarled and stuttered into silence.
    "I must tell you, comrades, of the words I have had with the colonel

of the enemy army. We must now take down the red flags and put up the white ones. We cannot fight any longer. We have nothing to fight with. We cannot use our hands against their cannons and machine guns. We have used all that we bought before the rising and all we captured. We must stop fighting. But that does not mean we are defeated!"

From somewhere in the ranks of the Legionarios came a baboon-bark of laughter. Ortega whirled around, his fists clenched. A row of bayonets glinted a dozen paces back. He turned back to Larra.

"But that does not mean that we abandon the class struggle, comrades. Our surrender today is but a halt on the roadside. Here we must stop, correct our mistakes and rest. We will rise again! We will be refreshed and renewed and rearmed! We will be prepared for the final battle which must end in the final victory of the exploited classes and the establishment here in Spain of a Socialist Republic!"

This time, the miners moved as one body. They surged slowly forward, bearing the priest with them. He stumbled, took a step, and flung himself against the shoulders of the men in front of him. A fist struck beneath his elbow, butting up his arm.

"Listen, comrades and red soldiers and lovers of liberty! Hear me! We have had a Spain of the blood-sucking aristocrats and simple-minded kings. We have had a Spain of crowns and thorns. We now have a Spain that calls itself a Republic. But soon, comrades, soon, we shall have a Spain that is a republic of Socialist workers! *Viva la República Socialista! Viva la revolución!*"

The roaring response struck at the sky. Thousands of clenched fists waved. Padre Ortega shouted until his throat ached and beat the air with his clenched fist.

"*Viva España! Arriba la República Socialista! Viva la revolución!*"

Colonel Bravo drew off his white gloves. He leaned forward and blew on the dusty desk top, then dropped his gloves on the clean spot. He gazed around the square, low-ceilinged room; his mouth puckered. The place was fit only for pigs. The walls were smeared, the electricity didn't work, the carpet was dotted with mice-droppings. The office of the mayor of this town. He had been shot by the miners for his politics. Why not for his filth?

The colonel drew the candlestick next to the blotter and straightened the sheets of paper before him. He took out his fountain pen, shook it until a dark drop formed on the nib, and began writing.

My little Carmen,

How nice it was to get your letter! I am surprised and saddened, though, because you say that you are lonely. How can this be, when Sister Angélica tells me you have many, many friends? I am sure you will be happy with them. I look forward to seeing you. It won't be long now, you know. We will walk down the Gran Vía together on Three Kings' Day. I promise it. You will have a new dress.

I know that you are not pleased about the apartment, but I got a very good price for it. We don't need seven rooms, now that Mama is in Heaven. Do you want seven empty rooms or to be at the convent with Sister Angélica and your little friends and a new dress?

Remember me in your sweet prayers.

Papa

The colonel sighed, folded the sheet and addressed the envelope. He smoothed the remaining sheet of paper and bent again over the desk.

Most Respected Sister Angélica,

It is my pleasure again to receive your letter! Naturally, as a man of affairs, I quite understand your concern about my daughter's tuition fee. How happy she is to be with you and her many little friends!

I have recently transacted some private sales that will enable me to place in your hands the sum you mention. At the conclusion of this most successful campaign against the enemies of Christ Jesus, I plan to request my annual leave. As you may recall, the papers take some little time to prepare. Rest assured that I will be in Madrid for the holy days.

God bless your generous heart and enrich your holy labors.

With every respectful devotion,

A knock sounded at the door. The colonel looked up. The room had grown so dark that he could not see beyond the pool of light cast by the candle flame.

"Come."

It was Gómez, his aide.

"Father Ortega of the parish requests permission to speak with you, Colonel."

"On what subject?"

"The prisoners, sir."

Colonel Bravo gathered his letters and thrust them into the top drawer of the desk.

"Have the lists been made up as ordered?"

"Almost completed, sir. Second company has relieved third company on guard duty as scheduled. Most of the prisoners . . ."

"Refused to give their names. I know, I know."

"Yes, sir. But they have been counted."

"Counted. Yes."

Colonel Bravo leaned forward and picked up his white gloves. He drew them on and flexed his fingers slowly.

"We shall let the priest worry about their names. All of Spain will know how many vermin were crushed in Asturias. The number is more important than the name, Gómez."

"Yes, sir."

"Bring more candles. Two glasses and some sherry. On a tray. I believe there are such things, even in this hotel for mice?"

"Right away, sir."

The aide turned to go.

"Were you dismissed, Teniente Gómez? I do not recall it."

"No, sir."

"But you understand and agree with me on the necessity of maintaining the highest of standards in military conduct?"

"Yes, sir."

"Good. You will bring the sherry and the tray. Then, you will admit Father Ortega. Then, you will issue a request for volunteers. Six Legionarios and six of the Moors. A captain to command. They will begin at midnight."

"Yes, sir."

"Then, Gómez, you will restrict yourself to your quarters. Then you will submit to me a request that your name be removed from the promotion list for a period of one year."

"Yes, Colonel Bravo."

The colonel rocked on his toes and hummed softly. He could see the emergency lights rigged at the *plaza de toros* where the prisoners were detained.

"Dismissed!"

"Take another little glass, Father."

"No, thank you."

Colonel Bravo poured his own glass full and tasted it.

"Not for every tongue, perhaps, but I enjoy an amontillado. It is a very clean taste. I enjoy clean things."

"Then you must find only the winds in Asturias to your liking, Colonel Bravo. Coal mines are dirty places, indeed. Which reminds me. What provisions have been made for . . . hygienic provisions, you understand . . . for the prisoners?"

"I have sent twenty-three shovels to the bull ring."

"I see. Then you do not plan any long period of detention for these men."

"No, they will not be detained long."

"I am deeply concerned . . ."

"As I am, Father, I assure you. A deplorable incident up at the mine. The offending Legionario will be punished."

"Why must we always punish? We must forgive."

"The Legion is not the Church, Father. Each has its disciplines, no?"

"And its disciples."

"Very witty, Father. And very true. Which leads me to make a request. You see? I offer you a glass of wine with one hand and implore a favor with the other."

Colonel Bravo moved his gloved fingers. The priest watched attentively. The colonel glanced away and let his hands drop to the desk top. He knew the priest's glance was fixed now on the motionless white hands.

"A favor, you said?"

"Exactly. Or a confirmation, if you like. The Legion has a burial detail, and the Church . . ."

"Has a priest."

"Clearly."

"I will serve."

"Excellent. You see that we agree. We must agree. We have our duties and we do them, Father. The Army and the Church have traditionally believed and acted as one."

"Not every tradition is a good one."

"A tradition that made Spain an empire is not good, Father?"

"Spain is not an empire, Colonel."

The colonel's white hands twitched as he stiffened with annoyance. The priest looked up and smiled. The spell was broken. Colonel Bravo emptied his glass and forced a smile to match the priest's.

"Quite so. I forgot. Have you noticed that it is easy to forget that Spain is a republic? For men in our positions, I mean."

"The people do not forget, Colonel."

"Indeed? What do they remember? You must tell me. Not now. Tomorrow. Tell me tomorrow."

Father Ortega stood up. Colonel Bravo examined him. He was short and stocky with wide, powerful shoulders. Sancho Panza in a soutane. Where did the Church get such fellows? Surely there were enough thin men in the country to more than fill the Orders?

"Where will this burial detail take place?"

"Behind the bull ring. In the cemetery."

"At what hour?"

"Midnight."

"I will be there."

"Captain Girona will accompany you. He is in command of the burial detail."

The priest walked quickly from the room. The colonel's gloved hand hung over the desk. He slammed his knuckles on the desk.

"Gómez! Gómez!"

The door opened.

"Yes, sir."

"That priest is not to leave the building unless accompanied by Capitán Girona and a military escort."

"Yes, sir."

"Has Girona found them?"

"Tomás Larra and his two brothers, Fernando and Carlos, are in the town jail in separate cells. Only two of the boys have been located. Jaime and the simple-minded one. They are in the town jail, too."

"Where is the third one?"

"Captain Girona has not yet been able . . ."

"Find him. Find him!"

"Yes, sir."

The slow bell boomed twelve times. Paco stood and pressed his face against the shutter. He could see twelve men in the mouth of the alley, the slot of stone that led from the bull ring to the cemetery. They stood at attention, bandoliers and bayonets silvered by the moonlight.

"Lantern!"

The captain's voice. Hard yellow light flared up, and shadows blotted the rank of waiting soldiers. To the left was a high mound of raw earth. Beyond, looming in the mists was the church, walls and spires of granite and iron.

"Prisoners!"

Soldiers brought them and thrust them down on their knees before the mound of new-shoveled dirt. Paco saw them. His cousin Jaime. His cousin Simple. José Zurrabán and Little García.

"Priest!"

He stepped into the brassy light, his hand raised in benediction and pronounced Latin words over the kneeling boys. Paco jerked away, his eyes stinging, his throat clotted.

The volley smashed through the night.

"Prisoners!"

Soldiers brought them and thrust them down on their knees, down on the blood-gummed earth. Paco saw them. His father, Tomás, in yellow pants and rumpled white shirt. His uncle Fernando, stupefied with the brassy glare, peering at the rank of rifles. His uncle Carlos covered his face with his hands.

"Priest!"

He stepped into the lantern light, his hand raised in benediction. Tomás flung up his hands and struck the priest aside. Padre Ortega stepped back, his knees bent and shoulders hunched as if to take the lash. He covered his priest's face with his hands and cried out in Latin. Tomás Larra waited until the priest was done. Paco could see his father's face stiffen, his father's eyes glare with rage. His voice rang off the stones.

"Shoot us, *hijos de la gran puta!* We go to our children, not to God!"

From the darkness came the order, the shout of the Foreign Legion, the echo from the night.

"Down with intelligence!"

The shadowed rank of rifles rose and leveled on the kneeling prisoners. Twelve dark fists worked the dozen bolts. The voice called again.

"Long live . . . "

The kneeling men went rigid in the golden glare. Tomás, his arms nailed stiff in space, Fernando sheep-gaping at the murderous row of rifles, Carlos and the priest, both hunched and both blind.

"*Death!*"

Paco saw his father lurch and lift, rising up to throw himself into the volley. The bullets lashed the kneeling men into a ripped heap that groaned and twitched on the red earth.

The priest fell forward slowly, as in a dream, to his knees. His hands still shielded his face. He shouted in Latin and his muffled voice pulsed through the lantern's golden glare, beat and slowed and beat again and stopped.

For three days, the Moors and the soldiers of the Legion came to the bull ring and took away the prisoners for questioning. At midnight, when the bell in the church tolled in the dark, the shooting began. When the gray light of dawn leaked through the crack in the shutter, the shooting stopped. There was a quiet time. Then different soldiers came to the bull ring and took away more prisoners to bury the dead and to dig new pits.

During the night, the smash of the rifles, groans, and silence. During the day, the scrape of shovels and the clink of picks in the hard earth. Then the dark again, and again the slow boom of the bell.

On the fourth day, the door opened and fresh, pine-scented air blew into the stench of the building. Three Legionarios stood there. Two had rifles. The prisoners whimpered and shrank away from them, then fled into a butting, elbowing, cursing mass at the far end of the room. The third Legionario had a pistol. He stalked slowly across the floor, pointing his pistol at one prisoner, then at another. When they flinched and ducked, he laughed. He moved them, herded them with his pistol. Paco knew him, the Legionario with pale green eyes. The snout of the pistol pointed at Paco's face. Paco did not move. Let the soldier shoot him. He was dead already.

"This must be him. We found him at last. Come on, you."

Paco held out his arms for the iron cuffs and the chain. The Legionario swung his pistol. Paco jerked his hands away. The soldier laughed again and shoved Paco out through the door. The three soldiers clumped down the stairs to the dirt courtyard. Paco blinked, dazed by the sunlight. The Legionario held out the pistol to him.

"Go ahead, *chico*. Take it. You know how to shoot. Shoot. Shoot yourself. Or shoot me. What difference does it make, eh?"

Paco looked at the revolver, hucked deep in his throat and spat deliberately between the soldier's dusty boots.

"Look. He's tough, this one. A hero! A bull ring full of Red heroes. Not many left, now. Come on."

They prodded him across the dirt court, through the gate and down the alley that led to the cemetery. Paco stumbled over the rough cobblestones. He felt nothing, nothing at all. The sun now touched his eyes weakly, for he had stared at the lantern light, the golden glare.

At the cemetery, a gang of prisoners, guarded by Moors wrapped in long cloaks, toiled slowly in the earth with picks and shovels.

"That's where you'll sleep tonight, hero. That's a bed for you and your brothers."

Paco spat again. The pistol snout stabbed against his ribs.

"*Un paseo* . . . a little walk first, eh?"

They walked up the road, past the twisted, leafless olive trees to the warehouse on the slope of the rocky hill. Women of the *pueblo* stood together in a dark, silent mass across from the building. Moors with rifles and bayonets guarded the big wooden doors. The soldiers took Paco into the building, down a short corridor and into a room.

In the room stood a man in the uniform of a captain of the Legion. Behind him, near a window, was the priest. In the corner, seated on a low bench was a woman dressed in black. Paco did not have to look at her. He knew it was his mother. Why did they bring her here? To watch. Then they would take him back to dig in the dirt with the others. At midnight, they would shoot him.

"Señora?"

"Capitán?"

"Is this puppy yours?"

Paco opened his eyes. He had not looked at her, but he knew that her face would bear no sign of suffering. She would give no one that. He waited for her voice. She spoke, steady, flat, insulting.

"Him? That one? *Qué va!* The best part of him ran down a drunk gypsy's leg."

"Señora . . ."

"What would you have me say, Father? Down the leg of a drunk priest?"

"Your mouth, woman."

"Capitán, I have my work to do. My washing . . ."

"Soon you will have no one to wash for, woman."

"Ehhh . . ."

Paco blinked, waiting for what would come next.

"Father Ortega?"

"I never saw him before. You are, permit me to say it, wrong, mistaken, Captain Girona. This is not the son of Tomás Larra. Just a beggar. I mean, merely to look at him . . . dirty little animal."

The room echoed with his voice and was silent. No one moved or spoke.

"Paco!"

But he was ready for them. He did not move or raise his head.

"Paco, come kiss this whore of a mother you have who does it with goats and gypsies."

He stared at the floor. He heard the boards creak as the soldier moved to him from behind. Paco slumped his shoulders and released his belly muscles just as the rifle butt pounded into his back, aimed at his kidneys. He fell forward, the pain washing up and through him, a pain he had never felt before that spilled like acid into his throat. He retched and thrashed on the sanded floor, but nothing came up. Now an ache like a hot stone filled his belly. He curled and cuddled it, gasping. The room tilted and swirled. Some black shapes skidded, faded into shivering bits, and settled down into the ache.

The black shapes were her stockings and the hem of her black dress. Her ankles were primly crossed. He saw her fingers flick at the dark stuff of her dress. Her voice, from a great distance, dropped down through the dull agony.

"Is that why I am here, Capitán Girona? To see you make this gypsy piss blood?"

The captain's voice, slow and cold dropped on him.

"Take this bag of garbage out of here. Shoot him with the others."

He lay on the board bunk, watching the Judas. Something had happened. He had believed that he was dead, but someone wanted to do something with him. They were not going to let him die so easily.

They had stopped where the roads came together. One of the soldiers held him. The other had gone away to talk with an old man seated on a cart. The burro blinked in the late winter sun. The old man had moved his hand. The soldier had taken something from him. He came back, grunted. Then they had carried him through the silent streets to the town jail, up the stairs, through the iron grate and into his cell.

Since then, from time to time through the aching hours, the plate over the Judas snicked, open and shut, like a camera. They were watching him. Why? Every time the plate snicked, he twitched. The sound skewered his back and snapped his head up. He cursed feebly, his body driven rigid, then shuddered down on the hard planks again. A pool of bloody urine dried on the floor. The bell in the church beat ten dull strokes.

Something grated in the door. Paco rose on his elbow. The door opened a few inches. Paco forced himself to sit up. His face felt cold, his head empty. He leaned forward, putting his head between his knees. Then he gripped the edge of the bunk and stood up. His soiled trousers slipped down to his knees. He pulled them up and stepped carefully forward. He could walk. He took another step, another. At every step, the door opened a few inches.

The face of the guard was white and slick with fear-sweat. He held a bit of rope in his shaking hands. Paco snatched it from him and belted his trousers. They had come for him an hour earlier than the others, that was all.

"Where are the others?"

Paco stepped out into the long, dim corridor, a shaft of bolted doors. It was cold and his breath blew in clouds. The guard whirled and hissed like a goose, batting at the air with his hands. Paco stepped back. Why did he have no boots, this guard? Why no boots?

The guard offered Paco his hand, then crooked his arm, pantomiming walking together.

"Your grandmother. I can walk."

"Sssssss!"

The guard fled softly down the corridor, stopped, and beckoned frantically. Paco looked back at the open door to his cell. So. That was it. They were going to shoot him for trying to escape, then show him to the others or hang him from a lamppost in the Plaza Mayor. Let them. What can they do to a dead man?

The guard waited for him at the grate. It was open. The guard held out a key. It slipped from his fingers and clattered on the floor.

"Mierda!"

He found it and gave it to Paco. The guard was drunk on wine, and blew sour clouds of steam into Paco's face.

"Go down the stairs. The lock turns to the left. Left, understand? El viejo . . . the old one is waiting."

"El viejo."

"Your comrade . . . Get out of here, for the love of Christ!"

Paco slipped through the grate and crept down the stairs. The key jammed in the lock. He whirled and looked up the stairs, looking for the squad of soldiers with their rifles, looking into the instant before they shot him down. There was no one. The guard had vanished. To the left, the guard had said, to the left. Paco wrenched at the clumsy key. The lock clicked. The door yawned open.

It was dark and cold, but Paco could smell the burro. He waited until he could make out the old man, el viejo, seated on the tailgate of the cart. Paco walked slowly across the alley. The old man lifted a tattered canvas cover. Paco half sat, half fell into the cart. The old man tugged the cover over him. The cart smelled of stale dung. The burro stamped, and the cart rolled forward. They went slowly, jolting, and made three turns, left, right and right again. They stopped. The old man whistled softly, a little melody, over and over. Paco shivered.

Boots stamped in cadence, beating on the stones. The slow bell boomed. The firing squad was marching to the cemetery. Paco clasped his knees and clenched his teeth. Now the betrayal, the harsh shout, the hands tearing away the tattered canvas and the wild, crooning cries of the Moors as they stabbed down into him with their ragged bayonets.

The heels clumped closer, and the last bell stroke faded. The boots marched on. The old man waited, clucked to the burro, and the cart moved again. They turned and started down a hill. The old man set a wooden brake. Paco could smell it burn as it rubbed on the wheelrim. They went on. The old man took off the brake. They went on for a time and then stopped.

The dark wind drove through the flimsy canvas. The tailgate clashed down. Paco crawled out. Something batted against his chest. He struck back in a blind panic, cursing, and snatched a piece of frayed rope. He tugged and felt his pants slide. He fell sideways, brushed through the old man's arms and hit the ground. He lay there, exhausted. The night roared around him. He sat up. The wind smelled of cold earth and resin, a mountain wind pouring down the slope of a hill. Paco could see lights in the distance, three bits of brightness ripped by the wind.

"Where are we?"

His voice surprised him, a shrill croak.

"At the crossroads. North."

"What are those lights? A barricade?"

"Moors."

"What is your name, *viejo?*"

"If I don't tell you, you can't tell anybody."

"All right."

The old man thrust a sheepskin jacket at Paco. It was too small, but the old man helped him and then shook a bottle in his face.

Paco drank some of the wine and nodded. The old man waved for him to keep the bottle. What was this? Sitting on the ground in a borrowed jacket that stank like a dead cat, drinking an old man's wine. The high stars wheeled in the windy sky.

I was dead. Now I am out here and alive. I am drunk, I think.

"Here they come!"

The headlights of an automobile bobbled down the slope of a hill, disappeared for a few moments and then streamed against the darkness, much closer. Paco stood up and leaned against the cart, holding the wine bottle by the neck, ready to throw it. The old man yelled something, but the wind whipped away the words.

It was a big sedan. It loomed on them, the lights boring down the wind-swept road. It shot past, the motor roaring, the tires spraying bits of dirt and stones, and the vacuum sucked at the sheepskin Paco wore. The sedan stopped, the motor murmuring. The gears gnashed, and the automobile shot back. The driver rolled down the window.

"*Hola, viejo!* Is this the road to Santander?"

"No."

"What road is it?"

"*Un momentito.* I'm trying to remember what to say to you."

"What's that?"

"He's right here."

"Say the words, you idiot!"

"I tell you I can't remember them, *cabronazo!* Something about France, no?"

"*Jesucristo* . . ."

The lights went off and the motor fuddled silent. Two men got out, but left the doors open. The old man struck his hands together.

"I know it's something about France, but . . ."

"That's all right, *viejo.*"

"When he asks like that . . ."

"Forget it, man. He has your money."

"Let him keep it. I have not earned it."

"You have done well. You are amazing."

"I am careful, that's all."

The old man walked warily to the sedan. The bigger man, dressed in a long overcoat and a hat came to Paco.

"Paco Larra?"

"Who wants him?"

"Get in the automobile. It's a long drive to the border."

The man looked off at the watch fires of the Moors. He seemed in no hurry. He held his hat on his head with one hand. His voice was heavy, slow. He shifted so as to block the hard, pine-scented wind.

"Are you badly hurt?"

"I can move."

"Let's go."

Something in the man's voice was good. He was to be trusted. Paco stripped off the sheepskin and gave it back to the old man. The old man patted him on the shoulder. Paco leaned into the dark gusts of wind and walked carefully to the sedan.

The driver started the car and turned around. They shot away from the old man, the burro, and the cart. They drove without speaking, very fast, the heavy automobile rocking and bounding over the rough highway.

The big man with the hat and overcoat lit a cigarette and held the match so that Paco could see his face, square and tough-looking with tired eyes and a broken nose. The man grinned and blew out the match.

"He thinks this is a race, the driver. Maybe he's a pilot, eh?"

Paco laughed and leaned back in the seat.

"So. I can laugh. It feels good. Who are you, anyway?"

"I'm from the Party. You call me Voget. And this is Barrone, an Italian comrade and anti-Fascist."

Voget shook Paco's hand.

"The Communist Party?"

"*Claro*. From Marseilles. We're going there. Our last trip. It's too dangerous crossing and recrossing the border like this. Somebody will check these passports, then, *pffft*, off to jail."

"You're taking me to France?"

"Now, yes. Your father got through on the telephone to Comrade Medina in Lisbon. Medina called me. Since then, we've been touring Spain, eh, Barrone?"

Voget took something from his overcoat and placed it in Paco's hands. It was a wallet.

"Now there are three of us. All French tourists. That's your new passport. You are my nephew . . . for the time being."

"You came here from France just to get me? I don't believe you."

"No, not you alone. There are others. Do you know of Juan Modesto?"

"No."

"Eugenio Lister?"

"Lister. Of course. He is known. The mason. Did he get away?"

"Some other comrades got him over the border two days ago."

"Good."

"We think so. But we think that you are worth the risk, too. The son of Tomás Larra. That name means something."

"I thank you for him. He was proud of what he did. He taught me much."

"How old are you?"

"Almost seventeen."

Barrone muttered something and shook his head. Voget lit another cigarette. The black tobacco smelled like a cigar. The car was hot, stifling. The wine roiled in Paco's stomach.

"*Por favor* . . . the window . . . some air . . . I feel . . . I never rode in an automobile before."

"No? Well, comrade, you will ride in cars and on trains and a ship and then on a train again. Don't worry. I'll be with you."

"All that just to get to France?"

"It's a long trip."

Barrone leaned forward, shaking his head. The sedan began to climb a hill.

"Tell the boy the truth. You'll have to tell him sometime."

"All right. First to France, yes. Then to Russia."

"Russia? Where in Russia? Why there?"

"Leningrad. Then Moscow."

"*Dios!* But what for?"

"To be with Modesto and Lister and the others. For your training. You must be trained to avenge your father and the others. You will go to a school, a military school for officers. It takes more than a few guns and some dynamite. Brains, not just *cojones*. And something else, too. Order, discipline. That's what the Party will teach you."

"For what purpose? It's all over now back there."

"For the next time."

"*La próxima.* Yes, all right."

Paco settled back between the two men. He felt safe and warm and sleepy. He dozed and woke and slept again while the big sedan hammered up the winding roads into the mountains. Voget and Barrone argued in French. Paco sensed it was about him. Barrone thought he was too young for this business. He fell asleep again and had a dream. He was walking in deep snow, carrying a gun and looking for someone. There were bodies in the snow. He struggled through the drifts from one to another, but when he got close, the dead men stood up and covered their faces and ran away. He woke up with a jolt of fright. Voget put a heavy arm around him.

"Take it easy, *chico*. That's all over now."

"My mother saved my life."

The automobile swayed and ground around a curve. The sky began to lighten. The kilometer stones whipped by. They drove through a silent town. Paco slept again.

When he woke, they were across the border and Barrone was singing some Italian song about a red flag. Voget jerked his thumb.

"You're safe, *jovencito*. You'll go back. Not to Asturias. What is there for you, eh?"

"Nothing. *Nada*."

"When you go back, you'll go to Madrid. Ever been there?"

"No. My father was there."

"Madrid remembers him. What did you want to be before all this? A matador, I suppose, right? You wanted a suit of lights."

"No. I knew what I was to be . . . a leader of workers. We used to read Lenin together at night."

Paco looked out of the automobile window. He remembered a poem that he had memorized for school. Some thing about *la dulce Francia* . . . sweet France. The road wound down a hill covered with vines. Even at this time of the year the valleys were green. The road ran down into the green, sweet valleys of France and on to Russia deep in snow . . . the road to Moscow and to Madrid.

"He needs a name, this matador of Fascists. Paco for his comrades, but what for the people, so they will know him?"

Voget nodded.

"Why not his province? Many of them take a name like that. Asturias. *El Asturiano*. How's that? It has dignity and will help them to remember the miners. El Asturiano. That's a name they will come to know. You like that, Paco?"

"Whatever you say, Comrade Voget."

Barrone smiled and began to sing again about the red banner. Voget spoke to the driver. The car rolled down the road.

Paco turned around. Through the rear window he could see the barren mountains. On the other side lay Spain. He turned around, satisfied with a single glance, something to hold in his mind. Paco Larra had lived and died back there. El Asturiano was here and now. It was the end of the beginning, and the road ran on to Moscow and Madrid.

The Ministry of the Interior listed 1335 killed in Asturias and nearly 3000 wounded. Ninety thousand rifles had been captured, along with other arms. Arrests were ordered by the Republican government. The prisons of Spain swallowed thirty thousand male and female political prisoners by the end of November. Café-rumors spread tales of murder, deliberate starvation, and torture. The city of Oviedo was a ruin. The leaders of the Socialists were imprisoned, along with the leaders of the Republic of Catalonia. Generals Goded and Franco were hailed as the saviors of the Republic. Asturias was compared to the Paris Commune by some, to the Russian revolution of 1905 by others. When the death sentences against those politicians convicted of rebellion were commuted to thirty years' imprisonment, the cabinet ministers of the Catholic Party resigned in protest. The government muddled through crises and scandals with no approved budget and nothing accomplished by legislation. The Cortes was dissolved and new elections were called for.

The Falange, the Carlists, and the Catholic Party combined with small independent groups in a National Front. The shrunken factions of the Center included the discredited liberals and the Basque Nationalists who had come to suspect the parties of the Right, even their fellow Catholics. The Bulgarian Communist Dimitrov at the Seventh Congress of the Comintern proposed alliance and joint action of the Communist Party with all social democratic parties, the creation of a Popular Front. Bourgeois democracy should be preserved until it could be replaced by proletarian democracy. Dimitrov made mention of the wooden horse that brought about the capture of Troy. Still, the Anarchists of Spain boycotted the elections held at last in February 1936. The Popular

Front promised reinstatement to those who had lost their jobs because of the Asturian rising, an indemnity to the victims there, restoration of Catalonian self-rule and continued social reforms.

By the end of two rounds of voting, necessary to establish a majority in disputed districts, the National Front of the Right held 134 seats in the Cortes, the Center, including the Basques, 55, and the Popular Front 278 seats. The Communist Party, showing unsuspected strength, outpolled the liberals, the Carlists, and the Monarchists. They had won 17 seats and were led by their Secretary, Dolores Ibarruri, known as La Pasionaria, a loyal supporter of Stalin.

Manuel Azaña in his first act as Prime Minister signed a decree of amnesty for all political prisoners. The citizens of Catalonia returned their imprisoned leaders to govern their republic. Press censorship, lifted for the elections, was clamped down again. Generals Goded and Franco were dismissed from the War Ministry, exiled, in effect, to posts in the Balearic and Canary Islands. An official State of Alarm was maintained by the government of the Popular Front. Despite Spain's large gold reserve, the value of the peseta fell.

Violence increased everywhere. Left extremists freed from prison repaid the amnesty with acts of vengeance against the Republic. José Antonio Primo de Rivera, a loser in the elections, increased the membership in the Falange and authorized provocations that could be blamed on the Anarchists and increase fear, while dramatizing the impotence of the Popular Front government. The two great trade unions, Anarchist and Socialist, took to the streets against each other, and rifle fire echoed in the darkness. The Communist Party shifted its growing strength from the Anarchists to the extreme factions of the Socialists. Banks and convents were bombed, churches burned. Murder, sniping and assassination became common.

General Emilio Mola was transferred from Morocco to Pamplona, capital of Navarre. In February 1936, he met with Generals Goded and Franco. They agreed together to support a military revolt against the Republic if power shifted to the extreme Socialists now flirting with the Communists or if the internal situation worsened to anarchy. Mola was an expert conspirator. A fourth general, José Sanjurjo, previously exiled to Portugal, traveled to Germany to confer with the military attaché at the Spanish embassy and with the chief of Nazi military intelligence. This was to be no comic opera *coup d'état*. Documents were circulated, outlining a double plot, the first military, the second civil. In all the provinces, public buildings were to be seized, especially telephone offices and arms depots. General Sanjurjo was named chief of the four-man junta. When a state of war against the Republic was announced, he would fly into Spain from Portugal. The Falange would help in the rising as civilian shock-troops and *agents provocateurs*. The link between the insurgent generals and Spain's Fascist Party was Serrano Suñer, Franco's brother-in-law. The commander of the Foreign Legion was an active and trusted member of the Falange. Mola's documents promised death and imprisonment to the leaders of the Anarchists, Socialists, and Communists and to known Freemasons, a declaration of war in the name of peace, justice and order. The date was set for the end of April 1936. Generals Goded and Franco left for their overseas posts.

The government closed Falange headquarters in Madrid and, in mid-March, arrested José Antonio Primo de Rivera. He was imprisoned in the seacoast town of Alicante. The situation got worse instead of better. Landless *braceros* seized private estates in the province of Estremadura. Strikes by the Anarchists and Socialists became continuous. A judge guilty of condemning a Falangist murderer to thirty years in jail was murdered. The celebration of the fourth anniversary of the Republic was turned into a riot by a bomb. Rumors spread everywhere. The country was being infiltrated by Comintern agents.

The generals hesitated. An important faction still remained uncommitted to the conspiracy. The Carlists of Navarre.

BOOK ONE

Sin Novedad
May–July 1936

We, the undersigned, Lieutenant General Emilio Barrera, in his personal capacity; Don Rafael Olazábal and Señor Lizarra, on behalf of the *Comunion Tradicionalista* and Don Antonio Goicoechea, as leader of the Party of Renovación Española, have drawn up this document so that there may remain on record what happened in the interview which they had at four o'clock this afternoon, March 31, 1934, with the head of the Italian Government, Signor Mussolini, together with Marshal Italo Balbo. The President, after carefully informing himself from the answers, which each of those present gave to his questions, of the present situation of Spanish politics, and the aspiration and state of the Army and Navy and the monarchist parties, declared the following to those there assembled:

1. That he was ready to help with the necessary measures of assistance to the two parties in opposition to the regime obtaining in Spain, in the task of overthrowing it and substituting it by a Regency which would prepare the complete restoration of the Monarchy; this declaration was solemnly repeated by Signor Mussolini three times, and those assembled received it with the natural manifestations of esteem and gratitude;

2. That as a practical demonstration and as a proof of his intentions he was ready to supply them immediately with 20,000 rifles; 20,000 hand grenades; 200 machine guns; and 1,500,000 pesetas in cash;

3. That such help was merely of an initial nature and would be opportunely completed with greater measures, accordingly as the work achieved justified this and circumstances made it necessary.

Those present agreed that for the handing over of the sum previously referred to, a delegate of the parties should be chosen, Señor Don Rafael Olazábal, and he should take charge of these funds and place them in Spain at the joint disposal of the two leaders, Conde de Rodezno and Antonio Goicoechea, for its distribution . . . between the two, in the form and at the time and in the conditions on which they may decide.

In the same way, it was agreed that with regard to the distribution of the first quantity of arms, the leaders in question should have what was necessary for the part proportional to the charge undertaken by each group and also for its transport to Spain.

Rome, March 31, 1934

(Signed) Emilio Barrera
Rafael Olazábal
Lizarra
Antonio Goicoechea

The face of the Man of Sorrow winced beneath the cruel crown of golden thorns. The gilt lids wept ruby tears. The votive candles glowed in silent crimson witness. A bell chinked. After a few seconds, the echo chinked through the cool, hushed gloom.

Pedro Alemany prayed erect, as his father worshiped in their private chapel. His hands clasped beneath his chin, his fingers twisted in the beads, he whispered his Pater Noster. His words seemed to him to hang there in the chill, gray air. He said the Pater Noster again, more slowly, placing another layer of faith on the first, building a bridge of words, his pledge and plea, between himself and the golden body spiked to the holy cross.

Pedro stood, steadied by the serenity of his mind and heart. It was that feeling, that inner calm, that was his faith. What flaw was in him then that this flood of peace drained away so soon? As soon as he lowered his hands, it began to leak away. In the instant that he thrust his rosary into his jacket pocket, all his nervousness rushed upon him. His fingers touched his *boina*, the scarlet beret stuffed in his pocket, and he turned, startled.

There was no one in the church. He stood alone. The rows of columns disappeared in the dimness. His foot scraped on the stone floor. It was not yet dawn. The windows of the clerestory were lead-colored, coffin gray; they had not yet their glory from the sun. Pedro walked slowly, steadily into the side aisle and stopped before the iron grill. In the niche, a plaster statue of the Virgin knelt in a bower of wax lilies. The stiff petals were coated with dust. He frowned. This, then, was the devotion of the Madrileños. An empty church and dusty lilies. His father had been quite correct. Only in Navarre was God loved. Only in Navarre did men keep alive the hope of God's servant . . . the king.

He felt it first, that shiver of the senses that touches the brain an instant before the ear hears. A dulled mutter of drums outside in the streets. His father had warned him of that, too, what to expect on this first day of May. A day of the people. *A celebration of dirty flesh, a triumph of apostasy, atheism and athletic clubs.* Pedro had seen the streets of Madrid clotted with little groups of men in overalls stringing banners and hoisting huge portraits of bearded, foreign faces, icons of their new gods: Marx and Lenin. He had walked from the Atocha railway station to the decent *pensión* run by the widow of the steward of one of his father's farms . . . the only place in Madrid fit for Christian youth, his father had said. And what had happened? Two filthy-faced children, boys of eight or nine years, had tried to sell him packets of contraceptives. When he spoke with them, they had laughed at his accent. *Rusticano!* one of them had sneered.

The drum sounded again, a long, low roll and then the double stab of the bugle, two notes, high, two more, lower, another pair, a parody at dawn of the opening of a *corrida de toros.* The sounds smeared flat. The voices of men laughed. There was a spatter of ironic applause.

Pedro walked down the aisle, slipped a peseta into the poorbox, and thrust open the small wooden door set in the huge slab of riveted iron and oak that shielded God and the Virgin from the distemper of socialism. The sun was up and filled the street with gentle warmth, an easy dawn that would heat to an oven afternoon.

A group of workers had formed, insolent with banners and placards and fresh-washed *monos* and coffee laced with *anís* at the corner café. They rubbed their behinds on the very steps of the church, the stairway to grace. They had drums and bugles, wine bottles, and fistfuls of shoddy pamphlets. Their banners were made of cheap sheeting nailed to slats. The slogans, daubed on with house paint, blurred through the flimsy cloth. Some sort of argument was going on as to who had the honor to drag this blasphemy through the capital streets: LA REPÚBLICA Y LA SOLIDARIDAD!

Solidarity of what? Republic of what? Slogan-slaves, church-breakers, self-styled educational reformers who wanted only to plunder the monastaries and poison the children of Spain with their foreign heresies. The February elections, despite the efforts of the decent and the devoted . . . his own father driven to threats of expulsion and foreclosure on the very tenants who had worked the vineyards for generations . . . this was the result of politics and "enlightened" thought, a mongrel Cortes, a whelping-house of "progress" called by the deceived and damned a Frente Popular—a Popular Front. A *façade*, his father often said over the estate sherry and almonds that grew in the kitchen-garden, *for the Bolshevization of Spain.*

Pedro snatched out his *boina* and drew it on, reckless of his carefully-combed and oiled hair. He stalked down the steps, his right fist clenching the rosary in his pocket. He must be discreet, avoid incidents. He had his mission, his message to deliver. It would not be tolerated by his superiors . . . some scuffle in the streets with the mud-brained and the misguided. If it was one thing the Carlists stood for, it was discipline. Faith and discipline, like the Christian knights.

"Hey, *camarada*, how goes it with Jesus and his Mamma?"

A few of them had turned. The banners tossed and jerked in the early morning air. The man with the bugle blatted the bull-fight call. Some children darted around, shrieking. Pedro tried to slip away before they turned on him. He clenched his fist until the beads bit into his palm. The words were torn from him. He tried to grind down his disgust with the knowledge of what he had to do this day.

"At least He knew his mother . . ."

"Ole . . . Ole!"

"Stick out your tongue, comrade. Did you have breakfast? A nice piece of stale bread?"

"Eh, come on, *estúpido*, let the kid alone. We're almost ready."

"Listen, comrade, change your hat."

Pedro pushed through them, his face lowered. The grinning faces made him tremble. Somebody grabbed at his beret, and he ran a few steps. He stopped. A little girl hooked the corners of her mouth with her fingers and waggled a pointed, pink tongue at him, her eyes crazy-crossed. Pedro shook his fist and shouted.

"*Anarquistas anticristos!*"

A stone skipped between Pedro's legs. He turned and walked away. The bugle blatted behind him. He turned the corner and nearly bumped into three women in black carrying a picture of the President of the Republic.

"Señorito, are we late?"

"What?"

"Not so fast. You'll tear it, see?"

"Ay, my feet already hurt . . ."

Pedro ducked under the picture and walked on. The police were out, but idle, chatting with the workers grouped at nearly every street corner. A gentle breeze fluttered the gold, fuschia, and scarlet banners slung across the balconies. Drums bunted and brassy music rose and faded, only to strike up again as he turned a corner. He saw barricades and gaudy posters, jostling groups with the red and black arm bands of the

Anarchist parties gathered around the pot of hissing oil where *churros* fried golden-greasy. A gang of schoolgirls with Socialist banners and red ribbons knotted in their braids whistled and called him, shrieking and giggling at their boldness. Pedro took off his scarlet beret and folded it carefully. He leaned against a newspaper kiosk and watched a delegation of construction workers march past, a comic procession of skipping, out-of-step, serious, fresh-shaved faces, razor-raw, with shovels shouldered like rifles, the polished steel bills threatening noses in the file that straggled behind while a union delegate, red-faced, bawled a cadence no one could keep.

He found an iron table beneath the trees on the island of a boulevard. He sat down, picking at his shirt. He was lost. Snare drums rattled and popped. On the house front facing him, half-blotted by the tender May growth of leaves, a rodenty Lenin smirked, a cardboard mask of vibrant tangerine.

"Coffee, sir?"

"Please."

The waiter brought a large cup of steaming *café con leche* and set it before Pedro. He idled, waiting, wanting to talk. Pedro sipped his coffee.

"A nice day."

"You're from . . . Asturias, señor?"

"Navarre."

"Very fine people in that province, sir. They are . . . responsible, you know? But, of course you know that."

"We have our ideas. We believe . . ."

"That's the whole thing! . . . pardon me, señorito, a customer . . ."

". . . that stability, crown and church . . ."

The waiter was gone. The street lay warm and empty. The morning sky was a brilliant blue and deep as grace. Pigeons flung through the green trees, wings clattering. A *sereno* in his gray coat and stick opened a dozen doors, his night face squinting and pale, and went whistling into a café, ducking under the half-raised shutter of corrugated iron. Pedro recognized the song. The night watchman was spilling into the blue morning the chorus of "The International." Pedro stood up. The toes of his new boots were scuffed. Across the street, the waiter smiled and held up one finger, then another. Two pesetas for a cup of coffee with milk? Pedro dropped two coins into the saucer, fingered a céntimo piece. At that price, clearly a *propina* was not necessary. The Republic, it seemed, wanted its waiters to be millionaires. Still, the fellow had some decency . . .

He dropped a céntimo into the saucer and walked away under the Maytime trees. A band played somewhere, a military march. He quickened his pace, smiling, and smoothed his jacket, patting the pocket that bulged with his *boina*. At the corner he stopped, getting his directions.

Surely La Castellana lay to the left? Madrid was all streets, houses, stores, cafés, gleaming trolley rails and political posters.

At home in the hills, they would be gathering in their starched white tunics, black breeches, dull-glossy boots and scarlet berets. Every Sunday after Mass and on specially selected days, the Carlists marched through the mountains of Navarre, rank on rank of red berets like mountain poppies, the white and black uniforms like photo negatives, the old and the young filling the pine-scented boulder-strewn valleys with their songs and the thunder-chanting of a hundred voices marching to the recitation of the Pater Nosters. Then, after the long march into the mountains . . . target practice with the Italian rifles, bayonet drill and, stripped to the waist, a hundred sinewed arms swinging up at once, lobbing rocks, the mock-grenades. Then, the prayers, the oath of loyalty to the absent king and the swinging march down to the crude tables set beneath the trees in the dying sunlight of the late afternoon and the wine and rough bread and thyme-scented lamb hissing fat on the grills. His father, in uniform, his beard and mustache purple, drinking from a wooden cup like any other man. The Movement, steadfast, loyal, devout from the Carlist Wars of the 1830s and after, too, more than a century of Spanish, pure Spanish . . .

A woman with bare arms and blond hair stood in front of him. Pedro stopped, stood at attention, felt himself flush and tried to sidle around her. His mind buzzed. Suddenly a band was playing very loudly, and a motorcycle battered and spewed exhaust fumes in his face. The woman's voice, shrill and eager, stitched at him.

". . . a young man of new Spain . . . equality of work, liberty of conscience . . . what of Spanish women? . . . deprivation . . . cloister and harem walls . . . latest . . . scientific . . . hygiene . . ."

Her lacquered nails plucked up something from an open cardboard box. She flapped a pamphlet in his face. He caught it, glanced at the limp sheets.

FREE ABORTION CLINICS

FREE WOMEN

He flung the pamphlet into the gutter. A squad of police heaved a sawhorse barricade onto the sidewalk. A mass of men and women, walking slowly, banners and placards tilting and jerking above red-wrapped heads poured down the street. Pedro stumbled into their ranks, elbowed and dodged, muttering apologies. The faces around him, sliding past him, men and women, old, lined and whiskered, young and work-lined and toughened were rapt, staring, joyous, unseeing. He tore a passage through them and fell free against a lamppost on the opposite side. He was sweating and rattled. The press of bodies poured on, quiet now, the shuffle of the feet the sound, bearing the banners of workers' syndicates, co-operative agricultural communes, women's leagues, youth groups. Then, without a signal, they began to sing their dreadful hymn, "The International."

The song rose up and up, urgent and heart-pulling, confident and vast. Pedro clung to the lamppost, gaping, feeling the song bound off the stones of the city. It struck into him, and he felt a sudden weak panic, a shredding of the soul. If he let go, tried to stand, alone, he would be slowly drawn by these beating words lifted so in hard-voiced harmony. If he tried to stand, alone, he would be swayed, dragged, until he fell in file with this overalled, red-bannered, stone-knuckled pressing mass, kneaded by its sweat and bare-armed, gritty power to bend or break, renew or ruin.

He shrieked, outraged, and shook his fist at the striding, singing crowd that overswarmed his senses.

"Stop it! Stop it!"

His words skipped like pebbles on the surge of sound. A broad, hard palm cracked between his shoulders. He clung to the lamppost, stunned and breathless.

"That's it, *chico!* For the Republic! Even the bourgeoisie!"

The worker pumped his hand, then ran back to the singing ranks. Pedro fumbled in his looted pocket, powerless, while a new, laughing girl in a snowy blouse and red neckerchief stuffed C.N.T. handbills inside his suddenly unbuttoned shirt.

"And you weren't afraid? Don't you see, Pedrito? Those mountain picnics in Navarre have done for you what reading and discussion have done for me. It's discipline. Discipline. So little and so much. Beginning at the font and ending at a barricade. That's our direction, the movement of our generation."

Pedro nodded dully and cracked his knuckles over his plate of melted flan. He had eaten little, and the first spoonful of the sweet pudding had gagged him. His knuckles popped. Then he remembered that Emilio detested any sort of nervous mannerism.

His cousin sat at ease and elegant, his somber double-breasted jacket freed to reveal a watered-silk waistcoat of soft yellow. Emilio smoked a cigarette with quick, fastidious gestures, brushing off the ash into a silver tray. A light breeze billowed the curtains behind him.

Emilio, the son of his mother's sister, was the only Madrileño in the family. Everything about him made Pedro feel provincial, clumsy, and annoyed. Emilio had an apartment and a new Italian two-seater garaged across the street. Emilio was handsome, with small, neat features, properly pale, the fashionable pallor of Castile. His hair, smooth and sleek, capped his head like a glossy helmet. His smooth lips parted and released a thin stream of smoke.

"Had enough? Lunch, I mean . . . not Madrid."

"Yes. It was very good."

Very good. How inadequate. How easily Emilio teased and flattered over the table on his rare visits to Navarre, turning the simple food into a feast, pinking the faces of the women, bending even his father to a rare smile. Only two years older, Emilio now somehow demonstrated a decade of difference between them. Of course, it was expensive tailoring from some shop on the Gran Vía, imported tobacco, nonchalant familiarity with the members of this and that *tertulia* at this café and that club, surface only, like the veneer of a few courses in history and philosophy at the University before he had grown "bored" with the chalky radicals at the Facultad de Filosofía y Letras. But he had changed, really changed, in the last year. The languid gentility had dried to a controlled, almost taut alertness. Had Emilio really changed or was he just a weaver of phrases? Had he, in truth, been "reformed" as he claimed by the Falange . . . the party he had "fled forward to" as he had written in a letter now more than a year old? Or had he come to use the opinions of the Fascists as he used his barber to straighten his hair? As much as he could, Emilio had made himself the mirror of José Antonio. When Emilio said "he," "him," "his," it meant only one man: José Antonio Primo de Rivera, son of the dead dictator and founder of the Phalanx Party.

"You'll be off this afternoon, then?"

"Yes."

"*Basta.* No more questions. Come, let's go out and look at the beast while the *chacha* cleans all this away. Have a cigarette? Tobacco *rubio*, from England. But I forget. Your father forbids it, doesn't he? That's something. You'll never know how much I wished my father had been like that. Forbid? He didn't know the word. Decent. Traditional. I had no help at all, you see, in making my life. I just drifted. Until I met *him*, of course. Then, I knew. And so it didn't matter that Papa had been . . . how does your father put it? . . . *the disappointing one*, that's it. In fact, the scandal of the family. Come on."

Emilio slipped through the curtains. His heels tocked on the tiled balcony. He flicked a handkerchief on the rail before setting his elbow and staring down into the street, eight floors below. Music, distorted and loud, a wrangle of brass, lifted on the breeze.

"These people are determined to ruin the siesta, that's for sure. Well, there we can agree with the Socialists. The tradition of indolence is one Spanish trait that must be abolished. By governmental edict, I suppose. *Abajo la siesta, arriba el trabajo!* I'll propose it at the meeting tonight. You'll come, of course. Or did Papa, el Conde, forbid that, too?"

Pedro joined his cousin at the railing. Emilio smoked, staring down into the street.

"No, *tío pesado.* He's more willing that I had my brains twisted by you and your friends than my morals corrupted at Chicote's."

"Oh, *no one* goes to Chicote's any more."

Emilio lit a fresh cigarette from the stub he pinched between his thumb and forefinger. He dropped the stub.

"May it drop down your neck, comrade . . ."

Pedro looked down into the street.

A sluggish blue serpent, flecked here and there with placards and banners. Emilio dropped a familiar hand on his shoulder.

"There it is, Pedrito. Doesn't look so bad from up here. The beast. The *mono*, minus the *sabio*. The monkey without wits. From here, just so many bodies in blue. With a single aircraft, a few bombs, eh? Would you care, really *care*? But is that the right way? *He* would say no, and in such a way that you'd be nodding that what's easiest is seldom best. You don't guide a beast with bombs. No. You put a harness on it."

"You have a harness from here to Puerta del Sol, Emilio?"

"A figure of speech. You Navarrese are so literal, if I may say so. It's one of your strengths, of course, and we need that. But you know what I mean. The Spanish animal *wants* a harness . . . really. That's what it's bred for. I say that the Spaniard knows and wants the bit and the check-rein, a tight stable, and good oats. You follow me? Because the Spanish worker is good. Yes, good. Good. I grant you he is confused, seduced, poisoned by his so-called leaders of this so-called Republic. Look, look at them in their collective costume."

Pedro stared down, dizzied by the height. The long lines of blue began to move, snaking forward. He strained to catch the melody that blared and echoed.

"Huh. 'The Marseillaise.'"

"Very popular, despite an abominable translation. Dressed in shapeless bags of blue coveralls, bawling out the words. Hardly the garment for the descendants of Conquistadores, the children of El Cid."

"You are . . . romantic."

"Am I? Then tell me. Do you believe in a Spain that is a nation of Panzas? A Madrid, the capital of an empire, filled with sandaled Sanchos all buttering their turnips with the fine words of Prieto and the rest of the simple-minded Marxists?"

Pedro straightened, shaking off his cousin's hand.

"We think . . ."

"I know."

"May I have your permission to finish?"

"You have. A true Carlist is finished when he begins. The king. Restore the king. I know it. He, too, agrees."

"Does he?"

"And we understand you, Pedro. Listen. We believe, like you, that there can be no Spain, no *real* Spain until the government is legitimized."

"The last elections, then?"

"They weren't *made* well. You know what I mean. Who can take the elections seriously? Does the burro vote on what field he will plow, the bull on which plaza he will die in? To hell with the elections! Spain is organic. Worker and entrepreneur, priest *and* poet, worker *and* manager. The Church and the crown *and* the Party!"

"Bravo. That's us. The Carlists."

"To you, forgive me, the king is all. We stand for an additional, meaningful ideology, the past *and* the future. When I say we must make a harness for the beast down there, I'm not forgetting that the bit terminates with the loop of the reins, just as the reins clip to the bit. Spain is not many, but *all* . . . Poh! I'm ranting, listen to me rattle on . . ."

Emilio relaxed, shook his sleek head, and puffed his cigarette.

"Too many meetings, I guess. Too many posters."

Pedro smiled and shrugged. Emilio paced away to a low chair beneath the striped awning and dropped into it, shaking his head again.

"You mean what you say, Emilio."

"We do. Exactly."

"It's good to listen to you. I'll be your stupid country cousin, and you can stuff me with your propaganda, a whole bellyful."

Emilio frowned slightly and pushed his handkerchief into his sleeve. "We're . . ."

Pedro caught himself. Not even to Emilio, his father had warned. The Falange was not to be trusted. Not yet.

"What?"

"How was Rome?"

Emilio sat up and nodded several times.

"Rome? Very exciting. Things are really moving. The Italian Fascists have taken the steps necessary for national unity. The Bolsheviks have been crushed, squashed like vermin. The Socialists have been—how shall I say it?—reoriented. And the spirit of the young people is wonderful. Wonderful! You'll see how we match it tonight at the meeting."

"And while you were in Italy, the Republic arrested your José Antonio."

"Pedro, what irony! It just shows you how they respect and fear him. Locked up in Alicante, that wretched little town. Of course, we still get his letters and instructions about learning the Fascist system of organization on the provincial level."

"You haven't been very successful in Navarre."

"A little missionary work. You Carlists can't do it all, you know. An alliance on the right is . . . Angela?"

Pedro turned. The girl stood in the open French doors, carrying a tray.

"Will you take the coffee here, señores?"

"Pedro?"

"I must say no. I have to . . ."

"Are you late? Take it away, Angela. We don't want it. Call a taxi. But I forget . . . Primero de Mayo."

"I'll walk."

Emilio waited until the girl left the French doors. Then he raised a dark brow.

"To Calle Alcalá?"

"To . . . find a shop. To buy a rosary. I'm sure there's one nearby."

"*Claro.* You can buy a lot of rosaries with a million and a half pesetas."

"I . . ."

"Tell your proud Papa that he should be more discreet. Was it wise to have his photograph taken at the *feria* . . . with General Mola? Old foxy-face."

They were in the foyer of the apartment. The telephone rang. The corner of Emilio's mouth jerked. He took Pedro's hand.

"*Ciao!* . . . And give my respects to Colonel Bravo."

"The colonel. I mean . . . I'm not . . ."

"We're old friends. Of a sort, you know. He thinks the Falange is a student club. They all do."

"I'm buying a rosary."

"His daughter, then. A little convent-pigeon, all soft feathers and big eyes."

"*Suerte.* Good luck. You know about the army, though. They think they don't need us."

"And you think you don't need *them.*"

Pedro ran down the marble stairs. He could hear the sound of a band playing out in the street. He ran down the spiral stairs into the music, whistling along with the blatting melody . . . Primero de Mayo, the First of May.

"Colonel Bravo, *por favor?*"

"Not here."

The porter stared past Pedro out into the Calle Alcalá. A group of Anarchists in their red and black arm bands paraded slowly past, singing:

> "Son of the people, your chains oppress you.
> This injustice cannot go on."

"But I was to meet him here. I had an appointment."

The porter nodded, still looking out at the passing workers. He tugged once on the iron grate, reassuring himself that it was locked.

"Then where does he live? I *must* see him!"

"I regret to say that I have not the honor of knowing who you are, señor."

"If your life is a world of grief,
Instead of being a slave, it is better to die!"

Pedro fumbled a card from his wallet and poked it through the bars of the grate. The porter read it, his lips moving. His eyebrows lifted.
"Forgive me, señor . . ."
"*Está bien.* His address, man?"
The porter drew a stubby pencil from his pocket and began to write on the back of the bit of pasteboard. His tongue slid along his lip as he wrote.

"Worker! Worker!
You shall suffer no longer . . . no longer!"

"They certainly can sing, these uncles."
"Eh, what? Oh . . . yes, and that's what they do best, you know. C.N.T. The colonel calls them Canalla ni Trabajadores. Very witty, no?"
"Is it far?"
"Not far. You go left until you reach . . ."
"*The oppressor . . .*"
"Damn them! Why can't they sing somewhere else? Keep to the right . . . *a la derecha,* señor."
Pedro laughed.
"To the right, of course!"

"Arise, loyal people,
At the cry of social revolution!"

The porter shook his head slowly.
"*Madre mía.* What is the nation coming to?"

The building was narrow and old. Pedro stepped through the archway into a cramped patio. A cracked, empty fountain stood in the center of a square of faded tiles in an imitation Moorish fashion. The colonel lived on the third floor. There was no porter, no elevator. A flight of stairs, foot-grooved and gritty, rose up into a darkness. Pedro sat on the lip of the fountain and squeezed his left boot. All this walking in new boots had raised a blister the size of a *duro* on his heel. For this sort of business he should have brought along his tennis shoes. He felt hot and uncertain as he glanced around. The windows opening on the patio were all shuttered, but he felt certain that he was watched. He kneaded his right boot. A blister there, too.
Remember, Pedro, that the military is a caste. They always have been. Their oath of loyalty to the Republic means nothing to most of them.

So, too, they will not bind themselves to us. They have their generals . . . Sanjurjo, Goded, and the little fat one, Franco. In our province, General Mola. You're making an offer of support, that's all. When they rise, we will aid them. We have agreed to that . . . but in a very loose fashion. And that is all. What we must know is the time . . . the month and the day. How soon? How soon? That is what you must bring back from Madrid."

Yes, Papa.

It has been very expensive. It is not cheap to bribe, to purchase information, I should say, from the military. But we have agreed to pay the debts of a certain Colonel Bravo. He is the man I was to meet before this idiocy of a liver began to . . . you know.

Yes, Papa.

You will not speak with him of this directly.

No? How?

You will speak with him about wine.

Wine, Papa?

Listen well, hijo mío. Any word or words he says twice . . . that is the signal . . . the code words of the conspiracy. For that we agreed to provide a dowry for his daughter, believe it or not . . .

Then I'll marry her and get the money back.

I trust you are joking?

After a fashion, Papa . . .

No member of our class would unite himself with the daughter of an Iscariot.

Yes, Papa . . .

Pedro stood up and brushed the seat of his pants. Well, there was no point in waiting. The pieces of silver had been paid. And now it was his duty to get full value for the Carlist faction of Navarre. He climbed the stairs, hobbling and leaning on the gritty banister, up to the third floor and pressed the bell beneath the polished slip of brass that said only BRAVO.

The door jerked open. Pedro pushed past a young girl in some sort of uniform. He held his card out to her.

"Here, chacha. Tell the colonel I'm here, eh?"

"I beg your pardon?"

"Listen, guapa, I'm late. Tell him . . ."

"You wish me to carry this to my father, señor?"

"Your . . ."

"Claro, my father!"

"María Santísima . . ."

He looked at the girl closely. He had done it, really done it. Bravo's now-dowried daughter, and he had thought she was the maid!

"It's not your fault. And it's not the first time, either. What are people to think? You and your *María Santísima* . . . Just *look* at me!"

Pedro felt his blush. He shifted from foot to foot, blinking and stammering, *bu-buh-buh*, unable to speak a sensible word.

"You're right. I *look* like the maid! He won't even let me have a mirror!"

The girl's harsh whisper, shaky with bitterness, whetted on the dull walls of the little, dim hall. She glared at him and gnawed furiously at the tip of her thumb, then tore her hand from her pale lips and swatted at the drab garment buttoned snug at her throat that fell, unbelted nearly to her ankles. Pedro could make out a few words in Latin embroidered on her collar . . . the motto of the convent Emilio had spoken of.

"It's the light, Señorita Bravo, believe me. If I had but the grace and wits to look . . ."

She thrust her face up to his. Startled, he stepped back and banged the door closed, bounded forward against her and clutched at her to keep her from falling.

"At what? My hair? They make us keep it like this. They have awful little caps they make us wear. The first Mother Superior a million years ago had scrofula or something and so we have to . . ."

". . . at your face, I should have known I was in the presence of a lady."

She seemed completely unaware that they were almost embracing. Pedro gasped and snatched his hands away from her shoulders.

"Lady. Our Lady of the Sorrows. See? Up here. The perfect name. Just perfect. You're the one from Navarre. Right? I thought so. Do you have any sisters?"

"Uhhh . . . yes, three, in fact. María, Concepción and Teresa."

"*Me llamo Carmen.*"

"Enchanted, señorita. Pedro Alemany *y*—"

"I know, I know. He's furious with you."

"Who?"

"My father, Don Pedro, my *father!*"

"I had to walk."

"He hates to be kept waiting. He was shouting just a minute ago."

"May I see him, please? It's very . . ."

"You know why he brought me here? Today, I mean. He heard something at the club . . ."

"I went there. They said he was . . ."

"Here. *Claro.* Where else does he go? To see me? Come on. The F.A.I., they were going to raid us, at the convent, you know. They're the Anarchists, a secret terrorist group. I said I hoped they did. Pzooop! Here I am. And he won't hire anybody. And so I have to stand around like an imbecile in this ugly rag and open the door for him! I haven't anything else to wear!"

Pedro nodded, completely bewildered. He whispered back to her, "That's a pity. There are some nice shops here, too. In Madrid, I mean . . ."

"I have a black dress. Two years old. It fits like a sausage skin and it's right up to—it's too short."

How long were they to stay like this, wrestling about and whispering like children in this bare box of a hall? Every time he moved, she rushed at him, waving her hands around. A real Juana *la Loca*. Some convent pigeon! Emilio must have met her during Holy Week in Seville.

"*Qué lástima* . . . that's a pity, señorita . . ."

He had felt her slenderness underneath the drab sack that covered her. She was standing so close to him that he could look down on the neat, bluish part in her thick, curly hair. She half-turned at some noise in the apartment. Her hair was pinned flat above small, very pink ears and drawn in an old-fashioned bun at the back of her neck. She spoke without looking at him, her harsh whisper jerked at him out of the corner of her pale lips.

"What's it like? Outside. He has the front room. Been there all morning. Watching. Like a cat at a birdcage. I haven't been able to see a thing. Any fights? Shootings?"

"God forbid. No, it's very quiet. Streets full of people carrying big pictures of Largo Caballero and Lenin. They sing a lot."

"I heard. You know the joke about him?"

"Lenin? What's funny about Lenin? These people *mean* it."

"The other one. That he's *muy largo*, all right . . . very slow-moving . . . but *no caballero* . . . no gentleman. That's funny, eh?"

"Very."

The pun was stale, months old. It must be a pretty well-run convent Bravo kept her locked up in.

"You don't look like any wine dealer to me."

"I am, I assure you . . ."

Pedro leaned against the wall, trying to ease his hot, puffed feet.

"And you're not army, either. I can always tell them."

"I'm sure you can. Will your father the Colonel see me, please?"

"Don't be so nervous."

"I'm not."

"You always rattle your fingers on walls like that?"

"Please, I . . ."

"It's very safe here. The whole building is filled with retired officers. It's a regular barracks."

"You must find that very reassuring."

"I find it very, very boring . . . oh-oh . . ."

A slow, firm step sounded from the back room of the apartment. The girl's hand shot out and stabbed Pedro in the chest twice as a bell pinged. She nodded and jerked out whispered words to Pedro.

"Thinks . . . not dignified to yell at me . . . Watch."

She folded her arms and leaned beside Pedro, her head against the wall, her shoulder touching his. He cleared his throat. Emilio had all sorts of stories about girls in convents, incredible anecdotes of delicious perversions and blasphemies. Here she was, rubbing herself against him. Maybe she was . . .

"Carmen? *Carmen!*"

She bounded forward and sank in a deep curtsy, her pink tongue poked out. Pedro snorted with laughter and looked up at the ceiling. She was deranged, this one, no question about it. A real crazy.

"Yes?"

"You may show the young gentleman in now."

"*Con su permiso.*"

Pedro felt a strange pang in his chest. He looked at her as she swirled up out of her curtsy and grinned at him. Her voice when she spoke aloud was as clear and sweet as the call of a mountain thrush. She had dark, wicked, tilted eyes and a mouth he now saw that would be soft as petals to kiss.

"You want to know what he was doing?"

"No."

"Putting on his medals."

"I think, señorita, that he is very wise to keep you locked up."

"Huh! The trouble is, that when they turn the key, I'm on the wrong side of the door."

"Would you rather be out there?"

They both stilled to hear the distant singing and the harsh call of cornets. She bobbed her head, grinning.

"Isn't that where you'll be? You and your comrades. Fighting for Spain?"

"*Claro.* Of course."

"Good. When it starts, look for me."

"Shall I?"

"I'll be the one in riding breeches kissing the wounds of a dying Anarchist."

"That's not funny, it's disgusting."

"When we at the convent talk about forgiving our enemies, we really *mean* it! . . . You should see your face, Don Pedro! You know what? You have no sense of humor. Come, this way."

She led him down a narrow, mean slot and left him at the only open door, ran on into the kitchen, curtsied again, and clapped the door shut, startling the smile from his face. He cleared his throat, wiped his palms on his lapels and stepped gingerly into the room.

Like the rest of the apartment, the room was small and ill-lit. The tile floor was clean and waxed but bare. On the walls hung a cavalry saber, a gilt crucifix, and a small, poor painting of a plump-faced young woman in a mantilla.

He was not easy to get at, this Colonel Bravo. Fond of sherry, but seldom beyond moderation. And despite years in Morocco no . . . no womanizer, if you take my meaning.

I understand, Papa.

Do you? Thanks to Emilio, I have no doubts. One bad grape in a basket, I've always said . . . But he gambles, this Bravo. It is the fashion in the Legion . . . They gamble on everything. And so . . .

I see, Papa.

"Have I the high honor of receiving the eldest son of the Conde de Gualvidal?"

Pedro bowed, not taking his eyes off the tall, broad-shouldered man standing before the shuttered windows. The colonel wore his hair cropped close, after the German fashion. His daughter had been quite correct. A spangle of medals hung on the colonel's dark jacket, a short-tailed Tyrolean coat with pale piping and buttoned cuffs. A hand of Patience lay spread on the desk, the discard pile neatly centered on a small Bible. The colonel gestured stiffly at a wooden chair. The colonel wore white cotton gloves, indoors, on this first day of May.

"I have the honor of addressing Colonel Bravo?"

"*Retired* colonel . . . and that by the grace of the minister of this thing that calls itself a Republic . . . retired, Don Pedro."

"But not inactive."

"Señor, I still see my duty and I do it."

"As does my father."

"May God shine on his endeavors in Navarre."

"And His rays reach you here in the capital . . ."

"The vineyards of your father?"

"They flourish. More even than last year."

"Indeed? More than last year. That is good indeed. Will you take a glass. I have an amontillado, dry as the flint of a musketeer. You are your father's son, with a Navarrese palate, I am certain."

"Perhaps later. It is warm in the streets, Colonel. And crowded."

"I have seen all that from my window. The police have kept order, at least, if not decency."

"We were talking of my father's vineyard."

"Yes, we were, señor. But first, your hand."

Pedro felt the dry pressure of the white gloved fingers. He matched the colonel's grip. They stood, face to face, crushing each other's hand.

He has many images of himself, this Bravo. Gentleman, warrior, patriot, Jesuit diplomat, Monte Carlo plunger. And he is, like many of his brother officers, a Germanophile. He has not heard the Italian proverb: He who loves an Austrian will die of carelessness. Hitler, the new Chancellor, is an Austrian.

Yes, Papa.

The colonel, satisfied apparently, released Pedro's hand.

"Seat yourself, Don Pedro."

"I will stand."

"Of course. Quite as you wish. You seemed tired, that's all."

"Not a bit. The crop this year will be nearly double the estimate."

Colonel Bravo stared with eyes that did not believe.

"Splendid."

"Much of this is due to the new machinery . . . from Italy."

"*Las máquinas.* They arrived in good working order?"

"I have been asked to inform you that the first tests were completely successful."

"In the tests, machines are always quite successful. When you take them to the fields with untrained hands, certain problems tend to reveal themselves."

"We anticipate no problems."

"I hope your optimism will prove to be infectious. These new machines will allow you to extend your operations outside of Navarre?"

That was it. The question that Mola, commander in the northern provinces, wanted to know. Would the Carlist units, trained and well-equipped, maneuver beyond the boundaries of the province?

When he asks it, give him an answer, so . . . sideways. Has José Antonio promised the support of the Falange? If so, has the army accepted this support? Find out, if you can. If not from Bravo, then from Emilio.

How, Papa?

You have five thousand pesetas. That will buy a good deal of brandy and champagne. Like father, like son. How is your liver, by the way?

"That depends, Colonel. On the weather."

"In Navarre?"

"No. In Alicante."

"The weather there is turning. Becoming better."

"And in Andalusia?"

"Very promising."

"And in Africa? Anything new or unusual about the grapes in Morocco?"

The colonel shrugged stiffly. His medals chinked.

"Nothing new, nothing unusual . . . *Sin novedad, sin novedad . . .*"

Pedro's heart bounded. That was it! *Sin novedad.* The insurgents' secret code. He felt faint, limped to the chair, and sat down. His head buzzed softly and his mouth was dry. The colonel walked stiff-legged to the desk. His gloved hand brushed over the hand of Patience. His fingers stole out and furtively moved a card from one rank to the next. He was cheating.

"There will be four shipments, then?"

"Four, yes, Don Pedro."

"And the date? The day and month is of much importance to my father and . . . his associates."

"It is not yet possible to give the date. You know, of course, how the harvest of grapes is. The action of the weather for a few days and suddenly all is ripe."

"But the month? One always can predict the month. From the day of the first blossoms on the vines."

"The first blossoms? Ah, long, long ago, señor. These grapes have grown very slowly."

"But steadily . . . like money in the bank."

The colonel jerked his head. His eyes glared for a second, before he mastered himself. Pedro felt an inner smile. The colonel had bull-broad shoulders, true. And, true, that meant strength, dangerous strength.

More meat means more room to plant the banderillas. Don't be easy with him. He's not the papal nuncio.

Yes, Papa.

"The month, Colonel Bravo?"

"In July."

"If we wait any longer, these grapes will rot, Colonel. But that is nothing new . . . *sin novedad.*"

"No . . . nothing unusual . . . *sin novedad.*"

The army would strike at the Republic in July, then! On the given day, he would stand with his father when they offered the Carlist volunteers to General Mola. On that day in July . . . *two months only!* . . . the "Italian machinery" would begin its work, cutting across the bull-hide shape of Spain, from Burgos to Madrid!

"Some fresh air, Don Pedro?"

"If it would not inconvenience you, Colonel Bravo . . ."

The colonel moved to the window and plunged his gloved hands down on the shutter-hoist. It racketed up, and sunlight shot into the room, with music and the murmur of workers still in the city streets and their song.

> "Son of the people, your chains oppress you.
> This injustice cannot go on.
> If your life is a world of grief,
> Instead of being a slave, it is better to die!"

Colonel Bravo rapped his gloved fist on the table, scattering the cards.

"Yes, better to die!"

"A choral group will never fight, Colonel. They have no will, no discipline."

The colonel released the shutter-hoist. The wooden slats roared down, sealing the room back to dim coolness and quiet. Pedro was shocked to discover himself standing, his fists clenched, and belly muscles taut. Colonel Bravo rocked on his heels, smiling slightly, and patting his gloved hands together. The floor was spattered with cards, bright rectangles on the polished tiles.

"Tell your father, the respected Conde de Gualvidal, to prepare his machines well. For when all is ready, we shall begin the harvest."

"In July . . . Thanks be to God."

"And we will crush and crush and *crush!*"

"The Spanish earth is thirsty. It can drink much."

"But I had nearly forgotten, Don Pedro! Our glass of amontillado! We will take it in the next room."

Pedro nodded. He had found out what he had been sent to discover. Why not chat awhile and taste a glass?

"You know, Don Pedro, it was during the last campaigns against the Riffs that I had the opportunity of witnessing the total absence of fear under enemy fire. Complete self-mastery!"

"Indeed? In the Legion, no doubt."

"One of the officers. A major in those days. Franco."

"Franco. We have heard of Franco, naturally."

"Now on duty overseas. In exile, actually, from this republic. They have good cause to send him to the Canary Islands. And he has good cause to . . ."

"Yes?"

"Nothing. One moment while I call the maid to clean up this disorder. Carmen? *Carmen!* Come here at once!"

Pedro sat down on the chair and stared at the playing cards scattered on the floor of Colonel Bravo's room. Outside, the music pounded in the sun-struck streets of Madrid and the hoarse-voiced crowds called to the *hijo del pueblo.*

Pedro dropped the coin into the slot and heard it fall, the machinery grind and suck. The keys fell and rose as invisible fingers beat out the melody. It seemed to be the only song the mechanical piano could play . . . "Madrid." Over and over, the notes struck against the low ceiling of the bar. Pedro hummed along. The melody pinked on steel bars, a bright chromium dribble. He shook his head.

"Piano, you're loud and fast. But you have no soul . . ."

El sabor que tienen tus verbenas
Por tantas cosas buenas . . .

For lots of good things . . . He had a belly filled with *cordero asado*,
baby lamb with crackle-shiny crust, sweet green peas with bits of onion
and bacon, a salad of lettuce that crushed juicy and crisp, rich with olive
oil and puckery vinegar, bread and Manchego, hard crumbling cheese so
sharp it nipped the tongue . . . and at least a liter of the best Valdepeñas. One could eat in Madrid, even on the first day of May. At least
the cooks and waiters weren't on strike or out parading.

"Da-dum-dum-dum. Da-dum-dum-dum. Da-dum-dum-*dum!* Da-dum-
dum-dum-da-dum-da-*dum!* Madrid . . . Madrid . . . *Madrid!*"

The others at the tables began to pound with their palms and sing,
more or less on key, but lagging behind the steely notes beat out by the
piano.

"*. . . la crema de la intelectualidad . . .*"

Pedro prodded his face gingerly. His cheeks felt stiff, numb-stiff and
warm. He was not used to drowning a meal with *vino tinto*. At home, he
never took more than a single measure poured into the silver goblet
that had been hand-chased for his great-great-grandfather.

He moved his hand to his jacket and touched his wallet. A shout
rose up from the table where Emilio sat.

"*La crema . . . con CAFÉ!*"

One of the waiters in bandit costume, short jacket, sash-topped trousers
and soft boots idled near the mechanical piano. Pedro hissed at him.
The waiter turned his sullen face.

"Take some cognac to the back table there. A whole bottle."

"Fundador?"

"Yes. Bring the bill to me. I'll wait here."

"*Sí, señor.*"

The piano sprinkled the final few notes, churned and stopped. Pedro
leaned on it and squinted through the smoke. They all looked the same,
these Falangistas, in dark suits, vests and striped ties, with smooth,
straight hair, young, eager faces . . . José Antonio fifty times. From his
prison cell in Alicante he played on them. His invisible hands rammed
and rippled over them and out came the same sounds, the same chorded
confidence at trip-hammer tempo, insistent, repeated and louder, harder,
surer every time. The sight and sound of Emilio and his Fascist friends
gave Pedro a heart-drooping sadness in his chest, a slew of melancholy so
strong he felt tilted, unbalanced. Their sharp, sure faces, elegant dress
and quick, puppety hands threaded to Alicante. Their voices, staccato-

hysteric, snatched through the blue, drifting smoke. Fifty faces gashed with smiles.

The meeting had been a great success. Ordered, meticulous reports and directives, motions, nominations, votes without dissension. A sense of compactness, cartridge-pouch unity, prolonged applause for lists of new initiates in Valladolid, Segovia, Ávila, and Toledo. The mass, throat-rumbled, stiff-armed declaration of loyalty to the party and the leader had slipped the leash of menace a notch. A bitter-faced leader of shock brigades loosed them more with his tales of vengeance against Madrid's Red front. Four Party members had been badly beaten by a Communist gang from Vallecas. The enemy leader was known, marked for "direct punitive action." A dozen were selected from a hundred volunteers. The vote was unanimous. The Communist leader called El Asturiano was to die.

Then Emilio had spoken. Even from his seat at the back of the room Pedro had been stirred. Emilio was easy, sardonic, almost negligent at first, then pressed steadily to a measured menace as he clarified two of the Party-leader's famous "Twenty-Seven Points" . . . the program for the renovation of old virtues and implementation of the "organic" design, the sheaf of arrows bound and bundled by human will that would create a new and perfect Spain. The immediate target of this iron-tipped phalanx was the young Communist called El Asturiano. Pedro caught himself nodding and once applauded before he shrank on his seat, angry and fuddled.

Pedro winced and glowered, shaking his head. They were wrong, all wrong in their methods. They lurched in darkness, brandishing slogans, reason gone to rage, whetted to stab. To think that they could so move each other that an auxiliary force of women, mothers, and *novias* had already joined and supported them!

When Emilio finished, glaze-eyed and shouting, the room roared back the Party song, and the chairs danced with the cadenced stamp of glossy feet. Cuff links sparkled on straightened arms as the words lifted from throats snugged with passion and silk cravats:

> "*Cara al sol* . . . *Face to the sun, wearing the tunic*
> *Which yesterday you embroidered.*
> *Death will find me, if it calls me*
> *And I do not see you again* . . .
>
> *Arriba! battalions and conquer—*
> *For Spain has begun to awake!*
>
> *Spain—United!   Spain—Great!*
>
> *Spain—Free!   España—Arriba!*"

And then, with the market-day gravity of cheese wholesalers or wine merchants, they had filed out, arm in arm, to get something to eat and drink.

Now Emilio beckoned to him, lifting his sleek head above the huddled shoulders around the table. The waiter was setting out the cognac glasses. Pedro puffed his lips and walked back to the table. He nodded and smiled uneasily as he slipped between chairs. He was accepted warily, on trust, out of their respect for Emilio, their spokesman. Faces turned to stare briefly, tipped to whisper as he passed. It was natural that they suspected him as a spy. His face was stiff with wine and smiles when he reached his chair.

"We thought you'd slipped out to some bordello."

"Me? No, no. Just listening to the piano . . . It only knows one song."

"We'll teach it some of *ours* . . . but you are offended?"

"No. Of course not . . ."

Pedro grinned and sipped his cognac.

"You like it?"

"Very nice. Strong, eh?"

Emilio shook his head too violently. He was about half drunk, Pedro sensed. He spoke in short spurts and laughed a lot. Pedro heard him begin some story about a woman who had three lovers. He nodded, paying just enough attention to know when to laugh appreciatively, and listened to voices from the next table.

"CAFÉ . . . CAFÉ . . . CAFÉ!"

A waiter glided by the table, bent and refilled the glasses.

"Did you march today, *camarero?*"

The bottle hung suspended over Emilio's glass.

"Yes, Señorito Emilio. I marched."

"U.G.T.?"

"C.N.T., Señorito Emilio. I'm an Anarchist."

Emilio nodded and chuckled.

"Pretty soon you'll be sitting here and I'll be pouring brandy, eh?"

"*Quizás*, Señorito Emilio . . . Perhaps."

"CAFÉ . . . CAFÉ . . . CAFÉ!"

"Emilio? Listen, Emilio, why do they keep yelling for coffee like that? They're all still drinking wine."

"Pedro Inocente. They don't want coffee. You see, what's-his-name here doesn't even pay attention. It's C-A-F-E. For *Camaradas! Arriba Falange Española!* Comrades of the Spanish Phalanx, arise!"

"Oh. A password."

"If you like. We don't have to hide ourselves."

"Right, Emilio. Every day we grow stronger. Why, up in Ávila . . ."

The song from the mechanical piano spiked at Pedro.

When Emilio squirmed around to talk with someone at another table,

Pedro tilted the cognac bottle and filled his cousin's glass. The waiter came by. Pedro snapped his fingers.

"Bring us some Anarchist champagne."

The waiter nodded, unsmiling, and drifted off across the blue-hung room. The song seemed to beat faster, a glittering gallop. Pedro yawned. It must be nearly midnight. One of Emilio's group spoke to him.

"You're from Navarre, eh?"

"Yes, from Navarre."

"How are things up there?"

"*Pues* . . . it goes well."

"That's pretty thick with Carlists up there, I guess."

"Solid. Thick as needles on the pines."

"That's a pity. If they'd come along, we'd really have something."

Pedro nodded and reached for an empty glass.

"Have a Fundador?"

"I'm at another table."

"Between comrades there are no other tables. *Salud!*"

"*Salud!*"

"How many do we have . . . really *have?* I've forgotten."

"Between you and me, we'll have five thousand when it begins. About the same as the Communists . . . minus one, of course."

"Of course . . . minus one."

The night air smelled sweet and pure. Pedro breathed slowly, deeply. The others jostled around him, shaking hands, saluting Emilio, joking and laughing. The sound of their voices rattled and echoed in the dark street. Pedro rubbed his smarting eyes and looked up at the wheeling stars, every one a medal pinned on an angel's breast. How many? Five thousand . . . about as many as the Communists . . . twenty thousand . . .

"*Buenas noches,* Emilio!"

Their faces bobbed around him. Someone shook his hand. Another. The piano jangled its brittle tune out into the darkness.

Suddenly, a body bunted Pedro against the wall. Emilio gave the man, dressed like a worker, a shove with the flat of his hand.

"Your mother!"

"And your grandmother!"

The worker stopped and turned around.

"Say that again?"

"Your grandmother, *trabajador* . . . *traba-joder!*"

The worker crouched and pointed his shiny fist. It rapped twice. Emilio's leg buckled and he sat down in the middle of the street. He picked at his stomach and made a high *uhhhhhhh* in his throat.

Pedro stumbled toward Emilio, tripped and fell forward, his hands flung out. A pistol shot flashed in his face. He jolted down on the stones, his ear ringing. Great playing cards of light fluttered on the street. He heaved up, blowing blood from his broken nose, and clawed at his cousin's jacket.

"Emilio!"

Emilio lay skewed on a card of light, his sleek head profiled in a coronet of bloody mush.

"Aquí Radio Madrid. Presentamos un programa de música popular. Nuestra selección? Unas de las canciones más preferidas en los Estados Unidos . . ."

> I push the first valve down
> The music goes down and round,
> Whoa-ho-ho-ho-ho-ho
> And it comes out here.

In Burgos, the officer cleared his throat.

"General Mola, I ask you for a declaration that you do not intend to rise against the government."

"I give you my word that I shall not launch myself upon an . . . adventure."

"Sixty-one murders in the last month. *Sixty-one!* And ten incidents of looted churches. Who loots churches? Decent Spanish people? No! Anarchists, that's who. Communists and Socialists and all the rabble that run with this republic! And who gives them the matches? Eh? I'll tell you, *amigo mío*, the Russians, the Bolshevik Russians, that's who!"

The telegraph key spit and chattered. The operator jotted the message on the pad, noted the time, and rolled a sheet of paper into his typewriter. He struck a match and lit a cigarette. Squinting against the smoke, he tapped out the message:

SIN NOVEDAD

Colonel Bravo carefully folded his newspaper—the last issue of *Ya* before its publication had been suspended by the government—and dropped it on the seat beside him. The train rolled on toward Seville. The carriage jolted and swayed through a switch, then picked up speed. Colonel Bravo stretched and yawned. How boring it was to travel by train, even first class in a reserved compartment! His hand moved toward his watch pocket. He picked up the newspaper again. The hours would pass. There was no point in looking at a watch. It was a matter of control, self-mastery.

He was dressed in a suit of light linen. His Panama rested on the luggage rack next to the single suitcase containing his uniform, binocular case, belt, holster and pistol. In his breast pocket was a letter of introduction from the Conde de Gualvidal to a wine merchant in a suburb of the city. Everything was in order.

The commander of the *Carabiñeros* General Quiepo del Llano, was also headed for Seville. Not by train. In an open staff car, a Hispano-Suizoa, driven by a chauffeur from garrison to garrison. A tour of inspection. Everything was quite in order, nothing unusual . . . *sin novedad.*

Colonel Bravo smiled. What a coincidence that Quiepo del Llano should have been appointed . . . at practically the eleventh hour . . . some disagreement or difference between him and Mola. Quiepo del Llano, with his fondness for drink. The Conde de Gualvidal with his vineyards in Navarre. A letter of introduction to a wine merchant. It was perfect, perfect!

The document from General Mola he had burned, along with other papers, in the kitchen stove, while the taxi waited in the street. Carmen had taken down his suitcase. The pages curled and crinkled to ash. Colonel Bravo knew every word.

The army would revolt, seizing key positions with the co-operation of the Civil Guards—the Asaltos—Falangists, Carlists, and other groups. The civilian volunteers would play their little parts. By the twenty-second of July . . . five days after the rising . . . the new regime would be installed. A Directory, consisting of a President . . . General Sanjurjo, without question . . . and four officers of the rank of general. Mola, naturally, Goded, the commander in Barcelona, Franco as head of the overseas garrisons and . . . could it be Saliquet? The Cortes would be suspended as a legislative body, the Constitution of 1931 abolished.

Colonel Bravo patted his gloved fingers on the newspaper. He could recall the very words on the pages he had burned. After a certain time devoted to preventive terror, a constituent assembly would be elected . . . How well General Mola had phrased it! . . . "by suffrage in the manner that shall be deemed most appropriate." Curiously, there was a whiff of Alicante and José Antonio in the following paragraphs. Laws not in accord with the "new organic system" . . . Mola must have studied the Falangist documents and proposals with care . . . or was it another sly ruse, a device to pull José Antonio's followers to the side of the insurgent generals . . . temporarily? . . . At any rate, such laws would be abolished also. Redistribution of land would cease, steps taken to weaken the holy orders would cease, the schools would be given back to the priests and nuns. All leftists, all Socialists, all those who . . . another fine phrase of Mola's . . . an admirable prose stylist . . . all those who "received inspiration from abroad" would be classified as outlaws and treated as such.

In five hours, the train would reach Seville. In five days, the Republic

would have been disposed of. In five months, forgotten. In five years?
The rank of brigadier, at least, in return for his loyalty to the army, his
faithful devotion to Spain.

"*Mierda!* You call that a trench? Dig, *dig!* It's not deep enough to piss
in yet! What if they start to shoot?"

A fly fizzed around the sergeant's head. He brushed it away, his green
eyes watching the sun-washed façade of the Residencia. He wondered if
soldiers crouched at the windows. He shrugged. If they were there, they
would shoot or not shoot. If they weren't there, then a trench had been
dug in the square outside the residence of the High Commissioner of
Tetuán. Somebody else's platoon could fill the trench up again.

The sun was baking hot. The Legionarios scraped at the dry dirt. Three
of them already were sprawled unconscious in the shallow pits.

"Water, Tiger? Sergeant . . . some water?"

"You want a drink? Open your mouth and I'll piss in it."

The sergeant pulled his tunic open. Sweat trickled in his beard. The
streets leading into the square were empty. The city lay in silence beneath
the vast, pale Moroccan sky. The shovels clinked as the Legionarios pryed
up cobbles, lengthening the trench. The sun struck off the Residencia,
a white that slit at the eyeballs. A buzzing gem crawled in the damp
tendrils of hair at the sergeant's throat. He walked carefully up to the
trench, shading the fly with his hand.

"Hey, Four Fingers. Sweet or sour?"

"What?"

"See. *La mosca.* Which of my tits will he fly to first? I say sour . . .
for your *duro*, man."

The soldier grinned and dropped his shovel. The others stopped digging.
In the silence, the buzzing of the fly sounded very loud. Four Fingers
nodded.

"You say sour? Why, sweet, then. For a *duro*."

"Let's see it shine."

The bet was more important than the trench. In the Legion, a bet was
more important than anything else. Even a direct order might wait until
a few coins changed hands. One by one the soldiers set down their entrenching tools and rested on the crumble-edged slot they had picked
across the cobbled square. They dried their faces and watched the fly. It
hovered, sizzling and glinting, before the sergeant's scarred belly.

"Tiger?"

"What?"

The Moroccan sun poured down on them.

"Didn't something like this happen back in thirty-one? I don't remember."

Tiger grunted, watching the fly.

"You don't remember. How could you, Shit-for-Brains? Yes, they tried something then. The officers."

"A revolt? What happened. I was in the stockade, Tiger."

"You should still be in the stockade. For always. What happened? We dug some trenches here and there. We got drunk twice in one day. There was some shooting. It didn't last long . . . shhhh . . . here he goes."

"He's going to land. Shut up."

"Where's the *duro*, Four Fingers?"

The soldier sifted a loose handful of shaggy tobacco and flipped the coin between the sergeant's boots.

"It'll be the same, then. Will we cross to Spain?"

"How would I know, *estúpido?* What do you care, for Christ's sake?"

"Remember Asturias? *Cold?* Jesus, you wouldn't believe it! We froze in those fucking mountains. And for what? To shoot some coal miners. For weeks we shot them. It wasn't even a campaign. It was target practice."

"Shut *up*, will you?"

The fly swirled higher. The soldiers watched, rapt, and muttered side bets.

"Sweet. A peseta on sweet."

"Taken. One on the sour."

"Sweet. Even money. Ten? Twenty?"

"Twenty on sweet."

"Come on, *mosca*, tear his right one off."

Four Fingers crept out of the trench and scraped the coins and bills into two piles. He crouched there, his eyes watching the fly. The sergeant glared at him.

"You scare him and I'll kick your balls off."

"There! Shit, he went away."

"Here he comes . . . shh. Easy. Land on sweet, you little mother."

"Sour . . . *Sour!*"

"Tiger?"

"What, for Christ's sake?"

"What's it all about? I mean, what's it *for*, this revolt?"

"What do you care for, man? As long as there's killing and some girls to screw and wine and stuff to steal. Eh?"

"*Shhhh!*"

The men along the trench hushed. The sergeant breathed evenly, slowly. He couldn't see the fly. He held very still. Only the little fly moved under the pale, smiting sky. He felt the fly settle on him and start to crawl. He grinned.

"He tickles."

"*Qué va.* Some revolution. We sweat like pigs and watch flies."

"Shut up. He's moving. Go for the sour!"

"The sweet, *coño*, the sweet one!"

The fly crawled. Some of the soldiers groaned and cursed. The sergeant moved his hand very slowly.

"Everybody satisfied? Fair is fair?"

The sergeant drew in his chin and looked down. The fly crawled over his nipple, just above the blue tattoo. Four Fingers handed out the money to the winners. His silver coin lay between the sergeant's boots. Tiger swung his hand and looked down. A tiny mess of blood and glitter was pasted to his chest hairs. He pulled up his tunic and drove the buttons through the sweat-soaked cloth. He bent and picked up the coin. A liter's worth of *vino tinto* at the canteen for the next three days. He flipped the coin and caught it.

"All right, you donkey turds, back to work. No water until the trench is waist-deep."

The soldiers began to dig again. One of the unconscious ones twitched. Tiger kicked him.

"Get up, you lazy bastard."

The soldier groaned and lay still. Tiger yawned. It was a dull business, this revolt.

> *I push the middle valve down—*
> *The music goes down around—*
> *Below, below, below—de-deleedee ho-ho-ho*
> *Listen to the jazz come out . . .*

The static crackled and fried like eggs dropped in hot oil. He twisted the knob and turned down the volume. Nothing but music on. American jazz. Even that was better than the marches they played for hours, without pity, on Radio Moscow. He walked to the open window and leaned on the sill. Down in the courtyard, some barefoot children played tag. In the winter their feet were bare, too. Lice grew in their hair, and their faces were dotted with flea bites. How old were they? Maybe nine or ten years. They were stunted, with weak, rickety legs and the pinched, addled faces of old men. He counted them. Nine. Maybe four would live through the next winter. A lot of babies died early. Then they seemed to be all right for maybe five years. After that, they went any time. Died or ran away to one of the other *barrios* to steal until they got caught. If they ran away, they never came back. What for? What was there in Vallecas to come back to? Lice, fleas, a stove without charcoal, no food.

At least the kids in Russia were well fed. Fat, even, from too many potatoes. But the government there looked after them. They were the future . . . the soldiers, Party members and workers.

We need money and food. How many young people in the slum of Vallecas were strong enough to carry a gun, march, and fight? Could you eat pamphlets? *Propaganda frita*, the worker's supper. And these kids played together. That meant their fathers were all members of the same union. The Anarchists most likely. Every few days, they had rock fights with Socialist kids down the street. Their fathers spent the long, hot days demonstrating, petitioning the government and shooting at each other . . . instead of at their class-enemies. Where was Voget? He was late, as usual. Half a lifetime in the Party, and he never even came to cell meetings on time. But why should he? Voget was Voget.

The kids froze, looking up the alley. Someone whistled.

He reached into the open bureau drawer beside him and took out the Luger pistol. He thumbed off the safety and held it just below the window sill. He whistled down to the kids, the first few notes of "Cara al Sol." Three of them shook their heads. Not the police then. He whistled the chorus of "Hijo del Pueblo." One of them shook his head. The others didn't know. They looked up at him.

He held out his left hand and rubbed the fingers together. They nodded and ran into the alley, yelping like puppies. He stepped to one side, hefting the revolver. It was a good angle. The stranger would step out of the alley, enfiladed on two sides.

He could see other faces in three windows across the court. A finger waved from side to side. *We can't see him.* The index finger out straight and stabbed down. *You shoot first.*

He clenched his left fist and held it out. *Okay.*

His small room seemed filled with the weak noise from the radio. It was stupid to turn the sound down. What would cover the noise of the shots? That's why he had them steal the radio for him the day after he went into hiding, the second day of May.

The kids spilled back out of the alley, running from side to side, screeching for pesetas. Not one of them looked up at the open windows. Well-trained. A bar of chocolate each tonight, if somebody had to steal a pocketbook or lift a wallet on the Gran Vía.

The man stepped into the courtyard. It was Voget.

He looked up and waved his hat. The kids looked up, and he signaled for them to get away. They scattered, screeching. Voget's heavy steps sounded on the stairs. He was stopped at the landing by the Tarradella brothers. Then, he came on up, slow and puffing.

"*Salud*, comrade!"

"*Salud* yourself. This is the pig house you hide in, eh? It stinks here, you know. Or do you? It took me two whole days to find you. What have you done to these people, *chico*? They sent me halfway to Toledo. How are you?"

Voget flung his suitcase on the bed and sat down. He fanned his damp face with his hat and lit a cigarette.

"*Qué calor!* Heard anything?"

"Rumors. The government ordered out some ships. Ramón Mola, the general's brother, is back in Barcelona. The Anarchists under Durrutti are standing by. Some Falangists have been arrested here and there. Nothing on the radio but this stupid music."

"Better than the love-sick cats usually screaming on the radio down here."

"You were in Barcelona?"

"Perhaps. Let's say I saw Stepanov. *Salud!*"

"*Salud!*"

"My God, you call this wine? I saw Stepanov. He would like the list."

"What makes you think I've got a list?"

"Because you slipped out of this hole and got to Valencia. For the meeting there. You're El Asturiano now, you know . . . a big shot. Stepanov knows you were there. To meet with the Socialists. Well?"

"True. There was a lot of talk about a *coup d'état* . . . you know how Socialists love to explain things like that in French . . . proves they've done their reading. Some of the other comrades went so far as to make a verbal agreement. To fake a rising on the Right, bluff the government into handing out arms to the workers . . ."

"You're kidding!"

"No. We have some dreamers here, comrade. They think Casares Quiroga is Kerensky. It comforts them to babble about the Petrograd Soviet."

Voget groaned and shook his head.

"I wish I had been there."

"I wish you had been, too, Paul."

"I was *in* Petrograd in seventeen. I *saw* . . . Well, forget that. It went like that in Valencia, eh? A *coup d'état* . . . oh, that's lovely. I'd like to see Stepanov's face when he hears that one. What did you get? I'm serious. What did you get? It was a hell of a risk to leave here. It's tight. No one can get through. Your own boys were on me the minute I left the Atocha railway station. Good organization, *chico*."

"I got . . . a list. From Álvarez del Vayo. A list of the Socialist Youth."

"You gave him?"

"A list of the Communist Youth."

"You idiot!"

"Not me. I got their list first . . . and a merger."

"It went through, then? You picked them up? . . . *all* of them?"

"Let's say the Socialist Youth elected to merge with the Communist Youth."

"And the leader? You?"

"Me."

"The Falangists knew what you were up, to, then! That's why they were going to kill you."

"No. I think they just wanted to."

"It was a stupid thing, shooting that *Falangista*."

"Would you have been happier if he had shot me?"

"Why did you do it yourself, Paco?"

"I need the practice."

"What if . . ."

"It was easy. He had a splendid funeral. We photographed them all out at the cemetery. We have a list of them, too. Both lists are in the drawer there. Take them to Stepanov. Make him happy."

Voget walked to the bureau and took out the lists. He held up the pistol.

"How many of these pop guns do you have, Jefe de Guerrillas?"

"Fifty-three, Oberleutnant. And three cases of Mills bombs. Where are the rifles, Paul?"

Voget closed the drawer and waved at the open window at the city.

"In the Montaña barracks. Everyone knows that. When it starts, go get them."

"Don't fool around, Paul. Where are the rifles? Stepanov promised . . ."

"You spoke with him?"

"Not *directly* . . ."

"Ah. Not *directly*."

"There *are* no rifles! That Russian pig!"

"You don't like our Soviet friends, comrade? Everywhere in Spain I see signs and banners that reassure me that the Soviet Union is the friend of the Spanish worker. And you, El Asturiano, leader of Communist Youth in the Madrid area, don't believe this in your heart and soul? Why, that's heresy! That's scandalous! That's . . . not unintelligent, in fact. You learned a few things in Leningrad, then. I thought you might."

"Will you be serious, Paul? Sit down. You make me nervous."

"I make *you* nervous? My God, you sit for two months in this stinking hole, not a word from you. I've got a man at the cemetery day and night looking over the stiffs dumped by the Anarchists, checking to see if one of them is you and you can sit there without even sweating on this day like a furnace and you say I make *you* nervous! Gives me the creeps just to look at your skinny, ugly face."

"Relax, Papa. I'll tell you something."

"I'm relaxed. I'm a pool of wax. A glass of jelly."

"Get back to Stepanov and the others . . . the ones you won't tell me about. Get them to *send the rifles!* Can you telegraph him?"

"Perhaps."

"Something's up at the Ministry of War. We have a comrade at the Telefónica. Many, many phone calls out of Madrid. A couple of ships are standing by. Telegrams from garrison to garrison . . . all with the same message."

Voget nodded and sucked dolefully on his cigarette.

"And you're just waiting?"

"Until I'm told what to do, yes. And given the stuff to do it with. Let's start with ten thousand rifles and a quarter of a million rounds."

"Dreamer. It would never get past Durrutti's gang in Barcelona. You're quite right, though. The revolt has begun. We got a phone call from Tangier this morning. Larache, Tetuán, Melilla, and Cueta, all gone over to the army. Tangier claims they heard a broadcast from the Canaries. Franco proclaimed martial law there. It's started."

"It's started. The government . . ."

"Will try to go on governing. As long as there is a telephone number they haven't tried, they will make telephone calls. Then, they will . . ."

The radio crackled and fizzed. Both men stood up, looking across the room at it.

"*Aquí Radio Madrid. Radio Madrid. Attention, people of Spain! Keep tuned to this station! Do not turn your radios off. Rumors are being circulated by traitors to the Republic! Keep tuned in!*"

"I think I *had* better send a telegram to Stepanov. The worst he can say is no. He'll have to check with Moscow. It'll take at least a day, maybe two."

"Two days? We can both be dead in two days."

"*Qué va.* Then you won't *need* the rifles, *chico!*"

They looked at each other and laughed, Voget with deep, belly-ripping snorts that brought tears to his gray lids.

"I . . . didn't think that . . . was funny, you know . . . until I said it. I'll send the telegram. Okay? But I'll get a train to France. I'll get some rifles for you, *chico.*"

"Good. The sooner we're in the streets the better."

"Tonight?"

"We can't do anything tonight. We'll issue what we've got and hit the nearest police station before the C.N.T. does. Ship the rifles to me. Use my real name. By truck."

"*D' acuerdo.* Get your people organized and ready to fight. I'll get through to Stepanov. If the Cueta garrison has really gone over to the rebels, their army will come across the straits at once. They will march on Madrid. Everyone knows that."

Paco stood up and gazed out of the window.

"Let them come. We'll be right here, waiting for them. Tell all the comrades that. We will fight. Give us the weapons and we'll make Madrid a fortress . . . and the tomb of Fascism."

"Concentrate all your efforts on making the fortress."

"Yes. I know. It will be the victors who build the tomb."

The radio fizzled and crackled. Music blared out into the room. Voget put on his jacket. Paco slipped his pistol into the pocket of his pants.

I push the other valve down—
The music goes round and round—
Whoa-ho-ho-ho-ho-ho
And it comes out here.

Wan yellow light, like pale and dusty banners streamed from the east windows and reached the altar. The bell tower gonged the half-hour. Padre Ortega stared glumly out into the church. The floor was a great plane of worn stones. From it, two ranks of columns rose and branched into darkness. The church was empty.

"*Ite, missa est.*"

He tried to make the call full, reassuring. His voice returned, a flat, bitter little echo. He sighed, genuflected before the altar, rose, and walked slowly down the center aisle. He looked at the first column, smoothed and slutted nearly black by countless hands as high as his shoulder. Today, this morning, nobody in Pilarmadre had come to take the Host. The two boys, the acolytes, had not served now in two days. From Pilarmadre to the provincial capital at Teruel to Zaragoza in the north, the people waited, watched and listened, not sure yet whether the churches would be sanctuaries, fortresses, or slaughterhouses. The mountains and valleys of Aragón were silent beneath the morning sun. Smoke from breakfast fires wavered up. Families sat at tables littered with coffee cups and bits of fried bread, communicants of a new order. They waited patiently for the voice to reach across Spain to them, the seven o'clock news broadcast by Radio Madrid.

Oretga stood for a moment on the steps of the church. The clouds brushed on the mountain tops, broke, and scattered. It would be another hot, dry day. The town of Pilarmadre waited, alerted and silent, each faction watching for the first move. The shock and confusion, hours of fuddled café rantings and scribbled petitions was over. The children and livestock had been penned up, extra food cooked, weapons gathered. The town Padre Ortega had been sent to serve had, overnight, gone from uneasy truce to a state of siege.

The priest walked slowly through the streets of Pilarmadre. The market place was empty, the stalls barren. At the corner, the *panadería* was shut; there was no belly-lifting odor of fresh white loaves. No herd of whicky-tailed, slit-eyed goats jostled outside the *lechería*, waiting to have their dusty udders milked into gleaming copper cans. The café chairs were stacked; the awnings were cranked snug against the corrugated iron shutters. The cement plant, now U.G.T. headquarters, had not sent up its feather of steam and shrill morning whistle. No files of workers hurried toward the wooden gates. They were already inside, told off into militia companies, waiting and listening.

Padre Ortega turned left. He heard the first shatters of static and then the hard, rapping sound of speech. He stopped and listened, but the radio was buried deep in one of the buildings. He could not distinguish the words, but the staccato urgency drove him on. He hurried now, but without direction, half running through the empty streets. He must be someplace, see what could be done to stop it, make them all wait, find a radio, telephone Teruel or his parents in Málaga. Breathless, confused, prodded by the voice that seemed everywhere, muttering behind shuttered windows, he ran through the streets that lay silent as a nightmare.

Outside the town hall, he saw them. Two Matford touring cars painted brown. A machine gun mounted on the balcony. One young Falangista there with the gun crew. The boy was raising the gold and scarlet banner. In a doorway, two Civil Guards with their long green capes and visorless, bicorn leather hats. They carried rifles with fixed bayonets. Several dozen soldiers—was that a platoon?—were in position around the railroad station. One of the Guardias saw him, smiled and beckoned.

"*Hola, Padre! Arriba España! Viva Cristo Rey!*"

The second Civil Guard pointed his rifle. Padre Ortega stepped back two paces.

"That's the new one, the Red from Asturias. Come here, Father!"

Ortega turned and ran, his head down, shoulders hunched against the bullet. They didn't shoot. He skidded into an alley, waited until his heart stopped pounding and then doubled back, skirting the Plaza Mayor, and headed for the cement factory. Then, very close, he heard the first sound of shots.

At the mouth of the alley, a rivulet of blood trickled over the stones, shooting and darting along the fissures and wagon grooves. The shots came regularly, one every few seconds, the flat smack cutting through the wrestling of flesh and monotonous cursing. In the arcade, a group of soldiers were shooting goats.

The kicking, skinny-legged animals were dragged from the panicked herd and wrestled down on a mattress spread on the road. A soldier with a hammer beat the squirming heads still. Another soldier shot with a pistol. Both were bloody to the elbows. A gang of soldiers fell on the dead animals and dragged them up into mouth of the street. They were building a barricade of dead goats, stacking the carcasses to make a wall. A signal rocket gushed up into the pale sky from the cement factory, flashed and banged. Then Padre Ortega saw the body of the dead goatherd hanging by the heels from the butcher's scales.

He stood up. The air snicked and clanged around him. He stared, puzzled, as holes appeared in an iron shutter. He ran for his church.

The aisles were filled with white-faced children, old women in fusty black, a few feeble-bodied men who cawed and clutched at his robe. The poorbox hung shattered from its pillar. The gypsy beggars of Pilarmadre whined and prayed at the altar. One of the acolytes, twisted in his robe and dazed with fear, trotted back and forth in front of the choir stall, tinging his bell.

Padre Ortega knelt for a few seconds, then rose. He seized the acolyte by the shoulders and shook him until the boy's hair flailed with the chatter of the bell. The priest's voice broke through the confusion of sounds. He stepped before the altar and stood in a shaft of golden light.

"Introibo ad altare Dei!"

His voice, exalted to a shout, rang from the stones. He stood before the altar with empty hands, the fingers damp with the blood of butchered goats. The congregation rushed forward, weeping and praying, and knelt with the beggars. Outside, a machine gun ripped, stopped, and began again its steady *tack-tack-tack-tack*.

By midmorning, Pilarmadre was silent again. Padre Ortega waited numbly at the main door. He was summoned shortly after ten o'clock by the young Falangist whose father ran a clothing store. Twenty soldiers were detailed to guard the church. The priest walked with a crowd of people to the town hall. There, he stood in the hot sun. The commander of the local garrison shouted from the balcony. The army was at war with enemy elements and winning all over Spain. The town of Pilarmadre, like the rest of the province of Aragón, was now under martial law. The people of the town were to go to their homes and stay indoors. Any civilians in the streets would be subject to arrest and execution. All private property would be safe-guarded. The municipal police were not to be obeyed, only the Civil Guard.

When Padre Ortega returned to his church, it was empty again. He heard noises and climbed slowly to the bell tower. There, on the plank platform, he found three young soldiers with a machine gun.

"Father! Hear my confession! I want to confess!"

One of the others laughed softly. The platform was littered with cigarette butts. The soldier who laughed tried to hide a can and hoses with his body, the cooling equipment for the machine gun. Ortega knelt, his chest aching from the climb.

"Where did you get the water in there?"

"We brought it . . . We . . ."

"You took it from the font!"

"That's all right, priest. This is war."

The ammunition belt snaked into the breech of the weapon from a wooden box. Padre Ortega picked up the box, his shoulders straining, and heaved it out through the window slot. The belt shivered and snapped. Hands grabbed him, and he punched blindly. The ammunition box burst on the church steps and flung out a glittering ribbon. Ortega cornered the laughing soldier and knocked him over the tripod. A hose-coupling snapped and the font water gushed over the platform. The priest crouched, his fists clenched.

"Get that damned thing out of here!"

The soldiers, one by one, raised their hands, palms out, surrendering. They looked terrified.

"I'll hear your confessions downstairs, not here. Now hurry up!"

"Yes, Father . . ."

"If you are not gone in ten minutes, I will report you as desecrators!"

He left them and started down the stairs. At the second landing, he sat down, faint and shaking.

In the sacristy, the young Falangist presented him with an order to report to Civil Guard headquarters. Ortega tore the paper to bits. The Falangist smiled and walked away.

The Civil Guards barracks was stormed by C.N.T. militia in the late afternoon. Two mechanics from the local garage drove a truck through the front of the railroad station and blew it up. The greasy smoke plumed over the town. The three young soldiers Ortega had driven from the bell tower were killed by hand grenades in the reception room of the town hall. The captured machine gun was used for executions until it ran out of ammunition. A group of U.G.T. militiamen came for the broken box and belt. The priest watched them carry it away down the smoky street.

The wounded began to arrive at noontime, all civilians. The only doctor was with the soldiers and Civil Guards. The priest asked for blankets and pillows. He put the women and children, mostly burns and cuts from broken glass, in the center aisle. The old people he gathered near the altar. The wounded militia he tended himself. Four of them died, and he covered their faces. He climbed to the bell tower and watched the fighting down near the cement factory. When he climbed down again, the gypsy beggars of Pilarmadre had stripped the dead militiamen. He draped the naked bodies with old choir-robes, to keep off the flies.

Four men in filthy blue coveralls, their arms cinched with red and black bands stood at the communion rail. They carried rifles, wine bottles and a wad of clothing. Padre Ortega stared at them warily. Perhaps the bottles were filled with gasoline, the cast-off clothing already ripped into wicks. They looked capable of anything or nothing, these Anarchists. They stood staring at him with dirty, expressionless faces and red-lined eyes. They stank of sweat and burned things. The old people gathered before the altar scrambled out of the way, hid behind the columns, and peeped out like children. Ortega set his hands on his hips and stared back at the milicianos, testing them.

One of them looked away and fiddled with the bolt of his rifle. Another smiled and drilled his nostril with a blunt finger. The other two met the priest's gaze. He saw neither fear nor respect in their faces.

"Yes, compatriotas?"

The one with the bundle of clothes was the spokesman. He looked older than the others, with a broad, sun-darkened face. His left eye was swollen nearly shut and gave his face a cunning expression.

"We took a vote, priest."

"A vote."

"It went against you."

"When do the people of Aragón vote *for* the priests? You know that I voted for the Republic in the last election."

It shamed him to say that, to remind them. It sounded like a plea. They nodded, first the one with the bundle, then the others, taking their cue from him.

"Alfredo spoke of that just now. He told us to bring you to the barricade. Some of the *camaradas* there want you."

The priest swung his arm slowly.

"There are many people here, as you see."

The one with the bundle shook his head stubbornly. The others shook their heads. Ortega wet his lips. For the first time that day he felt real fear. Not shock or surprise, but the cold seep of terror. He forced the words from his throat.

"I am not refusing to come. You have wounded men?"

"Some dead. Others are dying."

"It is over, then?"

"Over?"

"The fighting?"

"Yes, the fighting is over. The revolution, though, is just beginning. Alfredo spoke of that, also."

"Alfredo the barber, you mean."

They nodded solemnly. The congregation murmured, passing on the news.

"He who was a barber. He now commands our *columna*."

The one with the bundle glanced down dubiously at it and hunched his shoulders.

"Maybe you'd better just run for it, priest. You'll be shot later. We'll say you were gone."

"But that would not be the truth. I am here, as you see."

"Well, you will be shot later, no doubt. Too many kids here now, anyway."

The one picking his nose stopped and wiped his hand on his blouse. He sighed, bored and disappointed, and sat down on the floor. The leader shifted the bundle. He looked as though he wanted to throw it away. Ortega pointed at the bodies in the side aisle.

"There are many of your comrades here, too. Four of them are dead. I wrote their names in the parish register. To keep a record."

"A record?"

"For the history of this day."

They murmured and stirred. The congregation nodded approvingly. The workers stared around, sensing they had lost their initiative, and awed, not with the church, but with the mention of books, writing and history. Ortega pressed the point.

"You can read it, if you like."

"Later, later."

The priest sensed that he was shielded from their bullets only by the respect an *analfabeto* has for a man who can perform the mysteries of reading and writing. The one with the bundle thrust it to him, then snatched it back.

"You were with the rising in Asturias? In thirty-four?"

"I was there. Alfredo knows that, of course."

The bundle was shoved into his hands. He unwrapped it. A pair of soiled denim coveralls and rope-soled *alpargatas*.

"You're a Red priest."

"I am a priest who is a Republican."

Everyone looked at the bundle of clothing and the rope sandals.

"You are *bourgeois*, then."

"My father is a *campesino*, a peasant who lives near Málaga. An old man with no money but what little I can send him. I am his only son."

"That's too bad. Well, put on the clothes. You can't go down there, dressed like that."

Ortega nodded. They were not going to shoot him. Not now. Not here. That was something. He began to unbutton his robe.

"These are fit clothes for a priest who works in the Republic."

The words simply came from him, without conscious thought. What he said seemed true to him. He meant it.

One after another, the four militiamen smiled. Up went the clenched fists.

"*Salud!*"

He clenched his fist back.

"*Salud!*"

He felt a sudden twinge of modesty. How could he undress here, in the church, right in front of the altar, with a mob of children and old people, frightened mothers and this quartet of street fighters looking on?

He pulled off his robe, folded it and put it on the altar steps. He felt ridiculous. Standing in his singlet and shorts, black socks and shoes . . . it was worse than being naked. The children giggled. Shocked gasps from the women. Padre Ortega pulled on the coveralls. They were long enough, but too tight across the shoulders. He undid the top buttons, but then his chain and holy medal showed. Tongues clicked sympathetically. Ortega took off the chain and dropped it on his robe, sat down, kicked off his shoes and stockings and laced the *alpargatas*. He stood up, flushed and excited. From the back of the church came an *Ole!* and a patter of applause.

He walked with the Anarchist *milicianos* through the streets of Pilarmadre. It was dusk and the street lights came on, a little miracle of normality. A few cafés were open, crowded and joyful. Groups of workers, poorly armed, weary and exalted, patrolled the streets like gentle shepherds, keeping the curious from the town hall, the Civil Guards barracks and the railroad station. The station was still burning, and pungent smoke drifted over the tile rooftops.

Ortega walked freely, almost swaggering, filled with a fiesta mood. In his worker's clothes, he felt a security, a sense of oneness, comradeship with the people. He felt like hugging strangers, shaking hands. But he waited outside a tavern, while the *milicianos* drank a cup of wine.

If I start drinking, I'll end up like David, dancing in the streets, drunk and exposing myself . . .

He leaned against a building, washed with a new jubilation. For years, ever since he had taken his vows, he had worn the priestly robes, sometimes forcing himself to don the vestments that marked him. He felt safe, suddenly, for the first time in years. It seemed to him that his new comrades were filled with simple intelligence that thrust like a fist to seize the truth. Bullets were fired at the robe. It was more important to kill the symbol than the man. Now he had become part of them, as transformed as he had been when he took his vows. Twice, now, he had been ordained. If he died now, it would not matter. If they shot him, they would kill him as a man, not as a priest. And, somehow, that meant everything in the world. Truly, God was the people.

He could smell the barricade before he could see it. A sweetish, broiled stench of blood, burned fur, and flesh.

The market place was a ruin of heaped crates, sagging roof and bomb-blasted stalls. Bodies of men, some in coveralls, others in uniforms, the dead, the dying and the wounded lay in careless rows, the sprawled shapes stretched into shadows from the auto headlights. Somewhere in the belly of a broken café, a radio pulsed, beating out the same jazz tune he had been hearing for two days. He wondered what the words meant.

Broken glass crackled and skidded under the soft soles of his *alpargatas*. On the tailgate of a truck two women were tossing down bottles of beer to a gang of waiting men.

One of the *milicianos* nudged him roughly.

"Those two on the trucks. Whores from the house outside of town. Pretty, eh?"

Ortega turned away. He had known of the brothel for more than a year, but he had done nothing, nothing at all. Perhaps, now, he could go to them, talk with them. He shook his head, dismayed. Then he saw what had been raised in the streets of Pilarmadre.

The barricade was in three sections. Two parts of it clotted narrow streets, sealing off flank attacks. The third, longest section ran across the square and ended where a soot-shrouded taxi lay on its side in a guttering pool of smoldering rubber. The defense wall was low and lumpy, mottled gray and black, and crested with a dragon-frill of green and blue flies. Like ripples of gleaming tissue, the flies rose and sank, thousands upon thousands, with a fizzling roar. Beneath this gaudy, living crest, dainty black legs with small, glossy hoofs poked through paper sacks that leaked cement from the bullet holes. Fine powder drifted gray into stiff, waxy ears and frosted open, dull eyes. Ribs like bloody branches wore festoons of intestines. Blood, goat's milk, broken glass and cement dried in driblets, gouts, and batter pools crusted with brilliant, buzzing gems. In the center of this section, a red and black banner roiled on the smoky air, nailed to a pole driven deep into the dike of slug-burst cement bags and stiff, scorched goats.

"*Madre mía . . .*"

The leader of the *milicianos*, prodded his injured eye gently and spoke with a weary pride that reminded Ortega of museum guards and zoo keepers.

"First *they* put down a layer, see. But it was so low it didn't do them much good. We came out through the side gate down at the spur-track and hit them all at once. We didn't have many guns. It was the only way. Straight assault. Many were killed. Then we used the taxi. Brought out the cement, passing the bags from one man to the next. A chain. They came back with a machine gun and took it. But by that time we were in the buildings with gasoline bombs. We finished them off in the market place."

One of the other Anarchists nodded.

"It was done properly, with dignity. We had them look up at the mountains and the sky. Alfredo said . . . I forget what . . ."

"I'll tell it, eh? He said to each one . . . 'See how beautiful the world is? Look at the mountains, like the teeth of giants and the sweet sky blue and deep as the sea.' That's what he said. 'Sweet sky blue and deep as the sea.' That was good, that. Many of them cried. Some of us cried, too, without shame. Then, we made them look at the wall, the barricade, this thing of goats. And Alfredo said, 'And this is what you have made this world look like . . .' You know Alfredo reads a lot. But when he speaks . . . recites poetry, your heart splits like a ripe grape. 'This is what you want to do to us . . . to Spain. This cannot be allowed. And so we leave you here in your world, while we reach our faces up to taste the sky.' And then, we shot them."

"*Bam* . . . in the head with a pistol . . . Hey, here's Alfredo!"

Alfredo was dressed in baggy riding breeches and a red shirt. A toy telescope hung around his neck on a loop of twine. He had been wounded. His right arm and hand had been clumsily trussed to what looked like a broken tennis racket. He could only nod back to the clenched-fist salutes. Cement dust had coated his pomaded hair. His head looked covered with zinc curls. Sweat runnels lined his cheeks. He coughed steadily, tight, hard explosions that shook his thin, indoor body. The militiamen murmured respectfully and stretched out their hands to touch him or catch him if he fell. Alfredo ignored them. His voice was a dry, crusty croak.

"The people have won, priest. Some of the *camaradas* want you. A man dies before his habits do, you know. This will be the last of such actions for you. The church must be closed. We cannot have Vatican spies and that sort of swindle and corruption here. You had your turn. Now, it's ours."

"Alfredo . . . Capitán. The church is already filled with women, children and old people. Perhaps thirty wounded men, mostly C.N.T."

The barber nodded, looking over the priest's head at the evening sky. Flights of swallows swirled and dove, chittering through the smoke and noise, down to skim over the fly-seethed barricade.

"We have anticipated your resistance. Tomorrow, you will be tried by a People's Court and shot. It's only fair. The doctor will be tried tomorrow, too. He has already been shot for his many social crimes."

"Then who will care for the wounded in the church? Do you have a *practicante?*"

"I have telephoned Barcelona."

The *milicianos* nodded reverently. Barcelona was the center of everything to them, though none of them had ever been there . . . except Alfredo. Barcelona was the Anarchist's Jerusalem, the man called Durrutti, their Moses. Alfredo was blind and deaf with their dream.

"Oh."

"Hear the confession of the *chicos* here. Then, go to your church and wait."

"I will need help."

"Pray to your God, priest. This is the will of the people."

"I accept that. God is the people. But let me take those two women on the truck. They must know something . . . thanks to their profession."

"They helped us. They are accepted as good *milicianas*. Their past lives are forgotten. That place will be burned tonight. Never again will we have whores in Pilarmadre."

Padre Ortega nodded, stricken. What the Church had failed to do in how many centuries, this broken-handed barber meant to end, forever, in a single day. The priest's eyes filled with tears. God was the people . . .

"We . . . the people need them as nurses."

Alfredo lifted his shoulder. He was still looking up at the circling, swooping flocks of birds.

"They are probably diseased or something. The doctor would know."

One of the militiamen tapped his forefinger against his temple and shrugged. He went away to tell the women. Alfredo suddenly looked at Padre Ortega.

"So? Better a dead doctor than a live Fascist. You see the place here. People won't buy food from where all these men died. We confiscate the church."

"In the name of the people. Agreed. There is plenty of space for storage. Everything will keep dry in the winter months. The cellars are cool for the milk and cheese and the wine."

Alfredo coughed. Every hack shook him, and he dragged one foot through a gray puddle.

"Your resistance was expected. It has been entered in the prosecutor's testimony."

"Bring the market into the church, Alfredo. Don't burn it. It was built by the people of the town nearly three hundred years ago."

Alfredo seemed to consider this. He shook his head gingerly and winced.

"It is sufficiently inconvenient that the railroad station has burned. We want the money, of course. You must have millions."

"There is some money in the strongbox. Six thousand pesetas reserved to buy books for the school. Take it all."

"The criminal actions of the Church against the children of Spain have been noted in the prosecutor's testimony."

"As you say, Capitán . . . May I see the wounded?"

"You don't understand, priest, I am the prosecutor. *Me.*"

"Then we will meet tomorrow. I have much work to do."

Alfredo the barber nodded three times very thoughtfully. The last dip of his chin tilted him, unconscious, into the priest's arms. Padre Ortega lifted him. The bony body seemed to weigh nothing. He strode to the trucks, shouting.

"You women! Take Alfredo in the cab. Easy with him. He has lost much blood. You, driver, what-your-name . . . Rubio. We'll fill the truck with wounded and take them to the church. That's the hospital now. We'll need bedding, stuff for bandages, brandy to wash out wounds. And food."

The *miliciano* with the injured eye swung down from the truck.

"Did Alfredo give orders to . . ."

"*Claro,* he gave orders. He's bleeding to death, man. Hurry!"

"Well, that all sounds all right. But we'll have to have a meeting, first."

"A meeting?"

"Sure. We all have to vote on whether we'll obey Alfredo's orders or not. *Eso es democracia, no?*"

"*Magnífico.* Have your meeting while I see the wounded."

The two prostitutes helped Ortega place the wounded barber in the cab of the truck. The militiamen, about forty of them now, squatted in the gray, drifting dust.

Ortega walked into the shattered market place and bent over the first man he came to. He struck a match, half-hearing the *milicianos'* political wrangle.

"If Alfredo's dying, how will we hold the People's Court?"

"He won't die. The people's priest will take care of him. What's he for?"

"Let's vote."

"Somebody has to make a motion."

"I make a movement."

"In your pants, *hombre* . . . I can smell it."

The match sputted blue and gave off a whiff of sulphur. He shielded it with his cupped hands and held it over the face.

"*María Santísima, Madre de Dios* . . ."

The match caught and gilded the strain-stiff features of the young Falangist who had come to the church earlier in the day. Now he lay dying in a splintered fish-stall while swallows swung and darted like knives through the smoky sky above the town of Pilarmadre.

"*Y continuamos con nuestro programa de música popular . . .*"

> *I blow through here;*
> *The music goes round and round*
> *Whoa-ho-ho-ho-ho-ho—*
> *And it comes out here.*

Pedro hummed along with the music. He folded the little paper flag of red and gold over the milliner's pin, waited a few seconds for the paste to set, then carried the little flag to the map that hung on the wall of his room. The map was covered with tiny flags, from Corunna and Pontevedra along the north border of Portugal down to Salamanca and Ávila to Cáceres below the Tagus River. The line of gold and red looped west of Toledo and Madrid, dipped across Guadalajara southeast to Teruel, then up on an angle past Zaragoza and Huesca. Half of the border between France and Spain was already in the hands of those who could rescue the country from the Reds. A flag was planted on Majorca, another on little Ibiza in the Balearic islands. Down south, within Republican territory, two brave paper banners: one for Córdoba, the other at Seville. Pedro moved his fingers west through the Basque country, over Vizcaya, past Santander to Oviedo. On the map spot labeled Oviedo, he proudly thrust the pin.

The gong sounded for dinner. Pedro nodded with satisfaction at the map and took his dinner jacket from the *armario*. He looked at himself in the mirror over his dressing table. A tall, solemn-faced young man with rather large ears looked back at him. It was true, what people said of him. He looked much like the portrait of his father in the gallery, the painting done by an English artist on the Conde's twenty-first birthday anniversary.

The gong hummed again. Pedro heard his sisters rustle along the passage. They had been very secretive for days, in and out of the chapel and the sewing room. He suspected they were making some sort of farewell present for him. In the morning, he was joining his company. His luggage was already strapped to the back of the pony cart that would take him from the estate to the rally-point.

He opened the door and glanced back into his room. He felt extremely old and wistful all at once. On the wall was his confirmation certificate in a heavy silver frame. On top of the bookcase, two *banderillas*, the paper frills worn off long ago, the points filed blunt so he couldn't jab the barnyard dogs. From his first San Fermín. Could that really have been six years ago? A faded snapshot of a fat-faced boy on an equally plump pony. On the desk, his school notebooks and a wad of bright ticket stubs to local football games, an ink-stand, a wire-mesh fencing mask and a copy of close-order-drill regulations and commands written in German, a language he had great trouble reading despite two summers with an expensive tutor. The door to the *armario* stood open. A hunting outfit, some English suits, now mostly too small, his soccer jersey. He closed the door and walked down the great, winding flight of stairs.

His sisters, flushed and pretty as flowers in light tulle dresses and pastel mantillas—the very latest thing, it seemed—smiled to him as he crossed the parquet floor with long, swinging strides and stopped, his heels together sharply.

"My mother . . ."

He bowed over her hand and brushed the scented skin with his lips. He made a half turn, took his father's broad, hard hand in his and touched the heavy signet ring with mouth.

"My father . . ."

Curiously, it was his father's hand that trembled. Jacinto, the butler, opened the double doors. Pedro felt his mother's hand on his arm. She walked with him to her place at the end of the table and sat down, drawing her skirts in, her oval, fragile face averted. The girls said she had been crying, but there was little sign of it, perhaps a few fine lines around her eyes.

When he stepped to his usual place to her right, she shook her head.

"Tonight, you sit at the Conde's right hand."

Surprised, he glanced at his father. Where Teresa usually sat, Jacinto was setting out his silver goblet. Pedro bowed to his mother and walked the length of the table. The girls rustled down into their chairs, each of them making the furtive, nesting motions of women. Concepción, light hair burnished by the candles, rearranged each piece of silverware a millimeter. Then, she swept up her *servilleta*, snapped it open like a famished cavalry trooper, and spread it in her lap. Pedro heard his father suppress a groan. Concepción was a creature of little vulgarities with a secret longing to be a *rejoneadora*, the glittering star of *corridas* in the Portuguese fashion, thundering across the hoof-cut sand on a magnificent horse, planting *banderillas* and *rejones* in a great, black bull while thousands cheered, her mother swooned, and her two sisters were ill with envy. Pedro winked at her, and she winked back before dropping her chin for the grace.

His father's voice was husky, the blessing short. Pedro waited until Jacinto had seated his father, then sat himself. The long, low room, soft with candles and flowers, was very quiet. Pedro spread his *servilleta*.

"Will you try the trout, Papa? It took only an hour to catch them. Concha said she's never seen such plump ones."

"Of course, the trout. Tonight, everything! To the devil with my liver."

"Did you finish the map, Pedro?"

"Yes, Teresa. Thank you for making the flags."

"I wanted to do it."

"I don't see why there isn't a woman's auxiliary. The Falangists have one . . ."

That was Concepción. There was an awful silence.

His father waited until Jacinto placed the *jamón serrano* and melon slices, then cleared his throat shatteringly. Concepción sat very straight, her face expressing martyr's patience.

"It is not my wish to hear modernist views expressed in this house, Concepción."

"Yes, Papa . . ."

Meek, but with a wretched little sigh. Jacinto bent over and whispered.

"Vichy water or Perrier, Don Carlos?"

"Give it to the kitchen cats. Champagne!"

The butler backed swiftly from the room. The Conde de Gualvidal speared a chunk of melon. His mustache shivered.

"I am bored with drinking the rinsings from some Frenchman's washtub."

The girls giggled softly and worried at their food like bright mice. Pedro admired the flowers from his mother's garden. She admired his dinner jacket.

Concepción admired the rising *novillero*, Manolete, another of her "modernist" views. The trout, crisp-brown on a bed of garden lettuce was passed, with *salsa de almendras*. The champagne was tasted and approved. The Conde frowned.

"There are two matadors in the world. One of them is Juan Belmonte. The other is not this Manolo Somebody."

"But you yourself said, Papa . . ."

"It is my liver, Concepción, that is defective, not my memory. I may have offered some trifling praise for your little *novillero*. One must be generous . . ."

Fuming, Concepción ravaged her trout. Pedro grinned. Nearly every meal was like this, a *derribo*, a "knocking-down," as a test of bravery for young heifers to be bred. Concepción came to the table *buscando guerra*, looking for a fight, while his father sat in his high-backed chair, teasing, watching, judging. It seemed odd to Pedro that Connie had not yet understood this as an expression of his love. With the other two girls he was courtly, gentle.

The family ate slowly, with Pedro's mother guiding the conversation, avoiding the events of the past two days and ignoring the effect of champagne on bad livers. The long table dipped through the soft July night like a galleass from the Isthmus, deep with precious cargo, an expert pilot at the helm. Pedro was very grateful. He had feared a final meal of tears, reproaches and long, thunder-charged silences.

He devoured sweet, pinkish veal cutlets, saffron rice, and tiny peas from the kitchen garden. Jacinto filled his silver cup with champagne. His father's finger bunted his wrist.

"Damn your Vichy water, eh, boy? All right for grannies and sick girls. But this . . . this is wine! Puts bubbles in your blood. Just try drinking it in Mexico City, though. It gives the illusion of flight . . . a balloon ascension. Followed immediately by the wrong sort of women altogether, followed not long after by a visit from the police . . . of course, this was years and years ago . . . long before I met your mother."

Pedro nodded, dazed, drugged with happiness. He had heard the Madeira-and-cigars stories of his father's younger years, wild pilgrimages to the Barrio Chino in Barcelona, where, apparently, he had earned the nickname of El Horror de Navarra.

Jacinto brought a *bombón* . . . such an obvious indulgence to Concepción that even she noticed it and blushed with pleasure. A curt whisper from his father caused the popping of corks from the pantry and a cry of alarm from his mother. His father raised ferocious brows.

"An excess of rich desserts demands a certain astringency to shield the . . . ah . . . inner being."

"My husband, you are . . ."

She was quite unable to utter what he was. The girls shrieked with delight. Their mother, like Concepción, was not often at a loss for words. She flipped open a fan and dashed a limp curl from her brow.

"Very well, let the riot continue."

The Conde, pleased, snarled triumphantly, and Jacinto poured his glass foaming to the brim.

"Take a glass, my man. It will prolong your youth."

"A thousand thanks, Don Carlos. In honor of the Señorito!"

Poor Jacinto! A servant all his life, and he had never learned to hold his tongue. He was, as the Condesa called him in private, a "lamb from the hills," with both the gentleness and wrong-headed plunges against grace and good manners the phrase suggested. For nearly two hours, they had skirted the reefs of his departure for the war. And now the old fellow had done it. Pedro eyed his father.

The Conde dragged in a breath that seemed to stir the candle-flames and scatter the petals. Jacinto clung to the magnum, slack-jawed with dread for the four hundred-and-somethinged time. The ivory ribs of the fan at the table-helm snipped shut like the scissors of fate. The Condesa's glare would have flayed the hide from a mule. Pedro smiled and held up his cup to be filled.

"Thank you, Jacinto. I will drink to your thousands of kindnesses to me as a child."

Dios! That was worse still. The old man's eyes brimmed with tears, and he poured the wine over Pedro's knuckles. Concepción split with a cry of laughter. Jacinto grinned helplessly and mopped at Pedro's hand. The room shimmered suddenly, filled with the Conde's trumpeting laugh.

"Jacinto, you *buey!* Fill every cup! If we're to drink at your insistence, we'll do it right!"

The old man trotted from place to place. The Condesa hesitated, her palm floated over her goblet.

"Ana María Dolores!"

Pedro rocked with laughter. His father's mock-wrath, reserved in the cellars of his soul for the most festive of occasions, always caught her off-guard. She jerked her hand away from the goblet as though a thousand volts vibrated along the lip. Jacinto tipped the bottle, and the champagne rose bubbling to the brim. Even young María got a splash. The floor timbers creaked as the Conde de Gualvidal rose, steadied by Jacinto at his shoulder. The Conde scowled, and the butler skipped off to the sideboard where he threw sugar cubes about and rattled the coffee cups.

Broad and strong and deep, crisp-starched and hard-collared, the Conde stretched his dark sleeve down and seized his cup. His great, spotted hand closed it like a thimble. Pedro scrambled to his feet. He saw that the servants had gathered in the pantryway. They already had glasses and wooden cups, a *porrón,* too.

The Conde gazed over the table, his mustache working up and down, his eyes sweeping the room from pantry to the shifting billows of gossamer that blew on the night air.

"To the past, present and future king! The Christ, Jesus!"

"The Christ, Jesus!"

His mother raised her goblet.

"May He cloak this house with mercy!"

"With mercy!"

It was Pedro's turn. Something that was not too sentimental.

"And cure our ills. National and . . . personal."

His father gouged the room with a snort and dropped his spotted fist on the snowy cloth.

"Amén."

The voices roared.

"Amén!"

They drank. Pedro, after his father, flung his empty goblet away. Concepción smashed hers empty into the bouquet and ground her wrist across her lips like a stableboy.

His mother waited out the swirls and eddies, the surge and resurge of servants, gifts scattered over the table, whiskery kisses from the cook and old nurses, respectful bows and new boots from the *finca* hands and, final, tremendous and clashing, Jacinto's presentation of the sword of Gualvidal. He touched it with a trembling hand, the tassels, the hilt and the crusted scabbard, and placed it, safe, in his father's thick grasp. He looked into his father's face and saw the anguish and dread there.

"You will bring it to me, Papa. When we march in triumph through Madrid!"

"Madrid!"

His father breathed it like an incantation.

"To the *Palacio Real*. I will wear it during the coronation parade."

He was crushed to his father's starchy chest, scoured with whiskers right and left.

"So be it!"

By some signal he had missed in the blood-heat of the swirling moments, the servants were gone, out in the corridor, already subdued. His father coughed; his eyes flinched away.

"The . . . girls have a present, Pedro."

Teresa brought it, after some signaling and head-shaking and snuffling. She held it in her hand. He felt the weight of the steel covers, before she placed the pocket Bible on his palm. That was why they had demanded his uniforms . . . to widen the breast pocket so as to hold it and then to sew on the cloth, the Sacred Heart. He bowed to his sister.

"Go with God, my brother."

"Pray for me, my sister."

It was nearly too much for him. He felt a panic, certain now that Concepción would commit some final outrage like announcing she had been accepted as a volunteer parachutist. His father gave a wracking cough, a shotgun blast of sound. The Condesa picked up her fan and brushed a curl into place.

"The village priest is waiting in the chapel, my husband . . . my son. Please take us to him for his blessing . . ."

She moved, the spell was broken, the final meal of peace was ended.

"*Aquí Radio Madrid! Aquí Radio Madrid! Aquí Radio Madrid!*"

"Workers, anti-Fascists and laboring people!"

"Rise as one man! Prepare to defend the Republic, national freedom and the democratic liberties won by the people!"

"Young men and women, sound the alarm! Rise and join the battle!"

"Under the slogan, *Fascism shall not pass, the October butchers shall not pass!* Communists, Socialists, Anarchists and Republicans, soldiers and all the forces loyal to the will of the people are routing the traitorous rebels, who have trampled in the mud and betrayed their boasted military honor."

"The whole country is shocked by the actions of these villains. They want with fire and sword to turn democratic Spain, the Spain of the people, into a hell of terrorism and torture. But . . . *no pasarán!*"

"Working people of all parties! The government has placed valuable means of defense into our hands in order that we may perform our duty with honor, in order that we may save Spain from the disgrace that would be brought upon her by a victory of the blood-thirsty . . . butchers. Not one of you must hesitate for a single moment, and tomorrow we shall be able to celebrate our victory. Be prepared for action! Every worker, every anti-Fascist must consider himself a mobilized soldier!"

"People of Catalonia, the Basque country, and Galicia, and all Spaniards! Rise in the defense of the democratic republic, rise to consolidate the victory won by the people on February sixteenth! The Communist Party calls upon all of you to join the struggle. It calls upon all working people to take their places in the struggle in order completely to smash the enemies of the Republic and of the freedom of the people."

"*Viva el Frente Popular!*
Long live the alliance of all anti-Fascists!
Viva the People's Republic!"

Aquí Radio Madrid . . . This is Radio Madrid . . . *El diecinueve de julio de mil novecientos treintiseis* . . . July 19, 1936 . . . *Aquí Radio Madrid!*

That night, the workers of Madrid, one hundred thousand of them, like grains of wheat, rye, and barley, poured through the great stone sieve of Cybele, shook together and funneled toward the Puerta del Sol, the door of the sun. Beneath the torches, their faces were rust-red like the Spanish earth. Shaken and tumbled together, they lifted a sound that shook the stones of the city. One hundred times one thousand voices shouted for the tools, the iron and the steel, to harrow up to heaven the souls of their enemies.

SOL! SOL! SOL!
SUN! SUN! SUN!
ARMAS! ARMAS! ARMAS!
ARMS! ARMS! ARMS!

Carmen crouched on the narrow balcony and drew the light robe around her bare feet. She took from the pocket a box of matches and the package of cigarettes. Real tobacco *rubio* from America, in green and gold with a red spot in the center. Lucky Strike. She had looked up the words in an English-Spanish dictionary one of the girls in the dormitory used to translate hot passages from a book by an Englishman named Lawrence. The cigarettes were made by a labor syndicate in the United States that had won some kind of victory by sitting down. The punishment for getting caught was an unheard of number of Ave Marías, followed by expulsion. Smoking was a sin, the nuns said, nearly as bad as wearing silk stockings in bed after lights-out.

It was risky fun, a long wait until the lights flickered out, then tip-toeing from the dormitory down the hall past the nuns' cells, up the stairs to the attic and out the window. Eighteen nights running now, a new convent record! It was certain they would catch her soon.

She struck a match, burned her fingers, struck another and lit the cigarette. She puffed gingerly and let the smoke out her nose. If she inhaled, she felt drunk and sickened, debauched. She smoked, practicing elegant flourishes and looked out over the city. It was very exciting. All day and into the night, the fire brigades had been answering calls, mostly in the working-class districts. Classes had been canceled and everyone herded into the chapel for a long, hysterical session of prayers. Sister Angélica and the nuns were frantic with fear. The younger girls came down in fits of weeping. The Reds were burning one church after another, and the police, everyone said, had refused to send anybody to guard the convents. The police were in on a government plot. Good for them!

The convent gate had been closed and locked at sundown. The radio had been confiscated. Everyone had been talking about rape. One of the older girls thought it was a form of diarrhea. The windows had been shuttered and everyone sent to bed immediately after evening prayers. No one slept. Everyone talked, prayed, and wept. The nuns rushed in a dozen times to quiet them, which only made everybody worse. Finally, Sister Angélica sent the nuns to their cells. The convent moaned and whispered to exhaustion. It was safe, finally, to sneak out for the evening smoke.

Over Puerta del Sol there was an orange glow, soft and strange. The city stirred, a low, restless sound, and automobile headlights slid along the streets. Whole sections lay black. The night air smelled of things burning, and bells beat far away. Carmen pulled her robe around her shoulders and lit a second cigarette from the stub of the first.

She heard the men outside the wall near the orchard gate, then the clunk of a ladder. She cupped her fingers around the glowing tip of the cigarette and watched them, counting as their heads and bodies bobbed above the wall line. They were prepared. The first one up spread a mat or blanket over the broken glass that fanged the top of the wall. The others slid over and dropped down among the fruit trees. She aimed her forefinger like a pistol at them. *Pssh.* Another one. *Psssh.* Twenty-two. Twenty-three.

It was too far and too dark to see what they handed over the wall, but it took a rope and several minutes for each raising and lowering. She lit her last cigarette from the glowing stub and scrubbed the butt on the floor of the balcony. She smoked, amazed, but not really frightened. The men in the orchard were like a bad dream. They dodged from tree to tree, running clumsily, each one carrying something. They disappeared behind the classroom building.

The first smash of glass made her jump. Then a confused jumble of sounds, shouted orders and the crack and splinter of wood. She knelt, leaning out over the low railing. A ball of hot orange and then a deep *whoomph.* A long shadow lurched across the stained-glass window. Another flash and *whoomph.* The window disappeared, vanished. Flames squirted out through the sagging lead frame. She screamed. They had come, at last. They had come to burn the church and shoot and rape everybody!

She blundered through the dark rubbish of the attic and tugged frantically at the door before remembering that it opened *out.* She fell through it and crawled to the top of the tight circle of stairs that dropped down to the floors below. The convent bell began to *jang-jang-jang.* Something stuttered in the night. Again. She recognized it from a marksmanship contest her father had entered with the members of his club. It was an automatic pistol. The bell janged once and stopped. She gathered up her nightgown and robe and ran down the stairs, sobbing with fear.

Some of the girls and a few of the sisters were awake. She fled down the long corridor and into the dormitory. Fourth, fifth, sixth alcove along the left wall. Orange light now came through the windows. She tore the curtain aside and ripped off her robe and nightgown. Voices called and shrieked in the great dark room. Why in the name of God didn't they turn on the lights? Someone screamed her name over and over. She pulled on her cotton knickers and vest, then the drab jumper. She crushed on her shoes, unlaced, and swung aside the curtain.

The dormitory was a mad place of screaming, running girls. She timed a dash for the door, but was bowled over a cot. She clawed up again and ran. One shoe came off. She kicked the other free. One of the sisters, fully dressed, the one assigned to night-vigil, howled and grabbed. Carmen twisted free and fled toward the flight of stairs that went to the refectory.

The lights were on on the ground floor. The door to the refectory was open. The duty nun had forgotten to lock it. The room was bright, lurid with flamelight through the high windows. A sash sprayed into the room. She flung herself under one of the long tables, and lay in a stunned huddle. Something heavy tumbled on the floor. A *rock*, no— a blast of light, hot light and powder stink, and the hiss and smack of fragments. She stood up and ran, blinded by the grenade flash, into the serving kitchen.

It seemed safe there with the great kettles and pot lids like shields. She found a light switch and pulled it on and off. Like a photographer's flash, it showed her the cellar door with the key in the big, iron padlock. She slid across the room. The floor felt cold and greasy under her feet. She freed the key from the padlock and started down the stone steps. She could smell the earth-musty potato bins, sharp pickle-reek of onions in the salt barrels, pungent cheese. Off the main cellar was a low tunnel that ended in an outside door. She knew it well, the smuggler's route for forbidden cigarettes. She groped along it, listening to noises, voices, the dry smash of a rifle-shot. She fumbled her hand along the ledge until her fingers closed on the clasp-knife hidden there by Isabella, who had threatened to commit suicide the term before last until her parents married her off to a *teniente* of cavalry. The long blade was slick with stolen olive oil to keep it from rusting.

She opened the low oak and iron door. A steady, hissing roar filled the dark night. She half turned and blinked up at the sky. It was orange and filled with flying bits of stuff. Smoke swirled above the alleyway. A cat-squawl stopped her heart. She jumped back against the door, brandishing the key and the knife. The creature squirted off between two refuse cans. Carmen ran to the mouth of the alley and lay face down in the dirt. She edged forward until she could see.

A great gout of flame tore at the night, making a steady, seething roar, lighting the walls, the roofs and windows of the convent. The roof of the school building seemed to be burning, too. The main gate was wide open. Some men with rifles, flinching from the heat of the fire,

crouched behind a truck. She lay prone, in correct skirmish-observer
position, her heart thudding. She thumbed the lever. The clasp-knife
clicked open. The blade gleamed orange. She turned her head to look the
other way, down the dark street.

A steel snout. Bipod legs. The prong of a front sight. A fire-washed
face above the cartridge pan. The scream struck in her throat. She closed
her eyes as he reared up and dove at her over the machine gun.

He hit her, a solid, stunning blow that crushed her breathless.

An elbow rammed between her breasts and heaved her over on her
left side. Fingers ground her wrist. With a single snap, he shook the
knife from her grip. She scrambled feebly, staring at the fist clenched a
foot from her eyes. She nodded frantically and lay still. He lunged away
and back again. This time, he had the weapon with him, a Lewis gun.

"Lie still!"

She tried to roll away, and he hit her, a backhanded swat. Bright
flecks of light danced in front of her aching face. She heard him grunt
as he drove the legs of the gun in the earth. He wedged his knee
between her thighs and pinned her against the stone wall. She screamed
as he pressed the trigger. The Lewis gun spewed, a deafening shatter
and blue flames. The bright cartridge cases sprayed out into the street
and danced like locusts on the pavement. She lay still, terrified, as he
hunched against her, shifting his aim. She felt his slow rise and fall of
breath. The gun hammered again. He cursed slowly and stopped. They
lay together. He looked at her. He had a dark, tough face and a small
scar on one cheek, just under the eye.

"You all right?"

She nodded and began to cry.

"Shut up, eh?"

She felt his hand on her head, patting her like a dog.

"Listen, you got out. You're luckier than the rest of them."

"They . . . they came and . . ."

She pointed up the alley. He looked, a single glance into the darkness,
and shrugged slightly. Then he was on his hands and knees.

"Guardia Roja!"

Something stirred in the darkness down the road. He listened, his
hands on the Lewis gun, and shook his head. The flames from the burning buildings battered at the darkness. An automobile slewed at them.
He jerked her up to her feet and shoved her at the car. She skipped
through the spraying gravel and hammered on the door. It opened,
hands dragged her in, the Lewis gun spattered. She lay on the floor, her
hands over her ears. Hard boots ground on her legs and back. The auto
jerked into reverse, cramped in a half-circle and began to move forward.

A cartridge pan dropped on her.

"All right, Paco?"

"Yes. They aren't Falangistas. I was wrong. Anarchists, I guess."

"What's this one?"

"I don't know. I found her in the garbage alley with a knife. She says she got away out through the back or something."

"What will we do with her?"

"Take her along."

"Sure. Why not. Just what we need."

She squirmed over on her back. Voices muttered and feet waved over her. She sat up and pushed the flat cartridge pan onto someone's lap.

"Here. You . . . dropped it . . ."

His hand came down, caught her under the arm, and lifted her onto the seat. She clung to him.

"Don't hurt me . . . please."

"Hurt you? You can help load the *ametralladora!* She didn't even blink, this one, while I was shooting."

"My father is . . . an officer in the Army."

"*Jesucristo*, a spy. We got a spy!"

"What will we do with this one, Jefe?"

Carmen felt his hard fingers twist her head up. The car shot beneath a street light and on, swaying.

"What group is your father with?"

"He was with the Tercio . . ."

"The Foreign Legion. What *bandera?*"

"The fifth."

"Name and rank?"

"Faustino Bravo. Colonel."

"Where is he now?"

"I don't know. He got some mail and packed his uniforms and brought me . . . back there . . . and left me and said not to worry about anything and drove away. He didn't kiss me good-by. He never does."

The driver of the car spoke without turning around.

"We'll take care of that, *guapa*. Your father is the fifth? I'll be the sixth, then."

Another street light. His face was in shadow. He held her face close to his, without hurting her. She could feel his breath on her brow.

"What uniforms did he pack? Did you help him?"

"Yes. Summer-weight dress uniform. Binoculars, pistol and boots. Don't let them . . ."

"Don't be afraid. Anything else? Dark glasses, perhaps?"

"Yes, that's right."

"What railroad station? Norte? Atocha?"

"Atocha."

"You're telling the truth?"

"Yes."

"I believe you. Hold this stuff."

He released her and pushed the flat cartridge pans for the machine gun into her lap.

"Lucas."

"Sí, Jefe?"

"Turn down in back of Ventas. To the Red Aid place there."

"What for? We leave her there?"

"To get some clothes for her. She's coming with us."

"*Magnífico*. We can all take turns."

"As a hostage, comrade. Is that clear? To all of you?"

The men in the car muttered and nodded. She sat still, her trembling hands clutching the cartridge pans. The brass went slick beneath her palms. They came to a barricade of furniture, overturned carts, and stacked cobblestones. The driver honked the horn.

"Who wants to pass?"

"El Asturiano, four Red Guards, and this girl."

"El Asturiano is dead, *camarada*."

"You think so?"

He wrenched at the Lewis gun. Carmen shifted her legs. The bipod tore the hem of her jumper. She handed him one of the flat cartridge pans. He snapped it into place and opened the door. The Anarchist *milicianos* backed away.

"It is! It's him, *El Asturiano!*"

"It can't be. He was shot."

"Watch out, he's got a *máquina* . . ."

They drove through the barricade. A large group of men and women clustered around the automobile. The driver shifted gears and stopped abruptly. Carmen was flung against the front seat. The machine gun created a space of respect on one side of the car. Paco stepped down into it, cradling the Lewis gun in his arms.

"Where did you get those splendid rifles, *camaradas en la lucha?*"

"Issued by the government. We, too, are promised machine guns."

"Good. Without triggers?"

Laughter stuttered in the darkness. The driver raced the motor, scattering some children from in front of the car. The Anarchist sentries grinned and shrugged, shamefaced, fondling their rifles.

"We think it's part of a Fascist plot, El Asturiano. Fifty thousand rifles were issued . . . but only *five* thousand have bolts. The rest are like these."

"So I heard. You know where the extra bolts are?"

"We have our information . . ."

"Listen well. The bolts are in the Montaña barracks."

"Where those insurgent pigs . . . ?"

"Exactly. March with us to the barracks! Free the prisoners there, our

comrades! Seize the weapons for the fight! Rally point is Plaza de
España. We'll meet you there in two hours!"

The crowd shouted and waved clenched fists. He opened the door and
backed swiftly into the car, shoving the Lewis gun inside. Carmen pushed
on the safety, tripped the lever, and lifted the cartridge pan free and held
it. He dropped into the seat beside her.

"To the Montaña barracks! To Plaza de España. *Armas para la lucha!*
Arms for the struggle!"

The car shot up a dark street and wheeled around a corner, the horn
blaring, tires squealing. He leaned back, released a huffing breath, and
grinned.

"You can never tell with those types. Uncontrollables. Kiss you or kill
you. They don't know themselves what they'll do until they've done it."

"Are we going to attack the barracks, really?"

"What were the plans, comrade?"

"To go up into the mountains. With the rest of the Guardia Roja."

"For what purpose, comrade?"

"To fight the army of General Mola when they move on Madrid."

"Prime purpose. Secondary?"

"To infiltrate Segovia and beyond. To send a message off to the
comrades in France about the weapons."

"Have I indicated any change in these plans?"

"Well, no. But you just said to *them* . . ."

"What I say to the C.N.T. is what I say to them. What I say to
the Guardia Roja is the truth. Remember that, comrade."

"Yes, Comrade Paco."

"Let them attack the Montaña barracks. That's good. We have our
work to do in the mountains . . . Eh, Fermín! That's the place. Up the
street."

The car stopped outside a low, shedlike building. The sign letters
beneath the dim street lights were the color of old blood. RED AID.

"Now what?"

"It's open, isn't it? Wait here."

The driver switched off the motor. Carmen sat with the cartridge
pans in her lap, the heavy Lewis gun across her knees. He left the car
and walked into the building. The others lighted cigarettes and cupped
them in their hands. He did not approve of smoking, it seemed. She
closed her eyes. She felt very tired, suddenly.

The touch of a hand on her breast startled her out of a slurry doze.
She swung her arm, still clutching the cartridge pan, and felt her hand
pound into the man's ribs. He made an odd wheezing sound. The others
laughed delightedly. She shook the heavy brass pan at them.

"My father is my father! But I am anti-Fascist, just like you, so leave
me alone with your hands!"

"*Ole, chica!*"

"Hit him again!"

"Leave her alone, eh? Be smart. If she's anybody's she's *his*, see?"

"Sssst! Here he comes . . ."

He walked swiftly to the car and shoved a bundle inside. The driver started the motor again. Carmen tapped the cartridge pan on the stock of the Lewis gun, angry and nervous. A young boy brought a large, rattling box, put it in the trunk of the car, and saluted with a clenched fist. The men in the car saluted back. Carmen was relieved when she felt his hard body squirm under the legs of the bipod and press against her from the hip to the shoulder. He patted the bundle.

"Overalls, socks, boots, a beret, and a sheepskin jacket. It gets cold up where we're going, even in the summer. And a red neckerchief, so you don't get lost."

"I'll put it on."

The car pulled away from the Red Aid building.

"Where to now, Comrade Jefe?"

"The auto-park. There should be four buses waiting there. The Taradellas have brought the *chicos* up from Vallecas. We leave in twelve and one half minutes."

Carmen knotted the kerchief around her neck, tried the loose ends down the front of her jumper, but they were too short. She fumbled through the clothing and found the beret and pulled it on, stuffing her hair up into it. He sat watching her, and she felt her face flush.

"What was in the box in the back there? Medicine or something?"

"A frying pan, some pots and spoons, a grill."

"Oh."

"Can you cook?"

"Yes. We never had a maid. After my mother died, I mean."

"How democratic."

"No, my father needed the money to play cards with."

For some reason, he thought that was very funny and began to laugh. The others did, too. Carmen pushed the cartridge pans into his lap. Let him look after his own ammunition.

"What can you cook, *camarada hija de Fascista?*"

"Nothing, if you call me that. You can all starve!"

"*Qué va.* You have spirit. We'll call you Novia de la Guardia, Sweetheart of the Guard. What can you cook then?"

She looked down at the Lewis gun.

"*Sopa de ametralladora* . . . Machine-gun soup!"

They laughed and shook her hand and scrubbed her head with their fists and tugged at her red kerchief, and she was laughing and crying at the same time as the car shot from light to dark to light with the horn blaring and the tires squealing and jolting over the *tranvía* tracks.

They were at the auto-park. Three buses, loaded with armed men were waiting for them, the motors running, spewing exhaust fumes into the night. Everyone was shouting and singing. Horns blatted. The car slowed and swung left, leading the caravan. The buses lurched into motion.

She felt him give her something, pushing it into her hands.

"Your knife, Novia. With this gang, you may need it . . ."

> . . . *below, below, below . . .*
> *Listen to the jazz come out.*
> *I push the other valve down,*
> *And the music goes round and round,*
> *Whoa-ho-ho-ho-ho-ho,*
> *And it comes out here.*

The docks of Cádiz were dark. The mooring lines snaked around the piles and were snugged. The propellers of the gunboat *Dato* threshed foam. The ship shuddered and nudged. The gangplank slammed down and the order came back: *Shoulder field packs and make ready to disembark.* The engines rumbled, the water hissed and softened. The new night was still and dark, the moon not up. From somewhere in the city, a barrel organ chipped out a tune.

"*Cabo?* Corporal? Take your squad off the ship!"

Amil grunted. He did not like to speak in the Spanish tongue to the white officers. Better to have them think him stupid.

He squatted and slipped the pack straps over his shoulders, picked up his rifle and dropped the bandolier of cartridges over his neck. He stood up easily, despite the new weight. The pack was nothing. As soon as action started, he would throw it all away.

"Come. Here is land."

The others groaned and began to move around on the deck, pushing each other as they found their equipment. Hard, yapping voices shouted from somewhere up in the iron houses that formed the front of the ship. Amil stepped to the rail and looked out at the dark docks and the dim shapes of the city that lay beyond. It was bad, the night, wrong to try to do anything now.

The squad moved slowly, and he clucked to them. They had all been sick.

"*Cabo!*"

The captain was angry. Amil left the rail and unhitched his sheathed bayonet. He walked among his squad, beating them, all that he could reach. They were too weak to move away from him and hunched, struggling with their rifles and packs and crying to him for the love of

Allah to let them alone for they were sick and dying and the night was too dark and the wind was wrong.

At last, he drove them, beating at their legs, down the gangway to the dock.

"Make them move, Cabo. Get them off the dock. They are blocking the others. What do they want down there?"

"They try to wash themselves, Captain. They fear the sea and want to wash away the fear so they will be strong for battle."

While he waited, Amil took the banner of the *tabor* from the case and fitted it to the shaft. He was careful not to defile the flag by having it touch anything. It was hard to do, even with his rifle slung, but he did not want to walk into the night. If the banner, the beautiful soft thing, took his hands long to make correct, it would be light or the captain would become wise and let them all stay where they were.

"What's the matter, here, Captain Girona?"

"Same old thing. They won't move. Too dark, they're not purified, the wind is wrong . . . something. Try the ship's whistle or the siren."

"Right away. We've got to get them moving. The ones on the stern deck are beginning to panic. They think the gangway will not reach the land, that we mean to drop them all in the sea and drown them! Imagine it!"

"*Por Dios*, I'd like to! Get the flag out, you!"

Amil moved, sliding away from the kick he knew was coming. It glanced off his putteed leg. He raised the staff and shook out the banner and walked steadily with it down the gangplank.

On the dock the members of his squad still scrabbled in the darkness, their equipment clattering. Amil planted the flag, pleased by the boom of the staff butt on the heavy planks. He stood, his heart pumping every time the soft folds of the flag touched his cheek. He spoke to his squad.

"Listen to me. You are not yet on the land. This is a wooden road over the sea and not strong. You may all fall through into the sea. I have been here before. Here is a city and food and water. No movement, but all level and strong and safe, even in the dark. Beyond the wooden road is a level place and a fountain of water. I have been here before and know this fountain. The water is pure beyond anything in this city. One may wash and be cleansed and drink of it and be made strong. If you do not get up and move I will beat you all."

The men stood up, one here, one there, then two and three and more of them until they were all standing. Amil turned and looked up at the ship. He could see through the night, for his eyes were strong and he was not much afraid of the dark. The white officers were smoking along the rail. He could see the bright little lights of their tobacco in paper, where they burned them. He looked at them steadily, hating them all.

He had killed whites in the cold mountains of the north of this country and he had come back again to kill many more. All of this place had once belonged to the people, but had been taken from them by the whites. If enough of the whites were killed, the people would have the lands back again as it had been. He stood and heard their voices in the night, fat and cold like thick lamb-fat.

"Well, he's got them up. Bravo, Amil. He ought to be made a sergeant at least. We'll ask Franco. What did he say to them, anyway?"

"Something about water. He is crazy, you know, Amil. They all are, I think. But he . . . it's water with him. That and fighting. *Agua pura* . . ."

"Very interesting. We'll need a million gallons to get rid of the stink they've left all over the ship. Jesus, what a mess!"

Amil marched with the banner slowly, letting the others form into a column, then faster, setting a steady pace. He began to sing then, setting the cadence. The high notes came from him without effort and the others took it up. *Somewhere before us on this march is a fountain of stone and the water falls forever like crystal into a basin held in a maiden's hands. Never will her hands fail, for she knows from the whispers of the palms that we march to meet her.*

In the houses, the shutters creaked open over the windows and the screaming of the women began. Amil smiled in the night. That had not changed. The women screamed in the mountains, in the towns, and in the cities.

"*Los moros! Los moros vienen!* . . . *Aquí están los moros!* The Moors, the Moors!"

Tonight it was dark and things were wrong. But they were to march north, through the stolen lands. And as they killed the men, they would seed the women, as many as they could find, so there would be, when it was over, more of the people to take the lands and hold them, this time, forever.

Amil smiled in the night. One time only, he and some others had come upon a young girl at some place in the cold mountains. They had taken her by turns, holding her on her hands and knees. While one of them was in her, the others had bitten her white body all over her until the blood ran off her into the dirt. Amil slid his teeth together, remembering the biting of the girl. It was said that she had died later. He sniffed the air. He could smell dust and spoiled oranges and wine and then, the slight drop in the dark air, the cool feel of it. Water.

He leaned the flagstaff against the rim of the fountain and pressed it there with his knee. The others of the squad stood back, in respect, waiting for him to be done. He cupped his hands. It was dark and cool, delicious over his wrists and arms. He lifted and let it run and fall, splashing into the dark pool. A cool stream gushed out and struck his neck and ran inside his tunic, down his back and down his chest. He raised and held out his hands and washed and said a brief prayer. He was the first and no one spoke. The others were in line, ready to be herded like camels past the fountain by the officers. For them only a splash of the hands, a scoop and a gulp. Amil drank and drank and filled his metal water bottle. Then he stepped away, still holding the flag shaft with his knee and bound his turban around his wet, cool head.

"Is it always thus in this place, Amil? In all of Spain such fountains?"

"No. Not in all places. But where there is a fountain, we may wash and drink and pray and gather strength. There are many such places and so it is certain that we will win this war. We will march from one to the other or ride in *camiones* and when we have done the killing of the day, we will wash and drink. Every day that can be so, will be so."

"And then what? When it is done and we have won?"

A gush of wind snapped the flag across his face like a death sheet. He cried out and sprang away from the fountain, trembling all over. He looked around into the hateful night. It was a sign. He would die by water. Water would be his death.

"I know nothing more. Nothing."

"*Aquí Radio Madrid! Aquí Radio Madrid!* Loyal people of Spain. Continue to ignore false rumors and broadcasts of lies by the criminal elements of rebellion that still exist among us! Stand firm! All to the aid of the Republic!"

"There can be no question of the liberation of Barcelona from the Fascist elements and the continuing security and loyalty of the government of Catalonia!"

"The Captaincy General building on the Paseo de Colón has been seized. The first of the four insurgent generals, General Manuel Goded, has surrendered! His broadcast to this effect will be repeated at intervals of one half hour. General Goded has surrendered to the forces of the Republic! Barcelona stands fast against Fascism! *Viva* Catalonians. The military rising against the government there has failed!"

"Three enemy aircraft of the Breguet mark have been sighted landing at the airport in Seville. A telegram from the Triana district of that city reports that loyal workers are resisting frontal assault by elements of the Fifth Bandera of the Foreign Legion! Death to Fascism! All to the aid of the Republic!"

"Keep tuned to this station! *Aquí Radio Madrid!*"

The field at Marinha, Portugal, was small, not a regular airstrip. While the ground was smooth, almost level, it was surrounded on all sides by tall pine trees. A light, hot breeze stirred the heavy limbs and bent the treetops.

Ansaldo, the pilot of the aircraft, had protested about the suitcases. They were very large suitcases, of the finest leather, handcrafted at great expense to his passenger.

The propeller snapped over, flicking stiffly, then the motor snorted and caught. The airplane turned slightly as it taxied forward. A dust cloud whirled into the small crowd of Spanish friends and aides and a half-dozen uniformed officials of the government of Portugal.

Ansaldo, the pilot, tested the ailerons, the elevator flaps, and rudder as the small plane stopped, the motor roaring smoothly. The nose of the aircraft pointed east, toward the Spanish city of Burgos, its destination.

A thin cry rose from the dusty crowd, nearly drowned by the noise of the motor.

"*Viva Sanjurjo! Viva España* . . . Long live the Head of the Spanish State!"

The sun glinted on the narrow fuselage and slender wings of the airplane. Ansaldo gunned the motor. The fragile-looking craft rolled across the field slowly, then faster. It seemed to cling to the earth. The tires bulged and gave. The engine racket rose to a shrill snarl. Finally, the tail skid lifted free. Still the aircraft did not rise. It swept across the field, the sun gleaming on the wings.

The spinning wheels broke from the dusty earth, touched down, bounced gently, and broke free again. The propeller slashed a disc of silver in the hot, piney air. The plane slid through the sunlight toward the trees. The engine whined, wide-open, straining, pouring a dark feather of exhaust back along the slender fuselage. The great trees bent and swayed in the hot July wind. Aircraft and trees swung together, touched. The propeller bit and sprayed a cloud of shattered branches. The plane staggered in the air, shuddering, flinging bits of wood, battering at the treetops.

Greasy smoke squirted, a flash of flame and the dull, single concussive bump of exploding fuel. The airplane slewed sideways, out over the tall pines, the left aileron fluttering wildly, and plunged beyond sight, the motor spattering and blowing flames. A few seconds' fall, a fireball flashing through the dark pine trunks, a smoke cloud rising, blown up with the second explosion as the aircraft struck the earth.

In the gutted wreckage, witnesses to the accident found the charred body of General José Sanjurjo, *ex cathedra* Head of the Spanish State.

In Barcelona, General Goded, imprisoned, waited for his trial and execution.

In the north of Spain, General Mola, flanked in the eastern provinces, with the Basque Republic behind him and a salient thrust up from the south, cresting above Madrid, was forced to fight on three fronts.

In Morocco was the Army of Africa, thirty-two thousand veterans, and their commander, General Francisco Franco.

The Spanish national war is a holy war, the most holy war registered by history.

> Excerpt from a pamphlet distributed by
> the Spanish Catholic Church, July 1936

Franco and his people have no other ideal than their God and Fatherland.

> Cardinal Goma y Tomás, Primate of Spain

Q. *How long, now that your coup has failed in its objectives, is the massacre to go on?*
A. *There can be no compromise, no truce. I shall go on preparing my advance to Madrid. I shall advance, I shall take the capital, I shall save Spain from Marxism at whatever cost.*
Q. *That means you will have to shoot half of Spain?*
A. *I repeat, at whatever cost.*

> Interview with General Francisco Franco,
> Tetuán, July 1936, published in the London
> *News-Chronicle.*

I swear in the name of the beings who are most dear to me to dedicate my life to the democratic Republic, to the cause of the people, to justice and social progress. I swear by my blood to fight with determination and ruthlessness, to accept victory with joy and adversity with dignity. If I do not keep this pledge, may contempt, dishonor, and the inevitable punishments of military law come upon me.

> Oath of the Spanish People's Militia.

> *Los moros quieren pasar,*
> *Los moros quieren pasar,*
> *Los moros quieren pasar,*
> *Mamita mía,*
> *No pasa nadie . . .*

> The Moors want to pass,
> The Moors want to pass,
> The Moors want to pass,
> My little mother,
> Nobody passes . . .

A people which has arms and fights cannot be defeated.

Jacinto Benavente

"Name?"

"Kopa."

"First name?"

"Hans."

Something stirred in Voget's memory. He dipped his pen and wrote.

"Nationality?"

"German."

"Passport?"

"I have no passport."

"Refugee, then."

"I escaped."

Voget rubbed his tired eyes with his finger and thumb, shook his head slightly, and wrote again on the sheet of paper. Daudier, seated beside him, questioned another volunteer.

"Your name, comrade?"

"Kolodny, Kasimir."

"Polish?"

"That's right."

"You have a passport?"

"Yes. And a Party card."

"Good. Can you drive a truck?"

"No. I am a seaman. From Danzig."

"You jumped ship here in Marseilles?"

"Yes."

"Well, you can't stay here in the city. Ever used a rifle?"

"In the last war. For two years."

"We'll get you across the border as fast as we can, comrade."

Voget looked up. Kolodny, the Pole, stood fumbling with his cap. A big man, thick-necked, with a flat, simple face. When he smiled, his teeth looked like little pegs bedded in thick, pink gums. Daudier finished the form and looked at Voget. Voget nodded. Daudier held his hand out to the Pole.

"In the name of the Spanish people, I accept you as a volunteer in the fight against Fascism!"

Kolodny nodded seriously and twisted his cap, embarrassed.

Across the littered table from Voget sat Kopa, this thin, round-shouldered man with pale blue eyes, a broken nose, and a ragged auburn beard. He wore a shabby brown suit, a blue shirt open at the neck. His hair was odd, soft and uncombed, but short, as though growing out. Voget had seen that kind of hair a number of times on the heads of men fresh from prison.

"I know you."

"Do you?"

"You call yourself Kopa now? It was different before."

"A man must call himself something. Some name, I mean."

Voget offered a blue package of Gauloises cigarettes and a box of matches. Kopa nodded his thanks. He held the little box awkwardly in his left hand. The fourth and little fingers were crooked stiff.

"I knew you in Hamburg."

"I have been there off and on, yes."

"Right after the war. I was working at the harbor. Now I remember! You called yourself Kleist, then."

"Did I? What did they call you in Hamburg right after the war?"

"Red *Schweinhund* . . . other names."

Voget grinned and lit his own cigarette. It was late; the room was empty. Kolodny accepted the francs, the meal-ticket, and the hotel address from Daudier, who pushed the registration form to Voget and stood up, stretching.

"Well, that looks like it for today, Chief . . ."

"Go along. Keep an eye on that Pole. The people from his ship will be looking for him."

"I sent him to my hotel. Along with the others. See you at the garage?"

"Right."

Voget waited until his young assistant closed the door. He picked up the pen.

"Who was I in Hamburg? Let me see. I was Valois, later De l'Isle."

"Once you were Steegmuller, no?"

"That's right. Now I am Voget. Paul Voget."

The man called Kopa did not offer to shake hands. Voget frowned, annoyed. German comrades, even the best of them, had a way of keeping one at a distance. They all needed a trip to Spain—to thaw them out, if nothing else.

"You speak Spanish?"

"Yes. Some."

Voget wrote *oui* opposite PARLE ESPAGNOL. The paper was cheap, and the pen nib fuzzed and blotted. He picked at it with blue fingertips.

"We heard that you were arrested. Three years ago? In a concentration camp."

"Heinrich Kleist was arrested. But Hans Kopa escaped."

"May one ask how?"

"I had some help. There was another man with me. A comrade."

"Which comrade?"

The man who called himself Kopa blew smoke and shrugged.

"Beimler. Know him?"

"Beimler? Of course. He's in Barcelona."

"Well, we got out together. He killed the SS guard."

"How long have you been in Marseilles? Why was I not informed?"

"Two days only. I have no papers. I have been hiding."

"Paris? No, that would be too dangerous."

"Bordeaux."

Voget scribbled a note at the bottom of the sheet. Kopa smoked.

"I'll write to Comrade Duclos for you. We can take care of the pass-port. You know how to drive, of course."

Kopa nodded once.

"Where are you staying?"

Kopa shrugged, his shoulders hardly moving the shabby stuff of his suit.

Voget opened a drawer, took out a slim sheaf of franc notes, a ticket to a workers' restaurant, and a piece of paper with an address on it, a hotel out on the Corniche.

"When can you leave for Spain? Right away?"

"Yes. Why not?"

"How was . . . the camp? Bad, eh?"

"Bad enough. They have new . . . techniques. Slower, but more effective. If you break and talk, they kill you. If you don't talk, they kill you. There are not many left back there now."

Voget put the money and the ticket on the table.

"You'll go to Spain as a tourist. To the Worker's Olympiad."

"Driving a car?"

"A truck. You're a worker, aren't you? Would you rather fly by Lufthansa? We have been told that there are Junkers transport aircraft already in Morocco."

"How does it go in Spain, Comrade Voget?"

"We're holding in the Sierras. At Alto de León. More or less. Outside of Guadarrama, anyway."

"And Toledo?"

"We are still besieging the Alcázar. But the Basques took San Se-bastián. Albacete is ours. Valencia, too. Ever been there?"

"Yes. To eat the oranges."

Kopa's voice was soft, indifferent. Voget watched him.

"Kopa is your *real* name, isn't it? I just remembered."

Kopa shrugged and dropped his cigarette on the floor. He glanced up at the banner slung across the wall above Voget's head:

COMITÉ INTERNATIONALE DE L'AIDE AU PEUPLE ESPAGNOL

"I have managed to forget almost everything."

"I hope not, comrade. Beimler is forming a combat shock group. The Thaelmann Centuria."

Voget waited for some response. Kopa sat still, staring at the banner. He stirred and sighed.

"Who else is down there?"

"Codovila and Stepanov."

"Christ. Then it's true? What I heard."

"What did you hear?"

"That Vidali is going."

"Ah, Vidali. Well, he now calls himself 'Carlos Contreras,' and he has already gone. In Madrid, I think."

"And Singer—the Hungarian?"

"You *were* in Paris, then. You are well-informed, comrade."

"And Ercoli?—that's *his* new name."

"Comrade Togliatti will co-ordinate tactics with the Spanish Communist Party. He is not there permanently, though."

"Not yet, eh?"

The first glimmer of something like humor appeared in Kopa's eyes. He took another cigarette and lit it with his queer-clawed left hand. Voget felt uneasy. There was something about Kopa, something fatal. The German nodded and spoke again in his soft, indifferent voice.

"They go to see the Olympiad in Barcelona and to eat the oranges in Valencia. But not to Madrid, I imagine. Madrid is for the rest of us. One can get killed in Madrid. All the buzzards and crow fly south these days. Don't they know it's too late? We lost in Rome, Milan, Berlin, and Hamburg. How long do they think it will be before the Italian troops arrive, before the Nazis follow them? Or don't they care? Do they go for Spain—"

He waved his crippled hand at the banner.

"Or do they go for the Party?"

Voget reached for the application form. The franc notes, meal-ticket and address lay on the table in front of Kopa. The German had not touched them.

"I think we should forget all this. With a passport, you can go back to Paris. The Propaganda Department needs writers. In the old days, you . . ."

"I don't write any more. Not propaganda. Not anything."

"But you must know Muenzenberg and Koestler. There is genius in Paris, man. The literary world is reflecting the political situation that has arisen from the class struggle!"

Kopa smiled. Broken teeth showed through his beard. He blew smoke at the ceiling. Voget did not like his smile.

"Togliatti and Erno Gero in Spain? There is genius there, too. Comrade Stalin has a considerable supply of genius. Spain will get some artillery and tanks. They will get Italian tacticians and Hungarian commissars. To offset Trotskyite deviationalism, of course. Or is there another phrase one uses these days?"

Voget leaned on the table and said nothing. He could think of nothing to say. The German had thrown the Party clichés back at him. It was too long ago. Too much had happened. He remembered this slight, battered man as Heinrich Kleist, a tireless organizer on the Hamburg docks, talking endlessly to longshoremen, crane operators and seamen. He had been a writer, too, for the Party papers, a play opening in Berlin, a volume of poems paid for by some rich young woman, it had been rumored. And a street fighter, too, with gasoline bottles and a Mauser rifle.

Now, on a late summer afternoon in Marseilles, here sat one of Germany's *Moorsoldaten*, a "peat-bog soldier," an escapee from the concentration camps, the Gestapo, and the SS, an illegal entrant, wanted by the French police. He seemed a husk, a shell, perhaps more dangerous with his defeatism and cynicism than the local Fascists of the Cross of Fire movement. What to do with the man? Keep him close, watch him, rehabilitation through work, clerical staff, and then . . .

"Well, believe me, Comrade Kopa, there are no geniuses here in Marseilles. I am swamped, absolutely, as you see. More than eighty volunteers today. French, of course. Many students. Poles, Danes, two comrades from Finland. Three officers from the Czech army. Can you beat that? They left Prague to fight in Spain. Yesterday, a Dutch house painter and two of his apprentices. A golf professional from the Côte d'Azur. A group of Belgians, already organized, left for Perpignan two days ago. That place is jammed. Refugees, spies, everybody. I heard that two Englishmen rode across the border on bicycles. The volunteers are mostly workers. They have responded at once. It takes the intellectuals longer. After all, they have the handicap of university training to overcome. Except Malraux, of course. Between us, there are negotiations for twenty aircraft. Light bombers. The Potez model, twin engines."

Kopa nodded.

"Twenty bombers will be just enough to deliver the mail between Spain and Moscow. By way of Switzerland."

"Comrade Kopa, allow me to clarify your thinking. You assume, *tout court*, that there is a Party policy toward Spain. The Popular Front, a fusion of all socialist and liberal, democratic elements . . ."

"I heard about it . . . inside the wire."

"Look, Kopa. Stay here in Marseilles. You can help me. We'll talk. A great deal has happened. You've . . . been away from it, as you see. I am not a sentimentalist, but let's say for the old days . . . in Hamburg, eh?"

"*Ja, ja.* You'll have me filling out forms until I'm blind and sick with guilt, sending others off to fight. I'll get sick to death of it. I might as well drive your truck to Barcelona right now."

Voget shifted in his seat. He was uncomfortable from sitting too long. Kopa disturbed him. The money and the meal-ticket lay between them like a bribe. Yet, somehow, he must have Kopa. The others already gone to Spain were young or inexperienced, or adventurers, or running from bad debts, the police, their women.

"All I'm saying is that Moscow is obliged to consult the leaders of the Comintern these days. Moscow listens, and then . . ."

"I can guess the rest, *mon ami*. Remember what happened to us in Hamburg? Berlin? What happened in China? Ask Monsieur Malraux."

Voget spread his hands, palms up and dropped them on the table. "Stay here. After all, you've been in the forefront of the battle and—"

"I think that you read too much propaganda, Comrade Voget."

"Have you forgotten how to read? The newspapers . . ."

"They make me sick. Lies, all lies."

"The democracies, France, England, America . . ."

"Won't lift a finger. Blum is a coward . . . well-meaning, but afraid. The English have business interests in Spain. Everyone is obsessed with Bolshevism. Better Franco and the sherry on the table every night than a workers' republic. Now tell me what Moscow wants."

"I don't know."

"Yes, you do. Time. That's all. That's everything. Spain will give the Russians a year. Maybe two years."

Voget flushed angrily. He was not used to being lectured to, much less by Germans. He managed to keep his voice steady, but with an effort that did not escape the shabby, bearded man across the table.

"Then go to South America. The United States. It can be arranged."

Voget sighed and reached across the table. He blinked, surprised, when Kopa's stiff fingers snatched up the money and the ticket. His blue eyes still seemed fogged with indifference.

Kopa sat there, a threadbare German with a ragged beard to cover the identifying scars ripped on his face by Brownshirts with broken beer bottles, his fingers frozen by fractures, his blurred eyes. He was skin, bones, and scars.

It would have been better . . . better for the European worker, the Party, better for Kopa himself, even, if the SS had finished with him. Then he could be added to the long, long list, with Edgar André, Thaelmann and the rest. Better a dead martyr than a living wreck. Who would give him money to get away to Brazil or the United States? Officially, he was a criminal. Politically, he was no longer trustworthy. Actually, he might be dangerous. Why had he not gone to Spain with his comrade Beimler? Beimler was supposed to have escaped alone. Was Kopa lying? Was he a spy? Was his present freedom bought with betrayal of others still behind the Nazi wire?

No. The Nazis would have picked someone else. Someone from the Croix de Feu, a French Fascist. There were enough of them around. Kopa-Kleist wasn't worth anything, even to the Nazis. He was merely a survivor, nerve-shocked and crippled in spirit. Hans Kopa was all that was left of Heinrich Kleist, poet, journalist, worker, and expert sniper. Or was it that Heinrich Kleist was all that was left of Hans Kopa? Was this really Kopa? Or Kleist? Or just a numb wraith who had slipped through the barbed-wire fences, past the machine-gun towers, waded the swamps to elude the dogs?

"I—I can get working papers for you, comrade. You can get a regular job, here in Marseilles. Maybe that's best. Settle in. Save up. Then a boat for Brazil. A fresh start. Of course, I could write to Beimler. He's as loyal as they come. Between us, we'll—"

Kopa shook his head.

"No. I'm not diseased. I'm not sick that way. It's just . . . I want—"

"You want what?"

"I want to go to Spain."

"I don't think—"

"To hell with your truck. I'll walk. I walked across the border. I can get myself to Spain."

"Despite everything?"

Kopa nodded, more vigorously. The borrowed suit fit loosely on him, his beard looked fake, his hair made him look, somehow, simple-minded, but when he spoke, his voice had that odd, rasped toughness. The sound cut through the years at Voget from a dozen waterfront bars, on a bad connection, long distance from Party headquarters, over the churning of the presses running off the next day's special edition of *Rot Front*, from the cab of a truck delivering weapons from a secret, scanty arsenal.

"I'll go as a soldier. No Party rank. No propaganda department, no. None of that cultural attaché fakery. See, that's why I can use my real name now. The others, the ones that knew me . . : they're all dead. At least I think so. If they're lucky, they're dead. Even Beimler calls me Kleist. Be honest, Voget. Is it really a workers' government down there?"

"It could be. In parts, it is. In Barcelona, the C.N.T., the Anarchists run the city. In Madrid, it's the U.G.T. . . . the big unions, see. The Spanish Communist Party . . . well, I've heard that it's doubled . . . about ten thousand, say. Called the P.S.U.C."

Kopa shook his head stubbornly, both hands stuffed in his pockets. There was something now behind his eyes.

"I don't want anything from anybody. In the Party or outside. I just want to hold a rifle once again. After all these years I want to see, just for a little while, a true workers' state . . . before all the hyenas gather and the cowards sell out. Listen, it's there, isn't it? It's not all propaganda? It's true. It *has* to be true, sometime!"

Voget could not look at him. How old was Kopa? Thirty-eight? Forty? His voice, like an echo from the tar-black nights of Hamburg, that clenched-teeth snarl that had rammed the longshoremen back to the barricades.

My God, I used to sound like that, think like that, be like that . . . I cared, then. I believed, but I lost it. But him? They didn't beat it out of him; they beat it down into his bones.

Voget suddenly hated Kopa, like a sick man hates the cured. He wanted to lie to the German and detested himself for the dirty impulse.

The truth. He needs it.

"Yes. It's real. Now. For how long, God knows. They need everything. Weapons, men, leaders. If they are equipped well, properly led, and given support by the working classes in other countries—*if*. They will win. *If*. That's what I'm trying to do. Make that *if* small. Make it disappear."

"You haven't a chance, Voget."

"There's always a chance. England may—"

"No."

"Kopa, you make me hurt all over. Go to Spain. I feel a million years old and made out of mud. Go to Spain."

"What about the truck?"

"There are six of them. To take a shipment of weapons to a young Spaniard named Paco Larra."

"Another protégé? That's your speciality, I had forgotten. You types never give up. The pimps of the Party. You ought to work the Reeperbahn on Saturday night, Voget."

"Someone must do this work."

"And how do you sleep at night?"

"Perfectly. You will meet this Larra. He graduated first in his group from the Frunze military school in Russia."

"Too bad for him then."

"You will drive the trucks over the border as far as Lerida, then put the crates on the Madrid train, with some of your group as guards. Then drive the trucks to Barcelona. Do what you like after that. But I'd keep my mouth shut, Comrade Kopa. This is going to be a tough one."

"When do we leave?"

"Tomorrow morning. For Perpignan. Six men to a truck. Take turns. Don't lose the shipment. That Spanish kid is somewhere up in the

Sierras. He's counting on it. If he doesn't get these weapons, you'll never come out of Spain alive, comrade. Understand?"

"Yes."

"Then what's so funny? Shut up. I don't like the way you laugh."

"It's just that I thought that you, perhaps, might understand. I'm not going to Spain to live. I am going there to die."

Voget snatched up the pen and signed his name, then pushed the sheet at Kopa. The German was still shaking with silent laughter. Voget felt his flesh crawl.

Kopa signed, a surprising, elegant flourish. Voget loosened his tie. The room was stifling. Like a coffin. Why did Kopa have to come here? Why did he have to say that about dying?

"Comrade Voget?"

"What is it? Go away. Get some sleep. Eat a meal. Have a woman. What is it that you want from me, Kopa, for the love of God?"

The German's face was serious, but his bony shoulders shivered with amusement. Voget floundered with his papers.

"When can we expect *you* in Madrid, Comrade Voget?"

"Soon enough. Too soon. *Au revoir*, Kopa."

"*A bientôt*, comrade. Where will the trucks be?"

"They will tell you at the restaurant. *Bon appétit.*"

"*Bon repos*, Comrade Voget . . ."

> *Wir werden weiter marschieren,*
> *Wenn alles in Scherben fallt,*
> *Unsere Feinde sind die Roten,*
> *Die Bolshevisten der Welt.*

> We shall be marching onwards,
> If all else falls to pieces around us.
> Our enemies are the Reds,
> The Bolshevizers of the world.

Nazi marching song

Workers and anti-Fascists of all lands!

We, the workers of Spain, are poor but we are pursuing a noble ideal. Our fight is your fight. Our victory is the victory of liberty. We are the vanguard of the international proletariat in the fight against Fascism. Men and women of all lands! Come to our aid! Arms for Spain!

Appeal issued by the government
of Catalonia.

REBELS

REPUBLICANS

**DIVISION OF SPAIN
JUNE-JULY 1936**

It was a soot-and-lilac London summer evening, just twilight, with a dribbled line of pewter-colored clouds low and far away to the west. The gray, vast city throbbed with Saturday night traffic, crowded pubs and restaurants, the sidewalks splashed with the pastel shapes of women. It was a night full and murmurous, of easy rush, gentle power steered by bobbies in pot helmets, couples walking dogs on leashes, lovers sprawled on the park grass not yet damp, and the cheap glare of cinema lights. London summer with swallows spilling over Marble Arch, a barrel organ chinkling on the corner, a sidewalk artist and his cloth cap containing four big pennies, a worn sixpence, and a hopeful shilling, black, crooked arms of idle cranes hanging over the docks, a fresh packet of Players and just one more glass of oloroso sherry sipped in the front window of the club while the boys in the street cried the news from Spain.

Franklin Pierce Buckminster, in the left front seat of the open Riley roadster, stretched and lighted a cigarette, shielding the match from the gentle buffet of night air. It had been a long drive up from the Desmond country place in Kent, even with Peter Desmond, his English cousin, driving. Peter's brother, half asleep, sprawled in the rear seat, done in by the polo match. Frank stifled a yawn. His legs were stiff from the hard riding on borrowed ponies from the Desmond string. A good match, won six to four, the last two goals his, one a neat backhand from twenty yards out. He glanced at his cousin's long, intent profile. They were up to something, Peter and Harry. The weekend was strained, with conversation reined to the affairs of Buckminster and Desmond, London and Philadelphia, the polo match and the air show.

"Are you sure it's all right about this party, Peter? Will anyone mind if I crash like this?"

"Of course no one will mind! Steady on. Terrible fellows, bus drivers . . . think they own the King's highways or something. This is an opening of the Left Book Club. Think of yourself as a customer. Tom Coltringham is off for Barcelona on Monday, so it's a *bon voyage* party for him. Eric is expected, too. And it's a reception for what's-the-fellow, Lorca's friend who married the Spanish girl. A mob, in short, not Main Line, if that's what's bothering you."

"Who is Lorca?"

"Dear God . . . a Spanish poet. There's to be a reading. We've heard he was arrested."

"Poetry readings. Drinks and girls, I hope."

"Never a Left Book Club opening without lashings of drink. It's a rule, I think. And girls, of course."

"The kind that weave their own clothes and wear wooden bracelets, I suppose."

"I suppose. Harry?"

The younger Desmond thrashed upright and stuck his long face over into the front seat.

"What?"

"Nothing stronger than beer for you. That's an order from Tom. What with . . . you know . . . and we don't want a repeat of last time, do we?"

Harry frowned and jutted his long lower lip, the "Desmond lip," and looked even younger than eighteen.

"It wasn't my fault."

Peter passed a taxi and another.

"We went to the D'Oenchfields' for dinner. Harry went one over on the port . . . You know them, don't you, Frank? He's in the City. Anyway, Harry called Baldwin a bloody sod and a coward for not sticking up for Spain."

"Baldwin? Oh, the Prime Minister. No wonder things are sort of stiff. At home, I mean."

Harry groaned and rubbed his jaw. He leaned forward and jabbed Frank's shoulder.

"Tell me more about the air show. God, it must be wonderful to fly! I wish I could learn. Father won't let me. I have to stay in and swat for next term. Damn Oxford, anyway. I wanted Cambridge."

Frank nodded. Desmond Senior had let drop a few remarks about that.

"Your father seems to feel that Cambridge has gone Red. Bunch of Socialists up there."

"How was the air show?"

"All right."

Peter laughed and drummed his fist on the steering wheel.

"Ah, Americans. So enthusiastic. Childlike in their simple joy. You were going to buy a racer from that French fellow, weren't you? Saulnier?"

"He didn't make it. I asked everybody, but no one would say why."

Harry Desmond swatted the seat, and Frank shied from his enthusiasm.

"A racer! You were actually going to get one, Frank?"

"I thought I might go into the Bendix Trophy or the Thompson. Depends on business, of course. I've even thought about getting a commission and joining the Army Air Force. You two aren't the only ones who think brokerage and private banking is—"

"A bloody bore."

"A bloody swindle."

"Where are we, anyway? This doesn't look like Chelsea to me, Peter."

"Just the fringe. Can't you *feel* the difference? No, of course not. You're an insensitive Yank. I have no idea why we put up with you."

"Because I'm the front half of Buckminster and Desmond, that's why. Or I will be, one of these days. When that happens, watch out. I had a long talk this morning at breakfast with your father. He's fed up with both of you. It was a relief, believe me. All you two talk about is Spain, Spain, Spain."

Peter signaled for a left turn.

"Well, don't keep us both hanging. What did you talk *about?* The late indiscretion of Harry? The polo?"

"British neutrality."

The two Desmonds burst into laughter, Harry shaking his head, Peter making subdued snorting noises. Frank flushed.

"I don't see what's so goddamned funny about that! He's worried. Uncle Harry's worried."

"Don't tell me *you* are? You won't get your racer, I suppose."

"Look, Peter, Spain has the fifth largest gold reserve in the world, right?"

"So they say."

"This war business will knock hell out of European banking on one hand, but the bright boys will pick up a nice pile. We don't want to get snarled up in bad politics. Be reasonable. Let's stay on the side of the bright boys . . ."

"Who's *we?*"

"Drop it, Harry . . ."

"Well, Frank?"

"Buckminster and Desmond. Who the hell do you think? Why do you think Uncle Harry sent me over? To buy an airplane? I've *got* an airplane. Two, in fact . . ."

Peter Desmond braked and swung the motorcar into the curbing. He switched off the ignition and twisted around in the seat to glare at his brother.

"Here we are. Harry, take this colonial capitalist gently but firmly up the stairs, through the door, and turn him over to Tom. The cure may come late, but just in time to save him."

They got out of the car and stood together on the sidewalk. His two English cousins towered over Frank. He looked at a house, brightly lighted, the windows flickering as people moved back and forth through the rooms. Somehow, he had expected a slum section, a flight of splintered stairs, the smell of cabbage, and a garret studio. The house was three stories, semi-detached, brick, and respectable. All the lights seemed to be on; the place glimmered like a beacon. His false estimation angered him, like a fluffed forehand with the pony easy and straight and a free field or an overshot strip because he had neglected the push of a tailwind. He did not like to be fooled. It was bad enough in games.

"This Coltringham, the host. He's going to Spain?"

"His wife's named Naomi. You'll like her."

"And he's one of these damned Communists, of course. English style."

"Of course. English style, if you like."

"I don't. We've had the Wobblies at home and the CIO and you name it. He's an Oxford man?"

"Cambridge. Trinity College."

"Why in hell do all English Bolshies have wives called Naomi? Your father's right. The British Empire is going to hell and neither of you have the kind of friends he can invite to dinner."

Peter shrugged.

"That's too damned bad, isn't it? Very inconsiderate of us. We just happen to care very much, that's all."

"But *why*, for God's sake? What is Spain to you?"

" 'What is he to Hecuba or Hecuba to him?' "

"Lorca?"

"Shakespeare."

"He was probably a Communist, too . . ."

"He was a cell-leader in Stratford. Ben Jonson was a commissar."

"Frank?"

"What?"

"Listen, you will teach me to fly? At least take me up a couple of times with you?"

Frank stared uneasily at the house. He hadn't wanted to come up to London with his cousins, but he had more or less promised he would "talk to" them, somehow, put an end to this Spanish business and then cable Philadelphia to see if Peter could be eased into the firm's credit office there. And here he was outside a nest of hairy-faced bomb-throwers.

"Get me through this thing safe and sound and I'll do anything you ask. Within reason. I'll take you up tomorrow. We'll rent a Puss Moth somewhere. What the hell am I supposed to say to a bunch of Communists and Socialists, anyhow? We don't have anybody like that in Bryn Mawr!"

"More's the pity . . ."

"Done! I'll tell you what to do. First off, don't mention banking or polo. Second, offer to send around to the nearest pub for more drink. Third . . ."

"Come off it, you two. No one's going to hurt you. Talk to the women."

"What about?"

"Talk flying. Wave your arms and make low, gurgling noises."

They began walking up the steps. Harry grabbed Frank's arm.

"If you see me with a whiskey, strike it from my hands. Another bad booze-up and I'll be disinherited. To say nothing of what Tom'll say . . ."

"Who the hell is this Tom, anyhow? The Royal Pretender?"

"Why, no. A comrade."

"Jesus . . ."

They pushed into the foyer, and the crowd there separated them at once. Peter flipped his fingers and began edging toward the stairs. Harry bolted through an open door, his long face pale and serious. Frank stood still, bumped by men and women, stunned by the noise. The house seemed filled, bursting with people. The lights gleamed on walls bare of pictures. The room to the right had no real furniture, but secondhand-looking tables covered with books in toppled piles, hand-lettered signs and cigar boxes overflowing with coins and bank notes. Ashtrays smoldered, and there were empty bottles, soda-water siphons, and half-finished drinks.

"Village Bohemian . . ."

"Beg your pardon?"

"Nothing . . ."

Frank edged into room with the tables, sliding between men and women talking at the party-pitch that melted words into a sustained roar of sound that made the smoky air feel like a sponge. Middle-aged women in hats like salads shouted at boys Harry Desmond's age who looked self-conscious in workingmen's caps and cheap jackets. Most of them wore red neckties. They looked to Frank like Basset hounds with their tongues lolling out. Most of the girls seemed to be wearing the same cropped hair and the same Russian peasant blouse with baggy sleeves.

Frank tried to make his way out of the room and met Peter Desmond coming back with two glasses.

"Here. No fuss about ice, eh? There isn't any."

"There never is. Look. This is ridiculous. I don't know a soul."

"You don't have to. Buy a book. Karl Marx or something. Brian? Here's Brian. Brian, this is someone you and Sylvia must meet. Brian, Sylvia, Frank Buckminster. From America. A pilot."

Brian was a squat, red-faced young man with a new mustache and his jacket slung over one shoulder. His shirt sleeves were rolled above the elbows. He shook hands and grunted something. Sylvia was a tall, plain young girl in a yellow dress. Frank sipped his drink. It was warm as soup.

"I'm not a pilot, really. I have a plane in the States and Peter thinks it's very . . ."

Brian ignored him; Sylvia obviously didn't hear a word he said but smiled anyway. Brian shouted at Peter Desmond.

"We've all just heard that Roy Campbell is safe. He was there, right in Toledo when it started. With wife and kiddies, mind. Just got out. Near thing. Good mate, Roy . . . for a South African."

"Was he hurt?"

"No one knows that yet."

Frank took a large swallow of whiskey. Toledo was the city not far from Madrid that was in all the papers. One bunch of Spaniards had another bunch holed up in a building or fort there. Besieged or something. He smiled at the woman named Sylvia. She tilted her head to hear him.

"I think it's really great the way they're holding out in Toledo. Must be really something."

"I *beg* your pardon?"

"I say it's very heroic, you know, about the way the defenders are holding out."

"The defenders? In Toledo? In the Alcázar?"

"Sure. They're the Nationalists, aren't they?"

"The Nationalists? Quite."

"What's that? What's that?"

A pool of silence suddenly spread. Voices broke off. Several people turned around. The man called Brian set his glass very deliberately on the nearest table and handed Sylvia his jacket. He set his fists on his hips and stared at Frank. Peter Desmond was gone again. Frank was alone in a room full of strangers holding a glass of tepid scotch. Brian made an odd, rooting lift of the head.

"Well, now. You support the Nationalists, do you?"

"Sure, I . . ."

"Like to think you're joking. We'd *all* like it, I think."

"What's the joke? The Nationalists are supporting the government, after all . . ."

Brian threw out his hands, palms up and turned to the others to witness. He took two short, stalking steps toward Frank.

"Yes, I'd like to think this is a leg-pull . . ."

Frank finished his drink quickly and dropped the glass into his jacket pocket. He waited until the jeering at the back of the room stopped.

"With the Anarchists and Reds on the other side. Burning churches . . ."

Brian measured the distance between then. The room was very quiet.

"That much is true. Just forget the churches for a bit. The Left is loyal to the government they elected."

Frank hesitated, puzzled. He didn't dare look away for the Desmonds. Brian was ready to start punching. He shrugged.

"Then if they're loyal, what about the Nationalists?"

Sylvia plucked feebly at Brian's rolled sleeve. He shook her hand off.

"It seems to me, mate, that you've got yourself into the wrong bloody book club!"

"Brian, please . . ."

The others looked ready to help Brian throw him in the street. Frank slipped his wristwatch into his other pocket. No sense getting it broken.

"I don't really have much interest in politics. We've got our own troubles back home with That Man in the White House."

"Do talk on, Mr. Buckchester. This is fascinating."

"Brian, darling, *please!*"

"Just what *is* Roosevelt's attitude toward Spain?"

"I don't know that he's got one. Should he? After all, we had a war with Spain. Won it, of course."

"Imperialist grab on a fourth-rate power!"

"We'll swap you the Philippines for Canada. How's that?"

"In a pig's arse!"

"Brian, *stop* this!"

"Just trying to get at a few facts here, Syl. Fellow's spouting pure Fascism right to our very faces. Let's just have it out."

Frank unbuttoned his jacket and loosened his necktie.

"Pretty crowded, but we could move the tables . . ."

"Naomi will be furious. It isn't a bit fair. I don't think he understands. Do you understand, Mr. Franklin?"

"Nope. I said I'm not interested in politics and . . ."

Brian, red with triumph, shook his fist in Frank's face. Frank threw a half-hearted left jab that landed on the Englishman's shoulder and drove him back against the others. Sylvia shrieked softly, and Brian came back again, but stayed out of range.

"By God, you ought to be! Just because you've an ocean on either side doesn't mean that an isolationist policy can . . ."

Frank turned and walked from the room, directly into a solid mass of people in the front hall, all talking, all unaware of the near-fight. He laughed suddenly. It was all a bunch of nonsense. He put his watch on and sidled around, trying to find where the whiskey was located. Voices beat in his ears.

"Blum would have gone away with an entirely different feeling if he hadn't talked with Eden . . ."

"Eleven million signatures on the Peace Ballot or no, you can't tell me that the average member of the British working class isn't . . ."

"Churchill is openly against the Germans . . ."

"For traditional reasons, not ideological . . ."

"There isn't a single politician in the country who'll stand up for intervention . . ."

"It's premature, old man. Let the French go in . . ."

"What rot! Surely you read in *New Writing* . . ."

"If you ask me, the gloves are off at last. It's either fight them in Spain or right here in London . . ."

"You *are* thinking of going, then?"

"I have a few things to wind up . . ."

"Is it true that Cornford's already at the Aragón front?"

Frank climbed the staircase, setting his feet carefully between the couples seated on the steps. The roar of noise settled behind him. He stepped between two middle-aged men who were admiring a large sheet of paper one of them had just finished fastening to the wall with a roll of bicycle tape.

UPTHEREPUBLIC

"Sam Beckett sent it on from Paris. He says they're recruiting, too."

The upper hall was crowded, although there seemed to be almost no furniture in any of the rooms. No one seemed to know where Peter and Harry Desmond were and no one seemed to care. Another sign said LORCA READING. Frank maneuvered until he stood in the doorway. A young foreign-looking girl seated on a wooden box finished playing a guitar and set it down. Everyone applauded. The room quieted, and a man in a blue shirt and cotton trousers ruffled a sheaf of typed pages.

"First, I think, his 'Ballad of the Civil Guard' . . ."

"Seen the Desmonds?"

"Not in here . . ."

The man began reading. It seemed impolite to leave. Frank leaned against the door-jamb, holding his empty glass.

"Black are the black-shod horses.
Stains of ink and of beeswax
Gleam on the capes of the men.
Their deadly faces are leaden,
Therefore they never weep:
Hearts of patent-leather,
They come along the road.
Twisted, crooked, nocturnal,
They sow in the places they haunt
Sombre elastic silence,
Fears that trickle like sand.
They pass if they want to pass.
They hide in their muddled heads
An astronomical system,
Pistols for planets and stars.

O city of the gypsies! . . ."

Frank stood and listened to the poem. It was longer than he had expected. The only long poem he knew was "Evangeline," memorized for a sixth-grade parents' day. He sensed that the man read the poem well. Somehow, the images disturbed him, even though he didn't understand them. A young girl with her breasts slashed, tiled roofs smashing in the streets, huddled old women, and the troop of murderers riding away.

He stood alone, surrounded, jostled by other people. He had his own ideas about Spain—bullfights, orange groves, olive oil, and pretty señoritas with lace scarves and roses clamped in their teeth. Maybe the poem was the real Spain and the pretty girls were butchered in the streets of Granada. He felt vaguely that it was a damned shame and that somebody ought to do something to straighten out the whole business.

"A penny, as they say."

"Huh?"

He turned around and looked down into the face of a young, smiling English girl with very blue eyes, a pretty girl with her long hair in a single thick braid.

"For your thoughts."

"It's getting late for somebody your age to be up, isn't it?"

"It can't be. I keep this nest."

"You are twelve years old and should be in bed."

"Maybe. But I'm long past twelve."

"Sixteen?"

"You are a very charming chap. You *are* the American?"

"That's right. Frank Buckminster."

"Naomi Coltringham. You look parched. Come meet Tom. He's got the whiskey. Trying to save some for Eric and the others."

He followed her down the hall to the closed door at the end. He liked her at once. She shoved open the door.

"Got him, Tom. He was at the reading."

The room looked ready for a lecture. A brawny, sunburned man with a thick, black mustache was standing near a table. Some small chairs were scrambled in clusters. The man swung across the room, his bulk making the floor tremble. He swung one arm around the girl and thrust out a hand.

"Tom Coltringham. And you're Buckminster, the pilot. You met the missus, eh? Good. Peter asked us to keep a look out for you. They've gone, the Desmonds, for a bit of—well, getting on? You need a dirty great drink and so do I. Got some hidden right here."

Frank pulled his glass from his pocket.

"I was just wondering if it would help out if I sent to the pub for more?"

"Well, it would keep everyone here longer, and that's the great thing, isn't it? You see, the book sales are for the support of the Medical Aid unit."

Coltringham released the girl and produced a bottle of whiskey from under the table. Frank counted some bank notes from his wallet.

"Here. Would that keep things going?"

"Would it! I'll just ring up the Red Lion. Awfully kind, Mr. Buckminster . . ."

"Call me Frank. Everybody does."

She was gone, closing the door. Frank and Coltringham looked at each other. The Englishman held out the bottle.

"Damned pleased you can be with us. Say when."

"When."

"Drink to something? Somebody. Absent friends?"

He would have liked to drink to Naomi, but remembered Brian and Toledo and English reserve and didn't want to risk spoiling something new and pleasant.

"It will have to be Spain. Right?"

"To Spain!"

"To . . . Spain. I suppose you heard that I made a damned fool of myself downstairs. With somebody named Brian. About Toledo."

Coltringham laughed, throwing back his head. Frank grinned at him. He looked like a cross between a college professor and a stevedore.

"Did I not! Oh, you mustn't mind Brian. He's going through the difficult time now. Overcoming his class-consciousness and all that. The 'neo-prole' stage, as Eric calls it. Rather elaborately working-class. Refuses to wear underdrawers. That sort of silly stuff. Threatens people. Sylvia is quite sensible. Better too militant than the other way around."

"God, I don't know. I really don't understand all this. I never saw so many people so steamed up about anything in all my life. I guess it's more important to you people, but . . ."

Coltringham finished his drink and tilted the bottle again.

"But you don't think it's the correct thing . . . politically?"

"I never saw people like this in the States. Not . . . yet, anyway."

"Well. Where does one start? Many of us have been to Spain. Lots were at Trinity College and in the Socialist Club there. Or still are. We're committed, this way or that. The Party, of course."

"I don't understand how anybody would want to be . . . I mean, the papers here, don't . . ."

"Depends which ones you read. How do *you* stand on this? Can I ask? If not, forget it. But Peter tells me you fly. Any combat experience?"

"No. I just sort of buzz around. In light planes. Mixed business and pleasure and went to the air show."

"Business. Oh. You're the banker-feller. Funny, never met a banker before. Face to face, I mean."

"We're even. I never met a Communist, face to face, either."

"How is it?"

"I'll live."

"So'll I. Have a drink. You really bank? Wall Street and all that? You don't look it. Play rugger?"

"American-style. In college. I'm not a banker. It's like being a pilot. My Uncle Harry heads the firm on the American side. My father died a while back. I just play at it, I guess you'd say. I never seem to get very serious about anything. That's not so hot, I suppose."

"Just buzz around in aircraft. Sounds pleasant. While it lasts. Not much longer. Why not *do* something?"

"I will. Go back home. Get to work. Learn the ropes."

"And buzz around in aircraft?"

"And buzz around."

"Look. Seriously. To hell with your politics or mine. I mean this. You can buzz around in Spain and be part of this thing. Can you just turn away? It isn't *that* easy, is it?"

"I just don't think it has much to do with us."

"Us bankers or us people?"

"Us Americans."

"Then you think this is purely European. But you bankers have international concerns. How long do you think it will stay a European affair?"

"I don't know. What about it being just a Spanish affair?"

"That's not possible. Surely you've sensed that . . . may I call you Frank?"

"Sure . . ."

"Granted you're an . . . outsider. Granted a banker. Grant anything you damned well like, but I think you really do *care* . . . *something* . . . don't you?"

Frank shrugged.

"Sure. Okay, say I care. Grant that, too. I don't like wars. I don't like the idea of people being killed. I care that much. Anybody cares that much."

"Fair enough. Then you don't much like the idea that the Spanish people should be killed and their government destroyed?"

"Depends on the government and who's trying to destroy it. Right?"

"Right. Way back when, we British tried to destroy your people and your idea of government. You fought and won. Well, Spain is a democracy and the Army revolted against the government the people elected. Would you let the Army in your country pull that off?"

"Like hell! Roosevelt's bad enough."

"Well, then . . ."

Frank shook his head. He felt that Coltringham had trapped him by a maneuver so simple that it must be false.

"Let the Spaniards settle it. If everybody just stays out . . ."

The Englishman grinned again and nodded.

"That's just the point. *Both* sides have asked for aid. *Both* sides. Not just one. The Republic has asked France and Britain for support. War matériel. Guns, ammunition . . . and aircraft. You might just think on *that* for a minute. Aircraft?"

"Uh-huh. To buzz around in."

"Right. The Rebels . . . Insurgents, Nationalists, so-called, have asked the Italians and the Germans for aid. And they've been helped already. General Franco has been flying Moorish troops in from Africa in German transports. You've read that? Of course. About the Italian ships? The Savoia transports? Aircraft. Not to buzz around in. To ship in soldiers to overthrow the government."

"Damned smart idea, using planes like that. Smart cookie."

"Two Fascist powers helping Franco and the other generals on one side. France and England . . ."

Frank stood up and waved away Coltringham's offer of another drink. The Englishman took one of Frank's cigarettes. Frank shrugged.

"I got the feeling that England was going to stay out."

Coltringham flushed angrily.

"That sort of striped-trews diplomacy is a social crime . . . if it happens. You see my point? Democracies with the Republic, Fascists with the Rebels . . . and I hope to hell you aren't going to come back with that Mussolini-makes-the-trains-run-on-time muck. I shall chuck you about if I hear it, so a word to the wise."

"Tom, I don't *know* anything about Fascism. I don't know any more about Mussolini than what I see in the newsreels. A big-jawed Wop that picked on a bunch of darkies in Ethiopia while the League of Nations sat around and talked. Do I like the idea that he's going to pick on Spain now? No, not much. But it's basically a European affair."

The bulky Englishman pinched and fretted at his cigarette, snapping ashes onto the bare floor. Frank shifted about nervously and wondered where Harry and Peter Desmond had gone to and how soon they could all get away from this place. The two men stared at each other. Coltringham opened his mouth, scrubbed at his mustache and cleared his throat. Frank finished his drink.

"Sorry, Tom. I seem to be in the wrong place or saying the wrong thing or both."

"Well, I'll say I think your attitude a damned curious one. Been trying to think, you see. I can't seem to come up with anything that doesn't sound like damned foolishness . . . You know . . . Mr. - Buckminster - I - trust - your - views - are - typical - only - of - American - capitalists - and - not - the - American - working - class . . . Christ, I sound like *Brian!*"

Coltringham laughed, his head thrown back, his whole heavy-muscled body shaking. He snorted and wiped his eyes.

"Sound like Harry Pollitt, too. Damned if I don't."

"Who's he?"

"Secretary of the CP . . . Communist Party. In Britain, that is. Talks like that all the time."

"But you're a Communist."

"*Course* I am! Pollitt's a bore, all the same. Have a drink, lad. I like you, ruddy millionaire or no."

"I'm not a millionaire. But I'm not a member of the 'working class,' either."

Coltringham poured out more whiskey, eyed the level in the bottle and muttered about saving some for Eric and Eileen, set the bottle on the floor, shoved his arm through Frank's and towed him to the window.

"Want to show you something. Look down there."

Frank stared down into the back garden. It was nearly dark, but he could see people moving about, young men and a few girls, the girls holding two drinks or two cigarettes, while the men puttered with bundles and packages, suitcases and boots.

"Can you see well enough to count them? The chaps, I mean."

"Twenty . . . no, three more there . . . with, is that a tent? Twenty-three. Not counting the girls."

"Two missing, yet. Getting their gear ready. For what? For where? For Spain. Those aren't workers, Frank. They come from here and there,

to be sure. But they met at Oxford or Cambridge. Students and writers
. . . would-be, anyhow. How old do they look?"

"I saw some downstairs. Young. Eighteen, maybe twenty-odd."

"Right. Kids. Young Dickie Crashaw was to go along. His Mum
showed up in a taxi and cried all over the place and dragged young Dickie
away with her. Happened just before you came."

"Jesus, he must have been mad . . . angry, I mean. Sore."

"He was. He'll slip her soon and tag along. How old are you?"

"Me? Thirty-two, my next birthday. You?"

"Thirty-nine . . . Yes, I was in at the fag-end of the last war.
Infantry. Three months in the lines. Blighty-bullet in the leg. I was home
again when it ended. But see? I'm taking them to Spain. And how many
will come back? Half of them? Less? None of them? But they give a
damn. They'll go fight, even if they aren't workers. Even if they are kids,
students, and poets and still damp behind the ears. They care about
Spain. And, damn it, I care about them!"

"Then for Christ's sakes don't let them do it, Tom! It's crazy. They
look like a bunch of Boy Scouts down there. Camping trip."

"They do. Yes. That's what I thought of, too. But I can't *not* take
them. They'll go anyway. Better to have an old crock like me along. At
least I can tell them when to duck and how deep to dig. Besides, Frank, I
couldn't stay here. You have to *do* something. It's being willing to put
your miserable body right out there where your beliefs are. Yes, and get
them *both* shot at. They can kill the body. But the beliefs . . ."

"I don't have any. Not like that."

"Yes, you do. Come on. Don't be one of these tiresome middle-class
types who mopes about saying I'm-worthless-I'm-worthless, hoping that
everyone will say, oh, no you're not . . . especially women. Married?
That it?"

"No. No, I'm not married. Not even a girl, these days. The last one was
a bit . . . ah, tangled. She married another guy. Steady type. Not like me.
Now, your wife . . ."

"Naomi? We're not married. Funny, I thought Harry would tell you.
I couldn't, mate, don't you see? She's only nineteen. I'll be forty soon.
I couldn't do that. Taking these kids over is bad enough. Leaving one
behind would do it for me. See?"

"Yuh. I see."

"Come over here and take another look. You can just see them still,
before the dark blots them out. They'll be downstairs, yelling for beer
and arguing poetry. She likes that. I wouldn't want to keep her from it.
With me away, it'll be easier. She can find some skinny Byron and be
happy."

They sat on two chairs in the dark room, the bottle on the floor between
them. The whole house murmured with the movement of people up and

down the stairs, from room to room, the sound of voices steady as water rushing somewhere in the darkness. Coltringham cleared his throat, a hard, racking noise.

"I remember the planes in the last one. French Nieuports and Spads. We had Camels and a slab-sided thing called an S.E.5. Jerry had Fokkers, mostly. Easy to think what the lads called *them*, when they came over the trenches to strafe. I saw a triplane once. One of Richthofen's Flying Circus. Shot down behind our lines. We went back to look at it."

"I know the planes. I used to make airplane models. That's how I got interested in flying. Making models. Rubber-band ones, first. Then with little gasoline engines in them. I've still got them hung up in the office . . . the hangar where I keep my big ones."

"You really have a couple of aircraft?"

"A Piper Cub and an old Curtis biplane. I fooled around racing the Curtis. Never won anything."

"I'm damned. Always thought it was governments and armies that owned all the aircraft. Funny. Know what they are, of course. A flying platform for machine guns. Hard to hit from the ground. God, how they used to rip up the trenches."

"I've seen the movies. Errol Flynn. Basil Rathbone. *Dawn Patrol.*"

"Right. Every so often I can see these young chaps here out on a hill in Spain. No cover but grapevines and a few olive trees. Then you hear the engines and they come at you, diving down out of the sun. The dust-spouts go up all around and people are hit before you can hear the sound of the machine guns. The shadows slide over the ground, like stiff bat-shapes . . . and the whole platoon is torn up by then and bleeding and nobody even got a shot off at them . . . I can see it, Frank, I tell you . . ."

The room filled with golden, glaring light. Frank jumped up, blinking. Naomi stood in the doorway, her hand still on the switch.

"See it? How can you see a thing? Pitch black. I'm back from the pub and Meg's place, too. That's where Eric and Eileen were. Having tea and smokes at Meg's. What snobs, eh? Getting on, are you, old walrus?"

Coltringham stood up, nodding, rubbing his mustache and grinning.

"Yes, yes. Getting on. I was just boring Frank here with old war stories. Eric here?"

"God, Tom, you didn't hear a thing I said. Yes, downstairs. He has his papers and everything. Going to Barcelona. Journalist. And one thing more . . . Eileen's going, too. So there! Do you hear that? That settles *that* argument, I should think. If she goes . . ."

"Then all the more bloody reason for you to stay damned-well here, my girl. Listen. Tell Eric to have a drink on us. I'll be right down."

"He said he'll be right up."

"All right."

Frank edged toward the door, carrying his empty glass.

"Well, I think I'd better be going. Find Harry and Peter. You've been very kind. I learned something, Tom. Really. That's straight."

Coltringham came over to the door. He looked at Frank steadily.

"Then one thing more. I'd feel a hell of a lot better if you were up there buzzing around giving air coverage for us dust-eaters. More of those chaps in the garden will be able to come back if you fly for the Republic."

Naomi touched Frank's arm.

"You mean you *aren't* going to Spain? I thought when you came with Harry and Peter Desmond that it was all decided."

Frank shook his head.

"Oh, Lord, no. I mean, I haven't decided. And they can't go. Peter's going back with me to the States to work in our credit office. Harry's going up to Oxford. He's just a kid!"

Naomi looked at Coltringham. Her blond brows rose slightly. Tom shrugged his heavy shoulders. His grizzled hair looked golden in the light from the unshaded bulb.

"Like hell. You do as you must. But Harry and Peter are going over with me. I bought their tickets this morning."

"*What?*"

"I thought they told you. Peter's gone out to make arrangements about the motorcar, and Harry's gone to get his kit. He had a devil of a time smuggling the stuff out, I hear. Old man's had the wind up for weeks. Been watching him like a hawk. We're for Southampton tomorrow. Then 'fair stands the wind for France.' One last good drunk and one last . . ."

Naomi began to cry.

Frank tried to give her his handkerchief. He dropped his glass. It broke on the floor. Coltringham kicked the pieces into the corner, slouched to a chair, and sat down. The tears slid down the girl's face.

"Come on. Fetch him another glass and let's drink up. Do stop that, Naomi, won't you? Here, fighter-pilot, have some whiskey . . ."

"Listen, cut it out, huh? Don't be a bastard."

"And don't be a sentimentalist. It doesn't become you, Wall Street. Strictly business. Leave it to the Europeans. Right. We'll settle this. Come here and give us a kiss, hon. You want a drink, Naomi?"

She wiped her eyes clumsily with the backs of her hands, like a child. She found a glass on the window sill and held it out, holding it in both hands. Coltringham smiled, stood up, and kissed her on the brow.

"Good girl. Heard of Malraux?"

Frank shook his head angrily. He didn't like Coltringham now.

"No. Who the hell is Malraux?"

"Bloody famous Frenchman. Cambodia and China and all that. You've read *Man's Fate*, of course."

"No. My mother probably read it. I don't read much. I just buzz around, remember?"

Coltringham laughed and hugged Naomi. She gave him an ardent, girlish, smacking kiss on the corner of his mustache. Frank grinned weakly, his anger ebbing.

"That's more like it, Yank. Bit of spirits poured in us and a bit spits back out. Cheers! To Spain, then, and let's find out where in hell Eric's at."

"Cheers! To hell with Spain. I'm going back home and taking Peter with me!"

"That's what you think, fighter-pilot. Bring the bottle, mate. Meet the other comrades. Be good for your capitalist soul."

Naomi broke away from Coltringham and plucked the handkerchief from Frank's fingers.

"Damn. That's the third time today. I look a wreck. You're not dashing off? Let's you and me get out of this. It's nicer downstairs. So many people down there you can't think at all. You just . . . feel things and that's all right. It's thinking that . . ."

She slipped out into the hall. Frank hesitated and nodded to Coltringham, held out his hand to shake, waved it instead and hurried after her.

"Look. Don't abandon me. I don't know anyone here."

"I must see to the drink. The boys brought it round. Twenty buys enough to float the Royal Barge, I must say. And I should know. Daddy keeps a pub."

"Where? In the city?"

"God forbid. Down in Devon. He thinks I'm in typing school."

"You ought to be."

"Mr. Buckminster, I do believe you are shocked."

"Well, what the hell, you know . . ."

"Come buy a book."

"I don't want a book, Naomi. Can we . . ."

"Go somewhere quiet? I don't think that would be a good idea."

"I do. It would be a great idea."

"Great ideas are in books. Come on . . ."

They pressed through the crowded hall. He took her small, moist hand and held it loosely, pretending that she was leading him. Voices battered all around him.

"If patriotism is the last refuge of the scoundrel, then what in hell is pacifism? Answer me *that!*"

"How can you have a non-intervention policy when the Nazis have already intervened?"

"Stalin will not sit and do nothing. Help from the Soviets is just a matter of time. Probably already been decided on."

"Yes, leaving with Tom in the morning . . ."

"French shipping the stuff by way of Mexico. Cannons, ammunition and planes. Bombers. Long way round is the shortest way home . . ."

"Get some miners down from Asturias and plant dynamite in the Alcázar. One blast and the place is ours . . ."

"My gear's all set? Yours?"

"Get a Spanish dictionary. No, in the other room . . ."

The room with the book-filled tables was less crowded. The someone named Eric was in the room with the Spanish dictionaries, and most of the crowd had pressed in to see him. Frank asked and found out his last name was Blair.

"Who's he, Naomi? How did you get a name like that, anyway? You should be named Sally or something."

"He's a writer. My father liked it. Ugh. Sally is pretty Maughamish, isn't it? Here we are. Three-volume collection of Marx. Marked down, too."

"Uh . . . no, thanks. Pretty heavy to carry around."

"Pretty heavy reading. Here's something light."

She handed him a skinny, small book in a plain paper jacket.

"What's this? Something French?"

"Something Welsh. Poems. New. Somebody Thomas."

He put the book down and glanced at the table. A scuffled stack of something labeled *British Union Quarterly* . . . CAN YOU STOMACH IT? was just beyond reach. She pushed his hand away.

"You don't want that, I hope. Brian will really dust you up if he catches you with that."

"Oh, I thought it was something to do with medicine."

People came and went and got drinks and brought them back again and talked. There was no sign of food, but the beer was plentiful, the room was stuffy with cigarette smoke and rattling with talk.

"Of course they're burning the churches! Damned good thing. Even if Anarchists have no discipline, they're a damned sight better . . ."

"Did you read the *News-Chronicle* today?"

"No, anti-tank or machine-gun squad, I think. That way I'm sure to see action . . ."

"Look at Sassoon, Rupert Brooke, and Wilfred Owen. The test of being there. *Being* there. Enduring, seeing it, hearing and feeling it. I tell you, it's the risk that makes the artist."

"Yes, I'm for Spain. Damned right. That's all I can say. I'm for Spain . . ."

No one left; more people came. The rooms were filled with what seemed to be a permanent gathering of people who did not eat food, sit on furniture or sleep. They drank ale and talked about Spain.

Frank at last went over to them, not slowly, but at once, and happily, like a man swimming upstream who gives it up for a long, easy ride to the sea.

"What the hell, you know? If you can't lick 'em . . . join 'em . . ."

They were nice people, too, open, friendly, bursting with ideas and energy. He rode with them, lifted with the tailwind of triumphant-sounding talk, kiting on whiskey and beers beyond counting, feeling slightly drunk, red-eyed and enthusiastic. He began to accept books, pamphlets, newspapers, quarterlies, and shoddy little magazines of essays and verse by people he had never heard of but discovered he had just spent a half hour talking with. He gave out cigarettes and bottles of ale and got three dictionaries, seven *pensión* addresses. Coltringham appeared, burly and jovial and dragged Frank out from behind the table, and called him "my mate, Buckminster, the fighter-pilot from the States." Immediately, Frank found himself launched into a passionate defense of interceptor aircraft over conventional anti-aircraft cannon. He stood on a cracker box and made swooping gestures with both hands and motor and machine-gun noises. Everyone seemed to agree, somehow, that the critical height was ten thousand feet and there, the stuff from the ground couldn't hurt you.

Everyone wanted to educate him at once, on Spanish food and wines, places he "must see . . . between missions, of course." The history of Spain, the Armada, the only decent sherry, don't-take-a-chance-on-the-water, flamenco music, bullfighting, a German aircraft designer named Messerschmitt, some sort of trials going on in Moscow, a cheaper place to stay in London, a pub that *did* serve ice if they knew you were American, why the Popular Front concept would influence American politics. At different times in the long night, three different girls offered him "a place to stay" until he went to Spain.

It was all rather like a Winter Carnival weekend at college, or the night Prohibition ended, an elastic time stretching with no end, of easy friendships, the smell of beer and bodies, of laughter and hard, knuckle-cracking logic near windows thrown open to clear the smoke from the room, of maps plucked from pockets and strategic genius demonstrated with broken matches, all the emotion, washed aloft and held, like a thermal current, by brown ale bottles and a Spain that was not a place, or an idea, but a feeling, an emotion so strongly felt that not to go was to skulk in the *donjon* while the others buckled on the armor and rode to the last Crusade.

He liked them and was happy that they liked him and weren't afraid to say so. He felt some quirky bond to this house of noisy Englishmen. They spoke the same language, more or less, and all their talk lifted and drove him at once to a farther set of *what the hell, you know* than he had ever wanted to feel before. It was new and good to the point of wonderful. He found that he invited them to Philadelphia, "as soon as the goddamned war is over." And they accepted. All but Naomi.

It was long after noisy midnight when he discovered that Peter and Harry Desmond had returned. Harry staggered around in the foyer, hunched beneath the weight of a bulging knapsack. Peter had three sleeping bags already unrolled in the back garden, a number of aluminum cooking pots and utensils and a portable Primus stove.

"Well, well, well. About time. Where in hell have you two been? You'll have to get somebody to look after the car. We're flying back to Kent. Land on the south pasture. Rent a plane somewhere. I promised a couple of girls, see? Naomi won't come along though."

"Hmmm. Been a bit of thing here for you, hasn't it? Thought we might get to you. Up the Republic?"

"Goddamned right! Up the Republic! What about the car?"

"Did we not take care of it? Got a jolly fat price for it, too."

"You sold it? You *sold* the goddamned car? This hour of night?"

"Some little time ago, Yank. Secret negotiations. Just dropped it off. Had to have cash for it. Right?"

"Oh, Jesus . . ."

"Anyway, what would we do with a car in Spain? *Armored car*, I grant you. We thought of that. Gave it up. Have you met Eric yet? Tall, great, gaunt fellow with a new wife."

"He's with the ILP group. Upstairs with Tom again. Talking politics. P.S.U.C. and P.O.U.M. and C.G.T. . . . No, U.G.T. and C.N.T. and F.A.I."

"Great God, man, what have they *done* to you?"

"Nothing. Above ten thousand feet they can't do a damned thing."

"Then you've got nothing to fear. Girls?"

"Girls. But Naomi . . ."

"Uh-uh. Last time you were over here it was Giulia in that awful place in Bloomsbury. Listen, Franklin, don't get sappy and fall in love. Besides, Harry's already in love with her and so am I."

"Isn't *poum* slang French for shit?"

"Ask your flyer friend Saulnier."

"I'll ask Malraux."

"Come on upstairs and ask Eric. He'd know."

The rear room upstairs was crowded. Everyone huddled in sit-down-strike position on the floor, drinking the bad coffee from unwashed glasses and listening to Tom Coltringham and Eric debate the value of spontaneous militia groups inspired by a sense of class obligation and revolutionary discipline versus conventional military organizations or *apparat*, as Tom called it. Coltringham won the debate by a show of hands. More coffee and ale came up the stairs. As Naomi passed him, Frank reached out and touched the thick blond braid.

"Hi."

"Let go, hon, you'll have me spilling . . ."

Hon. He watched her sway between the crowded, huddled people, handing out bottles of beer. Midsummer Night at Daddy's pub somewhere in Devon. . . .

"The poem, Eric! The little fat man poem!"

"What did he say?"

"Says he's no poet and it's a pity Day Lewis isn't here."

"Is it?"

"There's a boy downstairs with a telegram for somebody who's supposed to be up here."

"You'll have to be more specific, comrade. Liaison breaks down somewhere near the first turning in the stairs."

It was too noisy at the doorway and out in the hall to hear much of the poem that Eric recited. Frank stood, leaning against the door-jamb, watching Naomi.

> "It is forbidden to dream again;
> We maim our joys or hide them;
> Horses are made of chromium steel,
> And little fat men shall ride them."

Harry Desmond butted him from behind. He was still strapped into his bulging knapsack and sweaty-faced from climbing the stairs.

"That's damned good. Literature *can* be good propaganda. 'Little fat man.' That's Franco for you. Bloody little Fascist sod."

"Shut up, will you? I can't hear with you chattering. Take off that pack before you pass out."

"Can't. Must get into shape. May have to walk the Pyrenees if the Frogs close the border. Been running five miles before breakfast for weeks. Oh, I think you've got a 'gram. Boy downstairs."

"Yeah, all right, in a minute . . ."

Someone bellowed up the stairs, and everyone in the hall turned around and *shhhhhed* furiously.

"Anybody up there named Buck Franklin or something?"

"That's me. I'll be right down."

"Oh, it's you, is it? It's fighter-pilot. Good show. Tell them we're coming over, will you?"

"Shut up in the bloody hall, will you?"

"My, my! Brian is feisty tonight, isn't he?"

"Don't tell me anything about Brian."

Harry laughed. "I heard you almost did ten rounds in the square circle . . ."
"Shhhhh!"

> "I dreamed I dwelt in marble halls,
> And woke to find it true;
> I wasn't born for an age like this;
> Was Smith? Was Jones? Were you?"

There was applause for Eric's poem. He bowed awkwardly.
"Hey, fighter-pilot, come and get your 'gram, won't you? The boy's been here for half an hour and says he won't stay, Spain or no Spain."
He crept down the steps cluttered with discarded glasses and ashtrays. The "boy" was nearly sixty, frail, and cranky-faced. He thrust out a book and the tissue envelope.
"Yer not one easy found, guv . . ."
"Not above ten thousand feet. Remember that."
"Sign 'ere, huh?"
"Here. Take this. Thanks."
"Say, any time, guv. Good news, I 'ope."
Frank opened the telegram and squinted at the top line. It had been sent to him from Paris, not from the Desmond family in Kent. It was not about the boys and the Riley motorcar, then.

VOLUNTEER SQUADRON FORMING TO FLY FOR REPUBLIC. 25,000 FRANCS PER MONTH INSURED 300,000 FRANCS HAVE RESERVED ROOM HOTEL GEORGE V POURQUOI PAS

SAULNIER

He read it through three times. A crowd of people butted past him, following Eric, Coltringham, and some others out through the open front door, down the steps to the sidewalk. He waited, smoking his last cigarette, until Tom and Harry and Peter Desmond came back. Harry had taken off his knapsack and Naomi was gently kneading his shoulders. Frank pushed the telegram at Tom Coltringham.
"Here. Read this."
Coltringham fumbled out steel-rimmed glasses and set them on his nose. He read and the grin spread across his face.
"Well, I'm damned. Malraux's doing, I'll bet a tenner. Listen! Listen, everyone! Hey! Hear this! The French are forming a volunteer air force to take war planes into the Republic!"
Everyone cheered and applauded, whistled and stamped until the floors shivered. Books slithered off the tables and plopped to the stained floors.

Peter Desmond clamped his hands on Frank's shoulders and shook him slowly back and forth.

"You can't say you won't go, Frank! Not now! Not with this! You *can't!*"

He grinned foolishly. Harry Desmond's mouth puckered as Naomi kneaded his shoulders where the pack straps had cut in. Tom handed him back the telegram. They stood there, waiting.

"Twenty-five thousand francs. How can you turn it down? You can be a decent chap, fight on the right side, give us air cover and get paid for it all at the same time! Live long enough and you'll have enough to buy your own fighter-ship."

"Uh-huh. Or I could get killed quick and will it to the Republic. Easy come, easy go."

"Frank, for all of us. You *are* going?"

"Well . . . What the hell, you know . . . For a little while, anyhow . . ."

"Good!"

"Hey! Hey! Up the Yanks!"

"I promised I'd keep an eye on you birds . . . just buzz around. Only one thing."

"What?"

"I can't speak much Spanish."

"Neither can we, old man, neither can we! We'll learn on the ferry going over tomorrow."

"Sure . . . what the hell, you know . . ."

BOOK TWO

No Pasarán!
August–November 1936

Colonel Bravo brought his white-gloved hand to the visor of his hat, grunted a greeting and walked into his office. As he closed the door, the clerks began typing furiously, the rattle of the keys like distant machine-gun fire. Bravo walked to the window. He stood there, staring out over the empty runways of the airport. Beyond the hangars, the new General Motors trucks were drawn up in a double row. All was ready there. In fourteen minutes, the first Junkers transports would fly in from Morocco. The morning sun was already hot.

Bravo fretted his fingers free from the gloves and turned to the wall calendar. The day was circled in red ink. August 5, the day of the Virgin of Africa. Under the date, he had written REISEGESELLSCHAFTSUNION—German for "tourist group," and under that HEINKEL (?).

He walked to his desk and sat down. At his left elbow lay two dispatch cases, one labeled HISMA, the other ROWAK. He opened the HISMA case and leafed through the documents. At the top of each sheet, the clerks had typed COMPAÑÍA HISPANO-MARROQUÍ DE TRANSPORTES, the title of the holding company created to market the war goods and services of Germany. Each sheet listed the number of the transport aircraft, time of departure from Morocco and estimated arrival time at Cádiz airport. The Moorish soldiers of the Army of Africa were listed as "passengers" with a cipher for their company and their *tabor*. Two *tabors* were due to arrive in eleven minutes, the planes landing at seven-minute intervals until 0945, five hundred and fifty Regulares, bringing the total of combat soldiers flown into Cádiz to exactly fifteen hundred. The

waiting trucks would transport them immediately to Colonel Yagüe at
the front. Everything was precalculated by the transport staff of the
German commander of the operation, General Von Scheele. The transport bills-of-lading were even cross-indexed by weight, time, fuel con-
sumption, distance and double-totaled in German marks and Spanish
pesetas with the due date for payment noted at the bottom of the last
page.

Bravo nodded approvingly. That was true German efficiency. He reached
for the second case marked ROWAK and opened it. What an impossible
language the Germans had! No wonder his staff laughed over their typewriters. ROWAK for *Rohstoffe-und-Waren-Einkaufsgesellschaft!* And
every sheet in the case had been obtained by an agent planted in the
ROWAK office. Whenever a German firm offered raw materials or
weapons to ROWAK as the central purchasing agency, a secret copy of
prices and profit percentage was forwarded into Spain to be checked
against the final pricing of the goods and materials sold through HISMA.
By this method, the Nationalist general staff could check and double-
check the price of German aid, without the knowledge of their new Nazi
allies. That was true Spanish cleverness. Three times in the last week he
had been able to reject outrageous charges submitted by FIAT. Fascists
or not, the Italians were not to be trusted.

Bravo lifted the case to place it in the office vault. It would hardly do
to have Kapitan Kurt Schmidt, acting local commander of "tourist group"
see the documents. He would know at once that ROWAK security had
been secretly breached, right down to the serial numbers on the engines
of the six Heinkel fighter aircraft designated for delivery, partially assembled, to Cádiz flying field at 1055.

As he lifted the case, Bravo saw the newspaper, neatly folded. He
glanced at it once. It was from the other side. The front page photograph
showed a woman standing on the running board of a truck, her right fist
clenched in the Red salute. How did it get on his desk? Who brought it?
Why?

Bravo strode to the safe, thrust the case of secret documents inside and
spun the dial. There. He sat down again and opened the newspaper. It
bore no name, only the imprint P.S.U.C. on its masthead. A Communist
paper, issued in Madrid, no doubt.

FURIOUS ASSAULT ON ALCAZAR!

MOLA REPULSED IN SIERRAS!

STRATEGIC REGROUPING AT CÓRDOBA

Lies, all lies. Typical Bolshevik spew. One of the staff officers must have
brought it in for a joke . . . or to curry favor. He had been unable to

conceal his disappointment at not being appointed to field command. Granted his knowledge of German indicated some sort of liaison post, but to be stuck here at Cádiz, a glorified quartermaster, a timekeeper for flying cattle cars? While Yagüe, an old comrade, to be sure, popular to be sure, even possessed of a certain rudimentary competence as a tactician . . . Yagüe had been handed field command? Had Yagüe negotiated with the Carlists? Kept watch on the Madrid Falange? This was his just reward for his services? Colonel by brevet in a staff post, commander of a gang of sniggering, clumsy-fingered clerks, with his major weapon a Spanish-German dictionary? Impossible to think it, yet it was quite as though his superiors did not trust him. What reason could they have? He had explained, in the most casual, joking fashion in the officers' *cantina*, how he had sold his Madrid apartment for a fat price, two days before the Rising. The money from the Carlist faction in Navarre was neatly accounted for. He had made a clever business transaction. Still . . .

Of course, there was the usual amount of politics in the background. The commander in Seville was Quiepo del Llano, of the Carabineros, an eccentric and a drunkard as well, while, he, Bravo, was a veteran of the Army of Africa.

Bravo opened the shoddy newspaper. He grinned at a Quiepoism that had escaped the proofreader. Instead of *miedo*, third line second column, the word was *mierda*. The Falangists were not filled with fear, but full of shit. Maybe it was *not* a typo. He smiled and glanced at the feature column.

> LA NOVIA DE LA GUARDIA ROJA
> ¿MILICIANA O "AMAZONA?"
> "SOPA DE AMETRALLADORA"
> PARA LOS ENIMIGOS DE LA
> REPÚBLICA!

He looked at the photograph. A young woman in overalls, with a Red neckerchief and a belt of machine-gun ammunition slung across her shoulders. She was smiling, her right fist clenched. Bravo stared, his heart jolting. His glance skidded to the photograph caption:

SWEETHEART OF THE RED GUARDS—CARMEN BRAVO

"Jesucristo Rey!"

Colonel Bravo slumped in his chair, his mouth open, one hand pressed palm down over the photograph. It could not be! It was a lie!

He lifted his hand. His fingers trembled. He gnawed his lip and stared again at the photograph. A mistake. Another typographical error. A filthy trick!

How do the young people of Spain answer the call of La Pasionaria? Have generations of witless nuns and prison-convents destroyed the sense of duty to the motherland and class-consciousness of the young women of Madrid?

"A thousand times no!" is the fierce response of beautiful soldier-patriot, Carmen Bravo, *novia* of the glory-drenched Red Guards commanded by that hero of the people, El Asturiano.

How can the youth of Madrid throw off the narcotic of political indifference?

"Leave home and join us in the Sierras!" is the prompt reply from the smiling lips of this young Amazon. Her fighting comrades cheer and applaud. Their favorite dish? *Sopa de ametralladora.* "Machine-gun soup."

"She is tremendous!" declares the now-famous defender of the Samossierra Pass. "She cooked for us, loaded cartridge-clips, stood regular guard duty, nursed the wounded and joined us in three attacks, one of them the night patrol when we captured the two Fascist machine-gun posts. How the men laughed then! Captured ammunition to us we call lentils for machine-gun soup!"

Although he declares that he and the soldier-*señorita* are but comrades-in-arms, are not arms made for embraces? Can love bloom on the battlefield? Do not the gentle tendrils of passion brush against the harsh vine of patriotic duty?

"The fight against Fascism and the defense of Madrid is paramount," declares the convent-runaway. But are her blushes from her family shame or called to her cheeks by the bold glances of the man who commands her heart?

My Own Father a Traitor

Supreme irony! This handmaiden of Mars was once bound to a rotting cross by an active conspirator against the Republic!

"My comrades in the Red Guards have showed human kindness and class-solidarity at all times. Yes, it's true. How to admit it? My father, Colonel Faustino Bravo, of the Fifth Bandera of the Tercio, betrayed the trust of the Spanish people by joining the insurgents quite early in their poison-plot against the Republic. I discovered, to my horror and disgust, that his word of honor was a sham, a pledge of lies to his so-called God. History must forgive him. I never can!"

From Convent to the Sierras

"It is impossible to know fear when the Red Guards go into action," she declares. "Why from the very first night when certain well-intentioned but misguided political allies set fire to the convent where I had been sent against my will, I have felt nothing but optimism and a hatred for our enemies. Life for the Republic, but death for all Fascists!" Here tears blind her beauteous eyes and she can but clench her fist in tribute to the people.

Bravo's fingers clawed the newspaper to a ball. He was shaking uncontrollably, and sweat leaked down his ribs, staining his tunic. He mashed the crumpled ball with his fists.

"Shut up! Shut up, you lying little whore! I forbid this, Carmen! Absolutely! Little pig! This is how you repay your own . . ."

He clapped his damp fingers over his lips. The walls of the room tilted. The calendar swung in a sickening glide, and saliva gushed into his throat. He dropped his head between his knees. *Quiet. Control. My God, I'm raving . . . I'll beat her, I'll . . .*

He heard steps outside the office door and lurched upright, his clenched hands locked against his belly. The crumpled newspaper, springing softly out from the wad he had beaten with his fists, seemed some spongy malignancy growing there on the green baize plane of the desk. He struck it off on the floor, the back of his hand toppling the telephone. He clattered the apparatus together, cursing softly. Knuckles rapped on the door.

"Pass."

Bravo sat stiffly erect, his arms clamped against ribs. Little beads of sweat tickled his chest hair and eyebrows. As the orderly stiffened and saluted, Bravo felt a weak wash of nausea.

"Yes?"

"I thought you called, sir."

"No . . . no . . ."

"I beg your pardon, Colonel, but do you feel ill?"

"I am never ill, *cabo* . . . Save your sympathies for others . . ."

"Yes, Colonel."

Bravo discovered, to his horror, that he was on the verge of tears. The orderly's boots creaked as he shifted impatiently, waiting to be dismissed.

"Who . . . who was in this office before I arrived?"

"Who was here, sir? Why, me and Zuloaga, first, then . . ."

Bravo's voice was a croak. He breathed deeply several times and then felt steady enough to raise his glance to the orderly's face.

"Someone not of this group. An officer. Who was he?"

"Yes, sir. A captain. He brought a newspaper. He said he was sorry to have missed you. Before we could stop him, he was in here and out again, just like that."

"What command, *cabo?*"

"Fifth Bandera, Colonel Bravo. We thought he must be a fellow officer and a friend."

"His name? No one gets by the front desk without giving his name."

The orderly could not help himself. He looked, once, just for an instant, at the floor. The newspaper had spread itself out into a low, wrinkled mound.

"His name, *cabo?*"

"Captain Girona. He said he served under you . . . in thirty-four, in Asturias. Said you'd remember him."

"Yes, I remember him. He was my aide."

"He's . . ."

"Go on. What?"

"He's aide to Colonel Yagüe now."

"Yes. I see. I understand."

"Sorry, sir."

"Dismissed."

It was several minutes after the orderly softly closed the door before Bravo attempted to stand up. The sensations of physical illness were gone, but he felt numb, stunned. He bent cautiously and picked up the newspaper. He looked again at the front page. How could she have done such a thing? He noticed that the photograph had been clumsily retouched to give his daughter a bulging bosom, to make the zippered overall she wore appear open nearly to the waist. He folded the shoddy pages, smoothing the wrinkles, and thrust it inside his tunic.

The sound of the motors reached him. He started, glanced guiltily at the wall clock and paced slowly to the window. The aircraft were coming in right on time. Something about the roar of the motors disturbed him. He looked and saw the first flight in the southern sky, a V of dark bits against the pale blue sky. For some reason, the Germans did not synchronize the engines on the Ju-52 transports. The sound of the motors was a deep, pulsing, a throb of racket that beat on the brain, *ur-ur-ur* like the burr of mechanical idiots. The dull, brutal spasms irritated Bravo. He forced himself to stand and watch as the German aircraft broke formation and circled in the landing patterns, losing altitude over the city of Cádiz.

The first Junkers came in, heavy, black, flat-sided as a freight car, the three motors battering, propellers like coins on the wing nacelles and the bulbous snout. The angular wings jutted stiff and graceless, the tips lopped square. The rudder, a clumsy, doorlike slab still bore the Luftwaffe swastika, the black witches'-cross on a blood-red ball. It settled, roaring, like a glutted bird of prey, the stiff, spatted landing gear awkward and heavy as a child's toy. The trimotor transport touched down and rolled slowly down the runway. Another one hammered through the air, landing flaps dragging like slats of lumber across the pale blue sky, exhaust pipes gushing dirty streams of smoke. Ugly as crates or coffins, black and graceless as a flock of crows, practical as flying tractors, the Nazi aircraft came bellowing out of the soft southern sky, landed and waddled up to the waiting trucks. The rectangular doors opened, and the Moors dropped from the bellies of the transports and fled to the waiting trucks. As soon as one truck was filled, it pulled away. The empty Junkers wheeled clumsily, engines gunning and spilling smoke, trundled to the take-off strip, rolled faster until the undercarriages bounced free and then beat away toward Morocco, sailing in stiff menace over the city of Cádiz. It took, Bravo noted, precisely seven minutes to unload each aircraft. He wondered, absently, why the precision of the Germans was punched into shapes so repugnant, angular and crude. The Junkers Ju-52 was an aircraft, a German machine. It had neither grace nor soul and made a noise like three steel cows.

At exactly 1055, the trucks pulled through the gates, six trucks, each ingeniously hitched to the rudder and elevator assembly of the Heinkel interceptor aircraft. The fighter-planes, propellerless and shark-nosed with round radiator gullets were trim, murderous, with mottled fuselages. Each truck carried the wings of the interceptor it towed. The HISMA papers stated that it took three Luftwaffe mechanics two hours and thirty-five minutes to refix the wings, struts and wires, an additional seventeen minutes for ground-testing and only ten minutes to fuel and arm the machine guns. Kapitan Kurt Schmidt would take the first Heinkel bi-plane up no later than 1400 hours. To assure this, the German pilot had sent his mechanics and equipment on ahead in a mobile machine-shop already parked between the east hangars.

A black Hispano-Suizo sedan stopped fifty meters from the operations building. A young officer in an immaculate foreign uniform sprang from the automobile and stalked swiftly to the main entrance. Bravo stepped from the window. His tunic crinkled as he smoothed his lapels. He went to his desk and sat, waiting, gazing blankly at his German-Spanish dictionary. The orderly knocked.

"Pass."

"Capitán Schmidt of the Reise . . . um . . . ge . . ."

"Reisegesellschaftsunion, cabo."

"Requests . . ."

"Show him in."

The German did not seem to enter the office but rather to occupy it. He was not there one instant, the next he was, like trick photography in the cinema.

He stood in the doorway, glittering, booted, brassed and buckled, slim, hard-faced and unsmiling, blue-eyed and milk-skinned, his right arm rammed stiff in the salute of the Nazi party.

"Schmidt, K. *Kapitan*. 245–567–662. Kondor Legion, Luftwaffe, re-porting for duty!"

Bravo stared and forgot to return the young German's salute. The airman's uniform was beautifully tailored, fresh and crisp. The man in-side it was a Teutonic male museum specimen, carefully selected for export to Spain, courtesy of ROWAK and HISMA—the bill for his services still-to-be-rendered to be submitted at some later date to be ac-knowledged and paid for in full.

"Welcome to Spain, Herr Schmidt."

The young man nodded once. Bravo gestured at the Heinkel aircraft and the trucks.

"Everything is in order?"

Kapitan Schmidt nodded once.

"A cup of coffee?"

The German shook his head.

"It is rather warm for coffee."

The aviator shrugged. Bravo wondered if his German was so bad that the young man did not understand him. He picked up his dictionary.

"I have been studying."

Suddenly, the young Nazi removed his hat, spun it across the room to the desk top and stepped to the wall map near the calendar. He set one fist on his hip and stood there, jaunty, glossy and smiling. His Spanish was harsh but rapid, a flat monotone.

"That is exactly what we are here for. We must study everything, profit from each error, improve every technique. This is ideal, ideal. Please be good enough to explain the military situation."

Bravo walked to the map.

"Today is August five. Tomorrow, General Franco will fly into Seville, leaving Orgaz in command in Morocco. Here, Yagüe is in command. An old comrade, a leading Falangist. Under Yagüe, here, here, and ap-proximately there, are Majors Asensio, Castejón and Tella, all veterans of the wars in Morocco."

"I have read about the wars in Morocco. Without the assistance of the French, you would still be fighting there. Go on."

"That is the military situation."

"How are the troops moved? What is your maneuvering?"

Schmidt ran his forefinger from Seville east to Granada, southwest to Ronda and directly north to Córdoba.

"How does one take these dirty tribesmen from here to over here and up, so?"

"Asensio, Castejón, and Tella each command a Bandera of the Foreign Legion, a *tabor* of Regulares, and a battery or two of artillery. A thousand men, more or less. Each, that is. Every force is equipped with truck transport. They drive from town to town. Preliminary bombardment for approximately thirty minutes."

"Your field pieces are obsolete. This is for purposes of terror, this artillery?"

Bravo paused, annoyed. He had published, at his own expense, a monograph on artillery, *The Effect of Indiscriminate Bombardment*, which argued the desirable effects of sporadic, undirected shelling on a civilian populace.

"A tactic proved most effective during the campaign against the Riffs, Herr Schmidt. Bombardment at random, followed by grenade and bayonet assault by the Legionarios and the Moors. Special burial details excavate to find the victims of revolutionary atrocities. For every dead man discovered, four or five members of the Left-wing parties are shot. The average time of pacification is slightly in excess of two hours per village."

"Why waste all that time digging up the dead? Surely the effect would be even more severe if executions took place at random?"

"To be effective, reprisals must appear based on justice."

The young German shook his head and laughed.

"Justice? For Bolsheviks? What an idea! Positively quaint!"

"The people understand."

Schmidt turned and stared at Bravo. The German had very pale eyes, almost gray. He was still smiling. His teeth were very bright and even.

"Do they? How interesting? We have heard that after the shootings you reopen the churches and wet the babies. True?"

"The unit chaplains perform baptisms and celebrate Mass."

"And the people understand, eh?"

"Yes."

"We have heard that these Moors castrate the dead. Is that understood, too?"

Bravo folded his arms across his chest. The newspaper beneath his tunic rustled.

"It is a ritual for them."

The German nodded and smiled.

"How perfectly disgusting. How soon is the city of Mérida expected to fall?"

"Soon."

"The siege at the Alcázar in Toledo will be lifted as your army advances on Madrid?"

"I believe that is the plan, yes."

Schmidt walked over to the window and looked out on the landing field. The teams of mechanics were at work on the Heinkel fighters. He turned abruptly, shot his cuffs, and stared accusingly at Colonel Bravo.

"It would be distressing to come all this way for nothing. Madrid could fall in a matter of weeks; the war would be over. Our equipment may not be tested sufficiently. What a waste!"

Bravo shrugged.

"Certainly the air transport of combat troops by your Junkers has been an interesting innovation."

The German was not listening. Alert as a terrier, glossy as a holly branch, he cocked his blond head and peered at the sky.

"Aircraft, Colonel? I was informed that most of Spanish war planes were in the hands of the Reds. These cannot be ours."

Across the sky, the airplanes were scattered like bits of tinsel. Bravo counted them. Forty-two. The German laughed.

"So. These are the White Eagles. Typical of Italians. Two days late and straggling out of formation. I should say you were most fortunate that Bolshevik aircraft were not in striking distance. Are we to believe that this flock of geese provided adequate coverage for the transportation of troops across the Mediterranean?"

The planes, like shiny toys, swooped down over the city. Bravo watched the aerial acrobatics, power stalls, Immelmann turns and glittering barrel rolls. A flight of three whipped in low, their double wings nearly touching, and snarled over the field in a mock strafing run. He could see the helmeted pilots in the open cockpits. Each of the Italian fliers wore a different colored scarf snatched stiff as wire. Schmidt sniffed.

"Clowns in a circus. Such behavior makes one thankful that these people are military allies only. They are incapable of understanding that what is needed here is controlled fanaticism. Italians are incapable of grasping ideologies. It is all emotion for them, a matter of the blood."

Bravo turned away, smiling. Now the newspaper beneath his tunic felt like a shield, an armored vest. What nonsense this young man talked! Did he think that Spain desired an ideological alliance with Germany? Did he think that ROWAK and HISMA supplied theories or matériel? If all Germans were this naïve, they would prove something of an embarrassment.

Another silver biplane banked around the flight control tower and sailed off across the city, upside down. Bravo picked up his gloves and drew them on.

"What mark of aircraft are those, Herr Schmidt?"

"Fiats. Good rate of climb, but underarmed and not so fast as our Heinkels."

"They are very beautiful, I think."

Schmidt turned and stared, his young face shocked and contemptuous. He shook himself like a drenched dog and raised his pale brows.

"Indeed? Beauty? I see there is much to be taught here."

Bravo bowed. The newspaper crinkled with the tilt of his body.

"Yes. And much to be learned. Let me show you to your quarters, Herr Schmidt."

The wall poster showed a map of Spain painted scarlet. From the center a lighthouse lurched like the campanile at Pisa. Golden smears, representing light rays sprayed across the plaster. The caption beneath the poster read SPAIN WILL BE A LIGHT TO THE WORLD! ¡VIVA EL FRENTE POPULAR!

Across the plaza, a red banner hung from the second floor of the Hotel Pilarmadre, expropriated by the Toros Rojos, the only militia group directly commanded by Alfredo. They were the source of his pride as well as his power. He had become fond of remarking that Pilarmadre must follow the example of Barcelona, not Madrid. The ex-barber insisted that the "Red Bulls" were not a secret police force, but rather "proletarian Chekists." As proof of this, he carried the pay roster in his pocket. The "Red Bulls" received ten pesetas a day, not a centime more, standard pay for all the militia groups in the area. Not that money meant much. Alfredo planned to declare money illegal on the day his wounded hand was fully healed. He had already prepared the handbills and the new posters: ¡DURRUTTI SÍ! DINERO NO! When the Anarchist columns reached Pilarmadre on their way to assault Zaragoza, the "Red Bulls" would make certain that the populace swarmed the streets to welcome the ex-bandit Durrutti . . . with empty hands. Alfredo had no intention of turning the *pueblo* over to Barcelona looters. The barber's radical politics stopped short of burning churches and plundering banks. Under Alfredo, churches became markets and money became unnecessary. And the "proletarian Chekists" now lived in the only hotel.

Alfredo had ordered the death of sixty-three men, twenty-eight women, and seven children. A piece of paper was tacked to the charred door of the old Civil Guards barracks every day at noon. On the piece of paper had appeared names and after every name the letter L and a full stop. Alvarez, Ramón L. Buñel, José L. Rodríguez, María L. L. for "liberated." The executions had taken place at night, out in the hills. Alfredo did not believe in the public display of bodies. He did not believe that his victims needed a priest, either.

Ortega fingered the work voucher in his pocket. The new rosary. And instead of the confessional, a visit to the voucher-clerk at C.N.T. headquarters once a week. Pieces of paper to exchange for goods. So far, he had earned two meals a day (burned malt "coffee" and fruit for breakfast, a rich dish of meat, beans and rice with a glass of wine at sunset), a pair of rope sandals and a cotton shirt. In his new position as supervisor of the public market, he worked from before dawn to noon. The rest of the day was his own, except that there was nothing really for him to do. Before July, he had dozed during the siesta, read his Office, then visited among the people of the parish. Now, there was nothing but the newspapers from Barcelona. He read, or pretended to read them at the Café Marx in the small square near the cement factory. The faithful, mostly women, came to his table, apparently to gossip and to hear him read. There, seated across the chipped metal table, they confessed their sins. Behind the screen of *Solidaridad, Clarín,* or *Red Star,* he listened and assigned penance and absolution. He could not think of celebrating Mass. The Host and the wine had been confiscated. The risk for the people was too great.

He sighed and sauntered down the street. He had become accustomed to his *mono,* the too-snug overalls he had put on in place of his priest's robe. The Barcelona newspapers were filled with boasts about the number of executed priests, even nuns. Thousands dead. An exaggeration, no doubt. Or was it? The bishops of Barcelona, Cuenca, Lerida, and Ciudad Real had been shot, the suffragan bishop of Tarragona, too. The nunnery twelve kilometers south had been set afire. One of the "Red Bulls" had shown him a scorched robe and told him a story.

One of the novices had been stripped and given a dress of purple with sequin stars stitched at the breasts. The girl had been very young and very pretty and so the "Red Bulls" had let her go untouched. Two days later, she had reached her native village. She had stopped to drink at the village fountain, and there family and friends had welcomed her. It was the purple dress with sequin stars that enraged them. Taking her for a whore, they had stoned her to death by the village fountain.

The young member of the "proletarian Chekists" had laughed in his face and had shown him a scorched robe he swore had belonged to the novice. And what had he done? Gone to his room and finished typing up the report for Alfredo, an Aquinian defense of the separation of Catalonia from the rest of the Republic, together with a fervent plea for Aragonese-Catalonian solidarity. All very formal, each of the saint's four conditions for the justification of revolution neatly argued: threat to the common good, necessary and approved by prudent men, the strong possibility of success . . . probable harm no greater by the probable harm caused by doing nothing and, fourth, the absence of any other solution. And he had signed his name. It was as though he had written the document in the young girl's blood.

Yet he believed in what people had quickly come to call "The Cause." The fear of Alfredo's Cheka was less than the fear the people had for the Civil Guard. Life went on, the local *campesinos* had seized the land and called it theirs, the people in the village paid only fifty per cent of the rents they had paid before, two young men from Teruel had come to open a school, all men greeted each other with the clenched-fist salute and called each other "camarada." The brothel was closed, a new water cistern had been dug, the workers were running the cement factory . . . and he was still alive. He could sit in the shade of the awning at the Café Marx, pretending to read the Party newspapers while sinners whispered across the chipped metal table. God was the voice of the people.

When he turned the corner, he saw the trucks parked before the church. The plaza was filled with people running back and forth, some of the men with their rifles, many more drunk and staggering. There was singing and a distribution of clothing, or so it seemed. On the tailgate of one truck, two men stood and threw bright garments out into a mass of women. He knew, then, what it was. These were Durrutti's militia, the columns so long promised, had been sent out from Barcelona to attack Zaragoza. Six trucks filled with drunken men, a few women, some rifles and a bundle of looted clothing.

He heard the sound of men running and stepped aside. Down the street from the Hotel Pilarmadre, the Toros Rojos were marching, led by Alfredo. Their banner jerked in the hot dusty air. They began to sing, but their voices were drowned by the wet shriek of the whistle from the cement factory.

"To the front! Republic or death! To the front! To the front!"

Alfredo trotted at the head of his column. The "Red Bulls" did not march in step, but they had new rifles, ammunition, and grenades on their belts. They were cheered as they straggled by. They smiled and waved their clenched fists. The oldest member of the "Toros Rojos" was nineteen. When Alfredo left them, they broke for the trucks and ran, knocking down the children who darted back and forth between the trucks and the church steps.

Alfredo saw Ortega, hesitated, and walked back. He set the butt of his rifle on the cobbles. The red kerchief around his neck was soaked with sweat. The cheap cloth had run. From the chin to the collar, Alfredo's skin was scarlet.

"Where have you been, man? I've had the boys out looking for you? We got the news by telephone. The army is coming! They're here!"

"I see them, camarada. I see six trucks."

"Right! They came to pick us up. We're joining the columns! To Zaragoza! We'll crush the Fascists there and go right on to Madrid!"

"Go then, but who will be in charge here?"

"Why, no one, of course! Pilarmadre will take care of Pilarmadre. It's human nature, isn't it? When this is over, we must think of a new name. This is a great day, a memorable day, historic, even!"

"Alfredo, are you taking these children to the front or are they taking you?"

The ex-barber squinted at the waiting trucks. The crowds in the plaza cheered as the "Red Bulls" swarmed over the tailgates and began scrambling and shoving for the position of honor: a seat on top of the cab.

"What do you mean by that? Everything is done together, by common inspiration."

Ortega leaned against the door-jamb. He could not keep his gaze from the scarlet smear on Alfredo's throat. It reminded him of a noose scar.

"Someone should stay here, *camarada*. Pilarmadre can't run itself, no matter what you say."

"And I say that you will go with us. It is your duty as a revolutionary citizen."

"Am I to go as a priest? As militia chaplain?"

Alfredo shook his head.

"Of course not. You will be director of sanitary facilities. You know these *chicos*. They shit anywhere, like alley cats. Unless proper revolutionary sanitary standards are maintained, they'll all get sick and be good for nothing. Get as many shovels as you can."

Alfredo walked to the first truck and climbed on the running board to make a speech. Ortega went to the church. It was empty. Where the confessional stalls had been, a plain wooden table stood. Sacks of rice and potatoes covered the altar. The figure of the Virgin had been removed from the side chapel; the niche was now the distribution center for olive oil and wine. He walked between the market stalls of vegetables and clothing. The vestry was now the storehouse of "community machines" . . . hoes, iron-tipped plows and mule harness, hammers, saws, a few pipe-wrenches, sledges, and pry-bars for maintaining the railroad bed and seven shovels of different sizes and shapes. Ortega picked up two of the shovels and carried them out to the trucks.

"*Hola!* Bury them deep, comrade! Shovel it on them!"

"That's it! Graves for the Fascists and bread for the people!"

He thrust the shovels into eager hands and went back for the others. He hesitated over a flabby pile of jute sacks. Filled with earth, they would be useful protection for the trenches. He gathered them up and stumbled out to the trucks.

The women from the brothel were in one of the trucks. They tore the sacks from him and flung them about.

"That's organization. Portable beds for Woman's Auxilary!"

"Hoo! How rough they are! Haven't you anything better? We're used to towels."

The crowd laughed, even the children. Ortega pushed through and found Alfredo.

"Listen, man, are you crazy? You can't let *them* come along! You know what will happen."

"So? Let it happen, then. They are volunteers now, not slaves of an economic system."

"Get them out of the trucks, Alfredo."

"You do it, *comisario*. We're distributing ammunition. Remember, there are many ways to fight Fascism."

Ortega shook his fist in Alfredo's face.

"You are a fool!"

Alfredo shook his fist back.

"*Viva la República!* To the front!"

The crowd cheered and waved their clenched fists. The truck motors started up. Ortega ran back to the church for the rest of the shovels. As he passed the niche, he took a liter of red wine and shoved it inside his overalls. Only one truck still stood in the plaza when he staggered out, carrying the shovels. The young militiamen took them. Ortega hesitated. Alfredo and the others had gone. He could see the dust clouds out on the highway. The door of the cab opened and an arm beckoned to him. Ortega climbed in and sat cuddling the bottle of wine. The arm moved to the gearshift lever, and the truck rolled down the street. Ortega could hear the "Red Bulls" in the back of the truck singing and stamping their feet. He looked at the driver. A thin, pale foreigner with a peeled forehead, bits of tissuey skin clinging to his broken nose. His arms were pink from the sun. Ortega held out his hand.

"Francisco Ortega."

The driver shook hands without taking his gaze from the road.

"Hans Kopa."

"You are from Barcelona?"

"Yes. Since three days. From *pueblo* to *pueblo*. We stop. Some get on. Some get off. Sometimes there is shooting, sometimes no."

"Are we winning the war?"

"War? What war? This is a carnival. A fiesta. We go from place to place with a fiesta."

"You are not a Catalán, then."

"German."

"From Germany? *Bienvenido* . . . welcome to Spain. You have volunteered?"

"I have come to Spain to fight. What do I do? I drive a truck in a carnival. The first day I drove athletes from the Olympiad games. Also some *maricones* . . . it is the word, no? Fairies from the *barrio Chino*. Dressed up like women. I mean it. We got rid of most of them. Here's the column."

He pointed. The road wound back and forth, doubling up the slope of a hump of hills covered with terraced vineyards. Loaded trucks crawled on the road. Dust drifted like fog over the vines. The air trembled with the sound of motors. Ortega choked and fumbled a kerchief over his mouth. He and the German shouted to each other.

"I have never seen so many trucks. Hundreds, eh?"

"Yes. I have never seen so few cannons. Old rifles, no machine guns, peasants with scythes and knives. No food or water. Every time we stop, the people must feed the column. Nothing is organized . . . except those women we picked up at your village."

"They should have been forbidden."

"Right. We've got enough whores along already."

"Disgraceful!"

"No, carnivals are beautiful. Freaks and fools and dreamers, a hundred colors, a thousand songs. It's like it must have been hundreds of years ago . . . like one of the Crusades. How come they didn't burn the church back there?"

"They just didn't."

"Did they shoot the priest?"

"No . . . not yet."

The long column of trucks groaned up the long slopes, cranked around the hairpin turns and crawled on. The interior of the cab was an oven. Dust leaked in through the windows. In the body of the trucks in front, the forms of the men were vague huddles, faces hidden in dust-caked kerchiefs. Every sweaty throat was daubed with crimson. Ortega pointed.

"What will happen to them when we get to the front?"

"They will be massacred. They will be cut to bits. The carnival will be over, the fiesta at an end."

"And then, comrade?"

"And, then? Why then it will begin."

"What will begin?"

"The war, comrade. The war will begin. And that will be very logical and there will be no beauty to it at all."

They stopped in the early afternoon. The trucks stretched all along the highway. They were some kilometers southwest of Bujaraloz. The militia troops climbed down from the trucks. They moved stiffly, bruised and weary from the long, dusty, jolting ride. They flowed into the olive groves, seeking the shade there, and sat and mopped the masks of dirt from their faces. Kopa had bread, *chorizo* and a piece of dry Manchego cheese. Ortega uncorked the wine. They found a tree and sat beneath it. The line of motionless, dusty trucks ran from the crest of one hill down through the olive grove, down into the little valley and the village below. It was very quiet, strangely quiet. The men ate what food they had and watched the skies for aircraft.

Kopa and Ortega ate and drank, passing the bottle back and forth. The German wiped his mouth.

"I would like to live in your country. Feel how hot the sun is! Here you feel the earth. She is hot and brown and silver-green, spread out for play, and the dust is like smoke in her heavy eyes. Look at the hills.

Stupendous shapes, like enormous knees. I could stretch myself across the belly of her plain and fall asleep between her big, dirty breasts."

"I think you must be a poet."

"I think I must be drunk. But she is beautiful, this Spain."

Ortega sipped some wine. He, too, felt drugged and drowsy, stunned with the heat and the harsh wine.

"Yes, Spain is beautiful . . ."

Kopa lit a cigarette and offered the pack. They sat and smoked. The German grunted.

"See these hills. The earth is stretched and taut as a tent, with those . . . bulls, I guess, eh? . . . they look like specks down the slopes. And the air is sweet with the lift of life. It will be sweet at the heart to be here, to try to lift and hold such loveliness . . . but it is so heavy that I think it will crush us. The hills of Spain will fall on us all. But I suppose you are ready for it."

"What do you mean?"

"Well, you're a priest, aren't you?"

"Someone told you?"

"I knew."

"I *was* a priest, yes. I don't know what I am now."

The German nodded and lay back on the warm, dry earth.

"That's all right. No one knows what they are right now. But they will learn. That's one thing a war does to you. I know. I was in the last one. That war made me a Communist. I wonder what this one will do to me."

Before Ortega could think of an answer, Kopa was asleep, sprawled in the shade of the olive trees, while the dusty caravan of silent trucks shimmered in the summer sun.

Frank looked at his watch. The fueling was taking too long; they would be late for the rendezvous. He shook the watch and put it to his ear. It had stopped. What the hell. For the last week he had been late for everything. He had missed the Dover ferry and, later the same day, the boat-train to Paris. The concierge at the little hotel in Rue Bonaparte told him that *les touristes anglais* had taken the train for Bordeaux. So he had missed Coltringham, the Desmonds, and the other English volunteers. The following day, he and Jean Saulnier were to have met André Malraux, the organizer of the volunteer squadron. Malraux had moved to a flying field to supervise training flights. Finally arriving at this remote place, an inactive practice strip with grass runways, they had learned that Malraux had moved again, but had left maps, orders, and a flight plan. The minutes slipped away, as the mechanics moved in the gloom like sleepwalkers.

He sat on a broken chair, sweating. Under his flying suit he wore two sets of woolen underwear. He was hot and nervous. His helmet was too small, a bad thing, because the skull swelled slightly at even medium altitudes. He stretched the leather and fumbled with his goggles, loosening the strap. He had run out of cigarettes; Jean Saulnier was briefing some other eleventh-hour arrivals, two German pilots and a Romanian, and no one spoke English. He jumped when the warning horn squawked. The chief mechanic sauntered over and jerked his head at the airplane.

"Ça marche."

"Okay . . . Merci . . ."

The heavy doors were rolled back, and the summer sunshine flooded the hanger. Frank stood up, clumsy in his suit and heavy boots. The mechanics kicked the wheel-chocks free. Two men pushed on the trailing edges of the silver wings, another boosted the tail. Out in the summer sun, the aircraft shone like an insect, the fresh paint still pungent on the light southwest breeze. Frank looked and wet his lips.

It was called a Dewoitine 510, an open cockpit, low-winged monoplane with a fixed landing gear. It was a slender, glittering, and fragile-looking thing, except for the radiator that jutted like a jaw. Two 30-millimeter machine guns, synchronized, fired between the two-bladed wooden propeller. From the engine nacelle to the cockpit firewall, the plane was sheathed with aluminum. From the cockpit aft to the rudder and elevator planes, the new paint had been applied over canvas. The wings, too, were fabric-covered. There was no armor plate around the engine, the cockpit, or the fuel tanks.

"Obsolete?" Saulnier had answered, "Of course. Really an advanced training craft, mon ami. You didn't expect this government to sell new ships to the Spaniards, did you? If you think your plane is bad, you should see what we're going to have for bombers! From the last war, I assure you . . ."

The controls were soft; the rudder cables stretched slack. The fuel gauge did not register. The stuffing leaked through the ripped leather of the pilot's seat. The wing fabric had been patched and patched. The frame was weak, with loose bolts, pulled rivets, rusty wire braces and rotten cooling hoses. The mechanics had seemed as glad to get rid of it as a bunch of secondhand auto dealers on Philadelphia's south side. The Dewoitine interceptor was pretty, slender, bright, and dangerous. Frank had never flown anything like it in his life, and there was no time left to practice. He would solo in the ship across the mountains, out over the Mediterranean to Barcelona, refuel, and fly two strafing runs over the lines near a city called Zaragoza and another place called Teruel. No enemy aircraft were anticipated. That bit of news had made everyone feel better. There were no parachutes.

The mechanics set the wheel-chocks. Frank pulled on his helmet and waddled to the interceptor, scrambled up the little wooden ladder and dropped into the cockpit. He stared at the instrument panel, dumfounded. All the gauges were in meters, kilograms and Centigrade. There was no artificial horizon, no bank-and-turn indicator, and the compass looked like something handed out for a Boy Scout hike. In the center of the panel were two thumb buttons, the safety, and fire for the machine guns. Which was which?

He looked to his left, out beyond the graceful wingtip with the blue, white, and red bull's-eye of the French air force. The other planes were out on the grass now, waiting like a flock of pretty birds. No one knew what the flight insignia of the Spanish Republic was, not even Saulnier. He had just shrugged. Let the Fascists figure it out. Frank kicked the rudder bar and slapped the stick back and forth against his knees. At least the ailerons twitched up and down. The warning horn blatted again.

He fumbled with the prime mechanism and the magneto lever, his gloved hands clumsy. The mechanic up at the propeller shouted, and he waved back. The wooden blades whicked over, the steel tips flashing. The motor wheezed softly. The mechanic tried again. The engine coughed, fired raggedly, like an outboard on a fishing skiff. Frank leaned the mixture. The motor stuttered and held in a hammering roar that shook the light aircraft from nose to rudder, wingtip to wingtip. The needles behind the gauge glasses shivered. Exhaust fumes whipped back in the propeller wash. He pulled his goggles down, tightened the seat belt and leaned out to see if the ground crew were standing clear with the chocklines ready to pull. Saulnier rolled out first, waving his clasped hands out over the canopy like a prize-fighter—the signal for take-off. The crew hauled on the ropes and he went rolling forward after Saulnier. The soft, lush grass flattened in the propeller wash. The morning sky was blue and empty of clouds. He sat in the cramped cockpit, deafened by the motor roar, his whole body shivering.

The signal rocket lifted up and bloomed, a bright, silent flower. Saulnier's ship shot forward. Frank counted slowly to fifteen and pressed the throttle open. The grass skidded toward him, the broad green slipping under the wings. The field was lumpy with little use. He nudged the throttle and felt the tail lift free. The wheels touched, bumped, touched again. Excitement slithered in him as the grass fell away below. He pushed the rudder bar, moved the stick and swung through the blue French morning in a gentle, banking turn. He opened the throttle again, and the fighter plane seemed to bounce up, the engine snarling. He tightened the turn and saw the green earth skid and tilt as he spiraled up and the needle rose in the altimeter. The struts shimmied and the wires howled and vanished, vibrating into gray blurs. His ears ached and popped. France dropped away. Houses and trees dwindled to dots, a village like a scatter of gravel; a small looping river lay like a bit of string dropped on green plush. The Dewoitine climbed like a gull, and Frank pounded the instrument panel with his fist and began to sing "Mad'moiselle from Armentières."

The mountain range rose up on the dull blue horizon before the formation was completely formed. In a straggling cluster, twelve Dewoitine interceptors, designed for day patrols in French Indochina, hammered through the blue sky, east to the coastline, then south, down the Costa Brava to Spain. Over the Mediterranean they spread and test-fired the machine guns. When Frank pressed the scarlet button, the fuselage shuddered in a new, choppy rhythm and the brass cartridge cases squirted up and flew away. The silver aircraft bored through the blue sky and there, down and starboard, beyond the blurring disc of the propeller, brown as an oxhide—there was Spain!

The fortress at Figueras was first a dull lump like a wen on the hide, then like a Christmas toy-soldier fort at F.A.O. Schwarz, then rushed up stone battlements, tilted towers and courtyards with little trucks and a red banner on the flagstaff as they shot over at 1500 meters, wing-wagging, and for a fraction of a second saw men waving up to them. There was the highway to Barcelona, more trucks filled with waving men and red flags, flurrying pin spots of color on the Spanish earth.

The fuel needle had been dancing on the zero long before Saulnier spotted the landing field and dropped down to it. They came in too fast for the short strip, and Frank hauled around on a wingtip, the whole frame creaking, a real Bendix Trophy pylon-buster, sure to please the bleacher fans, cut in front of Saulnier and down in a power glide over the stone houses that fringed the field. The Dewoitine touched down like a sandpiper on a beach, light and quick, right up to the fuel trucks, the motor spattering and snuffed, the bright blades flicking stiff, and then it stopped. Frank leaned his head on the canopy glass and laughed with delight.

His skull was ringing, and, half deaf, he sat and watched the others come in, the Romanian too high and too slow, stalling in, his goggled head whipping from side to side to see the tarmac booming up at him, nervous as a Bucks County housewife trying to park the new station wagon in time to meet the 5:05. He bounced so high he nearly nosed over, but caught it and somehow seemed to press the plane onto the ground and hold it there. Saulnier put his ship down like a man hanging up his suit, three points and not a crease or a wrinkle.

Frank did not see the man, but felt the weight of him on the starboard wing-walk. Square-jawed face, with thick hair, dark, neatly combed just off center, darting dark eyes and a sharp nose, a cigarette plastered to his lower lip and bobbing.

"You speak French, pilot?"

"Yes."

"That was quite something, that landing. Very pretty."

"Thank you."

Frank's body felt as though he had been tapped, lightly, from rump to skull, on all sides, with a badminton racket for three hours. His throat was dry, his nose ached. He pushed up his goggles and stood up. The man jumped down from the wing and stood with his fists on his hips. He wore a leather jacket, cavalry breeches and knee-high laced boots. His cigarette bobbed as he spoke, the blurt of words tearing off ashes and a film of smoke.

"Yes, very beautiful. But I wouldn't do it again, if I were you, pilot."

"No, why not?"

"Because the next time the wings will fall right off. That aircraft is over ten years old. Brrrt! Right off, I assure you. Have it filled and report to me at once for map reading, weather report, and combat instructions. We sortie in less than one hour."

He walked away, almost running, to Saulnier's ship. Frank edged down the wing-walk and dropped to the ground. Some men came up in a truck. They said something, waved their fists, and shook hands. Frank kept shaking his head. They wanted to know something and he could not understand them. One had a long, canvas hose and made unscrewing motions. Everyone was laughing and patting him on the shoulders, very lightly, as though afraid to do more than touch him. He understood that they didn't know where the gas tanks were. Neither did he. By the time they found the caps and air vents, Saulnier kneed him in the rear.

"Nice flying, *copain*. How do you like the old lady, eh? Like being in bed with your grandmother. Surprising what they can still do, no?"

"Who's that guy in the riding outfit, Jean? He bawled me out for coming in like that."

"That guy, you call him. That guy is Malraux, *mon ami*. You have just met your commanding officer. He was very impressed when I said you had never flown one of these before. He also believes you will be our first casualty."

"Not me. I was born rich and lucky and I'm going to stay that way."

"In Spain?"

"In Spain. What's Spanish for *thank you?*"

"*Gracias.*"

"*Gracias* for the gas, you guys!"

"Beautiful. Purest Castilian. Come on, I have to piss. These old planes are very severe on the kidneys."

Frank felt Saulnier's arm around his shoulder. They walked toward the nearest building.

"How are things going? That's really Malraux, huh?"

"That's him. Not well. We'll be at Getafe field near Madrid. André thinks the city may have been bombed already. Barcelona radio is full of news on this front and Catalán politics. It's hard to say. We'll find out soon enough."

One of the German pilots was waiting for them as they walked past his plane. He was an old Lufthansa hand with iron-colored hair and a bad limp from a crash at Hamburg in the twenties. He had a long, odd name and spoke some French.

"Congratulations. You fly in an air circus?"

"Yes. I wouldn't try a landing like that if I were you, though."

"No? Why so?"

"These planes are over ten years old. The wings will fall right off. Brrrt! Right off, I assure you . . ."

They walked with clumsy, spraddled steps toward the building. Saulnier looked back at the pilots who followed them. They all walked the same way.

"We should call ourselves the Pelican squadron. Very graceful in flight, but on the ground, so clumsy. Malraux wants a month's training near Madrid, but we won't get it. Not enough gas and not enough time. Combat training will be effected during patrols. That's to say, in combat."

Frank nodded and pulled off his helmet.

"That's to say in less than an hour."

The German nodded.

"Well, that's time enough for the engines to cool. Today we fly and fight. Tonight we make *Bruderschaft*. How do you say it in French, please? Or Spanish. Better, Spanish."

"*Camarada* . . . comrade."

"Good. Tonight we are *camaradas*."

"If the wings don't fall off."

"*Ja.* If the wings don't fall off. That is a joke, no?"

"Maybe."

The first sign of the front were the clots of animals tethered or corralled close to the roads winding across the rumpled, rocky earth that swung under the wings. Then, trucks of all sizes and shapes, some crawling like beetles in the dust, others parked or abandoned. The city of Zaragoza jagged grayly off the starboard wingtip.

Tufts of earth bounced and jittered down there, a faint and scattered winking of lights and bits and pieces of stuff seemed strewn and tumbled together. Saulnier slit through a pass, two hundred meters off the ground. Frank shied from the broken granite that shouldered up at him, great heaves of Spanish stone. He saw a filament of gold ripple out behind

Saulnier's propeller. He was strafing, but gone, as the lifting wing-slab shut him out.

He spun off, squinting at the mad compass whirling, possibly south or southwest and punched the red button. The plane shimmied for an instant. He Immelmanned back over what must be the battlefield they had come to find, bomb, and strafe. The other members of the squadron seemed to be up higher. He saw two circling, or the same one twice as he came up, pressed the stick forward and knuckled the throttle back a notch. The plane settled beneath him, whistling down with humming wires and the cataract of air tearing at him as he came over a ridge, belly pulled hard just above stall-speed, half scared, expecting another great wrinkle of earth to roll up from nowhere and smash him before he could haul up and bank away.

He flung up and over the cockpit rim, the belt biting his thighs, the engine vibration hammering. He could just feel the rudder bar, and he danced on it like Fred Astaire, pushing the tail from side to side while the blood bulged behind his eyes and his empty belly roiled. The smoke and clouds below shredded, and he could make out brown flecks of earth sliding beneath the wings. He pressed the stick forward.

It was a mob of little figures, clusters and strings that broke and scattered like ants, a bright bit of a flag, an upturned truck, some horses or mules, smoke, and mist sparkling with bits of orange flame and then, quite clearly, an astonished crew of men in blue uniforms huddled around a machine gun on a rocky crest strewn with what must be bodies. He knocked the throttle back and thumbed off two seconds of ammunition, the whole plane shuddering. Smoke and mist blinded him, and he cuffed the throttle open full. The propeller bit and the engine howled. Gravity rammed him back and down into his seat, the belt around him loose as he stared, slack-faced, at four star-bursts that shattered the canopy glass. Somebody down there had hit the old lady!

He hung in a blind, gray, wailing climb up away from the dark stones and red earth until his skull felt squeezed out and blood sprayed from his nose. He broke through the cloud layer and leveled off. He could see mountains, murderous rumpled peaks, off the port wing. His goggles smeared with pink film. He was high enough to see a city with what must be two cathedrals spiking the sky. A three-seater biplane in parallel course lumbered over the city. A single black bomb floated free, and the three-seater bounded up away from it. He banked away, pawing at his face with one soggy glove. He swung down and around, just off a spin, ruddered out of it and came in over the city, looking for the flash and wallop of the bomb. Nothing but rooftops and chimneys. He rocked gently up again, straight into the sun. There was Saulnier, shaking his helmeted, goggled face, pointing at the earth and waving.

Can't see. Forget it. Follow me.

Tepid, salty blood trickled down over his lips. He looked around and saw the rest of them strung out across the sky and the biplane bomber low and off to the north. It apparently hadn't hurt the city at all. He sagged back into the hard, shaking seat and let the Dewoitine batter on into the sun that daisied the bullet holes in the canopy. He was still rich. He was still lucky. He had flown combat air cover for an Anarchist offensive on the Aragón front where the mountains chewed the sky like molars. It had all looked like a cross between a riot and vast, disordered picnic with lots of trucks. He had triggered off maybe twenty dollars' worth of old ammunition at targets he couldn't see.

Dazed and drunk with fatigue and letdown, he dozed and droned into the sun. Finally Saulnier wing-waggled for landing. He cursed the Frenchman for expecting him to bring his frail protectress down out of the buffeting sweet blue to scatter her on the bony soil of Spain. He flew in, numb and terrified, as the dirt strip came up to him, certain that he was going to overshoot, letting the old fighter plane burr down in a long, soft glide. One jolt, and buildings like stone barns whipped past. Frank butted his glove against the safety button for the guns and then against the throttle. An enormous muff of hearing swarmed around him, the slow shimmy of a vibrating strut wire, the hiss of the radiator and ugly gurgle of cooling pipes. He could feel the rubber jumping of his heart and taste the salty blood gummed on his lips.

We made it. What the hell?

It was so snug in the broken, blood-sprayed cockpit that he sat there, patting his gloves together, breathing and listening to the ring and buzz of his ears. Three very gentle people lifted him out and set him on the ground. He tottered against the fuselage, then walked very slowly across a baking plain of raw dirt to Saulnier's ship.

The Frenchman was sitting on the wing-walk, stripped to the waist, his chest white as an unroasted turkey, smiling and smoking a cigar and chatting with his own ground crew. Frank waved one bloody mitt.

"Some fun, *camarada* . . . no shit . . ."

"No? Why do you think I'm taking off this suit? All of a sudden there was a *mountain*, baby, right . . . right *there!* Then I see you get hit. *Mon ami*, you are *insane!* You fly over a battle . . . *over*, understand? Not right down *into* it!"

"I went down there to see. I couldn't see a goddamned thing. Nothing. All that smoke."

Saulnier's voice seemed to float down from a great distance.

"Goddamn is right. You couldn't tell them apart, one side from the other. Hand to hand and everyone running. The bombers did nothing."

"That's right. Nothing."

"Eh? *Dieu*, you're wounded!"

"No. I came back up . . . too high. I got a nosebleed, that's all. Were we winning? The battle?"

"Eh, who knows? Ask a soldier, *no*. Ask his general, *sí*. Read a newspaper and learn nothing. You're all right. Listen, you fly beautifully, *mon ami*. Like a little silver bird. So calm, like you're asleep."

"Yeah."

Frank stepped back away from the wing, watching and feeling his hands slide and swing, leaden and useless at his sides. Little green lights of nausea pricked before his eyes. He swallowed down heat and dust and the reek of engines.

"Where are we, Jean? Did we lose anybody?"

"I don't know. We're all right. The others all stayed high. Ooof! I've got to get this suit off. What a thing to have happen, eh? My age, and pants full of *caca*, like my sister's kids."

Frank pulled his helmet off and rubbed his face. The three Spaniards who had helped him out of his plane were standing not far away, smiling at him and being very happy. Frank looked away from them, down at his trembling hands.

"Jesus, you know I could really use a drink. A cold bottle of beer."

"*Cabo? Hay una cantina?*"

"*No, señorito. Hay una taberna en el pueblo.*"

"Nothing here to drink. *Hay tranporte? Coche? Camión?*"

"*Nada. Un viejo con su burro.*"

"*Solamente?*"

"*Sí, señorito . . .*"

"An old man with a burro cart. We stay at a tavern in the nearest village, I guess. Tell the others, Frank, while I get some dry pants."

The pilots slumped in the shade, tumbled against the stone barn wall like discarded dolls. They pawed feebly at each other, shaking hands, patting faces, too tired to talk, but compelled to touch each other, lean together, bulky arms slung around each other's shoulders, slow hands very clumsy with exchanged cigarettes, eyes so dull with searching that they could barely see the Spaniards drawing the silver aircraft into line.

Saulnier appeared in a baggy blue coverall, riding on the tailgate of a burro cart. He counted off the first three men. Frank; the German pilot; and Sardou, the Romanian, rose and shuffled to the cart. Saulnier dragged them up and dropped them. They lay there, gasping. The cart creaked and jounced forward. Frank looked back. The other pilots seemed to be asleep. Or dead. Saulnier shook his head.

"I will have to say in my report that while the *esprit* is magnificent, the physical state of these pelicans is deplorable. Weak as kittens, all of you. A day's flying and look at you. A good course in physical training. We need gymnastic equipment, a three-kilometer run before

breakfast every day. A month of that, plus decent food and sleep, plus
. . . *Viejo*, are there women in this *pueblo* we go to?"

Frank turned his head. He could see the back of the old man, a blue
shirt stiff with salt, a faded red kerchief bound around his seamed
neck, a battered hat jammed down on wisps of white hair. The old
man clucked to the burro.

"*Hombre*, there are women. If there were no women, there would be
no *pueblo*."

"Young women? *Muchachas? Guapas?*"

"I saw guns. Those things you fly have guns?"

"Yes, two."

"You fly them for the people of Spain?"

"We are volunteers for the Republic. To shoot down the Fascist
aviones. For the people of Spain, yes."

The old man hesitated, then turned around and grinned.

"If that is true, then you will find young women, *guapas*, here in
Spain."

"I hope so. It has been three days now since last I . . .'"

The old man blinked slowly.

"You are French, then."

Saulnier laughed.

"Me. Yes. This one, German. This one, *no sé*. This *chico*, an
American."

The old man looked at Frank with mild, rheumy eyes.

"*Norteamericano?*" "North America?"

"*Sí.*"

"This is the truth? With his yellow hair? They have such hair in
"On him, yes."

"*Que cosa.* He will find many beds in Spain."

"Good. And me, *viejo?* What is my fortune in love, eh? Will I find
many beds in Spain, too?"

The old man thought for a moment. He shrugged and sighed.

"I was told as a boy that the men of France did not employ beds,
but preferred the action of animals and the positions, too. So I cannot
say, in truth."

Saulnier grinned and offered the old man a cigar. The old man refused twice, then accepted the tobacco and placed it very carefully
in the pocket of his shirt.

"For tonight."

"Will you return for our comrades?"

"No. I regret, but I cannot. I must cross the lines again tonight."

"To the other side? Why?"

The old man blinked slowly and waved one dry hand toward the east.

"There has been fighting. You saw it from the sky, no? Is that possible?"

"Yes. We saw it."

"Then, in two days will begin the burying of the dead. I go there with my burro and cart."

Frank sat upright, sniffing.

"What's that he says? He uses this cart for the dead? Is that what? Jean?"

"More or less. Listen, *viejo*. Is that what you do? You bury the dead?"

The old man looked at the French pilot and at Frank. The two others were asleep, and he did not include them in his musing stare.

"Not only the dead. I take away what there is no use for. I take away all those things that are no longer wanted. Some I put in the ground. Some I spread on the fields. Some, a very few, I keep for myself. You understand?"

Frank and Saulnier looked at each other.

Most Respected Father and Beloved Mother,

This day finds me well and safe. I write to you after the vesper service by the light of a lantern in a small house. We were engaged in battle three days ago, briefly, for perhaps two hours, during which time we routed the Anarchist horde and drove them back. We followed them, but were unable to advance far because of shortage of ammunition. Not weakness of spirit, I assure you! The Reds suffered very heavy losses, but we fared well, except in certain places where our lines were over-run. Our arms are far superior to theirs. My machine-gun squad fought valiantly from a well-chosen position among large boulders. The Italian weapons functioned very well. One of the Guardias Civiles positioned on our left said our Carlist volunteers were nearly experts with automatic weapons. We were quite puffed with pride by that. Imagine our feelings when our group received special commendation for valor on the field!

Some of this recognition falls upon my own shoulders, however unworthy. I have been selected to attend a school for officers, and I have accepted the honor. Although this will mean leaving my comrades, I have been assured that I will be reposted to a Carlist volunteer group when my training is completed. Duty and faith can both be served, with God's help.

We have Mass every day. It has become an obligation for the

Falangist volunteers, too, although I must say they were in-
frequent communicants when they first came into the lines.
Therefore, I have the opportunity to remember you both, and
my sisters, of course, in my prayers. May God give you all
health and peace of mind and our beloved Spain peace, too.

We get newspapers quite regularly and read the reports of
the glorious advance of our troops on Madrid with joy. Surely
the columns will cut off the city soon. Then it will fall, and
Spain will rise again!

I kiss your hands.

Your son,

Pedro

Dear Connie,

I am sending this by a comrade wounded enough to be sent
back for treatment. He has promised to deliver it in person, so
I do not have to worry about the censor. Be yourself the censor
and tell Mamma and Papa just as much as you think they
can accept. Wait, of course, until my last letter to them reaches
home. Give the bearer of the letter a hero's welcome. Poor
fellow, he needs it. He was shot in an embarrassing spot.

Tonight, we are all quite tipsy on bad wine, sentimental and
full of heroics and song. It is no fun burying the dead, even
when most of them are the enemy. A dead man is a dead man.
We bury Spaniards when we lay them in the ground. There are
the usual stupid jokes, stupid but necessary. One doesn't want
to think too much, you know. We call this work, the "fertilizer
squads," and the company humorists worry about the grass coming up red instead of green. Hilarious, eh?

The war is boring, dirty, dishonest and when the actual
fighting begins, frightening. Yes, I was afraid. The noise is terrific, the tension almost too much to bear and you cannot see
anything. The whole area was covered with such smoke and
dust. Our machine-gun squad huddled behind the rocks and
blazed away at anybody we could see, in range or not. We
used up a great deal of ammunition, the wretched Italian
machine gun jammed a dozen times and we had been in
dread for most of the day about a rumor of Red aircraft bombing and strafing our lines. I saw exactly one, very low. I could
have thrown a rock and hit him. Our gun, naturally, was
jammed.

We could see so little through all the smoke and dust, that

I ordered the machine gun moved forward. There seemed little real danger and we might well do some damage. So we went, like men moving a grand piano, over the rocks forward to some crude trenches. Some Falangists had perhaps a half-dozen kids in one section of the trench. They said they were the "Red Bulls" from Pilarmadre, down near Teruel. The Falangists brought a flag from somewhere and demanded that these children kiss it. One of them spat on it. I shouted, but it was too late. The Falangists shot them all in the back. Except the one that spat. I will not tell you how he died. You would not believe it.

This morning, we found eleven Carlists, from a Pamplona group (That's why we're drunk and singing "Adiós, Pamplona" for them). We wear, as you know, over the heart on our tunics The Sacred Heart with, often enough, the words STOP BUL-LET embroidered there. Each of the eleven corpses had been shot with a pistol—right through the heart.

We loaded them into a cart. Our "fertilizer squad" has a burro and cart, an old man from Asturias, I think, and enough shovels for all. We gave them a proper burial.

And so we won a battle, I guess. We are in defensive positions and short of ammunition, food, medicine and everything else. If this situation goes on much longer, the war will last forever, Madrid will never surrender and we will all grow old here. I jumped at the chance to go to officer's training school. Trench life is for pigs and peasants. We get the papers and laugh at the lies that are printed about us. What sort of fools do they take us for? We believe in The Cause. Is not that enough to get decent treatment and the truth? I guess not.

When I am located, write to me. Your packages are appreciated, believe me. I divide the food up, of course. Send tobacco and socks. Those things we all need, enough so there was some looting, especially from the dead of the so-called "Ghost" and "Ivan" battalions . . . the criminals from the jails in Valencia. It didn't seem ghoulish, just revenge. Their positions were cluttered with stuff they had stolen on their way.

Yes, some of the stories of women fighting on their side is true. Nothing so glamorous as that newspaper article you sent me, about Carmen whatever her name was. Very frankly, the Reds had some *mujeres de mala vida* with them. Don't get any ideas.

Kiss the other girls for me and argue with Papa. It's good for his circulation.

Your brother, Pedro

"Water! A river!"

The river was broad and smooth beneath the hot morning sun. On the other side was a town, walled with closed gates, and here and there a red banner clinging like a leech to a pole. The others, even the sickest, stood up to see this marvel. They murmured and pointed. The river was wide, very wide and smooth. It looked like the sea they had crossed on the ships, only not so blue and very smooth. Amil gazed at it, awed, and slowly scraped the dust from his face. He blew his nose into his fingers and wiped them on his tunic.

Sheltered by a low ridge, the new cannons were unharnessed, uncovered. The foreigners who fed them swarmed on the earth like ants. He saw one cannon slide back on itself. Then, in a little, came its voice. One after another the new cannons spoke. The town, walled like a well, trembled and smoked as the shells crashed into it. Amil watched to see if the shells fell into the river, defiling it, but the gunners were good and the cannons slide back on themselves and their voices beat like drums. The river lay broad and smooth beneath the hot morning sun.

The sun was halfway to the earth when the order came to advance. New ammunition was issued from the back of a truck. Nothing else was said, and so they marched toward the river. Some officers on horses rode alongside the column. It was understood that no one was to break ranks for the river. The sound of machine guns came from the town. Amil listened to two officers talking. The place was called "Badajoz" and five thousand "Rojos" were inside the walls.

Amil looked up, freed one hand and pointed at the beautiful river. The officer shook his head.

"After the attack. Tell them that. We went at the Puerta de la Trinidad once. Another time. Our *bandera* goes forward against the Puerta del Pilar. You follow us. Inside the walls is good water, but better still, in there you can drink blood."

Amil nodded. The Spaniards always talked about blood. The officer walked away, then came back.

"Your company was told yesterday? The colonel's orders? Colonel Yagüe has commanded that you leave the dead ones alone. No knives on the dead ones. Any one of you *moros* with *cojones* cut off the dead ones will be punished. Understand?"

The officer walked down the line, repeating what he said, while Amil shrugged away the questions of his comrades. Always after battle you cut the dead ones. How could you know how many you had killed unless you put the knife between their legs and cut off? It finished the wounded ones, too. They could not crawl away and make more enemies. The Spaniards talked of drinking blood and then gave foolish orders about not using the knives. It was stupid.

At the top of the hill, the column fanned out in support positions by company, leaving gaps for the armored cars. The sound of fighting was steady now. The Legionarios had a skirmish line forward supported by machine guns. They crawled across the earth toward a gap broken in the wall, not far from a fortified gate. The machine guns from the gate spoke and spouts of dirt danced into the skirmish line. There were soldiers at the broken place in the wall, too. The gap was dusty and fresh slides of stone fell down, gnawed loose by the machine guns of the Legion. An armored car rumbled by, and the Moors scampered away from it. A machine gun mounted in a turret fired until the gun jammed.

The Legion dead and wounded lay in the field. The Moors stepped over them, keeping the long line even, until the shout came. Amil stuffed his cape into his belt and ran. A few bullets hissed by him. He ran on until the shadow from the wall fell over him. He was directly before the gap. His squad came in around him, while the others knelt and started shooting up at the walls. Amil bounded over the broken stones. He stepped on a body and reached for his knife. He remembered the order and scowled. He climbed on, deafened by the explosions of the hand bombs. The Legionarios were down in the streets, dodging from doorway to doorway. Bullets spanged and howled off the house fronts. A gush of smoke, splintered shutters and stone bits belched from a second story. A dark figure slid from a roof in a shower of tiles and plunged down into the street. Amil looked to the right and the left. Something hit him on the neck, spinning him off-balance. He slashed back with his bayonet, a furious belly-rip that missed the bulky figure in Legion battle dress. A big, scar-faced soldier pointed a pistol and shouted.

"Down that street, you black bastards! We don't want you shooting into our backs!"

The Moors howled through the gap in the wall, trampling each other, bayonets held straight up, long shining needles through the ear-slamming racket and the sifting stone dust. Amil jerked his arm and ran to the left. His squad followed him. At the first street corner was a barricade, with no time or room to aim. Amil fired from the hip and flung himself against the heap of stones and furniture. It sagged and gave way, spilling him on top of someone. He brought up his rifle and smashed down with the butt. He missed and struck again, punching in bones and flesh. The others poured over the barricade, half crushing him, flailing, stabbing with bayonets, shooting, and screaming.

By the hour of near-darkness, Amil had used all but six of the cartridges he had been issued. His left hand was blistered from the hot rifle barrel. He had killed eleven men he had been able to see fall and three more with his bayonet. He did not count the prisoners shot inside the cathedral or three women caught in a cross-fire in the Calle San Juan.

Some houses were burning. No orders had been given to stop killing. The streets spattered with firing, stopped silent, and echoed again. The Legionarios had begun looting the shops and cafés and many were drunk and went in bands, singing and shooting. There seemed to be no officers. Amil went by himself, lost in the streets, sliding from doorway to doorway. Then he saw the light in the window.

It was pale gold, a rectangle in the bullet-chipped stone house front. The splintered door hung by a single iron strap, pinning the body beneath it. Amil crossed the street, his rifle ready. The dead man had been stripped to the waist. He was old with gray hair and his body was white and disgusting. His neck was dyed red. Someone had taken a woman's lip-coloring and made marks on the dead man's forehead. Amil knelt, curious, and traced the greasy markings. U.G.T. Above the second mark was the blue puncture of the bullet, and a seared spot from the muzzle flash. The tube of lip-coloring had been mashed on the tile floor. Amil walked into the house.

The first room had been wrecked, the furniture smashed, bits of broken stuff flung about, a puddle of blood sticky on a ripped carpet. Amil poked at a chair with his bayonet and walked out to where the dead man lay. There was no one around; no one to see. He slipped his knife free from the scabbard. At the turn of a dark flight of stairs, a slash of gold hung in the air. Amil straightened and stared. Holding his knife in one hand, he slung his rifle and softly climbed the stairs. The golden chevron floated toward him. He groped to it, reached out and touched a smooth, cool surface and saw his hand, another hand and the shadow of a hand. He grunted, understanding. A mirror, like a pool of water.

The house was silent. He held his breath and listened. No one. Outside in the streets, some shooting, but not near. He unslung his rifle and hefted it in one hand over his head. He let it fall slowly, deliberately, watching his dim reflection until the butt plate shivered the mirror into a brittle fall of blackness. Amil turned and walked toward and through the half-open door.

It was a big room for eating, with a round table and many small chairs with thin legs and cloth of plants and birds on the seats and backs. Over the table, golden-lighted, hung bits of stiff water on wires, swinging driblets and chains of water that sparkled and shimmered and made sweet chiming sounds like the play of a fountain. Amil stared, his mouth open, at the magic of the stiff fountain of water that hung on a golden chain from the ceiling of the room. He felt his legs quiver and sat down on the floor. He lay his rifle in his lap and sheathed his knife. He leaned back against the wall and stared up at the gleaming, shifting dream of water swinging pure and tinkling above the table.

He sat, stupefied, exhausted, fascinated, until full darkness came over Badajoz. He heard, faint and far away, the smash of rifles fired by the volley. He rose, drug-legged and clumsy, staggered to the nearest chair and knocked it over. He climbed up on the table. His boots scattered things that broke. He reached up his hands and clawed at the glittering strings and spurts. He cried out softly when he touched one stiff, sparkling bit. It had edges, flat places, corners. He tore it free with a whoop of joy. The whole fountain of gold-lit wonder clashed and swung sparkling, a dance of gorgeousness that made his throat ache. He bit the piece he had torn free. Whirling flecks of light and color sailed along the walls and skidded over the floor. His teeth clicked and skidded on the hard planes. Amil grunted. He licked the thing. It had no taste but was smooth and cool. So it was water, locked by some magic, a fountain fixed stiff by a dark spell.

He stood, swaying, dizzied by the loopy swing and cascade of gold and glitter. A lust crawled in him. He had found this splendid spelled thing. It was his. No wonder the man had been marked and shot in the head for his wicked keeping of this thing while Believers clamored with thirst and terror of impurity. Fury like combat-rage beat at his brain. He raised his rifle and drove the bayonet wildly up, again and again, until his face and shoulders were pelted with bits of plaster. The fountain in the air suddenly sagged down at him, a canting, wheeling clash of light and dancing pieces. A hunk of plaster tore loose and the fountain fell more. He clutched and snatched at the pendants and prisms, his hands greedy and reeling, trying to touch it all at once. He flinched back from a hot thing like an onion that burned inside itself. He pulled out his knife and wallowed with the clicking chains of dazzling light and struck at the onion-thing. It popped and vanished, leaving only a golden hole frilled with little teeth.

Amil put his finger in the hole. It bit him! He hung, swathed in chains of enchanted liquid and examined his hand. It bit him but left no mark. He wrenched down and fell across the table, staring up, his heart jamming wildly in his chest. A great dark snake drooled down from the hole in the ceiling, its head fixed into a cup at the top of the golden chain. That was the spell. It was guarded by a snake! The dead man down below was the keeper, the feeder of the snake that kept the water stiff.

Amil knew that he must kill the snake to free the fountain. He dropped to the floor and steadied his rifle against the edge of the table. It was a hard shot. The snake was thin and stiff and swayed from side to side. He fired three times. The third shot hit, and its blood squirted and smoked. It did not writhe or coil back, but hung, fizzing blood and the lights inside the onion-things winked on and off. It was wounded, dying. Amil dropped his rifle and climbed again to the table. He edged between the golden arms of the fountain, then flung himself on the snake, hacking and striking. It bit him again and again, until he howled and sawed and, weeping, slashed and killed the snake and came crashing down on the table in a tangle of shattered water and his own blood. He lay on and in his fountain, chanting with pride and joyous triumph. He had killed the snake and broken the spell. It was his!

It was very heavy and treacherous to carry down the stairs. The jeweled ropes and sprays and chains were dull, but chattered and pinged in the darkness as Amil toiled across the hall. He kicked the body of the dead keeper and spat on his dead face three times. Amil staggered out into the dark streets of Badajoz, bearing his treasure, his enchanted fountain, full drink and pious purity for all the days that Allah might grant him in this foreign war.

"Start motors!"

Schmidt glanced at the instrument panel. The inertia starters ground slowly. The starboard engine coughed and caught, then the port motor. The Heinkel bomber trembled, and the roar of the motors slammed back off the flat, rust-colored earth. Schmidt plugged in his radio headset.

"Ready for take-off. Navigator?"

"Ready, sir."

"Gunner?"

"Yes, sir!"

"Bombardier?"

"*Ja, Kapitan.*"

Schmidt could feel the chocks pulled free. The bomber rolled forward. The morning sun spangled the propellers to golden wafers. The aircraft jolted across the field.

"Spain. All this country is good for is for graves!"

Laughter spattered in his ears. Schmidt grunted. He had forgotten the radio was on. Well, a little joke was good for morale. He braked and opened the throttles, holding the throbbing bomber on the ground. The signal light winked in the control tower.

"Bravo!"

The Heinkel surged forward. Schmidt chuckled. How the Spanish colonel enjoyed playing with his little electric lamp! Every aircraft of the Kondor Legion took off to the flash of the light, with Colonel Bravo's "permission." The flight crews played the game, shouting his name. Bravo, Colonel Bravo. In the Wehrmacht, the man would be in charge of laundry and traveling theatrical groups.

The Heinkel hammered free, tons of steel, aluminum and wire, bombs and machine guns, oil, glycerin and water, fabric, cylinders and dials, fins, sights, bomb racks and doors, glass and chrome and bullets.

"Navigator? Air speed and course."

"Two hundred twenty-five kilometers per hour. Course north, northeast. Exact compass bearing to follow."

Schmidt turned the U-shaped wheel. Ten metric tons of aircraft drifted five degrees. Soft, heated air rose up from the barren plains. Not a pocket or a bump. Not a ripple. Like glass. The Heinkel seemed to hang in space while the wrinkled hide of the earth rolled beneath. The ship barely trembled when they test-fired the new machine guns. The blue minutes skidded past the steel and glass snout. Schmidt glanced at the delicate discs of the instrument panel. The needles hovered like insect wings. Time stretched, thrumming, elastic. The voice of the navigator startled him like the touch of a wire.

"Target sighted. Fifteen degrees to port. Turn five degrees starboard, *Kapitan*. We are already at bombing altitude."

The dull red earth wheeled. On the pale band of the horizon a dark, jagged smudge. The target. The enemy capital. The Bolshevik citadel.

"Madrid!"

The city changed from a ragged smear to a great dark coin flung on the dry plains.

"Bombardier?"

"Ready, sir."

"Time, navigator?"

"Two minutes, four seconds."

"Open bomb doors!"

The winch-motors whined. The Heinkel dragged and the engines labored. The bombardier began to talk.

"I see the park. El Retiro. One degree to port. Steady. A strip of green. That's La Castellana. I see the rail lines and Atocha station. Perfect. One . . . two . . . three . . . bombs released!"

A slither of oiled steel, and the Heinkel lurched up. Schmidt banked away, flying a long figure eight that would bring them back over the city. The bombardier lay on the catwalk, staring down through the glass floor of the nose. He started to chant as flashes of fire smashed the gray stones of Madrid.

"*Ja* . . . *ja* . . . *ja* . . . Right in the target area."

It seemed only a few seconds before the navigator handed him a slip of paper with a compass reading. Schmidt spoke to the bombardier.

"We have incendiaries in the rear bay. No target indicated. Drop from the center of the city toward the Vallecas section."

The city rose up to meet them again. Big, loose, dirty plumes of smoke above the railroad station.

"Hold speed and altitude, *Kapitan*. So . . . two and three. Releasing."

It felt as though the Heinkel was running over cobbles in a village street. The bay doors whined shut and the red light winked off.

"*Kapitan!*"

"*Was?*"

"I have a target. Two degrees to starboard. Request we strafe. That's the highway to Valencia."

"Very good. We will take photographs. Navigator?"

"Camera on and running, sir."

"We are going down. Gunner?"

The Heinkel, lightened, plunged toward the highway like a twin-engined interceptor. Schmidt flipped the safety off the wing guns, throttled back and leveled off, one hundred meters over the road. They ripped down the highway for two full kilometers, the guns hammering. Schmidt pulled the U-shaped wheel back into his lap and banked away.

"Camera off."

"Observe and report, gunner."

"We hit some trucks. Fires on the highway. An explosion, big, yellow ball of flame. It looks like the bridge is gone. Very beautiful, *Kapitan*. Very pretty."

Schmidt looked at his watch. Not bad. Four minutes over the estimated attack time. They could make it up on the way back to the base. The bombardier came up from the catwalk, swinging his helmet. He flipped open his seat and dropped on it. What *was* his name?

"Well done . . . Keppler."

"Thank you, sir. We really cut them up back there. A dozen vehicles hit. We got fifty to a hundred men. A conservative estimate."

Schmidt nodded. A good fellow, Keppler, as well as an expert bombardier, a credit to the Luftwaffe.

"Secure bay doors. Keep alert for aircraft and anti-aircraft fire. Estimated time of arrival is 1105."

They flew south. No interceptors. No anti-aircraft fire.

"Perhaps we destroyed more than a dozen vehicles, Keppler?"

"I'd swear we hit twenty, sir."

"Would you? Then why don't you fill in the intelligence report, eh, like a good fellow? I'll countersign it."

"A pleasure, sir."

The engines beat steadily and the sun streamed in through the glass canopy. A perfect morning, a perfect mission. Behind them, thick black smoke rose from burning Madrid.

"Do you play tennis, Keppler?"

"Yes, sir, but I'd be no match, I am afraid."

"How about a few sets before lunch? Work up an appetite."

Kopa sat on a broken chair, washing his socks in a tin basin and reading a P.O.U.M. newspaper. He turned the page with damp fingers. The motor pool was very quiet. The trucks were out, hauling food to Madrid. The sun was hot, the news was all bad. Even the Communist papers could not hide the failures, the losses. At the Alcázar in Toledo, it was a race against time. The besiegers mined and dynamited while the defenders starved and sniped. Every day, every hour, Franco's Army of Africa drove closer. The militia forces were falling back everywhere, outmanned, outgunned, disorganized. Every retreat was a "strategic withdrawal," every feeble counterattack that ended in disaster a "glorious punitive action."

And what do I do? Nothing. Kopa washes his socks. He sits in the sun, cooking in the Spanish oven. How much sun does it take to melt a German? When will I be "done"?

When the mechanics and drivers gathered at night for "political school," hours of argument and harangue, Kopa listened and said nothing. The Spaniards believed the newspapers. An act of faith. They had accepted him, and Kolodny, too, because of the trucks. The trucks from France were an act of faith. The lectures were frivolous, the teachers fools or innocents. Kopa listened and said nothing. He did not dare to speak.

An automobile came to the gate, and the P.O.U.M. guard lounged out of his shack. It was an open Matford touring car, black, with a red star painted on the side. As soon as Kopa saw the two men in the rear seat, he knew. In the fierce heat of the summer sun, they wore brown leather overcoats. They wore visored officer's hats. They had come for him.

Kopa wrung the soapy water from his socks, spread them to dry on a flat stone and stood up. They walked quickly to him. Both were young, with set, dark faces. They looked enough alike to be twins. The one on the left spoke.

"Kopa? Hans Kopa?"

"*Me llamo Kopa, sí.*"

"You speak Spanish."

"A little more each day. Thanks to my comrades."

"You are under arrest."

The guard was watching. So was the chauffeur. A familiar seep of dread filled Kopa's chest. He clenched his fists.

"By whose authority, comrades?"

"Brigade of Criminal Investigation."

The one on the right shook his head slightly and spoke for the first time.

"In the name of El Asturiano, military commandant of this area."

"May I bring my clothes? Leave a message?"

"No."

Kopa shrugged and walked to the car. The two men in brown leather overcoats got in, one on each side. They turned and drove out through the gate. The P.O.U.M. guard looked the other way.

They drove in what Kopa had come to think of as "the Spanish style," very fast, the horn blatting constantly, right in the middle of the narrow, badly paved road. No one spoke. Kopa stared straight ahead. The kilometer stones whipped past. At a crossroads, they came upon an old man and a burro cart. Both the man and the animal seemed stunned to sleep by the sun. But the old man raised his right fist in the salute of the People's Republic. Kopa saluted back. The man on his right struck down his arm.

"No signals!"

Kopa laughed and shook his head.

The one to his right blushed. Kopa watched him. It had been years since he had seen a man blush. A dull red tinged from the stiff collar of the leather overcoat to the sweat band of the officer's cap. It was stupid to make a secret policeman blush. A member of the Cheka might do anything to revenge his honor.

Kopa remembered the East Cemetery in Madrid. He had taken a truck there to collect clothing taken from the bodies. The ground was covered with nude corpses, men and women. In one corner, near the larger vaults, lay the bodies of four small boys, dressed in pajamas. They lay face down in the trampled grass. What had they done to some member of the Cheka? One of the dead boys clutched a worn picture book. Mickey Mouse.

The kilometer stone said CUENCA. The road switched back and forth up steep hills. The driver shifted gears with a ferocity that set Kopa's teeth on edge. That amused him. First they would question him, then they would torture him, then they would shoot him. And he was worried about the possible damage to the gears of a Matford touring car. That was Spain. The Gestapo chauffeurs were expert drivers. A few years ago, Kopa thought, I would have written a little article, a satire, on police chauffeurs for some illegal magazine. Very sophisticated and witty, confessing finally that my education in this area was not complete. I had never been taken for a ride by the NKVD, but surely that omission would be rectified during my next visit to the Soviet Union.

The touring car swerved off the highway and down a rutted dirt road through a well-tended vineyard. In the distance, Kopa could see the glint of railroad tracks. They hurtled on, raising a huge cloud of dust. Kopa was thrown from side to side. He reached forward and gripped the back of the driver's seat. Hands tore at his arms, a passion-seized face lurched at him, spitting in rage.

"No escapes! No escapes!"

Kopa shook his head and raised his hands. The touring car turned, slowly this time. Kopa could see a large, low stone building, a farm-house, and beyond it a grove of olive trees. The car stopped. The three men sat still. Kopa looked at the olive trees, moved, disturbed by their beauty, the slender leaves the color of tarnished silver. Olive trees, Monte Oliveti, in groves outside the interrogation center of the secret police. Even the geography, the very plants of Spain were an irony.

"*Fuera!* Out!"

Kopa climbed from the touring car. Clotted beneath the olive trees, clustered there, were men. Men eating bread, drinking wine. Men sleep-ing. Men reading newspapers. Men cleaning rifles and machine guns. On and on beneath the twisted silver trunks, hundreds of trees, hun-dreds of men, a battalion at least, preparing for battle. Kopa turned to the one on his left.

"*La Guardia Roja?*"

"*Claro.*"

The one on his right prodded him.

"No questions!"

They walked past guards at the front door, two young men in make-shift uniforms with splendid, tough faces. They saluted with clenched fists. The one on the left saluted back. Brigade of Criminal Investiga-tion did not.

Kopa was led to a small room without windows. An electric light, unshaded, hung down from the ceiling. There was a long table and three chairs in the room, a single chair across from the table. A man sat in the center chair, reading papers in a cardboard folder. He looked up. Another young Spaniard, but with a strained face and tired eyes. He was very handsome, very poised. Perhaps a man to be afraid of.

The two men in leather overcoats crossed to the table and sat down. They both gestured at the same time. Kopa sat facing them in the single straight chair.

It was always the same sort of room. Always a desk or a table. Always the single, straight chair. It might almost be *the* same chair, the identical room. The same faces. Identical questions. First, his name.

"How do you call yourself?"

"Kopa. Hans Kopa."

"Sometimes Heinrich Kleist?"

"Sometimes."

"Your papers."

The one on the right was Brigade of Criminal Investigation. He would handle the introductory formalities. Then the one on the left. Political Commissar. Finally, the young man in the middle with the tired eyes would write L. beside his name. *Libertad.* And a burial detail would be selected from the soldiers waiting beneath the olive trees.

"You have a French passport. How did you enter Spain?"

"I drove a truck loaded with arms supplied by the Communist Party of France."

"You are a German national."

"I escaped from a concentration camp. I have no German papers."

"You reported in Barcelona to Comrade Beimler and were directed to deliver the arms to the railroad station. You did this."

"Yes."

"Beimler gave you papers. P.S.U.C. papers. *Partido Socialista Unificado de Cataluña*. The United Catalan Socialist Party."

"Beimler gave me Communist papers. Yes."

The officer from the Brigade of Criminal Investigation leaned back in his chair. He was finished. He looked disappointed. He had not revenged his blush. The questions he was authorized to ask were annoyingly inadequate. The Political Commissar leaned forward.

"If you have P.S.U.C. papers, then why were you found at the *parque mobile* operated under the authority of P.O.U.M.?"

A good question. Why was a Communist with a group of Trotskyites? Had Beimler sent him there as a spy? Or was he guilty of apostasy? A very good question, Comrade Political Commissar. Comrade Brigade of Criminal Investigation is so filled with envy that his nostrils have turned pale as wax. The one in the middle, Comrade Silence, is waiting.

"I was driving a truck of food into Madrid. On the Valencia highway. We were stopped. Air raid. A plane came over, a bomber. Very low. He strafed the convoy. Many trucks were damaged. We had wounded. We went to this village. They are P.O.U.M. people there. They are allies. They helped us. They asked us to help them back. So we did it. That's all."

"*Verdad?* The first time? But you were with Durrutti's column in the advance on Zaragoza. First with the C.N.T., then with the P.O.U.M. This is very unusual . . . with P.S.U.C. papers."

Kopa shrugged. His mouth was dry. His hands rested lightly on his knees. It *was* unusual, not *very* unusual, though. The problem was precisely this: had he done something forbidden? Unusual, usual made no difference. The bizarre might be tolerated, and in Spain frequently was, while something very ordinary was suspect or, without warning or explanation, illegal.

"We had then six trucks. We had delivered the arms. We were empty. We volunteered to transport the Anarchist militia up to the front."

"You volunteered to take trucks provided by the Party in France to drive Anarchists to defeat at Zaragoza."

"That is one way to see it."

"There is another way?"

"We drove the dead back to Barcelona. I had a truck of wounded.

They all died. I unloaded the truck and went back. Three times. All died."

The man in the middle looked at Kopa intently and nodded once. Suddenly, he spoke.

"Is it true that Durrutti ordered the whores into railroad boxcars and had them machine gunned to death?"

Kopa blinked. He had seen the boxcars, empty. Splintered boards and the floors pasted with blood. He nodded.

"The women were venereal. Many of the men became diseased. The doctors suggested they be removed. The women. Durrutti removed them. In his own way."

The man in the middle nodded, once, and rubbed his knuckles over his right eye. The left eye, dark pupil and long lash-fringes stared at him. The man's voice was very soft, almost a whisper.

"One day I will . . . remove . . . Durrutti. In *my* own way."

The sincerity was what did it. The two young police officers could not conceal their feelings. They stared, astonished, horrified. Kopa looked at his knees. There was a long silence, before the young commissar spoke again.

"On the highway to Zaragoza, you passed through a town. Near Teruel. The name of this town?"

"Pilarmadre. We picked up some militia there. C.N.T. They called themselves Toros Rojos. "Red Bulls." A bunch of kids. They were very brave at Zaragoza. Many of them were killed."

"Just militia."

He knows, Kopa thought. Let him earn his pesetas, though.

"That's all."

"A lie! You made a rendezvous with the village priest!"

The commissar grinned ferociously. Kopa looked at him. The young man's hands tore wildly through the papers in the cardboard folder. Kopa could not stop himself. He grinned at the man in the middle and pointed at the commissar.

"He's new at this job, eh?"

The dark, drawn face suddenly split into a smile of pure joy. He did not laugh, but seemed to hold the pleasure inside himself, savoring it. The commissar's hands roiled up a sheaf of papers, plucked out a scrap and waved it. He was speechless with triumph. The man in the middle smiled and nodded once.

"We're all new at our jobs here. Except *you*. I think you have much experience. And so you see, we are obliged to find out exactly what your occupation is . . . the one you have had so much experience at."

"I didn't know he was a priest. He told me the second or third day. We were together during the battle. Afterward, he was very busy. We worked together taking away the wounded and the dead."

The commissar jumped up, shaking the scrap of paper at Kopa.

"Where . . . where is he? This priest. Tell me. At once!"

He was new at his job to be sure. He did not know where the priest was. Moreover, he didn't know how to find him. Kopa shrugged.

"I can't say for certain. He spoke of going to Málaga. His parents live there. He didn't feel safe in the People's Republic, even though he had helped the people in his village. He was very brave, but he was no fool, you see. Yes. He went to Málaga."

Kopa managed to keep his voice steady. He lied calmly, deliberately, as he had lied before, many, many times. Even the lies were the same. As soon as you learned what they didn't know, you lied. They knew you lied. And that was when they started to do things to you. Even there, even in torture, the police were unimaginative. They would begin, as usual, by beating him unconscious. The thought, the memories made him sick. The room blurred; the three dark, young, intent faces melted together.

Kopa remembered Germany. The cell. The stone floor slick with his blood, his urine, his vomit. The rope around his wrists, binding and biting his ankles. The filthy, stinking towel stuffed in the helmet tied over his face, stifling, blinding him. The sound, the unbearable sound of the Gestapo trooper kneading Vaseline into the thick leather whip, a slow, sticky, liquid sound. And when the whip was soft so it welted but did not cut the flesh, the others began to sing their song:

Let him scream, let him scream.

"To Málaga . . ."

The voice floated at Kopa. Yes, or Hamburg, Paris, Lisbon, Warsaw, Budapest, Prague. Yes, there, wherever you say. Wherever you want him to be so you can find him and do this to him, too, before you drag his shuddering, drooling hulk down into a cellar and blow his brains all over the walls. Except he isn't *in* Hamburg, Paris, Lisbon, Warsaw, Budapest, or Prague, you greasy-handed bastard! And he's not in Málaga, either. He's back in Pilarmadre, of course, where you're too stupid to even think of looking for him!

"Yes, Málaga. I'm quite sure."

"That's too bad."

The man in the middle. Kopa forced himself to look up. He was sick with terror. He could not stand it again. They would beat him. Then they would burn him with cigarettes again. And this time, he would break. They would make him tell the truth.

Kopa clawed frantically at his shirt. He was suffocating. It always got him. He ripped the buttons and showed them his chest. He stood up, holding open his shirt, and howled at them in German, his mind a white blank of fury.

"*Ja! Er ist nach Málaga . . . Schweinhund!*"

The sound of his voice smacked back into his face. He sobbed once. Tears broke from him. He swayed and someone caught and steadied him. He covered his face and his grief crushed him. They had won . . . without even touching him . . .

"*Basta, basta . . . fuera. Tú . . . también . . .*"

Chairs scraped and the door rattled shut. Excited voices shrilled outside. Kopa dropped into the chair. Two hands held him. He mopped his face. He was trembling uncontrollably. He opened his eyes. The dark, strained face was very close, sickened. He could feel the man's breath on his hot, wet cheeks.

"*Hombre* . . . My God, they did *that* to you . . . in Germany?"

Kopa looked down at his flat, dirty belly, stained and runneled with his tears. His brand. The mark they had set upon him forever. One day in a prison, the Gestapo had tied him down on a table. They had cigars and cigarettes. With the glowing tips, they had burned a swastika on his belly. They had crushed out their cigars in the little pit of his navel. The slick, tough scar tissue was dead growth on his body. Kopa could feel the young Spaniard's gentle, clumsy hands fumbling with the buttons on his shirt, drawing the cloth over the scars, but when the fingers brushed the swastika brand, he could feel nothing at all.

They sat for some time in the cool, bright room. Kopa calmed and touched his branded belly.

"Some show, eh?"

"You can make a joke of *that?* Those two *chicos* are outside being sick."

"That's because they are new at their job. One day they will laugh."

"*Que vida tenemos. No somos hombres . . . sino monstruos . . .*"

"Monsters are not afraid. We fear, so we are men. I was a monster, once. I was cured . . . by the Gestapo."

"This is a bad place. Come with me, Kopa."

They went together down a short passage and out into a walled garden where an iron table and some small chairs stood on a patch of scruffy grass. Kopa sat and looked at the silvery plumage of the olive trees beyond the wall. He felt completely empty, melted in the sun. He was made of wax.

The young Spaniard—his guard?—brought a package of American cigarettes, a bottle of wine and two glasses.

"Here. Drink wine and say nothing."

"One always says *something* . . ."

"It is not necessary, Kopa."

"*Salud?*"

"*Salud, camarada.*"

"*Y victoria?*"

"*Y pesetas.*"

"Money, not victory?"

"Right now I need money."

"Why?"

"You'll see. Later."

"The wine is good."

"Take some more."

"I'll get drunk."

"Go ahead."

Kopa looked across the table. The young Spaniard stared at him. Kopa drank more wine.

"Who are you?"

"Paco Larra."

"*El Asturiano.*"

"I am called that by some. For two years now. You smile. Why?"

"I expected some . . . ruffian . . . a bandit with a beard."

"And I expected Kopa to be . . . you know, with short hair, cut like so and a duelling scar on his face."

"I have other scars, as you have seen. And some that don't show. They are the worst. They never heal."

"I know. They never heal. You told them nothing when they did . . . *that*. Not a word. Right?"

"No. Not a word. Larra, your priest is in . . ."

"Pilarmadre? I thought so. I want to see him. If he's alone, some *pueblo* Durrutti will prove his loyalty to the Republic by shooting him. If he comes with me, I can protect him."

"Why would you do that?"

Larra looked away. A lizard crouched in the sun.

"He saved my life, that priest. He told a lie to save me. A priest."

"Recently?"

Larra sighed and picked up his glass.

"No. A thousand years ago."

"Before the civil war?" Kopa said. "In Asturias, then, no?"

Larra smiled again, as though tasting something delicious.

"In Spain, there has *always* been a civil war. There will always *be* a civil war. It's in the blood. We are not a nation. Spain is a gathering of tribes. Wait and see, Kopa. Wait and see. Spain is not Germany. And it's not Russia. You Germans are in for some surprises."

"So are the Russians."

"*Claro.*"

They sat for a moment. Kopa picked up the pack of cigarettes and opened it, took out a match. The Spaniard watched him, appalled.

"After . . . *that*. You are a smoker?"

"Of course."

"Incredible. Who sent you to Spain, Kopa?"

"A man named Voget."

"Paul?"

Suddenly, the Spaniard laughed. Softly at first, shaking his head, then loudly, beating his fist on his knee. He reached across the table and patted Kopa reassuringly.

"Forgive me. It is just very good, that's all. You see, Voget . . . Paul didn't tell me. A message missed us here, I guess. We heard from Beimler . . . about you. And so we hunted you down. You are a reckless man, Kopa. Don't you want to live?"

"I'm trying to learn that. It's hard."

"Not impossible. That priest. Father Ortega. He learned."

"He has a different system."

"Does he? I have not seen him for . . . a thousand years."

"Go to Pilarmadre."

"I can't. I must go somewhere else. A very stupid business. I have something else to speak with you about. Very important."

"Why me? I'm a truck driver who goes with the wrong people."

"Because Voget sent you. If he sent you I can trust you absolutely!"

Kopa looked across the table. El Asturiano, official hero, leader of the Red Guard. His pictures for sale in shop on the Ramblas in Barcelona and on the Gran Vía in Madrid. Except the pictures were of another, older man. His father? Probably. "I can trust you absolutely." Trust? Trust a cracked jar, a broken pot? Kopa closed his eyes. Beyond his lids, the sun burned red. How good it felt! How strong and even the sun was! It poured into you until the blood bubbled. "I can trust you absolutely." Paco Larra. A tough kid. But a kid. And a Spaniard, right to the marrow. Baked in the oven.

"Voget's name is absolute proof of loyalty. But you must understand, Kopa, that the case against you is not dismissed, but merely terminated. Stopped at this point. By my signature."

"How extraordinary. You are the man that fellow Josef K. could never find."

"Who?"

"A character in a book."

"I don't read books. Just manuals of strategy. Tactics. I come out here in the afternoons and drink coffee and read."

"Mmm-hmmm."

The sun beat down on Kopa. He breathed slowly. He heard the bottle chink on the glasses.

"Drink to *los ingleses*, Kopa."

"The English? Why?"

Kopa sat up straight, dazed by the sun. He lit another cigarette from the smoldering stub of the first and snapped the stub at the lizard. The creature darted off, a wrinkle in the grass.

"They have intervened? For the Republic? The Italians sank a British ship?"

"No. Not yet. Not so grand. But we have learned that there are more than one hundred volunteers. At Figueras. You know the place, of course. North . . ."

"Of Barcelona. We stopped there for gasoline on the way to Beimler with the weapons."

"One hundred Englishmen . . . all with military training. At Figueras. They are led by a man named . . . Coltringham. You know him?"

"No. Communist?"

"Yes. He was in the last war. I want him. I want his men. With me. Pay attention now. This is secret information."

"Everyone in Spain tells each other secret information. There are spies everywhere, too."

"We are forming a system of transportation from France to a place called Albacete, near Valencia."

"What for? The oranges?"

"To transport one hundred thousand international volunteers into Spain to fight for the Republic!"

"Is this true?"

"So you see, Kopa, we need men who have had experience . . . driving trucks, of course. Driving trucks."

Kopa sat blinking at the wine bottle, at the cigarette that smoldered between his fingers. He felt dazed, drugged by the sun and wine. *One hundred thousand volunteers.* The idea was too large for him at first. His mind kept pushing it away. It was not true, propaganda. Before, always, the thousands had dwindled to a dozen, a wretched handful to be abandoned, betrayed, trapped, destroyed, and forgotten.

He threw himself back in the garden chair, swallowed a glass of wine at a gulp and sucked greedily on his cigarette. His heart began to thud in his chest. He glared around, trying to find something real that could be drawn down inside, into himself to banish fear, to enable him to believe again. The olive trees!

His spirit floated over the stone walls and bounded in the grove of trees where frail shadows slid on the hard red earth. He saw and sensed the rusty soil of Spain matted like peat, clenched in the roots of a hundred thousand olive trees, the blue ceramic sky of Castile scribbled on by a forest of tough, thrusting branches, felt the dry, hot winds of Aragón pour through a billion slender silver leaves. The trees gave unctuous fruit with pits like flint. Ripe olives scattered to dry on tawny straw, crinkled-hided by the sun, pungent little hand grenades. A vast plate of granite pressed the golden sun, the clear fluid crushed free, amber and pure, overflowing the cup.

"One hundred thousand? From everywhere? *Mein Gott* . . . yes, yes! When, Larra, when?"

"Sit down, comrade. You will explode!"

"I am . . . I will . . . Finally, an army of workers . . . like a dream, but real. *When?*"

"For you, at once. For me, for the Republic, soon. We must buy time at Toledo, force Franco's army to halt. Then we will stop them, throw them back at . . ."

"At Madrid!"

Madrid would be the granite plate beneath the cruel force of the sun, the pressing-place where the fleshy pulp and bullet-pips would be crushed until the earth soaked slick. There he could stand, naked to the waist and show his shameful brand as a badge of honor earned at last. They would make Madrid a fortress and the temple of international socialism. A dream come true.

"Kopa? Kopa, come into the shade near the wall."

They carried the chairs and moved the table and huddled over the bottle and glasses like tavern cronies. The idea shimmered in the summer day between them, an incandescence they feared to look at too long. The dark young Spaniard stoked Kopa. The brigades of international volunteers became "they" and "them." All the Republic was "we." All the doubts, hesitations, and anxieties drained from Kopa. He wanted to drink, tear food, to dance and to sing. He forced himself to sit still, but a miracle of belief slugged in his veins.

"They will have their headquarters at Albacete. Frankly, they will get no training to speak of. We have no equipment to spare. More important, they must learn some Spanish and to accept and to obey their officers. Those with any military experience must be discovered promptly."

"Who have we named to direct all this?"

"A *troika*, as they say in Russia. Luigi Longo as Inspector General. The Italian, De Vittorio, as Commissar. The third, a Frenchman."

"Voget?"

"No. Paul has been involved in Central America, Brazil, the Argentine, and Mexico. The Comintern still thinks of him that way. They wanted a name, a star in the Socialist heaven. The base commander is André Marty. You must know him."

"I have met him a few times. Shortly after he led the mutiny of the French fleet in the Black Sea. Two horses and a mule hitched to our *troika*. Who named Marty? Thorez?"

"I heard it was *El Viejo*, The Old Man, himself."

"Stalin? That's possible. Perhaps with the two Italians, Marty will be . . . controllable. He suspects everyone and has a bad temper. I don't want to meet him again, but I suppose I shall. Where are your two *chicos* in the leather coats?"

Larra shrugged and filled the glasses.

"Gone. You will go with me to Madrid. I will arrange an *avión* to take you to Barcelona. Listen . . ."

Kopa heard the high wheep of a locomotive whistle. Larra finished his wine and stood.

"El Asturiano's private train. I take the Red Guards to Madrid, to show the people, then out to Talavera de la Reina. We will retreat from there to Madrid."

The Spaniard's face puckered in disgust. He shouted to someone in the house. A bell began to beat. Kopa followed him to a low wooden door set in the wall.

"Why retreat? We must stand and fight!"

"I know it and you know it. But the government does not. They think of El Asturiano's private train. There is even a bathtub in it. Come and see."

The two men walked out into a vast silver-green grove of olive trees. Kopa laughed aloud when the men rose up to meet them, settling cartridge belts, hefting rifles, stumbling over equipment like dancing bears. On every shoulder was a crimson Roman numeral one. Larra nodded and saluted them, his fist clenched.

"My battalion. The best in the regiment, which is the best in the Republic. We could take the Alcázar in two days, Zaragoza in three. But we ride in this *bicho* of a train and wave to children and girls. For morale. For nothing. It is stupid."

Kopa looked at the soldiers of Larra's Red Guards. They were unlike any group he had seen since coming to Spain. Every man had sturdy boots, a one-piece khaki field coverall with big grenade pockets, a light pack, an entrenching tool, and a French steel helmet. Each man had been issued six Mills bombs and a bayonet. Their rifles were Springfields, American make, but well kept. Kopa counted twenty heavy Hotchkiss machine guns mounted on wheeled carriages pulled by panting dogs.

"Dogs?"

"They don't take up room and heavy transport like horses. They keep you warm at night. They don't have any more fleas than the men and they stand night watch with the sentries. When we run short of food . . . we eat them. I learned more in Russia than just tactics, comrade. Tie dynamite to a dog's back and you have a very efficient anti-tank weapon. Chapiaev showed me that one. We spent a day together dynamiting dogs."

"Are those mortars?"

"Yes. That's what you brought me. Thompson machine guns and mortars. New. Voget negotiated the purchase through Mexico. He could negotiate the purchase of Mexico through Mexico, if they'd let him.

The Anarchists in Barcelona thought I was getting a shipment of irrigation water pipes. Your Pole told me all about it. He is a good man, an excellent liar, that Kolodny. Mortars are better than field guns for us. Easy to move, see?

"It comes, El Asturiano. *Mira, mira!*"

Larra grimaced. The soldiers were pointing. Kopa could see the locomotive through a gap in the far end of the grove. Several hundred men were already grouped there by platoons, waiting. They were very quiet, for Spaniards. Larra accepted a Colt automatic pistol and belt from a boy, apparently his orderly.

The locomotive wheeped again and came snuffing through a gap cut in the grove. It was the bad dream of a boiler maker. The locomotive was a great steel coffin spewing soft-coal soot, a blind box creeping on the rails, towing fifteen slab-sided cars topped by turrets presumably borrowed from some Spanish maritime museum. Larra planted his fists on his hips.

"I call it the Armadillo. Those *bichos* in South America covered with plates that eat ants. I go in back. That's in case the track is blown up. The *chicos* up front get killed. The whole thing is worthless."

"How fast can it go?"

"*Qué va!* Fast. With luck we'll get to Madrid two days before Mola, a week before Franco. This madness is from somebody in the government. Armored trains were very *à la mode* in Russia during *their* Civil War. Naturally, then . . ."

"Naturally."

They walked the length of the armored train. Hands waved out gun slits, and muffled voices called to Larra. The soldiers were pretending they were letters inside a postal box. Others were vegetables stewing with dog meat for some dish called *sopa de armetralladora*. There was a great deal of laughter and some singing. Larra climbed up the ladder welded to the armor plating on the last car and dove through an open hatch. Kopa followed him, laughing. It was a new carnival, and he was tipsy from the wine.

Inside it was nearly total darkness and hot as an oven. Larra switched on a light that flickered feebly. Kopa saw a full-sized bed, a desk, a gun case, the bathtub, washstand and shaving mirror, a closet full of field gear and, perfectly, a *bidet* filled with hand grenades.

"Welcome," Larra said, "*Estás en tu casa.* You are in your own home." Kolodny and I were in military school together in Russia. Kolodny's a tank instructor, really."

"Not a sailor?"

"Told you that, did he? What a liar! Shameless! No, he drives tanks, cannoneer, general repairs, and tactician. I had trouble getting the Russians to agree. Had to bring him in through France. Voget took care of it. No, Kolodny is a full colonel in the Soviet army. He escaped, actually. They're trying people for treason. Kolodny's not a traitor. To Russia. He's a traitor to Poland, of course, but that's his business, no?"

The armored train jolted once and began to move very slowly. Kopa stood at the window slit and watched the feathery branches of the olive trees. How beautiful they were!

"All you need, Paco, is your own air force."

"I agree. I asked Voget about it. He's going to speak to what's his name? . . . Malraux. I hope something will come of it."

"Yes," Kopa said, watching the olive trees stream past. "Yes, that would not surprise me. After today, nothing will surprise me."

The siren bellowed over the roof tops of Madrid.

"Carmen? Air raid?"

"Yes. Another one."

Out on the landing, doors slammed, as some of the tenants started for the shelter in the basement. Carmen pushed the light switch. The electricity was off again.

The morning song of Madrid . . . the siren blaring through the warm sky, the slow bark of cannons, the sound of doors like drunken drums and the slush and rattle of water in the pipes. The cannon shells cracked. Then, the sound of the motors, a faint rumble. More than one bomber this morning, three or four at least. The siren cried on and on.

Carmen wandered into the kitchen and yawned as she stirred the burnt malt and water that was "coffee." She blew the fire to life, added some charcoal and put two stale *churros* in the oven to heat. The sound of motors in the sky grew louder. She shrugged and lit a cigarette. A thin, far whistle, a pause, then a deep thump. The first bomb, not very close. The bathroom door crashed open and Teresa rushed into the kitchen wrapped in the hideous purple robe her *novio*, an artilleryman stationed at Huesca, had given her. Another bomb fell on Madrid. Teresa snatched Carmen's comb through her brassy hair. Roommates for months, they shared everything.

"You could set your watch by those *canallas*. That's out at the University. Why there? It's a wreck already. Put out that cigarette, Carmen, you'll get an ulcer! Coffee ready? Good. I've got surgery all day. A whole ward of abdominal cases. Full of morphine. They just lie there."

Another bomb hit, close enough to make the apartment building shiver. Carmen watched flecks of whitewash drift down from the ceiling. Teresa flung off her robe and struggled into her white nurse's uniform.

"Don't they ever sleep, those Germans? Put out that stinking cigarette. There was mail for you yesterday. Ministry of Interior. *Jesús y María*, now we'll have the newspapermen here again. A little article . . . ummm,

'The Life and Love of *La Novia*.' Subtitle. 'How exciting it is to share an apartment with the sweetheart of El Asturiano.' "

Carmen stubbed out her cigarette, peeled the paper, and dropped the tobacco shreds into a tin box. Enough to roll three more.

"*Qué mala, tú!* He's not my sweetheart!"

" 'We're just good friends.' Like in the cinema magazines, eh? Pah, this stuff! Remember how real coffee used to taste?"

"No."

The whole building shook, the saucepan skidded off the stove, paint and plaster bits rained down from the ceiling. The smash of the bomb drowned Teresa's cry. But she held her cup steady, away from her white uniform, and went into the bedroom.

"Hey, it's down in the next block! Just one place. But the whole top floor. *Ay, María*, why can't you shoot them down!"

The sound of the motors faded away. The smell of burning wood and scorched stone drifted through the open window. Teresa came back into the kitchen carrying a letter. Carmen bit into a greasy *churro* and opened the long stiff envelope marked with the symbol and initials of the Ministry of the Interior. Teresa poked her in the ribs.

"Well? You're in charge of Feminine Propaganda. La Pasionaria wants to know who does your hair. Largo Caballero has created a new post. He tells his government 'Gentlemen, we cannot win the war without female machine gunners.' "

Carmen wiped her fingers on a sheet of newspaper and read the letter again.

"No. It just says that I'm to report to the office of the Committee of Protection of Minors. I wonder what that means?"

Teresa shrugged, picked up her cap and smoothed her hair.

"I guess somebody found a place for you at the Palace Hotel with the orphan kids. Maybe they want you to pose for more posters. Like two weeks ago."

"No more posters. I told them at Party headquarters . . ."

"But you are *beautiful!* So heroic . . . so big in the front. You looked like a bureau with the top drawer pulled out. No one could possibly recognize you."

"But, Teresa, how was I to know that they were going to use my picture for a poster on contraceptives? I was so *embarrassed* . . ."

"Next time, *ask*. Poor Paco. Once you got out of his blankets, you've gone right to the devil, *guapita*."

"I've told you a thousand times that I was never *in* his blankets! Nobody else's, either!"

"*Ole! Virgen de la República. Qué lástima!* Me, I wouldn't have wasted a minute. Is he sick or something?"

"Of course not! Ten times I've told you that he's just not that way. He . . . *respects* me."

"Either he's got the clap or he's a fairy. Send him to us at surgery. If he has no use for it, we'll cut it off."

"You're terrible, Teresa!"

"You know what I think? This is Paco's doing. He has some false papers for you. They are good at that, the Communists. A birth certificate that says you're fourteen or something. Maybe a pass, a *salvoconducto* to get out of Madrid before we all get killed by this 'Government of Victory.' Run to the Committee and find out. Before it's too late."

"But I can't leave you! You're my friend, no? We're comrades together in the fight against Fascism and . . ."

"*Dios,* what nonsense you talk!"

Teresa blew her nose, three loud snorts, and grinned, then swung her hand and cracked Carmen on the hip.

"What nonsense I talk. A fourteen-year-old with that to swing. You have an indecent walk."

"I don't!"

"They'll have you filling sandbags at some orphan home while a company of U.G.T. militia get stiff ones from admiring your pretty behind every time you bend over."

"What things you say. You have no shame, Teresa!"

"No one would ever know the nuns once had a hold of you. I'm jealous, that's all. Run along."

"Teresa, you'll get a letter from your *novio* one day soon. I'm sure of it. It's just the mail."

"Of course. Just the mail . . ."

The honk of the all-clear signal, startled them both. Carmen snatched up her letter and her door-key and turned.

"*Salud,* Teresa."

"Until tonight, *patriota* . . ."

The sun was strong and warm. The bomb smell filled the street. Two blocks away, a team of men played a puny stream of water into a wrecked building. A small crowd, gathered there, watched quietly. No one was digging in the ruins. No one hurt then, most likely. She began walking in the other direction. A truck filled with militiamen rolled by. The soldiers called and whistled to her. She waved her clenched fist and smiled.

There was little traffic in the streets, but already the women were in lines, waiting for the market to open. Carmen walked past a line of small shops. There was a sign painted on each shuttered front:

NO HAY PAN	NO HAY TOBACO	NO HAY LECHE
NO HAY VINO	NO HAY CARNE	NO HAY ARROZ

In a workers' *cantina*, the radio was broadcasting the morning news. There was no way to conceal the disasters. The Italians had taken Majorca. The Basques had surrendered San Sebastián. In Andalusia, the city of Ronda had been overrun. Everyone knew that Franco and Mola had joined. Madrid was surrounded, although the highway to Valencia had not been cut.

Of course the Republic would win. Not right away, but some day soon. There were jokes about the new coalition, how the Communists had delayed joining until they had been assured that the Anarchists would have no cabinet posts and how the "Anars" had suggested that the Communists create a Ministry of Defeat, in order to make the government "truly representative of the human condition."

At the corner, Carmen stood in line, waiting with the others for a truck, another new joke. New ones, from Russia, they had an emblem on the radiators, THC, for Tres Hermanos Comunistas . . . Three Communist Brothers. There were lots of jokes. The workers of Madrid laughed away bad news, shortages, hunger and confusion. But they did not laugh at the air raids. Twice every day, the Fascist planes made widows and orphans in the streets of Madrid.

It was hard to remember what life had really been like *antes de la guerra* . . . before the war. Everybody said it, all the time. Before the war I was . . . or I lived . . . or we had . . . or I thought . . . Madrid had changed so! It had always seemed so beautiful, full cafés, crowded sidewalks, music, clean streets, flowers in the plazas and water splashing in the fountains. Now all the cafés were shuttered, the sidewalks nearly empty at night, even in the Gran Vía, and the fountain of Cybele was dry behind its shelter of boards and sandbags.

Whole groups of people had vanished: street cleaners, night watchmen, taxi drivers, flower sellers, the city police. Either the jobs had been declared "positions lacking in human dignity" or the men had simply gone off to the fast-shrinking fronts. Now you cleaned your own rooms and clothing, ate in workers' canteens and wore the blue coveralls and rope-soled sandals. Life was hard, but there was The Cause, and the city was democratic, "proletarian," as the Communists called it.

The truck came at last, overcrowded, but with room in the back to stand and hold on with both hands or better with just one, the other free to fend off the little "salutes" of friendship and comradely affection from behind and, sometimes, even in front.

The lower windows of a bombed-out apartment had been boarded over. Someone had daubed with black paint: ONE STATE—ONE COUNTRY—ONE CHIEF—FRANCO.

At her stop, she dropped down and waved her clenched fist in farewell to the man who had ranted in her ear for six blocks about the meeting of the Non-Intervention Committee in London. She did not really understand what made him so furious, but she had agreed with him. It all seemed very simple.

At a newspaper kiosk, she bought a Socialist and a Communist paper. It was necessary to understand these things, or at least learn something about them. She glanced at the headlines:

BALDWIN AND BLUM: FRIENDS OR ENEMIES?
CONTINUED SHIPMENTS FROM ITALY AND GERMANY
NON-INTERVENTION: MADNESS OR SICKNESS?

Carmen carried the newspapers into the office of the Committee of Protection of Minors. The building showed signs of bomb damage, and all the window panes were plastered with translucent tape. The office was a noisy, confusing place, quite unlike the disciplined Communist headquarters, or U.G.T. offices. Men and women in blue *monos* rushed up and down the halls, all talking, all waving pieces of paper for some-one else to sign, all calling for Comrade this-or-that. Carmen pushed through to the main desk and gave her name. She was told to wait. She opened the newspapers on a wooden bench.

She did not learn much. The Communists were suspicious that both Britain and France were hesitant and fundamentally insincere, not ma-neuvering to end the exporting of war-stuffs into Spain but merely making noises about it to pacify the leftist groups in their own countries. A new word was used in both papers: "appeasement." Even the So-cialist editorial suggested that the governments of Baldwin and Blum were afraid of Hitler's Germany and Mussolini's Black Shirts. Yet the Communists insisted that the People's Republic was ready to accept "real non-intervention." It took Carmen several minutes to understand that the Communists really meant that *no* legislation should be passed in *any* country that would prevent the *Republic* from buying arms. Facing this editorial page was a feature story with bad photographs, treating the growth of heavy industry in the Soviet Union. It was all muddled, a mystery.

Even if the news was bad or incomprehensible, the paper was needed in both the kitchen and the bathroom. She waited another hour, yawn-ing with boredom, then left the building and stood in line for an hour at the nearest *cantina*. She was lucky and got a seat at one of the tables. She ate a big bowl of beef cooked with *garbanzos*, white beans and bits of sausage. A canteen worker punched her meal-ticket and re-minded her to wash her tin wine cup and wooden spoon in the common basin. She donated a peseta to Red Aid and walked back to the office. This time, at the desk, she showed her letter and was handed a typed sheet. She was to report to the Palace Hotel at once to begin her new duties as "comrade assistant to orphan children." She waited outside the office until one of the Russian trucks stopped. She got on. Halfway to the Palace Hotel, the air-raid siren began to howl.

The high moan rose over the racket of the truck engine. The driver slowed and shifted gears, swerved to the left, directly at the long island of trees that split the boulevard. Some of the passengers began to scream. They were going to crash right into the trees. The front wheels bounded up over the curbing; the motor roared; the passengers were flung forward, then back. The truck lurched up on the island, sheltered beneath the flimsy canopy of branches that bore limp, parched leaves.

The long sweep of pavement was empty, black and shimmering in the afternoon sun. The cry of the siren sank to a sob, a moaning murmur. At once, there were two groups among the passengers, those who would stay in or near the truck because it was shelter and those who abandoned the trucks because they could be seen from the sky. Carmen was shouldered off the tailgate, fell on someone and muttered an apology. Men and women flitted in frantic haste across the street, the sound of their sandals an unnerving flabby pattering, like an invisible shower of rain in the sun-struck afternoon. On the long slender islands, every tree was claimed by three or four who knelt like penitents, pressing against the gray, harsh trunks. Wedged bodies squirmed beneath the trucks. The people around her waited, gasping, making the sign of the cross, eyelids crushed shut.

Carmen stared around, amazed. She had never been in the open during a raid. She sat down, drew the newspapers from the pocket of her coveralls and made a tent of them over her head. She felt safer at once, and when the anti-aircraft cannons began to fire, she tilted and craned to see the shell-bursts like black rags flung into the pale sky.

They came out of the south, a string of dots that did not seem to move so much as to swell. She did not hear motors or the shriek of the first falling bombs. The buildings, too close, shut off the view. The earth trembled, once, twice, a long shudder. The first plumes of smoke lifted. The planes changed course and the sound of engines was a ragged trundling far away. When they turned, she counted fourteen Junkers trimotors. They dropped more bombs. Carmen heard the high, wailing whistles. The ground shook, and then came the sound, a smothered deep whomp-whomp. The sky near the planes was sprigged with black. Stiff, ugly and invulnerable, the German planes wheeled high over the rooftops in formation, spilling bombs.

The bombs fell on Atocha, along the banks of the Manzanares River, and plummeted into the stone canyon of the Gran Vía. The earth heaved and shivered. The first concussive wallop struck her like a sea wave. It seemed to be one long, lurching explosion with spurts of flame stitching at her eyelids. Dust sucked up, and leaves shaken loose settled in clouds, skidding and tapping on her newspaper hat, batting like moths against her shrinking face. Stone and smoke geysered; her hat of newspapers whipped from her fingers. Flying stuff hissed and crackled in the branches of the trees. The bomber motors ground down on her. She tore at the hard earth with her fingernails. The dirt beneath her bucked, and she rolled, wide-eyed, on her back and stared up at the churning sky.

It ripped the length of La Castellana like a projectile, a silver spike. There were two more, close behind. They tilted, driving up through the smoke plumes, and she saw the red wingtips. A voice bellowed near her.

"Nuestros! Nuestros! . . . Ours!"

Ours? Yes, they *were!* Three interceptors, glittering wasps that swept up, whining, to sting the black vultures hanging in the sky. She could hear, very clearly, the tatter of their machine guns. Everyone rushed out into the street. The bombers disappeared behind an oily gout of smoke pouring up from the Gran Vía. The crowd groaned and gaped, stepping on each other's feet. Carmen clapped her hands.

"Get them! Get them!"

A cheer rose, beginning blocks away, and rolled up the boulevard. The crowds danced like frantic children, laughing and weeping. The iron formation of black bombers had cracked at the second blow! The trimotors were scattered, tilting clumsily in all directions across the sky. There were at least six silver planes darting and jabbing, wheeling, diving, guns firing. The street roared with delight.

"Ole! La Gloriosa! Mira, mira. Look at them!"

One of the Junkers staggered in the blue sky. A silver interceptor bored in so close it seemed impossible that the two planes wouldn't smash together. Smoke dribbled from the bomber's right-engine nacelle, and the propeller whickered slowly and stopped. The glittering monoplane, behind and above, fired another long, tattering burst. The Junkers skidded and began to fall in a sluggish spin, the two good motors blaring like tormented beasts. Pieces broke loose. The crowd hushed. The Junkers vanished behind the high buildings and boomed into the earth beyond the Manzanares River. The people of Madrid danced in delirium.

"Beautiful! *Estupendo!* Did you see it? He *got* him!"

The fighters drove the other bombers away. The all-clear honked. No one moved. They stared up at the smoke-smeared sky, waiting. Then, "He" appeared, flying low, back to the field at Torrejón. "He" was a gleaming monoplane, slender and fragile with fixed landing gear, a deep-jawed radiator and red-tipped wings. "He" swung over the city, very low, the engine throttled back. "He" was the always-promised, half-believed-in, seldom-seen one, La Gloriosa . . . the glorious air force that would sweep the Fascists from the sky. He was a foreigner, a comrade come at last!

Carmen looked up with all the others. Somewhere, a voice started to sing and the others took it up. "Himno de la República" swirled up from the smoking, broken streets to buoy him safely home. Carmen sang, her clenched fist raised, pivoting as the slender fighter plane whimpered over the trees. *Uno de los nuestros.* He waved back, a gloved fist. As the song swelled to a shout, he tilted his red-tipped wings in salute and was gone. But he would come back again. Because he was one of ours!

The song stopped. Thousands in the streets stared, rapt, in silence.

Then the truck motors coughed. The bells of the fire equipment dinged in the distance. The people of Madrid, the vast street crowds, the mass of blue coveralls and red kerchiefs, broke apart and eddied off, going back to the business of caring for the living, believing in The Cause, spying for the enemy and scraping through the hot rubble and bright fingers of glass for the wounded and the dead.

There was almost no resistance. The Legionarios killed thirteen militia and shot seven wounded prisoners. They looted the cafés and drank. They took six women into a garage and waited in line, talking and smoking. The German artillery was moved up to the abandoned airfield outside of town. The wind shifted at nightfall, and the Moors again refused to advance north of the town. Colonel Yagüe rode into the Plaza Mayor on a dappled horse. The U.G.T. headquarters was set on fire. A delegation of six nervous old men tried to surrender the town, but was ignored. Small bands of Legionarios walked through the empty streets. The executions took place at the railroad station, with one machine gun and a platoon of riflemen. The last to be shot were the six nervous old men who had tried to surrender the town. A victory Mass was said in the cathedral.

Tiger was drunk. They were all drunk. When the telephone rang, the others took rifles and started to shoot at it, but they were too drunk and missed. Tiger got up off the floor. The telephone bell jingled. Across the street some Moors had a woman. Tiger listened to the woman scream and the telephone ring. He picked up the receiver.

"*Dígame?*"

"*Oiga, oiga.* Listen. What is the situation at Talavera? What is the military situation?"

The woman across the street stopped screaming. She was dead, then. Four Fingers leaned over a wastebasket and vomited. Tiger blinked at the telephone and shouted into the receiver in Arabic.

"'Allah is a great god and Mohammed is his prophet!'"

"*Oiga?* Who is speaking? This is Madrid calling. This is Madrid!"

"Madrid is a bucket of shits and Reds."

"Eh? Who is speaking? This is the Under-Secretary of War. This is Hernández Sarabia!"

Tiger laughed and fell into a chair. He shouted into the telephone. "It is? Well, listen, Madrid. This is Sergeant González, 1st Company, 5th Bandera of the Foreign Legion, Army of Africa!"

The voice on the telephone made thin squawking sounds. Tiger listened for a few seconds. He yawned. He was drunk and sleepy. He tore the telephone free, staggered to the window, and threw it out into the street.

By dawn the next morning, all Madrid knew that Talavera de la Reina had been overrun. The last town of significance between Franco and the capital of the Republic had fallen.

At noon the next day, Sergeant González, 1st Company, 5th Bandera of the Foreign Legion, Army of Africa, was decorated for extraordinary gallantry on the field of battle by Colonel Juan de Yagüe y Blanco.

The British volunteers filled in the rear ranks. Coltringham could see the Desmond brothers, beyond them Brian, and, at the far end of the straggling line, Duncan, Whitlaw, Rouncey and their men. Between the British and the speakers' platform more than five hundred new arrivals had been driven together in a herd.

The weather had suddenly turned cool. The men shivered in light civilian clothes suitable for "sunny Spain." Only about half of them had received the makeshift uniforms issued by the quartermasters. As they gossiped, exchanged oranges and cigarettes, and tried to read copies of the Spanish newspapers, they reminded Coltringham of workers on strike. That's what they were, after all. Proletarians, workers, mostly French, this batch, with a sprinkling of Germans and Poles, even a few other nationalities, but all of them on strike against their own governments, all of them volunteers for Spain, asking only for arms and instructions. Then they would become soldiers. If there was time. There was very little time left.

The loudspeakers crackled. The waiting men muttered. They were bored with waiting, still exhausted from the long, slow train ride. Coltringham puffed his pipe and looked at the red banner flying on the breeze, high above what had been the barracks of the Civil Guards. There were still bloodstains visible on the floor and walls of the lower rooms. The Guardias had been massacred there.

André Marty was introduced. Predictably, there was sustained applause and a good deal of enthusiastic shouting from the French volunteers. Comrade Marty wore, as usual, his outsized beret.

Marty began to speak to the volunteers in French. Coltringham did not listen closely. He had heard speeches of welcome every morning for over two weeks. He had listened to the base commander's harangues against spies every night for the same two weeks. Marty had amazing energy. He never seemed to sleep and never needed to relax. Coltringham shifted uncomfortably. After morning parade came calisthenics, drill, then lunch. After lunch, small-arms practice. Except ammunition was very short. Except all the ammunition did not fit all the rifles. Except all the rifles were not even of the same make. There were Krag-Jorgensons, Mausers, Lee Enfields, some old American Springfields, and not enough of those to go around.

The day the first volunteers arrived in Albacete, aid from the Soviet Union began. Reports and rumors of Russian freighters unloading in Barcelona, Alicante and Valencia were passed around, believed in. Would there be time to get anything, men or munitions, to Madrid? How could they hold the defenseless capital against Mola? *No pasarán.* Good enough, a fine slogan. But where were the cannons, the machine guns, entrenching tools, food, bedding, trucks, barbed wire, tanks, and aircraft? Here were the men, but would they get to Madrid in time?

Interpreters spoke in German and Polish. Marty spoke again. Coltringham listened. His French was good enough to understand. Marty was hammering away at his favorite theme.

"The Spanish people and the Spanish People's Army have not yet conquered Fascism. Why? Is it because they have lacked enthusiasm? A thousand times no. Is it because they have lacked courage? I say ten thousand times no!"

The mass of volunteers applauded and shouted enthusiastically. The British volunteers clapped their hands and asked each other what Marty was saying.

"But I do say this. There are three things they *have* lacked, three things which *we* must have!"

"Political unity!"

Up went the clenched fists, a field of hard knuckles. Marty pointed to a short man in an overcoat buttoned to the chin, head bare to the bright sun.

"Military leaders!"

The man in the overcoat was called "Kléber," after one of the abler generals during the French Revolution. Although the propaganda unit insisted that "Kléber" was a naturalized Canadian, it was no great secret that he had been sent to Spain by the Comintern Military Section. His real name, Coltringham had discovered, was Stern.

Marty waited until the shouting and applause died down. He made a short, chopping motion with his hand like a cleaver.

"Discipline!"

He meant it, there was no doubt. The mass of men stood silent, watching and listening, glancing aside at the commissars wearing red arm bands. There was a commissar assigned to every company, a battalion commissar, a commissar for the brigade. The organization was modeled after the Red Army. What had worked in Russia could be made to work in Spain, despite the lack of uniforms and weapons, despite the difficulties created by four or five languages, despite the boredom, the weather, and the strange food.

"There are some who are impatient, who wish to rush off to the front at once."

Coltringham swallowed. He had submitted such a request two days earlier. The base commander was not pleased, so it seemed. Marty shouted into the microphone and slashed the air again.

"These persons are criminals!"

He was shaking with rage. Coltringham sucked his teeth. Very good, criminals, then. Get on with it.

"When the International Brigade goes into action, they will be properly trained men, with good rifles!"

Coltringham spat and scuffed the gravel. Comrade Marty spoke for a few more minutes. The loudspeakers blared out "The International." The volunteers sang, every man in his native language. Coltringham sang, too, at the top of his lungs. When the song ended, the men cheered and shook their clenched fists. Orders were issued again in French, German, and Polish. Morning parade was over.

A platoon of Germans stamped by. Coltringham stood aside to let them pass. The formation was good, cadence clear. Even though the men were dressed in floppy pants, random jackets and rope-soled sandals, they marched like soldiers.

The walls of the buildings were painted with slogans: PROLETARIAR ALLE LÄNDER, VEREINIGT EUCH! PROLÉTAIRES DE TOUS PAYS, UNISSEZ-VOUS! On the British Barracks, Harry Desmond had lettered, very neatly, WORKERS OF THE WORLD, UNITE!, but in so small a scale, so gentlemanly a hand that it looked like a public notice in a W.C. of the London underground. Harry had taken a ragging from the others and, unconcerned, had begun his "wall newspaper." Every day after parade, he pasted up articles from the Spanish papers, typed and hand-written notices and poems, slogans and pictures. Periódicos murales, the Spanish called them. Coltringham stopped to look. He grinned at a picture of himself and beneath it a caption in Desmond's handwriting "Wanted: dangerous criminal. Crime: enthusiasm." To one side was the front page of Mundo Obrero. Coltringham blinked.

Russian aid had begun to arrive! The ship Bolshevik had unloaded aircraft, tanks and ammunition in Cartagena. The ship Komsomol had unloaded ammunition, too, and more tanks. Tanks! That was something like it! Get them to Madrid in time, and General Mola's coffee would be damned cold before he got it. Instead of trenches around the city, a mobile strike-force of tanks, like a wall of steel!

Coltringham bounded up the steps into the boarded-off section of the barracks that served as his office. Harry Desmond pecked at a typewriter. Another man, unfamiliar to Coltringham, a German by his looks, sat waiting, holding a sheaf of orders. Was he someone from Ulbricht's imitation NKVD, one of the "Trotskyist-hunters"?

"Tanks, by God! They've sent some tanks! Tanks, Harry, Tanks!"

"Tom, this is Comrade . . ."

"Right. Comrade, have you seen *Mundo Obrero?*"

"I showed him, Tom."

"Good."

The German comrade nodded and smiled.

"Yes, very good. *Salud,* Comrade Coltringham. I am Kopa."

"Sorry. *Salud,* Comrade. Kopa, is it? What can we do for you?"

The German held out the papers.

"Sign these. Travel orders. Your group is moving out."

The papers declared that the English-speaking volunteers "having completed a course in military training" were to join the 5th regiment by a combination of motor transport and train.

"By motor transport? By truck? Where are these trucks, comrade?"

"They are being unloaded from the ship *Neva*. One hundred and fifty of them. More than enough for your men, I think."

Coltringham nodded.

"Harry, stop what you're doing and type up a general order. General inspection of men and barracks. Have Duncan see about the food ration. We leave at . . . um . . . 1600 hours. More or less. You know what Spanish transport is."

The German lifted the top sheet and pointed halfway down the next page.

"As you see here, Comrade Coltringham, the transport officer is myself. We will leave at *exactly* 1600 hours."

"You are transport officer for the 5th regiment, then?"

"On temporary duty."

"Where is the 5th regiment stationed now? We have heard nothing of them in several days."

"In Madrid."

"Madrid, eh? Damned good. Do they understand at Regiment what the situation is on arms and munitions?"

"All equipment will be issued at the troop train. All is ready, Comrade Coltringham. Bring us your British volunteers."

Coltringham thrust out his hand. Kopa took it.

"We are ready, comrade. Bring us your trucks."

At 1600 hours, Coltringham looked down the lines. How young they all looked, baby faces all sunburned and peeling! He set his fists on his hips and scowled at them.

"All right. You know where we're going and what we're going there for. You have empty hands now, but not for long. You're not good at drill, but I want a decent show. We came here as civilian volunteers. We leave here as part of the 5th regiment. I have spoken with brigade command, and have been assured that when sufficient numbers of British come here to Spain we shall have our own battalion. Until that time, we are combat troops for the People's Republic. Act like it. We have no brass band. But you all know how to sing. I have a favorite little tune. "Tipperary." I want them to hear it in Madrid! Forward . . . *march!*"

Coltringham marched through the gates toward the line of waiting trucks. As they passed the sentries, Coltringham brought his clenched fist to his forehead in salute. The British volunteers began to sing.

"It's a long way to Tipperary!
It's a long way . . ."

Four columns advanced on Madrid. General Mola, at his new headquarters in the walled city of Avila, announced that his "5th Column" of Nationalist supporters within Madrid would bring about the capture of the capital of the People's Republic.

Every day the Junkers and Heinkel bombers, the Italian Savoias and Bredas flew over the city and bombed. Every day La Gloriosa rose to meet them. The first Russian planes appeared, the stubby biplanes, immediately nicknamed Chatos, and a few barrel-bodied monoplanes with big radial engines, the Moscas. The Republican airfield at Getafe was bombed useless, the landing strips pocked with craters. The rescue teams counted sixty dead children at Getafe.

The 5th regiment pulled back. Italian Fiat tanks supporting Moors and Legion troops swarmed into Getafe. The next day, all buses and streetcars running to the suburbs of Alcorcón and Leganés were canceled. The terminals had been captured by the Fascists.

In the city of Madrid, the radios played day and night. General Franco made a special address to the civilians, announcing that the liberation of the city was near, and that his "noble and disciplined troops would respect all noncombatants."

Russian tanks with blond drivers rattled through the streets crowded with thousands of refugees, cattle, goats, herds of sheep. The Anarchist newspaper *Solidaridad Obrera* announced that the most transcendental day in the political history of the country had dawned. García Oliver was named Minister of Justice and Juan Peiro, who before the war had been a glazier, was given the post of Minister of Industry. Two days later, the "Government of Victory" the ministers, civil servants, and political leaders of all the parties, their clerks, dossiers, and files, including those of the Ministry of War were evacuated by automobile, truck, and train to the safety of Valencia on the Mediterranean coast. Only the Communists remained in Madrid.

**DIVISION OF SPAIN
AUTUMN 1936**

REBELS

REPUBLICANS

When General Miaja called for a defense *junta*, the Communists and their Russian advisors took over the executive offices of the city. The 5th Regiment was pledged to defend the city house by house. General Miaja demanded that 50,000 trade unionists be detailed for immediate service to construct defenses, trenches, and tank traps, and to fight in the trenches and behind the barricades they must raise.

The defense *junta* announced that the International Brigades had left their base at Albacete and would arrive at any hour to defend the city.

Dolores Ibarruri, La Pasionaria, spoke at a People's Front meeting. Her voice poured into the dark and dread-filled streets from loudspeakers:

"Spain will either win as a free democratic country or will cease to exist altogether. The enemy cannot be defeated by enthusiasm alone, by faith in the justice of our cause alone. War is an art and a science and must be mastered. Despite the heroism of the anti-Fascist fighters, the enemy has succeeded in dealing many blows because we lack organization, discipline and military science. These shortcomings must be made good, otherwise the enemy may pass.

"We must not conceal the fact that Madrid is in danger. The removal of this danger depends on the people of Madrid, and on them alone. The people of Madrid must remember the example of the Petrograd workers who in 1919 succeeded by their courage, endurance and discipline not only in repulsing but in destroying the large enemy forces advancing on Petrograd. All the proletarians in Madrid, men and women, must learn the use of arms. International democracy is on the side of the Spanish people. The working people of the land of the Soviets are on our side.

"They will not pass, the Fascists will not pass! They will not pass because we are not alone!"

BOOK THREE

The Siege of Madrid
November–December 1936

At Torrejón de Ardoz, the airfield lay at some distance from the Madrid highway and the cluster of low stone houses that made up the village. The twilight patrol came in from a strafing run over the Moors. They circled the field, wing lights winking, and settled to the earth.

Between the air base and the highway were fields picked clean at the early harvest and scoured by the cold winds of autumn. In these fields were dug shallow trenches or pits. The raw, red earth had been heaped carefully along one side of each pit or trench, forming a loose rampart that concealed six machine guns. The crews sat near their weapons, smoking and sharing a double wine ration with a platoon of men carrying Thompson submachine guns. The wind blew the cigarettes bright and shredded sparkles that whirled away.

Paco Larra sat in the rear seat of his command car with the Chief Political Commissar of Madrid, a Russian. Paco looked at his watch. The trucks from Model Prison were late. He glanced at the village. No lights in any of the houses. The men had been conscripted to fill sandbags and unload ammunition at the University. The women, children, and old people had been ordered into their houses and the windows shuttered. The café had been closed since noon. Torrejón de Ardoz was blind. But not deaf.

Paco glanced at the Russian.

"How many of them?"

"Perhaps three hundred. All those that were not transferred to Paracuellos or San Fernando."

"That's what you call it? 'Transferred'?"

The Russian nodded. Paco looked at the waiting Red Guards.
"It is a waste of ammunition."

"It is necessary," the other said calmly. "Have you forgotten Asturias? Your uncles and cousins and comrades? Have you forgotten your father?"

"You are so sentimental. You touch my heart."

"I give you an opportunity for revenge. Perhaps you might be grateful."

"This is a dirty job."

"I have said that it is necessary. Therefore, why talk of it? Look, here come the trucks."

"And now we do 'organization, discipline and military science'!"

Paco opened the door of the command car and got out. The Russian commissar looked up at him.

"You need to sleep more, comrade. I have some splendid pills. Allow me to give you some. Excellent for the nerves."

Paco slammed the door and walked quickly across the hard field. A convoy of trucks with dim blue lights crawled down the Madrid highway. Sentries with red flags at the barricade waved the trucks off onto a dirt road that rutted to the open trenches. Paco stood waiting until the trucks pulled in and stopped. Ten trucks with thirty men penned in the rear of each. Two Red Guards with submachine guns sat on the cab roofs, huddled in sheepskin jackets against the cold, their weapons pointed down at the human cargo. A group of riflemen waited. At Paco's signal, they yanked the bolts and dropped the truck tailgates and stepped back, forming a corridor leading to the trenches.

"All right. Get them out and down into the trenches. Listen, prisoners. You are to complete this series of trenches by dawn. When you are all in position, picks and shovels will be issued. The sooner you are ready, the shorter our work time will be."

The men climbed down, dribbling weakly over the tailgates and dropping to the hard earth. They were feeble from prison food and lack of exercise. Pale, rumpled and unshaven, they milled in the cold twilight and dropped down into the trenches. Only their shoulders and heads showed. The trenches were not really deep enough.

The Red Guards prodded the last men down into the pits with their gun butts. The trucks pulled away to one side, and the drivers turned the headlights on full. The trenches were blotted in dark shadows. Paco climbed up the rampart of loose earth and looked down. The men there were nearly shoulder to shoulder.

"You can see that this is insufficient for our purposes. Issue the tools and begin working!"

He stepped down. At once, the machine-gun crews heaved their weapons up and forward, grinding the tripod legs into the dirt. The men with the Thompsons cleared their guns and knelt. Paco raised his clenched fist.

All the truck horns began to sound at once, a ragged croaking that swept on the dark wind. The machine gunners opened fire, pouring bullets down into the packed trenches. The Thompsons stuttered. Spent cartridges squirted out into the headlight glare in golden streams. Sour blue flames danced on the machine gun muzzles as the gunners swung their weapons from left to right, slowly, mowing up and down the trenches. The truck horns blared, drowning the screams.

"Cease firing!"

The truck horns blatted on. The men with Thompsons scrambled along the rampart, firing short bursts. Paco saw two pale hands claw at the lip of the trench. One of the riflemen squeezed off a shot. The hands fell away in a patter of small clods.

The machine gunners cleared the unused belts, unsnapped the cooling hoses. Water from the cans trickled out on the loose earth. When the barrels were cool enough to handle, the crews carried the weapons, tripods, and water cans to the trucks. The Thompson gunners and riflemen scrambled up over the tailgates. As soon as the trucks were loaded, they pulled out, jouncing back up the rutted road out on the highway to Madrid. The lights dimmed, and the trucks drove away at top speed.

Paco climbed to the rampart and looked down. The bodies lay tumbled together, twisted like discarded dolls, flung about and ripped by the bullets. Here and there an arm moved, a leg lifted and dropped, a voice gibbered in the dark trench. Paco walked back to the command car. The Russian was smoking a long cigarette.

"Well done, comrade. What plans have you made for the burial?"

Paco snatched open the door and dropped into the seat.

"There are two tractors with scraping blades over at the airfield. They have agreed to come here and fill in the trenches. Late tonight. They have to use headlights and they're worried about a night air raid."

"Very good, comrade. You have created terror, a revolutionary necessity."

Paco spat in disgust and tugged the collar of his jacket up around his neck.

"I have created three hundred Spanish corpses. I have turned men who are soldiers into twilight butchers. What we have done dishonors us."

"You Spaniards will bungle your revolution with your sense of honor."

Paco looked at the Russian. They were really incredible, *los Rusos.*

"A revolution without honor is disgusting. Those men had wives, children . . ."

"They were Fascists, traitors, enemies of the Republic."

"They were Spaniards. Now they are dead."

The Russian tossed his cigarette out into the field.

"So? It amounts to the same thing. I think I must forget this little conversation, Comrade Larra."

"I think that I will not forget this night, Comrade Commissar."

"I would try if I were you, Comrade Larra. There is still the affair of the German. Comrade Kopa. A most interesting case of—how shall we call it?—political resurrection. He, too, is a man of honor. As you see it."

"And as you see it, Comrade Commissar?"

The Russian laughed softly.

"It grows dark. I can see nothing. Nothing at all. Tonight the darkness, tomorrow the dawn. You really must try one of my pills, Comrade Larra."

Paco leaned forward and rapped on the window.

"Driver. Back to the city."

"Where in the city?"

Paco leaned back and laughed shortly.

"To the University. The School of Philosophy and Letters. I am giving a lecture to the *chicos* tonight. On the ethics of revolution."

The battle broke at dawn on the seventh day of November 1936. Twenty thousand Nationalists, mostly Moors and Legionarios, struck at Madrid between the University City and the Plaza España, across the broad Casa de Campo. Artillery battered the middle-class apartment houses overlooking the shallow, rock-strewn Manzanares River. Shells smashed down into the Paseo de los Rosales, Calle de la Princesa and Plaza de Moncloa. Model Prison, the Don Juan Barracks and the Montaña barracks were pounded, and stones, glass, and twisted girders cascaded into the smoking streets. Russian tanks stationed at Puerta de Hierro ground and clanked toward the University. There the schools of Architecture, Medicine, and Agriculture were burning; heavy, sullen clouds rolled on the cold wind. The air-raid sirens howled, and the black bombers appeared. Masses of workers clogged the streets, heading for the Manzanares and the University. Ragged files and knots of men clambered over half-built barricades, stumbled deafened through the bomb-heaved streets. Children tore up paving stones and carried them to burro carts. A flight of interceptors ripped over the rooftops to strafe the Nationalists dug in along the Estremadura highway. Workers and militiamen fought from crude barricades, balconies, and rooftops. Light cannons bucked and blasted in a cold fog of smoke and stone dust.

In the Casa de Campo, the Fascist assault swept up the slopes of Mount Garabitas and was checked. Republican commanders sent frantic appeals for more men, more ammunition. The worker-soldiers were ripped by machine-gun fire, stunned senseless and bleeding by Moorish grenades. From the Royal Palace to the School of Science, Madrid burned and crumbled beneath the storm of bombs and shells. Men without rifles rushed into the shattered buildings to take up weapons from the dead

and wounded. The city shivered beneath a dun pall of smoke. Radio
Madrid cried through the crash of bombs and the slither of flying
shrapnel.

"Citizens of Madrid! Each of you has here on this soil something
that is ash; something that is soul. It cannot be! . . . It shall not be . . .
The mercenaries shall not enter as heralds of dishonor into our homes.
It cannot be! It shall not be that the Fatherland, torn, broken, must
entreat like a beggar before the throne of the tyrant. It cannot be! It shall
not be! Today we fight. Tomorrow we conquer. And on the pages of
History, man will engrave an immense heart. This is Madrid. It fought
for Spain, for Humanity, for Justice, and with its mantle of blood sheltered
all the men of the world. Madrid! Madrid! Madrid!"

And the city heard. And it rose and fought through the gray cruel
day until the night came down. The city heard, and the city, torn and
bleeding, held. The guns rumbled and fell silent. The Nationalists drew
back. They did not pass.

Outside the Palace Hotel, the street and the sidewalks were covered
with people, suitcases, carts, rolled bedding, lost families and abandoned
motor transport. The wounded lay everywhere, on blood-blackened
stretchers, torn heaps of blankets, up the main stairs of the hotel, in the
lobby and in what had once been the big, fashionable bar. Teams of
doctors and nurses worked in the gloom and sweet stench, stripping the
clotted bandages, cleaning wounds, stitching the gashed flesh. The hotel
roared with noise. Militia troops milled everywhere, cursing, bringing in
their wounded comrades, shouting slogans, street names, and promises.

Carmen came into the lobby with the burned children who had been
loaded crosswise on two stretchers. She struggled through the heaving,
grim-faced crowd and shouted for a doctor, for burn ointment, anything. She found a *practicante* with some morphine and rushed up the
stairs, jumping over and between the moaning wounded. Heavy gunfire
came from the University. She staggered down the hall. People rushed
by her, preoccupied, frantic, with white, set faces. The floor glided and
tilted. She could feel nothing from her hips down. Why not just fall in a
corner and sleep?

"Carmen! My God, you're still alive!"

It was a woman in an operating gown stiff with blood from the waist
to the neck. The woman rushed up and clutched her. It was Teresa.

"I thought you were dead! . . . Where have you been? Why did you
leave?"

"Some women came and asked me to show them how to use a machine
gun. They read the newspapers, I guess."

"Are you drunk? You look drunk."

"No . . . I don't know anything . . . I want to sleep. I'm so tired I want to cry."

"Come with me. I'll give you a shot of something. You're not hurt?"

"No. I was cut by some glass a few times."

"Were you fighting all this time? Did you kill any of them?"

"I don't know. Yes, I think so. It was hard to see and the shells kept hitting all around us. We did a lot of shooting. My shoulder is stiff."

"Let me see. A bruise from the gun butt. Drink this."

"What is it?"

"Bad cognac. I've been washing instruments with it. Some more."

"I just want to sleep. Please."

"Downstairs. In the burn ward."

A man in splotched white rushed up the stairs at them, waving his arms.

"They're here! They've come to us! The Internationals! *Los extranjeros* . . . the foreigners! At the foot of the Gran Vía!"

He rushed on down the hall shouting.

"Los Internacionales! They're here! Right outside!"

"Come on!"

Teresa ran down the stairs. Carmen took a deep breath and followed her.

It had become morning, bitter and sunless. They ran with the crowds that streamed toward the Gran Vía. The loudspeakers overhead chattered an order for total mobilization, blurted twice and went silent. The crowds surged on. Carmen stopped, buffeted by bodies, and listened.

In steady cadence, the beat of boots on the pavement and the sound of a hard, ardent voice shouting in the street:

"*Ein-zwei-drei-vier! Ein-zwei-drei-vier! Rot-front-rot-front!*"

Teresa waved frantically.

"Hurry, hurry! They're Germans!"

They came up the slope of the Gran Vía marching toward the new trenches, striding through the harsh morning to the front, unit after unit of International Brigade volunteers. The crowds packing the sidewalks and windows burst into applause and took up the cadence count.

"*No-pa-sa-rán! No-pa-sa-rán!*"

The front ranks were Germans, a battalion of them, solemn-faced, with blue eyes that seemed to stare far away. They carried new, oil-slick rifles and heavy machine guns. Their boots banged on the paving. They wore corduroy trousers, heavy sheepskin jackets and steel helmets. Their jackets were marked with a red K for their commander, Hans Kopa.

Teresa and Carmen hugged each other and jumped up and down.

"My God, they're huge!"

"They're *beautiful!* No *pasarán!*"

"What's *Rot Front* mean?"

"'Red front.'"

The Germans stamped past. Two young members of a machine-gun crew smiled and waved.

"Cheerio, girls!"

"*Ingleses?*"

"*Sí, sí! ingleses,* girls! I'm Peter, 'ere's me brother 'arry, and the fat one's Brian."

As the marching ranks swept past, Carmen caught a glimpse of young faces flushed with the chill air, steam in little explosions from smiling lips, lank hair trailing out from beneath a helmet worn at a rakish tilt. She waved her fist and called to them.

"*No pasarán!*"

The one with the tripod turned his head and waved his fist back.

"Bloody well right, *no pasarán!*"

The boots stamped on down the street. All along the Gran Vía second- and third-story windows popped open. Faces, arms, red flags appeared. Cheers and applause dashed in echoes. Here and there men and women wept with joy and wonder.

"*Mire, los franceses!*"

"Who are they? French?"

"Yes! *Commune de Paris* battalion. Tough ones, eh?"

Teresa stared and shrugged as the long lines lifted up the slope toward them.

"All Frenchmen look the same to me. Suspicious."

"About what?"

"Everything . . . Hurrah! *Vivan los franceses!*"

Carmen squirmed between two men who blocked her view. She stood wedged between them, while they talked calmly over her head.

"Comrade, look at those. Veterans from their war in 1914, I'll bet."

"Then they know how to use their machine guns. Funny, you know, to think that the last time for them they were fighting Germans."

"But they are brothers. Proletarian brothers!"

"That's class loyalty for you. I've always said it."

"*Verdad.* It is we who have brought them together . . . here in Spain."

The French volunteers were shorter, sturdy men, calm, compact in their sheepskins, unhurried and determined-looking. Each man in their ranks carried Mills bombs clipped to a broad leather belt. The grenades bounded to the tempo of their tread. They carried slung rifles, bright bayonets straight up, a picket of slick steel. The pavement, loosened by bombs and shells, trembled slightly as they marched by. Civilians and militiamen darted off the sidewalks to touch them, clap them on the shoulders. The moving ranks did not slow.

"What are these?"

"Why do they wear little round hats instead of helmets?"

"*Hombre*, they *have* helmets. Slung behind. See?"

"I have never worn a tin *sombrero*. It suggests lack of confidence."

"Then these must be Russians. Russians have much confidence."

They were heavy-bodied, slant-eyed men, thick through the shoulders and necks, with set, melancholy faces. They came on, row after row, thick corduroy pants, snug sheepskin jackets and dark, pounding boots.

"What battalion, comrade?"

The nearest soldier turned his face perhaps a centimeter and snapped back, his voice guttural and proud.

"Dabrowsky battalion! 11th Brigade!"

"*Qué va*, Russians . . . They're Polish."

"From where?"

"*Poland!*"

"Oh. *Viva!*"

Two squadrons of cavalry, also French, clopped steadily up the slope, the men easy on fine horses that drew much applause. Leading the horsemen was the commanding general of the 11th Brigade, "Kléber." He wore a long overcoat buttoned to the neck, with wildflowers sprigged in the buttonholes. He smiled and waved affably, ignoring the sound of cannon fire that stuttered through the dawn. His aide rode at his side, carrying a banner set in a stirrup socket. The blood-red flag roiled damp and smacking on the cold wind.

"*Vivan los Rusos!*"

Teresa pulled Carmen back.

"Are they Russians?"

Carmen shrugged.

"I don't know. Maybe. Why not? They're *everybody!*"

Two thousand officers, commissars, and combat soldiers flowed steadily down the stone valley of the Gran Vía, into Plaza España and on toward the trenches. They drove the sadness of loss, dawn-despair and the fear of betrayal before them in a roaring wash of noise, tossing banners and clenched fists. There was no pause for speeches of welcome, bouquets of limp, frost-nipped flowers from shy little girls, no bear hugs and wine from the militia, nothing but the rumble of boots beating on the stones of the city.

General Kléber dealt them like trump cards into the trenches, one brigadier for every four Spaniards, the British machine-gun crews spaced in the ragged trenches ripped in the Casa de Campo. The Dabrowsky battalion marched to bolster the Communist 5th Regiment at Villaverde. General Kléber assumed command of all the defense forces at University City.

When the artillery barrage lifted, the Moors rose up from their trenches with weird, yelping cries and rushed the Loyalist lines. Mills bombs ripped and stunned them. Ammunition belts skittered and jerked into the British machine guns. The Germans fired Mausers into the shrieking press of green uniforms and red caps that exploded through the ground fog, the stumped trees, and the tangled wire. The dim green figures hesitated, whirled and fled.

Artillery came down again, the slow, satiny rustle of heavy shells, the numbing shock of explosion with the red earth bounding up at the leaden sky. Shrapnel and fragments hissed and spanged, and the bottoms of the Loyalist trenches churned to a paste of dirt, urine, and blood. Stretcher-bearers crawled out between the ilex stumps and were blown apart by the grenades of Franco's Legionarios. Aircraft snarled and stuttered in the low clouds. A shattering storm of small fragmentation bombs swept across the Casa de Campo positions. German batteries blasted the buildings of the University and drove the bleeding defenders to the cellars.

The Legionarios attacked, singing their song, "My Bride Is Death." They were broken by rifle fire and streams of machine-gun bullets that popped and crackled around them. They fell back into their trenches, cursing, stunned by the fury of the Red resistance, unlike any they had met. They rearmed and rose again, howling and heaving grenades. The Germans, the French, the Poles, the Slavs, and the Spanish shot them into shocked and bleeding lumps that cursed and died in the swirling mists.

The long, bitter day crumbled into stricken twilight lit by the flames of Madrid burning in a hundred places. Wet fog drifted damp over the trenches, and Mount Garabitas vanished in the half-dark. General Kléber sent runners out wherever the telephone lines had been blown up. The Dabrowsky battalion hunched in their trenches, treading on a gravel of spent cartridges and shell fragments. The French hefted the cold, waffled iron of new hand grenades. The Germans rested, panting like hounds, and snatched pull-throughs the length of rifle barrels foul with mud and powder. The word passed from commanders to commissars. No smoking. Chocolate and brandy ration. Wire cutters. No ranks held in reserve. When the whistles blew, move and stay low, between the machine-gun positions. It is as dark for the Fascists as it is for us. If it's one thing they don't expect, it's what we'll give them . . . counterattack. Counterattack! Everybody! Now it's our turn . . .

Harry Desmond and Brian crouched in the pit, staring at the mud-smeared rifles and sharing a saucepan half-filled with gritty cold malt-coffee laced with cognac. Brian sieved the dirt through his teeth and swallowed.

"Christ, what stuff! Where's that Jerry?"

"Down the trench, I think."

"Have some muck, Desmond Two. Was Tom hit bad?"

"Upper arm. He's back. Saw him. Wish we had smokes. Brian, how many got it?"

"Chesbro, Porter, Angier. Never fired a shot, poor bugger. Sewell."

"Benjamin?"

"Him, too. Bled to death before Kopa could get him out. Foot kept turning around. Just skin holding it on . . ."

Harry closed his eyes. He felt cold, weak, and sick. He clutched his muddy rifle.

"Shut up, can't you."

"Steady, comrade."

"We're bloody cannon fodder, Brian . . . What's that?"

They flung themselves to the slot in the pit side, fumbling wildly with their rifles.

"*Cuidado!* Psst . . . carefully, please. It's me. Kopa."

"When . . . do we go over?"

"Right now."

The German stood up and whistled softly. The men down the trench stirred, a single, slow lurch. Kopa's voice carried through the misty night.

"Forward! *Para la Revolución y Freiheit! Allons! Vámonos!*"

Harry could not move. He did not feel afraid. He was paralyzed. If he left the pit, they, someone, would kill him. He had to stay where he was. He'd go, if Brian went. Brian lunged for the lip of the pit.

The German clambered over the parapet. Harry kicked over the saucepan and followed him. He could hear Brian and the others blowing and sliding in the mud. Kopa, bent double, began creeping forward. The mist dripped off Harry's helmet into his face. The field was craggy with shell-bits and torn roots. The men, dim, humped shapes, crawled and scrambled on the sodden earth. Harry bumped into Kopa.

"Head low. Down, like this, see?"

"Right . . ."

Kopa grunted and turned aside. Harry jerked away from a dead man flung down in the muck. They crept slower and slower. A terrible feeling closed in on Harry, an anguish of longing to get near something solid, a stump, a boulder, a heap of dirt. He grew worse, convinced that Kopa had betrayed them, that they were circling back toward the lines, that the militia would rise and smash down on them all. Something snagged his jacket. A faint rip came from in front. They had reached the Fascist wire.

Harry was exhausted. He lay down, very close to Kopa. The German thrust him away and fumbled clumsily in a muddy pocket. Harry squinted through the mist. How he wanted to sleep! Something pinked. Kopa lifted a strand very tenderly and lay it to one side. They waited. The men behind snuffled and blundered in the dark. Harry lay along the giddy brink of sleep and terror. The men squirmed closer, panting like winded dogs. Kopa moved again. Harry bit his lip and followed, dragging his Mauser. He longed to just let it go.

They crawled and crept, stepped like drenched cats over dark parcels of dead flesh. Harry kicked something and jerked away in horror. A shell, big as a melon, lay in a shallow pool.

The inner wire plucked and pinged. Harry groveled, shrinking from the volley that would tear into him at any second. How could they not hear? Kopa tapped him on the shoulder and handed him a grenade.

A flash and bang in the same instant that Kopa heaved up from the mud, his arm wheeling. A jabber of rifles spouting flames. Kopa's hand-bomb exploded with a blinding red smear of noise that lit up a parapet topped with sandbags like a string of sausages. Harry rammed his face in the earth. The brim of his helmet bit in the mud. When he yanked his head up again, his helmet stuck. He snatched at it and missed, something bobbled on the ground and went off in a single, searing lick of hot noise ringing in his skull. He rolled away over Kopa's boots, got to his knees and flung the grenade, without remembering to pull the pin. He raised his mud-slimy rifle and fired at the spitting parapet. The Mauser slugged against his shoulder. He rammed the bolt and heard a cartridge wheet in the breech. It was going to jam! It didn't. He squeezed the trigger, and the rifle kicked again.

The night was ripping apart, directly in front, to right and left and two paces behind. A blast of a grenade, the burr of a bullet.

"Brian! For Christ's sake!"

Brian was firing prone, his right hand working the bolt furiously. Kopa was kneeling, shooting with a pistol. He stopped and shouted. Three men behind Brian sprang up and careened through the lurid mist, their arms flailing. The grenades bloomed like bronze roses in the Fascist trench. A gap fell in the line of sandbags. Brian bucked to his feet, his bayonet ripping a furrow in the earth and all around Harry men were up and forward in a lumbering, crushing run. A Fascist machine gun sputtered to the left, a bluish-green flicker. Harry hit the parapet, the bags broke beneath the shock of his knees and the sand poured him in a greasy cascade down on a tangle of weapons, bodies and wooden boxes. Kopa lunged over him like a muddy bear, firing a pistol. More men piled down in, spraying wet sand. The crackling air flashed red. A Pole with a bleeding face lurched out of the dark and vanished again. But he was still there, shoulder-to-shoulder with Kopa. Harry worked the bolt and fired his rifle from the hip. The Pole roared forward, flinging a grenade down the Fascist trench.

The dark slot flared a vision of dark, caped figures with terrible bulging eyes skipping in the red air like bats. A skittering stitch of bullets and fragments, the muddy wallop of the concussion. Harry crashed against Kopa.

"*Was gibts?*"

"Hit. I'm hit! Leg."

"Bad?"

It felt like a hot nail in his thigh, then, suddenly, numb. Kopa pushed him down. Bullets smacked overhead, and pouty little holes spewed sand on them. Exploding grenades and a high flare lit the trench.

"Can't walk. Leave me a Mills bomb. Go on! Go on!"

"*Ja.* Here."

The Pole pointed down the dark trench and jabbered something. Harry smiled and nodded.

"All right, comrade. I'll watch for them. Right, right."

The Pole sighed, an enormous gush, wiped his mouth and planted a gritty kiss on Harry's brow. Kopa stood, turning this way and that, trying to sense the battle-danger. Harry felt a sudden tilt of fear in his chest.

"It's all right. About this, I mean. Kopa, do you understand? Take care of Peter. My brother. *Mein Bruder, Kopa?*"

The German flinched away from a mortar shell that exploded on the parapet, a deafening spang that spun up sand and tattered burlap. Kopa stared down on Harry, a glare of woe.

"*Mein Bruder . . . ja, ja . . .*"

"That's Peter. Don't forget!"

"I remember."

Harry nodded. A new pain filled all his left side, an oozing ache. He fumbled with his sheepskin jacket. The thick pelt inside was sodden.

Kopa and the Pole moved off, leaving him. He wanted to call to them, to crawl after them. They climbed up the trench wall and went off into the darkness, to join the attack that glared and crackled in the misty dark sky. Harry knelt in the trench, his elbow snugged gently against his seeping side. He breathed slowly and stared, dully, at his breath-clouds. He felt very drowsy and light-headed. He knew he was growing weaker.

"Hi, Desmond, saying your prayers?"

A tenor voice squawked from the broken parapet.

"No . . . posted here on trench guard . . ."

"Well . . . carry on."

"Righto, comrade."

Harry raised his right hand. The effort made the pain rummage in him. He watched, weak and dismayed, as the pain drew his fingers, curling them into the salute of the clenched first. He heard Rowle's voice in the night.

"Let him be. He's in a funk. Now he knows just what he's good for, the little sod . . ."

The voice was gone, shouting in French to someone about grenades.

Harry tried to stand up. He felt himself sliding against the trench wall, toppling forward on his face. His head buzzed drunkenly. He was growing numb. He caught himself and pushed down on the Mauser. He swayed back and nearly fell over. His eyes filled with tears. How long was it going to take? He cried out into the mist-swept darkness.

"*Secours! Socorro!* Help . . . help . . ."

His voice sounded in his ears like the mew of a lost cat. The attack sputtered and blasted, far, far away now. He knelt there, propped in the mud, breathing, waiting, numb, not afraid, but astonished. He wanted Rowle to come back. He wanted to explain that he was hit, just that. It was important that they knew this, that Peter knew it and all the others, about his side, his leg. To have "a wounded name" was . . . unfair. He slouched into a buzzing brood, moving his fingers on the mud-smeared barrel of the Mauser. He could just barely feel his fingers. In another moment, he would not know if his hand stirred or not. He was drifting in the darkness.

Then, he heard them. First, the stealthy plush and suck of their feet in the trench-bottom. Then the clicking mutter of their voices. They were Moors.

He had three cartridges left. He pulled the Mauser butt out of the mud and used it to nudge the grenade forward a bit where he could get at it. But he felt he would not be strong enough to pull the pin. The rifle was very heavy. The muzzle wobbled; he could feel his left arm dip and sag. He squeezed the trigger, and the rifle butted against his shoulder. A voice cried in the darkness and four blue flames popped. Two bullets struck him, one in the chest, the other in the face.

The meeting with the foreign press was held in what had been the dining room of the Hotel Pilarmadre. It was rainy still, almost sleet. Out in the garden, long dead weeds nodded stiffly between the melancholy little groups of rusty chairs and dripping tables. There was no heat, and the members of the Anarchist Anti-Fascist Militia Committee sat wrapped in blankets, smoking French cigarettes. There were two journalists, a fat, impatient-looking Frenchman and a woman from Canada in a rumpled tweed suit and rubber-soled shoes. The woman asked questions in good Spanish and then translated for the man.

Alfredo had ordered champagne brought up from the hotel cellar. From time to time, he reached out his crippled hand and touched the label of a bottle or rearranged the dusty glasses. Ortega listened, but watched the cold rain pelting on the weeds in the garden. The woman spoke.

"Then you do not disapprove of the Anarchists joining the *Generalitat,* the government of Catalonia?"

Alfredo thought and answered slowly, choosing his words. He was flattered by the attention of the journalists, but suspicious of them.

"We do not approve or disapprove. We accept certain necessary changes as part of the total revolutionary movement. We are co-operating with the Regional Defense Council.

"Will you support the Catalán government?"

"We support all anti-Fascist movements."

"Then you consider the P.O.U.M. and the Communists as your allies?"

"We all fight the same enemy."

The woman translated into French and the man scribbled. He was bored and flapped his notebook on his knee. Alfredo smiled and touched a glass.

"You see, on our side, there are various groups, but we are allies, comrades. On the other side, the Fascists, well, they are merely lined up. There is a great difference."

The members of the committee nodded and smiled, patted Alfredo. "Well said, well said."

The woman stared at Alfredo briefly, spoke with her companion and stamped her rubber-soled shoes on the gritty floor. Her breath swirled out and vanished as she spoke.

"But this new coalition, like the government of the entire country, has declared that its aim is to curb revolutionary indiscipline."

Alfredo smiled.

"How can there be indiscipline in the proletarian deployment of human nature?"

"I'm afraid I don't understand. Will you place the militia here in Pilarmadre under the command of the Catalonian government or the central government in Valencia?"

"The militia here is responsible to the wishes of the citizen-comrades of Pilarmadre!"

"What if those wishes conflict with the wishes of Barcelona?"

Alfredo flapped his crippled hand on the table.

"Durrutti is my friend! We will speak together and make some decision —in the name of the people."

The man grunted and said something. The woman nodded and leaned forward again.

"But Durrutti has gone to Madrid, to help defend the city."

"We remain here, to defend Pilarmadre."

"How close are the Fascist lines, now?"

Alfredo gnawed his lip and tapped the champagne bottle.

"Ten kilometers."

"And how many men do you have?"

Alfredo smiled.

"Everyone!"

"How many rifles?"

"Enough. Our major weapon is enthusiasm."

"A hundred rifles?"

"I cannot disclose such information, not even to such a charming foreign visitor."

There were sixty-two rifles and seven grenades. Alfredo had gone to Barcelona to beg for arms, but had returned with nothing. Ten kilometers away, the enemy waited for the weather to change. They would wait for weeks, until the ground froze solid. Then, they would come down into Pilarmadre.

"Do you expect help from the government in Barcelona?"

Alfredo shook his head.

"I do not expect help from any government in the whole world. We are the government here. We will defend Pilarmadre and the people to the last cartridge!"

There were four hundred cartridges, but only one hundred and eighty-three fit the rifles.

"And if you are victorious . . ."

"Of course we will be victorious! A thousand pardons. Forgive me for interrupting. The Señorita was asking?"

"If you are victorious, Pilarmadre will be a pile of ruins."

Alfredo nodded. The other members of the committee nodded. Their hooded heads bobbed up and down. Ortega thought of a group of monks at vespers. It was nearly dark. The Frenchman kept looking at the gold watch strapped to his left wrist. Alfredo spoke, tapping his fingers against the bottle for emphasis.

"The proletarians of Spain have always lived in slums, holes in the ground, caves dug in the earth. The workers here were born in ruins. At the time of victory, we shall know how to behave. We can also build. Was it not the workers who built the cities and palaces for the rich? Not only here in Spain, but in America, too. Everywhere. Very well, we shall make ruins. And then we, the workers, will build new cities to take the place of these ruins. Pilarmadre will be better! We are not afraid of ruins. Why should we be? We are going to inherit the earth, eh, Ortega?"

Alfredo's voice startled him. He jerked erect. The woman was staring at him, her face eager, her eyes curious. She began to speak, but Alfredo rushed on.

"The middle classes of the world will blast their own world into ruins, too, before they are swept off the stage of history. But they can't build anything. Just exploit. So we will have done with them."

The woman shook her head. She had thin, mouse-colored hair and fur on her freckled cheeks.

"But how can you have done with them, as you say, if you are willing to collaborate with the Catalán government? Are you not accepting as allies the *petite bourgeoisie?*"

Alfredo's mouth opened and closed. He made an odd little puffing sound. The members of the Anarchist Anti-Fascist Militia Committee made encouraging noises and lit cigarettes, a flurry of matches, papers and tobacco. With such intense activity, they clearly could not be expected to answer such a direct question. Who was this foreign woman, anyway? Why was there no photographer for the making of pictures, anyway?

Alfredo looked at Ortega pleadingly. Ortega smiled at the woman.

"We do not believe that we are collaborating with the *bourgeoisie*, señorita. We believe that they are collaborating with *us!*"

The members of the committee struggled to their feet, wallowing around the table in their blankets, all talking excitedly at once. Alfredo beamed at the two foreigners.

"Precisely! And now, the champagne!"

The Frenchman snapped his notebook shut and stood up.

"There's nothing more to be gotten out of these people. Come along, Beatrice. If the car sits out in all this rain much longer, it won't start. Then we'll be stuck here."

"Ortega. What does he say?"

The woman said something. Alfredo held up his crippled hand.

"We are not all simple workers here. No, we have a comrade who has been educated. Translate, Ortega."

"He says he is very sorry, but they must leave now, in order to carry your inspiring words back to Barcelona to be printed in the papers there."

"No champagne? No toasts?"

"The French comrade suggests that we guard the champagne until the day of victory. The champagne is for the people."

"Oh. Well, let us provide an escort. Members of the committee, an escort . . ."

Ortega closed the door and walked back to Alfredo. The ex-barber was seated before the bottles and dusty glasses. He stared gloomily around. The big room was nearly empty. A few strands of crepe paper snaked from the chandeliers and trailed on the floor, rustling and stirring in the cold draft that leaked through the broken windows. Clouds of blue smoke dissolved. A mouse scribbled in a dark corner. The portrait of Bakunin tilted on the wall above a battered buffet.

"Frankly, it did not go as I wished, as I had hoped."

"No. A pity, Alfredo. You tried."

Alfredo waved his crippled hand at the faded decorations, the tatters, cobwebs, and dust.

"The banquet is over, Ortega. Over before the main course was ever served. There is nothing for us now but empty dishes. Then, even the empty dishes will be broken."

Ortega sat down and lit a cigarette. Outside in the street, an automobile motor whirred. A weak cheer rose and died away. Alfredo lifted his head.

"Come, come . . . You spoke well. About building out of the ruins."

"Ah, but you knew I was lying. They knew it. Even, yes, even I knew that I was lying. That's something, eh? I can no longer deceive myself."

"It is necessary to make new plans, new programs."

Alfredo took a candle stub from his pocket, lit it, and dribbled wax on the table. He set the stub in the pool and blew on it. The flame wavered and threw shadows on his face.

"So? We announce a new banquet to replace the one that was never held? There is a limit to optimism, even here in Pilarmadre."

Ortega nodded. Every morning he doled out the food. A few potatoes, a handful of rice, a turnip, a glass of oil. One egg a week, a scrap of cheese. With the men of Pilarmadre away at the front, the harvest had been a failure. The charcoal burners had been conscripted and taken off to Barcelona. Now the women picked the hillsides for twigs. How they would live through the winter, no one could say.

"We still have credit for the cement, Alfredo. The last trainload went . . ."

"The Regional Defense Council in Barcelona accepted the cement as a 'free gift of the proletariat.'"

"You mean it was just taken . . . confiscated?"

"Call it what you will. We have no credit with the C.N.T. They promise to send milk for the children. One half-liter per child, per week. Nothing more."

"Why not?"

Alfredo shook his head and fumbled with the dusty foil on the neck of the champagne bottle.

"Alfredo, you cannot have lost confidence. You must not give in to despair."

"No lectures on sin. Despair is not a sin. It is part of the human condition."

"It is weakness. You cannot be weak. The others have come to depend on you, Alfredo. For them, you are the revolution."

"Open the bottle."

"Very well."

Alfredo watched Ortega pry up the wires. The cork popped and a froth of bubbles ran down the neck. Ortega wiped two glasses and filled them.

"*Salud.*"

"*Salud.*"

"To Madrid?"

"To Madrid. I should have gone. Now, now I cannot go. I must stay

here. That's what they told me in Barcelona. 'Go back to your *pueblo*.
We will send some foreign journalists. When you die, we shall make you
a martyr'. . . . Ah, it makes me sick. How the city has changed!
Only a few months, it was a real proletarian city. Everyone worked,
believed, wore the *mono*. Now? Huh! They turn the workers away from
the restaurants . . . 'Sorry, comrades, but the tables are reserved.' I spent
what I had on the black market. For medicines. I have eyes, man!
There is a lack of . . . trust. Less and less trust every day. This group
against that. The C.N.T. is losing importance. If it continues, what will
happen? I'll tell you!"

Ortega emptied his own glass and half-filled it. It tasted very good,
the champagne. Alfredo hunched forward and lowered his voice.

"It has begun already, in whispers. Soon, aloud. Shouting in the streets.
Then . . . *pam-pam-pam!* . . . the fighting will begin. The Communists
say, first win the war, then comes the revolution. We say, it is possible
to win the war and lose the revolution. You know what the Communists
say, then? Eh?"

"No, Alfredo."

"Nothing. They say *nothing*, man! But they go away and write your
name down in a book. My name must be in every book they have in
Barcelona. So you see? Here I am. I can't go to Madrid. Not allowed.
If I go to Barcelona, a suspect. Eh? Disloyal. Neo-Trotskyist. Me! *Me!*"

Alfredo slumped in his chair, shaking his head like a man stung by
flies. The two men sat and smoked and drank another glass of champagne.
The sleet drove against the windows. Alfredo shuddered.

"Listen to that. And I have to go up to the hills to inspect the lines
tonight."

"I'll go for you. They all know me."

Alfredo squinted across the candle.

"That's true. And they know you in Barcelona, too. They have some
special prisons in Barcelona. With two cells. One for you . . . the other
for me."

"The wine talks now. Not Alfredo."

"*In vino veritas*. Let me tell you what I feel. I don't know this, but I
feel it. In what you would call my soul . . ."

"You have a good soul, Alfredo. Blood can be washed away."

The barber's face was slick with sweat. His dark eyes stared uneasily
around the vast, cold room. The faded decorations sifted and rustled on
the leaking wind. Ortega stared. He wondered if Alfredo was sick. Or mad.

"Don't interrupt me. What I feel is this. We are betrayed. You, a
priest, should know what that word means. We are betrayed, as your
Christ was. We are betrayed as the Church betrayed the Spanish people.
Thirty pieces of silver, eh? Did you know that all the gold has gone

to Russia? No? It's true. To pay for the arms, the planes, the tanks, the guns. Who will get these fine new weapons? The P.O.U.M.? Never. Us, the Anarchists? You've seen the rubbish we have to fight with. You should see the Assault Guards in Barcelona with the new rifles, the fine boots, the machine guns. You know who gets the new stuff? The P.S.U.C. The Communists, that's who!"

"You told that woman that the Communists are our allies."

Alfredo spread his hands and stared thoughtfully at his stiffened fingers.

"A man in my position must say many things. Politics, I have learned, is the science of deception. Faith and falsehood. We are much alike, you and I. And that is why I cannot do it!"

"Do what, Alfredo? I don't understand you."

The barber twirled his wineglass, rolling the slender stem between his fingers. His breath steamed. He shook his head stubbornly.

"I cannot. If I did that, there would be absolutely nothing left. I would be obliged to hang myself. You know what they offered me? A submachine gun and two cans of ammunition."

"For what?"

"For *you!*"

Ortega leaned back in his chair. He felt great pity for Alfredo. How the barber must have felt to know that others more powerful believed his price was so low. Judas of Aragón.

Alfredo filled their glasses again. He threw himself back and glanced boldly around the dark room.

"Of course, I told them to stick it up. Way up."

"Be careful, Alfredo. Don't make enemies. The people here need you."

"All right! I know that. Even in coveralls, you can't stop, can you? Your advice. Don't you think I know they will wait, play with me like cat and mouse. Next they'll come to you. What will you sell *me* out for, eh? Your life. That's all. That's all they'll offer you. A chance to live."

"You could have killed me yourself."

Alfredo smiled bitterly and emptied his glass.

"Maybe I should have. Because they'll get to both of us. They'll let us, oh, you know . . . scamper around between the paws and squeak our little squeaks . . . but one fine day . . . *crunch, crunch!*"

Alfredo ground his teeth and ran his tongue out over his thin lips in a chilling parody of slaughter. He stroked his own neck, arched and purred. Then he threw back his head and laughed.

"You should see your face!"

Ortega felt himself flush. He fretted with his cigarette.

"I have never claimed to be a hero."

"But you're not afraid to die."

"No . . . I'm not. But I am afraid of being killed."

"That's too Jesuitical for me. Drink up."

"I mean, Alfredo, that I am afraid of pain. We all owe God a death, after all."

"You mean all animals die sometime. You don't like the *crunch*."

"That's it."

Alfredo's voice dropped harshly through the darkness on him.

"Blame the revolution."

"I blame myself. If only I had been . . ."

"Just don't blame me. I am just a man, not a force of history. You're just a man, too, Ortega. You're not the Church."

"No, of course not."

"As a man, a comrade, you will follow my orders. They offered me a submachine gun and two cans of ammunition for you. I told them you were in Málaga. Go there. At once. Tonight. I mean it."

Ortega sat staring at the candle. He nodded slowly. It had never been possible to doubt Alfredo's sincerity.

"I was very tempted, Ortega."

"I can understand that."

"With just one gun like that . . . Hell, I'm going to stay here and get killed with the others. By Christmas, surely. But with a good weapon and two cans . . . I could have taken a few with me, you know? That would have been a decent death."

"All men want that."

"Get out of Pilarmadre. The longer you hang around down at the Café Marx, listening to confessions . . ."

"I never fooled you there, did I?"

"They needed you, the people. They still do. I know that. But the bargaining has begun, Ortega. They are working out the price of the betrayal. If you stay here, I'll sell you, or you'll sell me. Or one of the Anti-Fascist Militia Committee will sniff the wind and sell *both* of us! I'm telling you. Here you cannot stay. Not another hour. Get out! . . . *Get out!*"

Alfredo's voice banged hollow off the dusty floor. Ortega saw him lurch across the room and slash blindly at the crepe streamers. The flimsy serpents threshed away and hung twisting slowly in the candle-gleam. Alfredo turned suddenly and rushed back at the table, his boots crushing the broken glasses. He thumped his ruined hand on the table and stared at Ortega.

"What I cannot understand, what I cannot grasp! . . . Ah, I don't *know*, you see? I don't know *why!* Why did we fail? What did we do wrong? Why are they turning on us? We carry the new world in our hearts! And for this, we are condemned? Why! Tell me, God damn you!"

Ortega stood up from the table. He felt lightheaded, but peaceful.

Wine usually made him like this, soft and contented, not maddened like Alfredo.

"Why? Think, my comrade. The new world in your hearts . . ."

"*Our* hearts, you fool! You're part of it. You can't escape that, you Red priest!"

"Our hearts, then. This sort of thing has happened many times before, my comrade."

"But this time . . . *this* time it was to be. To *be!*"

"It was . . . perhaps it still is, or can be. A dream is real, in its way. A good dream . . . what is more real than that? God bless you, Alfredo. You will be in heaven, my comrade . . . shearing the sheep of His pasture. The Barber of Paradise. I will watch you from across a dark trench."

"You make rotten jokes, priest."

"No worse than yours, militiaman."

"Huh! Where will you go?"

"To fight with the Basques. There, a man can be a priest and a Republican at the same time."

"*Vaya con Dios* . . . Go with God, my friend. An old man with a burro cart is waiting for you behind your church. He will take you across the lines."

"You have had this planned for some time."

"You didn't think I brought up the bubbly for those newspaper people, did you? *Qué fea!* I have never seen a more ugly woman. No, the wine was for us. For you. I had planned to get you drunk and roll you into the wagon. Listen . . ."

"What?"

"Well, there is some . . . some other wine, you know. Consecrated stuff. Three bottles. I hid it, see? I mean, you might want to . . . get back to work, you know?"

"Some Anarchist."

Ortega picked up the candles. The two men walked together across the big empty room to the door. Ortega held the candle high. Alfredo pointed. The chairs, the table, the broken glasses, and the empty bottle were just visible in the gloom. The sleet rattled against the windows like bird-shot and the crepe streamers lashed softly against the tilted portrait of Bakunin.

"The banquet is over. For us. All ready for them. All they have to do is change the picture."

"And put up one of Franco."

"Or put up one of Stalin."

The wind sucked the candle flame. It went out, and the wax stiffened on Ortega's fingers.

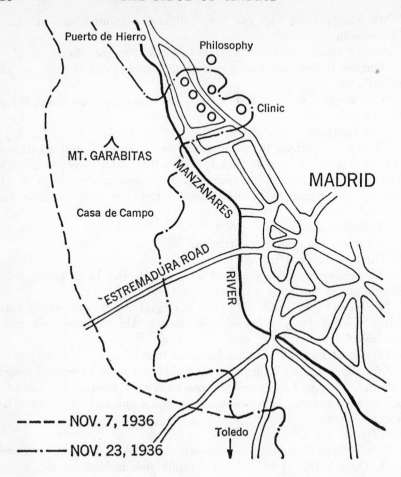

Puerto de Hierro

Philosophy

Clinic

MT. GARABITAS

MANZANARES

MADRID

Casa de Campo

ESTREMADURA ROAD

RIVER

– – – – NOV. 7, 1936

— · — NOV. 23, 1936

Toledo

"*Ça va?*"

"*Ça va*," Frank said. Jean Saulnier hung on the door, watching him and stroking his new mustache. The French pilot managed to look concerned and like an amiable pirate at the same time.

"Well, you look all right. Better than I thought. You were magnificently drunk last night."

"I know."

"And the night before that, too."

"And three nights ago."

Frank stood in front of the cracked mirror and combed his hair. He could hear the sound of motors. A flight of Chatos were taking off. He pointed with his comb.

"Is it that late? Almost eleven o'clock?"

"You sleep as magnificently as you drink, *mon ami*. It's ten-thirty."

"Stop . . . lurking, will you?"

Saulnier shrugged and dropped onto Frank's bed. He lit a cigarette and frowned.

"What is *lurking?* Something one does with women?"

"Something one does alone."

"Never . . . well, not since I was twelve years old. In those days I was the grand champion lurker in my *quartier* . . . perhaps the whole *arrondissement.*"

"I can well believe it."

"I spoke with the doctor, who said you were quite well. As a good Republican, he does not believe in miracles. However, he has looked you over and he has been twice to look over what is left of that Dewoitine. He is satisfied that divine intervention took place four nights ago. Malraux, on the other hand, says that it is all a matter of knowing how to fly an airplane. I believe that it is more subtle. It is a matter of know how to fly one *third* of an airplane. Perhaps less. You're smiling, Frank, eh? You *are* in good spirits. Good, good."

Frank turned and looked at Saulnier. The Frenchman smiled.

"Jean, I'd rather not talk about all that. Okay?"

"Okay."

Frank crossed to the window and looked out. The Russian biplanes were ranked at the edge of the field, the propellers whirling in the sun as the mechanics tuned the engines.

"I wonder."

"What, Frank?"

"If it's like being thrown from a horse. If you get thrown, you know, you get right back on, even if you're knocked silly. Otherwise, you lose your nerve. Maybe I ought to fly today."

"Malraux has given orders that you are to rest today. There will be enough flying. Only not at night. No, *not* at night. No one is capable of enduring again what you did to us."

"Relax. It was all because a few things happened to me . . ."

"I know. I know how it feels to lose a friend, a relative. When I flew for Air France. You never knew when it would happen."

Frank pressed his forehead against the grimy glass. It was cold out. The pane felt like a sheet of ice.

"But he was . . . only a kid, for Christ's sake!"

"Frank?"

He didn't feel like answering. He stood at the window, watching the mechanics and the aircraft. The pilots were ambling across the field now, accompanied by the Russian instructors.

"Frank? Listen. I found Peter Desmond. He's still alive."

"But Harry's dead."

"They could *both* be dead! *You* could be dead. You certainly tried

hard enough to kill yourself. Taking off at night without permission.
Intercepting enemy planes, shooting down three . . ."

"Two. I said let's not talk about it, Jean."

"All right. I have a car. We'll go to Madrid. Peter asked to see you.
You *do* want to see him, don't you?"

"No. Yes. Of course."

"Come on. I've got permission to leave, a *salvoconducto* for both of us,
everything."

"I don't want to go to Madrid. The weather is rotten. I don't feel like
it."

Saulnier shrugged.

"Then I will see Peter Desmond myself. He is curious about how you
won the medal and all the rest of it. He saw it in some newspaper, but
just the pictures, I guess."

"All right, Jean. Let me get my jacket."

"Good man. I knew you'd come around. Besides, we must see the lines.
How can we tell our children about this war when we haven't really seen
it at all?"

"Don't we have to have children first?"

"I can arrange that, too. Come on!"

The biplanes began to move, their engines making a terrific racket.
Saulnier lunged to the window and looked out.

"Watch the cross-wind, *chicos!* If it gets under the left wings, you
flip over, every one of you . . ."

Frank's feet twitched. He muttered.

"Left rudder, more, a little more . . . Hold the tail down, that's a
plane, not a sky-rocket . . . easy . . . *easy* . . ."

The Chatos swept forward and took off in flights of three. Saulnier
bit his mustache. Frank held his breath until the planes were well up and
circling to move into formation.

"Jesus, it always gets me to watch them take off in this kind of wind.
Only two crashes so far. That's pretty good from what I hear."

"I don't really trust those things," Saulnier said morosely. "There's
something. Something is not—how do you say it?—structurally sound.
There is a weakness in the top plane. Not that you'll have to worry.
You're going to get a new Mosca."

"Baloney. I'm a capitalist. They'll never give me a Mosca."

"I have it from a secret source. Consider. You have more planes to
your credit than anyone else. You are a *bona fide* hero, with a medal
and a bad case of nerves to prove it. Of course they'll give you one of the
new ships. Get a couple more Heinkel 51s and off you'll go to New York
to make speeches and sleep with debutantes."

"What's so hot about that? That's what I used to do all the time."

"How boring. No wonder you came to Spain to fly for the Republic. An excess of horizontal politics, eh?"

Frank turned away from the window and shook his head.

"Think about something else for a change, huh?"

"How can I? We've been here months and months and I haven't even . . . I tell you, the situation demands immediate remedy. I think that when these little *guapas* begin saying *no pasarán* that they include Saulnier!"

"You aren't whatchamacallit . . . *simpático*."

"I am *desperate!* I shall dye my hair blond. I might as well offer my balls to the 11th Brigade. As a new type of grenade. High explosives, you know? The car is this way, hidden."

The wind slashed at them as they walked across the field, leaning against it. They both looked up at the sky where gray clouds skidded and streamed.

"It's closing in."

"Miserable. Poor devils, trying to land in this stuff."

They ducked behind a hangar, out of the wind, and nearly toppled over into the strange, still quiet. Saulnier pointed proudly and stroked his mustache.

"My God. A Rolls-Royce."

"Precisely. An Anarchist Rolls-Royce, in fact, if you will note the flag on the staff there. Confiscated, of course. The Anarchists have not gone into production. At least not yet. Pretty little thing, no? I have always liked black and yellow sedans. *Salud*, comrade-driver!"

"*Salud*, comrade-pilots."

Frank and Saulnier climbed into the dusty luxury of the rear seat and sank back into the soft cushions. Saulnier picked up the speaking tube.

"To the University, *por favor*."

"*Al frente!*"

"*Sí*. To the front! He has an obsession, this one. You see he wanted to drive tanks, but they gave him this instead. Now with this jewel, he is not allowed anywhere damage might occur. You will see. So one must humor him. You explain where you wish to go. That, to him, is the front. Therefore, one always is going to the front."

The huge automobile started and murmured away from the airfield. Frank sat back, folded his arms and grinned.

"You have good taste, Saulnier. In motorcars, anyway. Where did you steal this thing?"

"I have it on loan. From a Greek. He has come all the way to Madrid in order to collect religious statues and paintings. He would also like to collect everything in the Prado Museum. I told him I would speak with Malraux about it. He loaned me this ocean liner to make everything more convenient."

"And where did this Greek of yours get an Anarchist Rolls-Royce?"

"He . . . ah . . . collected it."

"What else does this Greek collect?"

"Empty wine bottles. The last time I saw him he was surrounded by empty wine bottles."

"Swell."

The automobile rolled easily across the wind-stripped fields. Frank tapped on the window. Saulnier frowned and shook his head.

"There they are, Jean."

"Every time I see those damned pits I have to pretend they are potatoes or sugar beets or something."

"I was going to go back to the States when I found out what was buried out there. Really. I was packing my things, my stuff. Then that Spanish kid brought me the letter about Harry. So . . ."

"So you did what you did. None of us can understand how you managed to find the field in the first place, keep that old ship in the air in the second place and land in the third place . . . if you call sailing into a grove of pine trees landing."

"Any landing you can walk away from is a good landing," Frank said, imitating Malraux. "Some people are incapable of perceiving the aesthetics of flight. They do not hear the whisper of beauty in their souls and so they insist that the voice is silent. One can only pity them."

Saulnier chuckled appreciatively.

The driver pulled behind a convoy of trucks creeping toward Madrid. A man rode on every cab, watching the sky for enemy bombers. A smudge of smoke streamed away from the city, torn by the wind. Saulnier pointed.

"Incendiary raid again. They are trying to burn us out of Madrid. Stone doesn't burn, though. Stone is lucky. Like you, Frank."

"You think so? I think it's just because my number hasn't come up yet. That's about the only thing I've learned in Spain."

"What have you learned? For an American to admit he doesn't know everything is a wonder. Go ahead."

"Just that . . . well, how vulnerable everyone is. The soldiers, sure. But here, they bomb the civilians. Prisoners in jail get shot. Kids get blown up. You read stories about women fighting in the trenches. You hit one of those Junkers in the right places and you know not one of the men inside will ever hit the silk. They don't have a chance."

"And you fly a rotten plane in total darkness into a forest and walk away without a scratch. Not everyone is equally vulnerable. Or so it seems."

"I was *lucky!* Okay, so you're right. I was born lucky. Rich and lucky. But . . ."

"I have always wanted to be rich," Saulnier said abruptly. "Now I am more interested in luck. You know what, *mon ami,* you have really learned? That people really *do* get killed. They don't just die. Someone kills them, either very deliberately, or in an . . . how do you say it now . . . *à gauche* . . . in a left-handed sort of way. A war is a collection of horrible accidents, if you like. You really expected to get killed that night you took the Dewoitine up. Instead you killed others, some Germans, who were busily killing Spaniards because they are not quite ready yet to begin killing my own countrymen, the French. Look at the men in the trucks before us. They will get killed, some of them, and do their share of killing, too."

"Then it doesn't make any goddamned sense, Jean!"

The French pilot shook his head.

"I disagree, perhaps because I am a European, but perhaps merely because I have seen more people get killed than you have. My skin is somewhat darker than yours, but also somewhat thicker, I think. Your cousin Harry was killed in Spain, because he believed that if he didn't come here to fight, the Fascists would one day, perhaps quite soon, kill him in England, along with his brother, his father and mother, and so on. And you, too, must believe that it is better to fly a Russian plane over a Spanish city and shoot down Germans and Italians than to sit somewhere in the middle of a polo field watching Philadelphia go up in flames from an incendiary raid. Eh? The truth or not?"

"Sure, in a selfish way. But I remember once asking Harry why he really, *really* wanted to come here. And you know what he said? Because he thought it would be exciting, because he didn't want to miss anything, and because it had been a long, rainy spring."

"And you believe that?"

"Sure. You don't?"

"I believe it. But I believe that there are better things to believe in, too."

"Like what?"

"Like . . . well, you and me. We are friends, no? Very good. I believe in friendship. Between all men. This will be more possible, if we fight here in Spain."

"You sound like one of the speakers at the meetings we have to go to. Like going to church, only the sermon is about politics."

"The Fascists have no real political program. Only bullets and bombs."

"Uh-huh. But we have *real* politics. So it's okay for us to shoot those guys in Torrejón."

"François, you are impossible. Stick to flying. There, apparently, it is not necessary for you to think at all. You fly by the seat of your trousers. Promise me you will take no foolish chances in the trenches. No going over the wire to avenge Harry, or any of that nonsense. It isn't necessary.

It's already been done. It's being done a hundred times a day. Just be grateful to your luck and keep your head down. Look. See? The *camiones* keep right on going, but here we must stop. This is the front . . . at least for Anarchist Rolls-Royces."

Frank grunted and looked around at the battered buildings. Some military police waved them into an auto-park. Saulnier fumbled the papers out of his jacket.

"But, Jean, we're a long way from the University, aren't we?"

"Yes."

"How do we get out there?"

"Oh, by streetcar."

"You're kidding."

"Not at all. Consider yourself lucky once more. Poor old General Miaja rides out to inspect the lines on his bicycle. Don't laugh. It's the truth."

They got out of the car. Saulnier spoke at some length with the military police. The police spoke with the driver. A small crowd of soldiers and civilians gathered at the barricade. Frank leaned against the swooping yellow fender of the Rolls and grinned uneasily. Everyone seemed to be staring at him. Saulnier came back, smiling triumphantly, followed by the police, now also smiling. Everyone was talking at once and they all seemed to be smiling.

"Everything marches beautifully. We will have a military escort. These charming fellows are from the Guardias Rojas and will take us wherever we wish to go. Just take the pen, please."

"What for?"

"I have explained a few things. They have decided not to confiscate the Greco-Anarchist sedan. Point One. Point Two, they have agreed not to imprison our chauffeur. Point Three. I have discovered what is playing tonight at the cinema."

"What?"

"The Marx brothers. There!"

"Groucho and Harpo? No kidding!"

"*No estoy bromeando.* Now, then, put this on where everyone can see it, and start signing your name."

Saulnier dipped into his pocket and brought out a bit of bright metal and a red snippet of silk. The crowd began to applaud. The militiamen saluted. Frank swallowed and clenched his fist at his forehead.

"*Salud,* fellas . . ."

"*Salud, Francisco!*"

"You stole that damned thing from my bureau, Saulnier!"

"I collect them. There. Very gallant indeed. Wear it, idiot. You earned it. That medal is our passe partout. Free escort, free drinks, free meal tonight, free coffee and cognac, free cinema!"

The front, the first defense line around Madrid was nothing like Frank had expected, nothing like the pictures he had seen of warfare in illustrated histories of the war of 1914–18. The trenches ran from house to house, the broken buildings linked by planked-over tunnels, sections of road shielded by ramparts of rubble. Then, a long, irregular gulley, wide enough for six men to stand in, shoulder to shoulder, topped by sandbags and loose, rusty wire. Along this section, spaced a dozen feet apart, men with rifles watched the Fascist lines and shouted taunts.

"*Oigan! Maricones! Mariconcitos!*"

"*Qué haces? Jodiendo a los moros, como siempre?*"

Bullets whucked into the sandbags, and the men laughed. One of them fired back. The men seated in the hard winter sunshine in the bottom of the trench did not look up.

The trench turned out into a paved road again, shielded by a broken wall. Anti-tank cannon protected by more sandbags had been placed in the gaps. A gang of men passed ammunition boxes chain-fashion, laughing and joking. A machine gun fired out beyond the wall, and the bullets hissed harmlessly overhead. One of the soldiers was reading *Solidaridad Obrera* aloud, translating the paper into French for a half-dozen men seated around him, smoking and listening attentively. Frank stepped over some telephone lines. A bell chirped, and a man in a small dugout spoke briefly, shrugged and hung up. He came up out of the dugout, squatted, took out a clasp-knife and a hunk of sausage and began eating. He grinned and offered Frank a piece. Frank shook his head and held out a pack of cigarettes.

"*Tabac?*"

"*Merci bien!*"

"*Commune de Paris?*"

"*Non. André Marty. Brigade Douzième. Là bas, les Garibaldis.*"

"*Où sont les Anglais?*"

"*Suivez la route. Cette edifice là.*"

Saulnier was talking to some other members of the French group. He nodded when Frank gestured that he was going on. The road was littered with shell and grenade fragments, ragged chips of rusty metal. Frank followed the Red Guards up the wall to where the French lines joined the Italians. A shout startled him, and he ducked.

"*Le jeu! Le jeu commence!*"

A group of the French gathered and threw fingers, odd and even. The winners took rifles to a sandbagged section of the wall. The others followed. The Red Guards nodded and gestured for Frank to come and see.

"What sort of game is beginning?"

"Over there, the Tercio, the Foreign Legion. Listen."

The voice sounded very close, perhaps fifty meters or less, shouting in a mixture of French and Spanish.

"Hey, you Red shits! Why don't you show yourselves? Sons of whores!"

One of the French soldiers lifted his head and shouted back: "Your mother!"

There was a short pause. Then the shout came across the shell-gouged earth.

"And your grandmother!"

The soldiers along the wall sniggered as they worked their rifle bolts. One of the Red Guards drew Frank down into a rifle pit and pointed at a weapon with a long, thick, hexagonal barrel and a telescopic sight, a Czechoslovakian sniper's rifle with a bipod. Frank crouched and squinted into the sight. A line of bullet-punctured sandbags frilled with barbed wire, then a narrow slot. A dirty, bearded face appeared. The French began shooting. Frank could see the Legionario squint as the bullets hit around him. Then the face vanished, stuck back into the enemy trench. Frank looked at the Red Guard, who shrugged and grinned.

"Nearly every day they do this. For a bet, you see. A proof of courage. He must stand there for the count of five, while we shoot."

"They *let* themselves be killed like that? He was *hit*, that one!"

"Oh yes. Of course, we don't use this Czech rifle."

The voice shouted again from the Fascist lines.

"You're getting better, you French turds! Right above the left eye. Now it's my turn."

Frank looked again through the telescope. Another face appeared, tawny hair and beard and large, pale green eyes. The lips moved.

"It's me. Tiger. Come on and shoot! You'll never hit me, you Red frog-eaters!"

Frank could see bullets flick into the earth and punch holes in the sandbags. The Red Guard nudged him.

"Go ahead, take a shot. It's not part of the game, but then you're a visitor . . ."

The Legionario went on shouting abuse. Frank's fingers closed over the trigger guard. He drew a breath and released half of it, snugging the butt of the Czech rifle against his shoulder. He could see nothing but the circle of light, the cross-hairs like a web. Then, as his finger touched the trigger, the Legionario slowly and deliberately began to pick his nose. Frank watched. More bullets tore into the sandbags. Dirt flew into the Legionario's beard. The pale green eyes looked down at the end of the index finger.

"You stink, you French syphilitics! You couldn't hit a bull's ass with a mandolin! No wonder all your wives put horns on you! We're coming over tonight. Then you'll see some shooting. *Hasta la vista!*"

Frank stood up quickly and climbed out of the rifle pit.

"But you didn't shoot! You might have got him, too."

The Red Guard was disappointed. The shooting stopped. *Le jeu,* the game, was over. Frank shook his head. How could he explain that somehow he could not try to kill a man who was picking his nose? A man picking his nose was a man without politics.

"It wouldn't have been fair."

"Well, another day, eh? Yesterday we got seven of them. Then one of their officers came out to make them stop. We could hear them talking. Then the officer got up into that slot. He *had* to, you see. How can he command them, if he doesn't have respect?"

"So you got him, too?"

"*Claro*, we got him. *Los franceses*, I mean. The French are very good shots."

"And that's the game, huh?"

The Spaniard shrugged.

"It passes the time."

They walked on up the line toward the University. The Red Guards explained that some of the buildings had been captured by the Fascists, others were held by various units of the 5th regiment and the Internationals. Frank could see the great blocks of brick buildings with white stone sills beneath the shattered windows, the bombed laboratories and lecture halls. In the Clinical Hospital, the Germans of the Thaelmann Battalion had tossed grenades into the elevators and pushed the buttons, sending the grenades up to explode among the Moors, who were fascinated by the little room that went up and down.

That battered building with the shell holes punched in the sides and the roof torn away by bombs was the Casa de Velázquez. The Dabrowsky Battalion had fought there for two days and two nights. One company held the second floor until the final hand grenade and bayonet rush by the Moors. The company had fought to the last man. One hundred and twenty-two Poles had died in the Casa de Velázquez.

The road on which Frank and the others walked was too exposed to enemy gunfire. A trench, shallow at first, rutted down into the ground and became a dark, musty-cold tunnel, illuminated by a few feeble bulbs strung from the girder-braced ceiling. The tunnel broke through the basement wall of one of the buildings. It was warm and surprisingly snug. The dim rooms, foul with smoke and the smell of unwashed bodies, were carpeted with mattresses spread between chairs and a few desks. Men were eating, sleeping, picking the lice from their clothes. Rifles were stacked against the walls. Open boxes of hand grenades stood handy, just inside the doors. A medical team was working in one room. A few armed men lounged around, watching. Two of the wounded still waiting treatment were captured Moors. Their dark faces were stiff with terror. Every time the sheet billowed or lifted, they made soft, wet little cries. Frank bent to look at them. He had never seen a Moor although everyone talked about them.

The two prisoners wore dirty uniforms, cheap puttees wrapped from the knees to the ankles and some kind of canvas shoe. They had been stripped of their weapons; only one still had a belt. The other clutched his trousers in one hand, his turban in the other hand, a thin, smeared hand, like a bundle of bloody twigs. They looked like Negroes, but with straight, rather thin noses, and dusty, dark skin. They leaned together. The sheet lifted, and a stretcher came out. The two Moors whimpered, and a voice said, in English:

"You may think it's funny, and I may think it's funny, but mumps are mumps and the poor devil is nearly thirty years old. He'll be out of it just as long as if he'd drawn a bullet . . ."

"True. The comical thing is that none of us recognized the symptoms . . . until we took off his trousers. Mein Gott . . . like melons, they are. Get him out at once, eh? I have given him a shot of morphine."

"How is the arm, Coltringham? You haven't been in to see us."

"Getting on. All right, you lads. Take him out to the truck, eh?"

Frank reached to his breast and unfastened the catch. He dropped the medal into his pocket. Coltringham followed the stretcher a few paces, then turned back to stare down at the Moors.

"Here now, you two. Arriba! Smashed hand and a back filled with grenade fragments, I think. Caught them over at the Clinical Hospital. Again. Something going on there. Same group, you see. Those funny pieces of glass stitched up inside their jackets. We took them off. When you've done with them, ring me. The last ones seemed willing to talk . . . tell you anything to get back their baubles. I'm buggered if I can see why they set such store on pieces of someone's old chandelier . . . Who's that?"

"Me. Frank Buckminster. Remember? That party at your place last summer?"

"Frank! Yes of course! How . . . how are you?"

Coltringham beamed and held out his left hand. Frank took it, an awkward fumbling of fingers. The Englishman's right arm hung straight down at his side. Coltringham tapped it.

"Bit of a problem here. Hit twice in ten days. Same arm, damn near the same place. 'Bout an inch off. Good job I'm left-handed, eh? Well, we've been reading all about you in the papers. You've been . . ."

"Buzzing around . . . you know."

"Right. Time for a feed. Come along and meet the others. The literary society usually meets up in the library."

"You've lost weight, Tom."

"Good for me, but these medical types from Berlin are sending me back to Albacete."

The Red Guards hesitated, smiling and self-conscious. They all seemed to know Coltringham and to be pleased that Frank had found the Englishman. Frank distributed more cigarettes and exchanged salutes while Coltringham chatted.

"Dónde está su jefe? Cómo se llama? El Pequeñito?"

"Ahora está con los Thaelmanns . . . el Asturiano!"

"El Pequeñito, yo creo."

"Qué va! . . . el Asturiano!"

"Oh, perdone, Y la guerra?"

"No pasarán!"

The Red Guards saluted and left, turning down a dim corridor. Coltringham sauntered on, waving to acquaintances, saluting, dropping a word here and there. Frank trailed after him, grinning, and feeling like a parent taken about a boy's boarding school by the headmaster. Daddy's Day at Lawrenceville.

"They are a damned good sort, the Red Guards. Always give them a bit of a rag about Paco, their commander. First-rate soldier, especially at this sort of fighting. He goes out with them every night for hand-bombing. Lister's here today. Know him? Lister? He and Larra are cronies. Both from Asturias. Both were in Russia, too. Lister has a crack outfit. Big fellow for a Spaniard. Through this door . . . Here. This way."

The cellar of the building was honeycombed with rooms. Men came and went, slept and ate, cleaned their weapons, read and talked in the dim light and bad air. Coltringham waved his left arm.

"What's left of two companies of the Poles. Poor devils. Not one of them is quite whole. Kept in reserve now. Frederico? Hola! Good chap, company commissar for the Garibaldis. Having the devil's time with his teeth. Beautiful smile, did you notice, but behind the bicuspids, a perfect cesspool. He doesn't know it yet, but he's off to Valencia to have a full plate fitted. Malnutrition when he was a kid, I expect. Up these stairs, and keep right tight against the wall. There's a Moor across the way with a submachine gun and he knows how to use it. We've been after him for days, but he's a cute one . . . You *did* get Peter's letter? Of course. *Watch it!*"

They sank down on the gritty stairs. Something hit into the building. The staircase shivered with the muffled bump of the explosion. Three loud slams sounded from the floor above them, the hollow clink of discarded shell cases. Sunlight and cold air poured down through the open roof. Coltringham stood up and dusted himself clumsily. He looked dirty and very tired, with fatigue lines rutted in his unshaven cheeks. He peered around through his steel-rimmed glasses and listened. Explosions sounded, quite close, enough to shake the building. There was a long, loose clatter of falling masonry, and voices shouting furiously in French:

"Bataillon Commune de Paris! Vite! Vite!"

Coltringham grunted.

"Mortar shell. Started a fire, I suppose. That's one thing we really worry about. Fire. A lot would be trapped, or else driven outside. With no cover. They wouldn't stand a chance. See the landing there and that office? Took two hits a week past. Damned near burned us all out. We've got no water, see? None to speak of. A shovel and few buckets of sand. We used the carpets from the rector's office. Lovely Moorish things, soft as a kitten. Burned to bits, of course."

"That's the Hospital Clínico, isn't it? Over there?"

"Right through that hole in the wall? Exactly. Damned shame, isn't it. Splendid building once, knocked all apart. We burned them with gasoline bombs. Almost completely gutted. That heap of brick nearby, see it? Institute of Agronomy. Full of Moors."

"Where are we, Tom? Which building, I mean?"

"School of Philosophy and Letters. Very appropriate, we've all decided. Across the way they're shouting 'Down with Intelligence' and 'Long Live Death,' and here we are, poets and machine gunners, snug in our library."

Coltringham pushed open a door. It *was* the library, with dark carpets on the floor, a clock ticking softly on a wall. All the windows had been blown out and the cold winter air poured in over barricades made of books. Coltringham crossed the room, nodding to the soldiers sprawled on sofas, blanket-wrapped on chairs, crouching by machine guns and anti-tank cannons mounted at the shattered windows.

"Hello, John. Having a bit of a read? What is it today?"

The soldier looked up and smiled.

"A thing on the Lake Poets by De Quincey. Very good, too."

Coltringham pointed at a low wall of volumes neatly stacked on the floor.

"German philosophy and Hindu metaphysics. Just the thing. Very heavy prose, you know. Lovely thick bindings. Absolutely bulletproof. When it gets hot, we can crawl about from one spot to another and work the anti-tanks."

Frank looked around at the pocked walls. A poster, bright blue and orange, said: COME TO SUNNY SPAIN!

A rifle crashed at the far end of the reading room.

"Oh, damn! Missed him again."

The British sniper was seated in a leather armchair behind another barricade of books. He worked the bolt of his rifle, and the spent cartridge tinkled on the cold floor. Coltringham shook his head.

"Better knock off and have a sleep. You're on tunnel duty tonight. A long, hard dig."

"I suppose I might as well. He's gone to earth now, anyway."

The sniper leaned his rifle against the barricade of books and closed his eyes. His breath blew out in little clouds of vapor. A small, purple velvet cushion propped his shaggy head. He fell asleep at once. He looked like a Mongolian to Frank.

"One of yours?"

"Yes, indeed. Cornford. Cambridge man. Mother is a poetess. Writes some verse himself. When he gets off politics, he does some quite good things. Though I'm no judge, you know. I scribble myself. I believe you said they looked like Boy Scouts, Frank. Still think so?"

"No. They look like gypsies."

"Well, no one can wash, that's all. John, is Peter Desmond down the hall?"

"Next door, Tom. With the land mines."

"Good. Shall we?"

"Sure," Frank said. Almost all the British volunteers were quietly reading.

"It's damned funny, in a way," Coltringham said, "because every day has become so predictable . . . within a frame, you know. At dawn the scouts and snipers come in, the tunnel-diggers knock off, and the land-mine details are done. A nuisance squad is posted to do some sniping, and everyone sleeps until about ten-thirty. At eleven, there's either a bombing raid or artillery barrage for a half hour. It stops, and we all count noses. Then the fighting starts up. Like this. It will go on until half-past one. Luncheon. Never since we've been here have the Fascists made a move between two and four in the afternoon. Siesta time. Now that it gets dark soon, we have the evening meal, everyone gets told off into details for the night work, out go the scouts and snipers. Same cycle, day after day. It's a rat's existence, not heavy combat. We gnaw and nibble at each other. We haven't the equipment to drive them back across the river. They haven't the men to root us out of our holes."

"It's the same with us," Frank said. "Some of the pilots have taken their pay and beaten it back to France. Some were given the heave-ho. We've lost planes and men."

"But the Russian machines have arrived; we've seen them."

"Not very many. Intelligence tells us they're getting about four planes to every one we get. Tough odds to beat. We don't bomb during the day at all. We can't. Our old crates just get shot apart. We strafe and patrol at dawn and dusk, when the light's bad."

"But you're holding on?"

"Just barely."

"And the Russians?"

"I've seen a number of them. Training the Spanish kids. They're good pilots. Not very friendly. Stick to themselves. Of course, they don't much like the idea that I'm chief pilot for our group."

"Touch of envy there."

"No. I'm a mercenary. I've got a contract and get a bonus for every-thing I knock down. So we just nod and salute and drink at different ends of the bar."

Coltringham laughed shortly.

"I'm afraid that's standard no matter where you go. We think we're building a new kind of fraternity, comradeship, and you look about and the Communists have their meetings, their spots to eat, sleep and drink, Socialist types *their* private times and places, non-politicals still a third. The Germans sing a lot; the French complain; the Italians talk all the time or mope about, being homesick, and the Poles . . . well, they brood. Too many losses too fast, and now the Russians coming in."

"Tom, how is Peter taking it? About Harry, I mean."

Coltringham frowned and scraped his brow with dirty fingernails. The air smelled of smoke and cold ashes, a chill, sour odor.

"Here, see for yourself. Time to open the tuck-box."

Coltringham pushed open a door. Frank walked into what had been a small reading room. The empty window frames were stacked with sandbags shielding two Lewis guns. A sort of hut had been built in one corner of the room, like a child's hide-out made on a rainy day, furniture, boxes, rugs, and blankets tumbled together. Three men crouched around a Primus stove. Another squatted on the floor before a worktable made of a door. The table was covered with tools and bits of scrap metal and wire. The men around the stove stood up, smiling, showing teeth through grimy beards. The man at the worktable looked around. He was Peter Desmond.

Frank took a few steps toward him and stopped. Peter was bone-thin, scrawny in a stained *mono* and ragged jacket. His long, matted hair tumbled over his face, half hiding his eyes. He held a metal box of some sort in his hands.

"Peter."

"Hullo."

"Well . . . uh, you look *great!* Just *fine!*"

"Making a land mine. Always trouble getting enough spark to set it off. Must see the *dinamiteros* about it."

Frank could hardly hear him above the racket of gunfire. He squatted beside the work and smiled.

"The mad inventor, eh? Know anything about valves and carburetors? We can use a good man out at the base."

"Oh, I couldn't leave. I'm needed here. Who would do the mines?"

"Yeh, I guess you're right."

Peter gazed around the room absently and nodded a few times.

Coltringham swarmed over to them, bluff and hearty, dragging a blanket.

"Come along, you two and chin while we eat. Canned monkey meat, cheese, and the last of the tea and honey. Dormy feast, eh?"

"You go ahead," Peter said. "I'll just finish this."

Coltringham took the metal box from Peter and set it gently on the table. Peter sighed.

"Food. That's an order, comrade."

"Oh, very well. I can get right back to it, first thing."

"Of course."

Peter stared fixedly at the broken windows. He got up slowly and walked to the sandbags. Frank followed him. Most of the fighting seemed to be going on in other buildings. Republican artillery was shelling the Casa de Campo. Peter pointed with one skinny hand.

"That's why I must get on with my work. Every night we set the mines out a little farther. The Moors are deathly afraid of them. Play their drums and sing half the night, trying to conjure them up out of the ground. If we can just go on setting them, a bit farther every night, we'll push them back, you see. Back into their own trenches, then out of those. What's needed, you see, is not more artillery, but decent wire and batteries or a different kind of striker. Then we'll have all this clear and I shall find him . . . where he lies, you know. It was just a trench somewhere out there. No one remembers, really. Hardly expect them to. But they did bring in his papers, so someone must have found him. If they can, I can. Perfectly simple. Just a matter of making enough of these things to push them back."

"Right. I understand."

"The mines keep the tanks away, too. That's important."

"What you need is a Very Cunning Trap, like in *Pooh*, remember?" Peter turned away from the window, a thin smile brightening his face.

"A Very Deep Pit, it was. To catch Heffalumps . . ."

The smile faded. Peter walked slowly, almost shuffling, over to the Primus stove and sat down. He began to eat mechanically, poking the food into his mouth and sipping tea from a tin cup. Coltringham told funny stories about his grandfather, a Nonconformist preacher. Peter Desmond said nothing. The other English were consciously "being good" to him, but he did not notice. His gaze kept straying to his workbench. Before the hasty meal was eaten, he slipped away and began fiddling with wires. Coltringham lit his pipe and jabbed the stem in Peter's direction.

"Of course, I'm taking him with me to Albacete. He's become something of a wizard at those contraptions. Got to get him away from here. He's getting like Lucie Manette's father in the Dickens novel. Harry's grave is an obsession with him. He has to be watched on night patrols. Gets out too far and . . ."

The building shook with the crash of a direct hit that threw them all sprawling on the floor in a clutter of tin plates, crackling plaster and slopped tea. Frank rolled over, his ears ringing. The others rushed for the door. The hall was filled with vague shapes that plunged through the dust and smoke, all shouting. The reading room had been hit. The doors were blown off, and the British there moved like drunkards in the plaster haze. The blue and orange poster was gone. A large hole gaped in the wall. They piled the wounded onto carpets and took up the corners. There were three men hit by shrapnel, bleeding and groaning. Coltringham had them sent down into the basement. Frank followed as far as the stairs, then turned back. A cup, empty, stood on the workbench. Peter Desmond was gone.

He found Coltringham, finally, in one of the basement corridors holding an electric torch. In the feeble light, a surgeon was picking shrapnel bits from one of the wounded Englishmen and sponging away the blood.

"I'll see you, Tom. Take care."

Coltringham did not look up. He shifted the flashlight and shook it. "The battery's weak, damn it. There. What? Right. Very good. One of our own anti-aircraft shells, I should say. Straight down through the roof like that. Bloody fools. Happy flying, Frank . . ."

"Yeh. Peter's . . ."

"Don't worry, old man. He's one of us. We'll look after him."

There was nothing more to be done. Frank walked away, looking for the tunnel that led outside. Without a guide, he made a wrong turn and had walked fifty yards before he knew it. He was in a slot of broken masonry, twisted girders, and shell holes linked by tunnels. There was scattered firing, mostly machine guns, the occasional jolt of a light cannon. The men who had burrowed in this place were Germans, the Thaelmann Battalion, too preoccupied with short-range sniping to pay much attention to him. Their commissar very politely but firmly escorted Frank away from the headquarters dugout, back through the Thaelmann positions. The shooting had died down. It was two o'clock, siesta time.

The quiet was so unnatural that Frank found himself moving on tiptoes. He was unarmed and more or less exposed. After the incident of the shell dropping on the British, he no longer felt safe in this vast warren of rubble and trenches. Somewhere there was likely to be a Moor who didn't feel sleepy. The thought made the hair crawl on his neck. Where the hell was Saulnier?

He blundered along a trench littered with thawed excrement, spent cartridges, and tin cans. The men on duty there seemed suspicious, but too weary to do anything about it. If he wanted to find the Commune de Paris that badly, he could pass. The men wore red and black insignia. Some of Durrutti's Anarchists. The trench jogged to the right.

"Good afternoon, comrade."

A man, apparently an officer, held out his hand. Frank shook it. The man was another German, apparently, with blue eyes and blond hair poking out from beneath his helmet. Some sort of meeting was going on in what sounded like a dozen different languages. The men were gathered in groups around booklets and newspapers.

"What's this, a school?"

"Of a sort, yes. You *are* Buckminster, the pilot?"

"Yeh. Looking for a pal. Frenchman."

"Saulnier? He was our guest for *Mittagessen* . . . lunch. He is with his countrymen, collecting names of women in Madrid, I think."

"That sounds like him."

"But forgive me. Kopa, Hans."

"You run this school?"

The German gestured at the men in the trench.

"We take advantage of the day's lull to get on with our political indoctrination. Reorganization to create a real People's Army. These comrades, well, they are truly international. Belgians, French, Germans, Poles, Czechs, Bulgarians, some dynamiters from an Austrian anti-tank group, Catalonian militia, anarchists, too . . . they are very noisy, as you hear. Even some fugitives who came across the lines several weeks since. They are learning politics. They command or are commissars. It is very essential that they understand the new organization. A man must know what he's fighting for."

"Wouldn't it be easier to just fight and let the politicians worry about the rest of it?"

"Many here think as you do. But they are learning. No, a revolution makes war and politics one thing. That is the lesson of this century. Everyone must learn it. We must create a revolutionary morality for our side, don't you agree?"

Frank fingered the bit of metal and ribbon in the pocket of his leather jacket. He, a non-believer, had been decorated by the Communists. He shrugged. Kopa smiled.

"Comrade, would you be kind enough to say a few words? My men would like very much to meet you. They heard you were in the trenches. Our 'school' is very well attended today, as a result."

"Oh, I couldn't make a speech or anything."

"I will translate."

"Then you'd better fancy it up as we go along."

Frank stared down the length of the trench. A hundred faces of all ages, sizes, shapes, and shades were watching him. A political Ellis Island. The University of Madrid was creating a new kind of graduate. Kopa clapped a hand on his shoulder and introduced him in a torrent of syllables in several languages, all about international solidarity, the meeting of earth and sky, comrades in the air, other comrades on the ground, unified anti-Fascist striking force and a great deal more that Frank could not patch together from French and Spanish. When the German finished, there was a soft roar of approval and up went the clenched fists. Frank saluted back and cringed in embarrassment. His gold and crimson medal dangled from his fist. He shot his hand back into his pocket and stared, flush-faced at the men he flew over, the men the *Gloriosa* tried to protect from the Fiats, the Savoias, the Junkers, and the Heinkels. The sight of their faces, their steady eyes, moved him oddly. He had never thought of them as individuals, but as positions, lines, salients. Here now, on this cold, sunny day, in a sandy-bottomed trench between the Fascists and the shell-punched roadway, he saw them face to face, every face different, individual. Each man was that, neither more nor less than a man. If each man had stayed in his own village or city, rested in his own house or room, listening to the radio and scanning the papers, Madrid would have fallen at the first assault, the volunteer air force would have been scattered like autumn leaves, the war would be over. Yet these men, each one of them, for one reason or another, moving into something or away from something, had come to Madrid to fight in the ruined buildings of the University, the wrecked workers' houses in Carabanchel and Vallecas. Without them, it was likely that he would be back in Paris . . . or buried beneath the smashed hangars of Barajas or Alcalá.

He walked down the trench, until he stood surrounded by men. He tried to think of something else than the propaganda phrases, the worn words of the Republic. He swallowed once. Kopa, the German, nodded encouragingly, and he began:

"Well. I guess you all know that the United States is a long way from Spain, across the ocean. So far across the ocean that what happens here doesn't seem to mean much in America . . . except to some people. Maybe you know, too, that things haven't been going too well back home . . . although it always seemed to me that if Hoover had been given a real chance . . . What I meant to say is that something should be done to make . . . things mean something. I mean people should *care* . . . people should *want* to care. That's very hard, really. At least it's been very hard for me. Because I'm about as far from what everybody seems to call a proletarian as you can get. But, here I am, anyway . . ."

The men shouted approvingly and nodded their heads. Frank blinked in surprise. He wet his lips and plunged ahead.

"I had every break there was. A real señorito, as they say here. I guess I never had many what you could call real friends. Not . . . comrades, anyway. But now I feel like I've known the men in the squadron I fly with all my life. They're like you. French, Italians, Germans, some Russians, now, quite a few Spaniards. I hear there will be some more Americans soon. Communist Americans, I guess, so that ought to be all

right. But if we win here in Spain . . . I mean *when* we win here in
Spain, well, then I guess we can all go back home and live the way
we want to, only really giving a damn for somebody else that doesn't
even speak the same language or whatever, politics, you know and all
the rest. These other birds, the Fascists don't want that to happen, as
I understand it. But all I really want to say is this: if you keep doing
your job, fighting down here, we'll keep doing our job, fight up there.
Between us all, as . . . comrades, we'll win and . . . what the hell . . .
no pasarán!"

The buildings along the Gran Vía had been hit repeatedly by shells
and bombs. The lower windows were boarded over or sandbagged. Here
and there, the whole façade of a building had been stripped away,
leaving a multi-tiered stage set of sagging rooms and wet wreckage. There
was little traffic, and the *milicianos* on the crossings cursed and kicked
at the packs of scrawny dogs that scavenged and snarled in the gutters.
Frank saw a handsome Irish setter, gaunt-ribbed and hollow-bellied, a
German shepherd restless with hunger, dozens of droop-tailed mongrels.
"Where did all these dogs come from?"
Saulnier shrugged.
"Abandoned by their owners. Not many can afford the luxury of feeding
a dog. If the siege lasts long, not many will be able to afford the
luxury of eating one. Poor animals. They are not like cats. They can't
feed themselves, really. There's evolution for you. Bred for loyalty, dumb
as slaves, now thrown out in the streets to starve. I'm surprised the
Communists have not organized them . . ."
"A damned shame."
"Save your sentiments. There must be twenty thousand people in
the same condition, refugees from the Tagus Valley and from Toledo."
"I guess you're right . . ."
They walked on, past the boarded windows, the huge posters pitted
with holes from bomb fragments, the slogans and faded flags toiling in
the chill wind. Distant gunfire sounded like the thud of a heart. People
kept close to the building fronts. Frank and Saulnier were blocked and
jostled before another café. The place was crowded, with a triple rank
around the bar. One table was not occupied. On it sat a small sign, neatly
labeled RESERVED.
"Look at that. For some bigwig. General Miaja?"
"No. For General Mola. Two months ago he said he'd drink his coffee
here. They are keeping a place for him. A nice touch, eh?"
"Not bad. I wonder if they count the days?"
"I doubt if they do. But Mola does."
The motion-picture theatre was packed. A face like a mad sheep's
ringed with curls skittered across the screen. The audience roared when

the goat-gaited "colonel" buttoned, medaled, and booted like a regular officer swung away from the map table and stroked his brigand's mustache.

A child of five could solve this problem . . .

The subtitles flashed on and vanished. Frank grinned, tickled by anticipation, as the pause stretched out. Groucho, haughty as a *hidalgo*, scowled at his cowering subalterns.

Well, don't just stand there! Fetch me a child of five!

A group of militiamen stood up and cheered, beating their hands together. The picture careened on from one happy insanity to the next. Frank slumped in his seat, relaxed, laughing, and happy.

The audience applauded, and the lights went up. Frank sat there, unwilling to move. A low howl sounded somewhere outside. The audience surged into the aisles, as the lights flickered.

"Those dogs, huh?"

"What? No, that's the sirens. Come on. This is no place to be during a raid."

The crowd pressed them out onto the sidewalk. It was like being flung into cold water. The Gran Vía was dark, not even a flashlight. Footsteps spattered across the pavement, as the audience headed for the shelters in the subway stations. The sirens wailed across the heavy sky.

"Look!"

Above the city hung a band of dull red light rippled at the top by the moving clouds.

"Cuatro Caminos . . . working class district. Must have been hit yesterday. Those calcium bombs . . . you saw that one at the base . . . can't be put out with water. Just sand."

The sirens moaned and sobbed down, blending with a new noise, deeper, that seemed to press down over the city, a thick throb of motors, a single, solid endless groan in the sky.

"I've never been in a raid, Jean. I mean, from down here!"

Frank huddled, chilled, his thoughts scattered, waiting out the seconds before the first bombs hit. The street before him was empty, silent, waiting.

The explosion shivered deep in the ground, like a blast in a coal mine. Another, another, another. High explosives. Then a confused rattle of sound, a wild swing of a searchlight that swept the low clouds and the sedate cough of anti-aircraft cannons. The rattle sound again. Closer.

"Those the incendiaries?"

"Yes. Dropped by bundles."

Nothing hit close by. They left the doorway and began walking through the darkness. An ambulance raced by, the headlights a bitter blue, the bell beating. Now above the buildings, the first rose-colored flames. Another long, ragged rumble shook the sidewalk.

"Watch it!"

A bomb hit somewhere behind them, in the neighborhood. First the flash, then the jolt and the sound, then the cackling slide of roof tiles. Dark figures scurried by, heading away from the sudden, damp stink that gushed in the darkness.

The band of dull red over Cuatro Caminos spread across Madrid, until the jagged skyline was lit by a shimmering incandescence, a vast, trembling glare from horizon to horizon. Under the tile roofs punctured by the incendiary bombs, green flames licked and darted. A block of apartments, the windows gone stood like a vast griddle backed by roiling orange storms of fire. The cold wind drove restless little bands and flutters of scarlet everywhere. The streets were bathed in firelight. Beneath the roar of flames, the city scrambled and stirred.

Strange, glimmering figures heaved handcarts and staggered under mattresses and pieces of furniture. A cloud of searing sparks whooshed down on bodies tumbled on the stones. At the corner, like frantic ants, a team of firemen played a thread of water from a ladder down into a hissing caldron of fire.

A *miliciano*, his face and hands tinged rose, stumbled toward Frank, dragging a rifle. He shouted incoherently and pointed at a black building nearby. Something cricketed into the street. Frank stared, furious and feeble. From that building, snipers were shooting at the fire-fighters. He watched as the dark figures scattered from the ladder, rushed away and back again. The militiaman whirled off, cursing. Frank and Saulnier turned again and ran from the roar that swept across the shimmering sky.

Two racks of bombs, eight slamming explosions, a cloud of broken tiles raining down like sleet, a furious punch of flame and the heavy, slithering crash of a floor buckling and collapsing. The orange-sheened street was flooded with men and women, clotted with quilts and bedding, impassable with jostling herds of sheep tangerine-pelted and panicky.

"Let's try the basement of the Telefónica. This way!"

They ran again into a reek of burning wood and molten glass, under a sailing sheet of sparks. Bombs bit around them, on all sides now, vicious slams that sprayed every open space with flying fragments. It began to rain.

Women in black snatched at the stuff handed down the line by a salvage crew, a pot, a little broken chest, the morning-glory from a gramophone. A dozen bodies lay in a neat row on the sidewalk. Broken glass was everywhere. The people of the city crept on a pavement of topaz bits.

"There! Up there, the bastards!"

Like tin models trundling on wires, the Junkers slid steadily across the glowing sky, belly doors open, so low and loud that it seemed they must be gored by the pointed rooftops. They bellowed on, trailed by three Fiats. The incendiaries spewed from the bay doors like bits of excrement.

The bombers vanished, and the bombs pelted into the streets and houses. Green flames popped and sputtered, new growth of hot ruin flung down blind between the flaming furrows.

The tiny plaza opened to the right, off the street that led to the Telefónica. The plaza was burning, all the houses and shops spewing flames. In the center, a burro tugged madly on a smoldering length of rope, fell and scrambled up again, braying and kicking. The mane and tail hair crinkled and stirred; the eyeballs burned blind jerked up into the steam made by the rain pelting down through the roaring flames. The burro screamed at the scarlet world that roasted it alive, snatched a final, scalding breath and crashed to its knees, then rolled. The rough cobbles grated off hunks of charred flesh and bubbled hide.

Madrid burned. Three hospitals were in flames. The National Library burned. The Ministry of the Interior burned. Markets, shops, churches, houses, factories and museums burned. Atocha and Calle León, Cuatro Caminos, Velázquez, Gerónimo and Carlos, the Puerta del Sol, Calle San Margos, Fuencarral, Calle Martino and Calle Goya, Avenida Urquiejo, Plaza España and the Gran Vía. The buildings, like black bones, rose out of a great pool of scarlet, crumbled and fell silently into the lake of fire. The only sound was a deep, dreadful hiss, the Bessemer-breath, the blast-furnace gasp that blew iron and made it steel.

They drove slowly in a Matford sedan with a French journalist and a Canadian woman. At the Plaza de Independencia, Frank saw a huge banner with the hammer and sickle billowing in the throat of the brick arch.

"Pity about your car. Buried, you said?"

"Part of the Hotel Savoy fell on it."

Saulnier stirred in the circle of Frank's arm.

"Why are the lights so bright?"

There were no lights, just the dull orange glow from the fires. The Canadian woman looked into the back seat.

"How's your comrade? He seems quieter."

"Yes. Lucky for us you had that ointment."

"Oh," the woman said, "just Unguentine. I bought it for sunburn."

They drove through several barricades. The *milicianos* wanted to confiscate the car. The French correspondent thrust a fistful of papers; the Canadian woman translated; a whistle squealed and they rolled on. On the road to Barajas, Saulnier fell asleep, all at once, ducked down into his flight jacket. Frank held his greasy face from the window.

"You said you were in Aragón. How was it?"

"Boring, actually. I thought I had a priest, but he got away. We had to leave. The Anarchists aren't much, these days, and editors demand copy, you know. I saw a ghastly thing tonight. A woman holding a child.

But its head was off. That's copy, you see. Are you with the volunteer pilots by any chance?"

"Nope. I drive trucks and my buddy here pumps gas."

"I suppose you *see* the pilots, though?"

"Sometimes."

"We should talk. Aragón was such a bore . . ."

At last, the sedan joggled down the rutted road to the field. Frank held Saulnier's face away from the window. The French journalist flicked the headlights on. Someone shouted in the night.

"Turn those goddamned lights off! They'll shoot at us!"

The journalist snapped the switch and spoke to the Canadian woman. "You saw that? Ask this chauffeur what those trench things are for."

"Comrade, what are those trenches out there in the field?"

"Potatoes," Frank said. "Folks from Torrejón are planting spuds."

"In December?"

"The folks are very much for the Republic. Experiment in two-crop farming."

"Interesting. I never saw it tried in Alberta."

"I guess not, ma'am."

They jounced down the road until Frank could see the shape of the single building that served as *cantina* and operations huts.

"This is just fine. Thanks a whole lot. Come on, Jeannot. Wake up."

The woman leaned back and shook Frank's hand.

"Good luck, comrades. I'll just put you down as non-political. We'll meet again, I'm sure. We're here to really *do* Madrid."

"We must have photographs," the journalist said. "Of victims."

"*Merde!*" Saulnier said, thrashing upright. "I have been carrying my face in your shitbox of a car for two hours. Photograph me."

"*Out, salaud!*"

They climbed out of the car. It shot away across the field, the tail-lights glowing through the mist. Frank guided Saulnier into the operations hut. The squadron cook had malt-coffee steaming on the iron stove and a basket of bread bits fried in olive oil. Saulnier stopped and stood, sniffing, turning his head from side to side. Frank looked over the Frenchman's shoulder to see the new flight schedules. A new, neatly typed sheet was thumbtacked in the exact center of the bulletin board.

The notice was brief, written in French, and signed by the commander of the volunteers. All members of all squadrons and flights, ground staff, pilots and technical crewmen were, as of the date affixed, members of the Air Force of the People's Republic of Spain, subject to the same rules, regulations, and pay scale as officers, non-commissioned officers and enlisted men of the People's Army. All mercenary contracts were null and void as of this date. Bonus payments due would be honored at the end of the present month. Individuals with questions concerning their national status or passport violations should make application for an interview with the commandant. The new organization must be considered permanent.

Frank read it aloud. Saulnier listened, sniffing.

"*Merde.* They've done it. We are now Spaniards. Either that or clear out. Well, *mon ami?* Will it be Philadelphia for you and Paris for me?"

Frank looked out of the window at the gray, rainy dawn. The mechanics were already out in the hangars, pulling the motor covers off three Chato biplanes, readying the engines for warm-up. The sight of the planes brought back the feeling of solidity, of resolve.

"No. I'm staying here. Permanently."

"Let's say 'for the duration of the war.'"

"Go find the *practicante* and have him look at you. He's right down the hall."

"*Bien . . .*"

Saulnier walked away, trailing his fingers against the wall. Frank found a pencil in the pocket of his jacket. He looked at the flight schedule, crossed out Saulnier's name and wrote in his own. Saulnier pounded on the *practicante's* door. A voice inside muttered something.

"As soon as the fog lifts, we'll take off. Right?"

Frank nodded, as the door opened. The *practicante* looked at Saulnier and made a high, gasping sound.

"Right, comrade," Frank said. "Just as soon as the fog lifts."

The door slammed shut. Frank walked into the *cantina.* Someone was sitting in the only armchair, facing the stove. Frank saw the blue silk pajamas and leather slippers. The cook smiled shyly and poured out a mug of malt-coffee.

"*Buenas días, Señorito Frank.*"

"*Muy buenas, Marisela . . . gracias.*"

"*Pan? Un poquito, eh?*"

"*No tengo hambre, gracias.*"

He turned around and looked directly into the face of a gray-eyed man with short cropped blond hair. The eyes were odd, slanted like an Asiatic's, the face broad, flat and unsmiling. The man said something. Frank shrugged.

"*No comprendo, camarada.*"

"Do you speak French? Your name, please?"

"Franklin Pierce Buckminster."

"I have been waiting for you. All the night. You were in Madrid?"

"What's left of it."

"With Saulnier, another pilot."

"Yes. He was burned, second-degree, around the face. Who are you?"

The man bowed slightly.

"Dorlov, Ivan. Chief of instructors. You are to be my pupil. Can you fly a Chato?"

"I can fly anything with wings."

"You have not been checked out in Chatos."

"I've been too busy. I flew one a few times, maybe three. Before I crashed."

"I have seen the French aircraft. You were fortunate."

"Yes. Now, I am hungry."

Dorlov stared at him. Frank sipped his coffee. The Russian did not move.

"You are the chief pilot here, I am informed. An ace. Five planes already."

"After today, it will be six planes."

"Indeed?"

"I'm flying for Saulnier. He cannot see."

"Most commendable. But today you are my pupil. We will stay on the ground. Today you begin to learn about modern Soviet aircraft. I teach you to fly the Mosca."

"I fly early patrol."

Dorlov shook his cropped head.

"You do not understand. I am chief instructor. We make now a new squadron. Enough old airplanes from here and there. A new squadron of modern Soviet aircraft. Mosca interceptors. I have given orders."

"Yes?"

"Viriato, the Italian, will fly for Saulnier. You will report to hangar three at 0700."

"Very good."

"I begin then to teach you to fly the Mosca."

"How do you know that I won't go back to America?"

Dorlov nodded thoughtfully and scuffed his slipper on the bare floor.

"The squadron commander assured me that you Americans never quit when you are ahead of the game."

"Is that all he said?"

"No. He said that you would want to test yourself. After the crash. Also . . ."

"What?"

"Also that to teach you to fly the Mosca would be good propaganda."

"Do you think so?"

"I do not teach to fly the Mosca for propaganda."

"What do you teach for, then?"

Dorlov's gray eyes flicked at Frank and away.

"For the glorious Socialist revolution!"

The phrase came so quickly, so automatically, that Frank half-believed the Russian was joking. Dorlov's flat face turned away.

"They all tell me here that you are the best pilot the Republic has. The Fascists have Ramón Franco, the general's brother, and we have a capitalist sportsman. Life is droll. Until 0700. *Bon appétit.*"

Frank swallowed some coffee and watched the stocky Russian pad quietly from the room.

"Up yours, too, Mosca."

He sat at a table near the window and watched the early patrol take off into the mist. Viriato waved his fist from the cockpit of Saulnier's plane. Frank waved back. The sound of the motors faded, blotted by the mist. At 0655 he collected his flying gear and stopped again to look at the bulletin board. The *practicante* had grounded Jean, posting him on the sick-list. His own name was printed on a second sheet of paper, under the heading STUDENT PILOT. Dorlov had written it as BUKMISTER.

Amil lifted away the slab of concrete and looked down into the tunnel that led to the animal place where the bottles were. They had talked about it at night. The foreigners with the machine guns had no fear and fought until they were killed. Battle prayers and the amulets of hard water did no good. The foreigners in all their uncleanliness had a stronger charm that made them fight like devils. And he, Amil, had found their secret. They had animals and bottles of fluids. He had told a few of the company, but not the officers. They would not understand or would laugh at him. But they would see when the men of the company took the charm from the foreigners. One attack, kill them all, and be free of this place where the dead lay unburied and stinking and even the ground was not safe to walk on. Things buried there blew the legs off.

He pushed his rifle ahead of him and crawled on his belly, keeping his head low, so that his turban was not knocked off. The tunnel was long and dark. He crawled and prayed and crawled. At last he saw a dim gray light.

The tunnel ended in a boxlike room filled with pipes with wheels on them. There was a door and some stairs. At the top of the stairs, another door. He crept up there and listened. Nothing. No one. The foreigners came at night, then, to eat and drink and by these charms gain strength. He opened the door.

It was a place of long stone tables with small pipes and tubes of rubber. He tried the faucets. There was no water and a bad smell came from the other faucets. He turned it off. On the long stone tables were boxes with many little slips of glass and some heavy metal machines, like little cannons, with shiny wheels that moved the barrels up and down. In the drawers were boxes of knives they used to kill the animals with.

Yet they did not die, the animals, but floated in bottles, asleep. There were bottles of frogs, one of snakes, bottles of locusts and worms, all floating in beautiful bottles, asleep. That was the foreigners' secret. They had sleeping animals in bottles and so did not sleep themselves but prowled all night in the ruins like wolves.

There were other bottles, too, bottles beyond number, with foreign writing on them: FORMALIN, H_2SO_4, HNO_3, $C_{10}H_{14}N_2$. These bottles held the charms. The bottles had so much power that the foreigners left them unguarded.

Amil glided across the room to the cages. Someone brought food to the animals and water. There were rabbits, many rabbits, three cats, and a great many small, furry animals that squeaked and ran about. Amil did not know the name of this animal. That was because the foreigners brought them to this place and used them for strength. All was quiet. Amil left the animal place and closed the door. He crept down the stairs and climbed back into the tunnel.

The others were waiting in the trench. He told them of the place again and what they must do. The officers must not know.

They reached the tunnel, and again some did not want to enter. Amil lied to them and said there were things in the animal place that were not there, but were only memories of pictures that he had seen and stories that his father had told him. He would go first; they must follow. Then they would see wonders.

The tunnel did not seem so long. Amil squirmed and pushed his rifle ahead and hummed to himself. The others took it up and the tunnel began to sing. They came out of the tunnel into the boxlike room.

They praised Amil and thanked him, whispering and creeping up and down the room, turning on the faucets, twisting wheels and looking into the cages. Then they came back and sat down in a group around Amil and asked him what they must do.

Each animal must be killed, each with a single knife. That was the reason for the number of knives in this place. The blood must be gathered in the thin tubes that stood in the wire racks. Each of them must drink one tube of blood. That was the first part. When that had been done, he would tell them more.

They took the knives, each man one, and went to the cages and opened them, first the cats to see in the dark, then the rabbits to make the legs strong for running, then the nameless furry animals. It was done in silence, except for the rustles and squeaks of the twitching animals. They collected the blood, and each man drank. They left the dead animals scattered on the floor.

He told them that the foreigners took the skins off the animals and wore them over their hearts. The skins stopped the bullets because the blood was so strong. That was why the Spanish officers called the foreigners Rojos . . . Reds, because of the strong blood they had this

way. The men murmured and rose with their knives and skinned the
dead animals and put the skins over their hearts. They began to sing, very
softly, but Amil made them stop. He had decided that the foreigners did
these things in silence.

Then they ate the animals. Some had found the sleeping animals in
the bottles. Amil explained about them. For his wisdom, the men brought
him another animal, one of the nameless ones. He tore the warm slippery
flesh with his teeth, ground it and swallowed it, making his strength
double.

They brought out the bottles and marveled over the letters and numbers in gold. H_2SO_4, HNO_3. A very light blue bottle was labelled
$C_2 H_5OH$. Since it was the biggest bottle, it was the most important
and the most powerful as a charm. Amil said that he knew this was
true and sent them to get cups and vessels to drink with. He half filled
each of the drinking things and had each man hold his hands over his
vessel with the fingers spread. Then he poured the liquid over each man's
hands until the drinking vessel overflowed. This was how the foreigners
did it, and they all drank the pungent drink together, two cups each.

Amil knew he had been right, that the pictures that came to him
were true, because the men soon began to act holy and crazed. They
danced and sang, and Amil could not stop them. They flung the bloody
little carcasses at each other and began to smash things with their rifles,
laughing all the time. Amil began to break things, too, beakers, flasks,
bottles, and tubes. They opened the wooden boxes of little glass slips
and scattered them like chaff, delighted at the sounds they made in breaking. They fell on the glass-strewn floor and rolled there, laughing and
bleeding. It was true! They could feel no pain. The charm had worked!

And the other bottles held charms and powers, too. A rifle butt
whirled, the bottle broke and dozen of sleeping frogs flew out in a flood
of water that made the eyes hurt and stank. The men dabbled in the
stuff and sucked their fingers. Others began eating the sleeping frogs.
They broke more bottles to get at the sleeping animals. They took down
more of the bottles with the gold letters and numbers and drank of them
and threw the bottles like grenades. They staggered up and down the long
stone tables, fell over each other, sang and laughed and began vomiting.
They began to shoot at the bottles with their rifles and to chop up the
sleeping animals with their bayonets. The floor was slippery with foul-
smelling liquids, bits of animals and covered with broken glass. Amil
took up a small bottle with a death's head and bones on it. He recognized
the insignia of the Foreign Legion. This was what the foreigners used
to protect them from the bullets of the Tercio. He broke the stopper off
and filled his mouth. Now bullets and bombs and things that exploded
in the ground would never harm him. He swallowed it. Some of the
others were screaming now in their new holiness and strength, screaming

and tearing at their faces and bellies in the frenzy that the charms brought on them.

Kopa waited until full dark. By that time he had collected a small canvas sack full of vegetables and a few cans of sardines for the cats. The night patrol from the Thaelmann battalion went out through the wire to meet the *dinamiteros* from El Asturiano's battalion. After them came the land-mine team following Desmond. The young Englishman had deserted the train to Valencia and had returned to the University. No one had reported him yet. They needed him for the mines. After the land-mine team, it was possible to go out over the wire. Kopa was careful always to leave and return to the trench at the same time and place. He had been shot at four different times by nervous sentries. He carried the bag of food in one hand, a loaded revolver in the other.

The laboratories for the Clínica were away from where most of the fighting had taken place. Every night Kopa went there to feed the animals that had been abandoned. One of the English doctors kept promising to remove them to the city, but had not been able to requisition any transportation. They had a joke together about sending the guinea pigs out on the streetcar, each one fitted out with a little Communist arm band.

Kopa moved slowly, cautiously. The field was pitted with shell holes. Anyone might be hiding in them. He skirted each one, always moving at an oblique angle, guided by the bulk of the Clínica. When he was close enough to make the last dash to the end window he left unlocked, he groped and found a large stone. He flung it to his left with all his might. As soon as it hit, the Fascists opened up with rifles and submachine guns. Kopa hefted the canvas sack and ran for the end window.

The smell hit him like a blow. He grunted and gagged, hanging half in, half out of the window. A blast of chemical fumes made him cough. He dropped down into the lab, his boots spattering into a pool of slushy broken glass. He coughed and blinked. He breathed through his hands and squinted, his eyes smarting. The whole dark room stank of formaldehyde. He found the broken cages and the first body twisted on the floor. His hands trembled as he took out his metal cigarette lighter and pressed the lever. The flame dazzled him. He held it up over his head and stared. His jaw dropped. He walked a few steps and stopped. He gazed around. The Moors had invented a new horror. Kopa switched off his lighter.

"May God pity them . . ."

He could not stay in this place. He slopped back between the bodies and shattered equipment and bits of fur. He threw himself out the window, plunging like a diver into the cold, dark, pure December air. He slammed onto earth frozen hard as iron and lay there, gulping for breath. He knew he was going to be sick and rose to his hands and knees. He vomited and then stood up. He felt weak and shattered. Sweat poured down his face. He took out his revolver and headed slowly back to the Republican trenches.

The day his furlough began started like all other days for Pedro. The reveille bugle and formation at cold dawn, the march by companies to the mess hall, the solid meal of hot cooked cereal, eggs, bread with apricot jam, washed down with scalding coffee. There was little conversation. The news from Radio Burgos was strident but unconvincing. Everyone knew that Madrid could not now be taken by frontal assault. The weather had brought the fighting elsewhere nearly to a standstill. The Republican defense lines seemed to have hardened everywhere as the earth of Spain froze for the winter. The morning was gray, gloomy, with a promise of snow.

After breakfast, there was the policing of barracks, a perfunctory inspection by the officer of the day, a short break, and then morning parade. Since the camp had been set up near the railroad lines precisely for the purpose of dispersing troops and officers with leave-permits for the holy days, each morning parade was shorter, a mercy, since it meant standing at attention for less time in the bitter December wind.

Pedro packed his gear into a single knapsack and buckled his revolver belt over his greatcoat. He felt a trifle theatrical with the side-arm flogging his thigh, but officers on leave had been ordered to wear revolvers in public in order to intimidate "unreliable elements" of the civilian populace. Unreliable elements in Navarre? An absurdity . . . except to the Falange. To them, every Carlist was more or less suspect, ever since the Reds shot their leader, José Antonio. One month and one day had passed since the morning in Alicante when José Antonio's last request had been that the patio stones be wiped clean so that his brother Miguel would not have to step in his blood. The Fascists had forgotten already that two Carlists had been shot with José Antonio. He had become El Ausente, "The Absent One." The Carlist victims were not merely absent, but had passed into total oblivion.

Pedro shouldered his pack and left the officer's barracks. He stood in the lee of the building, out of the wind, and watched the Falangistas put on their morning show, a parade-before-parade, staged to show all others what real devotion, real patriotism was made of. They tramped across the frozen gravel, red-cheeked and serious, in a modified goose step they had picked up from the Germans. Pedro noticed a new face here and there. They spent every break, every fatigue hour recruiting in the ranks and seeking converts among the officers. They knew enough to leave him alone, but they did so not out of respect, but out of contempt. He watched the parade, sunk in a cold, sullen fury.

The ranks tramped and wheeled. The bugles and cornets were flourished, and the new banners broken open to the hard winter wind. They halted, a pause, the command, and the ranks knelt on the gravel, heads bared and bowed. Pedro folded his arms and scowled. Public piety was a new thing, relatively. Back in the summer, in the hot, confused days around Zaragoza, not even the constant threat of an Anarchist offensive had been enough to bring many Falangistas to Confession and Mass. But this group were "new shirts," recent members of the party. The chaplain finished the morning prayer. The kneeling ranks rose, and their local leader began to call the roll. One after the other, the "new shirts" shouted as their names were called. Then the big silence, the dramatic moment. The leader gazed up at the sky, at the compass points. Pedro thought he looked like a rooster on a village dunghill, and sniggered, coughed and blew his nose. The Fascist leader bellowed the big question.

"José Antonio Primo de Rivera?"

Two hundred voices shouted back, so loudly that the windows behind Pedro rattled.

"*Present!*"

A cheer and a hundred caps thrown in the air and blown by the wind. The banners were hastily furled, and the Falangistas scattered to the barracks to get a bit warm before the regular formation. The Absent One had been declared Present. Good enough. Now was it possible to get on with normal affairs, for the furloughs to officially begin? There were others who really were present who were eager to be declared absent.

"*Teniente?*"

Pedro turned and recognized one of the orderlies from Staff. The poor fellow had been sent out on the double without an overcoat and was trying hard not to shiver in the wind.

"Yes?"

"The major wants to see you before parade."

"Very good, *cabo*. I'll come at once."

"Thank you, sir."

The major was waiting for him. The major was a member of the Falange, too, but an "old shirt," and claimed to have known Emilio and others in Madrid and Valladolid well before the July rising. After a few glasses of amontillado, the major occasionally claimed to be among the first members of the Fascist Party in the old Regular Army. He managed to be both affable and distant at the same time, apparently in belief that this balance was proper when speaking with a junior officer recently handed his full commission, a junior officer whose father was a count.

"So, you leave us today for a bit, Lieutenant?"

"With your permission, Major."

"Of course, of course. I hope the ten days will give you rest and peace of mind."

"Yes, Major."

What was the fellow getting at? The major seemed somewhat ill at ease. A rather special-looking folder lay on his desk. The major lit a cigarette.

"Peace of mind is difficult to come by. As difficult as peace itself. I know your record of service, Lieutenant. There you have proven yourself, beyond cavil."

Pedro stood at ease, but with his hands locked together to keep them from trembling. He knew what was in the wind now, the whole stupid business of December 8. The letter from his father had obviously been opened, and not by the censor, either. Quite likely by the major.

"We can claim no credit for the route at Esquivias, sir."

The major shrugged generously.

"The finest cavalry can do nothing against tanks. Our new German machines will blow the Red tin cans to pieces. I was speaking of peace of mind. Yours, of course, and—indirectly—my own."

Here it comes, Pedro thought. My leave is canceled. For the major's Fascist peace of mind.

"I wish only to be . . . reassured, Lieutenant. To know that we are in a state of mutual understanding. May I explain?"

"Please, sir, yes."

The major opened the folder and took out several pieces of paper.

"I have here a request from a source more enthusiastic than astute. It is a request from certain officers, dated the eighth day of this month, that you . . . along with several others . . . be permitted to transfer to something called the Royal Military Academy."

There it was, out in the open. Was he to be punished or deprived because of the fervor of the Carlist colleagues of his father?

"I was forced to respond," the major continued blandly, "to the effect that I had never heard of such an institution, either through the regular chain of command or . . . other sources, political sources, to be completely frank.

"What you may not know, Lieutenant, is that this little affair was brought to the attention of the Generalísimo. Yes, Franco, himself. The Generalísimo pronounced himself disgusted with the concept, since it tends to disunity. In your own case, whatever good could come of it? You have been graduated as a cadet from an academy already. Are we to believe that with your combat experience, plus this schooling, that you need still more tedious hours in the classroom while Spain cries for young leaders? No, no. Of course not. Therefore, to set you at ease, you should know that the group of—local enthusiasts, shall we say?— met yesterday. The concept of a Royal Military Academy was abandoned by majority vote. You are quite free, Lieutenant, to pursue what I am certain will be an outstanding career within the framework of the Nationalist Army."

"Very good, sir."

The major nodded, smiled, and tore one of the documents to pieces.

"So much for that, then, eh? Much of my piece of mind is already established. What a marvelous thing it is to be able to dispose of such misunderstandings! One final thing . . . really trivial. You are a great reader, Lieutenant. One should rather say, an intellectual, happily uncontaminated by contact with university radicals and pedagogical riffraff."

"I was educated by private tutors. Reading is a habit with me. I am not aware that it has interfered with my duties, Major."

The Major created a shocked expression and raised his hands.

"Who can suggest such a thing? No, no. Reading is your habit. Very good—within reason, as you suggest. But there are good habits and bad habits. A bad habit can be a good habit carried to excess, do you follow me?"

"Not exactly, sir."

"Come, Alemany, you cannot pretend to be ignorant of the law of September which states that all books of a Communist or Socialist tendency must be destroyed as a matter of public health."

"I do not regard my private habits as a matter of public health, Major."

"Ah, how like the young! Such fire, such pride! But reflect, young man, on a more recent decree. Books, periodicals, and so on of any generally disruptive matter were ordered to be handed in within forty-eight hours. Yes, that's correct. Now it seems that you have a foot locker. And in this locker are certain books."

"A present from my sister on the occasion of my commission."

"How pleasant to be able to receive gifts in these troubled times. Fine volumes, I expect, too. For example? A title or two?"

Pedro wet his lips. The Major's small eyebrows were raised. He expected an answer, without stalling.

"A number of volumes by Unamuno."

"The Rector of the University of Salamanca is now under house arrest."

"He is an old friend of the family."

"Perhaps your family should seek new friends, Lieutenant."

"May I ask who among my brother officers informed you of the disruptive contents of my foot locker?"

"No, you may not," the major said rudely. "And I don't tolerate that tone of voice, my boy, so stop it. I command this base and every soul in it. I am not some steward on your father's estates! Turn those books in at once to the orderly, if you want your leave-papers and transportation slips."

"I . . . will do so, if you so order it. Since the volumes were a gift, perhaps it would be acceptable if I removed them? Took them home with me and left them there?"

"Hand them over!"

"Yes, Major."

"You are dismissed."

"With your permission, sir."

"Granted. Have a good furlough."

Pedro saluted. The major returned the salute. Pedro turned crisply and marched to the door.

"One moment, Alemany!"

"Yes, sir?"

Pedro turned around.

"What is *my* name, Lieutenant? My full name?"

"Major . . . Major . . . I don't know, sir."

"You don't *know* the name of the commanding officer on the base where you are stationed? . . . even temporarily. Extraordinary. And why not, if you please?"

Pedro stared at him briefly. The major's smile was stiff, cold.

"I have never made the least effort to learn your name, sir."

"And why not, if you please? That is rather unkind of you, I think."

"It was a matter of indifference to me, frankly . . . sir."

"It preserved your peace of mind, eh? Ever been to Aragón, Lieutenant?"

"Never, sir."

"An oversight I have taken care to rectify. You won't be coming back to dear old Burgos, *hidalguito!* I have posted you with a frontline unit. Near Teruel. Heard of that place?"

"Vaguely."

"But it was a matter of indifference to you, eh? The transport officer has a copy of your orders. You will proceed from the family estates to your new post directly. You will find my name at the bottom of those orders. I expect you will remember my name from now on, eh?"

The major laughed.

"Oh yes. I think you will recall my name from now on, Lieutenant."

Pedro walked to the door and bowed slightly.

"You flatter yourself, sir."

He closed the door.

The train left at noon. Pedro stood in line and bought food and a canteen of wine. At the station, he found the chief clerk, gave the man some pesetas and received back a reservation for three seats in a first-class compartment. First class was reserved for officers, anyway, but he did not wish to be crowded. He had never been able to sleep sitting up in a moving train.

The compartment was empty. The train jolted into motion. Pedro sat at the window. He noticed the flatcars in the freight yards, hundreds of them, each car loaded with fifty-gallon drums of gasoline and lubricating oil. Each of the cans was labeled: TEXAS OIL CO. Beneath that, in bright green letters: MADE IN USA. The train rolled on through the bleak suburbs. A band of filthy children by the tracks raised their fists in the Communist salute. Pedro felt the pistol on his hip. There were the "unreliable elements!" He grinned and waved to them. The train went on. He opened his knapsack and took out a volume bound in Moroccan leather, a novel, *Abel Sánchez*, written by the Rector of the University of Salamanca, Miguel de Unamuno. Pedro turned up the collar of his overcoat, propped his feet up and began to read.

He could not keep his mind on the story. He turned to the end-papers. There, neatly folded, almost worn to pieces by handling, were the newspaper photographs he had cut from *Solidaridad Obrera* and the other propaganda sheets put out by the Reds. The newest photo was a candid shot of a unit of the Communist 5th Regiment, the Red Guards, at some sort of rear-post bivouac. General Miaja, the enemy commandant at Madrid, was delivering a speech to a group of men, in honor of some sort of group citation for heroism in the defense of the University. The caption identified some officers with the International Brigades, guests, apparently, at the fiesta. Beimler and Regler, both Germans, Dumont, a Frenchman, and Malraux, the flier and writer. But one of the "comrades" was not identified. He stood at an angle, his face slightly turned, as though avoiding the camera. He was in position between the soldiers and the foreign guests, as though in some distinct relationship between them. Yet, even granted the distortion of the camera, he was physically *closer* to General Miaja than anyone else, hence more important.

Even in the gray winter light coming through the soot-grimed window, Pedro was certain. He had had a glimpse of that face once beneath a street light in Madrid, not far from the restaurant Las Cuevas de Luis Candelas. The sharp profile, with the nose straight, the mouth firm, the loose tendril of hair falling just so. Pedro was certain. This was the face of the man who had murdered his cousin Emilio. The face of Paco Larra. The name was the same, but the face was false, different, touched up in some way. El Asturiano. Another Absent One who was always present, here, there, everywhere, like a phantom, insubstantial, yet powerful, deadly.

The train rocked and jolted through the snow. The flakes were big and wet, at first, but fined out and became wind-driven clouds that would pile up, perhaps to real storm depth, shutting off the mountain roads. No doubt it was snowing hard in Aragón, too. When the train stopped to take water into the locomotive boiler, Pedro got out and kicked through the drifts to the station. There he bribed the operator and sent a telegram to his parents. He had written to them as soon as his leave application had been approved, but he had heard nothing from them. The operator looked at him through the iron wicket.

"Going home, Lieutenant?"

"Yes. To Navarre."

"I know it well. May I ask what village?"

Pedro told him. The operator pulled the thin hair on his brow out of respect. Then he glanced around furtively and whispered through the bars.

"Tell them up there to stand firm, señorito! Stand firm, get it? Say there's others who know we don't want some little Gallego Jew to rule Spain. Spain's a kingdom, right?"

"Of course!"

"For Cross and Crown, I say! You heard that Fal Conde skipped to Lisbon? Let him go, I say. As long as there's young gentlemen like yourself, we'll have our king back yet!"

"You are a good fellow. Yes, I'll tell everyone I see. For Cross and Crown!"

The operator beamed, showing toothless gums, and vanished. Pedro heard him tatting at his telegraph key. The station filled, as others braved the snow to buy whatever was for sale from the vendors. Pedro walked back to his compartment, kicked the snow off his boots and slumped in the corner.

He had never met Fal Conde, the leader of the Carlist movement, although he had heard him speak at the rallies. Now he was gone, an exile in Portugal. Lisbon must seem a boardinghouse, a *pensión* for discredited members of the Right Wing, all those whose hopes and plans for the future of Spain "disgusted" Francisco Franco, Jew from Galicia, middle-class, fat, with a high tenor voice, friend of Nazis and Italian Black Shirts. Pedro smiled and shook his head, hearing his father's tirade. The old man detested Gallegos, Cataláns, the Aragonese and Andalusians about equally. Some were Jews, the rest gypsies. Castilians, the Basques, and the people of Navarre were "true" Spaniards, although by what interpretation of blood-heritage, loyalty to the Church, or plain likableness as individuals Pedro had never been able to determine. It would be really "home," when he heard his father's voice again.

"May I? With your permission, Lieutenant?"

Pedro looked up. A priest stood in the doorway, his head and shoulders powdered with snow.

"Of course, Father! Come in."

He was young and solid, with a rather tough face, his burly chest snugged into a peasant's sheepskin jacket. Pedro noticed he wore army boots. They shook hands.

"*Teniente* . . . ?"

"Alemany. Padre . . . ?"

"Ortega."

"Ortega y Gasset?"

The priest smiled and shook the snow off himself.

"No, I am no philosopher. I only get in trouble when I try that, it seems."

"You look like you've been with the troops, Father."

"I have. And you must be on furlough."

Although the priest was some years older, he had none of the patronizing mannerisms Pedro detested. None of this "my son" business.

"Well, I am, too."

"On furlough from God?" Pedro asked, smiling.

"Oh, come on. That happens to us all the time. I mean, you know . . . we are not better than the rest of the parish. Of little faith."

"I think you're trying to scandalize me."

"Not at all. I am too tired to tell lies, that's all. Do you smoke, Lieutenant?"

"Off and on."

"I'm only off when I run out. Here, light up."

The priest rummaged in his jacket and produced tobacco and papers. He made several cigarettes very quickly with deft, dirty fingers.

"Hard to make on a moving train, you know. There."

Pedro smoked. The fellow really didn't look much like a priest. A deserter, maybe? Intelligence officer? A Falangist in costume? It was possible.

"Well," the priest said. "If it's all right with you, I'd rather not talk politics or about the war. Unless you want to tell me your adventures."

"No. I am looking forward so to seeing my home, my family again. By your accent you're not a Northerner, Father."

"No. I was born and raised in Málaga."

"A long way from here."

"Oh," the priest said, "I'm going to the Basque country. Touch the sacred oak."

"When the territory is liberated, freed."

"You mean it isn't free now?"

"I mean restored to Spain."

"Ah. I didn't understand you."

There was something odd about the priest. He was too bold, too big, too casual, not in the official jolly way of bishops visiting the school-children or sipping Madeira after a well-remunerated family baptism and certainly not in the rather clammy novitiate's Our-Lord-had-a-sense-of-humor-and-so-have-I preference for feeble puns and word-games. This one looked, sounded, and behaved like some tough from a factory. As Pedro decided to put his new companion to the test, the train started.

"I want to ask you a question, Father."

"Yes? Go ahead."

Again a kind of rough, dirty-nailed openness that Pedro could not help but find suspicious.

"I don't mean to ask questions to you about yourself. I meant to ask you a favor."

"Yes."

"Would you hear my confession? Right now? Here, in this compartment?"

"Of course," Ortega said. "I've heard confessions in stranger places than this, believe me. You don't have to kneel. I shall just look out at the snow."

He averted his face. The sight of his profile tore the words from Pedro. He told the priest everything, about his plans to turn his military career into a pilgrimage of vengeance, to track down and kill, if he could, by any means, the enemy of his country, his king, his Church, his family, himself . . . Paco Larra. He showed the priest his copy of the novel and all the photographs. The priest shook his head.

"This isn't a confession. You want permission to commit an act of vengeance on a single individual. You want to be absolved for a murder before you poison yourself with the act. You want an antidote. No. It's foolishness. You are young. It's a boy's dream you have. Forget it. Find another dream. You haven't a drop of repentance in your heart and soul. Have you?"

"None! Not for him."

"You would kill him without a flicker of conscience, if you could?"

"I would. And then I'd seek out a priest."

"Don't come looking for me. I have no absolution for bloody-minded children. You call yourself a Carlist and a soldier. Then in God's name *act* like one! This is no time or place for dimwitted romanticism. Haven't we had enough of that? . . . on both sides? There is nothing worse than a man who enjoys killing his enemies, who combines war with enthusiasm. I have grown weary praying for such twisted Quixotes. Not that I think pragmatic Panzas are that much better. Why don't you young people choose some middle way, instead of the extremes that have crippled poor Spain for five hundred years? It is not enough to have a dream, not enough to be strong-stomached or strong-willed. You must have reason and right on your side. You think you have reason to hunt down this man. Perhaps. But you have no *right* whatever to do it. You grant him the right to hunt you down?"

"He *did!* He hunted down my cousin Emilio and blew his brains out. He grants *me* the right to hunt him in turn."

"Two fools do not make a wise man. He had reason, too, he thought. But he had no more right to kill your cousin than you have to kill him. No one has such a right. Now put this rubbish away and look forward to the holy days. You're a good man at heart. Don't cripple yourself. Your family friend Unamuno is quite right. We have enough war cripples in Spain. Don't join those who go around shouting *abajo la inteligencia,* long live death. Eh? Come on."

Pedro snatched up the photographs and the novel.

"I knew it! You're not a real priest at all. You don't know the Confession. You're a deserter, a spy!"

"If you like."

"I'll turn you over to the police, you fraud!"

"Go ahead."

"I invited you in here. Now, get out! Get out!"

Father Ortega grunted once, stood up and left the compartment, slamming the door. Pedro stared after him, suddenly stricken. What if he had been mistaken? He had insulted a priest, indirectly the Church itself. What if the priest, in anger, had gone to find a police officer? There would be an investigation. His papers would be examined, perhaps his knapsack. Pedro lunged out into the corridor. Empty. Priest or no priest, the man was gone. The lights flickered, dimmed. The train ground and winced through a long switchback curve. Pedro tumbled back into the compartment, swept the book and photos into his sack and wedged it behind his head. He stretched out on the seats and tried to sleep.

The train crawled through the cold winter night. Snow ticked restlessly against the window panes. The carriage jolted and rocked. Pedro sat up and finished the rest of his canteen. The rough red wine buzzed in him briefly, then left him dull and stupefied, but still awake. He sat through a montony of dark hours, unable to think, unable to sleep, a state of jounced torpor that lasted until dawn.

The storm blew itself out, and the gray skies cleared. The sun broke at last above the sheared rocky peaks. The deep, clean, new snow glittered everywhere and tufted the dark fir trees like frosting. Pedro pulled down the window and let the brilliant cold day pour into the compartment. He hung out the window, delighted with the bold blue sky, the satin drifts, the sparkle spilling from the shaggy dull-green branches. He recognized a thrust of bare stone, a stream, blue-black and frilled with new ice, rutting down a slope studded with snow-laden pines like a clan of winter dwarfs in peaked hoods. The train rattled over a bridge, slowed for the long grade, and stopped.

Pedro dropped down from the carriage and waved his arm. Up ahead, the locomotive sniffed. A bell panged, and black smoke whuffed into the sky. The pistons blasted steam; the drivers rolled, and the train backed and banged into motion. Pedro waved again and stood watching. It drew away around the bend and was gone. The slow, gasping beat of the locomotive faded. The black smoke vanished up into the blue cold sky. He stood alone beside the empty track. It was very still, high, beautiful and desolate. The untracked snow lay everywhere, a solid drape of purity, cold and silent. The dense firs rose dark and stiff. The sun burned like a lump of gold in the blue sky. Pedro stood and breathed in the day. He had almost forgotten that his native province, his father's hectares, the family estates contained such simple elements; sky, stone, water, trees, all bathed in pure, numbing, resiny air.

A voice called and echoed, called again. Down the path, beneath the trees came two horses and one rider. The horses plunged through a chest-high drift, smashing the snow aside like surf. Pedro scrambled down the slope of the roadbed and swarmed to meet them.

"Connie! Is that really you?"

"At your service, teniente! We had to come by way of the high orchards because of the drifts! Pedro, oh, Pedro!"

She fell out of the saddle into his arms, laughing and crying and tugging at him, knocking his hat into the snow, covering his face with short, hard, cool kisses, her heavy cloak tangling both of them. He hugged her, feeling the slender, wiry body, and tickled her ribs to make her let go. The horses stamped and lipped the snow, raising muzzles frosted like naughty children gorging in a sugar bowl.

"Hey, hey, stop it now . . . come *on* . . ."

"Oh, so dignified we are, eh?"

She tried to wash his face with snow, an old trick made special by the fact that he hated it. He ducked away from her to the horses and mounted. A handful of snow spatted against his boot. She swung easily up into her saddle, her cloak flaring. She wore knee-length boots, a blue skirt, white sweater and a red kerchief knotted at her throat. She swung her tangled hair loose and smiled at him.

"So you've come back! The Prodigal. What makes you think we want you any more?"

"Going to a fiesta? Since when do you dress like that, señorita? That skirt is immodest. Where is your winter riding dress?"

She touched her skirt and her kerchief with quick, flirting hands and reined her horse around.

"I dress like this since I joined Auxilio Social. We all play our part, my man. I am the local secretary, in charge of everything!"

"A fine homecoming. My sister dressed up like a little Falangista. How's everyone? I haven't had any letters. Did you get my telegram?"

"*Claro!* The secretary of the Auxilio Social is well-informed. Everybody? Well . . . all right. Father's a little more . . . you know. Mother's in bed with a slight cold, nothing serious."

He came up beside her. The horses heaved through the snow.

"And you? You do everything, right?"

"Pretty much, yes. Someone had to take over, you know. It'll all very well for you to join up, that's your duty. But there is the hay to be taken in, the grapes to be harvested and all the other crops, taxes, manure for the fields, conscripts and volunteers leaving all over the place, the beef cattle and hogs to be slaughtered . . . we have a quota, now. Fixed prices and hand it over to the commissary officer."

"Ah, but the poor fellow is in love with you, so you cheat him right and left."

She giggled and nodded her bright head.

"He's an old walrus, but you're right. He *is*, a little, anyway. He ignores an occasional short weight, a few kilograms here and there, but, my God, I have every family on the place to feed these days. Too many women, refugees, you know. They come here with all their children. I can't pay them full wages, either cash or kind, because they can't do a man's work."

He rode beside her, delighted with her. Under the fir trees it was dark and cold. Her voice sounded to him like the calling of a bird, clear and impudent in the morning.

"And so you've soured the soil, left the fields full of roots and stalks, forgot to stack hay around the wines, didn't cut enough firewood and we're losing pesetas hand over fist. Ah, well, what can you expect? Take them out of bed, away from the stove or off their knees and what good are they?"

She struck at him with her quirt, angry and laughing at the same time.

"You . . . army loafer! I've made more money this quarter than the estate has yielded since *grand*father died! How do you like that? Big mouths and broad backs, but not a brain in the whole lot of you! I'll race you home!"

"In this snow? You're crazy . . . wait for me!"

"Go to hell, soldier!"

Pedro watched as his sister swung the big dappled gelding, his father's horse, off between two great fir trunks and out into a lake of unbroken snow. The gelding moved in great, surging leaps, chesting the drifts and leaving a deep, churned trail. He followed her, whooping like a red Indian.

They crashed into the front hallway, stamping snow, and breathless with laughter. Pedro was surrounded with smiling servants, deafened by their welcome, yelping dogs, slamming doors and the high, clear voice of Connie rapping orders out like the chief steward at tax-collecting time. A great fire of pine logs seethed on the stone hearth, and a bowl of *café con leche* appeared on a silver tray. Connie laced it with Fundador cognac and handed it to him.

"Drink it, my brother. Then off with those wet boots and upstairs to pay your respects."

"Where will you be? We must talk."

"Out in the stables. We're cleaning the stalls today. We've got plenty of time to talk. Go see Father and Mother."

He drank the *café con leche* greedily and warmed himself at the fire. Connie drove the servants away like someone herding geese. She came back with the bottle of cognac and a glass. She finished the remainder of his coffee, licking the sweet foam from her upper lip with the tip of her tongue and staring at him over the brim of the bowl. He sipped the cognac.

"It's colder than I remembered."

"Very. It's going to be a miserable winter."

"How you speak. Like some old peasant wife on the out-farms."

She shrugged and finished the coffee. He held out the glass to her and watched in astonishment as she tossed it off, swallowed calmly and wiped her mouth with her knuckles.

"Easy! You'll get drunk."

"Huh. I've been up since four! It's almost time for lunch, my boy. Move over. I want to get warmed up before I go out to the stables."

They stood shoulder to shoulder, backs to the fire. He looked down on her blond head.

"Well, you look very dashing, I must say. But surely you haven't really joined them, Connie?"

"I have. Father refuses to speak to me. Not a word in weeks. The silent treatment. First, I snubbed the Falange. They gave us a bad time. All sorts of inventories and threats of confiscation. So, I decided to co-operate with them."

"Temporarily. In the army it's the same."

"They outnumber us. Even here in Navarre. They've gotten to all the young people. All this José Antonio business. A martyr. The Cause. You know."

"In the army it's the same."

The girl looked up at him and shook her head slightly.

"It won't be temporary. Not in the army, not here, not anywhere. The Falange is permanent. So I joined the women's auxiliary. I attend all the Party meetings and I'm secretary for the Winter Help programs. Food, clothing, blankets, homes, work, everything. I know what is going on and I've been able to hold the estate together . . . so far."

"And Father tolerates this . . . in austere silence."

"He is dying."

She said it in such a matter-of-fact tone that at first he did not comprehend. He shook her roughly by the shoulders. She stared into his eyes and nodded.

"It has been diagnosed as terminal cancer. It was never his liver, so it seems. He was furious when he found out. All those wasted years drinking

Vichy water instead of Logroño. He drank champagne for breakfast for a month, just to catch up. But now . . . he can't taste it. Everything tastes the same. He drinks just to kill the pain. In two weeks, he will be on morphine. Then . . ."

"Can't they do anything? Operate? There's France, Switzerland."

"Nothing can be done. You cannot cure cancer by taking it to the Alps. That's T.B."

"Does Mother . . . of course she knows."

"Yes. The papers have been drawn up by the lawyers. You will have power of attorney. Luckily, you're of age now."

"I suppose that *is* luck. Mother . . . ?"

"I don't think she'll outlive him by much," Connie said evenly. "She has given up."

"I don't believe it."

"You'll see. She just doesn't care to go on living."

Pedro groaned and shook his head.

"Why didn't you write to me?"

"I did. I have. A dozen times."

"I never got a thing. I could have requested leave earlier. I have only a few days. Then I'm posted to some mountaintop in Aragón, thousands of kilometers from here."

"That's a disaster."

"Everything is a disaster! Father, Mother, the war, the Movement."

"You see we must talk. Very seriously. If you can't *be* here, I need your advice. I need your signature on everything. Because . . ."

She stopped and thrust her boot at a brindle hunting hound that had nestled down beside her.

"Go away, Chico, you stink! . . . Because they are leaving us. The old ones. Father's friends have been very indiscreet. All this foolishness of the Royal Military Academy. *Ay*, what a mistake! Fortunately the name of the Conde de Gualvidal does not appear on any documents. I've searched through his papers very carefully."

"My God, Connie, if he finds that out!"

"I have destroyed some things. Is that why you're being posted to Aragón?"

"Partly. There are other problems. It's fair to say that we Carlists are being redistributed so that we can be assimilated more rapidly into the Nationalist movement. Just like the Reds have spread their Internationals around. Everything is reorganization and solidarity these days . . . while we here fall quietly to pieces."

His sister shook her head stubbornly.

"Nothing of the sort. I will show you the books."

"Books? I mean the people, Concepción, *our* people."

"Well, we must accept it. We . . . you and me, *we* are going to be

'our people,' as you say it. I will allow nothing to change. Nothing whatever. I have even managed to keep the horses. I had to promise all of the
next spring's foals and twenty burros. *Twenty!* I must have a truck, Pedro.
Steal me one."

"Later, all this later. I must see Father. Both of them. I'll find you."

"I'll be in the stables."

She left him, striding quickly across the stones, her short skirt swinging,
the hound Chico bounding at her side. The door boomed shut. He waited
a moment, gathering himself. Connie had dumped disaster on him like
someone discarding dishwater. She had accepted it, everything, and
passed the sorrow on to him, as one who has no further need of it.
Obviously, she had already given her tears before the altar of the family
chapel. Now, she would supervise the cleaning of the stables.

"Welcome back, Señorito Pedro!"

It was old Jacinto, the butler, slightly more palsied, his dim eyes wet
with tears. He fluttered around, trying to pick lint off Pedro's tunic.

"We can't say how happy it makes us to see you again! These have been
sad weeks, sad months. If it weren't for the Señorita . . ."

"Yes. She is to be obeyed in everything. Without question. You will
tell the rest of the servants that is my wish."

"Ah, then, you will be staying on? We all hoped so. We prayed for
it."

"No, Jacinto. I will return to the front. But everything will be as it has
been."

"Ah . . . not quite, Señorito Pedro. Forgive an old man for saying
so."

"Believe me. Spain will stay as Spain has been . . . at least this part of
it. No wind blows strong enough to tumble the mountains of Navarre."

"True, true. I have taken the liberty of laying out a riding costume.
I thought something informal, after so long in your uniform . . . not that
it doesn't become you . . ."

"Thank you. Now go and inform the Count and the Countess that I
beg permission to see them."

"They are waiting in great impatience, señorito."

The old man shuffled off. Pedro watched him leave. Twenty years
my father's senior, illiterate, half in his dotage, and he will live on to
toast his bones and tell his grandchildren of what it was like in the old
days, while my father, el Conde . . .

He left the fire and strode to the main staircase. He touched the suit of
armor, the gleaming carapace of antique steel that another Conde de
Gualvidal had worn at the Battle of Lepanto in the time of Don Juan of
Austria. The lapped joints were a masterwork, cunning and strong. He
tapped the breastplate and heard the cold steel ring. That was old Spain.
Now we have tanks, blind crawling caterpillars of steel. The lances are

broken in the dust, and there are no vultures in the sky . . . Junkers
and Fiats, instead.

He drew himself up and pushed open the heavy oaken door. Sunlight
streamed into the big cold room. The curtains had been drawn back from
the huge, canopied bed, but the fire barely took the chill off. He walked
so that his father could see him. The sight of the wasted figure, the face
like a skull against the pillow appalled him. His mother was living a dream;
his father was fighting against the final nightmare. The only thing that
seemed alive was the dark, darting glance. His father's arm stirred. Pedro
bent and brushed his lips on a hand light as a bird.

"My father . . ."

"My son!"

Pedro straightened. His father indicated a chair by the bedside.

"Not too close. I find that I have begun to stink."

"Is it . . . bad, Father?"

"It is disgusting. I am rotting and can do nothing but wait until this
thing has done with me. Enough. You look thin, hard, dark in the face.
A campaigner. You like the life?"

"No, Father."

"A military career was once possible for a gentleman. No longer.
Well, this madness will pass. Jacinto, the poor old fool, blurted out, first
thing, that you were going back. That is not possible, of course. I will
dictate a letter today. There are persons of prominence and family. Fal
Conde . . . but I forget. Yes, you will go back, then. You obey orders."

"I obey orders. Even the orders I do not approve of."

"That is the meaning of obedience. I find that Concepción has not yet
learned this fact."

"She is magnificent, my father."

The head nodded, almost imperceptibly. The eyes flashed with pride.

"Of course," the Conde said. "It is expected that she be magnificent.
You must help her now. Your mother fancies that she is dying too, and
I suspect she will arrange to have that happen out of sheer will . . . and
feminine sentimentality. I had expressed my extreme displeasure at her
attitude. But, women . . . they get their way . . . damn them! Imagine
wanting to die . . . what a perversity! Tell me about you, my son.
I want to know everything. I dine on gossip. The only thing that has not
lost its savor."

Pedro talked; his father listened. A nurse appeared with medicine. The
Conde waved it away and demanded cognac. He drank two glasses, then
swallowed the medicine, his face contorted with displeasure.

"Go on, my son. What happened after that?"

Pedro talked about the Red tanks at Esquivias. The thin skin of his
father's face puckered.

"I know exactly how you felt. This thing came out of the mists at me, too. How sudden it is to meet death. How surprising! 'What,' we say, 'so soon? but I am not ready for you yet!' And then . . . then time slows down. I have discovered that it takes a lifetime to die."

Pedro told him of his temporary assignment to a German artillery battery firing on Madrid. To the Germans it was a test of equipment.

"It will take a long spoon indeed for this little Franco to dine at any table set by Herr Hitler. The bald Italian with the chin . . . he is a posturing fool. The Mediterranean an Italian lake, indeed! They are a nation of gondoliers and cobblers."

Pedro told him of the steady growth of the Fascist Party. The Count groaned.

"Your mother reads me the drivel in the papers. Primo de Rivera's son made a decent death. Better than his father . . . trotting from brothel to confessional . . . and right back again. God has spared me that humiliation, for which I humbly thank Him. I think you may be right. The Falange will be Spain's cancer. Perhaps in time that sort of cancer may be cured . . . or cut out with a knife."

"Then you think Concepción did the right thing? By joining them?"

"Don't be absurd! Her action is a flat betrayal of the family! A Gualvidal in the market place with these petty shopkeepers, middle-class riffraff? *Unheard of!* The girl has lost her wits. Find her a husband, I beg of you. That's what she needs. A stallion in the stall. She'll forget about politics and get on with the work here. She is very cunning, very strong, my little one with the bright hair. But she needs a man. Sooner than I thought. Take care of it."

"Yes, Father."

"Go on. Show me these photographs of this Communist anti-Christ from the coal mines. Thirty thousand were rounded up in '34. Why didn't the Republic shoot them to the last man, woman, and brat? Asturias is a dirty place, anyway. No one wants to live there. I say, track him down like the dog he is and let his blood!"

"Quietly, Father."

"I need one more glass of cognac . . . then I sleep. Not long, but enough. Thank you."

Pedro told him of the priest on the train.

"You are wrong, my son. He is exactly the type this sad old country needs. Not this gang of satined eunuchs. One of the great errors of my life was to allow your mother to select the family chaplain. This fellow now . . . I can't even think of his name . . . a bloodless little slug. Half of the clerics in this nation look as though they were born beneath a rock somewhere, the other half behave like clerks in some celestial savings bank. The people hate them because they are useless fellows. You should have taken this priest's name and address, his order, his superior's name. He is what we need, a blacksmith in a cassock. Believe in his God or he'll break your face. Leave his people alone or he'll bite them off you . . . Find him, bring him here . . . throw this slug out on his ear. Too bad there are not a million Ortegas in Spain . . . Go on, tell me more . . ."

The light breath came through the thin, pale lips. Pedro pulled up the blanket and stood. He tiptoed to the door and looked back. The dark eyes were open, staring at him.

"I'll be back later, Father. Rest now."

"As you wish . . . Conde de Gualvidal . . . You'll make a good one. You'll do . . . you'll both do, my little one with the bright hair . . ."

Pedro closed the door and leaned against the solid panels. He felt as though he had been struck, brain, heart, and bowels. He wandered, dazed, to his own room. The map with the little pins was still on the wall. A tight cluster of bits of red and gold around Madrid.

Pedro looked at the map. A bit of thread ran from Pamplona to Zaragoza to Samosierra to Esquivias to Toledo to Madrid to Burgos. There the thread hung, dribbling down the map. He moved a pin up into Navarre and pushed it in, wound the thread around it. He had covered quite a bit of Spain in six months. He looked to the east and found Teruel, the capital of Aragón. He drove a pin there and bound the thread to it. Then he fiddled with the loose end, swinging it, to see how far it would reach. How odd. Just short of the French frontier. *La dulce Francia* . . . sweet France. The Great War of 1914–19. They shall not pass!

No pasarán! No pasarán!

He hummed the tune, muttered the words to the Republican song:

> *Los moros quieren pasar.*
> *Los moros quieren pasar.*
> *Los moros quieren pasar.*
> *Mamita mía, no pasa nadie, no pasa nadie!*

The Moors want to pass, but, my little mother, nobody passes, nobody passes.

It was a proud song, a good song, a good Spanish song, new words to an old tune. But it wasn't true, because it couldn't be true. Somebody passed, somebody got through; there was no defense, no counterattack against death. Death passed, *mamita mía*, no matter how hard, how long you resisted, what you believed or hoped for. Death had passed through the forests, fields and family of the Conde de Gualvidal.

He thrust himself away from the map and tore off his tunic. He yanked the bell cord. Jacinto tottered into the room.

"Yes, Señorito Pedro?"

"Rubber boots, Jacinto! And a pair of old corduroys. Hold lunch back until we finish cleaning out the stables."

BOOK FOUR

Volunteers for Liberty
December 1936 – January 1937

In Barcelona, the Communists propagandized for the abolition of the the revolutionary councils favored by the Anarchists. Despite their few members, the Communists had achieved great influence in the central government of the Republic of Catalonia. The Party leaders had remained in besieged Madrid when Azana's fled to Valencia.

Russian cargo ships off-loaded trucks, tanks, field cannon, and food at Barcelona and Valencia. One and a half billion pesetas' worth of monetary gold was transferred from the Republic to the Russian seaport of Odessa. The Soviet Union's representative to the Non-Intervention Committee declared that his nation could not consider itself bound to any agreement to any greater extent than the other participants, by implication Italy and Nazi Germany. Count Ciano, Mussolini's Foreign Minister, conferred with Adolf Hitler in Berlin. The two Fascist states agreed to recognize the Nationalists as the official government of Spain— once Madrid capitulated.

President Franklin Delano Roosevelt urged congressional support for a bill banning arms shipments to Spain. The Embargo Act passed through the Senate by 81 to 0 and the House by 406 to 1. Generalísimo Franco remarked that the American President had behaved "like a true gentleman."

In the Soviet Union, more than one hundred members of the Communist Party were arrested for acts of treason and conspiracy. The NKVD began its purge of the officers of the Red Army and other "Trotskyites."

In ten days, more than 15,000 died when the Nationalists attempted
to cut the Corunna highway, the lifeline of Madrid. Exhausted, both
sides entrenched. Fighting slowed to stalemate.

They met at the Greyhound bus terminal in New York City on the
afternoon of December twenty-fourth. Schwartz arrived first, nearly an
hour before the bus down from Boston was due. He bought a copy of
the *Daily News* and a copy of the *Daily Worker*, sat down on a hard
wooden bench, and unbuttoned his overcoat. The waiting room was
stale and stuffy. Through the dirty windows he could see the crowds on
the sidewalks, the decorations and the lights. A Salvation Army band
played hymns on the street corner. He read about the CIO in the
News and about the defense of Madrid in the *Worker*. Comrades Ford
and Browder were to address an "Arms for Spain" rally at the Garden.
revolutionary councils favored by the Anarchists. Despite their few
   Schwartz had a list of names in the inside of his suit jacket. The
name at the top was WHITE, A. J. His own name was the last of five.
On the back of the sheet of paper was the address of an Army-Navy
store on Third Avenue, downtown. The others were all from out of the
city, so Schwartz was to take them to the store to buy equipment for
a "camping trip." After that, they were to do what White told them.
   A loudspeaker announced the arrival of the bus from Boston. Schwartz
stood up, holding a folded newspaper in each hand. He glanced around,
a conspirator, wondering if some of the other men in the terminal
were there to meet still other volunteers for Spain. It was hard to say.
Everybody looked pretty ordinary. He walked to the gate. He had been
told to meet the Greyhound from Boston, then wait until the bus from
Chicago came in. White would be on the Chicago bus. He was in
charge. The ship, the French liner *Normandie*, sailed on the day after
Christmas.
   The passengers came through the gate: a grandmother with two
children on walking harnesses scrambling and tugging like dogs, an
old man, a cluster of people, then about six men dressed in suits and
hats, carrying overcoats. Schwartz waited and lit a nonchalant cigarette
with trembling fingers. One of the men hesitated and walked over to him.
   "Hey, bud. You know where there's an Army-Navy store?"
   "Sure."
Schwartz walked back into the waiting room and sat down, staring
straight ahead. He ran over the list of names in his mind. A name for
an Irishman with gap-teeth, thin red hair, and green eyes who said,
   You-know-whey-ah-they-ahs-in-Ahmy-Navy-stoah?
   The man stood before Schwartz.
   "Gotta get a pack a butts. I'm all out. Stick around, kid."
   "Sure."
Schwartz was positive he saw *Mahoney, J*—that was the Irishman's

name—give somebody a high-sign. Five men moved together out through the exit. Three of them *saluted!* Schwartz jumped up and sidled over to the tobacco counter. Mahoney stuffed a carton into his jacket pocket and turned around.

"Hey, kid. What's up?"

"What's up? Listen, what's the big idea of the salutes, huh? For Crissake's, you want everybody in town to know?"

"But them's the Flaherty brothers, kid. Old friends, see. Relax."

"We don't need a *parade!*"

"I'm Jim Mahoney. Pleased to meetcha, kid."

"Norman Schwartz, comrade. We have to wait."

"What for? The Flaherty boys and them others is off to get their kit right now, then have a few, a good steak dinner, take in the shows and the bright lights, get it?"

Schwartz tried to stare the Irishman down. Mahoney shuffled excitedly up and down the dirty floor spattered with flattened cigarette butts and bits of tickets and chewing gum papers. He smoked and chewed gum at the same time. Schwartz cleared his throat.

"Some of the comrades must have the wrong idea. This isn't no circus, Mahoney. We're supposed to be inconspicuous."

"In where?"

"Like no one notices us, see?"

"Sure. Okay, kid."

"My name is Norman. After Norman Thomas. Call me Normy."

"Sure thing, kid. Well, shall we park the carcass here or . . ."

"We can have coffee or something. The Chicago bus isn't due for about thirty minutes."

"Coffee? Awright. Plenty of time to rush the growler later."

Schwartz didn't understand, but marched Mahoney to the lunchstand and ordered two coffees and two doughnuts. They sat on stools and began, slowly at first, to talk.

Schwartz smoked and played with his spoon and listened, trying, as he put it to himself, to get a handle on Mahoney's politics. The more he listened, the more handles there seemed to be, but the closest the Irishman came to politics was to declare, amazingly enough, his admiration for the boss of Boston's seventeenth ward, James Michael Curley.

Mahoney chewed gum and smoked and kidded the waitresses and talked through his nose, wide-mouthed and grinning, snapping the brim of a brand-new hat up and down. He was twenty years old and a worker in a Brighton steel warehouse. His only grievance against the system and the bosses seemed to be the fact that it was illegal for him to drive one of the overhead Shepherd cranes until his twenty-first birthday.

Mahoney offered the waitress a stick of Juicy Fruit and seemed annoyed when she refused. That got him off on the subject of women, a girl named Cathleen Sullivan from Dorchester. Mahoney had "talked off her bloomers" after nearly a year of trying, and now she had "a cake in the oven" and Old Sullivan with "blood in his eye," although it was true as "God made Paddy's pig" that Mahoney had been neither the first nor the last, but rather "the light of her life."

Schwartz nibbled cold sweet coffee off the tip of his steel spoon and shrugged, disgusted.

"You mean you volunteered just to get away? From this girl and her father?"

"Naw, now, kid, you don't know Mahoney. The day a Sullivan makes a Mahoney say 'uncle' ain't dawned yet. I could have stayed and seen it through, priests, relatives and all fought to a standstill. Yeh, and filled her up again, too, without ever a gold band. No, it wasn't that. Da was with the IRA, see?"

"Da?"

"My old man. Lost an arm at the Post Office during the April rising."

Schwartz nodded, mystified. He straightened on his stool, looked at the clock again and lit a cigarette.

"I was in the National Guard. You?"

"Nah. When's the bus, kid?"

"Kid" annoyed Schwartz. Mahoney was barely two years older than he was, yet treated him with a kind of genial contempt.

"Be here in a few minutes. We obey orders, see? Stay put. That's it."

"I get it. If the others don't show, frig 'em, huh? We'll take on the lot of them."

"We won't even get on the damned boat if this guy doesn't have the tickets for us. What's the IRA your father was in, a union?"

"Union? What the hell for? The Irish Republican Army, kid! Jeez, where you been? My old man fought the British, and when I read in the *Post* that the English wasn't gonna help out in Spain, I says to him 'The Irish must, Da. It'll be one in the eye for England and one for the priests as well.' 'Ram it up and break it off inside, Jimmy!' he says, and off we went to Oak Square and opened a keg of nails. Next day when I could see again, I talked around. About twenty boys were off, I went to the hall and seen this guy. He gimme a ticket and here I am."

"What do you know about Spain, Mahoney?"

"Not a Christly thing, kid. Why?"

"How can you fight, if you don't know what Fascism is?"

Mahoney rolled his chewing gum and stared at him. He put on his new hat, took it off and smoothed his hair.

"Well? An Irishman is a born fighter. Just point me in the right direction, kid, and watch me go to town. Hey, what's your last name? Schwartz? A Kraut name. You a Yid?"

Schwartz set his spoon down in his saucer, began to take out a cigarette and changed his mind. Mahoney knocked his arm.

"*Are* you, huh?"

"I'm Jewish by birth. But not by religion."

"Are you kiddin'? But who ever heard of Yids as fighters?"

"Ever hear of Barney Ross?"

"Sure."

"Well?"

"Name another."

"Norman Schwartz."

Mahoney laughed and clouted him on the shoulder.

"You're all right, kid. Hey, didn't that thing just say Chicago bus?"

"Yer *ahh-raight* yourself, Baloney. Come on, let's go."

"Baloney is it? Watch that stuff."

"Mahoney-Baloney."

"Watch that crap, kid."

Schwartz pushed through the crowded waiting room, trailed by Mahoney. It was like a game. Yid the Kid and Mahoney-Baloney. Schwartz stuffed his newspapers under his arms, drew his face solemn and waited outside the gate. Mahoney butted him from behind.

"Easy, comrade."

"Don't call me that no more."

"What? Comrade?"

"The other . . . what you said."

"Let's have a little discipline, huh, first."

Mahoney muttered and looked around at the women. The terminal was jammed now. Men, women, children, most of them carrying gay Christmas packages jostled against them. Schwartz could hear the Salvation Army band playing. Mahoney began to hum along and mutter.

"Come on, youse guys. Let's get outta here. Half the world's got a snootful, and we ain't even got our kit yet."

"Shhh, will you?"

The Chicago passengers poured out through the gate like cattle to market. Schwartz stood still, staring straight ahead, cool and aloof, furious at Mahoney. The Irishman bobbed and fidgeted, snatching his hat off and flailing it around, arguing and apologizing to people he struck with it. Schwartz spun around and grabbed him.

"Come *on!* Stop all that!"

"Where the hell are they, then?"

"I dunno."

A heavy voice spoke behind Schwartz, startling him so that he dropped his newspapers. Mahoney brayed with laughter.

"Can you tell me where there's any Army-Navy store?"

Schwartz bent for the papers, straightened slowly, seeing thick-soled shoes, dark pants, dark overcoat. He thought he saw brown gloves. He looked up into the face of a broad-shouldered, bull-necked man.

"You must be Mahoney, right?"

"Yeh."

"And you, comrade?"

"Schwartz. Normy Schwartz."

"Where are the others?" the man said, looking around.

"I dunno. You mean Durton and Cubeta?"

"That's right. No show, huh?"

"Not yet," Schwartz said. "You're . . ."

"Andy White."

Mahoney snorted and took off his hat. White stared at him evenly.

"Something botherin' you, buddy?"

Mahoney shook his head quickly and looked at Schwartz. White stared thoughtfully around the waiting room.

"Cubeta's a Puerto Rican comrade and Durton had a mustache last time I seen him. Well, they ain't here. Let's go anyway."

Mahoney signaled with his face and hands: *Is this him?* Schwartz shrugged and nodded: *I guess so.*

The man in charge of their group for the next two days was a six-foot-two Negro.

"I said let's go, comrades. We got places to go and things to do. Where's this store at, Schwartz?"

"Third. We take a bus."

"Right."

Schwartz and Mahoney hung on the straps in the crowded bus. White stood half hidden by the other passengers. He ducked from time to time to check the street signs. Mahoney whispered.

"This nigger's gonna take us to Spain?"

"Shhh! I guess so."

"I didn't know *anybody* was goin . . ."

"*We're* goin."

"Well, sure, but . . ."

"You can change your mind, Baloney, if that's what's got you."

"I never been with boogies, that's all. They keeps to themselves down on Columbus and Mass Ave. White, huh? Some name."

The Army-Navy store was nearly empty. White lead them through the cluttered aisles and asked for somebody named Maury. Maury appeared, a young man smoking a cigar.

"Yes, fellas?"

"We need outfits," White said. "Camping gear. Everything."

The clerk glanced at them and nodded.

"We sold quite a bit lately. Enough for maybe a hundred fellas."

Schwartz and Mahoney elbowed each other. A hundred volunteers! White nodded.

"We needs sheepskin jackets, good boots, shirts, pants, blankets, and all that."

"Well, we keep some camping equipment sorta ready-packed, you know? Down here. Everything fits right into a suitcase. Made out of fiberboard. When you're done with it, you got no loss, you get me? I mean, you don't want no pigskin suitcase for camping, right? Let's get sizes and see what we got."

Schwartz and Mahoney tore off their overcoats and jackets. The clerk measured them and another clerk flipped through piles of shirts and pants, all khaki-colored. Mahoney wanted cowboy boots. White shook his head.

"Cotton socks on first, wools over. Lace-ups and a big jar a Neet's Foot paste. Make sure they're big enough. You got ammunition belts and such?"

"At the back. Walter'll show you. Thought there was five in this party?"

White shrugged.

"Maybe they went on ahead."

"Arrange for the guides, huh?"

"Yeah."

It was dark when they were fitted to White's satisfaction. He stuffed an extra sweater into each of the cheap fiberboard suitcases and a rubberized rain jacket that folded flat. He took out a worn wallet and peeled off some bills, hesitated, and handed Schwartz a dollar.

"Go down the block and get three jars of George Washington Instant Coffee."

"Coffee? What for?"

"Do like I say. Just remembered it. Don't get lost now, hear?"

He grinned for the first time, a flash of big, square, white teeth. Schwartz took the dollar and hurried outside, half inside his overcoat. By the time he came back, Mahoney and White were standing on the sidewalk with the three suitcases. White unstrapped them right there on the sidewalk and placed the jars of coffee in each. He stood up.

"Buddy in the NMU told me that, before I left Chicago. He was just back from Le Havre."

"Where?"

"France."

White started up the sidewalk, striding easily, the suitcase swinging from his hand. Schwartz and Mahoney toiled after him, tilted and panting, past the tinseled windows through the red flicker and green drench of Christmas lights. The bars were filled and roaring.

"Where to now?"

"Get rooms," White said.

Schwartz and Mahoney looked at each other for the twentieth time since the Chicago bus had pulled in to the Greyhound terminal. Rooms for all of them?

"Where at?" Schwartz ventured.

They paused at a stop light. Traffic hissed past, honking.

"The Why-Em-See-Ay," White said calmly. "Where you think? The Plaza?"

"They won't let Schwartzie in, will they?" Mahoney said, watching the traffic carefully.

"I'll tell them Why-Em-See-Ays that he's a convert."

They marched across the city, Schwartz and Mahoney tottering and swinging the heavy suitcases from one dragged-numb arm to the other. When the lights were red, they asked White questions.

"You been to France?"

"Yeh."

"Can you *parlez-vous?*"

"Some."

"You musta been in the Army, huh?"

"Till I deserted . . . Light's green. For-*hard* . . ."

Deserted? Mahoney was wild with indignation. They had never told him he'd be tramping the streets of New York on Christmas Eve with a skinny little sad-faced Jew-boy and a buck-nigger who'd run off from Uncle Sam's own Army. The goddamned suitcase weighed a friggin ton. Why didn't they grab a taxi or break for a dish of suds? It was cold as a landlady's thigh, too.

"What was you in the Army?"

"A machine gunner."

"No crap?"

"Believe it or not."

"You ever been to Spain?"

"Yeh."

"In the *Army?*"

"Naw. On ships. I been a seaman. Still am."

"No foolin'!"

"Can you speak spick, comrade?"

White set down his suitcase and folded his arms.

"Now look here, you two. I ain't gonna play no more twenty questions, get it? I been to Bilbao and Barcelona and Cádiz. Mostly outta Shreveport. I worked railroadin in Texas and learned some from Mexicans there, doin some organizin on the side, like. Before I started workin freighters as a seaman. I'm thirty years old and I got a woman in

Chicago and two tads, both boys. That hold you till we gets to the Why-Em-See-Ays? Okay? Less march, then."

It seemed to Mahoney that they had walked for hours when he saw the YMCA sign in burning neon. Both his arms felt pulled loose at the shoulders. He was soaked with sweat and panting too hard to talk. He lay against the counter while White got rooms. The place seemed full of men of all sizes, many of them with cheap fiberboard suitcases, moving about in groups of four or five. White tossed him a key.

"You're in with Cubeta. He and Durton already been here and gone. Gettin tanked somewheres, maybe. Cubeta'll bring Ernie home all right. José don't speak much English, Mahoney, but then you don't either. You and me's roomies, Schwartz. Let's get this stuff up and go eat."

They had beer and steaks with french-fries and salad with apple pie and ice cream for dessert. White paid the bill. Schwartz, half buzzed on the beer, leaned back and swatted his belly.

"Some feed! And we eat free on the ship, huh? Lemme see the tickets, huh?"

White produced them from inside his jacket and put them down side by side between the coffee cups. Schwartz bobbed his head. There he was, Norman Schwartz, in a third-class cabin.

"How many in a cabin?"

"Four. We'll stow somebody somewheres else."

Mahoney lit a cigarette, dragged in the smoke and let it out through his nose slowly, like George Raft.

"Sure don't seem like Christmas Eve."

"It *ain't*, for me!"

"That's different. For you. I was thinkin . . . either of you notice a Catholic church around here?"

"Two blocks down. Turn left out the door. You comin back here, Mahoney?"

"Yeah. Well, I might take in a show somewhere. See ya around, huh?"

He went out. The radio was playing Christmas carols. Schwartz watched White count his money.

"Uh, maybe we should take in a show, too, huh?"

"Tomorra. Sleep tonight."

"Maybe I'd better go after Mahoney-Baloney. Keep an eye on him you know. He'll get lost. He don't know the city."

"He's goin to a Mass, Schwartz. You feel like tellin the beads tonight?"

"No," Schwartz said, "but a guy oughta look out for his comrades."

"His comrades, huh?"

White leaned back in his chair and stretched, nipped a cigar from some inside pocket and stuck it in the corner of his mouth. He lit it and sat smoking, his broad, pink palms locked behind his close-clipped head. His thick lids drooped. Schwartz flushed and shifted nervously.

"Lemme tell you something, Schwartz. What's your first name? Normy? Okay. Normy. I seen Mahoney before. Every place I been. He'll get himself to Mass tonight, then off to the nearest suds-shop. You don't worry about Mahoney finding no 'comrades.' Mackerel-snappers, they stick together, like . . . well, two Irishmen could find each other in the middle of nowhere. One be's the barkeep, the other his best customer. Somebody'll fetch him back, no fear."

"I guess you're right. It's just . . . he's a kid, that's all. Got no discipline. In the YCL, we always . . ."

"Yeh? Well, been a long way from Chicago."

"You goin back, to sleep now?"

"Yeah. And day afta tomorra I'll be on my way to Spain."

"How come you're goin?"

White looked at Schwartz, chewed his cigar and stood up.

"Cause I missed Ethiopia, buddy. I ain't gonna miss Spain. Let's get outta here and get some sleep."

Schwartz went to sleep at once, flat on his back and snoring softly. White punched up his pillow and lay propped, thinking. Most of the others came in when the early movies let out. He heard them walking up and down the hall, slamming doors and talking. They seemed pretty serious-minded, which was a good thing.

The room was clean and cheap and near the docks, near enough to hoof it, even if the weather turned bad. He stared up at the ceiling, wishing he had something to read. He had left a lot of good books back in Chicago, not just Party literature, either, but books he had picked up or bought or people had given him over the years, like Upton Sinclair's *The Jungle* and Norris' *The Octopus*.

The sisters at the orphan's home had taught him to read, one in particular, Sister Angelica, a plump, patient nun with a big white headdress who smelled of yellow soap. He had wanted to know about the big war in France, then, and she had taught him to read from newspapers, provided he knelt and prayed with her for the priests martyred in Belgium. But he hadn't really known about books, as such, except the Bible, until he had run off and hitchhiked across New York into Massachusetts to the knitting mills in Lawrence and Lowell. He had got there just after the big trouble with the Wobblies, and there were a few who had stayed on. He had got a job as a bobbin-boy and worked for more than a year. A white man named "Mac," a Wobbly with a scarred face and blue eyes like crazed marbles, half-wild from nightsticks in the head, had haunted the mills, a floor-sweeper until somebody caught him sticking up little posters of wooden shoes. It was the wooden shoes that made him look "Mac" up, finding him after a few days in a printing shop. The wooden shoes meant *sabotage*, wrecking the machines because they exploited people. Only he thought then it was "exploding" people. He had kept on about the wooden shoes, until "Mac" got a copy of a book called *Hans Brinker*, about a Dutch boy who skated in canals and didn't explode anyone. After that, it was a little red book of songs that "Mac" made him memorize. "Union Maid," the one about Joe Hill . . .

> *Don't waste time to mourn for me,*
> *Just go and organize!*

And the one he had liked best, because of the funny words:

> *There once was a union maid,*
> *Who said she wasn't afraid*
> *Of the goons and the ginks,*
> *And the company finks,*
> *And the soldiers on parade.*

Then one payday he had done what "Mac" asked him to, a handful of gravel and sand dropped into the spindle gears of the bobbin machine. The thread on every bobbin had snapped; he had been caught at once and dragged into the storeroom by the section foreman and the assistant timekeeper. They beat him good with their belts. The sound of the machines had drowned him out when he screamed. He still had scars on his back where the buckles had punctured him. He had crawled off to find "Mac," but the white man had been arrested. White's rent was paid until the end of the week, so he stayed in bed, drinking milk. Then he hopped a freight to Buffalo. Buffalo, Syracuse, Chicago, Pittsburgh, Philly, Detroit, Toledo, St. Louis. He worked ore boats in Detroit and lifted seaman's papers from a dead man he found in an alley. Three months later he was in Shreveport, an all-right place for jobs and for living, if you stayed in the colored section. He worked banana boats to Guatemala and Panama for a while and nearly died from a tarantula bite that left a little pitted hole in his left arm that he liked to tell his women was a bullet hole.

He heaved gravel and worked as a gandy-dancer in Texas with a crew of Mexicans. It was brutal work for a dollar a day, six days a week. He quit and joined the Army, deserted after six months, and went across the border. There was politics there, too, and he had helped blow up a mail train, but got cheated out of his share of the money. He shipped out of Vera Cruz for France and Spain. There were organizers and union men on all the ships. He ended up in New York at a school run by the Communist Party. They got him a union card in his own name, and he started to move around. He organized on the South Side in Philly, along the docks down at the river there and did so well that they moved him to Chicago. Four years in Chicago as an organizer, inside the CIO, but always for the Party. He had been lucky, jailed only twice, both short sentences, but by that time he was too well known and he stayed in the office mostly, except at nights when he was a grievance-man for restaurants and hotel kitchen help. He made thirty-two dollars a week, good money, and even wrote up a few things that got printed.

The Party had become his life. He wasn't the only black man in-terested, either. He met first dozens, then hundreds, always in the big cities, longshoremen, laundry workers, factory hands, yardbirds, Red Caps and porters on the sleeping cars, pearl-divers and pot-wallopers, coffee, brown, and black, dusty African purple, and some so light, "pinkies," that they passed as white men. He knew white men, too, organizers, secretaries, agitators, and dumb rank-and-filers. But they stuck together, white or black. They called him "comrade" and meant it, mostly. He liked many of them, worked hard with them and sipped beer and listened to ball games. The two times he got busted, the Party had a lawyer and got him off easy, ninety days and sixty days. When he was in jail they brought him books and Party newspapers. He organized half his tier the second time, and twenty-three of them came to Party headquarters and signed up, soon as they got out. That was when they raised his pay to thirty-two bucks, same as the white men.

The Communist Party was good to the black man and good *for* the black man. He went to meetings and marched on May Day and fought the cops. He voted and learned the way to talk right. The Party was serious, no fooling around, but the Chicago leaders were smart, too. They never asked him to go South, not even back to Shreveport. He was a Northerner, and they knew he'd just get into trouble or get killed. He didn't know how to act all meeky and muckle-mouthed like some cotton-chopper down in Georgia.

The Party hadn't told him to go to Spain, hadn't even asked or suggested. O'Brien had been surprised, not happy, had more or less tried to talk him out of it. They wanted him to go out to the coast, San Diego and the Salinas Valley to organize the Mex stoop-labor, first, and then work up the coast to San Francisco and Seattle, longshoremen and seamen, an important job, a really big thing. But he turned it down.

He could hear voices outside in the street, loud talk, laughter, and singing. He pulled on his pants and looked at his watch. Almost two o'clock. He must have fallen asleep or dozed off, anyway, with the lights on. He opened the door and stepped out into the narrow hall. He turned left and walked to the end where the window and fire escape were. He opened the window and winced away from the cold air. The city rumbled and muttered, flecked with bright lights. At the mouth of the alley, five or six men hung together in a weak-legged group, holding each other up and singing Irish songs.

"Hey, Mahoney! Mahoney! Come up this way."

He shouted for nearly five minutes before they finally heard him in between verse and chorus of "Galway Bay." A figure came wobbling up the alley and stared up.

"Who's 'at?"

"Me. White. Come up the fire escape."

"Bastid's locked us out. What kind way's 'at to treat sojers?"

"Who else is with you, Mahoney?"

"Ernie Durton and José."

"That's awright, then. Them others?"

"Friends. Good boys. They're comin along with us, see? All fixed up."

"Get rid of them. You three get up here before the night-manager calls a cop."

"A copper, is it? Where? Point me at him. Point me at him!"

"Stay right there. Don't move, understand?"

White cursed Mahoney softly and went back into the room for his shoes and overcoat. He could hear them singing again as he got dressed. He ducked out onto the fire escape and started down, cautious and cursing again, his heels gonging on the steel rungs. It was the kind with a counterweight on the last flight. When he stepped on it, it sagged down into the dark alley. He clung to the railing. It swung up again, just beyond the reach of the men waiting below. He moved out three more steps; the fire escape swung down and stayed. José Cubeta said something in Spanish and stood on the bottom step, pushing and pulling at the others. Mahoney began to sing.

"Mahoney!"

"What?"

"Get your ass up here! Tell them other bums to beat it."

"Beat it, bums."

"Jimmy, lad, another run through 'Danny Boy,' and then round the corner for a spot. The dark jintleman will hold yer ladder."

"Mahoney! José, get them two up here. That's an order!"

Cubeta pulled and shoved in the darkness. He seemed as drunk as the others and only identified Durton by stroking faces until he found a mustache. Mahoney seemed to be a happy drunk, not a fighter. When Durton went stumbling up the steel ladder, he followed, humming to himself. Cubeta pushed the other men away from the escape and followed. They swayed and scraped up to White on the first landing. The last section of the escape lifted up and clashed. A few lights were on now, and heads were out of windows, cheering them on. White drove them through the window into the hall. Schwartz was there, wrapped in a blanket, his dark hair standing straight up like a rooster's comb. He glowered sleepily at Mahoney.

"You oughta be court-martialed, Baloney!"

"Christ's blessing be on you on this, His birthday, Schwartzie! Hey, José. José-Can-You-See?"

"Not too good, man," the little Cuban said, leaning against the wall. Durton looked around smiling, as though he had arranged this little gathering all by himself. He insisted that everyone shake hands with everyone else. Schwartz refused at first, saying that he could not condone a breech of discipline. White flapped his arms.

"Get to bed, all of you. What the hell the Why-Em-See-Ays gonna think, huh? You three booze-hounds report to me first thing in the morning. Now go sleep it off. Ernie, gimme that jug."

"What jug? Huh? Huh? Wha' jug?"

"You got a pint on you. Hand it over."

"My mennecine. Doctor tole me take mennecine."

"Gimme it."

Durton surrendered a full pint of Four Roses. White gave it to Schwartz. Mahoney leaned against White.

"You know somethin'? There's a *Jap* comin' with us! Or maybe a Chink. I think he said Jap. Jack somebody."

"Off. Jack Off," Durton said and sat down. White kicked him once, and he stood up again.

"Just restin'."

"Go to sleep. That's Jack Shirai. He won't hurt you, Mahoney, relax."

They stumbled off to their rooms. Schwartz followed White, carrying the bottle of whiskey as if it were a bomb.

"I guess I'd better just pour this down the sink."

"Like hell. Tomorra's . . . I mean today's Christmas. Just put it on the floor, huh?"

"You mean you condone drunkenness on duty?"

"Now look, kid. No one's on duty, see? You just let me take care a this. I'll go see Phil Bard in the morning."

"Who's he?"

"The group leader."

"They oughta be punished. Discipline begins with the self."

"Yeah. Well, go to sleep, Schwartz."

"I'd really rather talk. There's a lot to talk about."

"Listen, it takes four-five-six days to get to France. You have time to talk all you want. I'm half froze and sleepy."

"Oh, all right . . ."

The next day, Christmas, was quiet. The men kept close to the YMCA, walked down to the dock to see the ship, went to the movies, ate in nearby restaurants and visited from room to room. Cubeta, who looked like a sick dog, Durton, and Mahoney were "talked to."

White found a teacher who had been a seaman, a lawyer from New York, a longshoreman, a writer from Milwaukee, a dressmaker from Seventh Avenue, an ex-Navy man, retired after twenty years' service and a young man from Tennessee with an engineering degree who could speak French. There were others that White didn't much like the looks of, but on the whole he was satisfied. The average age seemed to be around twenty-five; many of the men had union experience, mostly through the CIO. There were some members of the Party and some of the younger ones, like Schwartz, were in the YCL. He didn't ask about the rest. They had volunteered for Spain, as he had, and that was good enough. He was not the only Negro, either.

He went with Schwartz, Mahoney and Cubeta uptown to the after-noon show at the Roxy. Schwartz wanted to see the ushers do their close-order drill, and couldn't understand why the others weren't im-pressed. After the movie, they wandered around and looked at the windows. Cubeta disappeared to call his family in Tampa, and Schwartz finally found a bookstore, a secondhand place that was open because the furnace had broken down and the owner was worried about pipes freezing. Mahoney bought a Spanish phrase book and a little dictionary. Schwartz found a military manual dated 1885 filled with drawings of a soldier in a shako at port-arms, present-arms and parade-rest. White bought a guide book to Spain with faded photographs of Segovia, and a Boy Scout manual. Mahoney wanted to go to a taxi-dance hall, but Schwartz talked him out of it.

They broke up again at the YMCA. There was a note for White to come to one of the rooms for a cell meeting. He went, said very little, and listened. The group wasn't as well organized as he had first thought. Although Bard had been appointed leader, there was no real chain of command or responsibility. They debated for a while and then decided to run the outfit on a loose kind of trade-union democracy. The im-portant thing was to get everyone on the ship, through French customs to Paris, and then to a place called Perpignan near the border. They would cross the frontier, if there weren't any hitches, by buses supplied by French comrades.

They ate turkey dinners and went to bed early. Schwartz had been to a meeting of the YCL and was so hoarse from talking that he croaked.

The ship was supposed to sail at noon. They boarded the *Normandie* after breakfast, ninety-six men, all carrying fiberboard suitcases, climbing down the stairs and companionways to third-class cabins. They stowed their luggage and went up to explore.

No one seemed to know exactly who said it or why, and it didn't make a damned bit of sense, anyway, since there seemed to be no one else at all in third class, but the word got passed around that they were to pretend that they didn't know each other. They hung along the railing staring down at the docks and ignored each other. The sun came out, but the day was still cold, overcoat weather. They ducked in and out and moved to the stern and back, went to the bar, which was closed, and waited, pretending not to know each other. Mahoney looked out at New York.

"Well, it's grand place to visit, but I sure wouldn't want to live here, kid."

Schwartz turned pale with anger and went down to the cabin to read his manual. White smoked a cigar. They waited and waited. Doug Seacord, the young engineer from Tennessee, asked the purser the reason for the delay. Mahoney watched the gangways for police, convinced that "the joint was gonna be raided." The word went around by furtive whispers and scrawled notes that the tide was wrong, and they would have to wait until it turned.

There were a few others in third class after all, but no one who looked like an FBI agent. The volunteers sidled up and down the decks, trailed after the gong into the dining room, and ate, pretending not to know each other. Still the ship did not sail.

It was late afternoon, about four o'clock by White's watch, when the mooring lines splashed into the oily water and were snaked aboard by the French seamen. A tug showed up, frowsy-snouted and powerful, then another. Ponderous, almost imperceptibly, ship and dock separated, with the odd impression of the dock being somehow drawn away from the stationary ship. The *Normandie* eased out into the river. The tugs churned off, and the gulls wheeled and cried. They slid, the whole liner murmurous and vibrating softly, past the Statue of Liberty. They watched it. Some of them had never seen it. The ship began to roll in the winter sea. They stood at the railing until the land dropped below the ragged gray horizon. The lights came on, the vast dark hissed and smelled of the sea. The bar opened, and a few went in to have a drink. The gong sounded for dinner. It was another quiet meal. After coffee, White wandered down to the cabin and found Schwartz seasick. He sat with him for a while, then went up to the lounge. He sat and smoked a cigar and felt foolish and conspicuous. The right side of his face was tired from winking at everybody else.

The game of make-believe-strangers was over by the end of the first full day out. It was just too damned silly, and nobody else cared that they were going to Spain, any more than anybody could seriously believe that they were a group of tourists. In December? José Cubeta had brought a guitar. So had another volunteer. There were card games, pinochle, cribbage, and lack-luster poker, since no one really had enough money to make winning worth while.

Three days out, the ship's newspaper printed a statement made by the chairman of the House Foreign Affairs Committee:

> Chairman McReynolds . . . declared he would urge the Department of Justice to apply the section of the Criminal Code providing $3,000 fine or a year in prison for enlistment of Americans in a foreign war.

"Blackmail," Schwartz said, "crude and simple. What are we supposed to do, jump overboard and swim back, Andrew?"

"Whitemail, too," he said. "You better get out in the fresh air, Schwartz, you look pretty green around the gills."

"I wonder if my Aunt Sophy knows about this?"

"I wonder if Franco and Hitler know about this? Make *them* happy, I guess. See you at lunch."

Mahoney had disappeared. He and some of the others discovered some French showgirls up in first class. Mahoney was gone for a day and a half.

The days, gray, fairly rough, monotonous, passed. They docked at Le Havre on New Year's Eve. Word went around to have passports checked. They were told to say, if asked, that they were students on their way to the Paris Exposition. No one asked them anything. The French officials took the passports, stamped them, and waved the Americans on down the gangway to the customs shed. They formed into a single long line and slid their identical suitcases onto metal counters. The French customs officers ordered suitcase after suitcase opened. Inside were khaki shirts and pants, boots, socks, sweaters, rubber ponchos, ammunition belts, odds and ends of equipment. All books and military manuals had been left on the *Normandie* or thrown into the harbor. The French customs officers looked at the Americans. The Americans looked at the dim, vaulted ceiling of the shed, the damp concrete floor or straight ahead at the back of somebody's neck.

The Frenchman peeked into White's suitcase and gestured for it to be closed.

"*Vive l'Espagne,*" he muttered and made a mark with a piece of crumbling chalk.

"*Vive la République,*" White said.

They had agreed on the need for discipline and went directly to their hotel rooms. Not many went out to the cafés. They felt strange and exhilarated and reserved all at the same time. It had been impressed on them all to stick together, stay out of sight and not to shoot off their mouths. Even though it was New Year's Eve, no one was to try painting the town red. That was accepted as some sort of a joke. Most of the men were tired, anyway. They had slept little the night before, some because of a boisterous party organized by Mahoney and his new cronies, others, because of their first sight of the English Channel and the French coast.

They waited in hotels in a working-class district and were counted for train tickets to Paris. Breakfast was coffee with hot milk in it and oddly shaped rolls like crescents with sweet butter and apricot jam. There were very few shops open, and most of the volunteers were afraid to stray far from their hotels. White found a place that sold chocolate, and a *bar-tabac*. He brought his group of four and another group of five there in the afternoon. The men bought cigarettes and tried them.

"Jesus! El Cabbage-ohs."

"Guinea rockets, huh?"

"Everybody smoke these, White?"

"You can buy American smokes. They cost a lot more, that's all."

White tried out his French. It was good enough to get him a few packs of Gauloises cigarettes and a pint flask of decent cognac. In a surge of good will, he ordered a glass of white wine all around and one for the *patrón*. They drank to the success of the Paris Exposition. A *gendarme* came into the bar. The Americans looked at his uniform, then at White, and edged toward the door. The *patrón* of the bar smiled and waved good-by to White. The gendarme said something. The *patrón* shrugged.

"Oh, ils sont volontaires pour l'Espagne. Bon gars', eh?"

When he got back to the hotel, White learned that there had been an incident of some sort, not quite a fight, but an argument and a shoving match in a bar near the waterfront. It had something to do with the jars of George Washington Instant Coffee. Schwartz diagnosed it as the second example of Fascist dirty work, the first having been pulled by Representative McReynolds. White lay on a bed, reading a French paper, waiting patiently. Nothing much seemed to be happening in Spain. There was still fighting around Madrid, but no all-out assaults. There were rumors that both sides were building for an offensive soon. He translated for Schwartz and Mahoney. The Irishman was enthusiastic.

"Then we'll be in at the kill! We'll make it just in time, if we ever get outta this burg. No train today, huh?"

"Tomorra afternoon, late."

"Gay Paree. Boy oh boy!"

"We'll get there about three in the morning. Cathouses will be all closed, Mahoney."

What had touched off whatever really had happened was not the instant coffee jars, but a ship in the harbor of Le Havre, the SS *Washington*. The original crew was on strike, back in New York, and the boilers were being fired by a gang of French *jaunes*, the local word for scab. Word was out that the American volunteers were a full scab crew come to take the liner back to the States. The jars of coffee had been a coincidence, maybe. Mahoney thought so, but Schwartz saw another plot. It had been a seaman from the NMU who had told White to buy the coffee in the first place. Schwartz wrote a long letter to his aunt, describing what he called "a poison-plot already eating at the vitals of the National Maritime Union."

The train ride to Paris was dark, dull, and sleepless. Compartment doors were opened from time to time, as French comrades counted noses. Semaphore lights whipped by the windows. The train stopped, started, stopped again. The men ate sandwiches, apples, and candy washed down with warm beer. It was still dark when they pulled into the great smoky shed of the Paris station. Tickets south were bought and handed out to group leaders. They hung around the station, a few going out into the streets to look for an open café or restaurant. No bacon and eggs, just more coffee with milk and rolls with butter and jam. The Americans scattered in small groups, but didn't stray. They ate, bought more food and postcards. White wrote to Chicago.

Little Tomatoes:

Arrived safe and sound. Going south soon. Hugs and kisses for the kids. Tell O'Brien we made it.

Love,

Andy

Another train, more French comrades, but it was good weather and the men moved up and down the cars, visiting each other, making new friends, trying out the few words of French they had picked up. They stopped at Lyon long enough to buy beer and sandwiches from the station push-cart vendors. Then Béziers, and midafternoon, Perpignan. There was a lot of talk about whether the border was open or closed. It was open. The buses would be along after dark.

White and his group ate in a restaurant across the square from where the buses were to park. They were all nervous and noisy and hungry. Spain was just a few miles away. In a little while, they'd be across the border. They had thick, hot cabbage soup with tapioca in it, veal steaks with boiled potatoes, a bitter salad, wine, and good bread. White ordered coffee and paid the bill. Except for a small wad of Spanish currency, he was broke.

He sat half listening to the others talk. He gave the waiter his last few coins. The man shrugged and accepted. He jerked his thumb toward Spain and raised his brows. White nodded. The waiter gave the clenched fist salute of the Popular Front and the Spanish Republic. The others

saw him and fell suddenly silent. The fun was over, the holiday adventure of ships and trains at an end. They still had a long way to go,
but they would be traveling through the Republic they had volunteered
to help defend. That was real and unknown at the same time. Ninety-six
of them had sailed from New York. How many would make it back
home? They sat and thought about it. The waiter treated them to a
small glass each of mediocre cognac. No one moved, even when they
heard the sound of motors and saw the headlights shine on the windows
of the restaurant. A Frenchman opened the door and beckoned. White
stood up and reached for his suitcase and his overcoat.

"Let's move, comrades. Next stop's Figueras."

There was a delay, because the last buses were filled with volunteers
from other countries, Germans, French, a few Czechs. The dark figures,
the blue-uniformed Guardes Mobiles, walked up and down beside the
buses. White counted thirty of the French border police, but there were
more. Two came into the bus with flashlights and peered around. No
one said a word. There was no baggage examination. The passports
came back but were held. A few kilometers on they would be handed
over again, this time to the frontier guards of the Spanish Republic.

The barricade pole went up, and the buses lurched into motion. The
Guardes Mobiles waved flashlights and clenched fists. A nervous murmur
swept through the bus. Some windows were opened, and a few men
leaned out to return the salute. The night wind was cold. They rattled on
through the short no-man's land between frontier posts. Conversation
sprang up: the French guards were tough-looking babies, all right, but
good guys, sympathetic. If their government hadn't sold out to Non-
Intervention, those Frenchmen would be in Spain with their carbines.
Somebody started to sing: "There's a Long, Long Trail A-Winding." A
few voices took it up.

The stop at the Spanish frontier post was very brief. There was no
passport check. The buses stopped; two men in uniform with tasseled
forage caps and rifles swung on board each bus. They wore the red five-
pointed star of the Republic and seemed bored and businesslike. There
were no salutes. Everyone crowded forward to see the two Spaniards.
They accepted cigarettes and smiled. The lights went off, and the buses
moved on.

It was a disappointment, the ride through the night to Figueras. The
country, what little could be seen, looked exactly like France, grass, trees,
a few boulders, dark, silent houses. No sound of artillery, no searchlights
in the clouds, no troop movements, no sign of war at all. The two Spanish
soldiers seemed to know nothing of the war or they weren't saying. They
sat together in the door-well and smoked the cigarettes the Americans
gave them. The buses passed through a few dark towns, a minute or so of
shuttered shops and dark stone houses. The country was rolling, hilly,

and the road switched back and forth. The buses moved slowly. Voices dwindled in the darkness, a match spurted, a few cigarettes glowed. Somebody was snoring . . . Mahoney.

A car was waiting for them at the town of Figueras. They followed its red tail-lights up the hill to the fortress, a huge, black bulk that shut out the stars. There was a moat and a drawbridge, thick walls and a big courtyard. The buses stopped. The men stirred and collected their suitcases. Unshaded lightbulbs flickered in the night. They formed into a double line and stumbled off into the darkness.

They went down wide, worn stone stairs and narrow, dank corridors, gloomy and cold enough so that breath blew gray in the dim light. They went down and down into huge stone halls, empty and cold, ranked with iron sawhorses; on each pair sat three wooden planks and a loose bag of straw. Mahoney looked around.

"Where's the can?"

It was a bucket with a board on top. The place reminded White of a slaughterhouse. Big iron spikes came down from the ceiling. Some of the seamen in the group swore the spikes were to sling hammocks from, but to White they looked made to hang carcasses. One of the Spaniards showed them they could hang their clothing from the spikes. He pantomimed getting undressed and kept saying *media hora, media hora.* The lights would be turned off in a half hour. Word went around to hang up the Army-Navy clothing and to pack civilian stuff in the suitcases. It didn't take long. At the head of every plank-and-straw-bag bunk men who had gone before them had written and scratched names, addresses, pictures, and slogans on the stone walls. Schwartz saw five-pointed stars, the hammer and sickle, the inevitable nudes and everywhere:

Proletari di Tutti i Paesi Unitevi!

Prolétaires de Tous Pays, Unissez-vous!

and at the end of the big, vaulted cold chamber the words:

PROLETAR JUSZEWSZYSTICH KRAJOW TA CZEIESIE!

and underneath it:

Resist much, obey little

—Whitman

White looked at it gloomily.

"Polack comrades. This bastid Whitman must be an Anarchist. I hope he's dead by now."

"He is," Schwartz said. "*No pasarán.* I wonder what that means?"

"No pissin, the bucket's full," Mahoney said, rolling up in his blanket. He had a pencil in his hand and lay on his belly, his tongue between his teeth. He wrote his name and address on the wall. The lights flickered, and then many of them began to write on the walls. Schwartz had seen something and borrowed a pencil-stub. The sentence was scratched into the stone, very neatly, between his bunk and White's.

Things are in the saddle and ride mankind.

Schwartz scribbled beneath it:

Down with rear-rank defeatism! Workers of the World Unite!

The lights flickered again and went out. The men stumbled around, laughing and talking, finding their bunks. The huge room quieted. White lay on his back and wondered what it was all going to be like. He fell asleep.

The Spaniards woke them. They dressed slowly in their travel-wrinkled khakis with the price tags still on them. The room was cold. They clowned around, modeling their new uniforms, walking in stiff boots and saluting each other. They were led up stairs and corridors to a mess hall for a cup of white wine, hard bread, and black, bitter coffee. They waited in line to be registered and pick up their passports. They were asked two questions. Did they understand that they had volunteered for the duration of the war? What address to notify in case of . . . ?

They climbed to the stone battlements and looked back at the far mountains, the high peaks topped with snow. Back there was France. The other way was just plain-looking earth, no snow, a few fields and trees, a highway and a railroad line. They smoked and looked, and almost everybody said it was a goddamned shame nobody'd thought to bring along a camera to take pictures of them in their new duds. When the Spaniard came up, they plied him with cigarettes and tried to talk to him. He laughed, shook hands, and shrugged, beckoning them to come down into the courtyard.

They marched, or walked, to White's disgust. There was no way to even get them to keep in step, and after a little, he stopped trying. They thundered over the drawbridge and then down the hill to show themselves to the people of Figueras. Some kind of an announcement had been made, and the sidewalks and windows were crowded. They shuffled along, embarrassed and proud, some already limping in stiff new boots that were too small. They were tired when they trudged back up the hill and across the moat to the mess hall.

The two men at the end of each table were detailed to bring up from the kitchen in the courtyard washtubs of boiled potatoes and meat stew with garlic bits floating in it. There was nothing to drink but sour red wine. A Spanish officer read a speech of welcome, said something in French and again in German. They listened and applauded.

At White's table, the Americans were mixed in with the other volunteers. Everyone tried to talk, to make friends. He sat and listened, feeling odd and lonely. He chipped in the words of French and Spanish that he knew when the others asked him. He was surprised to discover that the

Europeans seemed to assume that *he* was French. They kept asking him what part of Africa he was from, and he told them Chicago.

Close-order drill for the volunteers that afternoon was first a joke, then boring. They tried to learn the commands in Spanish and couldn't. White drilled two squads, then three. He was a little nervous, and was glad that Mahoney was off at the other end of the parade ground. There was no trouble; the men were willing to *take* orders from him. That was okay. But they didn't know how to *follow* orders. There was nothing to do but laugh along with them, keep trying. He hit on a way of getting them to move in unison, if not in step. He got them to sing by starting the songs himself, first, "There once was a union maid," with a lot of dirty verses thrown in, and "Hold the Fort," which most of them knew.

The next day was cold, with a chill wind driving dark clouds across the sky. Trucks arrived, and they climbed on board, lugging suitcases. The train waiting for them looked too worn out to do anything but coast downhill. The wooden-walled coaches had broken windows, hard wooden benches. But they were moving out, that was the big thing. An excitement seized them. They shoved and wrangled up and down the aisles, all talking and laughing, begging oranges from each other, mooching cigarettes and singing songs. The whistle, a thin peep, made them laugh. They crawled out of the station about as fast as a man could walk and kept at that speed, which prompted "I've Been Workin on the Railroad" and "The Old Gray Mare."

There was nothing to look at but bare fields, a few stone houses, the sky so heavy with clouds that no enemy planes could possibly spot them, even if there were enemy planes. The coaches were freezing. They huddled in blankets and sang all the old songs they could think of and played cards with cold, stiff fingers.

At every town, and there seemed to be hundreds, they crawled and stopped, crawled and stopped, the same thing happened. They pulled into the station, usually just a shed roof, and the men jammed at the windows. The men threw cigarettes into the crowd and got back oranges. The children begged for bread. The locomotive panted. Bits of bread were traded for bottles or jars of wine, and more oranges. The floors were littered with peels. The master of the station rang his warning bell. The locomotive peeped. The crowd cheered, lifted their arms, a shoal of clenched fists, even the children so small their mothers held them up to see *los extranjeros*. The bell dinged, and the men in the coaches began to sing again: "Over There," "America," "The Star-Spangled Banner," and finally, at almost every stop, "The International," because the townspeople, men, women, children, and the peasants all knew it and would sing back in Spanish, their dark brown faces proud and happy.

The sands of the Costa Brava beaches were dull gray, the sea beyond like graphite. Tattered palms and mimosa flailed and tilted against the wind. If the window shutters were up, you couldn't see; if they were down, you froze. The train crept on through Mataro and finally Badalona, north of the Catalán capital. They saw the tracks multiply, the parallels alongside swooping away, back and under as they pounded through a switch. The houses became more numerous, a steady, but thin scatter, then two or three streets deep, finally what was recognizably the outskirts of a city with trees, factories, stores, awningless cafés, the first streetcars, bridges, and short, sooty tunnels. They creaked into a great shed and shuddered to a stop.

"Is this the front?"

"Barcelona."

"Jeez . . . Well, at least it's somewhere."

"What's up?"

"We march."

"Again? Where?"

"I dunno. Hand me my suitcase."

"How come we got no guns?"

"We ain't even to boot camp yet, dummy."

They were told off into columns and "paraded" into the city to the Karl Marx Barracks. The food was the same, the bunks as lumpy and hard. There was no tobacco, and they couldn't leave the barracks area. They were tired and dirty and sticky from the oranges. All they had seen of Barcelona was a few long, dim, gray streets with a few posters and pictures on the walls. Now, another train.

The train south became a slow torment, jolting, sleepless boredom. The days crawled past, chill and sooty, spine-aching hours just looking out the window with the sea on one side, the fields on the other. They tried to sleep, tried to sing, tried to read, but mostly sat and stared. The chocolate ran out; cigarettes got scarce. There was only bad bread, Spanish sausage that tasted red and soapy, some stringy corned beef packed in goo, and too many oranges. The men lay in the aisles, tried the baggage nets, slumped on the hard seats, exhausted but bounced and jolted awake. There was nothing to do but take it, think, if there was something to think about, and stare out the window. When the night came down, the blue bulbs went on, too dim to read by, but bright enough to keep you awake enough to notice that the sea had vanished. Legs cramped stiff from lack of exercise. There was nowhere to walk except out on the clashing, shifting plates between cars to piss down on the railroad ties that slipped by, trying to see how many you could hit. There was no drinking water, no water to wash or shave in. They lolled away the hours, indifferent now to the village crowds and the peasants. The slow train had hammered their enthusiasm out of them. In the blue night lights, the unshaven, bruise-eyed bodies lay tumbled like corpses. Everybody's temper held, not because of discipline, but because they were pounded too dull-minded to give a damn even if somebody stepped on them. It was like a cattle train, White thought, finally. He knew now how steers felt on the way to the packing plants. No wonder they went under the hammer so easy.

Albacete. Just before ten o'clock, January 6, 1937. They were there, at last!

The platform was crowded, but with soldiers, only a few civilians. A Spanish brass band smashed and blared at them, lifting them, the thump of the drum quickening. A fine, clear cold day, but bright with sunshine and a wind tearing at the flags and banners. They climbed down, weak-legged and rumble-bellied from too many oranges, but stirred up and waving their fists in salute at the Belgians, the Poles, the Germans, the French and the Spaniards who had come to greet them.

Schwartz marched, or tried to, in the front rank, right behind the local brass band. There was a winter bite in the clear, sunny air, and he stepped out, his back straight, his weariness and boredom forgotten. The sight of the other soldiers, Spaniards and Internationals, the sound of voices shouting from the sidewalks and windows, the low-gear growl of staff-cars and trucks with the three-pointed red stars and the insignia of the various units . . . B.I. 12, B.I. 13, B.I. 14 . . . filled him with the solid sense of belonging to a real army, not just a political group or students' club. This was the real thing, solidarity, seriousness, purpose. He swung along, his face, fuzzed with five days growth of light beard, set in a frown to hold back the tears of happiness that blurred the bright morning.

They were billeted at the barracks of the old Guardia Civiles. Even though the place had been scrubbed a hundred times, there were still dim stains beneath the grime on the wood floors. Back in June, the local people had massacred the garrison to the last man. Even Mahoney was temporarily subdued. He borrowed a knife and pried up a few splinters to send home to this father in South Boston.

White stared thoughtfully at the bulletin board. Every document posted there was written in French. Upstairs, he heard, voices spoke and shouted in French. Boots rumbled on the floor as the men up there roamed around uncertainly, trying to figure out where the French officers wanted them to go and what they were supposed to do when they got there. Before he went off to explore Albacete with the others he learned that there was only one English-speaking officer at the base, a Scot named Kerrigan, who represented the British and headed something called the Political Commissariat. There were no American officers at Albacete, and most of the English were stationed in Madrigueras, another town.

The French seemed to be everywhere, officers and men, drinking ver-mouth in the cafés, driving around in vehicles, flirting with the girls, all busy, all preoccupied, all speaking French. The Americans waited until the French went off to their own mess, then ate in the local cafés. The food was unfamiliar, drenched in olive oil, but tasted good. Famished, they wolfed it down in near-silence. Word went around that they were free for the rest of the day. This surprised White, but the others took it as a holiday. He watched them wander off for souvenirs.

"Well, after that train, the boys need a break. But it seems to me we gonna be like little lost sheep without Bo-Peep."

The next day, the Americans were lined up and registered on the rolls of the International Brigades. Each man gave his name and address, his abilities, stated his military service if he had any and what kind of work he had done in the States. The French officers and clerks were brisk, efficient. Rather than struggle with the spelling of names, they copied from bits of paper written by the volunteers. Some could speak a little English.

"*Service militaire?*"

"*Oui.* Yes."

"Rifle? Grenade?"

"Yes."

"*Chauffeur?*"

"Yes."

"*Bon. Chef?*"

"What?"

"You cook?"

"No!"

"*Non? Tant pis . . .*"

"No cook. *Soldat.*"

"*D'accord.* Next?"

They were loaded into Matford trucks and driven through winter-dormant vineyards and olive groves, the fields studded with clumps of dark green pines.

"Lookit them trees," one man said to Schwartz. "Like home. Sorta."

"Where's home for you?"

"Wisconsin."

"No kiddin?"

"Where's this place we're goin' to, you know?"

"Villanueva de la Jara."

"Willy-navy, huh? How far is it?"

"About thirty miles. We're gonna live in a monastery. Where monks lived."

"A monkey house. Don't that just beat all?"

The monastery was near the village church. Before dark, they climbed the sandal-scooped stone steps to the bell tower and looked out over the quiet, cold countryside. Around the town lay fields and hills to the horizon. Four hundred Spanish families lived in Villanueva and now, not quite a hundred Americans. There were four telephones, four radios that played, to the surprise of many, only Spanish programs, news broadcasts they couldn't understand and music they had never heard. There were no officers.

They organized on the same principles of trade-union democracy, debate and decision. All appointments were temporary, anything more formal was rejected out of hand by the French in Albacete on the grounds that duly constituted authority was missing. They deciphered orders of the day and directives, translated passages from military journals and wondered exactly what they were supposed to do to fit into what their French superiors constantly referred to as "the new People's Army."

The people of Villanueva were not like the happy crowds that had cheered them on the train. The men and women seemed hostile, suspicious. They seemed to be guarding something.

It was Mahoney who found the wine cellars underneath the village, long stone corridors and low rooms hacked out of stone, filled with dusty casks and tens of thousands of bottles. He burst into the bunkroom waving a liter in each hand.

"Jesus, boys, it's like a subway filled with hootch!"

Mahoney had paid for the wine. That had been part of the problem the villagers had had with the French volunteers, who simply took what they wanted. There had been drunken fights, and insults to the women and girls of Villanueva. Some decisions were made, voted on and accepted. Nobody was to take or "borrow" anything. Pay for the wine, the charcoal, the vegetables and fruit or trade with cigarettes. Don't try to pick up the girls. The local men don't like it. The French were a bum lot. Let's make these people forget all that. Let's show them what real international workers' solidarity is like. These people are comrades in the struggle. Treat them right, buddy, or it'll be your ass.

Weapons arrived, but still no officers. The Americans went out by squads to look at the weapons, a dozen or more rifles and two machine guns. White was summoned with the first group. He squatted and looked, then glanced out at the crude targets nailed up on the firing range fifty meters distant.

"I ain't so sure these things will reach that far!"

"They're Canadian. Ross make. Pretty bad shape?"

"I'll say. Rusted inside and out. Looka this bolt. Loose as a hot dog in a roll. Gimme a cartridge."

White loaded the old rifle, held it down on a sandbag with his foot, bent gingerly and pulled the trigger. The rifle fired, and the bolt kicked free, rutting a line in the hard dirt. White spat and picked it up.

"That'd lay some comrade's cheek wide open, take off an ear, or kill somebody dumb enough to stand behind him. We'd better bench-fire all these pieces before we let the boys use 'em. And them's the machine guns, huh? I'll be damned."

"The French said they work all right."

"This here's a Maxim gun," White said. "We used to fool with one, but never fired it. It's maybe twenty-five years old. Made about 1914. Hoo, looka that barrel. If you was an ant, you could roller-skate in there, it's so smooth."

"Will it work?"

"I guess. If it don't blow up. Or jam. They jam easy."

White and a work-crew stripped, cleaned and reassembled the few weapons during one afternoon while the others were out in the fields, learning maneuvers, battle formations for advance, oblique, fall back, and take cover. It was slow work. They had to clean the parts with sand soaked in olive oil, no wrenches and a single screw driver made out of a knife. White wrote up a requisition for spare parts and new cooling equipment for the old Maxim guns. When the weapons were finished, stacked and stored, he stood up and eased his back.

"Some arsenal. Hundred guys, eight good rifles . . . ones that work, anyhow, and a wore-out Maxim. And here we sit on a wine cellar in the middle of nowhere with no officers, yet. Man, oh, man. *Viva la Quince Brigada* . . . Well, it don't look good now, but it can't get worse, so it's bound to get better . . . I hope."

BOOK FIVE

Jarama Valley and Guadalajara
February–March 1937

Since the government of the Republic had officially closed all the churches, shot, imprisoned or exiled all the clergy, there was no traditional Christmas or Three Kings' Day, the day Spaniards gave each other gifts. Instead, Valencia had proclaimed "The Week of the Child," a nicely worded document that made every child in the Republic an honored citizen. If there were some who still thought of The Child and were discreet, the government would look the other way . . . at a display of floats and carnival figures on La Castellana and the Gran Vía, Mickey Mouse, Pluto the Pup, Felix the Cat, Donald Duck, Don Quixote, and Sancho. The Fascists across the Manzanares did not shell or bomb Madrid for the seven days, although there was sporadic fighting at the University and the war went on as usual east, south and north.

The toys, crates and boxes of them, sent to Malraux from France, had been delivered before Christmas Eve, unpacked and scattered around the big fir tree raised in the squadron *cantina*. The French festival of Réveillon had been celebrated with a special meal, really good wine, singing of carols and a dance with girls invited from Torrejón and Alcalá and a few from Madrid. It had been a good fête, ceremonious in the best French tradition with speeches, toasts, photographs and good wishes, hectic in the best Spanish tradition with flamenco music by two superb guitarists and a troupe of professional dancers. After that, there was jazz and dance music to the Victrola, a wind-up affair that squawked out Paul Whiteman and the Dorsey brothers. Frank had demonstrated the Big Apple and the Shag, solo, to great applause and had managed to teach some of the Spanish girls a few steps in return for lessons in the *paso doble*. Everybody had drunk a great deal and no one had spoken of Viriato, who had been killed over El Escorial or of the Breguet bomber with a full crew lost on a run over Boadilla where a British group attached to the Thaelmann battalion had been slaughtered. Frank had checked, afraid to hear the worst, but Coltringham's survivors from the University had been moved back to the new International Brigade camp at Albacete.

There was a new joke, the *communiqué* from Córdoba, where an attack had aborted. Saulnier had found it in the papers and made it up into a banner posted on the wall of his room, draped over the bits and pieces of the Caproni bomber he had shot down over the Corúnna road:

DURING THE DAY OUR GLORIOUS TROOPS CON-
TINUED THE ADVANCE WITHOUT THE LOSS OF ANY
TERRITORY.

The pilots, gunners, bombardiers, and ground crews walked the Spanish girls back to Torrejón. The last songs, the last kisses, and the buses and trucks drove away. Saulnier walked with Frank, arm-in-arm back across the rough fields beneath the wheeling winter stars.

"You know something? This is really a rather splendid war, don't you think? I mean, tonight, not tomorrow or yesterday. Right now."

"You're full of *vino blanco.*"

"Of course."

"You get checked out in the new fighters by Dorlov?"

"Yes. Also we went shopping in Madrid. The ruins of that Rolls-Royce have been removed. I nearly wept. Dorlov brought presents for his children. Like most Russians, he is a swamp of sentimentality. He even admits that he likes *you!*"

"We get on."

"Indeed. It is always exhilarating to hear your enthusiasm. Tell me, are all Americans addicted to those . . . um, primitive dances?"

"Sure."

"The birth rate in your country must be phenomenal."

"Not in Philadelphia."

"Ah. Well, I say this is a splendid war. Much better than I had thought. I really think we're going to win, despite Boadilla and what's going up with the Basques."

"We can lose a few. You only have to win one battle to win a war."

"Indeed? Military profundities. Which battle, *s'il vous plaît?*"

"The last one."

"Ah. Well, perhaps it comes soon. But you are glad you stayed on?"

"I'm glad."

"You had a good time tonight?"

"Sure. Fine."

"But you remember back home, perhaps?"

Frank stopped. The land ahead was sunken. They had come to the mass graves in the field. He tugged Saulnier away to the left. They walked on, stopped and urinated on a clump of weeds, Saulnier pretending he was firing a machine gun at a Heinkel.

"Christmas was always very . . . formal, you know. All the grownups dressed for dinner. Black tie. Relatives. But I was the only kid, you know. I had cousins, but they were all older. It was . . . lonely, really. I got sent to bed early Christmas Eve."

"To wait for Père Noël, of course. Me, too."

"The maid, a big, old colored woman named Bea, woke me the next day. I had my own tree, in a sort of nursery. With toys. Everything. The big tree was downstairs. That was for the grownups, too. I was allowed to hand out the presents to them, but they never gave me any back. I always had a ton of stuff, anyway. But I was always shut out. I remember when I was eight. My father gave me a hundred shares of New York Central Railroad. I gave him a tie rack that I made myself. Old Bea helped me. I found it in the rubbish two days later. I put it back on his bureau. Thought it got thrown out by mistake. No mistake. He put it in the rubbish again."

"That's very sad, *mon ami*. Depressing. I trust you did something violent?"

"I used the tie rack for kindling and set fire to the stock-shares."

"And what did he do?"

"I got sent to boarding school in New Jersey. A military school."

"Thus began an illustrious career. I wonder if there is any more wine?"

"All right. You want to come to the city tomorrow to hand out those presents to the orphan kids? Some of us are going."

"Where there are orphan children, there are nursemaids, no? How you say it? . . . Nannies. I will reconnoitre the nannies, eh?"

"Fair enough."

They rode in the cab of the Russian-built THC truck. Frank tried to teach Dorlov the words to "Jingle Bells," which Saulnier, beeping the rhythm on the horn, insisted was really a French song called "Dites-Moi Oui, Dites-Moi Non" with an indecent chorus that he bawled at the top of his voice. There was one truck in front, another behind, all loaded with presents for the children of Madrid.

"It's easy, Mosca . . . Try again."

The Russian shook his head and folded his arms so that he could see the gold watch on his wrist. Saulnier wore a gold watch, too. Frank had bought them in the city.

"I give up. Impossible. Who can speak your language? No one. Djinkle-Djinkle. Bells, of any sort, simply do not make such a sound. Where are we going, Comrade Saulnier?"

"Plaza de Ventas. To the bull ring there. It seems that it's the only place big enough to hold the children. There are thousands, Malraux said. I hope we have enough for them."

"I am an orphan," Dorlov said abruptly.

"Oh?"

"My parents were both killed during the Revolution. But I have three children of my own. Vanka . . . Ivan, he's six. Dmitri . . . we call him Mitya, you know, just became four. Josef will be two in April. I make boy babies only."

"I have never understood marriage," Saulnier said. "Even as a matter of practical business it's a poor affair. Like buying ten thousand liters of wine as an adolescent. One's taste changes, no? At the end, it will go sour, anyway."

"Spare us the cynicism," Dorlov said. "Your decadence explains why you fly so badly. You are convinced the Russian machine will disappoint you. You must be like this American."

"Him? He has glycol in his veins, not blood. You confuse skill with simple stupidity. A bad Russian habit. Look at your government."

"Drive the truck," Dorlov growled. "I will submit your name to the commissar."

The Russian was angry and remained silent until they reached the first barricade. Frank offered him a cigarette.

"I am fond of children," Dorlov said. "Children are good for the soul, as well as the strength of a nation."

"Could be," Frank said.

He had come to like Dorlov through admiration for his skill. The Russian was an expert pilot, with gold medals won in acrobatic contests and a citation from the chief of the Soviet Air Force. Despite the fact that they could speak together only in French with a few words of Spanish thrown in, Dorlov had quickly taught him to fly the new, radial-engined Polikarpov 1-16 monoplane so well that its maneuverability off-set its lack of real speed. The Mosca was barrel-bodied with short, broad wings and big tail surfaces, all engine, gasoline and guns, a stubby, tough plane made rugged for Russian landing fields not much better than the ones in Spain. The Mosca had a good rate of climb, but no glide at all. In a bank at full throttle, it turned so quickly that as Dorlov said, it could nearly eat off its own tail. You had to use the Mosca properly, the way it was designed. There were too many Fascist aircraft to get fancy.

"Tell me the truth, Comrade Mosca."

"Of course, Comrade Millionaire."

"You hit that German yesterday, didn't you?"

"Of course not. As you know, instructors holding commissions in the Soviet Air Force are not allowed to fly combat missions. As proof the machine-gun ports are covered with adhesive tape on every flight. To be examined by the Soviet military *attaché*."

"Who never leaves the Hotel Gaylord."

"That is his affair, not mine."

"I looked, Mosca. The tape over those guns was gone."

"It freezes in the cold and drops off."

The bull ring rose up like a Moorish coliseum of terra cotta, with blue and white decorative tile work. Around it lay a vast dirt parking lot, empty except for the buses. As soon as the trucks stopped, they could hear the sound of the voices of children, a sustained rustling shrill that carried out through the great arches and spilled into the cold afternoon. The men from the squadron carried the boxes and crates from the trucks out onto the big disc of hard sand and piled the toys in heaps. Frank looked around. It seemed to him that ten thousand children had come to the ring. He had never seen so many children together in his life. They were noisy, but very orderly, filing down from the tiered seats and out onto the sand.

Saulnier was in charge of all little girls and distributed dolls to them, hundreds and hundreds of dolls, a little mountain of blue eyes, jointed legs, china heads and stiff hair, a loose dazzle of bright colors tumbled around his boots. Dorlov handed out all trucks, autos, steam-shovels and wagons, anything with wheels. Two German pilots were in charge of games and coloring books and crayons. Frank stamped blood into his cold feet and swung his arms next to a heap of airplanes, metal and wooden models of all kinds, colors, and sizes. Someone had thought to have a band; three men in clown costumes perched on the *burladero* and made some thin music drowned out by the voices of the children.

Somebody from a government office made a speech. Malraux spoke very briefly, at top speed, as usual, explaining that the gifts were from all the people of Europe who sympathized with the sufferings of the children of Madrid. A woman, the wife of a trade union official, thanked Malraux in the name of the children. Frank stamped his feet, blew his nose, and watched the slate-colored sky. Another day in sunny Spain.

Saulnier handed out dolls in half-dozen lots, like a man selling chickens at Les Halles, surrounded by a shoal of waving arms. Dorlov distributed the wheeled toys, taking them off the pile without looking at them. He shook hands with each child and smiled, showing his aluminum teeth. No one came near the pile of airplanes though the nurses and women herded the little boys near the bright pile, and Frank flew a toy plane in each hand, making motor and machine gun noises.

"Errrrrrrrr. Eh-eh-eh-eh-eh. Boom! Hey, get 'em while they're hot. *Aviones.* Step right up here and get a free airplane. How about it, *chico? Mira. Mira, aviones!*"

The little boy, a skinny child with straight black hair and fine dark eyes, took a step forward, then looked up at the sky. His face twisted with fear. He shrieked and ran away blindly until a nurse caught him. She shook her head and smiled at Frank. She was dressed in a blue *mono* with a soldier's sheepskin jacket and a little white starched apron. Frank grinned and waved, staring at her. She looked very cute and odd, like a garage mechanic who had somehow gotten caught in a gigantic children's birthday party.

In a half hour, the children had picked the piles of toys right down to the sand. The clown-band and the other men of the squadron had gone out beneath the ring to the parking lot to play games until the buses arrived. In the hard empty space of the bull ring, Frank waited by the untouched heap of toy airplanes.

He kicked the sand and looked around the deserted ring. Depressed, he began to throw the toy planes back into the cardboard boxes. There were too many. The hell with them. He lit a cigarette, pushed his fists into his pocket and walked across the ring, through the gate and under the stadium. It smelled faintly of manure and musty straw. A sad tune drifted through the high, cold arches.

A girl was there, waiting for him, apparently. In the dim light, he recognized her. The cute one with the *mono* and the apron.

"*Hola.*"

"*Hola.*"

"I wanted to talk with you."

"My pleasure, señorita."

"They were afraid, the children. It's the air raids, you see. They think of the bombs and sleeping in the subways and what happened to their mothers and fathers."

He nodded, looking at her. She was short and pretty with dark, curly hair cut short, a small, straight nose, and no lipstick. She seemed very friendly, in no hurry to go anywhere. She smiled.

"I have seen your picture. In the papers. You have a decoration, no?"

"Yes. If you destroy the plane you are trying to fly and walk away alive, then they give you a medal."

The smile died on her pretty pink lips, then came alive again. Her whole face lit up.

"You make a joke. It's when you shoot down the Fascists . . . isn't it?"

She knew he was kidding all right. The apron still tied around her waist snugged the loose coveralls around her hips. She turned and walked with him, looking up at him and smiling.

"You guard the children?"

"I have about fifty. All day. We're from the Palace Hotel. You know it?"

"Yes, of course. My comrades stay at the Hotel Bristol when we come to Madrid. That's many children to guard. What's your name?"

"Carmen. Carmen Bravo. You are . . . uh . . . Buckminster, the pilot."

"*Book-ministro*, huh? That's a difficult name to say. Carmen Bravo. That's easy. Bravo, Carmen. Like the opera. You understand me? I don't speak Spanish well."

"Oh no . . . *no!* You speak very well . . . *very* well!"

"Where are all your *niños?*"

"The bus has taken them back to the hotel."

"Then you don't have to go?"

She shrugged one shoulder, walked a few steps and stopped, her face tilted down into the soft collar of her jacket. A gust of wind fluttered her blue coverall.

"Soon. I wanted to thank you. For the children. It was very kind of you. The girls liked the dolls, and I told the boys that the Gloriosa will protect them."

"Yes, protect them."

But she looked so small, framed in the towering arch. He reached out to touch her, but she stood too far away, her head still bowed, the chill wind riffling her hair.

"Turn around . . . please?"

"Why?"

"I can't see you. I wish to see your face again. You will go away."

She shook her head slightly.

"No. You're an American, they say. It is *you* who will leave."

"Turn around. Carmen."

She swung around, one boot toe scraping the ground, her hands set on her hips. He looked at her, amused and pleased. She had tilted, dark eyes and marvelous long, thick lashes. Her cheeks were pink from the cold. An odd pang of pleasure and pain lifted in his chest and seemed to run down the bones of his arms. The feeling made him laugh, a nervous little bark that annoyed him. He frowned and began to sing.

" 'Jeepers-Creepers, where'd you get those peepers . . .' "

She tilted her head to one side, staring.

"What is that song? Is that an American revolutionary song?"

"Yes. Very revolutionary. It is a song all about a pilot who meets a girl who guards children in a *plaza de toros*. He tells her she has very beautiful eyes . . ."

All the words came out in a rush. Suddenly, amazingly, the girl began to blush. He could see the color creep up from the shaggy collar of her jacket, tint her cheeks and burn across her forehead. He stammered at her in English.

"Look, I'm sorry. I just meant . . ."

"You are making fun of me."

She scowled at him and put her hands to her face. He sensed that she was ashamed to be caught blushing. She began to turn away.

"Carmen. Don't go. Stay here."

He tore his package of cigarettes from his coat and offered it to her. It was the only thing he could think of doing, and remembered as her small, cold fingers touched his that Saulnier said only whores smoked in Spain.

"Many thanks."

He struck a match, then another, but the winter wind whirling dust and bits of straw beneath the stadium blew them out. He cupped his hands. She bent over, the cigarette clamped in the corner of her pale mouth. The flame jumped; she puffed, making tiny grunting noises and lifted up, grinning at him. He brought her hand up and kissed her fingers.

"*De nada.*"

She backed away slightly, her face still mottled with blushes, and scrubbed the fingers he hadn't kissed across her thick, dark brows. Her hands dove into her pockets, and she fumbled with a pair of gloves, smoking the cigarette like a man without touching it. She looked like a tomboy, a kid trying to look tough.

"How many years have you, Carmen?"

"Eighteen. And you?"

"A few more than thirty. Too many years."

"Oh no. You look younger than that."

"You look . . . very nice."

They stood staring at each other, smoking nervously. They both began to talk at the same instant, laughed and stopped. He gestured for her to begin. She made a tentative humming sound and fiddled with her gloves. There was a hole in one thumb. He wanted to buy her a new pair of gloves.

"Are all Americans like you? I've seen your photo. But I never thought I'd meet you. Face to face, like this."

He groaned and shifted from foot to foot, frantically trying to think of something to say, anything to say. Bits of Spanish floated across his mind, the words for . . . shock-absorber . . . machine gun firing mechanism . . . crank-case . . . landing-gear strut . . .

"Have you been in air raids?"

She was polite enough to consider this as an important question, or not to laugh at him. She nodded, several quick little jerks of her head. She had abrupt mannerisms, quick and secretive, as though afraid to be seen or caught.

"Many times. You have eight Fascist planes, no? I read that."

She held up her gloved hands and counted eight.

"Have another cigarette? Please."

"Many thanks."

What was the word for gloves?

"You need new things for your hands. I will buy you some."

"Eh? Oh no."

She looked fussy and domestic, plucking at the apron knot and obviously cursing under her breath. At last, her coverall fell loose away from her hips. She rammed the apron into her jacket pocket. A group of men and women stood in the lee of the squadron trucks. She smiled at Frank rather shyly.

"Well, with great pleasure, Comrade Bookministro. And many thanks for the tobacco, too."

"Take the package. Please. My name is Frank. Like Franco."

"Ah? Oh no . . . *no!* Like Francisco. San Francisco. He was a saint . . . before the war."

"We've got cities in the United States named after saints. San Francisco."

"Yes."

"San Diego."

"Yes? That's nice. I must go back to the children."

"You haven't finished your cigarette."

"There. Poof! *Finito.*"

"Carmen . . ."

She turned away from him again. This time he reached out and touched her on the shoulder, and she stopped and looked at him. He couldn't tell what she was thinking. Saulnier plunged across the parking lot in a cloud of wind-whipped, scouring dust, his arm clamped around a tall, thin girl with dyed hair, cavalry boots and a long leather overcoat. For a numb instant, Frank thought the French pilot was absconding with some Cossack girl friend of Dorlov's. He and Carmen whirled away from the flying dust into an awkward, elbow-knocking embrace.

"Ah, here they are! Romeo and Juliet! Hero of the People's Republic, I have the pleasure of presenting Señorita Teresa Montera. *Guapita,* his real name is Frank Buck."

"Oh," the girl named Teresa said, "The one who tames animals?"

"*Claro,* look at what he just caught."

"Listen, Jean, just shut up, will you? Señorita Bravo . . . Jean Saulnier, a comrade from the squadron. *Con mucho gusto,* Señorita Montera . . ."

Carmen took off her glove and shook hands with Saulnier. When the Frenchman bowed over her fingers, she snatched her hand away, glanced at Frank, and flushed slightly. Frank felt his heart turn over. He ducked down to retrieve the glove she dropped and fitted it on her fingers, his throat filled with a sudden ache.

"Ah, what *politesse!*" Saulnier said, shaking his head. "You can easily see that he was a waiter in a chic restaurant. All this about banking and polo playing is a myth, so much poetry invented by his mother, poor woman, as she slaved over her washtubs."

Carmen looked blank, Frank started to get angry, and the girl called Teresa threw her arms around Saulnier's neck and hugged him. She spoke in good French, rapid and fierce, nuzzling at the Frenchman's ear.

"Shut up can't you? You have only to look to see that they are mad for each other. Look at their faces, you fool. My God, they look like survivors of an accident. I guess that's what it can be like, eh? Brrr, it's cold! I was never that lucky. Bed first, love second. Listen, she's only a kid. Is he a decent sort or some kind of gangster?"

Saulnier grinned fatuously and stroked his nose, staring at Carmen. She sidled closer to Frank, who looked around wildly. They had gathered an audience. About twenty men from the squadron, civilians and the other nurses were watching them, like some sort of circus. He stood there in the center of a parking while his cigarette burned his fingers. He threw the stub away, and Carmen shied like a pony. Saulnier's finger reached the end of his nose and dropped down to the new mustache that sprigged along his lip. The Frenchman nodded seriously.

"I would give my life for him. One of the best."

"Oh, for Christ's sake! This is too much. What the hell, you know?"

Saulnier beamed, his eyes glittering with malicious sentimentality. He swatted Teresa firmly on the rump and spun her around toward the trucks.

"Run along and play, children," he said in English.

"What did you say to them?" Teresa demanded. "I like him. He says absolutely nothing. Not a word. That's the best sort. You think she's pretty enough, don't you, Jeannot?"

"Pretty! *Mon Dieu!* Well, I mean to say that my own preferences are for tall blond women, but each to his own taste, eh? Come, we're going to Chicote's and drink whiskey."

Saulnier stopped and turned around. Carmen hid her face against Frank's shoulder. Teresa doubled over, pounding her knees and shrieking with laughter. Frank patted the girl gingerly. The other people standing around began to applaud. Saulnier bowed and gestured across the empty lot to them, as though introducing a vaudeville act.

"Come on, Carmen," Frank said. "I see a streetcar."

They fled, hand in hand, to the trolley stop and swung aboard. The streetcar was crowded. They stood silently, face to face, swaying together and apart with the rocking motion of the car. The day was darker, an early winter twilight. He tugged the shaggy collar of her jacket up around her chin. Her mouth moved in a stiff little smile, and she stared out the window.

Oh, you sonofabitch, Saulnier. If you've queered this for me, I'll . . .

It made the inside of his arms ache again, a kind of melting quiver, just to look at her. She touched his sleeve with her hand and turned tilted sleepy goat's eyes up at him. He wanted to kiss her eyelashes and her small, smooth pink lips.

"This is it. Our stop."

"Oh. Oh yes."

They swung off. He was lost at once. Nothing looked familiar. He saw broken house fronts, a wrecked and abandoned barricade, a few people trailing home from work, hurrying out of the cold and darkness, inside to the cold and darkness of unheated, unlighted apartments. A khaki sedan purred across a plaza pited with half-filled bomb-craters.

"When are you free, Carmen?"

"Later."

"Tonight?"

"Yes, at nine."

"At nine. Tonight. Good. Marvelous. Where shall we meet? At the Palace?"

"Someplace else, eh? I work at the Palace with the children, and it's a very sad place. Many, many wounded, too."

"That café where the table is reserved for General Mola? We'll have dinner. I have lots of money."

She shrugged.

"I usually eat in a workers' *cantina*."

"What's the name of that place that has the mechanical piano? That plays 'Madrid.' You know."

"Las Cuevas de Luis Candelas? If you like. Until then."

"I'll walk with you to the hotel."

"If it pleases you."

He took her hand. She freed herself. His heart sank, but she took off her glove and pushed her bare warm fingers back into his, squeezed and laughed softly.

"You have a cold hand."

"In my country we have a thing people say. It goes . . . uh . . . uh . . ."

God, I wish I could speak Spanish. I must sound like a moron. All I know is the words for airplane parts and a lot of dirty stuff.

"Yes?"

"Uh . . . *Mano fría, corazón caliente.*"

"That's beautiful . . ."

"You really think so?"

She nodded in her quick, furtive way. He was acutely concious of her, how close she was to him, the casual brush of her hip against his thigh. She had a bold, swaggering little walk that made men turn around appreciatively. He shortened his stride to match hers. At a corner, they stopped and he hugged her for a second and let her go.

"Why do you laugh, Francisco? Are you happy?"

"Yes. Now, today, I am very happy. It was just then. We are lost in our coats."

"I think maybe it's safer that way."

"You don't know half of it," he said in English, "I could get a job as a towel rack."

"What do you say?"

"I say I am sorry about my comrade. He made you . . . angry."
Frank nodded shrewdly. The Spanish word for "embarrassed" could
mean "pregnant." He had caught himself in time. Carmen was a nice
girl, he was certain, not a professionally "nice" girl like too many he
had met too long ago at too many Main Line coming-out parties, but
. . . nice.

"He looks at women like a *lobo* . . . a wolf. All tongue and teeth."

"He's French."

"*Claro*, he's French!"

"Forget him, Carmen."

"How you say my name! '*Cah-min.*' It's Carmen."

"And mine?"

"Francisco."

To say his name, the tip of her tongue flicked out softly between
her little teeth. She caught him looking and crimped her lips shut. She
obviously knew he wanted to kiss her. She marched on down the sidewalk, swinging her hand and his. They crossed the big plaza to the
Palace Hotel and walked between the ambulances to the steps. She
touched the bullet holes in the sides of the vehicles, elliptical punctures
made, obviously, by strafing aircraft. She shook all over and spat in the
street, wrenching free of him.

"*Qué canalla! Qué gordas!*" she shouted furiously. "Wounded from
the Corunna road! Red Cross on every roof and you see what they do!"

"I see. I've seen it before, Carmen."

"*Qué gordas!*" she repeated.

He blinked, surprised at the slang that meant "What fat shits!"

"*Claro.* I had a comrade in the squadron. An Italian. A good pilot.
Very brave. He played the violin. Named Viriato. His plane was shot,
you know. He jumped in his parachute. A Fiat caught him. Another
Italian machine gunned him to death.

She covered her face and shook her head, leaning against the ambulance.

"That's terrible. Have you ever jumped?"

"No. Not yet."

"You should touch wood."

"I'm lucky."

"Don't say that. Listen, I may be late. You understand me?"

"Yes. Late. All right. At the café. At nine o'clock. Okay?"

"Okay," she said, grinning at him. "Okay."

She began to walk up the steps of the hotel backward, both hands
clenched in the collar of her short sheepskin jacket. He followed her
up the stairs. A tough-looking *miliciano* clicked his tongue at her in
greeting. She turned and ran inside.

"Your papers, *camarada?* No papers? Then you have no affairs in here. Unless you look for wounded friends."

"No. What hour is it?"

"*Pues* . . . ten minutes after six, comrade."

"That's three hours!"

"To wait for her? A real *caballero* would wait three years and save up his *leche.* Go to the cinema, *camarada. Los hermanos Marx.*"

"Groucho, Harpo, and Karl, eh?"

"*Salud, inglés!*"

"*Salud, hombre!*"

He ran down the steps and headed for the Gran Vía. What good guys most of the Spaniards were! Good comrades. Three hours to wait until he saw her again. He went into the first shop that sold gloves and bought a pair, guessing at her size, leather ones, lined with rabbit fur. He wandered up the sloping sidewalk to Chicote's bar. The place was crammed with people, hot and smoky as usual. He found Saulnier and Dorlov and some of the other pilots and instructors drinking wine at the rear tables. They shouted to him. He squeezed through the crowd and shook Saulnier by the shoulders.

"Why the hell did you have to go and lose that Rolls-Royce, you dumb, goddamned frog-eater, you?"

"Heh-heh, no abuse or I'll break it off you and then what will you do? Ask Franco about the *voiture.* They were his bombers."

"Screw Franco."

"*Chacun à son goût.* Sit down and get drunk. My little blonde has just left us. I think we have reached an understanding. Neither of them are off duty until nine o'clock. That's time enough to get drunk and sober again. Comrade waiter, another glass! Dorlov has the Slavic melancholies. Teach him that song of the bells, Frank."

The Russian blinked slowly, as if testing his eyelids. He was very drunk. The waiter brought a glass and filled. Frank picked it up.

"To the Soviet Air Force. To the man who teaches others to fly the Mosca."

"You are . . . You are tremendously fortunate," Dorlov said gloomily.

"He is homesick. He misses his children. Talk to him. Cheer him up."

Frank took off his leather coat and placed the package of gloves on the table. Saulnier tapped the package with his finger.

"What optimism. You buy them in large amounts."

"Some *gloves,* for God's sake!"

The bar was so noisy they had to shout at each other across the table. He saw newspaper correspondents, staff officers from the Communist 5th Regiment, a Canadian doctor who visited the airfield once a week, a Spanish actress and her manager, but tonight, no other Russians.

"You know, Mosca, you ought to claim that Heinkel. You hit him first. He was going down when he dropped into my sights."

Dorlov blinked and sat upright, straightening his shoulders. He drank some wine.

"Forgive me. You were saying?"

"You ought to claim that German."

"I thought she was Spanish. You saw her first, comrade."

"What?"

"Your *petite fille*. I see her as . . . mmm, discreet, but with enthusiasm. You are tremendously fortunate. Make boy babies. They are the best. She has very nice . . . right around here. Not much up front. Not like Russian girls. You should see my wife. Like gun turrets, I assure you. What's her name, anyway?"

"Carmen."

Dorlov threw back his head and began to sing the *Habanera* from Bizet's opera in a rich baritone, snapping his fingers. The table quieted, then the others around. The Russian stood up. A dozen voices joined him. Everyone seemed to know the tune. Many sang *la-la-la* and clapped their hands, setting the rhythm. Dorlov stamped and whirled. The room sounded to the beat of his boot-heels, the crash of hands clapping. Dorlov frowned in concentration.

"My God," Frank said. "I didn't know he could sing. What a voice!"

Saulnier nodded and ordered another bottle of wine. The waiter moved slowly through the tables. Like everyone else, he was watching the Russian.

"Ah, you see. How happy he is! Love conquers all."

"Love."

"I said it. I am never wrong in such matters. Listen. I will tell you of the tragic story of one of my cousins. What began as a simple affair of the flesh involving the wife of a government minister ended in the scandal of the year. And for good reason. My cousin and the minister's wife were, one evening, riding together in a taxi when the lady, unable to restrain herself, began to perform on my happy cousin a certain act . . ."

Saulnier demonstrated, using his thumb. Frank nodded, half listening, watching Dorlov dance. He had stopped before the Spanish actress. The woman rose and flung away her shawl. She and Dorlov began the *Habanera* again. The men and women quieted to hear them sing. Saulnier went on.

"The taxi was moving, you understand, down the Champs to Place de la Concorde. The chauffeur applied the brakes in alarm; there was a minor collision, all at the very instant of my cousin's ecstasy. The lady, in her fright, clenched her teeth. The howl of pain was heard as far away as Chartres and Fontainebleau. Imagine the pretty confusion, if you will, when from the other *voiture*, in full evening dress stepped the lady's husband, the minister of government! The lawsuit that followed was most amusing. Everyone sued everyone. My cousin, despite the efforts of Swiss doctors, was marked for life by the experience."

"I'll bet."

"Moreover, it led to his bankruptcy. The whole affair had such nuances of joy and terror that he insisted on attempts to reproduce the incident. He purchased taxis in pairs, hired out-of-work actors and costumed them in full evening dress. Extensive alterations were made on his estate. Several kilometers of roadway were constructed, fountains, a bridge in replica, also a small obelisk of *papier-mâché*. Unfortunately, the minister's wife ran off to Brazil, and my cousin was forced to rely on certain *filles de joie*. Twilight auto-smashes became a weekly event, then more frequent until the driveway was littered with crippled taxicabs. How long could this madness last, you inquire?"

"I don't."

"As you no doubt know, the jaw muscles are the most powerful in the human body. One fatal evening . . ."

"Who's going to look after Mosca?"

"I should say his dance partner. She has gun turrets too. It's not lust with Russians, you know, it's nostalgia of the most Oedipal sort. With you, my friend, it is love. I have never seen a more acute case. You should see yourself. No, better not. The fixed, imbecilic grin, the vacant stare."

"She said she'd have dinner with me."

"Ah."

"Where they have the player-piano."

"Ah-hah! Well, you will understand if we . . . Teresa and I . . . don't join you? We have other arrangements. But you understand my point? The anecdote of my poor cousin. It is quite typical of your apparently permanent good fortune that the Rolls-Royce sedan was destroyed. Tragedy averted by accident."

"Why don't you shut up and go dance with the Mosca? That actress looks like she's getting tired."

"Of dancing, perhaps. Rumors persist that in other performances she is quite without mercy."

Saulnier reached across the table and patted Frank's cheek.

"*Copain*, you have a face on you that a man is born to wear only two times in his life . . . once when he is nursing. Look, here's Kopa! *Kapitan! Rot Front!* You know, I have been very prejudiced against Germans all my life. But Kopa is something. You should hear some of the stories about him. Courage is one thing, but with Kopa, apparently it approaches suicide. Kopa. Thaelmanns to the bottle! *Kommen Sie hier, bitte!*"

The German was wearing battle dress, corduroys, sheepskin, and boots, an officer's cap with a three-pointed red star. He smiled slightly and raised his fist in salute. People at the tables stared at him as he passed between them. Women reached out to touch his sleeve, his broad, chapped hands. A table of officers and commissars from the Dabrowsky Battalion stood up and saluted. Kopa shook hands with them. The Slavs beamed and nudged each other, offered Kopa a glass of cognac. He hesitated and drank it off at a gulp. Frank had not seen the German since the day he had visited the trenches at the University. It seemed long ago.

"What's he do, Jean? A commissar?"

"No, a sort of *liaison* between the 5th Regiment, the Guardias Rojas and whatever International troops are on their flanks. He supervises transportation and co-ordinates infantry with the Russian tankists. Also anti-tank. Speaks fair Spanish, good French, Italian, Polish, Russian, even your savage tongue. But you have met him. Here, Kopa, sit down, sit down. You remember Comrade Buckminster? Of course. We must drink to him tonight. It seems he has fallen in love."

The German sat down and took off his cap. His hair had grown out long and straight, blond streaked with gray. Saulnier poured wine. Kopa looked across the room where Dorlov still danced with the actress. He began to raise his glass. His hand shook slightly. He frowned and flexed his fingers, then raised the glass, steady now.

"Fröhliche Weihnachten . . . Merry holidays for children. We are all happy here tonight. Music and dancing. It is good to see and hear it."

"You're in from the front?" Frank asked.

"Bringing in wounded. To get ammunition. The roads are very bad."

"How goes it?"

"Not well. They drove us out of Boadilla and are on the high road to Las Rosas. We couldn't see their tanks and mobile artillery because of the fog. They have broken the front."

"*What?*"

"Miaja is out there. Some of our units have only blank ammunition. Against Moors with bayonets, tanks, and artillery. I am taking Lister's battalion out there tonight. We have asked for the 14th International Brigade. But I don't know. They are so far away. Down in Córdoba. I don't think they will reach us in time."

"What will you do?" Saulnier asked. "If we could only fly for you. But the weather is impossible."

"Exactly. What will we do? We will die at Las Rosas."

"Don't say that, Kopa."

"It is necessary," the German said. "We must stand somewhere and hold them. We will be destroyed, but we will stop them. If we fail . . . but we won't. We won't."

Dorlov and the actress stopped dancing. There was loud applause. The German struck his thick hands together a few times, absently. He seemed to be looking at something a long way off. Saulnier coughed nervously. Dorlov was invited by the actress to sit with her. A waiter scurried over with champagne in a bucket of ice. Kopa was very dirty and very tired. A smile lined his stubbled cheeks and crushed around his pale blue eyes.

"Russians are something, no? It is possible to admire them, to like them. But they are always themselves, somehow, always on guard, suspicious, even of each other. That's sad to see. How can we love them when they do not love each other?"

"Look at this one, Kapitan," Saulnier said. "He has just met a pretty little Madrileña. Is he in love or not?"

"Of course," Kopa said. "Spain is like that these days. One makes the friendship of a lifetime in a few days. In a week, a month, it is gone. Death makes love, creates it. Death destroys men and women, the lovers, but the love remains. We know this and so we can go on, you see? We, each in our way, love Spain. So Spain remains and will remain. Even tonight we have scars on our hearts. We can endure more wounds of the heart. It is our bodies that are so fragile and so few. That is why, out there, tonight, we are willing to stop the tanks with barricades of snow and frozen blood . . ."

The room had quieted. The nearby tables were silent, listening to the German's slow voice beating through the dense blue smoke. The men and women nodded and whispered. Kopa sighed and sipped his wine. He clapped Frank on the shoulder. He sat still, moved by the German's words. It was like hearing the statement of a condemned man who had passed the frontier of fear and stood beyond, looking back with pale, calm eyes. Kopa's smile was gentle, knowing.

"I must agree with your comrade. You have something of the look of a prize-fighter who has just discovered he is not destined to win the championship. You would rather be, like him, somewhere else. But don't worry. At fifty meters or so, it's hardly noticeable. I did not know that the Russian comrades had sent us some of Diaghilev's troupe of dancers."

"He's the best goddamned pilot in the Republic," Frank said.

"He has an extraordinary sense of balance to be sure. May I ask the name of your young lady?"

"Bravo. Carmen Bravo."

"Indeed?"

Kopa looked puzzled for an instant and removed his hand from Frank's shoulder.

"She is the daughter of a Fascist colonel."

"I don't give a damn who her father is. I'm just having dinner with her. I just met the girl."

"A critical case, as you can observe, Kopa. Highly infectious."

"Carmen Bravo."

"You know her?" Frank demanded, suddenly panicked. Half the women in Chicote's were staring at the German officer. Kopa shook his head.

"I know *of* her. Through a mutual comrade, the commander of the Red Guards. She fought in the mountains with them in the beginning. Later, here in the city."

"That . . . kid? You're mistaken, Kopa. She is just a little girl!"

"Spanish women stop being little girls at about five years of age. The Red Guards call her La Novia, sweetheart of the battalion, like your Madelon, Saulnier, in the song."

Frank sat back in his chair, took a deep breath and blew out his cheeks in a long groan.

"Oh," Kopa said. "Don't misunderstand. It's just that the commander of the Red Guards has a sort of brotherly interest in her. At least, I think that's all. With Larra it is very difficult to tell exactly. He was in Russia for two years, you know. That changes a man, even a Spaniard."

"Well, what the hell," Frank said. "You know? . . ."

"She is, they say, quite superb. As a person. And very pretty. *Petite*, eh, Comrade Saulnier?"

"An *hors d'oeuvre*. An *amuse gueule*. Delectable."

"You see?" Kopa said. "Everyone approves. Now, of course, it is the young lady's move. I wish you the best of everything, my friend."

"Love," said Saulnier, "is like a game of chess. No . . . not at all. What am I saying? *Cuidado, hombre!*"

Dorlov hurtled through the smoke and crashed against the table, up-setting the glasses. He saluted Kopa, who bowed in return, rose and shook hands. Dorlov beat their locked hands on Frank's head.

"Why do you sit here, Comrade Capitalist? Calculating your invest-ment. Saulnier's right. You have no soul, boy."

"You are plastered. Leave me alone, or I'll kick you."

"You are Kopa, of course. Delighted. This one here, this American, I have taught to fly the Mosca. You must see it to understand. In the Soviet Union he would be a general by now. And his girl, this girl. At the bull ring. Today. A public spectacle. In my country, looking at each other like that is forbidden by law. And correctly, it makes everyone else very nervous. That is why we are drunk. Waiter, more wine! I will bring Anita over to this table at once."

"Another time, Comrade Dorlov," Kopa said. "I have a driver waiting. I had heard that Lister was here, but he must be back in the trenches."

Frank stood up, dragged on his coat and picked up the package of gloves.

"I'll come with you, Captain. I need some fresh air. I'll see you guys back at the base. Where are the trucks?"

"At the Hotel Bristol. We'll sleep over. The weather's too bad for flying. We can never help enough. I am sorry, Kopa. If we could, you know that Malraux would give orders at once to get every machine in the air."

"Of course. I understand. It is men we need at Las Rosas. Men and ammunition. A *bientôt*, comrades."

"*Suerte*, Kopa."

The murmur followed them across the crowded room, as people stepped aside to let them pass.

"*Suerte . . . Suerte . . . Mucha suerte . . .* Good luck . . . good luck . . . *Suerte compañeros . . . Suerte compatriotas . . . camaradas.*"

On the sidewalk, a mud-smeared command car waited. Kopa held out his hand.

"We have heard that nearly four hundred Americans have arrived in Albacete now. They plan to build to battalion strength, then join us. We have always expected Americans. We have been waiting for them."

"If you ask me," Frank said, "I think that man Roosevelt was scared stiff about the Catholic vote. Otherwise, the United States would have backed the Republic here officially."

"The Atlantic Ocean is not only deep, but very wide, my friend. That some Americans have heard and answered . . . that is good. We knew you could not betray us."

"Maybe as many Americans will come here as you Germans."

"We are closer. We have been betrayed, betrayed ourselves. We must put an end to this, here, in Spain."

"We can do it! Give us a few more planes, some decent tanks and . . ."

"That's true. We need the matériel. We have the people, no?"

"I'll say."

"And you . . . you, you know, are one of the people now. One of us."

"I guess so. It just sort of happened."

"How it happened is not important. Only that it did."

"Oh, it did, I know it now."

"No, you won't betray us. It is in the air, like a fog over Europe, a poisonous fog. There will be more of it, not less. Man cannot live in such a deadly mist. Better to breath awhile the clean, pure air and die than to exist in a poisoned fog. Well, I give speeches on the sidewalk, it seems. What next? I am very tired. Two days now, no sleep. Go to her and be true. There is nothing to be afraid of, I promise you. Nothing at all. Good-by, comrade."

"*Auf wiedersehen*, Kopa!"

"Yes, that's better, isn't it? Until we see each other again."

The sedan pulled away from the curb, U-turned, and drove away into the night. Frank watched it go. He felt lonely and depressed. Two hours stretched before him. He began to walk the streets of Madrid. It was dark and cold. Militia patrols on the street corners. He walked on to the Palace Hotel. The same *miliciano* was on duty there.

"Back so soon, *camarada?* No cinema?"

"No. I've seen *los hermanos Marx.*"

"I have seen them twelve times. Also the Shirley Temple film. You have heard the news?"

"What news?"

"The front is broken."

"Not true. I have just been with one of the officers. Lister's battalion is going out. Also the 14th Brigada Internacional."

"Even they have traitors."

"What do you say?"

"The whole of Madrid knows it. Major Lasalle, the commander of the French. The Marseilles Battalion. He was a spy for the Fascists. He was tried and shot. A spy, a traitor. Who can you trust these days?"

"Yourself, comrade."

"Exactly. That's why I am an Anarchist. And a good Republican, of course."

"Who accused this Major Lasalle?"

"Why, another Frenchman. André Marty, of the Internationals."

"I see. What hour is it?"

"The eighth."

"*Gracias. Salud.*"

"*Salud.*"

He sat in the café, beside the table reserved for General Mola, and drank bad coffee, read a newspaper and smoked. At nine o'clock, the door opened. He looked up, his heart thudding. She marched into the place, high heels rapping, and snatched a shawl off her damp, dark curls. She wore a military overcoat, belted tight. Several men greeted her. She looked around, a single, quick glance that swept the room. She walked to the table. He stood up, making a great clatter. She sat down and unbuttoned her overcoat. She wore a modest wool dress of lilac color.

"Am I late?"

"No. Not at all. You look . . . like springtime."

"Good! May I have a drink?"

"And what do you drink, Carmen?"

"Pernod."

"Pernod! That's pretty strong stuff."

"I like it," she said firmly.

"Two Pernods, *camarero.*"

"*Sí*, señorito."

Frank offered her a cigarette and took her hand. He felt stupid and apprehensive. All the things that Kopa had said churned around in his mind. He wanted to tell her many things, but he knew his Spanish wasn't good enough.

"I saw your friends," she said, when the waiter brought their drinks.

"Oh?"

"At the apartment. The Frenchman, Saulnier, brought champagne and some Russian and Anita Rodríguez, the actress."

"I see."

He didn't. They toasted each other and sipped the Pernod. She giggled suddenly.

"What's so funny?"

"Well, by the time I left, they were . . . in bed, you know. Not altogether. Two and two. Only the Russian was asleep, I think."

"My God. I should have known it," he muttered.

"What did you say? Will you teach me some American, Francisco?"

"Yes, of course. I was apologizing for my friends. Saulnier is *mal educado* . . . badly brought up."

"So was Teresa. They were all laughing and singing. It was very gay . . . very sophisticated . . . and . . ."

Her voice wavered, and she looked at him quickly, her long lashes fluttering, and looked away.

"And what, Carmen?"

"And . . . and I've never been out at night with a man in my life. Alone, I mean. Not even *once!*"

She did not cry, because there were people around and, apparently, because she had simply decided not to cry. He looked at her.

"Carmen? Tell me something. The truth."

"Yes."

"Have you ever had Pernod before?"

"I used to steal my father's."

"I see. You look tired and hungry, yes?"

"I am always tired and hungry. Everybody is."

"Then finish your drink and we'll go to the place with the piano."

"I could eat a burro, hoofs and tail."

"That's probably what we'll get."

"Will you tell me about America, Francisco?"

"I'll try."

"I have only seen it in films. It looks . . . very different. Horrible." She laughed suddenly.

"I shouldn't say that, eh? I meant to say 'different.'"

"That's okay."

"Okay. Promise you won't talk about the war."

"I promise. Finish your drink."

"I never get drunk, don't worry. I have a soldier's head."

"And cold hands?"

"Maybe. You are very *simpático*."

"Thank you. We go now?"

"We go now. But first you must pay, no?"

They fed pesetas into the mechanical piano, ate horse meat and boiled turnips with a bottle of wine. For dessert there was a spoonful of rice pudding sweetened with honey. He asked her to dance, but she refused. She didn't know how. They walked back through the dark streets, groping hand in hand.

"I can't go back to the apartment. I will sleep at the Palace Hotel. And you?"

"At the Bristol."

"Is it nice?"

"Noisy."

"Oh."

They stopped at the corner of the Palace Hotel. A gang of *practicantes* and nurses were unloading ambulances from the front. The trucks were covered with wet snow. Flashlights bobbed in the darkness, and the wounded groaned. She began to tremble violently and clung to him.

"I don't want to go in there! I'll be helping. I don't want to see their faces. They are Germans, now. The Thaelmanns. They just give them morphine and wait until they die. Francisco, will you take me with you?"

"Huh?"

"To the Hotel Bristol."

"No, Carmen. That wouldn't be right."

"No . . . Will you see me again?"

"Of course. The weather is bad. We don't fly. Tomorrow night?"

"Yes. Same place. The café. It is your custom to kiss, no?"

"Yes," he said, and kissed her.

Villanueva   Feb, 1937

Dear Da

Things have got better with us Abraham Lincolns, more than 400 now. We have a regular Dr., named Pike, a movie-show machine we all chipped in for (but no Bank Nite) and some officers the best is Merriman, 2nd in command. The James Connally outfit that was with the British took a vote and most came to join with us. There CO is named Ryan and he is some baby. They have been in Spain some time and done some real fighting. The night they come to us we had a fiesta (party) with good food, *vino* and songs. So yrs. truly isnt the only

Irishman. One of the songs they sang was Clancys Wooden Wedding and, Da, when they sang it out about Big Jim Mahoney neat as a pin he brought a cradle for to rock the baby in you should have heard the guys all laugh. They kidded me a real lot and I had taken a drop you know and got into a fight with someone for calling Schwartz a yellow sheeny. Stember, he's what we call the comic-star for the outfit and some others all members of the Com. Party had me up the next day and chewed my ass. They said I got IRA and IWW ideas that are no good these days. I got guard duty and books to read and lessons like in school. I decided Id show them what a real Boston boy can do and learned it and got to be best in the field too with the rifles and the dummy grenades and all. I wanted to get in the Tom Mooney Co (machine guns, 2 old ones only but they work ok) they wouldn't let me and I was pissed. Then they made me a section leader in the third rifle co. It was White who fixed that I learned. He is an ok guy alright, a section leader to and so is Schwartz. I have worked my section there asses smooth and we are the best in the co. if not maybe all of the Lincolns. We have lessons on politics every night and these Com. Party guys know a real lot. White says I can maybe join in a yr or so if I prove myself. So I try every day like hell because I remember Da what you told me about if you cant lick them join them but White says that is negative thinking and it takes more. He is an ok guy alright and plenty smart, nigger or not, only they all say here colored comrade. It has snowed some and everybody says we are going to go up to the lines somewhere because a big bunch of wops came over with tanks and guns and its real bad for the republic now. I hope to hell we fight soon I will show them all you bet. Send me some papers and cigs if you can. How do things look for the Red Sox did they make any trades yet?

> Your son,
> Jimmy (section leader for the Abraham
> Lincoln battalion)

Out on the flight line, a rocket popped. A dozen Italian Caproni bombers began to move, stirring one after the other like heavy hornets. They slid down the runway and lifted clear. Four diesel tractors were towing bomb trucks out to the Junkers trimotors. The German and Italian bomber squadrons flew in rotation from dawn until twilight, two hundred kilometers to Málaga, unloaded their explosives on the smoldering city and cruised back. There was no anti-aircraft defense at Málaga, and the Republican interceptors were north in the Jarama sector. The bomber squadrons flew from Seville to Málaga on a fixed schedule like a railroad. There had been no combat losses, and none were anticipated.

Bravo stopped at the daily report board, the news from the fronts typed out in German, Italian, and Spanish. In the north, the Basques were still retreating. Málaga was doomed. The young Italian general Roatta, hero of Ethiopia, had moved his Black Shirt armored columns to Ventas de Zafarra and dominated the highway running north to the Republican capital at Valencia. The Nationalist warships *Canarias, Velasco,* and *Baleares* were shelling the coast line while the German battleship *Graf Spee* cruised in international waters on patrol. The Anarchist commander at Málaga, was not going to defend the city. The 13th International Brigade at Murcia had not been shifted to break the siege. The Reds were abandoning Málaga without a real fight.

The office was quiet, a few clerk-typists pecking out routine fuel and ammunition reports. The morning mail had come in. Bravo carried two heavy envelopes to his desk. The first, an answer to his request that a full squadron of Spanish pilots receive training in the new Messerschmitt interceptor aircraft, had been routed to General Hugo Sperrle, commander of the Kondor Legion and referred in turn to Kapitan Kurt Schmidt for comment. The carbon sheet had been preserved by the Spanish typist:

> All Spanish student-pilots are without exception mechanically incompetent and confuse conceit with courage. Since, with these inferiorities, they cannot learn to fly our aircraft well, let them be trained at some other field in Italian aircraft, most of which are obsolete in any case.

General Sperrle's letter was polite: the new machines were relatively untested, some difficulties had been reported in the hydraulic systems and the shell-ejectors for the nose cannon. Until these problems were corrected to the satisfaction of local squadron flight operations officers . . . and so on. Bravo dropped the pages. He was quite powerless against this sort of thing. The Germans had their own ships, crews, mechanics, and instructors. Spanish personnel were allowed, grudgingly, to watch and to listen. The Italians imitated the Nazis. Seville airfield might as well be Hamburg or Milan.

The second letter was postmarked Marbella, a seacoast town some twenty kilometers south of Málaga, sent from staff headquarters of the Duke of Seville, commander in that area, a Bourbon aristocrat. The letter was short and correctly courteous. While there were no field commands of infantry available at the present moment for an officer possessing the high qualifications of the most respected Colonel Bravo, an intelligence survey of the aerial bombardment of Málaga and the effect of sustained attack was imperative. Puzzling discrepancies between the claims of the Kondor Legion, the Italian high command and observed results had already reached the attention of the Generalísimo. Therefore, the Duke of Seville had requested the general staff of the Army of the South to post Colonel Bravo, present liaison officer at Seville air base, to temporary duty as field intelligence officer to the brigade the Duke of Seville had the honor of commanding. Colonel Bravo was encouraged to make use of transport from the Seville area motor pool and to report at his very earliest convenience.

At last. There was no point in waiting until the order cleared through staff. The papers could be forwarded to him. He was free. Once attached to field headquarters, his experience, loyalty and influence would be rewarded. Success at Málaga would mean promotion for the Duke of Seville to brigadier. Some officer of high qualifications would be selected to replace the Duke. Certainly the rabble of Falangist "new shirts" would be passed over. Then, then . . .

Colonel Bravo called the motor pool and requested a staff car. He dictated a directive to his immediate subordinate, authorizing that officer to accept all responsibilities for services and supplies to the base. He wrote brief notes in his own hand to the Italian and German wing commanders, informing them of the change of command. He stood at his window, quietly and completely satisfied, looking down on a football game. He saw Schmidt, limber and fresh, running and passing the ball. *Macht durch Freude*—Strength through Joy, the Aryan sportsman, a walking recruiting poster for the Luftwaffe. Bravo's white-gloved fingers trembled on the window sill. He phrased a portion of the intelligence report he would write for the Spanish high command, copies in German and Italian to be released on the level of all squadron commanders:

> All German combat-crews are, without exception, lacking in the imagination necessary to convert striking power to tactical victory and confuse conceit with courage. Since, with these inferiorities, they cannot learn the meaning of our Hispanic crusade, let them be removed to some other field, with the Italian aircraft . . .

No. It would never be allowed. He would never write his report in such a fashion. A simple statement of the tactical effectiveness of Spanish artillery, supported by photographs, a simple statement of the tactical uselessness of the German bombing, accompanied by more photographs of craters in an open field, a dead mule, a smashed barber shop. That would be enough. Schmidt would have ample time then to improve his football.

Photographs. Bravo went to his safe and took out the secret file. He turned the shoddy pages ripped from *Mundo Obrero* and *Solidaridad*. It had pleased God to allow his enemies to practice a sadistic, but absurdly futile form of vengeance. At first, their plot had been a nerve-scraping torment, then dwindled in effect to a minor nuisance; finally these enemies had placed in his hands proof of their own dishonor. The circulation of enemy propaganda through the regular or military mail services had been declared a crime punishable by death. Here, in the folder, was evidence enough. The photographs of Carmen. A deliberate attempt to discredit his loyalty to the Nationalist movement on one hand, an effort to destroy his morale on the other.

The latest one showed her, arm-in-arm, smiling into the face of some new man, a blurred face, neither ugly nor handsome, in flying costume with a pair of goggles hanging around his neck. The caption and article below were typical Bolshevik drivel. The little whore was in love again, this time with a "Hero of the People's Republic," symbolic of the blending of two cultures, two revolutionary spirits, a love triumphant that prefigured victory on all fronts and the emergence of a new, modern Spanish state. Sickening, sickening.

It was Carmen, without a doubt. No one else with those dark, stubborn eyes, those smiling lips he could not see, even in a bad photograph, without feeling an urge to strike her in the face. Her short, curly hair, vaguely French in fashion and unspeakably vulgar, had been retouched before printing to accentuate the "Amazon" look that was fashionable in the Republic. Let her sleep with every international "volunteer" in Madrid, a gang of criminals, morphine-addicts and venereals. As a final reward for her disobedience, her face, rotten with syphilis, would be used as a prophylactic poster.

He swept the pictures into his briefcase and telephoned Ronda to confirm quarters for himself and the chauffeur. He was perfectly calm as he went about his last little affairs, ordering triplicate typing of all significant documents, a final check on the gasoline and ammunition lists, a sealed set of instructions to his replacement describing the system by which documents were collected from German and Italian sources. All was in order.

He took lunch alone in the officer's mess, and drank a half bottle of good Valdepeñas. The fall of Málaga was imminent, but the Italians, despite nine full battalions of Black Shirts with artillery and tanks, made no move to press an assault to overwhelming victory. Roatta was afraid of another Madrid, a slaughter in the rubbled streets and ruined houses. The Germans were all robots, the Italians cowardly swine. When Spanish troops marched into Málaga, he would accompany them. When final victory was attained over the Bolsheviks, somewhere in the records of the military tribunals the folder of photographs would lie. The guilty ones would be dead, all of them. The past would be forgotten, forgiven and decency, loyalty, and ambition justly rewarded.

Colonel Bravo stepped into the Hispano-Suizo sedan before the siesta quiet was shattered by the sound of bomber motors warming up for the 1400 hours run over Málaga. He passed through the checkpoint at the entrance to the field. The sentries saluted. Colonel bravo saluted and smiled. He was free. He instructed the driver to take the highway to Ronda. He could pick up a field kit there, run through the hills to the northeast and come into the city with Roatta's Italian armor. By nightfall, he could reach the headquarters of the Duke of Seville with the first fragments of the report discrediting the Black Shirts and minimizing the effectiveness of the Kondor Legion.

The roads were clear, the chauffeur skilled. Colonel Bravo requisitioned a field kit and obtained an official photographer at Ronda. He had the driver stop near a broken barricade, changed into field dress and was photographed standing on the barricade looking east through his binoculars. Here was an honest photograph. Caption: NEAR THE FRONT. He changed poses until the photographer had used up one role of film.

There was no sign of action, but the roads had been torn by tank treads. The villages seemed abandoned. The sedan swept on toward Antequera, over narrow dirt roads, empty beneath the cool, clear sky. They shot over the crest of a hill. Before them the road ran straight down into a broad, shallow valley and to a stone bridge across a river bed filled with shadows. A long plume of dust lifted up and hung in the golden afternoon.

The highway north to Almería looked like a strip of flypaper clotted with struggling insects. The flight of Messerschmitts had passed over the burning city to the south. At two thousand meters' altitude, the Italian tanks and motorized artillery were clearly visible, like bugs crawling on the earth. From the fringe of Málaga north, the Black Shirts had set up road blocks. Only women and children were allowed through. Down on the long beaches, the execution squads were shooting the men, uniformed or not. The waves came in, broke and creamed over dark specks that tumbled in the shallows.

Flight orders were precise, as always: *Strafe vehicles Málaga-Motril. Test-fire cannons.* The Messerschmitt squadron had been armed with explosive bullets for the 20-millimeter cannon that fired through the propeller hub. The cannons had jammed, as the result of engine heat and expansion, but new baffles had been installed. The sea was very blue, the sky clear. There was no ground fire whatever, not even when the squadron broke and made low runs over the highway and railroad. Schmidt wagged his wings and climbed. The others scattered, each man to seek targets. It was rather pointless and boring for one plane after another to strafe the same sections of road, the same burning trucks.

Schmidt circled inland. He could see the others, like sharks in a shallow clear sea soar up, wing over, and dive again. He dropped the throttle and cruised. The new planes were splendid, fast, strong, well-armed and maneuverable.

Low, bare, rolling hills slid beneath the square-tipped wings. Here and there a few stone barns and houses. It was a miserable country, Spain, with dirty, inefficient people and bad food. It was only when the country was considered, as it should be, as a huge target, a testing ground, that it made any sense at all. Some of the hills must hide the few Republican lice shaken out of Málaga. Schmidt pushed the stick forward, and the aircraft slid down through the blue air. He glanced at the compass, the fuel gauge, his watch. Time for a long look, then northwest to the rally-point at Antequera. The squadron was to reform there and fly into Seville, a matter of minutes. He still had a half drum of cannon ammunition.

He saw the automobile, alone, moving very fast almost directly east along a dirt road, raising a long line of dust like a piece of soft brown yarn. He climbed three hundred meters and looked around. No getting caught by something dropping out of the sun this time. Why was the vehicle here, between Roatta's force and the Spanish troops to the south? It was brown—Spanish then—not black like the Italian equipment. The thing scuttled like a beatle dragging a bit of yarn.

An exercise in advanced ballistics, velocity, air speed, direction, trajectory. A good lead, the nose raised, a single burst, right at the stone bridge. Schmidt tripped the cannon-trigger, and the interceptor shivered as the cannon fired *crong-crong-crong-crong*. Stone dust sprayed up from the bridge. The driver tried to brake, the sedan skidded on directly into the little storm of explosive projectiles. Schmidt saw the pale flash, like an electric spark, that lifted the sedan off the ground and then the gush of flame as the vehicle broke through the abutment, smashing stones and mortar. He flew through the concussion bubble, and the Messerschmitt bounded up, full-throttled for Antequera. Schmidt banked and looked back. The bridge was a fleck, the dirt road a dim stroke on the earth, the burning Spanish staff car a bright petal fluttering in the dark shadows of a dry river bed.

He would write in his report that the nose cannon had functioned perfectly.

The trucks were parked in a big circle, the radiators against the wooden barrier of the bull ring. The speeches were over. Cold twilight hung over Albacete. Somewhere up near Madrid, the Fascists had punched a big hole in the Republican lines. The breakthrough was in the Jarama Valley. If the Fascists were allowed to keep going, to exploit the opening, Madrid would be surrounded, cut off completely. The Abraham Lincoln battalion was being sent to Jarama to help plug the gap.

Field equipment was distributed. First, case after case of rifles slobbered with protective grease. The men sat on the sand of the bull ring and stripped the stuff off with their fingers and shirttails. The rifles were American manufacture, Remingtons, but two different lengths. The long ones were stamped with the double-headed eagle of imperial Russia, the shorter ones with the hammer and sickle of the Soviet Union. Every man who got a rifle was handed a leather belt with three cartridge boxes and a long French stiletto bayonet, not flat like a knife, but triangular. Mahoney fitted his on the muzzle of his rifle and lunged, driving the long blade into the sand.

"Jesus, now, they're real toad-stabbers, huh?"

He laughed and jabbed the sand twice more. The other members of his section, watched him.

"Jim, ain't we gonna get our helmets like the rest?"

"Go get one if you want. They ain't no damned good."

"Regular steel helmet, Jim. Made out of regular steel."

The others nodded. It was good to think about, a helmet of steel that protected you. Mahoney laughed scornfully.

"Thin as bum-wad. They got no liners. A helmet's no good without a liner."

"Who says?"

"White says."

"Oh."

The men in the section were not sure what a liner was, but if Andy White said a helmet was no good without one, they believed it. They squatted in the cold dusk and scraped the thick grease from the Remingtons, laughing and joking. Somebody trotted up to them.

"The Hose says come get your ammo."

"Okay. Let's go, you guys."

"The Hose," José Cubeta, leader of the Cubans attached to the third rifle company, waved to Mahoney from the back of one of the trucks. They got in line, eager, excited. They were to be issued one hundred and fifty rounds each in three heavy, reassuring packets that fit snugly into their new cartridge belts. Between the stacked ammunition and the first man, sat one of the B.P.s, base police, a Frenchman. Mahoney stepped up.

"Your passport, comrade."

"What for?"

"Security. First, passport, then bullets to kill Fascists."

Mahoney pulled his passport from his pocket and flung it into a box.

The B.P. nodded, and Mahoney was issued his ammunition. The others in his section did the same. The heavy packets made the belts sag over their hips. They swaggered back to cleaning their rifles. It grew dark, and still they waited. Schwartz found Mahoney.

"You hear that Merriman and Seacord and Johnny and Steve got battle commissions?"

"No foolin'? Hear that, you bums? Battle commissions! Yahoo!"

"They get to keep the rank, if they don't get . . . you know."

"You give that Frog yer passport, Schwartzie?"

"Well . . . no, I didn't. They gave me the ammunition, anyway."

"I guess it don't mean nothin. Who's that bunch over by the gate?"

"Dr. Barsky from New York. Some nurses, too. Very nice girls."

"Yeh?" Mahoney said. "Guess I'll go innerduce myself. We got plenty a time. Hey, baby, help out a hero."

He strolled away into the darkness. The men around Schwartz laughed.

"Jimmy figures he'll get laid."

"Jimmy always figgers he's gonna get laid."

"Whatta we need a doctor for? Nobody's sick."

"Whatta we need a doctor for? Listen to that."

A truck whirred and snorted, another and another. Mahoney came running back, excited and waving his arms.

"All aboard, you guys, all aboard! Here we go!"

Schwartz ran back to his section. In the dim light from the single bulb jerking in the wind at the main gate, he saw some of the officers from the base, shaking hands and talking with his men. André Marty, wearing a huge beret, Colonel Vidal, and Kerrigan, the Base Commissar. Kerrigan shook Schwartz by the hand as he clambered up on the tailgate.

"Good luck, boy."

"Thanks."

The truck pulled away. Outside the bull ring, the wind hit them. They broke out blankets and huddled together. It was a long, long, cold, bone-slamming ride over bad, twisted roads. They stopped to refuel twice and the men dropped down to urinate, stiff and clumsy, wrapped in their blankets, some clutching their greasy rifles. They got back on the trucks and drove on. No one could sleep. They were moving up to the front. They stared through the darkness, looking for it, listening for cannons above the dull roar of the truck motors.

At dawn, grey, misty and cold, they reached and passed through the town of Chinchón. They halted along the road. The men stayed in the trucks. There was nothing to eat, no coffee. The word went around that the brigade had a new commander, Čopic, a Yugoslavian. The grease on the rifles had thickened in the cold. The stocks and barrels felt like bacon fat. They looked around. There was nothing to see but mist and low, rolling hills covered with weeds and dry grass. They shivered in their blankets and waited.

White appeared, big and easy, his dark face serious. He leaned over the side of the truck.

"Word just come from Bob Merriman. This truck gets down and stands spread out on the right. Everybody takes five rounds. Test fire these rifles."

"Whatta we shoot at? We at the front yet?"

"Uh-uh. Got ten kilometers to go. Just loose off at the hills there. Then clean the rifles."

"Huh? With what?"

"How do you clean these things, anyway?"

White pulled out his shirttail and tore off a strip.

"Make a pull-through, like this. You got shoelaces, right? Tie em together, drop it down the barrel and pull the hunk of shirt through. That's the best we can do."

"Okay."

Mahoney hefted his Remington and pulled the bolt back. His fingers were greasy, and he dropped the first cartridge, wiped it clean, and dropped it a second time. He rolled it on his shirt and slipped it into the breech, eased the bolt forward. The cartridge disappeared. He heard something click.

"Load," he said. "Make it snappy."

He watched Schwartz and the men of that section. Up came the rifles, a wobbly line. Schwartz shouted, and the rifles crashed. Mahoney jumped, startled by the ragged volley. The echo came back, damped by the morning mist. The men in Schwartz's section looked surprised and happy. They patted their rifles and grinned at each other. Mahoney grunted.

"You see that, you guys?" he said. "We're gonna do better, see? When I say *aim*, point at that hill there. When I say *fire*, squeeze, all at the same time. Get it? Awright. Ready? *Aim!*"

He watched them as he lifted his own rifle and snugged the butt against his shoulder. He was shivering from the cold and nervousness. The muzzle bobbled all over the place. He took a deep breath of the chill, wet air.

"*Fire!*"

He squeezed the trigger and closed his eyes. The rifle smashed him in the shoulder, rocking him back on his heels. It nearly slipped from his fingers. He looked down the line.

"You guys shoot?"

They nodded, grinning, with rather dazed expressions. Mahoney looked at his rifle. How did you unload it? He worked the bolt, and the cartridge fell out at his feet. Sure enough, the pointed bullet was gone. He took another cartridge from his belt and fed it into the Remington.

"Load up! . . . Ready? . . . Aim . . . *Fire!*"

He kept his eyes open this time, or tried to, but flinched when the rifle went off, kicking his shoulder again. He stared at the hill, expecting fountains of dirt to blow up into the sky. All up and down the highway, the other men of the battalion were firing. It sounded like the Fourth of July. Mahoney shouted happily and loaded and fired off his five cartridges, bent and gathered the spent shells and put them in his pocket for souvenirs.

"Mahoney's boys is ready and spoilin' for it!" he said, rubbing his shoulder gingerly.

They waited. All morning. It got a little warmer, but not much. They got a soup ration and some bread. Officers from Chinchón came out and looked at them. The men looked back at the officers. One of them carried a little gold-headed stick under his arm and had bright polished boots. He was Nathan, an Englishman, Brigade chief of staff, and seemed very cheerful when he told them about the artillery and the aircraft and the machine-gun fire they would run into on the road to Morata, the next stop. At three in the afternoon, the trucks were refueled and they moved on.

The bombers hit them just outside of the town of Morata. They stood packed in the trucks, watching the dark specks in the sky. The specks swung around and grew bigger. The trucks stopped, brakes jammed on. The men swarmed over the sides and ran out into the fields. The officers were shouting for them to lie down, hit the dirt. They flung themselves onto the muddy furrows, turned their faces and watched the sky over their shoulders. They couldn't hear the motors at first, and the first bomb hit before they knew it had been dropped.

"Them Krauts can't bomb for shit," a voice said.

Schwartz looked around, raising his head an inch. Another bomb hit down the road. Andrew White was lying on his back, his hands locked under his head, watching the planes.

"Germans?"

"Yeah. Oh-oh. Watch *out!* Here they come!"

"Whatta you mean?"

Schwartz looked up. Three Heinkel bombers hurtled down from the gray sky and roared at the convoy. Schwartz saw the dark line of the wings and three bright circles, the twin propellers and the glass nose of the nearest plane. Something hit the dirt between him and the man to his left, another and another thing, a wet, popping sound, and the planes hammered over and were gone, lifting up into the sky.

"Stay down! Stay down! They're coming back!"

The planes turned, banking, their motors a dull hum and swung until all that showed again was the dark wing line, the propeller discs and the glass and steel nose. Schwartz, propped on his right elbow, his mouth open, watched them swell in the sky. Bits of the road skipped up into the air and the popping sounds in the wet earth began again. He looked at White, angry and astounded.

"What the hell are they trying to do, *kill us?*"

White began to laugh as Schwartz flopped back, face down in the mud. The German bombers snarled over them, machine guns hammering. White heard the hard smack of a rifle-shot, a voice cursing, and then another shot. He looked around. Jim Mahoney was kneeling in the mud, firing his rifle up at the German planes. He pulled the trigger and his body jerked from the kick of the weapon. The big, broad-winged bombers boomed up into the sky, turning tightly in formation. White sat up. Mahoney was still kneeling, his rifle butt down in the mud, staring up at the planes. He pointed.

"I got one, sure's hell!" he shouted, "Look!"

There were no casualties, not a man wounded. Mahoney was reprimanded half-heartedly, by the battalion commissar. The men got back into the trucks, excited, singing and shouting. This was more like it! Bombers, enemy planes, strafing, and nobody so much as touched. The men were counted off, and the trucks checked and counted. There was one truck missing, a big French Matford with twenty-odd men and the battalion files, records and organization sheets and rosters. It had simply vanished, somehow, somewhere between Chinchón and Morata. They never saw the truck, the papers or the men again.

But it was a good afternoon, with the men shouting from truck to truck as soon as they could hear the cannons, like thunder, bumping and growling up ahead:

"Hey, what are they tryin' to do, *kill us?*"

Mahoney's section was nicknamed "The Irish Anti-aircraft."

They saw tanks painted with red stars moving toward their base at Perales, another town not far from the lines. The Americans hung over the sides of the trucks and cheered and shouted. The turrets were open, and each hatch-opening was filled with what seemed to be identical bodies and blond, oily-faced drivers.

"Hey, comrade! *Salud*, buddy! *Comprendy* English? You a Roosky, Mac?"

The men in the turrets grinned and saluted with the clenched fist. "*Salud! Da, da.*"

"Hey, they *are* Russians!"

"Looka them goddamn tanks, huh! We got good stuff. Looka that one go."

The tanks, treads making a steady, clattering racket, swung off, the men in the turrets still waving and smiling. And then came the brief winter twilight and the quick, starless dark. The trucks stopped. They were there. They had reached that place everyone always talked about—the front.

It was black, black and cold, but a night filled with noise, the soft, faraway bunt of cannon fire, the high slither of a shell directly above, the chuckle of stones down an invisible hillside, the mean, intense whir of a mortar round and a red stab of light, the whistle of steel bits in the black air, the hard batter of a machine gun.

White found that every time he moved, his section snuggled around him. Everything was tight and taut and dark, everything crammed together and nervy. He finally got them to string out and follow each other by sound up the iron slope of a hill. He followed some men from the machine-gun company. Every so often, they set down a tripod, and he trotted forward toward the clank and the heavy breathing. They crossed a railroad line, stumbling over the tracks. The dark night hissed, swished, and sizzled. Machine-gun bullets, but fired too high. They scrambled up the slope and along the steep crest of a hill.

"Dig in along here. Deep. This place is going to be under fire in the morning."

"Dig?" White said. "With what? We got no tools."

"You've got bayonets, helmets, and hands, haven't you?"

"I guess so."

They dug. They picked, scraped and pried and cursed, gouging little pits and scratching up hunks of frozen earth, lumps with ice crystal that numbed their hands. Tattered, muddy figures stole past in the darkness speaking French, English, and Polish. The Americans burrowed and raked. The morning did not break upon them but leaked through the cotton-colored mist, a morning of brown, broken earth, bleeding fingers and cold coffee from a British kitchen. The hills of Jarama rolled up from the mist, not hard, stony peaks, but rounded, rumpled together like a brown sea, frozen waves of earth sprigged with ruined olive groves, pocked with craters. They could not see the forward positions held by the British, the other Internationals and the Spanish. But ahead, some 1500 meters, less than a mile, they could see the rutted lines, the shell-lopped silvery trunks of olive trees, the timber balks laced by rusty wire and the sand-bags like a string of lice clinging to the raw flank of Spanish earth—the trenches of the enemy.

They sat, weary and disoriented, and looked. Their own lines, shallow scrapings of the night, wandered along the west face of one hill and around the northern hump with battalion headquarters over the crest to the rear, safe from anything but mortar fire. The machine-gun company scrabbled like gophers, trying to dig pits for the four Maxim guns. They sat and smoked damp cigarettes and drank gritty cold coffee and when it became really light enough to see decently, the cannons on the other side across the valley started to fire, a slow, sporadic booming and the first shells came over, swift and silky across the sky, like someone ripping rotten cloth, and the earth shook and bounded up in muddy cypress-shapes, each hit a sluggish leap up of frozen dirt and the searing whistle of fragments.

"They don't really mean nothin," White told his section hopefully. "They just tossin a few, a lot like a pitcher in the bull pen, see? Loosenin' up, like. I guess they know we're here somewhere's but how much and . . ."

He ducked as some light stuff fell around him. A forward position was gone, but no one hurt. They came up the slope, hands and knees, and fell into the first hole. An enemy machine out in the mist swept along the hill and then a crackle of rifle fire. No one shot back. There was nothing to shoot at, just the mist and the muddy earth. By midmorning, the artillery stopped. The Abraham Lincoln battalion had two dead: Charlie Edwards, shot through the head by a rifle bullet and Misak Chelebian, a New Yorker, blown apart by a direct hit on his slit trench, his head cut from his body. Both men were buried, and the trenches and rifle pits were dug deeper and wider.

The two forces, Rebel and Republican, had stood face to face in the Jarama Valley, a stiffened sea of frozen, rolling hills that shut off battalion from battalion, rain-drenched slopes littered with broken olives and dead horses and ripped at each other day and night for two weeks. Pavlov's Russian tanks cruised and rumbled, the gunners pounding the little Fiat tanks to burning junk to be smashed themselves by German anti-tank shells howling flat between the narrow buttock creases of the slick, cold mud. All the new planes the Republic had were driven like mules, flogged up into the dripping skies to tear at the clumsy Junkers dribbling fragmentation bombs down on the battleground.

For seven hours on the twelfth of February, 1937, the British held a slope outside of San Martín de la Vega. North of the British were the remnants of the French *Sixth of February* battalion, north of them eight hundred men of the Dimitrovs. South . . . south of the British position, for three full English miles, there had been no one, nothing, no defense at all. German medium tanks and the little, machine-gun spitting Fiats, supported by Italian mortar squads and German heavy machine guns plunged at the scatter of Internationals. The French machine guns over-heated and jammed, and the French ran. A dozen Russian tanks with twenty minutes of gasoline left in the tanks came up to plug the gap. The British and Poles had rifle ammunition and holes in the ground. They had no hand grenades at all. The Poles were driven from their trenches five times by Moorish infantry. Five times they came back with bayonet counterattacks, and the last time they held. The position was called "Suicide Hill."

The Thaelmann battalion lost its commander and commissar. The

Edgar André had every officer killed. The Commander of the Dimitrovs was killed, as were almost all of the officers of the Sixth of February battalion.

The Spanish reinforcements arrived, then the 14th International Brigade, then, by truck from the base at Albacete, the Americans, the Abraham Lincolns.

Of the French, there were one hundred and fifty survivors of the original eight hundred, the Dimitrovs had less than two hundred men. The British counted one hundred and twenty-five of six hundred who had marched into the Jarama Valley. The American volunteers held the hills near Morata and listened to all the stories, dug, and ducked shells. On February 22, they moved, shifted along the line into the trenches the Dimitrovs had held with bayonets. The Republican commanders planned to counterattack across the Jarama on the twenty-third, a bayonet assault by the Americans of the Abraham Lincoln battalion.

Schwartz could feel the broken macadam road through the soles of his soggy boots. The other two companies had gone forward into the black night with canteens wrapped in their shirts and carrying their bayonets. They seemed to have walked away straight into the muddy slopes. There was no moon, no stars. Schwartz had a pocket compass that glowed pale candy green, as though bits of a Necco wafer had been scattered under the crystal cover. Behind him, the men of his section shifted and breathed. Schwartz was convinced that the essential thing about command was confidence, but what moved him across the road into the cold solid dark was a new kind of fear.

"Follow me," he said in a hoarse whisper, and started in what he hoped was a southwest march. Someone pulled at his sleeve.

"Where's the friggin' trench, Norm?"

"If we move oblique, we'll cut right across it."

"You sure?"

"I'm positive."

They walked slowly, a blind shuffle. Schwartz slipped his foot forward, like a man testing thin ice, eased his weight on it, slipped his other foot out, balancing himself with his rifle. He smelled the trench, the dank, sour mud stench. The lip broke beneath his boot, and clods dropped to the trench bottom. He turned and walked along the trench. It was deserted. The Poles of the Dimitrov battalion must have pulled out.

A human voice gurgled in the night. Schwartz stopped, every nerve quailing. He held his breath, feeling his heart joggle, and listened. The sound of voices seemed to come from above and away, a kind of fumbling gargle that floated through the dark. Schwartz dropped to the ground. The section collapsed, a pig pile strewn along the trench lip, the men tangled together. Schwartz hooked out his arms so that his rifle lay in his elbow crooks. He began the belly-crawl, worming his way over the cold mud on his knees and elbows. Someone breathed on him, a warm gush against his face.

"Schwartzie, what the hella you doin?"

"We better infiltrate this area. Belly-crawl. Pass it on."

"Belly-crawl, pass it on."

"Belly-crawl. Pass it on."

The section began squirming along the abandoned trench, back toward the macadam road. It occurred to Schwartz that he could slide down into the trench and walk, but he decided not to try. The hair on his neck crawled. Somewhere in the night the Moors were talking to each other; a squad of skirmishers had worked across the valley into the trenches. If they could only crawl along until they found the machine-gun company, it would be okay. He grunted and wiggled forward. His knees and elbows began to hurt.

It sounded, at first, like water falling on rocks, or the surf at Coney Island. The ground before him and off to his left lightened as moonlight came through a torn hunk of cloud. The mud shone like silver. Schwartz looked around. He could see lines of men, shoulders, helmet-covered heads, rifles and bayonets. These men were sitting there in the dark, applauding. Schwartz and his section were getting a solid round of enthusiastic applause. He scrambled up to a seated position, his wet legs tucked under, and began poking around as though he had lost something and had come down close to the cold mud in order to find it. The men along the moonlit parapet exploded with laughter. Schwartz saw hundreds of men pointing and applauding and laughing.

"Okay, fellas," Schwartz said, his voice half throttled by embarrassment. "I guess we can get up now . . ."

Voices called to them from the trench parapet. The applause still sounded through the night.

"Allons, camarades!"

"Qui est là? Bataillon Escargot?"

"Non, non. Ils sont L'Escadron Serpent! Vive les Serpents!"

"Well," Schwartz said slowly, picking the mud off his elbow, "I guess we hit the wrong place. These guys must be the Sixth of Februaries."

"Yeah," someone said in a flat, disgusted voice, and blew his nose.

Schwartz led his section back to the macadam road. He saw a figure waiting there wearing the visored cap of an officer.

"Where the hell have you birds been?"

"Lieutenant," Schwartz said, "we scouted down the line and made visual contact with French comrades."

"You did, huh? Well, get your asses up next to the 24th Spanish where you belong!"

"Yessir," Schwartz muttered. "Come on, fellas, it's this way."

They held a line of shallow trenches north of the surfaced road all the next day. Food and cases of hand grenades came up by mules. There was not much food, but plenty of grenades. They passed them from hand to hand and waited. They lay low, peeping from time to time between the broken sandbags at the Fascist trenches that ran on an angle about six hundred meters away across a shallow valley. They lay in the cold mud and fiddled with their long bayonets and waited for orders to be given.

The mail came up with the hot food from Jack Shirai's field kitchen. The trenches were deepened and pushed forward to a shepherd's stone hut only two hundred and fifty meters from the enemy lines. They filled sandbags and installed new machine guns that came up on the trucks. Mahoney was blamed for "showing-off" during the movement. Some of the others tried to walk in the open too and were hit. White was called away from the machine guns by the battalion commissar to see a man killed by a sniper, a house painter named Alonzo Watson. White went away and came back and sat in the trench for a while. The other men left him alone. Watson had been a quiet guy, a thin man with black skin.

The next day the sun shone, and the enemy artillery shelled the lines. The battalion officers went in to Morata to a brigade operations meeting with General Gal. They came back with maps and promises of artillery support and bombers for an attack the following morning. The Fascist shells had killed and wounded an even dozen men in the trenches. Mahoney was uncomfortable and loud and gloomy.

"Just you wait, that's all!" he kept repeating. "This is a jinxed sector. Goddamned battalion of machine guns over there, three rows deep, all strung between with barbed wire. Wops and them Arabs, too. How come we got a friggin Hungarian for a general, now? A Hungarian, fer Crissakes! How come we got the only section of road that's wide open, huh? Fifteenth Brigade fuck-ups, that's what, and it's gonna get worse before it gets better."

"Can it," White said. "You don't go round here bad-mouthin and bringin down morale, hear? If you can't dig or fill sandbags, then shag on down and fetch these comrades some coffee."

Mahoney glared at him and sniffed disgustedly. He sat for a minute and borrowed a cigarette from White.

"Listen. They ain't gonna send us out there, huh?"

"We follow orders. This ain't Boy Scouts."

José Cubeta was cleaning his rifle with olive oil saved from a can of sardines. He looked at Mahoney and shook his head.

"Don' gimme no sad Irish shit, man. This outfit gotta have *optimismo*."

Mahoney spat and wandered off down the trench and began shouting.

"All you fuck-offs what ain't doin nothin come up here and help us guys what is!"

"He's awright," White said. "Just nervy, that's all. He don't like gettin shot at."

"Hey," Cubeta said. "Poor him. Wait till tomorra, huh?"

Schwartz sat in the sun, reading. It was quiet, siesta time, and the Fascists had laid off the nuisance-firing. A shadow passed over the pages of his book. Schwartz read on, hesitated, his attention broken by the shadow blotting the page, went back to the top and began again.

QUESTION: *What is War?*

ANSWER: *War is an act of violence intended to compel our opponent to fulfill our will.*

QUESTION: *What is the primary aim of war?*

ANSWER: *The primary aim of war is to disarm the enemy.*

The shadow continued to distract him.

"I'm outta smokes, Mahoney. Move, huh, I'm tryin to read."

"Sorry. But I'm not Mahoney. I'm Comrade Rosenbaum. Milton Rosenbaum, to be precise."

Schwartz looked up and saw a thin, homely face with deep acne scars and a wad of curly hair leaking out from under a tasseled forage cap. Rosenbaum wore a wrinkled set of Army-Navy seconds with a blanket pinned Dracula-style around his scrawny neck and trailing down to the mud. He wore a musette bag around his neck like an oat sack for one of the pack mules. Schwartz would not have been surprised if Rosenbaum had plunged his snout down and started to munch. Rosenbaum's sad, friendly, hesitant gaze made Schwartz get up.

"Conrad Rosenbaum, huh? You from the city?"

"*Comrade.* I joined the Party last year. The Bronx. Odd, isn't it that one reads Von Clausewitz, a political and psychological enemy in order to learn, not about the enemy, but—paradoxically—about oneself. Certainly that must be the very nature of war, especially a civil strife such as this. Ideological opponents, imbued and fanatic, slowly imitate each other, learning to exchange roles. Curious, but it argues that we shall become fascistic in nature while *they* adopt our deep feelings of comradeship and solidarity."

Schwartz blinked. He had not heard talk like this for what seemed a long, long time.

"You go to City College?"

"University of Chicago. It's very progressive, especially now with the CIO. You *are* Sergeant Schwartz?"

"Yeh. Whatta you want, Rosenbaum?"

"I've been assigned to this section. As a replacement. We just came up from Albacete."

"That's a nice town."

"I really wouldn't know," Rosenbaum said. "We were only there two days and one night we were bombed."

"*Bombed!* They bombed the *base?*"

"The town. The civilian populace suffered heavily from unjustified Fascist aggression. Frankly, I was terrified."

Rosenbaum eyed the book greedily and shifted from foot to foot. He had legs like a wading bird, wrapped in khaki puttees, and enormous new shoes with white laces.

"You had lunch?"

"Of sorts. Oriental-kosher."

"Don't make fun of Jack."

"The cook? I didn't mean . . ."

Schwartz gazed at Rosenbaum appraisingly.

"How much training have you had, Rosenbaum?"

"Call me Milton. Well, none at the base. Then we came up on trucks. Seventy of us, give or take, you know. Lunch. Then an English officer talked to us for about an hour. Springdale?"

"Captain Springhall. That's *it?*"

"We were issued rifles, and some of the comrades shot at a hill."

"Did *you?*"

"No, Sergeant Schwartz. I was not given any ammunition."

"Where's your rifle at now?"

"An Irishman took it from me. We have another lecture, it seems. With a Comrade Stember? I'm not good at names."

"He's the comic-star."

"What?"

"Battalion commissar. Tell him to get Mahoney to give you back your rifle. You're gonna need it."

"An attack tomorrow, we were told."

Rosenbaum gangled up to the nearest rifle-aperture and looked out, sniffing heavily, his nostrils working like wings.

"It looks rather like a vacant lot," he said, interested and alert. "That's a tank out there, isn't it? All burned. How much do they cost?"

"That one cost us four guys. Three Spaniards and the Russian driver."

Rosenbaum nodded and plucked at this cape.

"Well, *All Quiet on the Western Front,* anyway. I have a good deal of equipment to bring up. Pack, helmet, overcoat and so on. I'll see Comrade Stember about my rifle and bayonet, too."

"You do that," Schwartz said. "That would be a very fine idea."

A bullet flicked into a sandbag four inches from Rosenbaum's face. He inserted two fingers in the hole, right up to the knuckles.

"It's good to be with a veteran command," he said. "I'll leave you to your Von Clausewitz, Sergeant. I'm going along now."

"You go along and get back here. What are you doing?"

"Saluting you."

"Forget it."

Schwartz watched Rosenbaum amble down the trench, the tassel on his cap bobbing. The others in the section began to laugh. Schwartz pulled on his shirt.

"So he looks funny. So he's *here* isn't he? He could be back at Chicago making posters. But he's here. Let's have a little comradeship, huh? Get some shovels. Battalion staff is moving up and Merriman wants a trench dug for the telephone this afternoon before the *transmisiones* get here."

The men off duty got up and went for the shovels. Schwartz put away his copy of Von Clausewitz. He shook his head.

"Milton Rosenbaum from darkest Chicago . . . *Madre mía* . . ."

The cigarettes glowed and faded, glowed again. Merriman was talking to Brigade on the new telephone. Runners came up from the kitchen with big clay jars filled with cold coffee and some hard bread. Schwartz showed Rosenbaum how to soak the bread in the coffee. The new recruit stretched out, stiff as a poker, his helmet-covered head wedged on one side of the trench, his huge feet touching the dew slick far wall. The men of the company moved up and down, stepping over Rosenbaum to pick grenades out of the wooden crates. Everybody stripped down loose and easy, tightened belts, buttons and laces. Rosenbaum reared up and ambled about wearing a huge pack and blanket roll bound over a thick overcoat several sizes too small. The helmet kept tilting over his nose. When he walked, it bounced on the springy hair that matted his long head.

The firing started with the machine-gun company's signal: *Shave-and-a-haircut-two-bits* rapped out with 30-millimeter bullets across the valley at the enemy trenches. Schwartz and his men pressed against the sand-bags, firing through the slots. Rosenbaum had his bayonet fixed and waved it around. Schwartz took the rifle from him and sent him off to watch for the Russian tanks that had been promised. A Republican battery began to fire in a slow, disinterested fashion, and the enemy fired back with anti-tank cannons and heavy machine guns.

Mahoney ducked and squinted along the trench. The top row of sand-bags disappeared in a shower of flying earth and bits of burlap.

"Jesus, Mary, and Joseph!" he muttered. "Get the guns on them, huh, before they chew us up."

The men in his section saw, too. José Cubeta trotted by on his way to the Cubans.

"Slow it down, Jimmy."

"You seen that, Hose? They got them heavy German machine guns over there, huh? Where's the artillery? Where's the tanks? Where's the planes?"

"I dunno. They put a signal out for *aviones* and two guys got killed. Out on the road. Cut all to pieces. Shit, man, this is bad! *Malísimo!* We gonna go out there?"

"My ass," Mahoney said. "My Irish ass we're goin' out there!"

The firing slowed, almost stopped, and started again, heavy from the British and Dimitrovs, but not much from the Spanish. The Spanish Brigade moved out. Two armored cars came up from Morata and fired machine guns. They were hidden by shellbursts from the enemy anti-tanks and drew back. The Fascist machine guns swept up and down the lines.

"*Aviones!* Planes, planes!"

Three aircraft appeared in the gray sky. Rosenbaum watched them.

"Air cover. That's good."

Schwartz looked at his watch. The fire fights had started up two or three times, now, he had lost count, and the artillery fired until they drew a barrage and then limbered up and moved and fired again. They seemed to be overshooting. Schwartz kept his men down low in the trench. The enemy machine-gun bullets ripped and gnawed and whished overhead.

"They got two-three lines of nests over there. The Mooneys glassed 'em. One line stops to load and cool, the next starts shootin. Sit tight. I don't think we're goin over. It's *crazy!*"

Schwartz nodded and the runner darted away. Schwartz moved as close to the battalion command post as he dared. He could hear Captain Merriman arguing in English with someone at Brigade. The command post was being raked by machine-gun bullets. He heard Merriman shouting that the Spanish Brigade was not out and attacking, but had been pinned down and cut up and had come back into their trenches. Anti-tank shells hit and caved in a section of the trench. Schwartz crawled back to his men. They looked at him questioning. He shrugged, pointed at his watch and showed six fingers twice. It was noon, and the enemy machine guns were still firing steadily all along the line.

White smoked the last of his cigarettes and fumbled with the belt. A shell hit the stone hut again and dirt sifted down on him. There was only a single belt left for his machine gun. A runner stumbled up the trench, shouting and gasping in Spanish.

"What's he say, White?"

"He says . . . he says some English officers came up here and everybody's goin' over."

"All right. Fire off the belts, take grenades and rifles and move on out! We'll make up the second wave."

"Yeah," White said. "If they get a *first* wave out there . . ."

A group of officers, some carrying pistols, came out of the half-wrecked command post. Schwartz saw Merriman and Springhall, the Englishman. Merriman jerked his arm up. Schwartz stood up. They all stood up. Merriman heaved himself over the parapet of tattered bags, scrambled to his hands and knees and waved his arms again. The Englishman bounded up, took four steps, and the side of his face burst open, showering blood on another man.

"First aid!"

Merriman went down, staggered by a burst that caught him in the shoulder. The stretcher bearers swarmed up over the sandbags. Schwartz ran away from the bloody parapet down into the field.

The shout went along the line that Seacord was now in command. Twenty running strides from the machine-gun hut, Seacord and two Spanish runners were killed.

Mahoney's section was tumbled together with some of the 1st Company. Bill Henry, who had taken over from John Scott, was hit, punched up straight-legged and back-pedaling, and knocked flat. Mc-Grotty fell behind Henry and raised up, waving his hand. Bullets hissed over him. Mahoney took thirty-one men out of his section of trench. Seventeen made it past the two dead officers to the thin shelter of the olive grove.

José Cubeta was hit and killed by three bullets in the chest, another in the throat before he took a step forward. He dropped back into the ruined trench as bullets slashed into the other Cubans.

White saw whole squads go down, a section line well-spaced with bayonets at ready rise up and melt, run forward at every step dropping, until a dozen or less sprawled behind the olive stumps. He thought he saw Mahoney's red hair. He ran for the grove and fell over the wounded of 2nd Company. The day was a solid mass of sound, bullets like fire-hoses on a city street, spatter of rifle fire, the rip and blast of anti-tank cannon and the cheepy buzz of shrapnel. White ran, a dazed, delicate hopping over bodies. A groan locked like a bubble in his chest. He held his rifle in one hand and covered his groin with the other. They got him before he reached the grove, once in the hip-meat, once in the left thigh and a final, fiery rip through his left calf. He let the groan out in a high squeal and crashed on his face. The sky opened, and rain poured down. He lay there expecting to die. He could tell where he had been hit; the holes oozed and dribbled on both sides. His hip was a jelly of loose meat. An explosive bullet. He muttered and rolled over on his belly. He tried to crawl and fainted. He found his rifle and began shooting.

Something tapped on his boot. He looked around. Some English officer was tapping at him with a swagger stick. White looked at him dully. The officer crooked his finger and pointed through the bullet-whipped sheets of rain. White dragged up his shirt and patted his punctured thigh. The Englishman bent over, holding the swagger stick behind his rear with both hands. He nodded once and gestured *go on firing*. He walked away, stepping over the torn earth and bodies and dodging the hunched and hurtling teams of mud-plastered stretcher-bearers who burst through the rain, heaved a man onto the canvas sling, and wallowed off. White watched the English officer standing near a tree, going through the same silent conversation with somebody from 2nd Company. Then he turned and strolled off, like a dream, into the pelting rain. White went on shooting and waited for a stretcher-crew to find him.

Schwartz lay in the dark trench, his head wound bandaged, his left eye covered with a gauze pad. His broken arm was set in a splint pulled from a grenade carton. People kept coming up to touch and talk with him. His head buzzed and dribbled, as though he had water in his ear from swimming. He kept crying and the pad over his eye was soaked loose. Tears and blood sheened down his muddy face. He moved his lips, but he could not tell whether he was hearing his own bleating voice or the voices of others.

"Goddamn criminal bastards sonofabitching comic-star never moved his ass and pointed a goddamn gun and said get back out there frig you okay now Schwartzie I never saw stuff like that not a goddamned plane there was so two of them what the hell good did they do they got the Hose did they the idiots every idiot from Brigade shoulda been made to go out there we never had a chance every goddamn officer in the whole company dead everybody dead and so many bullets you couldn't take a step some never made it over the friggin top I told you take it easy now kiddo you'll be okay where's Milton who Rosenberg I dunno if you get a friggin Hungarian are you hit too yeah who's that White where are we communication trench gonna get carried out Jimmy's here but Bob and Paul and Charley and Joe and Bill are dead I seen em but they got Merriman out I can't see at all now I'm going blind I think yer all right it's them goddamn bastids at Brigade that oughta get their balls ripped off for sendin us out like that with no nothing not a goddamned chance to just get killed and cut up because some dumb goddamn ignorant and pissy-eyed blind sonofabitch at Brigade thinks Merriman wasn't tellin the truth or thinks the boys is yellow and so he says get up and go out there and they never did give us nothing no more really than the last time but a few lousy seventy-five rounds fired asswise and no bombers oh shit what a goddamned dirty thing to get us all killed like this we never had a real chance at all . . ."

More than two hundred bleeding, broken men were hauled down a rain-soaked narrow path through the moaning night to a field station for bandaging, plaster-of-Paris temporary casts, and morphine needles. They lay in the night rain, numb with shock and the cold, until the trucks came to take them to the hospitals.

Up across the Morata road, from the bullet-riddled sandbags of their own shallow trenches down into the battered olive grove where shell fragments froze and rusted in the muck, and up the long slope to the triple trenches and the enemy machine-gun nests, one hundred and twenty-seven bodies were scattered in the queer, stiff sprawl of death.

Three quarters of the American, Irish, and Cuban volunteers of the Abraham Lincoln battalion had been wounded or killed. One hundred, by rough count, had lived through the attempted assault on the Fascist lines untouched. They manned the few operative machine guns, spread out along the ruined trenches with mud-fouled rifles, and volunteered throughout the sleepless night to crawl across the shallow valley and drag in the dead.

There was no food, no dry clothing, no fires, no coffee, no warm blankets. The steady, pelting rain changed to flying slush and then to stinging sleet that lashed down over the Jarama Valley from the mountains in the north. At last the dawn came up on the wreckage of the Abraham Lincoln battalion. A detailed report was forwarded to the International base camp at Albacete. The list of casualties was suppressed, the failure of the assault disguised, a general statement issued over international wire services and the first headlines appeared in American newspapers:

AMERICANS FIGHT IN SPAIN!

YANK SHOCK-TROOPS IN VIOLENT GOVERNMENT OFFENSIVE!

VOLUNTEERS SPEARHEAD JARAMA ATTACK!

AMERICANS FIGHT IN SPAIN!

Ten days after the disaster in the Jarama Valley had settled into sullen trench-vigil broken by raids and counterraids, a second major offensive to encircle Madrid was launched from the northeast. The first objective was the provincial capital of Guadalajara. The destruction of the Republican field forces there would force the weakening of the Jarama defense line. With the Jarama breached, the insurgents and their allies would advance and meet at Alcalá de Henares like two jaws of a vise. Madrid, its defenders, the hopes of the Republic would be crushed. What Franco and the Moors, Mola and the Carlists had failed to do in eight months, General Mario Roatta and the Corpo Truppe Volontarie would accomplish in a matter of days. Madrid would be another Málaga.

Sixty thousand troops were shifted to the assault area. The right wing, *banderas* of the Foreign Legion, Moroccans and Carlist cavalry, was commanded by General Moscardó, hero of the besieged Alcázar at Toledo. The main force was composed of four divisions of Italian troops, the Black Shirts, the Black Flames, and the Black Arrows, plus the Littorio Division. General Roatta had two hundred and fifty medium and light tanks, one hundred and eighty pieces of mobile artillery, a flamethrower company, a full brigade of German infantry, four companies of heavy machine guns with transport, a motor pool of seventy trucks for each battalion and sixty-two aircraft.

Opposing Roatta's force, the Republican line was held by ten thousand men of the 10th and 2nd Divisions and twenty-two artillery pieces of mixed caliber.

General Roatta issued a statement to his Italian troops:

> I have the honor to communicate to the commands and troops of all the units under my orders the resolution adopted by the Fascist Grand Council on March 2, 1937:
>
> The Fascist Grand Council expresses its solidarity with National Spain and greets the armed forces of Franco, whose victory will mark the end of all bolshevik designs on the West and a beginning of a new period of power and social justice for the Spanish people, which is bound to the Italian people by ancient ties of language, religion and history.
>
> The Fascist Grand Council in sending its greetings to the armed forces acting under the orders of his Excellency, Generalísimo Franco, has in mind, above all, the 50,000 comrades who are fighting on Spanish soil under the Fascist emblems and for their glory.
>
> Officers! Volunteers! The greetings which come to us from the Mother Country through the Fascist Grand Council, the highest spokesmen of the Italian nation, fill us with pride and emotion while fresh victories await us!
>
> Let us be worthy of such honor, and with gratitude and determination let us utter the cry which is the symbol of our faith and our aspirations to victory!
>
> Hail to Il Duce!
>
> A noi!

The Italian artillery shelled the Republican lines for two hours. The tanks and armored cars of the Black Flames roared through the breached, abandoned trenches. General Moscardó captured the towns of Castelblanco and Gogoludo. The sky was the color of coffin-sheathing. The wind changed; the temperature dropped, and the Fiat tanks slithered and churned across a crust of frozen mud, the navigators in the open turrets blinded by sheets of stinging sleet. The assault force struggled toward Guadalajara, slowed but not stopped. The towns of Almadrones and Alaminos were captured.

Paco Larra bent over the map. It had been drawn by Muera, chief of staff for the new 4th Army Corps of the People's Republic, copies made in Guadalajara and rushed forward by staff car, truck, horseback, and runner. The map, thumb-tacked to the table, and held at the corners by his pistol, a coffeepot, and a bottle of cognac, might as well have been of the dark side of the moon. He had never been, even as an observer, in this section of Spain, and the cartography classes of Frunze military school in Russia had never been presented with map problems like this.

The field telephone chittered, and his aide shoved scribbled notes to him. Scattered bands of the Republican 2nd and 10th Divisions had rallied outside of Gogoludo and ambushed some of Moscardó's cavalry. That force had hesitated, then turned in toward the center where the Littorio Division skidded and crawled down the highway, unopposed. On the second highway, roughly parallel, more massed columns of trucks, tanks, and artillery poured in a sluggish thrust at Brihuega, the biggest town northeast of Guadalajara. The Fascist forces were funneling together, compressed by the steep, snowy slopes, limited by the few roads still open. They groped forward now, half frozen and blind without their observation aircraft, directly toward the ragged semicircle spread across the valley.

Paco picked up a pencil, glanced through the scribbled slips of paper, and marked Cipriano Mera's 14th Anarchists on the flank of the Thaelmann Brigade. East of the Germans, in the exact center, were the Garibaldis, with the Spanish troops of Lister and El Campesino dug in the fields and farms around Brihuega. In the gap between the Garibaldis and Lister's left, Paco printed GUARDIA ROJA and beneath that DINAMITEROS. He hesitated and added a question mark. Until the runners came back, there was no way of knowing where his troops lay or where the Englishman had positioned the dynamite squads.

The small stone house groaned. The March wind drove sleet against the windows like shrapnel and roared through the pine trees, dulling the thunder of the guns. He walked to the window and scraped the cold, chalky frost with his fingernails, melted a section with his hand and looked out. A sentry coughed and stamped and swung his hands against the bitter wind. Paco frowned and went back to the table.

The greasy lines, pencil flecks, and arrows meant nothing to him. Frost sheathed the windows, but for the men out in the lines it froze rifle bolts. Across the room a bright fire of pine logs seethed and crackled. Outside, the snow slashed into numb faces, stung the watering eyes of exhausted men, and muffled the racket of motors and slow-creeping treads of the Italian tanks butting through the drifts the wind scooped in under the dark groves of trees. Through the door was a deep, soft bed. Outside, it was flirting with death to drowse in the shelter of a low stone wall. A clock ticked on the mantel.

He could not concentrate. A safe small voice pushed at his brain; shame tasted like sugar on his tongue. It was good here, snug and safe, a place to play with maps and pencils, sip good coffee and cognac, talk on the telephone, and sleep. The colonel dreams by the fire and can imagine the thaw of spring. He scribbles and sips and pities his soldiers bayoneted by the wind. What was such pity worth? Not a céntimo. His body was warm enough, but his mind had congealed. His hands trembled in rage at his comfort. He was trapped in this place, smothering, suffocating.

He lunged across the room and tore open the door. The wind struck at him and sent the papers on the table up in a whirling scuffle. He breathed in cold, clean air hard as iron.

"Pepe, get my horse. I'm going up to the lines."

The wind howled through the pine groves. A company of riflemen struggled against it, marching with their hands clamped under their armpits, faces hidden. The sound of battle roared on the wind; artillery, machine-gun and rifle fire. He rode along a rocky crest and saw shells falling. Broken trees rose with each orange flash, sailed in a cone of flying snow and needles and settled again. The low, cold sky slithered with artillery shells.

He could see almost nothing, and the sounds blurred together, a roaring clatter that rose and fell on the wind. He drove his horse down into a grove of trees held by a French machine-gun company. Neither the men nor their officer seemed surprised to see him. He left his horse and walked in the direction they pointed to, a clump of pines.

The Garibaldis were dug into the snow, a thin line with a few machine guns. He dropped down behind a fallen tree. The Italians were waiting, watching and listening. One of them pointed out into the narrow field. The road ran across the field, elevated like a railway.

"They will come along that. The tanks."

Paco nodded. The Italian who spoke was an old-looking man with frozen whiskers and weeping eyes. He was a *teniente*, lieutenant of this company.

"How old are you, comrade?"

"I have forty-eight years, Colonel, but never a winter like this."

"Where is the Englishman I sent you with the dynamite squads?"

"The brothers? Back at their monastery."

He jerked his head toward a cluster of ruined trees.

"Twice today we have stopped the iron pigs, the little Fiats. The French over there shot them up with machine guns and turned them. The *inglés* and his religous brothers blew them to hell. But we have to pull back each time. They know where we are and bring up artillery. We go back. They come on. We catch them again."

Paco went back to the cluster of trees. There, white-shrouded figures huddled around boxes, kneeling and squatting in the snow. They did look like monks, dressed in snow-robes made from bedsheets with peaked hoods and belts of dynamite fusing. They looked like penitants in a Holy Week procession. Each of them had an unlit cigarette either cupped in one hand or pressed between chapped and bleeding lips. These were his *asturianos*, coal miners from his province. They pulled off their hoods when he walked among them. He counted twenty-seven of them. There had been forty, plus Desmond, their leader. They were young with tough, wind-flayed faces and red, weeping eyes. He pulled the hoods up to cover the faces and the eyes.

"They work, eh, these things? Like I told you."

They were watching the road, but they nodded.

"They never see us, *jefe*. Not until too late. Then, *poom!*"

"Where is Desmond?"

"The *inglés* is cutting fuses."

A shell whistled overhead, another, three more. One of the *dinamiteros* nodded.

"Ansaldo tanks. The medium ones. They have cannons. We have these."

He reached under his billowing robe and brought out three fat orange wands wired together and fused. Paco nodded. The fuses were three centimeters long. Three seconds from ignition to explosion.

"*Adelante, dinamiteros!*"

Paco saw Desmond kneeling in the snow. The Englishman held something in his hands. The dynamiters waded to him, plucking up their skirts like peasant women. They bent over Desmond's frost-split, bleeding fingers and lit their cigarettes, then trudged on over and through the Garibaldi rifle pits and out into the field of wind-whipped snow. Paco was the last in line.

"Give me fire, comrade."

"Here."

A metal cigarette-lighter fluttered between Desmond's palms. Paco looked at him. The young Englishman had dead-looking eyes and a face to frighten children with.

"Get up. Do you know me?"

"El Asturiano."

Desmond's face was dented with slick little scars from the forehead to where his lip at the left corner ran out in a long puckered slash across his lightly bearded cheek. Saliva had frozen there. Even as he looked, Desmond drooled from his ripped mouth. He was a deserter, technically, from Coltringham's British *columna*. He had joined the Red Guards in the fighting at the University. A land mine he was defusing had gone off and left him with this face. The Asturians were afraid of him; he commanded them by dread and gestures. He could speak very little Spanish.

He got up at once and pulled his hood around his face, hid his lighter away and ran the waterproof strip of fuse between his fingers. His thumbnail bit down on the fuse, marking centimeter lengths as precisely as a machine. He began walking. Paco followed him through the snow to the low wall of fallen trees. Desmond slid down beside the Italian *teniente*. Paco squatted a few paces away and gazed at them.

The Italian had a thick, square, good face beneath his beard. He was dark and solid in his dirty sheepskin and worn corduroys. The Englishman, hood and robe, crouched, amorphous and white like the smear of a photograph negative.

The low beat of treads and motors blew on the wind. Out in the narrow fields, the *dinamiteros* lay down in hollows they scooped in the snow. They cupped their cigarettes in their stiffened hands and blew smoke into the snow that kissed back cold against their lips. The first tank appeared.

It was an Ansaldo, broad and blind, clanking and creaking forward, the turret turning, dull and curious, the cannon snout probing and exhaust blowing up blue. Two other medium tanks followed it. Paco could see the rivets on the slab sides, the packed snow drop off the churning cleats. The tanks, engines wallowing, snuffed with their cannon snouts like wary elephants. The first tank fired at the slope where the French lay, a long, rippling spray into the dark, close-ranked pines. The French did not fire back. Paco looked at the Italian officer. The *teniente* spread his forefinger and thumb, measuring the thickness of armor plate on the Ansaldo. He grinned and nudged Desmond.

"Just right for you, San Pietro."

The tank turret chattered and the barrel hole pointed at the Garibaldi lines. Desmond and the *teniente* ducked. The muzzle lit up, and a perfect smoke ring floated out and vanished. The shell hit in the trees, lopping one that settled, sighing and flinging snow. The engines fuddled, and the three tanks shifted gears and lumbered forward, blind and snorting.

White monk hoods lifted above the level of the wind-whipped snow. Cigarette tips nipped the fuses. The robed figures bobbed up, heaved the clumsy orange bundles and dropped down, invisible again. The Italian officer and Peter Desmond began counting.

"*Uno* . . . one . . . *due* . . . two . . . *tre* . . . three!"

The first tank chattered over the bundle fizzing on the highway. A yellow flash bulbed underneath the slow treads. The bow of the tank rose in a coffee-froth of dirt and snow, lurching and rolling on the concussion. A hunk of embankment sailed across the snow field and broke apart. The tank nodded, stricken, and rolled over on its side, the plates buckling like cardboard, the treads racing. Cleats and a great, sprocketed wheel floated out into the snow. Then the earth behind the last tank vanished in a leaping thunder of snow and frozen mud, but too far back. The two Ansaldo tanks turned and headed toward the Garibaldis in a roaring plunge, machine guns spitting blue, dancing flames.

White figures rose up from the snow, hooded and wind-shivered, out-lined against the rusty bulk of the leading tank. They threw orange bundles under the rushing bluff snout and dove away into the drifts. The port tread scaled out like a broken fence, flying away from the explosions. Snow boomed out and up, hung on the wind an instant, and hissed away. The tank settled, groaning and snapping, as the machine gun stabbed down blindly into the pit of tumbled clods. Heavy things broke and crushed inside the tank. The machine-gun barrel twitched and stopped shooting.

The third tank heaved around broadside to the Garibaldis and boomed through the deep snow, the cleats chattering and the tank bulk sucking it up over the stern as far forward as the slow-wheeling turret. The cannon fired, and the tank wrenched in a big circle and headed for them.

The Garibaldi riflemen and Lewis gunners lay in a white dream, frozen by the thing that came at them, warty and bellowing, the bow machine gun whipping from side to side. Paco saw the canvas cannon-gasket on the turret crumple in on the recoil and the treads tearing through a blue cloud of snow. He felt Peter Desmond move, and saw the Italian *teniente* grab for him.

"No, no, Pietro!"

Desmond waded down a drift, both billowing arms raised, holding a rust-colored bundle with a bright point of fizzing flame running down the fuse that flailed with every slow-plunging, skirted stride. Desmond dove straight at the tank, still holding the dynamite-bundle, and vanished in the scalding smear of light that sucked the snow off the field and blew it up in a whirling white column that drifted off into the dark, tossing pines in a single, brain-stunning blast.

Ibarra Castle, as it was called by the peasants and village people, was a big, low, flat-roofed country house. The Loyalist Garibaldis held the woods on one side, a Franco-Belgian unit had slipped around to the rear. East and west, the counterattack roared in the dusk, German and Spanish infantry following the tanks of General Pavlov. It began to snow again. Paco's staff car, coming from recaptured Brihuega, brought coffee, three cases of Mills grenades, and ammunition for the Lewis guns. The company commander of the Garibaldis distributed the weap-ons and sat on a stone sipping the coffee and brushing the snow from his beard.

A ripple of noise came from the dark building. Bullets crackled into

the trees, and branches dropped down, spilling snow. The Italian lieutenant jerked his head.

"A new kind of automatic weapon or submachine gun. They have one
at every window. And it's getting dark fast."

Paco nodded. In another half hour, the attack would have to be
called off. He creased the propaganda leaflet in his hand, folding it into
a paper glider. He tapped it on his knee.

"How many of your compatriots surrendered because of these things?"

"Perhaps thirty. Most of them along the road from Torija. They had
been run over by the Russian tanks and there was no fight left in them.
They picked up the leaflets and walked up to us. They had shot their
officers. They wanted food, not money."

Paco glanced at the words printed on the wing of the folded paper
glider.

"Fifty pesetas for every man. One hundred if they bring their weapons."

"That's more than most of them are worth," the Italian said sourly.
"Compatriots. Black Shirts. You know, some of them were told they
were going as garrison troops to Ethiopia. They didn't know they were
coming to Spain until the ship docked at Cádiz. But they had a fine
time at Málaga. A holiday on the beaches. Shooting civilians. Well, now
we've got them running and holed up here like rats. Mussolini-lovers.
Corpo Truppe Volontarie. You know what your men call them, Colonel?"

"CTV. *Cuándo te vas* . . . 'When are you going?'"

"Is that a tank or the sound truck?"

"The truck," Paco said. "The road is too narrow to get a tank up
here. We could use one, or some heavy artillery, but the guns are too
far back. They'd never get here in time."

"Let's hope this thing works."

"It has been explained to the prisoners?" Paco asked.

"They volunteered," the Italian said bitterly. "That's what they are.
Volunteers. They will volunteer for anything. Shit on a plate and they
will volunteer to eat it."

"When they stop talking, wait as long as you can. Then send up the
rocket for the Franco-Belgians."

"As you wish, Colonel."

The sound truck was a big mottled Russian van with a speaker-horn
on the roof. It lurched up under the trees where a dozen Black Shirts
squatted on the snow-dusted needles watched by some Garibaldis and
few Red Guards. The door of the cab opened and a man dropped
down.

"Where is Colonel Larra?"

"Here. Is that you, Kopa?"

"Yes. You wanted a program of dance music, no?"

Paco embraced the German. The soldiers grinned as they wrestled and pounded each other.

"I saw the Thaelmanns take Trijueque, Kopa. With the bayonet. It was not badly done. You're not hurt?"

"Today there have been miracles happening, and so, of course I am not hurt. I have been rounding up prisoners and looking for you. Brigade staff is in a fury. Muera said to me: 'What does he mean going to the lines like this? Who does he think he is . . . an anarchist?' I am to bring you back. At gun point, if necessary."

"First we take this place. Is the truck ready?"

"One moment."

Kopa pulled away and walked to the rear of the van and opened it. The deadly ripple of submachine-gun fire sounded again. One of the Garibaldis kicked a Black Shirt.

"Get them to come out of there, understand?"

"I'll talk, I'll talk to them."

"Sing like Caruso, but bring them out."

The speaker-horn whistled and crackled. Then Kopa began to speak in Italian very slowly, every syllable thundering out through the dusk. The men around the sound truck were driven away, clutching their ears. Sound waves shook snow from the pine branches.

"*Comrades, workers and peasants from Italy. Listen to me. Why are you here, fighting against us? Do you want to die in this place? For what? To keep fellow workers and peasants of Spain from living a free life under the government they elected?*"

Submachine-gun and rifle fire came from the Ibarra Castle. The bull-deep voice boomed through the shadowed forest and across the blue snow.

"*Comrades, you have been misled! Some of you have been tricked into coming here. We are free men! We fight for what we believe in. Noi siamo Italiani di Garibaldi!*"

The Italian lieutenant stood beside Paco, his fingers in his ears.

"Shall we get the prisoners?"

"Yes. Quickly."

The lieutenant waved his hand. The guards herded the Black Shirts into line at the back of the van. Kopa's voice roared again.

"*Listen, comrades. We have already many of your friends who have surrendered to us. Don't believe your officers. Don't believe what they tell you about the Reds. Listen to your friends . . .*"

The speaker-horn squealed again, and the lieutenant winced.

"How far does it carry, this thing?"

"At full volume, more than two kilometers."

"If the wind is right, they can hear him in Rome!"

A new voice sounded, high, breathless and excited. Kopa must have taken the youngest prisoner of the lot.

"Hey! Hey, it's me! It's Riri!"

"Riri." The lieutenant said, "For the love of God. Riri."

The young prisoner babbled on, the words squawking out through the broken branches.

"It's not true what we were told. It's all lies. They didn't shoot us!"

"We're short of ammunition," the *teniente* said.

"We got money, just like they promised. You saw their planes today. Well, they've got tanks, too. Big ones! And a general is right here with us. He's going to attack the castle. Don't be idiots. Over here there's plenty of food and wine and nice warm blankets. Come on out, boys! Come on over to this side. To hell with Mussolini! Long live the people!"

"That one," the lieutenant said, "belongs on permanent assignment to the propaganda section. Food, wine, and blankets. See? I told you. They'll say anything. Look, it's really getting dark, Colonel."

"The rocket. Send it up."

Another voice tittered and boomed.

"Angelo Bertelli. Angelo? This is your cousin, Giuseppi. The place is completely surrounded. In front, fellow Italians. Come out the front way. If you stay there, you'll get killed for nothing."

The rocket shot up into the sky and powed. The Garibaldi assault line exploded with rifle fire by the volley, aimed at the second-story windows. The Red Guards went forward in the snow, running and diving, getting up and running again toward the wall that closed in the front courtyard. In the darkness, bullets from the first and second floor windows smashed along the top of the wall. The first grenades sailed into the court and exploded, lighting up the twisted trees of an orchard. The Fascists inside the court threw grenades back. Muzzle flames played on the second-floor sills.

Paco lay in the snow, firing a Lewis gun. A wounded Red Guard passed him a new can of ammunition. He fired again. The lieutenant stood up in the snow.

"Avanti! Avanti, Garibaldi!"

The assault by the Italians and the French burst across the tracer-flicked snow. The Red Guards were supposed to hold the front line and provide a cover-fire. Paco saw them get up, all at once, and run forward. Two waves of men struck at the wall in a frenzy, shouting and lobbing grenades. They seemed to lean in against the enemy fire and claw at the wall even after they had been hit. Voices wailed and hooted through the snow.

"Carlos, don't stay in there! Don't shoot! They are our comrades!"

The battle roared up again. The moon shone down suddenly on thick files of men clambering over the low fences and ditches of the formal

flower gardens. A full company of Poles with fixed bayonets were joining the attack. They swarmed at the big, low building through a huge,
slow, moonlit drift of little snowflakes. There was a sudden silence.
It lasted a minute, two, three. A series of explosions inside the building,
then some scattered shots. The Poles knelt and fired, a single, smashing
volley. There was no return fire.

Paco could hear the singing. At first he thought it was the Garibaldis
and the French, but the words were too muffled. The singing was *inside*
the building. He stood up and looked at the dark, battered façade. A
piece of sheet or a pillow-case flapped at one of the windows.

"They are surrendering! That's 'The International' they're singing!"

From the dark woods, the voice thundered, first in Italian, then,
Spanish, French and Polish.

"Cease fire . . . Cease fire . . . Cease fire . . . Cease fire."

The mechanics pushed the Dewoitine 510 out on the frozen, wind-
lashed field. Dorlov pointed to it.

"I have assigned her to you again. She has been rebuilt. For training,
of course. But today, we fly everything with wings. There is slightly less
than five seconds' worth of machine-gun ammunition already loaded
and, as you see, some small bombs."

"I see," Frank said. "Dorlov's Air Circus."

The field was covered with old aircraft, some flown in, some dragged
there in trucks and reassembled. He counted three Fokker mailplanes,
a British Airspeed, with square holes hacked in the fuselage to mount
hand-held Lewis guns, a Koolhoven biplane, some twin-seat De Havil-
lands, antique Breguets the English-speaking pilots and gunners called
Break-Aways, a tattered Corbina and some other light planes owned
before the war by the aristocrats and señoritos of the Royal Sporting
Club.

"Well," Frank said, "I soloed in a Jenny. That's all we're missing."

The Madrid air commander, Cisneros, had gathered every prewar relic
in the Republic, automobile mechanics from as far south as Jaen, and
some machine-gunners who had never been in a plane in their lives.
For three days they had all worked and practiced in the sleet and snow,
waiting for the weather to change. The ceiling had lifted to one thousand
meters. Eighty-one aircraft, counting the rebuilt Dewoitine, the biggest
air fleet the Republic had ever flown in battle, were scheduled to take
off at 1300 hours to bomb the Black Shirt columns stalled near Brihuega.
For bombs, some of the planes carried wooden boxes of hand grenades
fitted out with contact fuses and sections of steel rails from the ruined
freight yards of Madrid. The cold air racketed with the sound of old
motors. Saulnier was arguing with his ground crew, shouting and waving
his arms. He walked over, wiping oil from his face.

"I have been patient with those animals long enough, Dorlov! I have explained that my motor will march only if it is lubricated with a mixture of castor-oil and the stuff drained from the trucks. The engine will march for exactly one hour and twenty minutes. I tested it yesterday. These burros have burned half of it already. The motor will seize up, and Saulnier will descend on Brihuega."

"Use olive oil," Dorlov said.

"Give me one of the Chatos. I will bless you as a saint."

"None of the new aircraft. You know the orders. Stay on the ground then and go see your girl friend."

"Where can I get seven liters of olive oil?" Saulnier demanded.

"Try the cook."

Saulnier ran off between the hangars. Frank looked up at the sky. Low, dirty-looking clouds raced on the wind.

"It's going to snow, Mosca."

"Of course it's going to snow," the Russian said angrily. "Also it will play lightning, thunder, and earthquakes. Probably a flood. Get into your ship. I want you to show these others how to take off in this wind. There is no time left. It's now or not at all. We did everything. Lengthened the runway. They take off with the wind and it will blow you right over the Fascist positions. On their side of the mountains there is rain and sleet and no visibility. They can't get off their fields. Get going!"

The Russian shook Frank by the shoulder and shoved him in the direction of the Dewoitine. Frank trotted out to the plane. The left wing had been covered with new canvas and the controls had been strung with telephone cords. The radiator leaked and the fuselage had been so twisted by his crash into the trees that the rudder bar had to be held forward just to fly it in a straight line. The four bombs slung loose between the landing-gear struts were dropped by the "Dorlov Device." Over the target, he had to cut eight pieces of rope with a clasp-knife. The bombs were already fused. If he cracked up on a tail-wind take-off . . .

"*Preparado?*"

"*Sí*, Francisco. Give it to them."

"We will."

He climbed into the cockpit and knotted the scarf around his throat, tugged down his goggles. He could see Dorlov watching and tapping at his left wrist. It was time for take-off. Dorlov shook his clenched fist. Frank saluted back as the mechanic snapped over the new propeller. The engine spit, backfired, and caught. The old French interceptor shuddered from nose to tail. Frank waved the chocks away. Off to his right, three of the Breguet bombers were rolling down the wind. He opened the throttle and pulled out in front of them. The sky above looked like dirty suds. He ruddered out on the runway and could feel the wind shake the old fighter. He clicked the throttle open and shot forward, the wind driving behind him, lifting the tail surfaces too high, too soon. He butted the throttle, trying to feel the plane, ignoring the runway that skidded past.

"Oooooh, *Jesus!*" he said and pulled back the stick.

The Dewoitine lifted, the new wing low, and skidded up into the air. He circled the field and looked down on Dorlov. The Russian waved to him, a sad, sweeping farewell. Dorlov had been grounded by orders of Cisneros himself. The first Italian prisoners and a truck filled with documents had arrived in Madrid to be shown to the correspondents as absolute proof of German and Italian violation of the Non-Intervention Agreement. The Republic did not want a ranking Soviet Air Force officer shot down and displayed in Berlin or Rome.

They flew just beneath the clouds, sometimes disappearing in the low shreds, three by three and spread far apart to avoid collisions. The roar of motors shivered and stirred the snow on the valley floor and shook it from the pine trees. The open fields were covered with battle wreckage, and the dark hills were pitted and torn. The main road looked like a shivering strut-wire to Frank as he dove down on it. He butted the throttle back, and the old interceptor shook less. He could make out a column of trucks, tanks, and armored cars, some headed toward him, others scattered along the shoulders, more heading away. He took out his clasp-knife, held the stick between his knees and sawed at the first four cords. He saw canvas-shrouded guns, ammunition, and fuel trucks, ragged lines of infantry. He flew over them and cut loose two bombs. The plane slid into a snow cloud. He felt machine-gun bullets hit. He dove again, blind, the plane creaking, snow striking his face, his goggles, whirling into the open cockpit.

The cloud broke, but the snow came down still. He flew low, lower, two hundred meters off the snowy ground and sawed loose the last two bombs. He looked back and saw them flash as they burst on the highway.

He circled, watching the rest of the planes waddle in and drop their loads. The bombs bloomed in the snow. Three times, he flew over the valley and strafed the motorized columns. He saw Russian tanks in neat lines driving forward and firing steadily, a few signal strips staked out and fluttering on the ground, a cross of Lorraine, a huge L for Lister's brigade, an orange arrow pointing northeast. The Dewoitine snarled and lurched, the left wing dropping, buffeted by the gale. His guns were empty, and the windshield was crusted with ice. He swung again over the valley and saw a loose horseshoe shape of artillery, Republican cannons, firing through the mist, throwing a barrage ahead of Pavlov's tanks. In a grove of trees, trucks with red crosses painted on the roofs were loading wounded.

A red banner flailed on the staff in the front court of Ibarra Castle.

The building looked hardly touched from the air. An odd van with a thing like a flower growing out of the top was parked inside the walled front courtyard. He tilted his wings and swung back over the valley to rendezvous with the bombers. His face went numb and he flew with his left arm flung up as a shield.

They came through the streaming clouds, tilting and staggering, bounding and dropping as they fought the headwind and swung in a scattered convoy toward Madrid, a fleet of antiques, rusty mailplanes, patched bombers, and hay-bellied Breguets waddling over the hills while the little sport aircraft were blown like bright leaves around the heavier Fokker and De Havilland transports. Exhaust smoke spilled in dark streams from worn, clattering valves, fabric torn by ground fire raveled and blew away on the snowy wind, rusty wires howled and creaked.

Down on the ground at Barajas field, Dorlov and the others were waiting. The air commander for Madrid would be there, cursing the iron-colored clouds overhead and straining for the first glimpse of a plane coming down through the fine snow. Dorlov would be humming the Soviet Air Force song:

> Higher and higher and higher
> We rise despite hate and derision
> Each whirling propeller sings
> We defend the Soviet Union!

It was too bad Mosca had to miss the biggest mission ever. "Come, Josephine, in my Flying-Machine," but, what the hell, they had made it over the target and they were going to make it back to the base, too, despite leaky tanks, cheap cognac for antifreeze, blown gaskets, ground fire and a full gale driving snow in their faces.

Tremendous, that's what it was! The *Gloriosa* and, by God, we can fly anything, anywhere and bring it back. Wait until I tell her about this one. What have you been doing, Francisco? Well, Carmen, today we took a little run out over Guadalajara and blew up part of an army.

The highway was blocked with burned-out Fascist trucks and riddled armored cars, stalled Fiat light tanks and the bigger, battered hulks of Ansaldo models. The pebbly shoulders of the road were lumped with the frozen bodies of horses, mules, and men. Out in the cratered fields the litter lay everywhere: blankets and sleeping bags, helmets and rifles, canteens and crates of hand grenades, shattered field telephones and drums of wire, pots, iron kettles, mess kits, ruined boots, an altar, officers' dress tunics with new ribbons from Ethiopia and Málaga, mail sacks, soggy magazines, smashed typewriters letters marked with Italian stamps *. . . I can only pray to God and all His saints that you will come back*

soon and move to Rome like you promised. We can be married in the
spring . . . Armando, my son. How we miss you! Why have they taken
you to Spain instead of Africa? Papa doesn't understand but I am knitting
you some nice wool socks . . . How empty and cold our bed is these
nights, my husband! I pray every morning and every night for you, my
darling . . .

The Red infantry, stumbling forward after the advancing tanks found
Biretta pistols, Zeiss field glasses, and mortars still in the shipping
crates, machine-gun barrels fired so hot that they lay in perfect, circular
sheets of ice where they had been dropped and had melted the snow
which froze again in amber watch-crystals. Case after case of rifle ammunition, the bright brass cartridges in the crusted throats of shell holes
like the pollen in flowers of mud, a perfect anti-tank cannon screened
by blocks of snow, the ammunition stacked neatly, a small tractor
hidden in a gully nearby, a dead officer in the snow, his brains and
blood flecking a drift, the whole emplacement covered with little signs
fastened up with pink ribbons, written in bad Spanish: UNO REGGALITO
DE SUS COMPANEROS LOS CAMARADI DE MILANO. A pine tree was covered
with frozen underwear, forty-two wind-wrung legs and crinkled seat flaps
sitting in the branches over a tin box of condoms and a wad of booklets
on venereal diseases. A blackened Breda observation plane that crumbled
beneath the boots of souvenir-seekers, the fuselage and wings sieved by
ammunition that had exploded. A truck of gasoline with hoses and
shoulder-packs and brass pipes, flame-throwers that had never been used.
Three hundred cases of big sardines in tomato sauce stacked in a pyramid.
A dump of tobacco and cigarette papers like a manure heap. The
valley, hills and highways held a vast junkyard, burned, broken and
flung aside, half-buried in the easy sweeps of snow that eddied and
whirled away. The vehicles, the frozen flesh of animals, the boxes,
barrels, crates, cartons and jars were marked with Fascist emblems and
the big, black letters: CTV. Corpo Truppe Volontarie . . . *Cuándo te*
vas? When are you leaving, those who can still move, who can still run
away?

In the little serving kitchen where the wineglasses had been iced and
the bowls of local fruit dusted with chopped mint from the kitchen
gardens, the lieutenant of the Garibaldis bled to death, covered with
blankets, the ice melting in his rough beard. Paco and Kopa knelt by
his stretcher, putting cigarettes to his slack lips and taking them away.
The *teniente* let the smoke out his nose in little snuffs. His chest
burbled when he inhaled.

"I was at Caporetto in the Great War," he said, in slow, careful
Spanish, "when the whole Italian Army retreated."

"Easy, comrade," Kopa said. "The doctor will come to you soon. I know him. You'll be all right."

The canvas stretcher squeaked as the *teniente* shook his head. Ibarra Castle was filled with the wounded and dying, Belgian bicycle salesmen, Polish farmers, French factory hands, Spanish peasants, Croats, Bulgars, and Hungarians from the Luckacz brigade. In one room were the Moors and some Black Shirt officers who had been shot by their own men.

The *teniente* puffed on the cigarette. Underneath the ripped blanket, his bowels made a loose liquid sound, air and juice. His dirty lids fluttered.

"I am from Tuscany, myself," he said. "I used to teach mathematics at a school for boys, but the Black Shirts got me thrown out. How was I to care for my wife and three little ones? I went to France. Then here. These Fascisti fought like men, most of them, eh? Not all Italians run away. Our boys fought even better. Is that correct, Colonel?"

Paco nodded and took the cigarette away. He fretted the end off where the *teniente* had wet it.

"Without the Garibaldis, the center would have broken," he said. "You are brave comrades."

"I saw the new graves out in the orchard."

"The doctor will be here soon," Kopa said.

"It should be perfectly understood that Italians fought Italians here. And fought well on both sides. Let them know it . . . not like Caporetto . . ."

The *teniente* heaved and coughed. Blood burst from his lips and nostrils and ran down into his filthy beard. He was dead. Kopa pulled the blanket over the dead man's face and stood up.

"I never even knew his name," Paco said.

"It doesn't matter now. Nothing matters for him."

"I want to see the others. The Red Guards. My *chicos*."

They walked through the wrecked rooms of Ibarra Castle. The parquet floors were covered with bits of broken glass. There was no electricity, and the first-aid teams worked by the light of candles and kerosene lanterns. Huge shadows roamed across the bullet-pocked walls. The Italian defenders had used the furniture for barricades. Snow drifted in through the ruined windows and dusted the silk brocade of slug-ripped armchairs and dainty carved sofas.

The wounded had not been sorted out by battalions, except for the Black Shirts and the few Moors locked in a small salon on the second floor. Stretchers lay everywhere in the halls and corridors. The kitchen had been converted into an operating room because of the stoves to sterilize equipment. The German doctor, Werner, a Jewish refugee, probed for bullets and grenade fragments, clamped blood vessels, stitched and swabbed, bandaged and set broken bones on the big oak central

counter. The floor was slippery with blood and littered with limp morphine tubes. He whistled a Viennese waltz; a nurse held a flashlight;
his rubber-covered fingers moved and flicked a grenade fragment into
an omelet pan. Above his head on a rack of iron hooks hung cleavers
and carving knives, soup ladles, wire whisks, and wooden spoons.

"Hello, Kopa," he said. "Don't block the light, please. Who let you
in here? Can you get us more wood and blankets?"

"I have already sent for them."

"You mean well, Kopa, but you are very slow. With all the windows
out, this place is freezing cold. We'll have a run of pneumonia, anyway,
but wood and blankets . . . they are a comfort, you know. Good evening,
Colonel."

"Good evening, Herr Doktor," Paco said.

"You want to know how many Guardias Rojas, eh? I don't know.
They bring them to me. I do what I can for them. I don't ask them
what their battalion is. Look here."

The doctor paused and waved his slick rubber hands at the form that
bulked the bloody sheet. The wounded man was covered from the forehead to the feet. Werner's hands disappeared into a rectangle of gleaming clamps and soft pink intestines. Paco swallowed and looked away.

"You can't look, eh? Grenade fragments in here and pieces of bone
from the ribs and hip-crest. If I do nothing, he dies. If we are lucky, he
will recover. That is, he will walk with a limp and live on boiled rice
and milk. Then he will die. But from cancer, perhaps, or heart failure.
Lift the sheet and look at his face."

Werner's fingers moved. Another bit of iron pinked in the omelet pan.
Kopa slid back the sheet. A nurse stared at Paco. All he could see was
her eyes. He bent over the wounded man.

"Well?" Werner demanded. "One of yours? French? Italian? German?
Polish? Bulgarian? Eh, eh? All you can be sure of is that he is not
Oriental. What if he were face down and I was picking this rubbish
out of his buttocks? Could you tell then? They don't all have marks on
them like Kopa here. The Gestapo didn't brand them all. But you,
Colonel, you have set your own mark on them. Not with a burning
cigarette and a whip. But your own mark, just the same. Here, take
this!"

Werner held a shiny little scalpel out to Paco and waggled it.

"Go on. Take it!"

Paco held the little knife, still warm from the sterilizer. Werner pointed
across the kitchen at four loaded stretchers, the wounded men shrouded
with blankets.

"Why not carve your initials in them? Go ahead. Slice a five-pointed
star or a hammer and sickle. Or do the job properly. Cut their throats!"

The nurse stared at Paco, her eyes all he could see above the mouth-mask, below the white cap. Paco handed her the little scalpel. She dropped it in a sterile bath and handed Werner a sponge. Paco backed away. Werner wiped with the sponge, again humming a Viennese waltz.

"Get out of here, now," he said softly. "We are busy and you are just in the way."

Paco stopped in the corridor and leaned against the wall.

"Still want to see your *chicos?*" Kopa asked.

"Yes, of course."

"I will see about the wood and the blankets."

"Is he always like that?"

"Werner? Oh yes. He has been awake for sixty hours now. The nurses say he sleeps standing up while they finish bandaging. He is too kind, you see. He says that makes him a bad surgeon. He had a huge practice in Germany. Before the Nazis."

"Now he has a huge practice in Spain."

"Yes."

Paco borrowed a flashlight from a *practicante.* The intern walked with him between the stretchers and pushed open a door. The room was dim and filled with wounded, the floor almost covered with them. The walls echoed with their groans, terrible low mutters of agony, pain-whimpers and frantic, brainless shouts. Paco moved the beam of the electric torch over twisted, dirty faces, dull, wild eyes, trembling lips. The air was thick with a latrine-stench. The men thrashed and plucked at themselves in the reeling darkness. The moans and cries, their litany of suffering, beat on Paco's ears. He was deafened, weak-legged. His head felt light and cold.

"What . . ."

"Abdominal wounds. Bayonets, bullets, hand grenades, broken glass."

They groaned and cried and crushed their teeth together and wept and screamed and cursed. Paco snapped off the torch. The intern guided him out of the room and shut the door. Paco wiped his face. He was sweating, a cold drench on his face and chest.

"How many will live?"

"None."

"Not one?"

The intern shook his head.

"No. We can do nothing for them."

Paco walked across the gritty floor and down the main staircase. He met a squad of prisoners bringing up firewood and blankets. They smiled at him, timid and frightened. Kopa was waiting by the open door. They walked out of the Ibarra Castle and kicked through the new snow to the sound truck. The moonlight, pure silver, drenched the courtyard. The fruit trees looked like candelabra. It was very still and beautiful.

BOOK SIX

*The Almonds and the Oak Tree
April 1937*

Two of the biggest brindled dogs he had ever seen stared down the broad steps of the Villa Paz.

"Hi, fellas," Mahoney said uneasily. "Pretty big, ain't they?"

"They are great Danes," Coltringham said. "They were left here by María Cristina de Borbón, the previous owner."

"Do they bite?"

"No. At least, not so far."

The Englishman grinned at Mahoney and scratched under the plaster of the cast that covered him from the waist to the neck and ran out, encasing Coltringham's shoulder, elbow and arm as far as the wrist, where it ended in a gauze cuff. He walked with a cane to support the weight of the cast and was sweating slightly in the sun. The dogs stared down dourly at Mahoney and lolled thick, pink tongues. Coltringham pointed with his cane.

"We call them Franco and Bruno. Fascist pups. Your friends are on the second floor, front. Thanks, lad, for the . . . ah, lemonade."

Mahoney slipped the cognac flask into the Englishman's pocket.

"Keep it until I get back. I got another in my shorts."

"Very enterprising," Coltringham said. "Best tradition of the IRA. Your father would be proud of you."

"He is already," Mahoney said, eying the dogs. "You're sure these big mutts don't bite?"

"They eat nothing but *paysan d'Irlande*. Never fear, Mahoney. *Adelante* the Quince Brigada!"

Two patients in pajamas and heavy sweaters appeared on the stairs and stopped to pat the huge dogs. They came down, walking carefully, and went along the gravel terrace that looked across to Castillejo. Coltringham said hello to them, and they waved. He touched his cane to Mahoney's rump.

"See? They're perfectly harmless. Up you go, lad."

"Yeah."

"Give my best to your colored comrade. Good chap. We've had long talks on trade unionism. He's much better."

"Who? Oh, yeh. White. You know Schwartzie, too?"

"Norman? Indeed."

"He can see okay?"

"Bad skull fracture. It's the student, Raven . . . lost both his eyes when that grenade went off. Terrible thing. Stone blind for life."

"That other guy never shoulda pulled the pin," Mahoney said. "You never pull the pin and then hand a grenade to somebody else. You ast me, I figure they dropped it. Then when Raven was bending over, it went off."

"Both eyes. And so young," Coltringham said.

"He was crawlin around when we found him. Well, I'll see ya, Captain, and we'll have a touch. I'll drink with an Englishman."

"Very good," Coltringham said. "Glad you're broad-minded. I'll keep the . . . ah, nerve syrup safe inside me cast here."

He watched Mahoney climb the stairs, edge around the two great Danes, flurry two nurses at the entrance and vanish into the villa, doing a little dance step. The nurses trotted down the steps, starched, rustly and smiling.

"Good morning, Captain. Who's your Irish friend with the fast hands?"

"A Dublin pickpocket," Coltringham said. "'Jimmy the Dip.' You look lovely, my dears."

"How's the plaster vest, Captain?"

"Bertha, my love, a bit breezy under the arms, but otherwise, Savile Row tailoring."

"It's coming off tomorrow."

"Thank Christ," Coltringham said.

Mahoney had stripped two big vases of mimosa and was carrying a big, frail, dripping bunch past the nurse on duty. He winked at her and sailed on into the ward, his sunburned, peeling face thrust through the soft golden blooms.

"Don't get up, you lazy bastids, it'll split yer stitches, you sons of bitches!"

There were twenty beds in a big sunny room with glass doors that opened out on a balcony, wedged open to let in the cool, sunny air.

He saw White, the big man's face and hands black against the sheets, one thick leg trussed to a splint, pink palms locked behind his head.

"Well, well," White said. "Normy, wake up and say hello. Look who's here! Mr. Back Bay, his own self."

"Jimmy!"

"Whatta you say, Matzoh? When are you comin back?"

He threw the mimosa branches on top of White, who giggled like a girl and thrashed around.

"Get these things offa me, Jim, they *tickle*."

Schwartz, very thin and pale, held his nose.

"It's not bad enough, I gotta have hay fever from Mahoney-Baloney."

"Watch that shit," Mahoney said dangerously, laying cigarette packages across White's chest. "These here are tanks, see? The Luckys are the Moors. They came at us like Orangemen the night of Saint Patty's day. Here's us, the Lincolns. British like so. Here's the trench. Got it? When you gonna get out of here, you bums? We been *busy*, for Chrissakes!"

He had the whole ward for an audience and a flat pack of the battalion newspaper, *Our Fight*, to shower over them. He told them about the fourteenth of March when a fine Irish lad named Hourihan had led a charge down two hundred meters of broken trench with only the adjutant of the first company, Wolk, killed during the counterattack.

Schwartz shook his head. His skull had been shaved from the left ear to the crown.

"Bob Wolk? That's a goddamned shame. He was a nice guy. You know Raven's here. We go to read to him every day."

"I heard," Mahoney said. "We put his letter to Coop . . . you know, Phil Cooperman, well, we put that on the front page of the *Daily Mañana*."

"Huh?" White said. "Wall newspaper, huh?"

"Lissen," Mahoney said. "While you bums been laying here playin with yer dummies, we been *busy*. We got radios in the trenches. We got a ping-pong table."

"A ping-pong table! Mahoney, you're shittin us."

"Softball."

"I'll bet. Yers was never too hard, Jimmy."

"Up yours, comrade. Volleyball, only you gotta be careful when you jump up to spike see, cause the guys across the way shoot at the ball. I mean, you go up, see, and, *whee-fizzy*, the stuff comes over. You want books, you big-brains, huh?"

He was skinny and worn-looking, nervous and gay with an elegant haircut. He did a little tap dance, skidding and laughing between the beds, pulled faces over the covered bed-pans and threw the mimosa blossoms around until the nurse made him settle down. White laughed until his belly ached and passed out the cognac that Mahoney had smuggled in. It was good to see him. He was some young kid, tough and brassy and busting with news.

"We lost *sixty guys*, fer Chrissakes! *Disappeared!* Down south some-wheres. The French frontier's closed. They gotta be mountain-climbers, I swear. They come over the mountains, now. A guy showed me his passport. 'Not Valid for Spain.' Stamped right on her. Ain't that a bitch? We found them guys, though."

"You find em yourself, Mahoney? Or did you have help?"

"Aw, come on, Baloney. Give us a break!"

"Well, there was a few other comrades here and there . . ."

"Catch that! 'Comrades,' huh? Who told you that one, you dumb mick?"

"Yer ahss. I never said I did everythin' myself, did I? There was other guys. Listen, us Lincolns been in Jarama longern anybody! Decent outfit gets drug in for a couple weeks in the line, then hauls-ahss out and some other suckers take their place. Us? Sh-i-i-i-t! *Quince Brigada's* been in them trenches so long now, anybody the snipers and artillery don't get is gonna croak of old age! We found them guys, though. I just drove a truck down to Pozoblanco and . . ."

"A *truck*? They got you in Transport, now?" Schwartz said. "I didn't know you could drive?"

Mahoney shrugged.

"I learned on the way down and back. It ain't hahd, fer shit's sake. I just tole the comic-star I wanted to increase my commitment to the anti-Fascist struggle, thassall."

The men in the ward stared at him, open-mouthed and silent. Schwartz cleared his throat thoughtfully. Mahoney lit a cigarette and stared out through the French doors.

"Besides," he said, "truck drivers get around, see? And get to meet these Spanish cunt."

"Ohhh . . ."

White began to laugh, rolling his head from side to side on the pillow.

"You can always tell an Irishman," he said. "But you sure can't tell him much! 'Commitment to the anti-Fascist struggle.' Mahoney, you got no shame!"

"Least I ain't lying here beatin my meat. When you gettin out?"

"I'll be up walkin in four days," White said. "Schwartz, too. Tell the comrades to hold the line till we get back. Won't be long."

"Married?" Paco said. "You want to get married? Who is the man? Why? When?"

"I want to get married because I want to get married," Carmen said calmly.

"Impossible," Paco said, glaring at her. "You are too young."

She made a rude little noise and lit a cigarette. He looked at her, his heart sinking, heavy with anger. With her new freedom, she had behaved like too many other girls and now it had come to this. It was his fault. He should have sent her away to Valencia, even across the frontier to France.

"Tell me the truth. Is it necessary, this marriage? Have you . . . I mean, *are* you?"

"Of course not! How can you think that?"

"I don't see why you go on living with that Montera slut. She's a bad influence on anyone."

"You are a puritan," she said. "I'm not pregnant. What if I were? That's my affair, isn't it? I've done most of the things you asked me. Go here, move there, do this, do that. But I have some life of my own, you know. Oh, Paco, don't be angry with me!"

"I'm not."

"You are, I can tell."

"Carmen, believe me. I am not angry with you. It's just . . . Who is this man, anyhow? If it is some old lover that Teresa has thrown off, then I forbid it."

"You forbid it? And how will you do that, Generalísimo of Public Morals?"

"There are ways," Paco said darkly. "Certain people who can be spoken to . . ."

He looked away, trying to control his anxiety. He was not jealous. He was not in love with her, not in that way. But ever since he had found her at the convent she had been a special favorite, a sort of best-loved younger sister, someone to cherish and protect and worry about. He did not want to surrender this privilege to some total stranger who wanted to take her off to bed. He smiled bitterly.

"Who is the lucky fellow?"

"It might have been you," she said. "I don't know what happened."

He felt a pang in his chest, as though she had stabbed him. He forced himself to shrug carelessly, but his hands were trembling and he thrust them into his pockets.

"I have enough trouble without a wife," he said roughly and cleared his throat. "Damned cold I picked up at Brihuega. All that snow."

"You never tried to keep me for yourself," she said. "If you had, I would have . . . you know. Well, you know what I mean. But you didn't."

"I knew exactly what I was doing, Carmen," he said. "There were a hundred and fifty of us up in the mountains those first weeks."

"Thirty-one days," she said. "And there were a hundred and sixty-three. I ought to know, I cooked for all of you."

"And you were the only woman . . . girl, along. An impossible situation. So I made it that you belonged, in a way, to all of us. That way there could be no jealousy, no fights, just comradeship and . . ."

"No love. I think you must be afraid of love, Paco. You hide from it."

"I have no time for little sentimental affairs. I have the battalion, soon a brigade. We are reorganizing. I have part of an army to worry about. I am responsible to the people, to Spain."

"To Spain. There are times when I am very sick of Spain."

"Don't talk like that. I know you. The food is bad. When you eat well, you are cheerful enough. Don't confuse The Cause with your empty little belly. You've lost weight and it's rather becoming."

"What? You are insulting me. I came to see you to have a serious talk and you tell me that I was fat."

"Not fat. Plump. Who is he?"

"An American."

"What? A *foreigner*? You want to marry some foreigner?"

"Now you will ask why."

"Why, Carmen? Foreigners, well, some of them are good men. Excellent. The best of comrades and first-class soldiers. Like Kopa."

"I don't know Kopa. I don't love Kopa."

"Love. What do you know of love? Look, these volunteers have come here, but they will go home."

"He had a chance to leave with no questions asked. He stayed."

"Who? I ask you, but you don't tell me his name."

"Buckminster. The pilot."

"Him?"

"Yes. Why do you say it like that? *Him* . . . and make a face?"

"The photograph in all the papers. The two of you. I should have guessed then. You wish to marry a man or a 'Hero of the People's Republic'?"

"Paco, you cannot envy him for a few photographs and a medal! Such things are propaganda. I do not wish to marry a photograph and a medal. I wish to marry a man because I love him."

"And him? Perhaps he wishes merely to marry the girl on all the posters. A souvenir of Spain to show his American friends. He doesn't love you. He's just lonesome. You can never tell with foreigners. They are very different, you know. Different language, customs and culture and . . . all the rest of it. People, generally, do not marry foreigners. Women, I mean. Men seem to."

"Oh, I understand. It's all right for you to marry some stupid German blonde, but Spanish women must marry Spanish men. From the same province . . . after all, the Andalusians are all lazy and have Moorish blood; the Cataláns are mongrels and don't even speak the same language; the Basques are peculiar, *almost* as bad as the Gallegos who don't have any money, anyway, and so why don't you marry some *nice* boy that we've already picked out for you? You Spanish men. Narrow-minded, conceited . . ."

"Now who's being insulting? Well, surely there's no rush. Think about it for a few months . . . or longer. Get to know him. Remember that you are young. You don't know men. You had a decent family."

"Oh yes, very decent. Marvelous. I really enjoyed every minute of every day. Be serious, Paco."

"I mean . . . things were *well done* . . . as they should be . . ."

"You used to tell me that the *bourgeoisie* fouled their own nests, corrupted their children, poisoned them with religious superstitions, kept them from contact with the lower classes, bred snobbery and social indifference and *now* you say such things are 'well done . . . as they should be!'"

"A father has the obligation to protect his daughter. It is the duty of a brother to defend his sister . . ."

"Against what? Spanish men?"

"Every young woman needs to be protected," Paco said slowly, triumphantly. "Protected against *herself!*"

"Ah. Oh! Eh, that's a good one. You, the son of an Asturian coal miner think exactly like some *hidalgo*. We men are so irresistible, so handsome, such lovers, that if the women of Spain are not kept from us by force, the poor stupid things will all ruin themselves. Bah, you men. It is only from the waist down that you are true Communists. There, you are all equal."

She punched him in the shoulder. He laughed and shook his head.

"I don't know where you get such ideas. How did you ever learn such things?"

"I spent a long time in convents. While the other girls were praying, I was thinking."

"If men are all Communists, as you say, and where you say, then what are women?"

"It's easier for men. To be a woman is extremely difficult . . . The politics is very complicated. You don't have politics, you below-the-waist Communists, just . . . a weapon."

He stared at her, shocked, scandalized. It was indecent to sit in public and speak in such a fashion.

"Carmen. I forbid you to talk like this. Stop it at once! Come, let's walk for a bit."

"Of course, Paco. Anything you say, Paco."

He frowned at her mockery and stood up, flinging a few pesetas on the table to pay for their coffee. The waiter rushed up and shook his head.

"Oh no, Colonel Larra. Please, the hospitality of the *café* is yours. Here, El Asturiano never pays, *never!*"

"Keep it," Paco said. "A *propina* . . . a tip."

"That implies inequality between . . ."

"I am learning about inequalities and equalities from the Señorita."

"We have been honored by your presence, Señorita Bravo! My wife keeps all your pictures in the newspapers."

"Do you have daughters?" Paco asked suddenly.

"Three," the waiter said, shaking his head morosely.

"You encourage them to read articles about Señorita Bravo?"

"Frankly . . . Well, I am a simple man. Not antiprogressive, but . . ."

"That's what I thought," Paco said. "Come along, Carmen."

They walked up the Castellana. It was a fine day. Carmen looked around happily.

"It feels safe, now. After Jarama and Guadalajara. Madrid knows it is not to change. They can't make us surrender. They can't surround us and cut us off. They can bomb and shell us forever. It is still dangerous, but we are safe."

"Ummm," Paco said. "He is not young, this American."

"About thirty. He has lovely soft, fine hair. Like a little boy's."

"Where does he live in his own country?"

"In a city called Philadelphia."

"*Qué barbaridad!* What does that mean, anything?"

"The city of the love of brothers. Something like that."

"Well, it sounds like a very proletarian place. That's good. He is a republican, then?"

"Definitely."

"I wish he were a Communist," Paco said.

"Oh, he is," Carmen said softly, "I can tell when he kisses me."

"What's that?"

"Nothing."

"If he's not in the Party, then he must have some sort of religion."

"Some sort," Carmen said. "He tried to explain, but I wasn't very interested."

"He's not a Catholic?"

"No."

"That's good. He would insist, then, on a church and a Mass and all the rest. You would refuse, of course."

"Oh, of course."

"Well, if he comes from a proletarian place, Madrid can more than match it. Is he an intellectual?"

"No. He is a pilot."

"That's too dangerous. Find someone else to marry. A quartermaster."

"But I *love* him, Paco!"

"You said that before. Watch out, you'll fall in that bomb crater. He has declared himself? His intentions are for marriage?"

"He loves me. He has said so. In fact, that's about all he does say lately."

"You see? A man in love loses social awareness."

"But isn't that what he's supposed to do? Maybe only with Episcopals."

"What is that word?"

"That's what he says his religion is."

"What does it mean?"

"I'm not certain," Carmen said. "I went to a library and looked it up. They are Protestants who oppose the Pope and the Orders but have bishops."

"If he wants to be married by a bishop he is without luck. Here in the Republic, there *are* no bishops. Either shot or driven out, and the masses are glad to be rid of such parasites! How can you be against the Pope but for bishops? I don't understand."

"Me neither. But that's what he is. He refuses a militia ceremony. He has seen some and he says he wouldn't feel really married."

"He will if he marries you. Poor fellow."

"Paco, that's the nicest thing you've said all day. You will help me . . . us, then?"

He shrugged, stopped and looked at her. How pretty she was, small and fine! No foreigner could ever appreciate her. What gave them the right to come to Spain and take the women, anyway? What sort of comradeship was that?

"And if I don't?"

"I will live with him."

"You do that, and I will never see you or speak to you again!"

"Please, Paco. Help me . . ."

"I'm trying to, for the love of God!" he shouted.

She began to cry. Other people on the street stared at them. Paco patted her clumsily.

"Come, come. I said I'd help, didn't I?"

"If you're going to behave like this, then I don't *want* your help. You're cruel and you shout. Worse than my father, sometimes . . ."

"I say I'm *trying to help!*"

A pair of *milicianos* with carbines slung over their shoulders sauntered toward them deliberately and saluted.

"Some kind of trouble, Colonel?"

"No, no trouble," Paco muttered furiously. "It's just . . ."

The two *milicianos* looked at Carmen admiringly and did not move.

"If there's any trouble, señorita . . ."

She shook her head and began walking, very rapidly. Paco hurried after her. The two soldiers began to laugh.

"Carmen, wait!"

"I'm going home."

"Well, that's it," Paco said. "Where will you live? You can't just go off to the United States. They speak American there, not Spanish. Everyone will hate you."

"We're going to live here in Spain."

"How?"

"He has money. After the war he is going to open a factory and build aircraft. He and Saulnier, a comrade in the squadron, they have already discussed it and it is settled. Francisco has the money and Saulnier is related to some people in France who already make airplanes. Cousins or something. He was a test pilot for the firm at one time."

"I see. Well, the Republic will need aircraft after the war. To defend itself. That sounds all right. His family agrees to this?"

"His father died some time ago. His mother allows him to make his own choice."

"But there must be some arrangement. Between their advocate and . . . we must get a lawyer, at once! For the marriage settlement. Did your father provide for you?"

"May I never forgive him," Carmen said. "The day before the Rising he took every céntimo from the Banco España. He had sold everything."

"There is nothing? No property? No land, a farm somewhere? Not even a small orchard of olive trees, a few vines?"

"Nothing."

"*Qué va*, a marriage! How? In my part of Spain there is *always* an arrangement. Girls don't *get* married if they have no dowry! A poor man's curse is a dozen daughters. You never told me this. Why not? This makes it very difficult. I must speak with him, this Francisco at once. Perhaps a loan. I don't know anything about this, though. We were all miners, you know, and . . ."

"Paco. Listen to me. He *has* money. Enough for both of us. He has already rented a place near the field where he flies. Not for long. That's why we must be married soon. The squadron is being moved to the Aragón front."

"Then you'll never see him again. He'll run off and leave you."

"No. I will go with him. I have notified the authorities. When the orphans are moved to Valencia, I accompany them. From there, I will be posted to the nearest hospital for internationals. He is already taking out citizenship papers. His government has done something about passports, he says. So he is going to become a Spanish citizen and live here forever."

"Well," Paco said, bewildered. "If you have done all this, why do you need me?"

"To arrange the wedding and to stand up for me."

"Yes," he said. "All right. Episcopales must be pretty close to Católicos, though. I can't get a bishop, but maybe a priest. Would a priest do?"

"I'll ask him. We must have all kinds of things, I think. In Philadelphia, marriages are things of great ceremony."

"A brigade of the 5th Regiment will make ceremony enough!"

"And his friends . . ."

"A squadron of pilots, too. There is usually a marriage trip, isn't there? I remember they used to leave the village on the train for Oviedo. Some of them . . . on the, what do you call it? *Luna de miel.*"

"Honeymoon. Yes. Except it's very hard to travel. He had an automobile, but lost it in a raid."

"No one has automobiles in Madrid any more. Not even General Miaja. He has a horse and sometimes a bicycle! Well, there is the Red Guard motor pool. Or the armored train. What about . . . I have still the place in Cuenca, the *finca*. Would that do?"

"That would be wonderful! I *knew* you would help. Are you certain about a priest? I know there used to be one down near the Puerta del Sol. He was working as a bartender. A fat, timid one."

"Someone shot him. After Toledo fell."

"Oh."

"But I have an old friend. From Asturias. He's across the lines. I know about where he is."

"How? You have spies?"

"Of course. They spy on us, we spy on them. I'll get him. As for the wedding arrangements, they will be taken care of. I will call you when I find the priest."

"It's late. I am on duty. Call me."

"Of course. *Salud.*"

"*Salud, Paco. Te quiero!*"

She ran across the street. He stood for a moment, watching her. She did not look back. She had beaten him. He had surrendered. He felt very sad. He had never had sisters. When the other *chicos* had been flirting with the girls during the evening *paseo* in the summer months, he had been reading Bakunin and Marx with his father. No sister, no *novia*, no daughter. Carmen had been, for a little while, all three. Now, she demanded that he give up what he had hardly possessed, that he simply hand her over to some foreigner. He had agreed to the loss. Better to give her up in a decent fashion than to have her run off with this foreigner. After all, they weren't gypsies! Before the war, she would have had a wedding as elaborate as her father could afford. The military always gave big weddings, it was said, thus revealing how much they had stolen from the regimental funds. Very well, a wedding with a fiesta. There was a little chapel on the *finca*. Madrid was not safe, but Voget could find Ortega. Paul had forged documents stating that he was a newspaper correspondent from Switzerland. Voget could cross the lines, find Ortega, and bring him to Cuenca.

Kopa was on leave. A little reunion had been planned, Kopa, Voget and himself. He would present the whole plan to them at dinner. It could be done. It should be done in the right fashion, too, with flowers and music. A Spanish woman married once and forever.

And it could be done. Everything seemed to have slowed down after the rout of the Fascists at Guadalajara. Madrid was shelled only from time to time. He could organize everything out at the *finca*, create a few hours of happiness, and make one Spanish girl a bride. He should be pleased. Why was there a kind of soft pain around his heart? This American must be—what was the word?—scrutinized, yes. His acceptability as a husband for Carmen must be examined with great care. If there was anything, anything at all, no matter how small, he would forbid this marriage. It would be his *duty* to forbid it. He would be unable to forgive himself if he did not make a thorough examination. Carmen's happiness was at stake. Not a moment to lose.

He went to Communist Party Headquarters and demanded a telephone. He called another office, Military Intelligence and Security. *Seguridad* would know.

"*Dígame?*"

"Colonel Larra of the Guardia Roja, 5th Regiment. You have information on an American pilot stationed at Torrejón? Name: Buckminster. B-U-C-K . . . That's right. Francisco, I believe. When did he arrive in Spain, under what circumstances? What is his loyalty record? Yes, of course I know he was decorated for heroism. I have seen others receive decorations. I know what some of them are worth. What are his politics, family background? What? Don't try to pull that shit on me. You have an informer with every foreign group. I want to know everything. I want a copy of everything you have. No, I'm not opening a formal investigation. This is personal, for my own information. Yes, I'll wait. I'll stay right here. You know the number. Very good."

He waited an hour and was summoned to the telephone.

"Colonel Larra?"

"Yes."

It was a different voice. He recognized it.

"This is Jiménez," the voice said. "Chief Political Commissar. We have met, you will recall. At Torrejón?"

"I remember."

"You have requested certain informations from *Seguridad*. Of a certain volunteer pilot. For personal reasons."

"That is correct."

"Ah. How unfortunate. Security does not release information for personal reasons. A formal charge must be presented to them, in writing."

"This is foolishness."

"Security of the Republic is *tonterías*, Colonel Larra?"

"I want to know if he is a good comrade. He wants to marry . . . a friend."

"A friend? The daughter of Colonel Bravo, recently deceased."

"He's dead? We didn't know."

"Machine gunned near Antequera. Buried with full military honors, the funeral attended by aristocrats and other Fascists."

"I am not interested in the dead colonel. I want to know about the American."

"Security cannot release that information."

"Who can? Put me in contact."

"You *are* in contact. I can release anything to anyone."

"I would be grateful."

"*Yo también*, Colonel Larra! For a piece of information in return."

"What do you want?"

"This special comrade of yours. Kopa. He was made commissar."

"He served in that position temporarily. Recommended to me by Hans Beimler."

"Too bad Beimler was killed. We could check on it. You signed an order appointing Kopa as commissar?"

"No. We didn't do things that way, then. There was no time. We were fighting, not making out papers."

"Did Kopa *request* such an appointment, Colonel Larra?"

"Not to me."

"But to Beimler. They knew each other. From a concentration camp, no? In Germany."

"Perhaps he requested it, perhaps it occurred to Beimler first. I don't know. And Beimler is dead."

"Yes. Well, if you don't have the information, I am afraid I cannot help you."

"What is it you want, Jiménez, eh?"

"Perhaps this. That to the best of your knowledge Kopa requested appointment as commissar to Beimler. Beimler spoke with you. You, pressed by the responsibilities of command, accepted. Then just list the dates Kopa served in this temporary capacity. We're merely clearing our files on everyone."

Yes, Jiménez, but for what purpose?

"You could do that, Colonel? A copy of the file on the American will be forwarded to you as soon as I have your little statement . . . Oh, don't forget to sign it."

"And if I don't forward my little statement, no copy."

"No copy. But a little statement into *your* folder, Colonel Larra, that you refused a routine request from the office of the Chief Political Commissar of the Madrid area."

"Do you really waste the people's time and money with such activities?"

"That would be for the people to decide, no?"

Paco hesitated. All the Russian wanted was a statement of the truth, really. No one could be harmed. But what was contained in the American's dossier? Madness in the family? Chronic illness? Trouble with the police?

What he half hoped, half feared to find was a statement that Buckminster was already married with a family back in America. Either way, yes, true, no, not true, it was something he had to know. Not for his own sake. No. For *Carmen's*. It was her happiness alone that concerned him. Was Buckminster married already or not? That was everything. What Jiménez wanted was nothing . . . really.

"All right," he said slowly. "I'll have the statement on your desk within an hour. The messenger can bring back the *dossier* on the American. Agreed?"

"Agreed," the Russian said, and hung up.

"It's beautiful!" Teresa said. "So white and pure and . . . beautiful."

She reached over the back of the chair and touched the silk wedding gown on the dressmaker's form. The fabric rustled softly. The seamstress, her mouth full of pins, knelt on the floor, making a final adjustment to the train.

"Do you think people will know that it's made from a parachute?" Carmen asked.

"Of course not," Teresa said. "My God, are you really *that* small around the waist?"

"It's pretty tight. I can hardly breathe."

"Well, you won't wear it very long. A few hours. Put something on. You're indecent standing around like that."

"Real silk stockings and this thing that holds them up and holds me in! Where did Saulnier get these things?"

"From a brothel, most likely," Teresa said. "Is there any beer? I have a thirst, and my *head* . . . It was quite a party. Anita will be fine. A few hours' sleep, that's all she needs."

"I don't see why I wasn't allowed to go to the party," Carmen said. "I've been locked up here for days. Worse than being in the convent. 'Don't go outside, you'll catch cold. Don't do this, don't do that.'"

"He's just nervous, that's all. Paco said he'd give you a wedding, but it happens to be the one thing he knows absolutely nothing about. Either they don't have weddings in Asturias or they don't teach about them in that school he went to in Russia. Voget *did* bring the priest yesterday?"

Carmen nodded and sat down on the bed, her legs straight out, admiring her new silk stockings. She lit a cigarette and smoked, blowing blue billows out into the morning sunlight that filled the bedroom.

"We had lunch together out in the little garden. He was very hungry, poor man. He's very *simpático*. We walked down through the olive groves as far as the river and walked some more and back again. It was nearly dark when we got back. He went off with Kopa last night, and they went fishing this morning. Old comrades, it seems. Every one is an old comrade, and they keep locking me up. I'm not going to run away. I *want* to marry him!"

"The squadron is not going to fly over and drop roses," Teresa said. "They don't have the gasoline to make a 'reconnaissance flight.' Everyone knows, it seems, even Cisneros, the air commander. Dorlov wanted to make a parachute jump . . . you know the kind where they fall for thousands of meters and then open the thing just in time? You don't? Well, we got him to promise he wouldn't, anyway. Instead, he took some mechanics out and picked every almond blossom between Madrid and the front. I swear. They filled a whole truck. I suppose I'd better go down and place them around. I need a beer first, a big cold bottle of beer. Maybe two. Hey, can you smell it? They've started cooking the steer!"

"What steer?"

"The one Kopa shot. He went out to some *ganadería*. Since there are no *corridas* in this thing of a Republic, there are no fighting bulls. The breeders raise them as steers. But Kopa didn't have any requisition, and they turned him down. So he took a rifle and went hunting. *Pam!* Into the truck with it. Carmen's wedding feast. He got everything. Wine, even champagne for the toast. Sugar and white flour and fresh eggs. Concha, the cook for the squadron, came down on the back of a motorcycle with all her kids in the side car. You should have seen them. The chapel is being cleaned. The animals have been taken out. I'll see that it is scrubbed with lye and water."

"How *is* he?"

"Who? Oh, the groom? Fine. He wants to see the priest. They should talk, I guess. His Spanish is a little better. He has a new mechanic— Pavito. Maybe Pavito should talk with the priest. Just as long as he keeps away from me."

"Who, Pavito?"

"No, the priest."

"But he's very nice, really."

Teresa yawned. The dressmaker stood up, made a few adjustments, tweaks, sudden pinches and folds. The wedding dress stood like a great doll on the wooden form, the arms out stiff, the train caught up on a wire loop. Teresa touched it again.

"It's beautiful. Look at that lace."

"That's real French. Alençon. It must be fifty years old and just *look* at it! Perfect! You will be more beautiful than ever, señorita."

"Thank you, señora. It's the dress that makes the bride," Carmen said.

The dressmaker gathered up her thread, scissors and pin cushion. She stood eying the dress, and nodded, satisfied.

"I can't do much more with such short notice," she said. "I wonder, señorita. He is a *real* priest? If I could just see him, for a moment, you know."

"I'm sure you can. As long as the people in the village don't know about it. That would be very dangerous. He could be denounced and arrested."

"I know," the woman said, her pale lips twitching. "I remember . . . When you are my age . . . the Church is . . . well, you could hold on, even through the worst things. But then, the Republic took it away. Oh, don't misunderstand me! I'm loyal to the Republic. I have two sons with the 5th Regiment. One, the youngest, is with Colonel Larra's Red Guards. But, well, you young ladies wouldn't remember. But I'm old. I remember the time in Barcelona, oh, forty years ago or more, when the Anarchists opened the graves of the priests and nuns and danced with the corpses right in the streets . . ."

"Ugh!" Teresa said. "Come along, señora. Let's leave the bride to herself. This is supposed to be a happy day. No more of that talk, now. I expect you might like some beer. It's thirsty work, kneeling in the sun there."

"Well, I wouldn't mind a *caña*, to tell the truth . . ."

The two women left her, and Carmen fell back on the bed. She finished her cigarette and the dregs of a cup of *café con leche*, real coffee and real milk! She lay among deep feather pillows, idly twirling a strand of hair and listening to the preparations for her wedding. The house sounded to women's voices, the cook, Teresa and the dressmaker. Apparently Anita was awake, too. Carmen heard the actress moan, a husky, soft Andalusian voice. Anita was going to dance with her partner at the fiesta. Anita and Antonio. They were famous in Mexico and all over South America, and they were going to dance at her wedding. Outside, in the hard, bright sun of an early spring day, warming now, but it wouldn't last, the men, truck drivers, soldiers of the Guardia Roja, and the pilots from the Pelican squadron laughed and talked as the whole steer turned on an iron spit above a great bed of charcoal. Inside, the wedding was the affair of women; outside, of men.

Somehow now, it seemed like a very bad idea, a mistake. Why had she said yes? Because of the funny, formal little speech he had made to her, something he had obviously memorized and blurted out in his bad Spanish? Because he was lonely, as Paco had said, obviously alone with a kind of melancholy reserve? Even though his Spanish was not very good, she was convinced that he did not ever talk a great deal. Not like Saulnier, who never stopped. He and Teresa were a splendid pair. They were lovers from the first night together, and Teresa was crazy about her "French parakeet," as she called him. Teresa had no intention of marrying Saulnier, though. And he never talked of it. It seemed that everyone understood that they were lovers and that was right, but that they would never marry, which was correct also. Why, then, did everyone think that she and Francisco would be happy only if they were married? She didn't think so. What if he, too, had changed his mind?

"He can't do that!" she said, sitting up, terrified. "He can't! He said he *would!* Where is he? We must talk about all this. Just to make finally, completely sure."

She swung off the bed and tried the door. Locked! Like an animal in a cage.

"Let me out! Let me out of here! I want to see Francisco!"

"Not a chance," Teresa said. "Go back to sleep. You won't get much tonight."

"Teresa? I have to talk with you. There are a lot of things I don't *know!* Things I should know how to *do!* Please come and explain to me."

"Later. We're all coming in to help you get dressed. Relax."

"I can't relax! I won't go through with this! I don't know him! I'm not ready! You're all making me do this!"

"Eh? Two days ago you were like a bitch in heat. You never should have talked with that priest. Get back to bed, close your eyes, and use your imagination."

Teresa was standing in the hall, her arms filled with branches of flowering almond. Frank tried to help her, but she pushed him toward the door.

"Go away, please. They are down at the river. Go away and stay down there until we send a boy for you."

She rushed away to the kitchen, shouting. Frank went outside. Bright dew lay on the ground, soaking the dead grass flat in thin, brown strands. New grass just showed, pale green, slender spears glistening in the sun between the silver trunks of the old olive trees. The first leaves had broken bud along the twisted branches, and new, pink shoots and crumpled soft tendrils tipped the shaggy vines in the vineyard. He heard birds singing and the dull clatter of sheep bells from beyond a stand of ilex trees. He followed a path until he could hear the river. He came out on a high bank.

The water rushed over black stones, breaking and foaming, running fast, swollen and strong with the melted snow, clear and chill blue in the deep, whorling pools. He walked along the bank through a patch of soft moss and tender fern and then a little field of wildflowers just in bright blossom. He found Kopa, fishing, with another man who looked to Frank as though he might have a small business down near the Philadelphia Zoo fixing tires and automobile radiators. He was fishing, too, with a long, wooden pole. Frank waved and called to them.

"Have any luck?"

Kopa pointed at a wicker basket. Frank looked inside. Eight trout about two feet long lay on a bed of wet fern, beauties, plump and firm, their gills still gasping. Kopa had a strike. Something as long as Frank's forearm broke the surface of the pool, and the tip of the pole drooped and shivered. The line straightened, throwing silver drops, and zipped in the water. Kopa played the trout skillfully, holding the rod-tip high, letting the fish run and jump, tiring him, working him slowly into the bank. A final rush; Kopa bent and caught the line and lifted the fish out, whistling in admiration.

"He is fishing, you see," the other man said. "I am drowning worms. You must be the American. I am Ortega."

"A pleasure, *Padre*."

"We are catching the first course for the wedding dinner. Broiled trout with almond sauce. Is it good? I have never eaten it. That is the second basket. A boy took the first one up to the kitchen, filled up to the top. Want to try?"

Frank shook his head and sat down on a dry rock.

"I'll watch."

The priest was dressed in corduroys, rubber boots, and a raveled sweater. His head was not tonsured, but covered with thick, stiff dark hair. His face was burned dark, like a peasant's, from the winter cold and wind and mountain sun. He crouched on the bank, moving his pole, and spoke over his shoulder.

"I spent much of yesterday with your young lady. You are a very fortunate man, I think."

"Yes, I think so, too."

"We talked of . . . oh, everything. For hours."

"It was good of you to come. Brave, I mean."

The priest lifted his shoulders.

"Nothing. This is the safest place in Spain."

"It seems like it. For a little while, anyway."

"Yes. Nothing lasts, of course. That's why good things, when they come, must be treasured. We Spaniards are good at living hour by hour, for one day at a time. You Americans they say, live for tomorrow, always anticipation."

Kopa splashed up the bank and dropped another trout in the basket.

"Better there than a thousand years in the past, like the Germans. *Hola*, pilot of Moscas!"

"*Salud*, matador of fishes!"

They shook hands. Kopa gazed down the river, shaking his head. He seemed drunk with happiness.

"Never have I seen such fishing! I wouldn't have believed it! Every pool is filled with them and hungry. The boy who came with us said that only the owner fished here. The people were not allowed to. It was a crime, theft. Let me see your bait, Father Ortega. Ah, you have too much. They don't know what it is. Just one worm, a nice, fat one, like this . . . so, see how he wiggles? Now, try it."

Kopa went down to the next pool, whistling and singing. Ortega sat down an the rock and accepted a cigarette.

"Your wife is a member of the Faith, of course. I heard her confession yesterday. You are a Protestant. You know, I never met one? We used to read, at the seminary, of course. The topic was Heresies. We used to have great arguments about Martin Luther. Luther always lost. That made me feel bad. He was a great man. Do you believe in God?"

"Yes. I'm not very religious, *Padre*."

"Neither am I," Ortega said. "But I love God. Not just the idea of God. But God."

He pointed at the sky, the river, the trees and bankside, at Kopa casting in the next pool and at Frank.

"I am a bad priest," he said. "I see God in the wrong places. But I cannot help it. For me, they are the right places. I have been living on the other side, you know. God's side, so they claim. The Church is over there. Here, the people. I crossed the lines the day before yesterday. As a correspondent."

He rolled the word over his tongue, tasting it, and smiled.

"Correspondent. One who answers to the fitness of things. One who adapts. That is me. I have invented a new variation of the sin of disobedience. I don't mean to disobey; I just find things and respond to them as they are. You know, I have been preaching to the villagers and peasants. About this. They come to hear about the saints. I talk about correspondence. They think I am crazy. Perhaps I am. A Red priest."

"That seems right to me," Frank said cautiously. "I don't know. I'm not a Catholic. Maybe it's the war."

"*Silencio!* Today, no one talks of that!"

They turned around. Paco Larra ran down the bank, followed by a boy struggling under the weight of a wicker basket.

"I have been driven out," Paco said. "Those women are in complete control. They dominate everything. I ran like a rabbit, but not before I brought some beer. Kopa! *Hay cerveza fresca!* You don't fish, *Padre?*"

"Kopa fishes for everyone. I spoil his pleasure. He wants me to catch as many as he does. I don't, and so that bothers him and he has less pleasure. So, I stopped."

"Take a bottle. From before the war. There's no beer at all now, you know."

"*Qué lástima*," Ortega murmured, pushing up the wire loosening the porcelain stopper. "How do people live without it? Beer is a necessity. *Salud!*"

Kopa came up the bank with more trout strung on a willow branch. He flung himself down, took a cigarette from Frank and a liter bottle from Paco.

"What a day!"

"Cease-fire has just been announced by the colonel, here," Ortega said. "I think I will declare the same. Let us not talk of the war or of religion —in Spain it's practically the same thing, anyway. Today we talk of food and drink and the spring weather and the mysteries of women. Or, you talk, and I will listen. Well?"

"Let's drink the beer and sit in the sun," Kopa said. "After this winter, I never thought I'd feel sun like this again. What a country! For four months you freeze in order to enjoy melting for the other eight. In Germany, people are still skiing and skating. Let them. Give him some good advice, Paco. You present him with his wife. Inform him about Spanish women."

"What can I tell him?" Paco said. "He's older than I am."

"Then you are sufficiently ignorant to be an expert and he old enough to be full of doubts. Say something and watch him nod."

"Spanish women are like horses. They need a firm hand on the reins and a touch of the whip from time to time."

"That sounds like Saulnier," Frank said. "Where is he, anyway?"

"He and Voget are arranging for the band," Paco said.

"A band?" Frank said. "For the dancing?"

"And before. But Kopa and I have decided on all the arrangements. The ceremony, Padre Ortega. Decorations and food, the women. All you have to do is stand there and say yes."

Paco looked at him threateningly for an instant, then grinned and clicked beer bottles.

"*Salud.*"

"*Salud*, Colonel Paco."

The morning spilled away like the river, bright and filled with noise, a few hours of sloppy clothes, beer and easy talk and fishing lessons until the wicker basket with ferns was filled and the *chico* took it away to the kitchen. The sun grew stronger, and a few birds sang.

My bachelor party, Frank thought, amused and happy. A German refugee, a Catholic priest, and a colonel of infantry, the father-of-the-bride, who is probably not quite twenty years old.

He lay on the bank, his eyes closed, the sun beating red through his lids, and remembered other weddings, Main Line affairs, at which he had been an usher in morning coat, striped pants, boutonnière, and hangover, or the best man, same outfit, same condition. Groom's family and friends on one side of the hushed church, bride's family and friends steered to the pews on the other side, the smell of flowers, the sweet drone of the organ, the sunlight falling through a saint of ruby, blue and golden glass, the secret rustle of dresses, the giggly near-hysteria of bridesmaids, rice and rose petals on the red carpet leading out to the rented Packard sedans. Afterward, the country club reception with champagne and always the same orchestra playing the same music, or champagne and the same orchestra playing under a striped marquee in the broad green smooth yard of a Bucks County estate. He had always expected exactly that sort of marriage and reception himself. Instead, a smuggled priest, a farm filled with soldiers, and a Spanish girl for a bride.

He wondered if he were making a mistake. This was the second time in his life he had ever done anything on impulse. The night at Tom Coltringham's when he had agreed to come to Spain, and now this. How could it be a mistake? Everything *before* Spain was a mistake. He had simply existed before, everything comfortable, predictable, secure. Now he was alive, uncomfortable most of the time, poorly fed, awake and asleep at crazy hours, howling up off the runway at dawn while the rockets powed in the mist, every day of combat flight stripping his nerves, near-collisions, the swarming terror of being hit, the blood lust of hanging on tight, pumping the guns empty into some dark bulk wheeling and twisting in his sights, the slow suffering of watching the Chatos come down at dusk, counting them, counting three, two more, a last straggler, three comrades lost, forever, and praying that it wasn't Sismondi, or López or Dorlov or Saulnier. He was bound to them, his comrades, his blood-brothers, although they seldom talked about it. But it was there, solid as iron, something you could feel.

"What are you thinking of?"

He opened his eyes. The father-of-the-bride. Paco Larra. He doesn't really like me. I've come to take away his girl. I'll be lucky if he doesn't knife me at the altar.

"Carmen. I am very pleased that you have agreed to the marriage."

"It is the correct thing for her."

"It is the correct thing for me, too."

"Therefore, it is done. You will live in Spain, she tells me."

"Yes. I would like to live here. Or some place like this. You have a splendid *finca*."

"It is not mine," Paco said. "It belongs to the people."

"Of course. I could arrange for investments. Agricultural machines, perhaps a school of agriculture. Electricity from the river."

"You would do that?"

"Yes. We could make a co-operative. Democratic, too."

"The Anarchists have tried experiments like that," Paco said, without enthusiasm. "There are other possibilities."

The father-of-the-bride. *Of course, son, it's nice to be on your own. Some fellows make quite a decent living in the insurance business. We'll see how it works out. If it doesn't, there's always First Bank or a good brokerage firm on The Street.*

"There are other possibilities. I know something of aircraft."

"*Claro.*"

"The Republic will continue to fight Fascism."

"Always."

"Therefore . . ."

"*Aviones.* A better possibility. The Party will take care of agricultural development, but we lack technicals in this country. We make very few things. But they learned how in the Soviet Union. We will learn here."

"There are great possibilities."

"Very great."

They seemed to have exhausted all possible topics of conversation. The war was forbidden, politics was muddy going, and Carmen too close to the heart.

"I have heard that you are lucky."

"I was born lucky."

"That is good. The Russian, Dorlov, tells me that you will take a squadron into Aragón."

"I will be in charge of planes and pilots. Someone else will command the squadron. Dorlov, perhaps."

"You will not fly so much?"

"That depends."

"Yes."

Voices whooped from the olive grove and the vineyard. Paco stood up, obviously relieved at their appearance.

"*Mis chicos.* They come to swim. Take a bath, so they will look elegant. I brought down the battalion barber."

"I might have my hair cut."

"It needs it," Paco said and walked away.

"Señorito?"

A boy stood staring at Frank.

"Yes?"

"I am told that it is time for you to dress yourself."

"*Muy bien.*"

The band members, clutching their antique instruments, dressed in worn, somber suits and red kerchiefs in place of neckties, arrived on burros. They had been auditioned, rehearsed and fortified with anisette and coffee.

"Not quite ready for the Salzburg Festival, perhaps," Saulnier said. "Everything they play seems to come out as 'The International' or the Republican hymn. But they have *brío* . . . spirit."

"I can smell it from here," Kopa said.

"Rehearsal space was at a minimum. We used a rather damp tavern. The trip out here has refreshed them. They are eager for musical combat. Just look at them."

"Yes," Kopa said. "Well, keep them out of the sun until it's time to go. They lead the parade across the fields to the chapel."

"The victim?"

"Is there with the priest."

"No one is guarding him? He may escape, seek asylum in distant lands."

"I don't think so. He has on his blue suit and he managed to find the ring without difficulty."

"He will drop it. I will help him. A shave first, a light cologne, my Savile Row suit. The soldiers look first rate. It is the squadron members who depress me utterly. Regard them. A convocation of bottled-water salesmen. The annual convention of Lithuanian snowshoe repairmen. I will speak with them officially and then individually. You are quite ready here, Kopa?"

"Quite ready."

Saulnier rushed off into the house. A light explosion of women's voices sounded immediately.

"Like a fox in a hen house," Voget said. "The wine is chilling. I have seen to it, and the door will remain locked until after the ceremony."

"Let's go see the cooks."

They walked together into the olive grove. They could smell the roasting steer. Wooden tables were spread with pots, pans, cleavers, and knives. The great brown carcass turned on a spit and dripped on the glowing coals. Voget tasted the basting sauce and approved grudgingly. The cook smiled grudgingly.

"You have to watch Spaniards. They would put garlic in ice cream."

"You have made the arrangement for getting Ortega back across the lines?" Kopa asked.

"Everything is ready. I have my credentials. I report the war in the north for a Catholic weekly newspaper. There is an automobile, a certain railroad tunnel, a path and a guide, another automobile. I'll leave him off, cross into France, and come back again. I'll be in Valencia in seven or eight days. You'll get a report of everything I see. Not that it will do much good. The Basques have almost no artillery. We tried to send some in, but the Non-Intervention fools stopped the shipment. The British are alarmed. What to do? They have merchant steamers in St. Jean de Luz with cargoes, mostly of food, for Bilbao. The Nationalists, as they choose to call themselves, have a naval blockade. To run the blockade and be accused of violating the agreement they have just signed, or to yield to the blockade and surrender the sovereignty of the seas? If the British ships are stopped or sunk, if a warship of the Royal Navy is fired upon? A nice little problem for the English government. They argue about it constantly. The War of the Spanish Obsession, they call it. As a result, anti-tank guns and howitzers from Czechoslovakia are still on the docks. Clearly labeled DENTAL EQUIPMENT. The Basques are doomed."

"Then we must not talk of them."

"Words are nothing," Voget said. "I'm sick of talk."

"Have you seen the bride?"

"Yes. I have always thought of Spanish women as fat with furry lips. She is charming. Except for the hair. I do not like women with short hair, curly like that. Like being in bed with a *caniche* . . . a poodle."

Paco, in new dress uniform and boots polished like mirrors, his throat bound in a scarlet neckerchief that matched his beret, was pacing in the hall. Outside, the double file of Guards stood waiting, surrounded by the pilots in civilian clothes. The band members phooted and scraped like insects.

"No more time, you women!" Paco shouted. "Do you know it is almost eleven o'clock?"

"We're almost ready!" someone cried.

The breeze washed through the almond blossoms that filled the hall. He snapped off a few petals and nibbled them, then wiped his face. The cautious *clock-clock* of high heels sounded in the upper hall, and then Teresa and Anita rushed down, holding their skirts and mantillas and trying to struggle into long gloves and talking incomprehensibly at the top of their voices. He stepped out in front of them, blocking their rustling plunge out into the sun. They dropped their skirts and smoothed themselves, preening like birds. The dressmaker appeared, mouth full of pins, stumping along on her knees. Anita and Teresa fiddled with gloves, whispering and giggling. Paco set his fists on his hips.

"Listen to me, señoritas. This must be with dignity. This is not night clubs and a day with the *rusticanos*, get me?"

"Yes, Colonel Larra," Anita said.

"With dignity," Teresa agreed.

"Immense dignity. More than has been seen for fifty years! A hundred. So behave yourselves. Or I'll pack you off to the Barrio Chino! Outside, now."

Demure as does, they stepped out into the sun. The Red Guards breathed like bellows. Paco glared at them. High heels struck down the stairs. Paco waved his hand.

"*Música* . . . but with dignity."

He turned around. Carmen in her wedding dress stood in the hall, clutching the great flounce of her train, her face white with terror and rice powder.

"Oh, Paco . . ."

"*Cuidado,* now. It's all right. Take my arm. So. The veil is very nice. Flowers, ready. Hear the music? It's for you, *querida.* Everyone is waiting."

"I can't . . ."

"What, an army brat? Thirty days a *miliciana* in the mountains?"

"Thirty-one days . . ."

"Cooking Sopa de Ametralladora. The Red Guards are waiting to see their comrade, La Novia."

"*Adelante!*" she said abruptly. "Forward march!"

She saw the walls as high as the ceiling covered with a mist of almond blossoms, the shaft of golden light falling through the open door, a double line of boots and khaki and crimson and shining steel, beyond it a dark blur and the path, newly mowed, across the fields. Music struck up, viols, French horns and *serpentinas,* an old Castilian love song.

She walked with Paco, her hand light on his hard arm, beneath a canopy of raised rifles with a crest of sparkling steel bayonets. She saw the faces of the Red Guards, young, sun-brown, raw from the razor and very serious. Captain Kopa waved an almond branch, and the village band moved off, out of step, but in tune, leading the way down the path. Kopa fell in behind, with Teresa on his arm, then Anita and Antonio. The rifle butts clashed and slammed on the cobbles. Boots crushed to the cadence of the music, and the pilots all cheered and followed the marching Guardias. Children from the village darted around, shrieking and twittering like swallows. The sunny breeze whipped the veil across her face. The procession moved, *con dignidad,* across the field to the chapel.

"They are *en marche,*" Saulnier said. "Hear the music? What a day! We shall all tell this to our grandchildren. Excuse me, Father, I was not including yourself."

Ortega did not hear the Frenchman. He was pleased with the chapel, a small but high-arched old building, the worn stones of the floor covered with fresh river rushes on either side, forming a center aisle. New mimosa and almond branches burst from heavy iron wall sconces. The altar was bare, a simple stone slab. Above it, a crucifix, carved long ago by some forgotten craftsman, The Lord with a peasant's face and heavy, muscular body that accepted the nails, but denied suffering. The face was set, determined, almost defiant.

How strange and good it felt to move in a robe again! To smell dusty stones, see sunlight on an altar, to look into His face! He knelt to pray.

I commit another offense against You. The sin is mine, Lord, not theirs. They are innocent and wish to live together according to Thy holy will. I will marry them according to the Faith, Lord, and pray that he will convert. Be gentle unto them, Lord. Let fall on me the punishment for this addition to my sins . . .

He stood. The American was close at hand, waiting. The music came through the open door, then the bride, white and veiled, the colonel removing his beret. The little chapel filled quickly. The village band waited on the steps. At a signal, they began to play the Hymn of the Republic. The stones of the chapel rang with the voices of men singing, triumphant and reverent. Ortega's mouth opened. He lifted his arms and sang with them, deeply moved, his throat hot and choked. The bride and her sponsor came slowly forward. Beneath her veil she was smiling. The American took her, and the colonel hesitated, and stepped back. The hymn stopped. A sweet hush filled the chapel. The ceremony began.

First fillets of broiled trout dressed with lemons and slivered almonds with chilled local *vino blanco,* then the roasted steer, brown and rich-crusted, rare and juicy with squadrons of dusty bottles of Logroño, red wine with a dryness that left a pang on the tongue. Bowls of chick-peas cooked with wild onions and baskets of miraculous white bread made from real flour, clumsy trenchers heaped with a salad of wild sorrel and new river cress, baskets of Valencia oranges like cannon balls and a pastry log, *brazo de gitano,* gypsy's arm, a sweet crush of crust between the teeth and a filling of raisins, apricots, and hazel nuts drenched in wild honey.

Paco toasted the bride and groom. Frank responded with their thanks to the Red Guard and threw his glass over his shoulder. Kopa brought the best wishes of the international volunteers. Saulnier praised the beauty and artistry of the bride's maids. One of the Guardias Rojas praised the courage and skill of the Gloriosa. Padre Ortega drank to an end to the fighting and the brotherhood of man. Dorlov proposed the destruction of Fascism and the power and wisdom of the Communist Party. Voget drained his glass to the village musicians, makers of harmony. The floor was covered with broken bits of crystal and scattered almond blossoms.

The musicians tuned up. The Red Guards began to clap in cadence and called for the bride to dance. Saulnier hung over the leader of the village band, sweeping his arms through the air. They struck up a waltz.

"This I can do a little," Carmen said, taking off her veil. "We used to practice in the convent with chairs. Holding them out and going round and round. We gave it up for Lent, of course."

Frank whirled her slowly. She forgot her nervousness and followed him easily, holding her train. They went around the floor and around again. The soldiers watched, entranced, beating time with their wine cups.

"Ole! Ole! La Novia! Viva Francisco! Ole!"

The musicians struck up again. "The Music Goes Round and Round," in waltz time. The bride swung and circled with Kopa. Saulnier groaned and shook his head.

"All Germans dance with the arm *so.* Like they are pumping water. My turn."

"Irene and Vernon Castle," Voget growled. "It comes of a thousand evenings wasted in *cabarets-dansants.*"

"You are jealous," Teresa said.

"Of bourgeois decadence? Hardly."

"Well, then?"

"*Voulez . . . ?*"

"*Avec plaisir.*"

Carmen sank into her chair, gasping and fanning her face.

"*Basta . . .* Enough. How many pilots make a squadron, four hundred? I am exhausted."

The musicians collapsed, red-faced and mopping. A chair was brought out from the table and set like a throne. Antonio escorted an old man with a guitar to the chair and bowed respectfully. Anita rose, sliding the *castañuelas* over her thumbs. The crowded room hushed. The old man struck three chords, a long flailing thrum, and began to play. The music rose from the guitar slowly, a scatter of silver notes, a melody repeated, a harmony, then counterpointed, faster, faster. Anita rose and glided out on the floor, the castanets churring softly. She threw back her head and shoulders. Her nostrils flared, and she stared scornfully across the floor at her partner. Antonio stood straight, his elbows pressed to his sides, pinning his short bolero, his slender legs clamped stiff. His dark face was haughty, threatening. Suddenly, Anita and Antonio crashed into swirling, stamping motion, and the wine danced in the cups. The guitar shivered and rang above a staccato, syncopated, hollow stutter the old man beat somehow with his hard, brown palm. Antonio stalked her, arched and hammering with his heels, half encircling Anita, his strong fingers clicking in still a third tempo as she spun free, her skirt with its bright petticoats frothing around her thighs. Paco Larra bounded to his feet, clapping his stiff fingers into his right palm. A second guitar boomed and skimmed behind the old man's delicate race of driving harmonies torn from the blurred strings. The whole room shuddered to the leashed splendor and elastic fury of the dance.

"Wow!" Frank said, awed.

Carmen watched, her mouth open, a dazed, drugged expression lazy in her dark eyes.

Voget bent over and whispered to Padre Ortega. The priest nodded once, without looking at the Frenchman. The dancers crashed and whirled. Anita's hair tore loose and spilled across her face. Antonio crowded her. She struggled, surrendering fiercely to his rutting rhythm. He drove her, blocked her, cornered her at last and she flung with him, their arms laced and shivering as the castanets rocketed and their heels beat in unison, stopped for a heart-snatching instant, and then slammed into stuttering frenzy as they wrenched and held a posture, Anita crouched, pliant and open beneath Antonio's rigid, suspended thrust, and the sweat from his dark triumphant face dripped down on her staring eyes, her open, exulting lips. A single string cried and sank to a whimper. The room exploded like a bomb, a concussive blast of noise. Anita sank to the floor, her face pressed against Antonio's thighs.

Frank saw the priest slip from the table. Voget was already in the hall. A staff car stood at the door, the motor running silently beneath the roar of noise that came from the main room. The priest glanced slyly at Frank.

"You comprehend the meaning of the dance, I think."

"An old dance," Frank said.

"The oldest dance there is," Ortega said.

Frank stripped off the watch on his wrist and placed it over the priest's brawny forearm.

"With a million thanks, *Padre.*"

"Impossible," Ortega muttered, struggling and clawing at the gold band.

"I shall be insulted. One must correspond to time."

He backed away, his hands raised, pleased at the wine-charged blurt of Spanish that came out, somehow, perfect in verb tenses with the Castilian crispness that ended any possibility of further discussion. He marveled at himself and the nature of the language he could use. Ortega smiled, pleased and stricken, staring at the slender golden wafer with the crystal face. He held it to his ear.

"I hear the feathers of an angel. One of the Powers."

"Come," Voget said gruffly, "it grows dark."

A body bumped across the hall. It was the dressmaker, on her knees. She wailed and clasped at Ortega's hand, trying to kiss his fingers. The priest bent over her, nodding gently to the lament that shook out of her trembling lips. Her eyes rolled blindly, and she beat her fist in the sign of the cross.

Paco tore them apart. The woman fell sobbing to the petal-strewn floor, one hand lashing a string of beads. Ortega crouched like a boxer, hunched and powerful. Paco's hand snaked out, clamped and twisted the priest's wrist up before his face, holding the watch in front of his eyes.

He spat something at Ortega, who growled back, straightened, and then both men embraced. Voget jerked his head. They all ran for the command car. Kopa sat beside the driver, a submachine gun in his lap. Voget and the priest dove into the car.

"*Adiós!*"

The car shot away beneath the ilex trees. Paco and Frank looked at each other.

"Come," Paco said. "We shall be missed. The others will notice. It is impossible to trust everyone here. If they ask, say he's gone to take a piss. Priests have to piss, just like the rest of us."

"He is some man," Frank said.

"No one in Spain would have done this thing," Paco said, "only Ortega. It was crazy but an enormous thing. That is Ortega."

"That is you, also, Colonel Larra."

Paco looked at him, not giving a centimeter. He shrugged, a hard flirt of his shoulders.

"There are others," he said.

But you can't think of any right now.

Frank followed the slight, strong figure back into the house. The dressmaker still lay on the floor. Paco lifted her like a rag doll and shook her gently.

"That is enough, woman. You have seen him. If you speak a word. One syllable, understand? I will kill you and eat your heart."

He flung the woman away into the dark passage that led to the kitchen, turned and stalked into the smoky clamor of the main room. The village band began to play a *paso doble*. Paco snatched up a wine cup and drained it.

"*Vino!* Give me wine!"

A *porrón* appeared, the odd-shaped glass drinking vessel of Spain that reminded Frank of a hospital urinal, an open, tubelike throat, a flask body and a pointed, slender spout. Paco held it by the throat at arm's length and tilted it. A stream of wine shot a full meter into his open mouth. His throat jerked as he drank the *porrón* empty and threw it against the wall.

"*Otro!* One for Don Francisco!"

Not a *porrón*, but a *bota*, a leather bag filled with wine, a half-liter goat-skin with the fur inside and a horn nozzle thrust at him by one of the Guards. He twisted off the cap. The music played. Everyone was watching him.

"Here goes nothing," he said grimly, and raised the *bota* up and out, squeezing it. The harsh wine spurted over his teeth onto his tongue and trickled down his gullet. He swallowed and nearly choked, squinting his eyes. He worked his hands on the *bota*, wringing it like an udder to hold the stream steady. The band played. He swallowed and swallowed.

"*Ole* . . . Go *americano!* To the last drop!"

His fingers touched the horn nozzle. He snatched his arms in and sipped up the last squirt, scrubbed his mouth with the back of his hand and tossed the empty skin into the crowd. The soldiers pounded him on the shoulders and plastered kisses on his cheeks.

"Anybody want to see me do the Shag?" he shouted.

"*El Shag?*" Anita said. "No, go to your woman. Mosca and I will show them."

The band began to play "The Music Goes Round and Round" again. Antonio watched Dorlov and Anita dance, a pitying smile on his lips. Frank pushed through the crowd to him and shook his hands.

"Many thanks, Antonio. You are a great artist."

"Yes," the dancer said, "I know."

Frank retreated, running a gauntlet of enthusiastic Guardias and pilots. Their faces swam at him through the blue air. He fell into his chair beside Carmen, who was talking in a low, earnest voice to Teresa.

". . . and after *that*, it is up to him," Teresa said. "Oh, *here* you are!"

"Yes," Frank said. "Jean is looking for you."

"Is he? Yes, yes, of course. Well, until later, eh?"

"*Hasta mañana*," Frank said firmly. "Until *tomorrow*."

"Possibly not for several days," Carmen said.

Teresa was snatched off to dance by one of the Spanish pilots. She waved good-by. Frank and Carmen waved back. Someone touched Frank on the shoulder. Paco, the father-of-the-bride.

"I think you had better go now," he said grimly. "This *fiesta* begins to lack dignity. Some girls from the village have arrived, but not enough to go around."

"Then the *chicos* will have to take turns, no?"

"Francisco!" Carmen murmured. "*Qué escándalo, tú!*"

"*Vámonos*," Frank said, standing up and taking her hand.

The band stopped and began another tune. The Red Guards began to sing and gathered together near the door, their hands held behind their backs. The song was hard and strong, threatening.

"Oh-oh," Frank said, but Carmen was smiling.

The Guardias moved together toward them, now singing a two-part harmony. Two of them held ropes of garlic in their hands.

"What's this, Carmen?"

"A song from Asturias. They bring the *ajo* to put around our necks."

"That's what I'm afraid of," Frank said. "Then . . . *chkkkk*."

"Oh no. It is to keep away witches and demons."

The soldiers sang and draped the ropes of garlic bulbs over Carmen's head, then his. Frank kept his face straight. The Asturians were very serious and sang very earnestly. Paco held two almond branches in his hands. The song stopped when he raised them. Paco sang the first line, and the soldiers responded in a hard, strong chorus. Paco tore the petals off one branch and sprinkled them over Carmen.

"Each petal is a happiness that they are wishing me."

When the branch was bare, Paco handed it to Frank. The chorus rose to a fierce shout, and the soldiers all laughed. Carmen looked at him with her dark, tilted eyes.

"And that is for you to beat me with when I displease you, my husband."

The soldiers applauded. Paco handed her the second branch. He stood there for an instant, brought his hands to Carmen's face, bent and kissed her lightly on the forehead. Tears sparkled in her eyes. Paco then lowered his arms, not touching her, embracing the air around her. The song sank to a rough whisper. Carmen touched the branch of blossoms.

"Each petal is a *niño* I will give to you. They say that we shall have as many sons as grow on this branch and each will become as strong and straight as the trees in the mountains of Asturias."

Paco's arms encircled her full, silk-draped hips. He stepped back, as though holding all her beauty, invisible, but there, within his arms. He turned slightly and flung it all in Frank's face. Frank flinched as though he had been struck and lunged forward, as Paco turned and stalked away through the Guards. Carmen clung to his arm. The soldiers sang, and her face said *Forgive him, please!*

The singing soldiers followed them to the hall and up the stairs. Carmen kissed her fingers to them. The pilots swarmed around with the village girls, shouting and waving their clasped hands like victorious prize fighters. Anita and Teresa were weeping like babies. Saulnier lounged against the wall, stroking his mustache. His right lid dropped in a heavy wink.

At the top of the stairs, Frank turned and held out his hand, palm up. The soldiers stopped; the song ended. The Red Guards nudged each other, grinned and muttered, sniggering and making lewd gestures. Carmen blushed. Everyone laughed, and she hid her face. Frank scooped her up in his arms and swung her around. She clung to him, outraged and laughing.

"What are you doing, you *loco?* Put me down!"

He swung her again, a soft wash of swinging train and skirts lifting over her silk knees.

"This is an old *American* wedding custom," he said. "*Muy simbólico.* I have captured you and carry you away on my horse, you see? Now, this door here. On one side . . . ah, ummm . . . innocence. On the other side, marriage. This is to show that I will carry you forever in my arms . . . I turn the key to lock out strangers . . ."

"Oh, yes. No strangers . . ."

"And I put you . . . where you belong."

He dropped her gently on the big, broad bed. She looked at him anxiously.

"Francisco . . ."

"What, Carmen?"

"Are you sure that door is locked?"

"I have the key right here. See?"

"Umm," she said. "Throw it in the corner somewhere and help me out of this dress."

DIVISION OF SPAIN
APRIL 1937

At first, only the spire of the church showed through the mist. The town of Pilarmadre lay sleeping beneath a thick, white blanket. The morning was very still. Then, the wind began to blow, no more at first than a shifting in the air, then cool, irregular puffs baffled off the slopes of the rocky hills.

"We are ready, Captain Alemany," the sergeant said.

He pointed down the slope where one of the howitzers was hidden in an arroyo, only the snout showing above the lip of the gully. The gun, and another covering the road east to Barcelona had been moved into position at night, packed across the mountains on mules and assembled. Pedro lifted his binoculars. Now he could see the gray bulk of the cement factory and the flag poles outside the hotel near the Plaza Mayor. The black Anarchist banner flapped heavily in the breeze.

The assault force, two companies of the infantry legion of Our Lady of Monserrat, with a detachment of eight machine guns, ringed the town from a farm overlooking the Barcelona road to the arroyo on the slope to the southwest of Pilarmadre. There were two enemy positions to be over-run, outposts manned by eight and six *milicianos* each. The bridge to the Teruel highway was certainly mined. It was a question of whether the first attack group could reach the bridge before the defenders blew it.

"Stand ready," Pedro said. "You have range and bearing on the hotel?"

"Sí, *capitán*. We'll shake those straw-guts out of their beds."

The sergeant ran down the slope, agile as a mountain goat, and dropped over the edge of the arroyo.

Pedro watched the world contained in the bright disc of the binocular lenses.

"Fire!" he said.

Pedro swung the field glasses. The howitzer fired, and the other gun across the valley sounded like an echo. One shell fell in the Plaza Mayor, a gray geyser leaping above the second-story windows. Part of the tile roof of the hotel bulged and broke up into the air. A window went out, and smoke and plaster dust puffed out through the hole. Rifle fire crackled. The enemy was firing. A solid smash. His own troops, by volley. The enemy rifles popped back like firecrackers during San Fermín. The volley crashed again.

They were across the bridge. One squad milled around the first houses, kicking the doors open, another scraped frantically in the earth around the abutment, looking for wires. Dark figures appeared in the streets of Pilarmadre, running and carrying rifles. The machine guns were firing down by the cement factory.

The town was taken in fifty-eight minutes. Smoke streamed up from the hotel and a few houses that had been set on fire to drive snipers out onto the roofs. Sheets, pillow-cases, anything white hung from second- and third-floor windows. A machine gun stood on the front steps of the Ayuntamiento. The telephone wires had not been cut, and the bridge was undamaged. Rifles fired down at the cement factory and hand grenades went off, muffled by the thick walls of the building. The roads were sealed off. At every position, Pedro's infantry stood guard over a few men with their hands raised in the air. Most of them had not been armed. They had merely run away from the falling shells. Pedro rode into Pilarmadre on his horse.

The Plaza Mayor was crusted with broken tiles. The square was quiet, the air thick with dust lifted by the bombardment. Half of the roof of the Hotel Pilarmadre was gone. Two soldiers with slung rifles lowered the black flag. They grinned as Pedro rode by on his way to the post office. One of the soldiers rubbed his backside with the Anarchist flag. Three dead men lay on the steps.

The soldiers had broken into the post office. The telephone operator sat at the switchboard, terrified.

"Get me Teruel," Pedro ordered. "You men, take the proclamations from my saddlebags and start putting them up."

Pedro notified his battalion chief of staff that Pilarmadre had been captured.

"What? Already? Why, very good. Very good! Take every precaution, Captain Alemany. The trucks with reserve troops won't reach you for several hours. We hadn't expected such quick success. Many losses?"

"Very few, sir. Three killed, eight or nine wounded."

"That's all? My God. I shall request a full report, Captain. Some attack! Put a patrol out on the Barcelona road."

"I have, sir. As soon as everything is secured, I intend to open the riding school. With your permission."

"Absolutely. The population is to be pacified at once. You have my verbal permission to proceed with this. Arriba España!"

"Arriba España," Pedro said. "You, cabo, remain here with the operator. No calls in or out, understand? I will be at the hotel."

"Very good, sir."

The lieutenant of A Company was receiving prisoners at the Plaza Mayor. The captured rifles, shotguns, and pistols had been gathered in a loose pile. The lieutenant showed Pedro a hand grenade fashioned from a tin can.

"Look at this thing, Captain. It's filled with marbles. Marbles. The kind kids play with."

"Put it down. How many prisoners do you have here? About eighty?"

"Almost to the man, sir. The cellar of the hotel has been secured. Shall we take them there?"

"At once. Every male of sixteen years or older is to be arrested. The military tribunal will convene as soon as the names are taken. You have the records from the Ayuntamiento?"

"Yes, sir. These are C.N.T. swine."

"Where is that barber? Alfredo? Have you got him?"

"He's already at the hotel."

Pedro looked at his watch. "The tribunal will sit at 0930. That gives you an hour and a half to identify these people and check them against the C.N.T. lists. We aren't going to get any support until about 1200 hours, if I know Transport. Spread the word to the men that the battalion is in the next valley and coming right on. The church was not damaged. No resistance there?"

"None. We caught them sound asleep, sir."

"Good."

"Do you think we'll get a citation for this, Captain Alemany? I mean, it was beautiful, the attack."

"Perhaps."

"Maybe even a promotion, eh?"

"No one is promoted for cleaning out a stable, Lieutenant. That's what we're here to do. Quick and clean. That's all."

"Yes, Captain."

Pedro rode to the church and dismounted. A dozen old women in black crept out of an alley, hesitated for an instant, then rushed on him. He reached for his pistol, and they halted, fluttering about like ravens.

"Thank God you've come, General . . . How we waited and prayed! . . . Yes, praise be to Jesus and the Virgin! . . . You won't leave us? . . . Did you bring a priest? . . . Thank God it's over!"

They all talked at once. He buttoned the holster-flap over his pistol. They rushed at him, gabbling and stroking his tunic.

"Get back to your houses, mothers," he said. "The war is over here. We are the Regular Army. A priest will arrive. A Victory Mass will be said at noon. Go along now."

They scattered, cackling and crossing themselves. Pedro climbed the steps and opened the door of the church. The interior was dark and cool. He stood for a moment, blinking, letting his eyes adjust.

On the altar was the Anarchist trinity, three photographs, huge, mounted on cardboard with gilt frames. Bakunin, Buenaventura Durrutti and the local barber, Alfredo. The choir stalls had been wrecked, the confessionals removed. Slogans on painted bed-sheeting were strung up between the columns. The place had been used as a market, a slaughterhouse, and a public latrine. Pedro walked through the rubbish, his face pinched against the smell. A skinny goat was tethered in a niche dedicated to the Virgin. It stared at him with yellow eyes and bleated. He walked to the altar and knocked down the pictures.

In the sacristry was a small wooden table. On it lay a stack of pamphlets on birth control and a large carton of male contraceptives. One of them, blown up into a balloon, lay on the floor. There was a poster on the wall: PEOPLE'S HEALTH CENTER. He tore it down and ripped it to pieces.

On the front steps he bellowed at a passing patrol.

"You men! Get in here and clean up this garbage! The battalion chaplain will be here soon. Remove everything! There's a goat. Take it away."

The informer showed himself early. There was always an informer at every town retaken. Sometimes a man, occasionally a woman, always religious and full of stories. They smiled a great deal and were very humble and sometimes had papers or a journal of some kind. This one was a man, bald, about fifty years old with spotted hands and bad teeth, the pharmacist of Pilarmadre. From the very beginning, he had been a secret supporter of the Rising, but—and this was his feat of cunning—

because he was an old crony of Alfredo's, they were both professionals, one might say, dwellers on the fringe of science, he had realized his position and had *pretended to be one of the strongest supporters of the Republic!*

"How clever of you," Pedro said. "And this deception worked?"

Of course they were *mal educados*, Alfredo's followers, but practicers of terror. For months he had aided them, patiently waiting for this day. He had documents, photographs. There was even a picture of himself. No, two. With a firing squad. Posed, of course.

"Of course," Pedro said. "What became of the priest? The Red. Ortega, I think?"

Haunted by his sins, the priest had fled. A man of unspeakable vileness. A pervert, it was almost certain. Too fond of children, if the captain took his meaning. A coward, a drunkard, probably a drug-addict.

"Then why wasn't he shot by Alfredo?"

An excellent question. One often raised. Others, all liars, every one, would swear that the priest was a true friend of the people. False. Utterly, completely false! He stole great sums of money, insisted that the young men of Pilarmadre join Durrutti's column, forced women into accompanying the troops as prostitutes . . .

"I thought you said that Alfredo closed your place?" Pedro said.

True. That was the fashion of the Anarchists. Every brothel was a convent, every convent became a brothel. Young girls were seduced every evening at C.N.T. headquarters. The whole town was mad for sex.

"Are you married?" Pedro asked.

There were no decent women in the town, he said, before the Rising or after. Once, as a youth, he had proposed to the niece of the owner of the cement factory. Her father, a vicious type, had actually threatened him, forced him out from beneath the balcony, so to speak, completely misinterpreting his intentions. Since then, he had given himself to religious readings, scientific journals and The Cause. He expected to be defamed. He had many enemies. The people were very provincial.

The brothel was a shabby, two-story stone building near the railroad station. Pedro shot the lock off the door with his pistol.

The place was musty-smelling. To the left of the hall was a ruined parlor-salon with a mechanical piano and fat, dirty chairs and sofas. There were pictures of nymphs and men with goat legs on the walls.

"Upstairs, Capitán, there is a room with a mirror on the ceiling. Another with a huge bathtub. Want to see them?"

"No," Pedro said. "I want to see only the room you told me of. Where is it?"

The pharmacist led him down a hall and opened a door. The room was empty. The floor was stained and pieces of plaster had been crushed on the boards. In the corner was a sheet of canvas the size of a small rug.

"Look at the ceiling, Capitán."

Pedro looked. The plaster was cracked, broken through in a dozen places as though someone had kicked a football up hard enough to shatter the masonry.

"I don't understand," Pedro said. "What has this to do with anything?"

"This room was used by Them," the pharmacist said, sucking his teeth. "For interrogations. Can't you see the pencil marks? They used to tie them by the feet, so. Then one arm behind the back, tied to the belt. They gave him a pencil and put them in the canvas here. They said to them, 'Write your name on the ceiling.'"

Pedro stared. He could see loops and scrawls, broken lines, a fairly distinct ANTON.

"They threw them up in the canvas? To the ceiling. You saw this? When did it happen? Early?"

"No, Capitán. Late. Only in the past few months. It was closed, this place. Locked up. Curiously, they did nothing like this until after the priest left. He must have told them just how to go about it, don't you think? Alfredo is quite mad, now. You will see. He carried a machine gun around with him everywhere. But today he just lay in bed and did nothing. Very strange, no? They were tied, so, and thrown up at the ceiling. It took as long as ten minutes, sometimes. Broke their faces. There would be bits of plaster packed into the eye sockets. Like smashed melons. The heads all soft."

"How many?" Pedro said.

"Twenty-three. The bodies were thrown in the river. All men, no women."

"How many did you actually see?"

"Four. They were just battered to death against the ceiling."

Pedro looked at the pharmacist. The man was sweating and sick-eyed.

"Which end of the canvas did *you* hold?"

"They *made* me do it! If I didn't, Alfredo said they'd do it to me!"

"There weren't twenty-three. There were four. And you helped throw each one of them."

"I have all the documents, papers, everything, Capitán! You mustn't believe the others! I can tell you everything! The truth about everybody!"

"Bring the piece of canvas. We shall need it as evidence."

"Of course, Capitán. There must be legal procedures now."

"We call it 'riding school.'" Pedro said. "What happened to the women of this place?"

"Oh, they are around. Some of them. A few, really. Others were shot, you know, by Durrutti himself."

"I heard the story. Listen, I want you to find these women. Get them here."

"Here? But it's *closed*. Forbidden."

"Look," Pedro said. "I have two companies of infantry who haven't seen a woman in three months. You want me to turn them loose in the town like Moors? Get me the *putas* who used to work in this place. At a *duro* each man, they'll make their doweries in a week. A full battalion is going to be stationed here. As pharmacist, I suppose you can supply whatever is necessary. There are articles that were in the church that you must have some knowledge of."

"I am a good Catholic. They made me do it."

"Bring that sort of thing here. I don't want sick troops on my hands."

The military tribunal, Pedro and the two lieutenants, sat in the ballroom of the Hotel Pilarmadre. Crepe streamers dangled from the ceiling like red and black pythons. The pharmacist sat at the end of the table.

"Name?"

"Silvestre, José. A farmer, Your Excellency."

"He's lying, Capitán. There was Silvestre, a farmer, but he was very religious and was shot in the early days. This one is not even of this place. He came back in the trucks after the attack on Zaragoza. He is named Riado or something like that."

"Were you in the F.A.I.?"

"I am a farmer, Your Excellency . . ."

"In a blue suit and alligator shoes?" Pedro said. "What crops you must raise on your *finca!* An alligator farmer. Begin the lesson, *cabo*."

The corporal flapped the stiff riding crop against his palm. He nodded, and the other soldiers held the bound prisoner back against the column near the orchestra stand.

"Ever ride a horse?" the corporal asked, smiling.

"I am a farmer, Your Excellency . . ."

"Seen one of these?" the *cabo* asked. "The captain wants to know if you were in the F.A.I. I'm going to help you remember."

The *cabo* raised the riding crop. The prisoner flinched, rolling his head against the column. The *cabo* waited an instant, and then struck the bound man as hard as he could across the face, at eye level. The man screamed and slid down the column until he sat on the floor. He kicked his feet on the polished planks.

"Yes?" the *cabo* said. "*Sí o no?*"

"Don't waste your time, Corporal," Pedro said. He addressed the defendant. "By the testimony of impartial witnesses and the confession you have just dictated to the secretary of this tribunal, you stand guilty of crimes against the Spanish state, the Holy Roman Catholic Church and the people of this village. As chairman of this tribunal, I defer to the votes of my subordinates. Your verdicts?"

"Guilty."

"Guilty."

"You are therefore sentenced to death. As a professed atheist, you will not require the attention of a priest, who is not yet here anyway. Take him out and get rid of him. Next!"

It went on all morning. There were no more left in the cellar of the hotel. Only the barber, Alfredo.

The *cabo* went down into the cellar, out into the garden, and came back.

"The sergeant said he's sorry, sir, but they're down to the last belt on the gun. And what does he do if they are sent up to the Barcelona road and the reserves aren't here yet? He's not doing anything, just pointing this out, sir."

"There is a truck, isn't there?" Pedro asked. "Lieutenant, didn't you find a truck?"

"Yes, Captain."

"And gasoline?"

"Twenty liters, Captain Alemany. In wine bottles."

"Tie this Alfredo hand and foot. Put him out on the Plaza Mayor."

"Yes, sir?"

"And then run the truck over him," Pedro said. "That will teach him to defile the house of God with his photographs. This tribunal is dismissed, having completed its function, which is the administration of social justice and the re-establishment of order in this area."

The pharmacist scuttled suddenly from the room. Pedro struck the last name off his list, closed his folder and sealed it.

"Lieutenant, see to the truck. Now, you, *cabo*, come here."

"Yes, Captain?"

"Go after that pharmacist. Find him. He will be in the Plaza Mayor, talking to someone. Take four or five liters of gasoline. Have the pharmacist show you to a certain house. Down by the railroad station."

"You want this house burned down, sir?"

"No. Take the pharmacist there. But come back alone. With the empty bottles. Understand me?"

"Yes, sir. But . . ."

"What?"

"This pharmacist has been a great help in identifying enemies of the Spanish people. If I may point this out, sir."

"We have shot eighty-one persons. Each of them spat in his face. If he lives, that pharmacist will be the mayor of this place. That would not be agreeable to me. Consider that I have given you an order."

"Very good, sir."

As Pedro finished lunch, the first motorcycles roared into the Plaza Mayor. The reserve troops had arrived. The civilian populace was in the streets, waving Nationalist banners of red and gold made of paper taken from the stationery store. The battalion chaplain rode in an open staff car, his hand raised, blessing the people. A platoon of Pedro's soldiers roasted chickens over a bonfire of books.

"The execution of the barber had great psychological effect," the lieutenant said. He had not touched the food on his plate.

"Did you burn the body?" Pedro asked. "Do not drink any more wine."

"Yes, sir. Along with the other, the pharmacist."

"Well," Pedro said, "we have cleaned every lump of dung from the stable, then. It is like moving into a place where there has been a plague. After we are done, the germs that cause disease have been destroyed. We will purify Spain, Lieutenant, little by little."

"Yes, sir. There was really only one thing that bothered me today."

"And that was?"

"The barber. Alfredo. He began singing when we tied him up. Just lying there, face up on the plaza, while we filled the truck with gasoline and drew lots for the driver. You must have heard him, sir."

"I was in the church, praying for the soul of my dead father."

"Oh. Well, you know the song, I suppose."

> *"Man is a brother to man.*
> *He will win his citizen's rights.*
> *Earth will become a paradise*
> *For fatherland and humanity."*

"He sang that?"

"Over and over, sir. Some of the men watching, it brought tears to their eyes, you know? I mean there he was, with the truck a dozen paces away. I got the men into the truck, but they kept dropping off over the sides, and he kept right on singing. Finally, I just told the driver to go ahead, and we drove the truck right over him. He went on singing right up to the instant the front wheels crushed his chest. It was . . . very psychological, the effect, on everybody."

"Who drove the truck, Lieutenant?" Pedro asked.

"I did, sir."

"That's what I thought," Pedro said.

They sat watching the motorcycles circle around the square. The civilians watched them, blank-faced, flapping the gold and red paper flags.

Pedro leaned across the table, half shouting to be heard above the roar of motors.

"Understand me, Lieutenant. I am sorry that we ran out of ammunition for the barber. Mad dog or not, he believed what he believed. The informer, he believed in nothing. He had no loyalty, only little itches.

No one is a man who has fleas for a conscience. Spain is better off without them both, as a bull is healthier without ticks."

"Ticks grow in the grass of the fields, Captain Alemany," the lieutenant said.

"About this time of year, back home, we burn the pastures and the open fields. Fire purifies, kills the weeds and insects, and the grass comes up richer and greener. The animals are healthier for it."

"Animals . . ."

"Men are animals," Pedro said. "Social animals. Come, surely that is self-evident. Man is not equal, but divided into species, like the animals. Clever, stupid, vicious, or good. The clever and strong must see it as their duty as the servants of God to rule the others fairly and justly, to destroy atheism and criminal socialism, to teach the lower species to obey. Out of obedience comes first usefulness and, finally, virtue and honor. That way, only that way, will man ever be happy. Isn't that what everyone wants—to be happy? Here, today, we use the harshest methods to make happiness possible for future generations. We are like stern fathers, that's all. Do you think I take any kind of *pleasure* in this?"

"I know you *don't*, Captain," the lieutenant said. "You are a very honest man, sir, if I may say so. It just bothered me. The truck, and him singing."

"Never do that again," Pedro said. "I don't pull the trigger on the machine gun in the hotel garden. You should not have driven the truck. The men must do it, all of them, together. That way, they all feel responsible."

"They all feel guilt, sir."

"If you like. Guilt and responsibility, the sense of each, they are very close, it seems to me."

Pedro stood up and walked to the balcony. The motorcycles were gone, and the first reserve troops were marching into the square. They were singing a Carlist marching song. Pedro pointed down into the plaza. The booted feet slammed on the stones, right across the wet scrubbed spot where the barber had died.

"Listen, Lieutenant Gallador! There's a song for you."

> The Requetes of Spain,
> Marching off to war,
> Always sing a Salve
> To the Virgin of Pilar!

The company commanders walked out before their men. The soldiers came to attention, hands slapping hard, boots grating on the stones. The commanders shouted.

"Tell these people who you are!"

The soldiers roared back in a single voice:

"*Los Requetes de España!*"

"Tell them what you believe in!"

The troops responded, a bellow of noise:

"All for one, one for all! *Dios, Requete y Falange!*"

"Your commander!"

"Franco! Franco! Franco!"

"*Y José Antonio?*"

The soldiers howled:

"Present!"

Pedro turned to his lieutenant and spread his hands.

"There you are. We will have no more trouble in this town. Come along to the Victory Mass, eh?"

Guernica was thirty kilometers from the front. Ortega had passed through the lines at Marquina with three farmers returning to their homes after selling sheep to the quartermaster of a Navarrese brigade. Prices were high due to the scarcity of food and the flood of refugees moving west to Bilbao. The farmers had seen the artillery and tanks. They did not believe that the Ring of Iron, the fortifications around the Basque capital, could hold back the army of General Mola, the "Navarrese hangman," as they called him. The Basques would fight, but they had no chance of victory. Until peace was declared or Bilbao surrendered, the best thing to do was to stay out of the way. Ortega took their advice and walked directly north, then crossed a river and turned west. The region was mountainous and from the high slopes he could see the ocean, the Bay of Biscay, a dark blue line on the horizon. He walked on, seeing only an occasional shepherd. He had hoped to reach the town on Sunday, but the mountains were steep and his boots were worn paper-thin. He limped along the stony paths worn by sheep and goats, keeping away from the main roads.

The town was legendary, not only for the oak tree, the symbol of Basque freedom, but for the sword of the famous warrior-knight Zumala-cárregui and a very old guitar preserved there, said to have belonged to the poet and musician Iparraquirre. The Basque names amused Ortega. He grinned and said them over aloud again and again as he walked, rested his sore feet, and walked on again. A legendary place, he decided is one where no matter how many days you keep walking toward it, it never gets any closer. If I get to this place, I will never leave it.

He wanted to confess. He wanted to talk to one of the Basque priests. The farmers had told him that it was true, what he had heard. The Basque priests were all Republicans and went with the soldiers into the lines, not merely as chaplains, but to take part in the fighting. Every monastary, too, had brothers who hunted mountain goats. They knew the hills and mountains, every path and track and were experts with rifles. Ortega smiled, imagining a monk with his shaved skull, sandals and loose flapping robe stalking a mountain goat with a rifle and a telescope.

The air was clean and cool, and a few butterflies danced over the wildflowers. Ortega chased them and caught one. It sat on his thumb, moving its wings slowly. It was the color of old paper. He blew on it, very gently, and it fluttered away. He groaned and got to his feet. He looked around and saw a cloud crash silently against a high peak, break apart and pour like water over the huge gray, splintered stones. He had never seen such a thing and shouted, waving his arms like a spectator at the football match. Was the cloud winning or was the mountain? On the lee side of the peak, the cloud drifted, silent, white, and then there were two clouds. Ortega was delighted.

"It's had a baby!" he said, and laughed. "So that's how they do it."

He walked on. Today was Monday, market day. The town would be filled with people from sunrise to dusk. No wonder the Basques wore heavy clothes. Here it was, almost the end of April, a full sun, and it was quite cool. He remembered Málaga and the long, muggy days and nights. There were only two seasons in Málaga, his father had often said: summer and rain.

He was certain that they were dead. In an odd, twisted way, he was glad. They were with God, he was certain. They had been good people, quiet, soft-humored, expecting so little of life that his father had given his only son to the Church with a smile and his blessing. His mother, he remembered, always made *sopa de mariscos* on Mondays. It was her conviction that the fishermen spent all Sunday drinking and running up debts. They needed money to pay off what was chalked against their names on the café slates and were glad to throw another *calamar* or a flat, gray *gallo* on the brass scale, or add another fist of blue-brown whiskery mussels into a cone of paper. What did we eat on Sundays? He couldn't remember. Nothing in the morning, of course, fasting until they took the bit of the Host. He remembered kneeling between them and the winey breath of the priest saying: *Here is His Body, take and eat.*

In the raw stones, bitter herbs and clean air of the mountains, so far away in time and space from Málaga, why did he see now the Holy Week procession? Across a dry dunged field of thistles swayed the statue of Our Lady, crowned with a fringe of gold. The rich women of the city gave their jewels to Her. She waded through the kneeling people, stiff and smiling, dressed in silk and diamonds, rubies and emeralds like the glittering skin of a snake from her wooden fingers to the shoulders. The priests surrounded her, in vestments of gold embroidery, shielded from the golden press of the sun by parasols of purple worked with damask lace, swinging censers of silver and glittering filigree. The narrow, stinking streets were washed with the silken banners of Christ rolling between the jeweled croziers. He felt again the gnaw at the heart as he watched acolytes with lace collars, train-bearers no older than himself, boys in soft violet soutanes carrying pearl-crusted boxes of relics, the bones of those who had suffered and died and now lived with Christ. They swarmed across the meadow of his memory, and the cool mountain wind chanted in the pines.

He remembered walking home, holding his father's hand, calloused and tough as a turnip and hearing the voice say in sad wonder: *They say that our monstrance is worth a million pesetas. Imagine that! A million!*

How shocked he had been to see the nuns dressing the statue of the Virgin, the raw wood, bolts and hinges and wires that lay beneath the rich robes worked by the novices. The nuns had chattered and giggled like girls, playing catch with a bracelet of rubies loaned by the Marquesa of This, a necklace of three hundred pearls from the Contessa of That. He had never spoken of such things to his mother and father. It would have been like spitting in their faces.

He stopped to drink from a spring that broke from the mossy stones and had stroked the granite smooth to spill into a pool. The bank was notched with the hoofprints of sheep or goats. Perhaps the monks with their rifles and telescopes drank here, too. He was afraid of spoiling the watch the American had given him. He wore it strapped up under his shirt, almost to the elbow. It would be very odd indeed to be seen wandering through the mountains with a gold and crystal watch bound to his wrist by a gold band. He would certainly be arrested and questioned. He unfastened the strap, admired the clasp, and placed the watch on a stone. He bent over it and watched the little hand, fine as a hair, creep around the dial. He wound it gingerly and listened to the secret beat of life, the tick of the minutes unwinding.

He saw the town at midafternoon, gray and spired, lying in the floor of the valley. Dogs rushed out of the few farmhouses to sniff and bark at him. He passed women on burros returning from the town. They had bartered all morning, offering their fresh eggs, dozed away the siesta, and now returned with a bit of veal, a bunch of onions, an orange hand of carrots, a turnip or two and a silver bulb of garlic. He saw carts pulled by oxen with heavy eyes and noses like wet snails, a herd of scuttling, uddered goats, a man carrying a wicker-barred crate of chickens on his head. Down there in the valley was the oak tree, the sword and the guitar. Ortega crept down the road, mincing along the shoulder, trying to find soft spots to set his blistered feet.

He had never been much for literature, but he remembered one rainy afternoon sitting in the window of the seminary library, trying to decipher a book of Basque poetry. He had memorized the first line:

I pray that God may grant me the grace to end my life in this beloved soil.

The road was covered with people, Basque men, women and their short-legged, sturdy children. He watched them, shy and smiling. They spoke to him in their dialect. Can they tell that I am a priest, even in these rags? No, they are just being polite on a market Monday. I might be a customer, a cattle factor, a seller of buttons and thread.

Church bells clanged, just as he reached the first clusters of stone houses. He stopped, surprised. It was too early for the angelus. Perhaps it was a special vesper service. He pushed up the sleeve of his shirt. It was much too early. Just half-past four. Perhaps a funeral, then. The bells jowed and battered, gonging through the cool blue afternoon, then, abruptly, stopped. Ortega walked on slowly. The cobbles of the street chewed at his feet like molars. He saw a restaurant, a kettle of oil at a *churro* stand, smelled the hide and straw-dung of the cattle pens. He wondered where the oak tree was, the *Árbol Guernicano*, almost sacred to these Basques. I will have to buy a beret. But first a glass of white wine, a small loaf of bread, and a bit of fried fish.

The air thrummed. It reminded him of the morning on the river-bank, the stiff tremble of the fishing line in deep water. People were looking at the sky. He stopped, jostled by the crowd, and glanced up.

"*Aviones! Aviones!*"

He had seen enough aircraft to recognize them even at a distance. They were German planes with blue bellies and mottled wings and bodies when they rolled over and began to dive. A practice run before they swung across the mountains to Bilbao? He watched them. What could they be doing in the sky over Guernica?

The air seemed filled with them, flight after flight, V-shapes, the motors like the angry buzz of hornets. The people in the streets looked up and began to run, not fast, almost walking to the shelter of buildings. Ortega heard the voices of women calling for their children and the outraged lowing of cattle prodded under an arcade. A thin whistle ended with a brightness, a bump, a column of smoke at the other end of the town. A Heinkel roared over the market place, glittering spots on the front edge of the wings. It whipped off away, roaring and chattering. It was shooting down into the street at the people! Bombs fell everywhere. The earth shook. Everyone began to scream and run. A whole house vanished in an instant. Bullets stitched and howled off the cobblestones. A burro plunged and brayed, showing bloody teeth. Children, insane with fear, crashed into Ortega, spun away, and ran. Ortega stumbled back against a building. A terrified horse dragging a splintered wagon floundered between the stall. The *churro* kettle tilted, and smoking oil spewed into the market place, bubbled and burst into fat flames that skidded between the worn stones. The street was suddenly pink with tile dust, and choking-dry. Dark figures ran and ran. A stiff shadow slid along the street and the cobbles from gutter to gutter spanged and spurted, and the running men and women fell down.

Ortega ran for the fields and stopped, clinging to the rough wall of a burning house. He saw the fields covered with people running, running, and the blood blew on the grass as the planes ripped over, machine guns rattling. The crowds milled and rushed back into the town.

Dark things, black-finned, fluttered down, turned and plunged into the narrow streets. Walls blew out, and fire seethed and crackled. Whole sections of street squirmed up in orange shocks of sound, and the cobbles peeled off and sprayed like cannon balls. Ortega looked up and saw a bomb as big as a coffin slice through the roof of a clothing store. The blast knocked him flat, and he lay beneath a soft pattery horror of burning bits of cloth while the pavement under his belly twitched like a fly-bit horse and a woman ran by, holding the stump of her left arm. Part of a wall leaned down and buried her in a rumpling wave of stone and dust. A roof beam scaled down the street like a straw and seemed to suck after it a thin sheet of fire like a burnished plate or a flying knife blade. A bomb hit, and a body sailed up out of its shoes and swam in the hot screaming air and popped like a crushed bug against a house that folded down slowly, spilling beds, pictures, and chairs into the open maw of a steaming crater.

Ortega crawled and plucked at the smoldering stones and charred beams that jumped away from his bleeding fingers. He snatched up a child and raced into a courtyard. He fell into a tangle of chairs and lay gasping, the child's neck pumping blood on his shirt. He staggered up, mopping himself, blind and weeping. Glass poured down into the patio like a shower of bright water. Something fell like a sack. He did not turn to see what it was.

He was lifted by the billowing bright wave of explosion that struck him deaf. He lay in the rubble of a café, the blood leaking from his ears. He could not move his legs. His arms were pinned across his face, and he bit and butted at his hands. A black bat-shape flicked along a whitewashed slab of wall. Through the webby shatter of the watch crystal, he saw the golden whisker, motionless. The plaster of the ceiling rushed down silently to bury him alive.

Voget remained in what had come to be called "Nationalist" territory for much longer than he had expected. He had been sent to spy on the formation of a state, not the movements of an army. He remained at a cheap hotel in Salamanca and watched and listened and read. He sent information to the Comintern in the form of regular dispatches to a new Catholic weekly newspaper, always submitting his copy to the local censor, never protesting when a statement was penciled out.

It was quiet, rather dull work. Only the actual writing of dispatches gave him any pleasure. It was an elaborate cryptograph constructed in French, for the local censor read that language easily, with letter-symbols and syllables convertible into Russian:

Ramón Serrano Suñer, early leader of the CEDA Youth, who merged that group with the Falange in 1936, is a man of remarkable physical charm, sensitive, loquacious, and witty. In manner, he little resembles Generalísimo Franco, who is reserved, laconic and traditionally devout. Serrano Suñer's hatred of the Republic is the result of personal experiences, imprisonment in Madrid, a daring escape and the loss of two brothers at the hands of the Red executioners. General Franco meets frequently with his brother-in-law to discuss the political future of Spain. Their wives meet constantly. Local officials and military authorities, Falange and Army are drawn together, perhaps as opposite poles of a magnet, a situation that seems to be creating a new type of regime, called by the Salamancans cuñadísimo, super brother-in-law.

Cuñadísimo was easily twisted to *coñodísimo*, a Spanish indecency the enemies of each man repeated endlessly. It was the single joke of the city. Salamanca was a nervous, overcrowded place, with every faction jealous of every other, a city of secret meetings, pistol shots at night, sudden arrests, and decrees issued by the Falange one day and countermanded by Franco the next. The Fascist Party of Spain and the Carlists were defeated, absorbed, by a bold double maneuver. Hedilla, leader of the Falange after the execution of The Absent One, José Antonio, was arrested. Immediately, Franco issued a decree combining the Fascist and Carlist movements, with himself Generalísimo of the Nationalist Army, as head of the new party. Franco had never been either a Carlist or a member of the Fascist movement. Now, he ruled them all, or appeared to. This was *cuñadísimo* in practice, for Serrano Suñer was named Secretary General of the new party.

It seemed to Voget that the new coalition would not last. Like oil and water, the Fascists and Monarchists had been shaken together, but would soon separate again. Even the new party uniform was a daily problem, an exercise of Spanish pride in every hotel lobby and on every street corner. The Falangistas wore the red *boina* as seldom as they dared, while the Carlists dressed with great formality, in order to avoid being seen in the Fascist blue shirt. The Nazis were not happy, either. The German ambassador remarked that the Fascist leader in Spain should be a man of the people, not an ambitious lawyer who dressed like a fashion plate.

The Comintern was not interested in clothing, blue shirts, and red berets. What direction would the new state take? Was there a real ideology or merely a provisional *junta?* Voget watched and listened and read. He interviewed the less powerful, the Falangistas, Carlists, and army officers of the second and third rank.

The Spaniards admired cleverness in others, but especially in themselves. They talked; Voget listened. They were wittily evasive; Voget was dull-witted and easily confused. They were short-tempered and quarrelsome; Voget was patient and sympathetic. It took weeks, but he got what was wanted.

The Nationalist Rebellion had been not an action but a reaction against what it felt to be the criminal tendencies of the Republic and the atheistic menace of Communism. The new state, gathering together all supporting elements, driving all opponents into limbo, would be a new Spain. The new Spain would be the Authoritarian State, the truly modern state, the only form of society capable of carrying out the education and reorganization of the Spanish people. The Authoritarian State would be based on national tradition and Catholic confessional faith. Political relativism and political atheism were rejected absolutely. The Authoritarian State was the embodiment of the great and unchanging principles, the permanent truths of Spanish political life.

As far as Voget could learn by a sort of discreet stupidity, this government by brother-in-law generally ignored the advice and offers of political assistance made by the Germans and the Italians. Franco or Serrano Suñer or both had no intention of creating an imitation state, modeled on those created by *Il Duce* and Hitler. Franco wanted the military support of Germany and Italy, not ideological intervention in the future of Spain. If Franco did not despise the Germans, he did not seem either to trust or admire them. But he let them test their weapons on the Spaniards who opposed him.

What about Guernica? Was this the Authoritarian State as military strategist? Did *cuñadísimo* extend to approving the destruction of undefended villages crowded with civilians? Whose idea had it been? Voget learned that the selected targets had been missed and the town bombed at random.

The Nationalists first denied bombing the town at all, then admitted that some bombing had taken place, then accused the Basques themselves of dynamiting the sewers, finally attempted to blame the Republican Air Force for the incident, declaring all reports to be Communist propaganda. There was a final touch of cynical absurdity. A German pilot, captured by the Loyalists, claimed that the word *Garnika* written in his diary under the date April 26, was the name of his girl friend in Hamburg.

The Kondor Legion officers were glum, even over the many glasses of cognac that Voget bought for them. They seemed in a funk, unable to understand why so many of the Spaniards despised them. Weren't the Basques the enemy? In cipher, Voget stated his belief that the

Kondor Legion had lied, more or less, about the extent of the raid planned. A vague plan of operations had apparently been submitted to General Mola but not to Franco. The Germans had decided to destroy a target of no military significance largely as a military exercise.

Voget received back an answer from his "editor." While the Carlists and the Fascists quarreled in Salamanca, the Anarchists and Communists had begun to kill each other in Madrid, Barcelona, and at the French frontier. The "Anars" were linked with the Trotskyite P.O.U.M. against the Catalán government and the Communist Party. The usual May Day demonstrations were being canceled in some parts of Republican Spain. He was to return to France at once and proceed from there to Barcelona. Voget recovered his laundry, reserved a train seat, and paid his hotel bill. It was Republican Spain that was now being ripped to pieces by its two parties, the Anarchists and the Communists. When the fighting began in Barcelona, it would be a battle to the death. After the shooting in the streets stopped, it would begin in the jail cellars. There would be no mercy by the victors. And Voget knew which party was going to win. The "Government of Victory" was going to be destroyed.

For weeks he had been listening to political gossip, rumor and slander. He had pretended not to understand, to be indifferent, to be amused. When the train for the French frontier jerked into motion, he lay in his seat, stupefied with relief. The compartment was jammed with Spaniards talking about how soon the big seaport of Bilbao would surrender, when the war in the north would end. Voget sipped cognac and smoked and pretended he did not understand Spanish. He stared at his reflection in the dirty glass of the window, thinking.

All his adult life, Voget had been an activist, what was now the literary fashion to term "engaged" in politics. He had been one of the ringleaders of the mutiny of the French army in 1918 and had escaped being shot only by surrendering to the Germans. In the prison camp, he brought into being an Internee Council, a group that used their own hunger and defeatism to wreck the morale of their guards. When the time seemed right, Voget organized a breakout. Most of the prisoners headed west, back to France. Voget headed east and entered Germany with French troops, deserted again and went to Hamburg by way of Berlin. In Berlin in the terrible, "starving winter" of 1919, he had joined the German Communist Party and had fought in the streets of Hamburg beneath the red banner. After the defeat, Switzerland, then Russia, then Switzerland again, Vienna, Rome, and Milan until the Black Shirts seized power, then Mexico and Central America. He had been interrogated by police and had killed police, published clandestine newspapers and wrecked opposition printing presses, dynamited railroads and banks, stolen arms, clothing, medicine, and food and given it all away. For nearly twenty years he had been just powerful enough, given that latitude of personal initiative that enabled him to see and judge those in the Party more powerful than himself and to know that only in the center section, neither too low nor too high, was there something like freedom. The closer one moved to the top of Party hierarchy, the more one was a prisoner of dogma and tradition, the more one was "Russified." At the very top was Stalin, all-powerful, and serving a life sentence of guileful orthodoxy.

"It is better to be at the waistline," Voget had once said. "You go in a notch, out a notch, but always you are holding the pants up. Don't be a trouser cuff; you get pissed on. Don't try to be a necktie. A noose is a noose, even if it's made of silk. Live at the waistline, and you've got a fair chance of going right on living. The fashion for belts never changes."

What he had seen in Russia over the years had acted like a slow toxin in his system. Despite his wanderings, he always considered himself a French citizen first, a Party member second, a state of affairs that he never mentioned to anyone and took care not to demonstrate by any action or even in his relationships with women. He liked Spaniards and their Central and South American descendants. He could not believe that increased Russian influence at a time when the Party in the Soviet Union was being purged would prove to be anything but a disaster in the end. He knew the Russians well enough. They would sacrifice Spain to delay Hitler. If, by a miracle or a world war, the Republic survived, it would be only as a sort of serf state, Poland on the Mediterranean. It was a saddening thought, but the Spaniards by their own fanaticism seemed to be asking for it. Like their Russian allies, the Spanish regarded compromise as a sign of weakness. Neither people were democratic by tradition, both believed in and behaved by traditions and doctrines of power. In Madrid and Moscow the strong had the duty, the obligation to rule, the weak to submit. The Inquisitor's rack, the NKVD knout. And he was a go-between for both. The belt was part of the rack and the beating-table, the strap that served to pin the suffering flesh to the bloody boards. Soon, perhaps very soon, Voget knew he was going to be forced to choose between France and the Party. His fate was to be decided not in Bordeaux, but Barcelona. He was going to be put to the question himself: which, Voget, the Party or the people?

The train to the French frontier plunged, shrieking, into a dark tunnel and soot black as death blew against Voget's face. He lay back in his seat and gave himself to motion, to movement. He was going somewhere to do something, as he had done many, many times before. But this time, his ticket was good only for Spain.

The rumor spread very rapidly. The American volunteers had been taken from the Jarama trenches and, along with the British, moved to Alcalá de Henares to join in the May Day fiesta. Frank and Carmen walked to Plaza San Diego with Saulnier and Teresa to see the parade.

Alcalá was filled with people, military and civilians, the streets bright with flags and banners. The bars and cafés were open and bursting with customers. Bands played, and children ran and shouted. Carmen and Teresa wore red kerchiefs and carried paper flags. They walked ahead, arm in arm, chattering and laughing.

"Well, *mon ami*, you get on, as the saying goes? *Ça marche bien?*"

"Sure. Everything's fine. I wonder if I can see these fellows from the Abraham Lincoln battalion?"

"You look thinner. Your wife is as sleek as a cat. Often the way, I've noticed."

"Look. It's a holiday, right? Lay off, huh?"

"Domestic bliss seems to have done little to improve your personality. You fly patrols, neither better nor worse than before. You go to your *casa*. You come back the next day. It's not the same. You have gained a wife, but we have lost a comrade."

"I'm touched, Jean. You really move me."

"Bah. You have no sentiment. Or do you? Will you miss Dorlov, now that he's been ordered back to Russia?"

"Of course I'll miss him! I thought he was going with us to Aragón until two days ago. He volunteered to fly for the Basques, but got turned down."

"That is not why he is returning to the Soviet Union."

"No? What, then?"

"There is the reception tonight. You are planning to be there?"

"He invited me . . . us. Sure, we're going."

"Good. Ah, the band. Here they come!"

Some other units came first, then, the Americans. Before the Abraham Lincoln battalion, two men marched carrying a huge wreath with a red ribbon that trailed to the pavement. A Spaniard held his rifle vertically. There was no mistaking the nationality of the man who carried another vertical rifle that supported the other side of the wreath. Carmen clapped her hands and jumped up and down.

"Francisco, look! It's them, isn't it? Is that an American?"

"What else could it be?" Saulnier said. "Americans are like Orientals. You can't tell them apart. Be careful, Carmen. *Les nuits, tous les chats sont gris.*"

"What does he say, Teresa?"

"He likes the wreath. The flowers are beautiful."

At the top of the wreath was a broad plank painted in the colors of the Republican flag, red, gold, and purple, and the words EN MEMORIA. The two men carrying the wreath passed very close.

"What part of the States are you from, Mac?" Frank shouted.

The soldier turned his face and grinned.

"Bahstin," he said. "Bahstin, Mass."

"*Vivan los americanos! Viva la Quince Brigada!*" Carmen shouted. "Remember the day last winter, Teresa? Remember when the first ones came into Madrid?"

"Latecomers," Frank said. "Us real volunteers were already here, weren't us, Jean?"

"I try to be prompt. Machine-gun company, eh? Look, a *noir*. Another. The big fellow must have been wounded in the leg."

"A what?" Frank said. "Oh, *noir* . . . black. Yes, I guess so."

"Even he looks very American," Saulnier said. "Perhaps it is because the others seem to be the color of mud and sunburn. What does the sign say, stuck in the muzzle of the gun?"

"*Nosotros pasaremos,*" Frank said. "We shall pass. We . . . we Americans. Damn, but that sounds funny! They look all right, though. As good as anybody else and better than some."

"I would agree," Saulnier said. "*Viva la Quince Brigada!*"

The Abraham Lincolns did not march very well, but they looked like front-line troops, fresh-shaved but still dirty, with patched uniforms of ski pants bound at the ankle and stuffed into worn boots, faded shirts and jackets. Not much spit-and-polish. They looked tired and tough and happy.

The crowds on the sidewalks applauded and cheered.

"You know something?" Frank said. "I'm really proud of those guys! Not just a dozen or so pilots, but infantry and gunners and the whole works. A real battalion. It's too bad people back home can't see them. If that man in the White House . . . oh, forget it."

"These must be the British," Teresa said. "They look very shabby, but they pretend it doesn't bother them. Also, they march quite well."

"That is how one always tells the British," Saulnier agreed. "Do you see someone you know, Frank?"

"Yes," Frank said, dismayed. "Coltringham, with the second company of infantry. The one with the glasses. My God, I'd hardly recognize him! He's been hurt since the University fighting. Tom! Tom Coltringham! Hey! Too noisy. He can't hear me. We'll get him later. After the review."

The review was not a success. It "smelled wrong," as Saulnier put it. The soldiers, raw-faced and trench-dirty, stood at attention in an open green field. General Gal rode down the lines on a beautiful horse. His uniform was clean, freshly pressed, his insignia and medals shining. He spoke to the battalions in turn from the back of his horse, his voice unemotional, a flat, rapid staccato, pausing briefly while another officer interpreted.

"Doesn't he get off that horse?" Carmen asked. "What does he think this is? The Spanish army from before the war?"

"I don't think he's making much of an impression," Frank said. "We Americans are a pretty lively bunch. If they liked him, they'd give him a cheer, at least. He looks at them; they look at him. It must be what happened at Jarama. They don't like him. Hell, *I* don't like him."

"No one likes Gal," Saulnier said. "Except Gal, of course."

The 15th Brigade marched back into Alcalá by a different route and were dismissed in front of a ruined church. Frank and Carmen listened and watched.

"This pleases you, eh?" Carmen said. "Your face is splitting in two."

"I like to hear the sound of their voices. American voices. They were very quiet coming back. Let's go meet some of them."

They wandered from bar to bar. The Americans were drinking cognac and talking. They seemed casual and perfectly at home, but rather subdued. They seemed to gather by sections or squads. Frank took Carmen by the hand. Suddenly, he felt very shy. He did not know exactly what to say to them. He hesitated and walked on until they found a small place in a side street. The Americans looked a little happier there and talked a little more loudly. Frank recognized the soldier who had carried the wreath.

"Hello, Bahstin," he said, holding out his hand, "I'm Frank Buckminster from Philadelphia. Let me buy you fellows a drink."

The soldier grinned and nodded. He had a strong grip.

"That's a damned good idea, comrade," he said. "Mahoney. Jim Mahoney. What outfit you with?"

"Spanish Air Force. I'm a pilot."

"Sonofabitch. Hey, *alférez!* Blanco. White! Come here and meet a pilot from Philly. This your girl? Some cute doll!"

"This is my wife. Mrs. Buckminster," Frank said.

"Pleased ta meetcha," the soldier said. "You from Philly, too, Mrs. Buckminster?"

"Okay," Carmen said and shook hands with him. Frank laughed and shouted for the waiter. They met Logan from San Francisco, Herklemeier from Wisconsin, Johnson from Dallas, Rosenbaum, very tall and thin, from the Bronx, Schwartz a sergeant from Brooklyn, and a big Negro from Chicago who was the *alférez*, the lieutenant. Frank was surprised.

"How long have you been an officer, anyway?" he asked.

"A week or so," White said. "Promoted from the ranks. Just like most everybody else."

"Well, congratulations," Frank said awkwardly. "Have a drink?"

"Just one more, comrade. Somebody's gotta keep an eye on Mahoney-Baloney, here."

"Watch that sh—watch it. Lemme getcha another drink, Missus Buckminster. Schwartzie, don't pull no rank on yer old buddy. Find another *señorita* for yourself."

"Okay," Carmen said.

"Take it easy, Jimmy," Schwartz said. "You shoot down any planes, Buck?"

"A couple," Frank said. "You guys looked really great out there. Really. Brought a lump. Right here. It's very queer, you know? To hear you fellows talk. You just . . . *talk*. Pure American. It sounds funny, sort of. I haven't heard it in a long time."

"It always sounds that way when Mahoney opens his big bazoo," the Negro officer said and punched Mahoney in the shoulder. "Comrade Mick from Beantown."

"I just call a spade a spade," Mahoney said and punched White in the chest.

"I was in Philadelphia, once," Schwartz said. "My aunt took me to a Party rally there. Then we went to the zoo. You live near the zoo, comrade?"

"No, comrade," Frank said. "I lived somewhere else. Now I live right here."

"No foolin?" Schwartz said. "Better here than where we been."

"Pretty bad, huh?"

"Not so damned good," Schwartz said. "We been in those trenches for so long we're going to take out a lease. Over two months, not counting hospital time. We are slightly used goods, you might say."

"I've flown over the Jarama a few times," Frank said.

"Don't go way," White said. "Stay up there and keep them German ugly-birds off our necks. Only anti-aircraft we got's Mahoney. *Oh-oh*, he's got that look. He's gonna sing—watch it, comrades! The Irish Nightingale's loose again!"

The soldier called Mahoney was standing on a chair. The bar echoed to groans and catcalls. Mahoney bowed gracefully.

"Respondin to popular request, I am gonna favor you birds and our guests—specially the lady—look, you bums, get away from her, she's married, fer Crissakes!"

"Sing, Jimmy-boy. Get it over with."

"Normally, I gotta full band . . ."

"Normally, you gotta bun on! Sing!"

Mahoney cleared his throat and started the song. The other men in the bar took it up. The tune was an old one, "Red River Valley," sung in a doleful tenor wail by Mahoney, supported, more or less, by Schwartz and White singing in harmony. It was all done very seriously and struck Frank as very funny.

> There's a valley in Spain called Jarama;
> It's a place that we all know too well,
> For 'tis there that we wasted our manhood
> And most of our old age as well.

> From this valley they say we are leaving,
> But don't hasten to bid us adooooo!
> Cause though we'll soon make our departure,
> We'll be back in an hour or two!

> Oh, we're proud of the Lincoln Battalion
> And the marathon record it's made
> But if you would do us the favor
> Take our last words to Brigade:

> "You'll never be happy with strangers,
> They will not understand you like we . . . *like we,*
> Sooo, remember the old Jarama Valley
> And the old men who waited patiently . . . *pay-shunt-lee!*"

There was great, ironic applause. Mahoney bowed and blew kisses to Bronx cheers.

"Some old men," Frank said. "Is there anybody here over twenty-five?"

"Just me," White said. "Thanks for the drink."

"We've got to get transport," Frank said.

"I know what you mean," White said. "I think it's about time you got your missus outta here, anyway. These birds been in the lines too damned long, you know? Keep shootin down them ugly-birds, comrade."

"*Salud,*" Frank said. "How long are you going to be stationed here?"

Rosenbaum hunched his bony shoulders.

"Gal only knows," he said. "*Salud.* A very genuine pleasure. We generally only see a few journalists. Of course, there was one day when Comrade Mahoney came running up the trench, absolutely red-faced with news and dragged me out of the dugout by the feet—not that I fit in there too well, anyhow—and said 'Rosey, Rosey, guess who's down at headquarters? I just seen him, big as a bear at Franklin Park.' So, naturally, I said 'Who?' And Mahoney said, 'Why, you dumb bastid, the famous writer—*Hemingstein!*'"

"Ernest Hemingway?" Frank said. "Say, I'd like to meet him. I've read a couple of his books."

"Come back. Maybe we could talk," Rosenbaum said. "Schwartz and I could use a fresh point of view."

"Maybe Hemingstein will come back," Frank said. "*Salud*, Rosenbaum! Take it easy, you fellows!"

"Hey, comrade, leave her here!" someone shouted desperately.

"Okay," Carmen said.

"Come on, *mi mujer*. Let's go."

"Yes, my husband," she said. "*Adiós, camaradas!*"

"Saloo, honey!"

"Come back, comrade!"

"We'll try," Frank said.

Mahoney was singing again, and the others joined him.

> "We're the Lincoln Battalion, by cracky,
> And a bunch of brave bastids but whacky,
> And we held down the line for two months at a time . . .
> And we fucked Franco, Il Duce's lackey!"

"Isn't that the word I asked you about the other night?" Carmen said brightly. "The one you said they didn't use much in Philadelphia?"

"That's the word," Frank said. "I wonder if we can find the British or Saulnier or Teresa or anyone?"

"I like Americans," Carmen said. "Very *simpáticos*."

"They really are," Frank said. "I like Americans pretty well myself. American men and Spanish women, okay?"

"Okay," Carmen said. "My God, that was terrible cognac."

"But good music."

"Oh yes. Very good," a man's voice behind them said. "But we have slightly different words."

Frank turned around.

"Hello, Yank. How's the air force?"

"Hello, *Tom!* How *are* you?"

"Better—and worse. I bought a bit of a one. Three here in the shoulder and upper arm. I'm rather creaky, still."

He stood in the center of the street. Spanish and American soldiers of the Quince Brigada walked by and saluted with the clenched fist. Coltringham held his fist at his belt and nodded back.

"See what I mean? Come along. We have a decent bottle in a back room, one street over. Thought I heard someone shout at me."

"I shouted at you."

"That's what I thought. You're all right. You crashed, but that was back awhile, when . . . Let's have a drink. Bring the young lady."

"I'd like to," Frank said. "I'm married to her, and she doesn't have much of any place to go but tag along with me. Carmen, this is Captain Coltringham of the British Battalion. An old comrade."

"A very old comrade," Coltringham said, in Spanish. "My congratulations, señora. If all the women of Spain were as beautiful as you are, the war would be over tomorrow. Either that, or it would go on forever. Your husband is a famous pilot and very brave."

"I know," Carmen said. "And he is very fortunate to have comrades that are even more gallant than they are courageous."

"What a lovely little piece of ass!" a soldier said. "Steady on there, Captain Tom!"

"Watch your language, Ian, or you'll get six of the best!" Coltringham said angrily. "They can't help it. Sorry, Frank."

"Well," Frank said. "Sure. She doesn't understand much English yet anyway. At least I hope not."

They sat in the back room of a small, sour *taberna* and drank wine. Carmen sat smoking and listening. There were other Englishmen in the room. They looked at her and said polite things and looked at her some more. She did not understand much that was said.

". . . and dove with a whole bundle of sticks right under the bloody Eyetalian tank. And that was it."

"Jesus . . ."

"El Asturiano, believe he's Colonel Larra now, sent me note on it all. He was right there. Said the Ansaldo would have crushed right over the Garibaldi position. As it was, Peter got the tank."

"Both killed," Frank said. "My good God."

"Don't go taking any planes and trying to shoot down everything in sight," Coltringham said. "That won't do. We must be very steady now and not foolish. There aren't enough of us left."

"What about that fellow I nearly had a fight with that night? Brian?"

Coltringham shook his head and rubbed his nose.

"Boadilla. I think we had less than twenty at the end of the day. Brian was not one of the lucky ones. Funny. We all thought he was noise and no grit when we first came over. That he'd take off. Came of a good family, Brian. We should have known. Got so we called him 'Brian the Bold.' Wasn't that so, lads?"

"One of the best. Brian liked to mix it up. He really did."

"We heard a lot about the British at Jarama," Frank said.

"Did you?" Coltringham said with a flicker of pleasure. "Well, we did what we could. I have never been so windy in my life."

"How can we ever tell, Tom?" one of the others said. "I'd like to know for one. If I see the symptoms, I'll run like a rabbit."

"Well, I was," Coltringham said. "Absolutely windy. I *couldn't* run, it was that bad. My legs wouldn't work right."

"Nothing the matter with your trigger finger, old lad."

"A reflex," Coltringham said. "Besides, there was no place to run to. It was safer, actually, *in* the trench than outside. The poor Poles learned that. Brave devils, those Poles. Can't understand a word they say, but they fought like hell. French, too."

"Did you see the Americans in action?" Frank said.

"The Lincolns. Oh, yes. We saw what happened."

The others nodded and drank their wine and looked at Carmen, waiting for Coltringham to go on.

"It was a criminal thing," he said, slowly. "There should have been an investigation. Merriman was quite correct, his superiors completely wrong. Misinformation does nothing to counteract basic stupidity. General Gal should have been relieved of command on the spot. He killed a lot of your countrymen, wasted them."

"I gathered that they don't like him," Frank said cautiously.

"They are very solidly proletarian," Coltringham said. "Give them a commander they trust and watch out. He's a fool, is our general of Brigade."

"How is the battalion commander?"

"Čopic? Competent. Nothing flashy. He does the best he can. They need a good Yank field officer and staff. New commissar joined them. First-rate man. Right?"

"Right!" the others agreed. "No comic-star there. Just came in and you can feel the difference. Wait until he tangles with Gal."

"I'd put a quiet quid on Nelson," Coltringham said. "He's a battler, so the Yanks say. A Philadelphia lad, too, I think. Though I doubt that you and Nelson traveled in quite the same circles. He's more slaughter-house and shipyards. I spy a French comrade—and his lady, of course! Saulnier, isn't it? It must be. Come join us. Daryl, fetch a chair for the lady, there's a lad."

Saulnier and Teresa shook hands all around, but refused the wine, with regrets. The squadron truck was ready to leave for Madrid, and it was the only truck.

"Run along," Coltringham said. "We'll meet again soon for a real chin-fest. Yes, yes, of course. With the greatest pleasure, señoritas. À bientôt, comrade. Take care of yourself, Frank, my boy. I mean it. If I get out of this business with a whole skin, I'll follow your lead and get married, myself. Move to Wales and take up poaching. Yes, salud! Salud . . ."

Frank walked with Carmen to the truck, climbed in beside her and sat down. Teresa leaned against Saulnier and closed her eyes. He put his arm around her. Carmen touched Frank's face.

"Are you all right, Francisco?"

"I'm all right. I feel bad about Tom—the English captain. He looks and acts like he's lost everything. Maybe he has. All killed."

"The wounded are always like that," Saulnier said. "For a time, they lose all *esprit*. When the body mends, so does the spirit. The *anglais* is not a young man. He heals more slowly."

"Both my cousins dead," Frank said. "I'll have to write a letter to England. Harry rotting in a trench somewhere in the Casa de Campo, and Peter blown to bits at Guadalajara. They were going to be my future partners in the firm, for God's sake! Two *kids*. Two young English kids. Where is this party for Dorlov, anyway? At the Gaylord? I hope they've got plenty of vodka."

"No, it's to be at a room in the Palacio Real. Two rooms, actually. One for the new Russian generals to meet and drink with the old Russian generals. Every week there are new Russian generals. In the other, Party officials and commissars, friends and comrades and the guest of honor. There will be music played badly by a string quartet and waiters in old *smokings*."

"The Tuxedo Ball," Frank said.

"Maximovich will be there, head of the Russian Delegation. There will be champagne. Russian champagne."

"Good," Frank said.

The party for Dorlov was just as Saulnier had described it. The large outer room held several dozen officers, some in uniforms, others in bulky dark blue suits. They drank vodka in small glasses and did not talk very much. The officers in uniform stood facing the officers in blue suits. They shook hands, toasted each other and drank, then changed partners up and down the lines, shook hands, toasted each other and drank.

"A traditional Slavic folk-dance," Saulnier said. "The Kremlin gavotte. The Moscow minuet."

The interior room was crowded, hot and noisy. Waiters tilted across the carpets with full trays; the string quartet scraped and hummed behind a clump of dusty palms; the air was filled with smoke and laughter. There were Germans and Spaniards, a few East Europeans, a dozen women, all Spanish, and the members of the Russian Delegation in bulky blue suits and neat ribbons pinned over their breasts. The surviving officers of the volunteer squadrons were there along with the Russian instructors and Spanish pilots who had replaced them. Everyone talked at once and laughed and drank champagne.

"It's warm," Saulnier said disgustedly. "Only a Russian drinks warm champagne. Look at the Mosca."

Dorlov looked compact, strong and elegant in a new suit of dark gray, a snowy shirt and a neat, figured tie. His black shoes glittered. He was drinking champagne and being congratulated. He perspired and smiled.

"Why, he's elegant!" Teresa said. "I don't see Anita, though."

"I found him a tailor," Saulnier said. "I picked out the cloth, the shirt, the cravat. I made him leave the woman wherever he leaves her these days. *Pfui*—this stuff is mouthwash, that's all."

Dorlov broke away from some Spanish officers and came to greet them. He was very glad to see them. He shook their hands over and over again and kissed Carmen and Teresa on both cheeks and laughed a great deal.

"Maximovich will be here in a few minutes," Dorlov said. "It is all very wonderful, no? I come here as an instructor, no? To teach . . ."

"How to fly the Mosca," Frank said. "Yes."

"I make a squadron of Chatos, all Spaniards. Another. Finally, the Mosca squadron. I write up and submit my report . . ."

"*Et voilà la Croix de Guerre,*" Saulnier said.

"No, no," Dorlov said. "I expect no reward. I have a place reserved on a ship from Barcelona. We land at Odessa. Let me show you the presents for my children and my wife."

They followed him to a chair against the wall. His presents were in cardboard boxes stuffed with tissue and tied with red ribbons. He had a miniature steam engine made from a used anti-aircraft shell, a book of pictures, a photo guide to Madrid, a plaster model of the Royal Palace.

"You see?" he said, turning the model to show them the scarlet ink spot. "Right there. That's the very room we are in now. So they will know where this reception was held. A good idea, no?"

"Very original, too," Saulnier said. "X marks the spot."

"For my wife!" Dorlov said, triumphantly, shaking out a fur jacket. Carmen and Teresa stroked and admired it. Dorlov wiped his face. He seemed as happy as a child, himself, and bent to spin the flywheel of the little steam engine. His hand was trembling, and he took a glass of warm champagne and downed it.

"Also for her," he said, opening a long, narrow box.

Half-buried in the tissue was a Flit gun. Dorlov sprayed it, pumping the handle, on the chair.

"Against the mosquitoes," he said, grinning. "The little *moscas*. It is an American machine, correct?"

"'Quick, Henry, the Flit,'" Frank said. "That's a very *unusual* present, Comrade Dorlov."

The room stirred. Someone important had arrived. A heavy-set man, middle-aged, stood alone, smiling faintly, holding a glass in his hand.

"Maximovich," Saulnier said.

Everyone turned to look. Dorlov gripped Frank's arm above the elbow, brought his face close and scrambled in the pocket of his suit.

"Listen, comrade," he said, quickly, "I want you to know that you are the best pilot I ever trained. Who was not a Russian, of course."

"Of course," Frank said.

Dorlov took out a package wrapped in brown paper and dropped it into Frank's pocket.

"That is for you. So you don't forget Dorlov. Listen, I leave Madrid tonight."

"I thought it was tomorrow."

"Plans have changed. Don't open it until later. Promise me that. As a comrade."

"As a comrade," Frank said. "Okay."

"Okay," Dorlov said. "You will understand then."

"Understand what?"

"I cannot keep Comrade Maximovich waiting," Dorlov said.

He wiped his face and hurried away across the room, made a stiff little half-bow. The whole room gathered in, drifting closer, taking new glasses from the waiters. The string quartet hushed suddenly, like startled insects. The leader of the Russian Delegation handed Dorlov a glass of champagne and then made a speech in Russian. Frank strained to hear, but Maximovich was talking directly to Dorlov, as if no one else was present. He seemed like a father congratulating his son.

"What's he saying?" Carmen asked. "I can't see anything."

"Well, that Comrade Dorlov has brought to Spain the best . . . something . . . of the Soviet Air Force. Something, something, heroic tradition . . . Communist Party, that's easy enough . . . revolutionary something . . . He's saying that he did a good job and he will be rewarded in the Soviet Union."

"Oh. And now they kiss each other and cry, eh?"

"Dorlov is crying. Yes, now they are kissing each other."

"Why do Russian men kiss other men? Worse than the French."

"What's that?" Saulnier said.

"Let's get out of here," Frank said. "This is Mosca's big night. Fur coats and Flit guns and speeches in Russian. Can we get transport back to the base?"

"Let's try the motor pool," Saulnier said.

Frank touched the package Dorlov had slipped into his pocket and wondered what it was. He waited to open it until they had returned to the base and Carmen had set out the coffee around their wooden table, littered with dinner dishes.

"Real coffee," Saulnier said. "Where did you get it? Black market, of course."

"Of course," Carmen said.

"I like decent coffee," Frank said. "And I can afford it."

"Voilà," Saulnier said, "illegal and immoral. Therefore, delicious. What's that you've got?"

Frank set the package beside his cup and shrugged.

"I don't know. A present from Dorlov. He said not to open it until later. I was going to wait, but . . ."

He pulled open the paper. Something rattled in a wooden box. Frank slid open the top. A gold watch lay in a nest of cotton.

"What the hell is this? He bought *me* a watch? No . . ."

He took it out and looked at it. The second hand crept across the face. He turned it over and looked at the engraved initials and the date 12/25/36.

"This is the one I gave to him. That's funny. He said so I wouldn't forget him. Listen, remember the night he danced at Chicote's? By God, that was something . . . I don't get it, though. He buys his wife a Flit gun and he gives this back to me. What's it supposed to be for, a *memento mori?*"

Saulnier nodded and set down his coffee cup with a sharp click. "Exactly. You have guessed it."

"Guessed what?"

"When the ship docks in Odessa, the secret police will arrest Dorlov."

"What? What for?"

"Political crimes. He has been denounced as a Trotskyite."

"Here? In Spain? That's crazy. They just gave him a party to tell him what a swell job he did!"

Saulnier nodded. Frank stared at the watch. He felt cold all over.

"Don't be confused by the champagne and the speeches," Saulnier said.

Frank dropped the watch, horrified.

"You mean they *knew* that Dorlov . . ."

"The Russians there all knew it. That's why they gave him the party. That's why Maximovich made the nice speech."

"Jesus Christ! And Dorlov knew. They're going to shoot him? They *are*, aren't they! That—that's *disgusting!*"

"*Francisco*, sit still!"

Frank jumped up, knocking over his chair. He pointed at the gold watch.

"Take that goddamned thing away! I never want to see it again! When did you find out, Jeannot? Why didn't you tell me? I could have *done* something, *talked* to somebody!"

"Exactly. And that is why I did not tell you. Dorlov spoke to me himself. So I took him to a tailor and bought him a suit, a shirt, a cravat and some new shoes."

"God—that makes me sick. We could have . . ."

"Done nothing. If you had tried, they would have taken him to Model Prison tonight and shot him there. Sit down. It's better this way."

"But he just *stood* there and looked so goddamned *happy*—like a kid. And all the time he *knew*. And the others knew. And he never said a thing. Jesus . . ."

"What is this about Dorlov?" Carmen said. "Jeannot, what are they going to do to him?"

"Don't ask, don't ask questions," Teresa said, and began to cry.

Saulnier pointed his finger and cocked his thumb.

"Oh no!"

"*Pam!*" Saulnier said, dropping his thumb.

"It was a dirty, disgusting, goddamned . . . how can they *do* something like that? Huh, just tell me that, will you?"

"Because they are Russians," Saulnier said.

"On May Day," Carmen said.

"An unintentional irony," Saulnier said. "Unless it was Maximovich's idea of a joke."

"Joke!"

"The Stalinists have their own sense of humor. Is there any more coffee?"

Frank picked up the chair and sat down in it, holding his head and staring at the box, the little nest of white cotton and the gold watch.

"So I wouldn't forget him. No, I won't. Not the Mosca. He was quite a guy."

"Yes," Saulnier said. "As you say—quite a guy."

Frank reached out his hand and snapped the lid of the box shut.

"I feel lousy. Bring the cognac, Carmen."

"What do you mean you cannot honor this requisition?" Kopa demanded. "Everything is in perfect order. Checked and double-checked."

The Spanish captain shook his head.

"*Tengo mis órdenes,*" he said, and shrugged.

Kopa stared at him. Sometimes the Spanish were stubborn as burros. If they had their orders, like this one, that was final. Sometimes, though, they obeyed only the orders of the *corazón*, the heart, and gave up supplies and equipment that had not even been on the requisition sheets. The windows of the office overlooked the vast, piled floor of the Barcelona warehouse. Spanish workers were opening crates and boxes.

"*Mira,*" Kopa said, pointing. "Right down there. The heavy machine guns and the ammunition. You know what it's for, and here are the papers that say exactly whom it is for. And this paper is my authority for transport by truck. This is the motor-pool ticket. Here is my authority to bring the equipment to Madrid. Look, my name. And *this* name. You know it?"

"I know that name. El Asturiano."

"You know that name," Kopa said. "Then you know that he needs twelve machine guns, replacement barrels, and the ammunition that is requested, too."

"I know that name," the Spanish officer said nervously. "And I know your name, too."

"What, exactly, are your orders then?"

"I give you nothing."

"*Hombre*, this is for the Madrid front!"

"The front is everywhere. Pardon me. I have other affairs."

"Who is chief of ordnance these days? Garrocina?"

"No, no. *Está al fresco*."

"In the cooler. In jail?"

The Spanish officer blinked.

"For the enormity of his crimes against the People's Republic," he said rapidly and stood up, shaking his head. His hand dropped to his revolver holster.

"Who replaced him?"

"Colonel Kolodny."

"Who?"

The Spanish officer repeated the name until Kopa understood.

"Well! *Muy bien!* Where is he?"

"Not here. Inspection tour."

"*No lo creo*. Where is his office? The old one of Garrochino?"

Kopa snatched up his papers. What a stroke of luck! Kolodny, the Polish "seaman," the tank commander who had come down from France in the trucks! He walked up the corridor. The Spanish officer reached for the telephone and bent over it, speaking rapidly.

Kopa waved his papers in the face of the startled clerk-typist and strode through the swinging wooden gate. The door was shut. He pounded on it with his fist and turned the knob.

"*Hola*, comrade!" he said, "Kolodny, it's me! Hans Kopa!"

Kolodny was seated at a desk. His broad fat cheeks twitched and his teeth, set in bright pink gums like pegs, were bared.

"Get out!" he said in German. "Get out at once! The police are already at the front gate, Kopa!"

"Police?"

Kolodny moved, lunging up from behind his desk, scattering papers. He dove at Kopa and seized the German's arms and shook him.

"The Cheka, man! Quick, the fire escape!"

The Pole hurled Kopa through the door to the outer office. The clerk-typist sprang to his feet. Kolodny swung his arm like a cleaver, and the Spaniard ducked.

"No one came in here! Tell the police that! No one here!"

They ran down the long hall. Kopa shouted in German.

"What is this? I've come for the machine guns!"

"They make many arrests. Run, run! No, to the right. Get out of uniform. Hide! Telephone me here tonight. Just where you are."

They burst out onto the fire escape. The alley was empty. Kolodny pointed at a low wooden fence and a street, some barbed wire and an armed patrol.

"Turn left. No, right. Turn. Run for it. I tried to warn you, but you changed hotels."

"There's been a mistake!" Kopa said.

Kolodny looked at him and shook his head. Kopa nodded and ran down the fire escape and pounded the length of the alley. He vaulted the board fence easily, tore off his tunic and stuffed it into a broken barrel. He unbuckled his revolver belt and dropped it down a sewer-grate and pushed the pistol into his pocket. He ran along the wire. There was a sentry shack. He gripped the pistol that flogged his thigh as he ran, curling his fingers around it to weight his fist. The sentry heard him and turned, sliding the rifle off his shoulder and fumbling with the strap. Kopa knew that the sentry would have the rifle on safety. He dove on the Spaniard, swinging his pistol-loaded fist. His hand crashed at the base of the man's neck. The sentry gave a squealing grunt and fell sideways, his rifle sliding on the stones. Kopa scrambled over the sentry and fell against the steel gate. He stood up and steadied himself, put the pistol back in his pocket and tripped the heavy latch. The gate swung out. He pushed open both panels and sauntered into the street, yawning and picking his nose.

There were four of them with rifles and an officer.

"*Manos arriba!*"

Kopa raised his arms into the air and stood there panting.

BOOK SEVEN

*The Brunete Offensive
July 1937*

On the third day of June 1937, the aircraft carrying General Mola to the city of Burgos crashed on the fog-shrouded slope of Buitrago. The "Navarrese hangman" was dead. José Antonio, founder of the Falange was dead. General Sanjurjo was dead—also in a plane crash. A rumor spread that a time bomb had been placed in Mola's aircraft. Of the four insurgent generals, only Franco still lived. Franco said of the dead man: "Mola was a stubborn fellow!" General Dávila was named to command the Army of the North in the final assault on Bilbao and Santander.

In the Republic, Largo Caballero resigned as Premier. President Azaña named as head of the new "Government of National Unity" Dr. Juan Negrín, a German-trained physician, once Professor of Physiology at the University of Madrid, later Minister of Finance in Caballero's "Government of Victory." Negrín was not well-known, except as an efficient administrator with an excellent education. He had been responsible for paying the Soviet Union for military supplies and food shipped into the Republic. He had no personal following, therefore no enemies. It did not take long for enemies to appear.

Negrín was Premier, total Premier, shrewd, dictatorial, energetic, with an appetite for food, wine, and conferences in the middle of the night. Himself a member of the Socialist Party, he was supported by the Communists. Posters appeared on walls and wooden fences, chipped stucco and stone:

RESISTIR ES VENCER!

In Madrid, the names of streets were changed; The Gran Vía became Avenida de Rusia, the tree-shaded Castellana, Avenida del Proletariado.

Negrín planned to fight and to win the war. The Anarchist complaint that it was possible to win the war and lose the revolution was considered to be a statement that it was preferable to win the revolution and lose the war. The government headed by Negrín in Valencia sent final approval to Generals Miaja and Rojo in Madrid. For the first time since the Rising against it in July of the previous year, the Republic of Spain went on the offensive.

The staff meeting was held in a building located north of the El Escorial-Madrid highway, the final briefing before the attack. Juan Modesto commanded the infantry of Lister and Walter's men, including the 11th International Brigade and the 46th Division. The other prong of the assault was headed by Jurado, who had checked and then routed the Italians at Guadalajara. Jurado would direct the 13th International Brigade and the 15th. A huge map hung on the wall. The chief of staff moved a long wooden pointer.

"A triple assault at Quijorna here. In the center. Cañada. Here. Finally at Villafranca del Castillo up here. The center penetrates through Brunete directly southeast, so, and meets the other forces moving west from Villaverde. The junction should be effected at the banks of the Guadarrama River five kilometers east of Navalcanero. In sum, like the pinch of a gigantic claw, crushing all the Fascists together and destroying them west of Madrid!"

Paco groaned silently. Another map. The trouble with maps was that they were never like the earth they were supposed to represent. The room was sweltering. Perspiration dripped from every face. The brigade and battalion staff officers smoked nervously. This was going to be a real tango, the "Big Tomato" they had talked about for months.

They had heard it before, a dozen times, twenty, forty times. Every time that they heard it, it sounded better, more certain, even easier to accomplish. On a map you could accomplish anything. But this was July. The weather was hot and getting hotter.

"Any questions? Now is the time. The eleventh hour, comrades."

"About the Quince Brigada. Aren't they under strength? More than a hundred days in the Jarama."

"The 15th has been reinforced by a fresh battalion in combat training for two months."

"A Spanish battalion?"

"No. Another group of Americans. Jorge Washingtons. They are well-equipped. There is a Spanish battalion, also the Franco-Belgian and the Dimitrovs."

"What's left of them . . ."

"What about aircraft? How many tanks will we have?"

"Aircraft? Central command reports one hundred and fifty bombers and interceptors at full combat readiness with ample reserves of gasoline, ammunition, and bombs, both demolition and fragmentary. All pilots and bombardiers have received full instructions.

"Our own tank corps has in position and in reserve one hundred and twenty-eight tanks with ammunition, gasoline and reserve crews, drivers, mechanics, and turret gunners."

A rumble spread through the hot, airless room, a few low whistles of amazement and approval.

Paco raised his hand.

"Comrade Larra?"

"Just this," Paco said. "I mean it without insult. What if the second claw, the other half *does* not or *cannot* move?"

"Would you repeat that?"

There were groans and gestures for him to sit down. Paco flushed angrily and pointed at the map.

"It's easy on a piece of paper. But what is going to happen if the troops striking west from Madrid to meet us don't move? There's a defense line and the Tercio from Getafe field to the Casa de Campo!"

"It will be broken."

"*No lo creo*," Paco said. "I don't believe it."

There was a brief, shocked silence. He had committed heresy. He had said he did not believe in the tactic of the offensive thrust. Angry murmurs rolled in the room.

"Then go back to your mountains and screw sheep, *chico* . . ."

"*Qué va*, he doesn't believe it! . . ."

"Tell it to Miaja!"

The staff lecturer smiled and patted the air reassuringly.

"Please, comrades. We have just heard the final word from the Leningrad military academies. Thank you, Comrade Larra."

The officers laughed. Paco sat down and stood up again at once. A hand pulled at his shirt and there were whistles. The staff officer was elaborately, ironically polite. He gestured for silence.

"Yes, comrade?"

"It is twenty kilometers from here to the Guadarrama. On the map."

"Approximately, comrade. Your question?"

"Call it double the distance, given the terrain."

"If you like. Your question?"

"Do you believe even our best men can fight and walk from here to there with a single canteen of water? What provisions have been made to bring the men water?"

"Comrade Larra, in complete respect for your training, may I point out that the attacking infantry will be moving relentlessly in the direction of one of the larger *rivers* of Spain?"

Paco stood there, picking his damp shirt from his chest, while the laughter rose up and shook the room. He opened his mouth to speak. The other officers quieted, waiting for his final absurdity. He gave it to them.

"What if the river is dry?"

"Piss in it, *sincojones!*"

Paco sat down, red-faced and furious. The meeting broke up with more laughter, salutes, a round of applause, the rumble of boots on the floor. He sat still, waiting for them to leave. They walked around him, shaking their heads and snorting with laughter.

"*What if the river is dry?* That's a good one, eh?"

"Anybody got a cigarette?" White said softly.

A little ripple of amusement slid away down the dark. The men breathed heavily and eased equipment. White shook his fluttering leg. It acted up on him when he stayed on it too long or marched like this.

"How about we throw fingers and send a guy out for beer?"

Laughter came up out of the darkness like a gush of wind. White shifted his rifle to the other shoulder and kneaded his thigh. He was glad that the darkness shielded him. He was worried about the leg. Below the knee it felt stiff, as though it might knot in a cramp.

He listened to the artillery thud in the dawn mist, the heaviest firing he had heard. He looked down into a blurred open space below the ridge. A flame stabbed and another and the sound bumped his ears. Heavy ones. The new 105s. He scrambled up the slope. They were late, maybe two kilometers behind.

"Come on, you guys!" he shouted, "Let's go, let's go! We're gonna miss it!"

The land rolled off to the south, a broad plain slashed by the dry ravines that Mahoney called "nun-cunts." An ammunition dump or gasoline depot had been hit near Cañada, and black smoke lifted up. A flight of big, fast twin-engined bombers came out of the sunrise mists, twenty of them, Tupolev SB-2 "Katyuskas" with red bands on the tips of the long wings. Then a whole squadron of barrel-bodied Mosca fighters. The bombers were manned by Russian crews of the 14th Group. White had met some of them during the fiesta at Alcalá. The planes hit two villages about five kilometers away. Bright points of light, a long pause with smoke and dust pluming up into the pale sky, then the rolling boom of the explosions.

"That's really kinda nice," White said. "You know? Makes me feel comfy. Boy, it's gonna be a hot one!"

The tanks went out, spread far apart, rolling slowly, each set of treads ripping up a dust cloud. The turret guns fired at the villages, over the cavalry that appeared again and again, always in a different place, low hunched riders and the horses tossing over the hill crests and vanishing again. The George Washingtons went down the slope and out into the field, following the tanks, but not too close. White watched the Washingtons start to shed their equipment. Off came the packs, blanket rolls, jackets and mess kits. The plain was scattered with cast-off stuff. White nodded. They learned fast. You can't fight weighed down by the stuff it takes to live in the field. The Washingtons spread out in attack formation and followed the tanks at a steady walking pace. The first enemy artillery shells, overshooting the tanks, spouted in the plain. Everything was going good. Just like watching a movie from the balcony. All you needed was some popcorn and a girl to feel up during the previews.

"Oh-oh," White said, sitting up straight. "Hey, don't turn them tin cans off like that! Run right on through that shit. Get in there! What's the matter with those mothers, anyway? They all want to live forever? Now they gonna take off and leave the Georgie Washes pinned down out there, for Christ's sake!"

The tanks were turning, creaking and clanking, out from beneath a low, shell-flashed, drifting bank of red dust thrown up by field guns. The morning was stiff with the steady crackle and split of small-arms fire, like a thousand work-gang cooks breaking kindling. The word came down the line. Get ready, we're going out to help the Washingtons. White nodded and massaged his thigh. It was a long walk on a damned hot morning with a bum leg.

"Check your stuff, comrades!" he shouted. "Everybody up offa your ass. Fix bayonets and load rifles!"

Everybody began shouting, and the battalion spilled down the pine slopes, kicking up sand and needles. The sun hit like an opened oven. Sweat rolled down White's face. He reached for his canteen and shook it, astonished. It was empty. Empty, and he didn't remember even taking one drink during the night. Empty, and it was only about seven o'clock in the morning with ten miles to walk.

Mahoney's company was strung out for a thousand meters, exhausted, formationless, wandering weakly across a dry plain that looked as though it had been flung down from the pale, searing sky and smashed into a hundred pieces. The men crawled slowly up little rutted slopes and half fell, swayed, and staggered on down into gravel gullies filled with weeds burned brown. Empty canteens rattled and clanked. They were lost somewhere between the captured town of Cañada and the Guadarrama River.

The plain, folded and fractured, broken and then worn, drove them back and forth, a thousand paces east or west in order to move thirty paces south, toward Brunete, where, somehow, Lister's infantry held and waited for the flanking units to come up. It was hot, hot and hopeless. The sweat evaporated on the skin before the men could lick their salty arms with swollen tongues. They frothed like driven cattle and saw things. Somewhere on this baking field of earth and weeds there was a place, an orientation point. If they could find it, Mahoney could plot by the sun and the bit of paper he had for a map and lead them to a road and the British company they were supposed to reinforce.

No one spoke. They walked slowly and stopped, hunched over with belly cramps, collapsed suddenly, and picked for crumbs in their empty pockets. They had missed the food trucks. They had not eaten in thirty-six hours.

Where was Division? Where was Brigade? Where were the British?

Everything looked the same. A weed tuft that broke to dust and seeds beneath the frayed rope sole of a sandal. A heap of wind-scoured stones. The crusted lip of another ravine, a dry moat to creep up on, scout, walk around and on.

Where was the orientation point? Where was the road?

They could hear the sound of artillery, see the planes skidding across the pale sky, a dust cloud hanging over what must be the town of Brunete. They walked on.

It was hard to breath. Mahoney's tongue, swollen and plastered with a sour white scum, bulged out between his teeth. His dry nostrils were half clogged with dust. His face felt flayed, and his vision blurred double. He could not talk. When he reached the lip of the long gash in the earth and looked down, he did not believe that the weeds were green between the boulders, that the earth was dark with moisture. He waved to the Spanish scout. The boy walked over. They leaned against each other and looked. Mahoney made a scooping gesture with his hand. The Spanish boy nodded and sucked in through his cracked lips. Mahoney gestured digging with an entrenching tool. The boy made a circle with his arms and nodded. Mahoney drew his pistol and fired twice into the air.

The water seeped into the hole. It was the color of weak coffee. Mahoney bailed with an aluminum spoon until the helmet was filled. The men drank, slurping the dirty, iodine-treated water off the spoon, each man taking five spoonfuls before passing the helmet. It was late afternoon. Someone handed him another helmet. Mahoney rolled back on his belly. His mouth still felt like cotton waste, but his tongue was smaller and he could talk.

"Awright," he said. "This here's the point, awright. The road's three kilometers that way. Let's go."

They had scooped out and shared enough water to give every man about a pint, Mahoney thought. Mahoney put out a triple point and formed the company into a loose column. They began walking, winding southeast across the barren, baking land.

"*Aviones!*"

Mahoney could see the road, the dusty trucks and the straggling columns of infantry. The planes came out of the southwest, just below the unbearable brightness of the sun. He waved his arm.

"Take cover! Take cover!"

The company scattered into the *barrancas* and huddled down between the bigger stones or pressed against the steep walls. Bombs fell, jolting the dry earth. Pebbles shook loose and cackled down between the sun-crisped weeds. The hot air shivered with the roar of engines, and dark shadows flitted across the ground. The planes climbed and turned, came back and bombed and strafed again and went away. The futile snapping of rifle fire from the road died away. Mahoney stood up and climbed to the lip.

"Come on," he said and started walking. Dust sifted down, fine as talcum, a cloud blown up by the bombs. One of the trucks was burning.

Mahoney felt the bullet-pop, the crack of air against his eardrum and dropped to the ground. He squinted between and over a rubble of stones. He saw two heads along the line of a ditch.

"Quince Brigada, you bastids!"

"Your royal arse you are!"

A slug plowed off a stone, spraying fragments.

"Cut it out, you friggin Limey!"

"Yank? Are you Yanks there?"

"Yeah."

"Oh."

Mahoney lay on the hot rock ground, waiting. The two men in the ditch stood up.

"Sorry, chums."

"Yeah," Mahoney said.

The air was reddish-gray, a dust-sifting twilight. The truck burned on the road, and except for a few men scattered in a perimeter defense, the British lay tumbled into the dry ditches or wandered around, weak and stricken. Mahoney saw face after face rutted with tears, sunburned flesh showing through the caked dirt. Two first-aid teams milled up and down the road with stretchers. Mahoney spread his company out with the British defense perimeter and then walked on into the road, looking for a familiar face.

"Who's in command here, Limehouse?" he asked a soldier sitting on the ground. The soldier pointed at the road. Burning gasoline seethed and rumpled around the wrecked truck. The flames melted the white background and ate away the bright, broad red cross. Bodies and broken stretchers had been heaped in a ditch, a dark tangle of smeared canvas

and dead flesh. Mahoney jumped the ditch and fell heavily onto the road.
The enemy planes had bombed and strafed the British dressing station
and ambulance.

"Where's the comic-star of this outfit, pal?"

The bandaged head turned. Two reddened eyes looked at Mahoney
through a wet slit in the dirty gauze. The eyes blinked twice. Mahoney
stood up. All around him, the British were stirring, coming in, the
limping wounded, the riflemen, the loaders from the machine guns
still bent under their boxes of bright belts like hod carriers, here and
there a wasted, sun-scorched face with a rough beard under an officer's
cap. Mahoney stepped in front of one of them.

"Ain't you Captain Lloyd?"

"Later. He's called us."

"Mahoney of the Lincolns. Got any water? Food? Where's Major
Coltringham, anyway?"

The British officer looked at him, vague-eyed, and nodded thoughtfully.

"That's just it," he said, and nodded again.

Mahoney stared around. At least a hundred men had come together
in a loose mob that filled the whole road, blocking it. They all looked
south where a smaller knot of men stood near a stretcher, but carefully
to one side of a medical crew.

"Hit last night. Grenade, you know. Lost blood," the British officer
said.

"You guys been bombed before. Plenty." Mahoney said. "What's goin'
on? Don't let these birds bunch in like this. What if them *aviones*
come back, huh?"

"We waited here for you chaps," the officer said. "Too long, too
long."

"We been lost all day!" Mahoney said. "Just like everybody else. I
never seen anythin' like this 15th for a frigged-up outfit."

Mahoney was not conscious of walking. Like the others, he drifted down
the road. No one listened to him or stopped him. He came to the
second circle of men, officers, one commissar and the stretcher.

"Lieutenant Mahoney of the Lincolns," he said.

"Decent thing," someone said, and shook his hand.

Mahoney looked at the stretcher and recognized the man lying on it.
The face, without the steel-rimmed glasses, looked naked. Coltringham's
torso was bare, double-bandaged. Beneath the armpits, across the hairy,
slow-heaving chest, the belt of gauze was dark purple, crisp and flaky,
yesterday's wound. What looked like an ordinary towel lay across the
stretcher, covering Coltringham's belly and groin. The boot had been
blown off his left foot, or cut off. A tourniquet was knotted below the

knee, and blood dropped slowly from the crushed and clotted toes. Mahoney sucked breath between his teeth.

"Bomb?" he whispered.

"Yes . . ."

"He's . . ."

"Going fast."

Coltringham rose to his right elbow before the corpsmen could press him back down on the stretcher. He shook them off and peered near-sightedly at his bleeding foot, touched the saturated towel with his fingers and sniffed. He pinched and rubbed the bridge of his nose. It was very quiet.

"I hope you all had the good sense to take care of the other comrades first," he said distinctly.

"Yes, Major, sir," the corpsman said and bit his lower lip. He looked at the circle of officers and shook his head.

"Ian. Ian?"

"Yes, Major Tom. Right here."

"Get the men off the highway at once. Send back to Cañada for food and water as soon as it gets dark. It is getting dark, isn't it? Rather dark, I mean?"

"Rather dark, sir. Yes, sir. Food and water."

"Lloyd?" Coltringham said. "I've lost my glasses. Can you look about a bit?"

"We'll find them, old Tom. Just rest easy."

"Of course," Coltringham said.

He lay back on the stretcher and blinked, looking straight up at the sky.

"It was a plane, wasn't it? Bomb, I mean."

"Yes, Tom."

"Leave me right here. Orders are to push on. To the river. And across. You have the maps."

"Yes, Tom."

"Then get on with it."

Most of the officers were bare-headed. Mahoney dragged off his cap. Coltringham grimaced and felt his brow and cheeks.

"If you bleeders don't mind, I think I'd like a bit of a song," he said.

"A song?"

"What? . . . oh, a song . . . he wants a song . . ."

"Sing me out of this one and into the next," Coltringham said quietly. "Fair enough?"

There was a sudden, dusty, shuffling rush as the rest of the British came up and stood bare-headed in the dusty gloom. An aircraft snarled off to the west, heading for Madrid.

"I think," Coltringham said, "I think we all know "Tipperary," don't we? Good . . . well . . . sing me off, lads. One and two and .. . ."

Coltringham began it, his fingers beating time on the bloody towel. The officers joined in, off-beat and shaky-voiced. Mahoney swallowed. All the British, well and wounded, began to sing:

> "It's a long way to Tipperary;
> It's a long way . . ."

Mahoney walked slowly back across the rutted, hard-baked field. He sat down on the lip of a *barranca* and looked down at the men waiting there.

"What's goin' on, Jimmy?"

Mahoney shook his head. Behind him, near the road, a volley of rifle fire crashed once, twice, three times.

"We gonna get water and chow, Jimmy?"

Mahoney nodded.

"What's all the singin and shootin for, Jimmy? Where the hell a ya been?"

"To a funeral," he said. "I been to a British funeral."

The alarm clock jangled. Frank rolled over in the damp sheets, fumbled, and found the button. The spring unwound, and the bell dwindled to a feeble churring before he snapped it silent. He rolled on his back and lay looking at the ceiling. It was already hot; his chest and legs were slick with sweat. A truck rolled by in the street. The sound faded. He wondered what day it was.

Carmen lay on her side, facing away from him, asleep. Damp dark curls were plastered to her neck. She breathed evenly, quietly.

He lay still in the big, lumpy bed. The dawn light came through the slatted blind and touched the open door of the big armoire. He could see the dim, dummy shape of his flying suit, flat and spectral, headless on the wooden hanger. It was a beautiful suit, made of soft glove-leather, that had been taken from an Italian Fiat pilot he had shot down near El Escorial. He couldn't remember when. A month before? Right after May Day? Sometime. The other pilots in the squadron had wrapped it up in a big package and had given it to him for a *bautizo* present. They thought it was a great joke, the mistake that had been made on his new passport.

His mouth was dry and his teeth felt covered with fuzz. His head felt stuffed with dirty wool. Another dawn, another hangover. Dawn, operations hut, then out to the hangars, the morning mission, then back, white wine and malt-coffee, bitter and black, while he wrote up the report, totaled the gasoline and ammunition figures, listed the enemy

kills and the squadron casualties. Then, the siesta, an hour sprawled
on the hard cot in his office, sweating and nervous, out to the flight
line again. The second combat mission, another report, all the papers to
the Air Ministry, the motorcycle rider with the next day's mission sheets
and maps. Waiting in the *cantina*, drinking white wine and malt-coffee,
rolling loose cigarettes, watching the dusk sky until the last patrol came
in. Then what the pilots called the *tertulia*, the long gab-session while
they talked and he asked questions and tried to make sense out of
what they had seen and done. Then, while they went to the *cantina*
to eat, he wrote the report for Intelligence. By that time it was dark,
and he was drinking bad cognac, "Franco's revenge" as Saulnier called
it. When the report was ready for the motorcycle rider, he handed it
over and went out to see the mechanics. He and Pavito talked over the
repairs that ought to be made, the repairs that *could* be made, gasoline,
oil, and ammunition supplies. Then, finally, he checked out with the
night-officer, made sure the four pilots of the night-patrol were dressed
and 'chuted, ready to wait out the darkness until the first flight. He got
on his bicycle and pedaled to Alcalá. Sometimes Carmen was waiting
for him, sometimes not. They drank bad cognac, ate what there was to
eat. She was not a good cook. He drank more wine, and they went to
bed.

Then, he dreamed, wild, senseless dreams, nightmares of fire and
falling. He saw the faces of schoolteachers and boys he thought he had
forgotten. He wandered through garden parties and debutante cotillions
where dead men danced with girls he had known at Penn. He dreamed
in French and in Spanish and was flung, shuddering and drenched with
sweat, clutching the sheets and crying out in the darkness with Carmen
shaking him gently, talking to him, rubbing his neck or holding his head
between her small, naked breasts.

He was falling apart. They all were. They flew too often, drank too
much. Everybody's nerves were shot. The Fascist planes outnumbered
theirs. The Italian fighters and bombers they "dominated," as the Spanish
pilots said. But the Chatos were sitting ducks for the Messerschmitts.
The Russian biplanes were too slow and too fragile. The German pilots
had learned to shoot at the top wing, the wear spot in the structure.
One day—when?—they had lost five in as many minutes over Brunete.
There were no more planes from Russia to replace them.

He pulled the damp sheets away and sat up cautiously. He felt
awful. He found tobacco and cigarette papers on the table beside the
bed. His fingers wouldn't work properly. He ripped the paper and
spilled the tobacco. He stood up, groaned, and padded out through the
little living room into the tiny, tile-walled kitchen. He opened the stove
lid and looked inside. A few coals glimmered. He put a pot of water
on to heat. He found the bottle of *anís* in the living room, poured

out a glass of the colorless, sweet and raw stuff and drank it, then another. He lay in the dusty armchair and looked around the room. They tried to keep it clean, picked up, but they were never home long enough.

The table was strewn with dirty plates where flies buzzed, saucers filled with cigarette butts, wineglasses, and an empty liter bottle. The *anís* steadied him. He cleared the table and carried the stuff to the kitchen. Smoke leaked from the stove, and the water hissed. He found the burned malt and threw some into the pot. There was a piece of stale potato-flour bread. He opened the oven and stuck it inside, found the little pot of marmalade and the last chocolate bar. He set out two dirty cups, two saucers and two spoons and walked back to the bedroom.

He knelt over Carmen and brushed his stubbled chin on her bare shoulder. She made a soft, snuggly sound, stretched like a cat and rolled onto her back, her dark eyes blinking rapidly. He pulled the sheet down to her hips and touched her nipples with his finger.

"*Muy . . . buenos . . .*"

He slid his hand down her belly and tugged gently at the crisp, dark fur.

"*. . . días.*"

She reached up and pulled him down on top of her and kissed his nose, his eyes, and his right ear.

"*Hola*, Francisco."

"Time to get up," he said. "For coffee. The truck will be here soon. There go the planes. Hear them?"

She nodded. The sound of aircraft engines drummed in the dawn, as the first patrol took off, circled for altitude and formation, then swung off toward Madrid and Brunete. He kissed her damp neck and her shoulders and her breasts. She ran her thumbnail down his spine.

"Get off. I have to go *pipi.*"

She squirmed out from beneath him, strode to the window and snatched up the blind, an ear-shattering racket. The day was already blue. She turned around.

"Look at you," she said. "Shameless one."

"Yes," he said. "Look at me."

"I'll be right back," she said.

She rattled around in the kitchen, talking to herself and humming. He rolled a cigarette and lay smoking, waiting for her. She came back with the cups and the bottle of *anís*. She poured some *anís* into the cups and handed him one, taking the cigarette from his fingers. She perched on the edge of the bed, sipping the malt-coffee and smoking.

"Come here," he said.

"Oh yes," she said. "Always in the morning . . . like a rooster. *Qué va . . .* what a husband."

She left him to wash herself and came back dressed in her *mono* and sandals, her wet hair tied in a red kerchief. She took his flying suit, helmet and goggles from the armoire and placed them on the bed.

"Your boots, Francisco. Where are they?"

"Under the bed, I think."

He pulled on a pair of cotton khaki trousers and a shirt while Carmen rolled his flying suit into a ball and tied it with string. He pulled on his socks. She helped him with his boots, kneeling on the floor and tugging. They did not speak. He put the flying suit under his arm, picked up some tobacco and cigarette papers and walked to the door. She hugged him with all her strength and let him go.

"*Con Dios, mi amor.*"

"Until tonight."

The *sereno* stood on the sidewalk, holding back the usual little gang of skinny children. They set up a mewing cheer and clapped their hands, broke away from the night watchman and surrounded Frank, touching his legs and hands, stroking the rolled-up flying suit. The *sereno* tried to drive them away, clucking and shaking his head apologetically. Frank swung on the bicycle, waved and returned the children's clenched-fist salutes and pedaled down the street into the blue morning.

By the time he reached the operations hut, he was drenched. The squadron was awake, the mechanics at work down at the hangars; armorers draped with belts were loading the guns on the Moscas. Sentries, ground crew and the newer pilots saluted.

"*Muy buenos*, Capitán Libro!"

The squadron meteorologist waved at the worn map covered with swirls, arrows and figures and shrugged.

"The same, Capitán Libro, always the same. Very hot, steady up-draughts over the central plains, no cloud cover. The wind, as you see, very weak, from the south. The first patrol has gone to look, but it will be the same as yesterday and the day before that. It is impossible to see the target area."

Frank nodded. He knew that the offensive was losing impetus, that heavy reserves had been brought up by the Fascists—one rumor said thirty battalions. Another rumor had it that Brunete had changed hands twice. Lister's infantry still held the town, but if the whole area was hidden, they could give him no air cover, no tactical support. Down in the dust clouds, men would tear at each other until they died or dropped of exhaustion and thirst. All the Gloriosa could do was patrol and engage, harass the Heinkels and Junkers, drive them off, try to lure the Messerschmitts away from the Republican salient to dog-fight. The German pilots were hungry for "kills." Usually, they broke off their strafing runs as soon as they spotted Republican planes in the sky and came up to fight.

"Well," he said, "if there's no cloud cover, we'll use the dust. It is big enough to circle in, say four planes? In close formation? We could make an ambush."

"Perhaps," the weatherman said. "I am not a pilot. There would be great risk flying close in such obscurity. You could try it, Captain. We have one curious report. I have never heard anything like it."

"What is it?"

"The river has gone dry. The Guadarrama River is without water. A whole river. The weather, the sun has evaporated all that the men and animals did not drink. I remember distinctly being told that such things were not possible. But the instructors at the institute of science were old men. Perhaps they meant that they could not recall such a thing happening."

Frank carried his suit to his office and untied the bundle. He dropped the bits of string into a desk drawer. The drawer was nearly filled with pieces of string; it looked as though a bird was building a nest. On the exact center of the desk lay his new Spanish passport. He opened it and looked at the picture. Typical passport photo, a sour, unsmiling face. Underneath was his new name: Libro, Francisco. Under the printing, he had signed it: Francisco Libro.

He had left the business of the passport to Carmen, who had a friend, a girl from the convent, who now worked as a clerk-typist at the Ministry of the Interior. The whole idea had been to get Spanish papers, citizenship and passport, to replace his American passport, now "Not Valid for Spain" by act of the United States Government. "Buckminster" was hard for the Spaniards to say. It came out "Book-ministro" or something like that. Carmen had confused the typist by explaining that "book" was *libro* in Spanish, but "buck" meant money or male deer. Somehow, it had all become a silly joke among two girls and the typist had written in LIBRO. Franklin Pierce Buckminster had been removed from all official papers, right down to leave-permits and the pay roster. Franklin Pierce Buckminster had vanished from Spain, from life. Francisco Libro had been born, at the age of thirty-two. *Abajo* Buckminster, *viva* Libro. A goofy business that would take months to straighten out after the war.

Every day, before he dressed, he debated with himself over the passport. The Republic treated German and Italian pilots in the same fashion as Spaniards shot down behind the lines, with one exception. All their documents were forwarded to the League of Nations or to the international Non-Intervention Committee, in order to prove that Germany and Italy continued to violate the treaty they had signed. The Spanish pilots were simply imprisoned for the duration. On the Fascist side things were different. Non-Spaniards were treated as criminals, or so the stories went. Saulnier had tracked down two French pilots and had learned that they had been shot, one by Italian infantry, the other after a "trial" held by a local Falange organization. Both the pilots had had French papers. There was no reason to believe that the Fascists would not shoot an American. Every day, he shuffled the passports on his desk and ended the debate by putting them both in the spacious pocket of his captured flying suit. Why not hedge his bet? If he got shot down, let the Fascists figure out who he was.

"*Muy buenas, matador de Capronis!*"

Saulnier wandered into the office with two cups of malt-coffee.

"*Muy buenas, picador de perros,*" Frank said. "Thanks."

Saulnier fanned himself. His face was wet, perspiration runneling down the fatigue lines pulled in his unshaven cheeks. His mustache sprouted like dark weeds along his lip.

"Listen, *elegante*," Frank said. "Visit the squadron barber. Refresh yourself. Make a fine appearance. Someone in the squadron must preserve dignity."

"I have decided to grow a beard," Saulnier said. "We fly today."

"When the first patrol comes in, I'll take a flight over. We won't use the Chatos until it gets dark. Tonight. We'll just lose them."

"And if the Ministry orders all aircraft over the lines?"

"The Chatos all need engine overhauls. I have had the papers all typed up."

"If a commissar comes on the base and sees those ships sitting in the hangars . . ."

"I know, Jeannot . . ."

"You are not protected any more, Capitán Libro. The American, Buckminster, would have been reasoned with. The Spanish citizen, Libro, will be denounced, perhaps arrested. Don't you know what's going on, *chico*? This Russian, Jiménez, is a crazy one. Not crazy-good, like Dorlov. Crazy-bad. What will all your friends in Philadelphia think, if they learn that you are shot as a Trotskyite obstructionist?"

"They'll think I died of a blocked intestine."

"Very funny. Nothing like wit at seven in the morning."

Frank stood up. They listened. Saulnier shook his head.

"Only two coming in," Frank said. "They were told to stay away from Getafe. The anti-aircraft . . ."

"They are Spaniards," Saulnier said. "They do not believe in anti-aircraft cannons. Anti-aircraft cannons lack dignity. One flies over them to establish the correct relationship."

"One gets one's ass blown off and loses a ship we can't replace!"

Outside the *cantina*, the pilots and ground-crew teams stood looking at the hot sky. Two Chatos circled to land.

"Look at his wing. On the right. Chewed up, see?"

"Why does the other keep cutting the throttle in and out like that? Overheated?"

"No. He's losing oil. See the smoke. His oil line is hit."

Frank pushed through the waiting men, turned and looked at them.

"You see?" he shouted, furiously. "I give orders not to fly over Getafe! You see what happens? Four planes up, two come back. You do not own these planes! You fly them, but they belong to the people! To the people, understand? An order is an order. We will have obedience in this squadron! I will punish those who disobey! Understand?"

The pilots stared at him and nodded, slowly, then looked back at the sky. The Chatos were coming in.

"Get the fire equipment out there!" Frank said. "Send those pilots to me as soon as they land. Pavito, add those Chatos to the repair list."

"*Muy bien, capitán.*"

Frank walked back to his office. When the two Spanish boys reported to him, he listened to their clumsy lies, shaking his head until they told him the truth. He ordered them grounded and wrote a report of their disobedience to the wing commissar, adding all their lies to the report. If they were lucky, the commissar would stop their pay for a month only, a meaningless reprimand, since no one had been paid in anything but food coupons for the last fiscal quarter.

The Moscas had the shabby, hard-used look of combat aircraft. It was not possible to patch the bullet holes in the plywood-and-aluminum fuselages. The ripped metal was bent back with pliers, the plywood plastered over with canvas, doped, and glued. The sun and the dust had blistered and buffed off the paint on the bodies and wings. Raw wood and metal shone through in blotches. The tires had been worn smooth, and the exhaust ports were foul and smeared with black stuff that drooled and baked in the July sun. Pavito, the head mechanic, did his best. What he could not salvage, he stole. What he could not replace, he manufactured in the machine shop. The stub-winged, stocky, big-tailed Russian interceptors were Pavito's special pride. He detested the Chatos, flimsy, under-engineered, dangerous things that wasted time, money and lives. The twin-engined "Katyushka" bombers awed Pavito. The Russian mechanics who maintained the bombers were his idols. He admired them as a village tailor might admire the *couturiers* who served film actresses. He did not trust any pilot in the fighter squadron. They were loud, careless children who ruined in minutes the aircraft he had spent days rebuilding. Pavito loved the Mosca aircraft. After the war, he wanted to go to Russia. That was his dream.

Frank stopped at his plane.

"Pavito, who painted the nose of that aircraft?"

The mechanic looked accusingly at Saulnier and gnawed his black thumb.

"*El francés,*" he muttered. "*El fantástico.* He comes here last night with his brush. I told him we have no paint, no time to paint. He paints. He makes the Mosca have a red nose. Like a drunkard. That is a joke. For Frenchmen to laugh at."

The nacelle of Saulnier's interceptor was scarlet, a great, bright ring. Frank buckled on his parachute.

"Jean, get a wire brush and scrub it off. What the hell, you know? They can see you ten kilometers off with that red snout. This isn't Von Richthofen's Air Circus, for God's sake! You'll have all these kids painting their ships when they should be sleeping."

Saulnier waved his helmet. His face was bright red, soaked with sweat.

"The sight will instill terror into Fascist hearts," he said. "Saulnier, the blood-drinker, is in the sky. Italians will vomit from fear. Germans will curse, grow careless, and come under my guns."

"How much *vino blanco* this morning, Jean?"

"Enough," Saulnier said. "Not too much. It's just the heat. I'll be all right when we get up."

"Maybe you'd better stay down," Frank said.

Saulnier shrugged.

"I owe you a flight. Remember the fire-raid on Madrid? I got burned, no? Trying to save a burro. I missed my turn. This morning I make it up. The ledger will be balanced."

He ducked under the wing and ran to his plane before Frank could answer. Down the line, the motors wheezed, churned and spattered to life. Frank climbed up and dropped into the cockpit. The parachute bulked uncomfortably in his back. He wriggled down and fastened the belt, opened the fuel line and worked the primer-pump. He moved the stick and kicked the rudder bar. Pavito had tightened the control-wires. The fuel tanks were three-quarters full. The propeller snapped over and the big radial engine caught at once, a deep, deafening roar. He released the brake and rolled forward. The chunky plane trembled. He knotted the white scarf around his throat and zipped up the suit. He was suffocating in the heat and engine stench. He did not wait for tower clearance or for the engine to warm. There was not enough gas. Every minute on the ground was one minute less over Brunete.

They flew around Madrid, avoiding the anti-aircraft batteries in the Casa de Campo. Brunete was below them almost at once. The river was dry, like a dead snake parched in the sun. The wind poured around him. Over the fighting, the cloud of dust rose straight up into the sky. Five bits of silver skidded out of the cloud and came straight for them. Messerschmitts! Head on.

Saulnier came in, his red-nosed Mosca hanging off the starboard wing. He grinned and pointed. The others bunched up, their defense against the German nose cannons and machine guns. Frank raised his fist and pulled back the stick. Smoke squirted out of his gun ports. The flight of Moscas were "duck-shooting," as they called it, filling the sky with loose lead. The Germans never swerved from their attack pattern. They would fly into the stuff like mallards over the Chesapeake. Frank dropped his arm and plunged the stick forward to the instrument panel. The Mosca dove, a gut-lifting plunge for the earth. Stuff hit back at the tail as the Germans swept over, stiff, elegant and deadly like a school of sliding sharks.

Frank dove into the dust cloud and through it. The Messerschmitts were so fast that they would make their banking turn to come back over the streets of Madrid.

Bright little bits of stuff sailed past the Mosca, like hot tiny bubbles, slow and pretty, floating up through blue oil. Anti-aircraft. The plane was hit again and again, light taps, sharp small jolts and creaks.

The Messerschmitts were back. Four of them. They slit through the dust cloud, heading south, pack-hunting. He was too far away to hit them; and they would outrun him. He swung after them, the wings groaning as he wrenched the Mosca around at full throttle. If they lost their prey, they would circle broadside to him. He could fire a burst and go over them, turning with them, but outside their turn. The German planes were better than the German pilots. They flew by the book.

He saw the red-nosed Mosca lift up above the broad, dry twist of the Guadarrama. The Messerschmitts slid toward Saulnier, letting him climb up into their gunsights. Smoke bolls puffed and vanished from the cannon snouts, and Saulnier was hit before he knew they were on him. He kept climbing, almost straight up, and the Messerschmitts tore the Mosca with machine-gun slugs. Saulnier's plane trembled and hung there, squirting feebly at the German ships that knifed through the pale sky above him. Frank barreled after them, holding a near-collision course with the still-climbing Mosca.

"Dive! Get down, Jeannot!" he shouted.

He saw, dream-clear, the bullet-starred windscreen and shattered cockpit, smoke streaming back from the scarlet nacelle, gasoline spraying in white clouds from the punctured wing tanks and a hand clawing at the seat belt.

"Dive!"

But the red-nosed Mosca was above him, when Frank was half through his turn, ruddering tight, pulling *inside* the circle pattern of the Messerschmitts. The Germans, intent on Saulnier, did not see him. He poured a three-second burst into the leader and saw the Messerschmitt roll like a harpooned dogfish, silver flight-skin scaling off into the sky. It dropped off, propeller whickering, falling, upside down. Saulnier's plane, a red blur, slanted crazily, still climbing, barely under control.

They banked and came back. Frank fell off, tailing the Messerschmitts. Now if he got caught inside their circle, they could get him on their way back to Saulnier. They might break, one or two, after him. Saulnier could climb and jump.

They didn't. The silver shapes tilted tight against the sky. Saulnier's Mosca leveled at the same altitude and headed toward them. A figure struggled in the cockpit. Jeannot was pinned against the seat by the propeller-wash. Then the figure vanished, the Mosca rolled over, spewing smoke. The figure plummeted down free. The blunt, bright-nosed fighter hung in the sky and fell directly into the flight path of one of the Messerschmitts. The German twitched, a wild dip, too late. The collision was a golden flash in the sky and a spray of glittering fragments. The shock wave bunted Frank's plane. He lost control for an instant and plunged. He saw the white parachute dome open over the dry Guadarrama. He shouted, amazed, a burst of joy.

Then the two Messerschmitts broke formation, one in an Immelmann, turning around and up, doubling back above him and diving. Frank snapped the throttle back and drove the stick against his left thigh. The Mosca turned on its side and dropped like a stone. The Messerschmitt made a pass and missed. Frank slapped the stick across the cockpit and leveled off, looking around frantically.

Saulnier hung in his chute, one wounded arm down slack, the other dragging down on the chute lines. The scalloped dome of silk buckled and fluttered on one side as the pale, hot air spilled. Saulnier was sliding down on Brunete, falling and sliding into the big, dry billows of dust and battle smoke. Saulnier began to *dance in the air*, his legs kicking, curling up to his belly and snapping out! The parachute snapped full. The Messerschmitt droned by, stiff and easy, brass cartridge cases spilling back in the wash like golden roe.

The dark figure, still and slack now in the harness, dropped down into the dust. The chute lifted on an updraft for an instant and then sank into the dim, great cloud and disappeared.

The two Messerschmitts, gleaming like razors, slashed across the morning sky, south for safety.

Frank flew, numb, stupefied, around and around the lifting cloud of smoke and dust, circling over Brunete until the fuel needle shivered a millimeter above the zero. Then he banked away toward Alcalá.

It was the siesta, and the Fascist guns were silent, cooling. Over Brunete a great, dry, choking cloud of dust pounded up into the sky by the enemy shells hid the sun. From the cemetery to the cratered highway, men rose up and staggered in the dim, dry twilight that came at noon. There was nothing left of Brunete, no streets, no houses, just a dusty, mounded field of stones smashed small as gravel.

Paco ordered the bunker evacuated and walked out to supervise the burning. The dead lay in heaps, stiff and bloated, their faces, eyes, and broken mouths covered with stone-dust. They looked like statues flung down, shattered on the earth, things of granite. In this deafened dusk, stones smelled of sweet decay, and the gasoline that gurgled over the faces, the rigid, blackened arms and chests, spread a reek sharper than putrefaction. The cremation details, swathed to the eyes, gagged and stumbled as they stacked the bodies and spilled the gasoline.

Matches sputted. Little trails, damp on the flinty soil, flickered and danced toward the stacked, soaked dead. The gasoline ignited with soft, hissing explosions. Tattered uniforms flamed and fell away. Beneath the great pall of dust, the air shimmered and black, fatty smoke twisted up like cypresses. Dead flesh roasted, bubbled and charred. A grenade forgotten in the pocket of corpse, exploded, a dull grunt that scattered broken bits of the cadavers across the pocked earth.

Beneath the black, rich smoke that rose from the burning dead, the survivors crept away, retreating from Brunete, a march of scarecrows to Cañada. The forgotten hand grenades burst in the flaring heaps, and dark scraps rose and sank in the pale flames.

Here and there, bearded, filthy, shell-stunned men crouched and gibbered in their holes, staring at the forest of smoke that marked where Brunete had been. Commissars and corpsmen went to them, spoke gently, and led them, weeping, away into the twilight.

The Red Guards moved like drunkards, supporting each other, too stupefied to speak. Six hundred and eighty-five men had attacked from the El Escorial-Madrid highway. For twenty-one days they had fought and thirsted and starved and died at Brunete. Paco counted them as they lurched past him. Seventy-four men. The Guardia Roja had been destroyed at Brunete. He turned and followed them. He had no tears; no man weeps in a nightmare.

The dry, battered, fissured earth was a junkyard. The roads had been obliterated. Smashed cannons, gutted tanks, and burned-out trucks squatting in pools of melted rubber. Everywhere, the dust-drifted rubbish flung away by the dead, the refuse of the ruined army: blankets, boxes, canteens, helmets torn into sieves. Clouds of flies sizzled over the picked carcasses of ammunition mules. Crows glutted too fat to fly stalked and stabbed between the shell craters.

They walked very slowly, the columns growing: Campesino's men, some of Lister's, stumbling fragments of the 3rd, the 16th and the 68th brigades, all moving north, the only sound the shuffle of their feet. Beside the columns, the stretcher-bearers. Over everything, the great cloud of dust that shut out the sun. Behind them, the faint, muffled bursts of the grenades and the low, menacing factory-hum of the Fascists.

They came to trucks, scores of dusty, battered vehicles with riddled cabs and peeling tires. There was no water, no food, no ammunition. The rear-guard units had been herded away, out into the fields. They squatted and stared at the trucks.

The corpsmen helped the men of the broken battalions into the trucks, packing them in, propping those too weak to stand, separating the wounded, flinging the useless rifles over the tailgates. The trucks started and crept north in a long single line, swinging off the pitted road, up into the fields and back again.

Paco saw the broken aircraft between Brunete and Cañada, wrenched skeletons of aluminum, punctured fuselages and shattered glass, crushed and twisted wings: A Junkers trimotor, a Fiat biplane, upside down, a mottled Heinkel fighter, the wreckage of Chatos and splintered Moscas.

He saw a field hospital, three riddled tents painted with red crosses, an abandoned ambulance, a sterilizer, an operating table tilted into a slit-trench. Out in the fields, a black plume of smoke wavered up from a *barranca*, and a dry gust blew the smell of roasting flesh at him.

On a dull-golden slope between the twilight and the day where the great cloud dispersed, the column halted. The sound of motors sank. Radiators hissed softly. Most of the men in the trucks were asleep. A motorcycle wobbled down the line, the rider shouting. His voice slid at Paco from a great distance. The motorcycle stopped. The rider got off. He climbed on the running board and put his head into the cab. Paco stared at him.

"Colonel Larra?"

"Yes."

"Come with me, Colonel. At once. There's a mutiny!"

Mutiny. The word meant nothing. He knew only that he had heard it before, that the motorcyclist expected him to understand it. He nodded. The driver of the truck was asleep, slumped forward over the wheel. The door opened. Paco got out.

"What do they want with me?"

"There are Asaltos . . . Assault Guards and some tanks. I was sent to find you. You are in temporary command."

"Of *what*, man?"

"Of the force to put down the revolt."

"What group?"

"The 13th Brigade."

He tried to remember. He walked to the motorcycle. The rider turned the machine around. How could there be a revolt? A mutiny? All the men were asleep. He shook his head.

"We have no such group. No Spanish thirteenth. Go away."

"No, Colonel. It's the 13th Internationals!"

Paco shrugged and turned back to the truck.

"Find General Gal. Or Jurado. Or anybody . . ."

"Colonel . . . you must come with me. I was *sent* by Jurado."

"Oh."

Paco climbed on the motorcycle. The driver kicked it and the engine roared.

"Hold on! The road is bad."

"Yes, yes . . ."

Paco twisted his hands in the motorcyclist's belt, leaned forward against him and fell asleep. He woke and dozed, slept and woke as they jolted and churned. It seemed to take a long time. They stopped at a tent. Someone shook him.

"Yes, yes," he said.

People in white were supporting him. The motorcyclist shook his head.

"He's out on his feet, can't you see? Give him a shot."

"Impossible. Who is he?"

"El Asturiano, commander of the Red Guard."

"You are lying. He is just a comrade of yours, this *chico*. Go away."

Paco looked at the man in white. A doctor.

"I am Colonel of the Guardia Roja. Give me some stimulant. There is a mutiny among the Internationals. At once!"

The doctor blinked slowly and nodded.

"Yes, Colonel. *Practicante*, get alcohol, cotton, hypodermic needle. Caffeine and dextrose."

"Do you have a telephone line here, Doctor?"

"Yes, Colonel."

"I must use it. You, motorcyclist! Back to the road and get me a command car, an officer's tunic and a pistol. From one of Lister's officers or commissars."

"Yes, sir."

He sat on a stretcher while the *practicante* swabbed cool alcohol on his arms. The doctor gave him two injections, and he fainted. When he woke, he was lying on the stretcher with stuff from a bottle dripping into his arm. The motorcyclist sat on the stretcher with a tunic and a pistol.

"Take this thing out of my arm. Let me up. That's an order."

He dressed and walked to the next tent. He called Army Corps headquarters. He spoke and listened. It was true. The 13th Internationals had refused to obey an order to return to the lines. They were still at their last reported position, but Kriegger had lost control over them. A small force of Assault Guards had been sent to the area with four light tanks.

Paco demanded more troops. No, the George Washington battalion had ceased to exist. They had been incorporated with the Lincolns. The British battalion? It had ceased to exist. The 6th of February? Destroyed in battle. He had a free hand. Quell the mutiny, arrest the leaders, round up the entire brigade or what was left of them and ship them up to the Madrid highway at once.

He put down the telephone and walked out to the staff car. His arms hurt, and he felt nervous. They rushed off into the heat and dust.

The Assault Guards had the 13th Brigade surrounded on three sides, but were out of rifle range. The four tanks blocked the dirt road leading north. Paco drove to the top of a crest and looked through binoculars.

The mutineers were sitting in the shade of some broken buildings. There were not many of them. Very few seemed to have rifles or weapons of any sort. A smaller group, the officers, no doubt, and the commissars were at a slight distance. Between the two groups stood a few men, four or five, some kind of delegation arguing with the officers.

He remembered that the 13th was made up of Slavs and Polish volunteers. He would have to speak to them in Russian.

Paco drove to within pistol range, got out of the staff car, and began walking. He tried to remember words in Russian. His brain felt light and empty. He seemed to float over the ground. He recognized Kriegger. The commander had a revolver in his hand. He ran out toward the small delegation, stopped, and pointed the pistol at one man and shouted something. The soldier shook his head. Kriegger shouted again. The soldier shook his head a second time.

Paco saw the spat of smoke from the revolver. The soldier fell backward and lay in the dust. The men rose up from the broken buildings, howling like animals. Kriegger swung his pistol and began walking back to the group of officers. Paco ran for the staff car.

The Asaltos, heavily armed with grenades and submachine guns moved into the area, slowly, deliberately. Paco sent the staff-car driver off with a request for ten trucks. The tanks chattered up the road, the cannons pointed at the mutineers. The Poles and Slavic volunteers surrendered. The Asaltos drove them at gun-point into the trucks. Colonel Kriegger climbed into the staff car, wiping the blood from his face. He spoke bad Spanish, with an Italian accent.

"They tried to kill me!" he said. "With their hands!"

He lay on the seat, trembling.

"Why did you shoot him?" Paco said.

"I am the commander!"

"You are a fool."

"They should all be shot! Every one. Shoot them all! Where do they go now?"

Paco shrugged and yawned. The stuff the doctor had given him was wearing off.

"They go to the Russians," he said. "There is a re-education camp near Alcalá de Henares."

"I must make a report! I am a good Communist. Former deputy from Trieste. Good Party member!"

"Then the Russians will listen to you. They will shoot the ones you name."

"Good, good!" Colonel Kriegger said. "The swine."

"Yes," Paco said. "They are swine. *Claro*, they are swine! Back to the highway, driver."

"It's just like I thought," White said. "You get to the Pearly Gates and somebody sticks out his head and says 'No room in here. Get back where you was.'"

It was dusk. The men lay on the soft carpet of dry needles beneath the big pine trees. White could just make out the big, pale gateposts that gave the place its name. A cigarette tip glowed. A tin spoon rattled and scraped on a mess kit.

"What the hella you talkin about?"

"We got orders," White said. His legs gave out and he fell to the springy, scented ground.

"Bullshit."

"Yeah. Bullshit. Yesterday we got bombed by them bastids. Today they left us alone. What orders?"

"From Division. That German, you know, Klaus? He read this order."

"*What* order, fer Crissakes?"

"We're goin back to the lines, fellas," White said. He lay back in the pine needles and began to laugh. The men stirred in the dusk, cursing and calling to each other, gathering in around him.

"Coupla days ago, we got *six whole hours* sit-down time!" White said. "Ain't that plenty? What the hell, we ain't been doin what you'd call *much* . . . just a fire fight, hold a ridge, take a road, counterattack with no machine guns, march all night, patrol here, drag-ass over there, attack at night, toss some grenades around . . . that ain't much."

"They want us to go *back*? What the hella you talkin about?"

"You'll see," White said. He sat up.

"You'll hear," he said. "Chapaiev said the Dimitrovs are done in. Crespo says his Spanish boys'll never make it . . . not that it's so far . . . just back to Quijorna . . ."

"*Quijorna!* Fuck you, buddy!"

"Like I say, not far," White said. "That one-eyed Frenchy we got sends a *teniente*. Kid just stands there, lookin like he's been kicked in the nuts and he don't say *one* . . . *Goddamn* . . . *word!*"

"The hell with them others. What did Steve say?"

"What did *he* say, for Crissakes?"

"Were you spying on them?"

"It's near dark," White said. "I just was *standin* there. So they can't see me, right? What am I supposed to do? Make the sun come back up again? I just *heard*, that's all."

"We ain't goin! Right, fellas?"

"Bet your ass we ain't!"

"The lines broke," White said. "We won't hafta move. Them Fascists gonna be right on top of us pretty soon, anyway. Something happened with the 13th. I dunno. You generals figure it out."

"That's all crap."

"Lines broke two days ago," White said. "Or you guys forget that?"

"What did he say?"

"That's what he *did* say. Steve told them that if the line's broken then we're goin' back, that's all. Gimme a smoke, some good-and-loyal-old-comrade-buddy-general. Andrew always gets the real good news while it's hot, huh?"

"Let Nelson go hisownfuckinself!"

"I never seen you out ahead of him, comrade," White said. "Except in the chowline."

There was a little laughter, not much. Somebody gave him a cigarette and a match. He struck it on his boot and looked through the flare at Mahoney.

"Thought it might be you, Jimmy. Thanks."

"You goin' back?"

"Not finished with my good news," White said. "You know Wally, the British boys' commissar, right?"

"British battalion, shit," Mahoney said. "I counted them Limeys this mornin. Not a real honest-to-God *section!* Whadid *he* say, Tapsall?"

"He says to Steve that he knows bloody-well right that we won't *go* back."

The pinewoods sounded to a half-cheer, half-growl. White sucked on his cigarette and nodded. Mahoney poked him.

"Whadid Steve say to that?"

"Oh, not so much. Just that he'd get us all together . . ."

"For *what?*"

"Oh," White said, "so he can tell us we're goin back to Quijorna! So form up and let's get up by that big rock and hear him tell it."

The men of the battalions that made up the Quince Brigada gathered slowly in the darkness, sitting and crouching around a huge boulder. They lit cigarettes and waited, tense, uneasy, refusing to believe what they had heard. They smoked and talked among themselves in four different languages, in English, Spanish, Czech, and Slavic. It was impossible, they told each other, impossible. Where there had been nine hundred Americans in two battalions, there were two hundred and eighty in one battalion. There were only eighty-eight Frenchmen alive out of three hundred and sixty. The Dimitrovs numbered less than one hundred out of four hundred and fifty. Captain Crespo passed out extra matches in the dark so that his Spaniards could see as well as sense each other. Of four hundred and fifty, he now commanded slightly more than one hundred. Tapsall, the British commissar, had supervised the physical welfare and political loyalty of three hundred and sixty men. There were, as everyone in the brigade had learned only thirty-seven Englishmen left alive. They sat and smoked and shrugged and shook their heads. Impossible.

Klaus from Division headquarters climbed to the top of the boulder. He read the order to return to the lines in German, English, French, and Spanish. Here and there a match flared and lit a bearded, dirty face. A man coughed. Cigarette papers whispered. Klaus climbed down from the huge stone. Steve Nelson, the Lincoln's commissar, climbed up to take his place.

White sat smoking. He could not see Nelson. The commissar's opening remark that they were going to "discuss the orders" was drowned out by boos and Bronx cheers from the darkness. Nelson shouted down at them.

"Listen. Just listen to me! The lines are just a short walk . . . a few kilometers, that's all! What if they break . . . tonight?"

"We ain't goin back, Steve, and you know it!"

"Get down and shut up, comic-star!"

"How about you rank-and-filers shuttin up so we can hear what he says? Go ahead, Steve."

The cigarettes glowed and faded in the darkness. Up on the massive boulder, Nelson coughed and cleared his throat. His voice was rough and weary, familiar, the harsh half plea, half command to man the picket line one more day, to hold out against the cops until the strike was won, till the bosses gave in. They had, many of them, heard that same urgent, angry voice shouting at line-ups on the waterfronts, in hiring halls and Party offices, police vans and jail cells.

"Listen to me, you guys, will you? If the lines break tonight, the Fascists will go all the way to the highway, all the way to El Escorial! If the Spanish troops behind us, out there, can't hold, the Fascists will bust on through to Madrid! Tomorrow!"

The glowing cigarettes pulsed and died, flushing orange on cracked and peeling faces, lining faces like masks. Dark mouths croaked.

"Yeah? Then go on out and talk to *them!* Tell em to lay off us!"

"Don't ask *us* to go back!"

"You go back. You and them fat-asses at Division go back!"
"Shove it up, Yank! Shove it up and break it off!"
"*Nous ne sommes pas d' esclaves!*"
"*Ta gueule, assassin! C'est les stupidités commes ça pourquoi nous avons perdu la guerre!*"
"*La boca, valiente!*"

White sat and smoked and listened to the voices in the darkness pelting Nelson with abuse. In daylight, the loudmouths would have said nothing, then grumbled bitterly behind Nelson's back. Now they were safe, shielded by the night. It was a bad moment. Were they a battalion still or a beaten mob? Were they solid, tight, or had they given up?

Nelson stood up there, invisible, too, and took all their weariness, cynicism, and despair. White imagined him nodding thoughtfully, listening, but letting all the crap run off him, calm, canny, and set-jawed, figuring out the right words. White grunted. He had seen enough picket lines dissolve in the rain like cardboard, meetings break up in disputes, shoving matches, and fist fights. Nelson was letting them get it all out of their systems at once. He knew how to handle even this. No wonder he was the biggest man the Party had sent to Spain.

The shouting stopped, yelped up again, died off to sour mutters, the flare of matches, and fresh cigarettes. They had told Nelson where to get off, but none of them had moved. Nelson's hoarse voice was sympathetic but unyielding.

"I know you're all tired. Everybody's tired."

Someone near White yelled back over a chorus of Bronx cheers.

"We're too goddamned tired to move anywhere, Steve!"

Now the voice from the rock dropped on them like a whip, striking exactly the spot they all nursed.

"I know it. And I don't give a damn *how* tired you are! Understand? By tomorrow morning, we'll either get driven out of here, or we'll die here. *Right here!* Tomorrow! We don't have a choice. We've *got* to go back. We don't have a chance if we stay here."

There was a short, stunned silence. Voices muttered in Spanish, Czech, and French, as the men who spoke and understood English translated for their comrades. Hundreds of cigarettes winked and twitched as the battalion thought it over. White waited. He was convinced, but there was always a rear-rank lawyer, egged on by his buddies, a one-man grievance committee. The voice rose up, typically, from way back on the fringe of the crowd.

"Bullshit! We got a choice. It's if we go back that we ain't got a chance! Why don't you tell us the truth?"

That did it for most of the men. You could call Nelson a goddamned slave-driver and a know-it-all sonofabitch, but you couldn't call him a coward and you couldn't call him a liar. As White gathered his aching legs under him, two or three cigarettes lurched up in the darkness, jerked and circled, drawing, unconsciously, closer to the boulder. Some others were standing, too, sticking up for Steve, as White pushed himself, groaning, to his feet.

"He just *did* tell us!" someone shouted.

"He's right!"

White puffed his cigarette and exhaled. He had learned to go tippy-toe with angry white men, even Party members, comrades. He spoke easily, softly, to the men of his own company.

"Course he's right. If we stay here, they'll come and get us. If we go get them before they move, they'll never get here. That's simple enough."

He had his own back-row lawyer, but he didn't recognize the voice, maybe somebody from another company or one of the Washingtons.

"Says who?"

"Says me."

"It's Andy White, fer Crissakes. You can't *see* him. Who else would it be?"

There was a little laugh, tired and uneasy. The voice cried again at him.

"Go get em, pal! We'll bury you!"

"Uh-uh," White said. "I'll come back and shovel pine needles on your dead puss. We been hit hard before. We been tired before. We been in places first and out last, right? What about Jarama?"

"First in and last out, huh? What you think we're talking about . . . Cathouse nooky? Screw you, comrade!"

White looked around. There were more cigarettes head-high, moving in the darkness like fireflies. Here and there, others came swooping up.

"I'm goin back and fight," White said, flatly. "That's why I come here and that's what I'm gonna do."

A nasal, Boston-Irish voice sneered in the darkness.

"Stop the bellyachin, you dumb bastids! Whadda ya wanta do, live forever? You ain't *that* tired. Yer *yellah!*"

Now more than half of them were up. Mahoney had hit them in another weak spot. The cigarette tips glowed and skidded everywhere. Voices shouted all around.

"What part of the line busted, them *marineros?* We'll show em some Yew Ess sojerin!"

"*Marineros? . . . Eh, hombre, maricones!*"

"We gotta go back."

"Vote! Vote!"

"This ain't no time for trade-union politics, comrade."

"Ah, that's what you pricks in the Party always say! Take a vote!"

"It's an *order,* you dumb bastids!" Mahoney shouted, his voice cracking with anger, "you don't vote on an order!"

"We do on this one, Mahoney-Baloney."

"Watch dat shit," Mahoney said.

"Look," White said. "When you joined this outfit, when you volunteered you *done* your votin. You said yes then. Everybody in my company go get your stuff and draw ammunition."

White dropped his cigarette stub, crushed it with his boot heel and limped away from the boulder. The argument was still going on, but the decision had been made by most of the men, more or less at the same time. They would go back.

He flung himself down and leaned back against the rough column of a pine tree. He listened to the wind sing thin and easy through the trees. Men stumbled and groped in the darkness, tired and talked-out, but gathering their helmets, canteens and ammunition belts.

"The judgment of the citizens of Athens," a voice said. "Pass out the hemlock."

"Rosenbaum?"

"Naw. Guildenberg."

"You been so quiet these days I thought you'd been killed, Rosey."

"It's a matter of hours," Rosenbaum said, dropping down in a loose clutter of arms, elbow and legs, covering White with a shower of dry needles.

"If I had a candle, I could finish my autobiography. At chapter two. The condensed version. Schwartz used to say a great thing about Lenin . . . you read Lenin not for the subject but the *style!* Isn't that great?" He'll be okay. Got hit real bad, though. He'll be okay."

"We coulda used Schwartzie up there," White said. Most of the time he didn't understand Rosenbaum, but the skinny kid was tougher than he looked and good-humored like most of the college kids in the outfit. Rosenbaum shook him.

"You know this is insane? I mean, it's *crazy!*"

"Uh-huh."

"I thought only *Spaniards* voted to get themselves killed."

"Other folks think that way, too, Rosey. It's happened before."

"Yeah, but not to *me!* Perhaps you have a certain racial fatalism."

"I got sore feet and weary ears," White said. "White folks go on and on and on, like mammies at a fish fry. Some of them comrades . . ."

"Hey! Hey, you bastids! It's all off."

"That's Jim Mahoney!" Rosenbaum said.

He struggled up on his long legs and galloped off into the darkness, whoofing once as he hit a pine tree. White groaned and limped after him. The rest of the company scuffed and groped on up to the dirt road. Mahoney was there with a Spanish runner, a box of matches and a piece of paper. In the orange flame, Mahoney's face looked like a piece of

raw beef, half skinned, half covered with a beard like Brillo. He thrust
the piece of paper into White's hand.

"Read it!"

"It says . . . Not so close, you'll burn it up, Jimmy . . . Uh, uh . . .
'The Spanish comrades have ex . . . extricated themselves from encircle-
ment and have the situation in hand.'"

"Is *that* what it says?" Mahoney demanded. "Extricated . . . ain't that
when they cut off yer nuts? Them poor bastids . . ."

"Right! Right!" Rosenbaum shouted, clutching his baggy trousers at the
fly and prancing in a long, loose-footed circle.

"Those Spanish comrades got their situations right in their hands!
Yahooo!"

"We don't go back? We don't hafta, Andy?"

White handed back the note. He sat down in the road and grinned
at Rosenbaum.

"No," he said.

He fell flat on the road and kicked his heels.

"It's a jubilee time! Lift me up, point me at the water and I'll walk
on it! It's a goddamned miracle, that's what! Who says the 15th's a
frigged-up outfit, huh? We got lucky!"

They yelled and wrestled and punched each other around. White got
up after a bit and walked back to his blanket with Rosenbaum. He
breathed the air, feeling as he had when he had been let out of jail.
Rosenbaum sidled around him, walking backward and bumping into
trees.

"You're not as fatalistic as I thought," he said. "Listen. Tell me something?"

"Right now, Rosey, I'll tell you any damn thing you wanta know."

"Do you think Zlotnick's as good a cook as Jack Shirai was?"

"*Huh?*"

"Do you think . . ."

"I heard you. That's a helluva question. You always ask the damnd-
est . . . I saw Jack get killed. Stepped right out into machine-gun fire,
everybody yellin at him to stay put . . . with a big grin on his face."

"Yeah, yeah," Rosenbaum said impatiently. "But is Zlotnick a better
cook?"

"You still fuzzed about them bomb fragments in the soup, Rosey? We
told you that was mule stew, kosher-style. It *always* got bitty pieces of
bombs in it. How come you ask me, huh? Do I ask you questions like
that, huh?"

"Well," Rosenbaum said, "it's important, really. Tomorrow, there'll be
breakfast, see? And lunch. Maybe even dinner. You see, I figured that
we were all going to get . . . you know, and now that I know I'm

going to live and eat breakfast and lunch and maybe dinner, it's very important . . . because I can *worry* about it, see?"

"If that's what bein' Jewish is like, then I'm glad I'm colored," White said.

"But . . ."

"I get you," White said. "But I'm *tired*, Rosey . . . Come and ask me tomorrow night, okay? I'll tell you then, when I've thought on it. Bring some *vino* and we'll talk it all over. Okay?"

"Soitenly," Rosenbaum said. "Why not?"

The dainty, embroidered *fauteuil* was set too close to the pale gleaming slab of marble. Voget cramped his legs to one side, his boot knocking the chromium leg. The brandy danced in his glass. He felt hot, heavy, and uncomfortable. Thick imitation-zebra curtains shut out the sea sounds and smell of Barcelona Harbor. The walls of the room reminded Voget of marzipan. In the soft light that spilled down from secret fixtures, the dozens of framed photographs seemed pinned to slabs of candy. His own reflection, diminished by space, glittered at him in an oblong mirror that rose from the rococo mantel of a tiny fireplace to the vaulted, plaster ceiling strewn with rose garlands twined in love knots. The mirror was blue, like the carapace of some exotic beetle. Voget felt that he had somehow wandered onto the set of a certain kind of motion picture.

Kolodny sat comfortably, his broad rump buckling the soft, brocaded pillows of an armchair in the shape of a swan. He sipped brandy, smacked his lips and set the balloon glass on a Chinese lacquered table. Kolodny wore a royal purple silk dressing gown over a loose shirt and cavalry breeches. His feet were broad, plump, bare and dirty. Voget lit a cigarette and dropped the match into the mouth of a malachite toad.

"I am going to ask you one question, Comrade Colonel," he said. "I will ask you this question twice only. Here is the first time: Where is Hans Kopa?"

Kolodny's hand trembled slightly as he raised a cigar and plunged the wet tip like a stopper between his lips. He shrugged, and the purple silk stretched across his heavy shoulders creaked.

"I don't know, comrade."

Voget leaned forward and moved his brandy glass a millimeter.

"Thirty-two days ago, Hans Kopa brought a requisition from Colonel Larra of the Guardia Roja of the 5th Regiment to your ordnance warehouse. At 1618 hours Kopa, now dressed in civilian clothes, or at least some attempt at disguise, was arrested by the Barcelona Cheka. In the street behind your ordnance warehouse."

Kolodny shrugged, gnawed his cigar, and drubbed the carpet with his bare heel.

"You know more about this than I do, Voget. These things happen in Barcelona. It's not good to talk of them. I promise you that the requisition for the 5th Regiment will be honored and shipped as soon as we have transport. Eh? That's fair enough. Come, relax. What do you think of my apartment, eh? That chair you sit on is Louis *Quinze*. Genuine! Everything is deluxe here, have you noticed? This used to belong to a film actress. I'd show you the bedroom, but my little kitty-cat is in there sleeping."

Kolodny laughed slowly and the cigar smoke leaked in blue streams between his gapped teeth.

Voget looked across the room at the Pole and smoked his cigarette.

"Marshal Tukhachevsky and seven other senior generals in the Red Army were arrested recently in Moscow and Leningrad and charged with acts of treason. They confessed to intrigues with Germany and were sentenced in the name of the peoples of the Soviet Union to be shot to death in Lubyanka Prison."

"More brandy? But you haven't touched yours. My little *minette* drinks only champagne, would you believe it? It makes her sleepy, though."

Voget brushed his cigarette on the green maw of the stone toad.

"As part of their confessions and self-accusations, a great many names were mentioned and put in writing by Marshal Tukhachevsky and the other generals. Secret meetings along the Polish frontier were alluded to. During the maneuvers of 1935. Several members of the NKVD were cited as witnesses. Two of them are now here in Spain. Orlov, of course, and another man who calls himself 'Jiménez.' This 'Jiménez' was seen in Barcelona recently. Can you imagine where?"

"At the cinema? All Russians are crazy about the cinema."

"Not recently. I was speaking of thirty-*three* days ago. The day before Kopa was arrested."

Kolodny tilted the brandy decanter. The liquid poured out over the top of the lacquer table and dripped silently to the carpet. Kolodny raised his empty glass to his lips and stared into it.

"I'll wake her up in a few minutes. She is fifteen years old and knows how to—*faire le pompier*, is that how you say it?—Do the fireman, eh?"

"The day before Kopa was arrested, 'Jiménez' was in your office. At the ordnance warehouse."

"Oh yes! Routine inspection visit. Look here, Voget, I thought you wanted to have a drink and talk over old times. Be a decent fellow and stop all this, eh?"

"We are talking over old times," Voget said. "A month in Spain is like ten years in another country. Look at what has happened here in Barcelona. First the "Anars," then P.O.U.M. Catalonia is a Russian province. What about those maneuvers, those meetings on the frontier, Kolodny? How long did you tell them the Polish Army could hold out? A week? A day? Three hours?"

Kolodny lunged up out of the swan-shaped chair, thrust his fists into the pockets of his dressing gown and stumped to the windows. He tweaked away the zebra-striped curtains and peered down into the street.

"No one even knows I'm in Barcelona," Voget said. "Officially, I am at International Brigade headquarters in Albacete."

Kolodny whirled around and flung up one heavy, purple arm. His bare, shaved skull was covered with tiny, golden beads of sweat.

Voget pointed at the radio.

"Doesn't that thing there get Radio Seville?"

"We listen to dance music," Kolodny said. "My *minette* is mad for the dancing."

"Then you have not heard that the 13th Brigade mutinied at Brunete?"

"*What?*"

Kolodny clapped his hands on his bare, slick skull and crashed down into the swan chair. His broad, flat face was pale, and his hands slid down his cheeks and plucked at the lapels of his dressing gown.

"That's . . . impossible! They are Polish patriots . . . old comrades and friends . . . It's a lie! Are you sure? Listen, we're good friends, right. You wouldn't lie. What happened? Tell me."

"They were sent to Alcalá de Henares, the birthplace of Cervantes. Comrade Orlov has his headquarters there. It is called a *re-education camp*. They have such places in Poland, no?"

Kolodny made an odd, high, strangled sound and broke his glass. Voget stubbed out his cigarette.

"Alcalá is an odd place. All the streets there are *sens unique*. One way. The trucks go into Alcalá filled with men, but they come out empty. Very odd. There is a rumor around that Orlov and André Marty consider all Polish volunteers no longer trustworthy. Of course, it's only a rumor, but after what has happened in Russia to a field marshal and seven senior generals . . ."

"It's hot . . . I'm sweltering . . . too much brandy, not enough fresh air . . ."

Voget reached into his tunic pocket. Kolodny tore the dressing gown off and flung it on the carpet.

"When all the roads are marked 'one way,'" Voget said, "it's nice to know that there are papers all prepared, transportation available, highest priority clearance, comrades and friends waiting . . . in Paris, say. Papers and railroad tickets. Like these."

Voget placed the passport and a railroad ticket on the marble slab. He tapped the passport with his finger.

"All this needs is a photograph. The train ticket is prepaid and lacks only the date. But they can stamp that at the window. Papers like these, good any time at all . . . like money in the bank. Better, even."

"How do I know . . ."

"I got you into Spain," Voget said. "I can get you out."

"How do I know . . ."

"You don't," Voget said and smiled. "You'll just have to trust me, eh?"

Kolodny groaned and kneaded his face, snatching up his jowls until his peggy teeth gleamed in his thick, pink gums.

"This place is not right for Kolodny," he said. "Barcelona, it's a nightmare, a brothel run by gangsters. Arrests everywhere. I live from day to day. Maybe next week a tank battalion on the Aragón front, maybe . . ."

"Maybe," Voget agreed.

"It is incredible," Kolodny said. "You cannot trust *anyone!* Not a soul!"

"Hard to imagine," Voget said, stroking the malachite toad. He watched Kolodny pick up the decanter and drink from it, his thick throat jerking. The Pole gasped and swatted his chest, then squinted across at Voget.

"What is so important about this Kopa? What do you, a Frenchman, care about a damned German? It's . . . it's *unnatural,* that's what!"

"We all have our . . . tendencies," Voget said. He struck a match, grinned through the acrid smoke and moved the passport two millimeters. Kolodny was crouching in the swan chair, watching him. Voget blew away the smoke.

"And now it is time to ask my question the second time," Voget said. "Where is Hans Kopa? Tell me where he is being kept, right at this moment, and these things are yours."

"You think I'm afraid, don't you?" Kolodny said. "Well, I'm not. I'm thinking about that poor kid in there, only fourteen years old."

"Fifteen," Voget said. "I don't answer questions, Comrade Colonel, I ask them."

Kolodny stood up and walked unsteadily to the table. He reached down for the passport. Voget held the booklet down with his hand.

"He's in the basement of the Hotel Falcón. The old P.O.U.M. headquarters. The P.S.U.C. Cheka just rounded them all up, all the Trotskyites and locked them in there."

"You're lying," Voget said. "I've already checked about the Hotel Falcón."

"In the lowest wine cellar there are a number of small rooms. They are used as cells. For solitary confinement. I saw him there."

"When?"

"Tuesday."

"Three days ago. He was alive?"

Kolodny nodded.

"You identified him," Voget said. "For 'Jiménez'?"

Kolodny hesitated and then nodded, slowly. Voget lifted his hand and shoved the passport and ticket across the table. He looked away and picked up his brandy glass.

"How long have you been living in this apartment, Kolodny?"

The Pole turned away and padded like a bear across the carpet to the bedroom door, the passport and ticket clutched against his damp shirt.

"Since Tuesday," he whispered. "Only since Tuesday."

Voget tossed off the brandy and nodded once.

"Of course," he said. "Of course!"

The light was blinding, unbearable. The tears poured from his twitching eyes. The voice beat at him from behind the light. The voice spoke to him in German, flawless, precise, as though played on gramophone records.

"First, the matter of your identity. Are you Kopa or Kleist, both or neither? A double agent or an impostor? Your claim that Comrade Hans Beimler knew is most convenient. He is dead."

Kopa nodded. They had reached, at last, the summing-up, the necessary final illusion. They knew everything, since they had created the evidence. He knew nothing, not the place, not the day, not the hour.

"Second, although instructed to deliver the trucks purchased by the Party in France to Comrade Beimler, you utilized these vehicles to supply not the Party here in Catalonia, but ideological enemies, the C.N.T. So much for your sense of loyalty."

Kopa nodded. The sooner it was over the better. He wanted only to be left alone in his cell. The heel of his left boot was missing. Odd they hadn't noticed it. He had pulled out the nails in order to scratch on the wall, forming the letters by touch alone.

"Third, during this traffic in treachery, you took as a passenger a fugitive priest from the town of Pilarmadre, an enemy of the Republic, and knowingly aided and abetted his flight from justice at the hands of the people. This same priest was last seen on a railroad train in the province of Navarre in conversation with a captain of Navarrese infantry. It is, therefore, obvious that you served as part of a Fascist intelligence ring."

Kopa nodded. It was possible. It could be true. Or false. It made no difference. Not now.

"Fourth, at the time of your first arrest, you had deployed the missing trucks and drivers and mechanics at a P.O.U.M. motor pool under the pretext of repaying favors for repair work done by Trotskyites and others of that type, proved by their words and deeds to be the implacable enemies of the anti-Fascist movement. In an attempt to deceive the Madrid Cheka, you somehow contrived to deliver the vehicles and technicians to the 5th Regiment. Chief among your confederates at this time was Felix Kolodny, nationality Polish, politics, Eastern-opportunistic. The fact that you have denied his knowledge of your clumsy maneuver only increases the guilt that will inevitably fall and crush him in his turn."

Kopa nodded. Yes, they would crush Kolodny in his turn. If they could catch him. Perhaps he was already imprisoned, in this very building. There was no way to know, no way to learn. The cells on either side had been emptied. No messages could be tapped out on the stones, whispered across the narrow passage.

"Fifth, the document you have seen. It states quite clearly that after the death of Hans Beimler in Madrid you used his name, deliberately, poisonously, to influence your superiors, themselves suffering the strain of unceasing combat, to grant you appointment as temporary commissar and chief of liaison between the Red Guards of the 5th Regiment and whatever volunteer battalions were flanked on either side. You have confessed to delivering lectures on both political and military subjects to Spanish and non-native combat troops on so many different occasions that you cannot now recall the exact number."

Kopa nodded. True. He could only remember the faces and some of the names. He could not even remember what he had talked about.

"The document is here. You have seen the signature. Colonel Paco Larra. You agree that the signature is authentic."

Kopa nodded. The signature *was* authentic. It was the document that was forged. Badly forged, too. Like most men educated to literacy by priests and pamphlets, Larra was an expert grammarian and rather vain about his handwriting. The document was typed and contained errors in case agreement, verb tenses, even gender.

The light was blinding, baleful, and the voice spoke from beyond it with the dry perfection of a machine. Since the words were without meaning, in any human sense, it was necessary that the performance be without flaw.

Kopa sat weeping and indifferent. He had been starved and drugged, beaten and ignored, cast into darkness until he did not know day from night and then hauled, like so much rubbish, to this place of the light and the voice. The charges against him were as false as the tears that flowed unceasingly from his dazzled, aching eyes. He had told them nothing. There was nothing to tell. They had separate dossiers, one for the priest, one for Kolodny. No doubt there were other dossiers. Certainly they had one for Paco Larra, another for Paul Voget. What a waste of time, money and energy! A form could be printed up, with spaces left blank, an all-purpose accusation, good for all persons, all crimes, all nations, all parties.

Kopa raised his hands. The cuffs were tight on his wrists, and the short, rusty chain clattered. The room was stifling. The room was always stifling. It smelled of blood and urine. It always smelled like that. He tore at the buttons and stripped the rotting cloth from his chest.

The voice spoke from behind the dazzling bulb.

"Sixth, you are charged with self-mutilation, a cowardly attempt to avoid front-line service in the People's Army."

Kopa nodded. He felt his face move strangely, pulled by something in his chest and belly. His lips grew taut and curved, his cheeks creased. It occurred to him that he was smiling. The Sixth was indeed the best, and, surely, therefore, the last.

Suddenly, he was laughing, howling, his belly knotting. He beat his hands on his knees, and the chain clashed against the numbing cuffs. He laughed, and tears, real tears, flowed from his crimped lids, and the light and voice swam away in a crimson pressure that sprayed out in laughter and filled the small, stinking room.

He could not stop. It was in him, like a gas, a bubble beneath the ribs. It squirted up, little, convulsive heaves and gasps, and he was off again, screaming with laughter, mad with it, like a tickled child. He was weak, heaving, drenched with sweat. His sweat was uproarious. He went off into another fit. His fit was too funny to resist. They were waiting, patiently, for him to stop. It was so hysterically simple. Why didn't they beat him again? Their patience was excruciatingly comic. He laughed as he had never laughed before in all his life.

At last, he stopped. He was empty, wrung. He stared with dry, smarting eyes, directly at the hot, white light. Now, he could just make out the dim shape. It was a man, after all, not a machine or an instrument.

"We have seen your cowardly belly. Be certain that we will decorate you on the other side. Take him away."

Kopa stood up, before the hands touched him. The writing on the wall of his cell was almost finished. The man was not a Spaniard. After such laughter, a Spaniard would have shot him out of hand, perhaps on the spot. But this one was incapable of rage, indifferent to tears or laughter. The execution would take place according to schedule, not a moment earlier or later. There would be time to finish what he was writing with the nails pulled from his boots. That alone was important, now, the bite of a steel sliver into stone, the inscription on a cell wall.

Kopa nodded to the blinding light, to the voice from behind it.

"*Danke sehr*," he said. "Thank you very much."

The door boomed shut, and the boots went away. It was dark again and cool. He sat down and wrenched off his boot, pried the heel off and brought it up to his mouth. He set his teeth on a nail and worried and twisted. The other nails tore his lips. He could taste the blood, feel the ripped, flimsy tissue with his tongue. The nail pulled loose. He held it between his thumb and forefinger, both calloused and creased. He scrambled across the damp floor and knelt there, running his fingers over the stones.

For a long time, he did not know how many hours, he had written it on his brain, tracing it there in the soft pulp, printing on his memory, erasing, changing, trying out new words, phrases. In Spanish? French? For another time, he had believed that it could be done in Latin. He had had a childhood of canticles, plainsongs, hymns, responses, and prayers. In other prisons, other cells, he had recited poetry, including hundreds of lines of *The Aeneid* and parts of Ovid.

He had decided, finally, on English, that mixture of old Germanic and the tongue of Rome. It had been very difficult, wrestling with the demons and angels of spelling and syntax. In other prisons, he had kept a regimen of the body, setting-up exercises. In this place, he scraped a poem on the stone wall in a language he did not know well and could not pronounce without making an American smile.

Perhaps it had been that American, the pilot, who had married the pretty little Spanish girl on a blue, windy day in Cuenca that caused him to choose English. That had been one of the happiest days of his life.

He knelt in the darkness, running his fingertips over the stones, listening to the grit of the steel on the granite. It was not a very good poem, perhaps not a poem at all. It had neither rhyme nor meter. It was just lines graven on a damp wall. They would not be able to read it, decipher it. For them, it would be Sanskrit, not worth the effort to deface with a maul and chisel.

He knew it by heart, in all the languages he had learned, and had written it in the language he knew least of all. He had used the nails of his boots to save his mind, to accomplish the final emptying. When they came for him, he would be ready. They would shoot a scarecrow, tear a dry husk with their bullets.

The New Thermopylae

Born in distant, timid, weary fatherlands,
We came to find among the rocks and olives
What had been misplaced, not lost, but put aside
Beneath the counters or buried in a ditch,
Stuffed into a mattress, a pillow, a ledger.

In November-grey Madrid, we heaved up, singing,
With our Spanish brothers and their shawled
And stubborn women a barricade of wincing flesh
Against the bayonet, the bullet and the Bible.

We drank fire and fear gnawed at our guts;
Fog and cold crawled on us like lice and rats.
We had been the most brittle of all things . . . men.
We became, in Spain, the strongest of all things . . . men.
Our bandoliers hung on our shoulders like garlands;
Our love was sweated in the trenches, forged into iron.
We were welded, each to each, in a narrow place.

We stand or sit now, waiting, void, dumb,
Soldiers of the cells, the ranks of the condemned,
Peasants and cowards, workers, volunteers,
Comrades of the boot and hose, our insignia
Given us by the gristle of the whip.
We are the battalion of the battered ones,
Flogged beyond fraud and forgery to silence,
Sphincters, fists and faces clenched against the dawn.

When we fall, bathed in piss and blood
At this new Thermopylae, they will fling on us
The riddled banners, the shrouds of solidarity.
Then, they will turn, mirthless as hyenas,
And giggle to the dupes and deceivers both
That it was we . . . *we*, who came to fight in Spain,
We, who betrayed the dark-eyed, dreaming people
And their republic of the human heart!

It was done, but his fingers stroked on against the stones. He could not kneel. His joints would lock. They would think he had been praying in the dark.

Kopa nodded. It was true. What did a man cut in stone but a prayer against time?

His fingers rubbed, chafed and bled. The stone dust pasted with his blood. He swayed and shivered, dropping his arms to let the pulses beat again through the quaking muscles. He did not know whether it was dark or light. He did not know the hour. On a single stone above the doorway, he scraped with the final nail torn from his boot heel. At last, exhausted, trembling like a beast of burden, he opened his raw fingers and dropped the worn bit of steel to the invisible floor. On the single stone, he had cut two lines, this time in German. He traced his cenotaph and smiled.

ALLES FÜR EIN: NICHTS.
EIN FÜR ALLE: ALLES!

Should he sign it? He bent for the steel nail, found it and straightened. Kopa or Kleist? Why not H.K.? No, not at the last, the little vanity of the author. Leave it unsigned.

He flung away the bit of worn steel and nodded, empty and sated. He spoke into the darkness from the darkness.

"The case is closed. The judgment begins."

Boots boomed in the corridor. A key scraped in the lock. Kopa carefully tucked the tails of his shirt into the loose waistband of his beltless trousers. He grinned in the darkness as the door swung open.

"Right to the end," he said. "Even when there's no audience. We never give up, *never!*"

BOOK EIGHT

Pilarmadre and Puerta del Sol
August–September 1937

Full dark, the dry earth cooling from Gibraltar to the Pyrenees. 2200 hours, military time. The horses and mules have been fed and watered, the trucks and tanks refueled. The guards in the trenches, the listening posts and the hilltops long for tobacco and sleep. Ten o'clock at night. In Nationalist territory and in the Republic, in the offices of both governments, in the cafés and homes, in the staff headquarters, the soldiers' *cantinas*, in episcopal apartments and in brothels, the knobs are turned, switched on, the dials already set; the tubes warm and glow orange. Ten o'clock. All Spain stops to listen to Radio Seville, to hear General Quiepo del Llano.

A blare of music, the Nationalist hymn. The sound of papers being shuffled, the scrape of a chair. The music fades. Quiepo clears his throat. Then, a deep, rumbling, liquid belch. All Spain smiles.

> "Buenas noches, amigos y amigas! Aquí Radio Sevilla! Aquí *General Quiepo del Llano! At the hour of ten. First, my deepest apologies for the recent change in broadcasting time. How many thousands of kind letters we have received! How typical was the vile abuse, the slop-pail flung at me by the* canalla *who howl their Bolshevik madness over Radio Barcelona! No, my many thousands of friends, your Quiepo was not ill. No, my pitiful enemies . . . how proud I am to have such enemies! . . . I was not drunk. What's a few glasses, Ask Negrín, physician to your venereal Republic! No doubt he sits listen-*

ing to me, right now, sharing the finest champagne with his Russian friends and conspirators and commissars and all that rabble . . . Where was I? Oh, yes! About the change in broadcast time. I will explain it.

"Some time ago, I had the extreme pleasure of receiving in my private quarters here in the beautiful city of Seville, a delegation of beautiful señoritas. It seems that my broadcasts gave them only thirty minutes at their windows with their novios, a mere half hour of whispered words and burning, yearning glances. What? Only thirty minutes for flirtation? Impossible! Every half hour Negrín and his Russian friends dream a new, mad vision. Every half hour children starve! But here in the Nationalist state, every half hour a brave young man, a hundred, a thousand join our noble cause and a hundred, a thousand beautiful women fall in love with them and pledge their secret treasures on the day final victory is won!

"And, speaking of women, how do the eminent Señores Blum, Daladier and Chamberlain rest these nights? Eh? Has not Madame Blum been absent these warm nights? No doubt she puts into practice her husband's maniacal theories of socialism. Equal distribution, no? The chauffeur, the gardener . . . Sleep well, Monsieur Blum! Have you all heard, too, that a special commission of architects has been summoned to London? True! I have it on the very best authority! Mister Chamberlain has requested that the main doorway to the House of Parliament be widened. It is such an inconvenience to him, poor man. He has to turn sideways when he enters . . . to avoid catching the tips of his horns!

"How do you enjoy frozen horse meat from Russia, you poor people of Barcelona? Are you sure, quite sure that it is horse meat? An interesting story has reached us. It seems that certain packages of food were sent to the starving Republic from some misguided souls in France. Naturally, such criminal support of the regime of bandits is illegal. But these packages were sent in care of the Communist Party headquarters in Catalonia and from there to the Red Help center in Madrid . . . for the starving children who perish every day in the worker's paradise . . . but God will receive them . . . Where was I? Oh. When the children tore open the packages, what did they find? Stones. Stones and sawdust. A little gift from their Communist brothers in Barcelona. Among thieves, there is no honor, none at all . . .

"Now for dessert this evening, I had . . . Guess. A great, thick slice of chocolate cake with butter-sugar frosting. What richness! What flavor! Can you remember, my poor friends in

*the almshouse you still call a Republic? Can you remember
sugar? Coffee? The real stuff? Café con crema? And then, the
finest of cognacs!*

"*No wonder we are winning this war, eh? We eat here like
human beings, like the Christian warriors of old! We do not
root in the fields like pigs. Our children flourish, our girls are
beautiful and our young men strong and eager for the final
battles. How long can it take? Bilbao falls. The Basques are
defeated. Soon Santander will surrender, and the war in the
north will be over. How long then, Valencia? How long, Barcelona? How many days are you willing to starve as slaves to
your Russian masters, Madrileños? Why wait? Cross the lines!
Come to us. Our hands are open. Our hearts are generous. And
our tables . . . come and taste and drink and forget this madness! Look at your maps. Your Republic is shrinking as fast as
your bellies. Look at the Aragón front. See? Teruel. Teruel, it
points like a dagger at Valencia! One thrust . . . Ahhh . . . and
the battalions marching beneath our banners shall bathe in the
blue waters of the Mediterranean. Like an orange on a severed
branch, Valencia will fall into our pocket! Only two minutes
left? Then good night, all, especially that delegation of beautiful
young ladies who visited me with their sweet petition. The door
to my office always stands open to you. I will listen for the secret
rustle of your little skirts, eh?*

"*And now if my wife and daughter in Paris happen to be
listening, I should like to say that I hope they are well and to
assure them that we here in Seville are thinking of them.*

"*Viva Franco!* Arriba España! *Long live the Republic! No,
no . . . I mean, long live the Nationalist State, of course! To
the gallows with Negrín! How long can you last, Madrid? Barcelona? Valencia? Tomorrow night, dine on fresh disaster and
desertions while I read you the menu from another restaurant.*
Arriba España! *Viva Cristo Rey, Hitler y Mussolini! And
a very, very good evening to you all. This is* Quiepo del Llano,
Radio Seville. Buenas noches señores, señoras y señoritas!"

Pedro snorted disgustedly and turned off the radio. The others in the
junior officers' *cantina* were still laughing, repeating words and phrases,
the treasures of the evening broadcast. The laughter faltered; the grins
faded. The room was quiet, stuffy, blue with smoke. They looked at
him. Pedro trailed his fingers over the radio knobs, trying to look as
though he had intended to change stations and had twisted the wrong
knob by mistake.

"Hey, Romero, don't you find our Quiepo amusing? Where's your sense of humor, man?"

"Every night," Pedro said. "Listening to that drunken buffoon is like washing your face in urine. Do it long enough and you get to like it. You forget what water, pure water, is like."

"But it's all a joke! What else are we to *do* in this place? Go to the brothel every night? The girls there listen to Quiepo, too. They love him."

"I'm not surprised," Pedro said. "He dishonors our cause with his spew."

"Tell it to the Minister of Culture!"

Pedro hesitated, his hand on the door knob. He decided that he had already made a sufficient fool of himself. He walked out into the streets of Pilarmadre. The town was quiet, the streets dark and empty. A dog barked as a patrol marched through the Plaza Mayor and on out to the fortifications. The night was still warm and smelled of dust. A light breeze seemed to shift the blackness beneath the steady stars.

He turned and walked through the side streets, sliding through the slots in the unmanned barricades, until he stood on the bare earth that sloped south to the new concrete emplacements. He could see the glow of cigarettes. Although it was forbidden, the sentries regularly smoked on duty. The men, like the officers, simply couldn't take the war seriously. The nearest Anarchist positions were twenty kilometers away, on the east bank of the Río Gallego. Pilarmadre had been taken from the Reds, reinforced, carefully fortified under the supervision of German engineers —and forgotten.

Pedro sat down. He could see the curved glint of steel rails, the tracks that ran to Zaragoza, like the edge of a knife blade. A horse kicked and whinnied in a stall. Pilarmadre slept and dreamed.

Off to the east was the enemy. Twice Pedro had dressed in a stained *mono* and sandals and crossed the river at night. Peasants with rusty rifles and home-made grenades, that was the People's Army on the Aragón front. Twice he had submitted a proposal, a plan to breach the Anarchist lines. The chief of staff had shuffled the pages, glanced at the maps.

"That's the stuff, my boy. Fine, fine! Your ambition does you great credit. Yes, quite feasible. Well, all in good time, eh? Have you heard Quiepo's latest? Of course, one shouldn't mock a superior officer, a general, but last night he said . . ."

The August in Aragón drowsed away. Pedro drilled his company until they hated him, read manuals and technical journals until his jaws ached from yawning. He rode out across the bare, sandy plains in the cool dawn and sat up late writing letters to his sister. Connie's latest was folded inside the pocket Bible he wore over his heart.

How odd it is, still, to turn around in an empty room and realize again, always with a slight shock, like touching a wire, that he is dead . . . Exactly one hundred days ago. I wonder if I'll ever get used to it. I suppose a father never really does die.

Very dry for the last three weeks. Not a drop of rain. We are too few now to irrigate the fields as before. My little burros can't pull the water-wagon, much too heavy. We work with buckets on the vegetables in the morning and after sunset, but the sun has baked the ground like bricks. We will only be allowed two-thirds of the vegetables, anyway. The rest is a levy for the army, of course. I sold the dogs to an artillery officer, for the same one who came last month to commandeer the saddle horses. He was good enough to leave me two, one more than I can feed. Do you pray for horses in the army? We do at home.

He did not tell her what he prayed for. He had shown her the tattered photographs. The spies in Madrid had forwarded to brigade headquarters every bit of information they discovered—and it was a great deal. After the slaughter at Brunete, the Republic had pulled back, nearly to their original positions. They were reorganizing, shifting troops not north, but east. To Aragón.

From where he sat on the bare, baked mound, he could see the rolling horizon like a scribble of ink that blotted the low border of the star-strewn sky. More than one hundred kilometers from Huesca to Belchité. Beyond the river, the Reds were gathering: Juan Modesto, Lister's 11th Division with three brigades, González with two brigades. The reports of the spies stated that the 15th Internationals, the Americans and the English, were to move east soon. Somewhere beyond the river, his wrecked Guards rebuilt with fresh volunteers, was Larra, El Asturiano, Emilio's murderer. The Communist newspapers with their usual mixture of slander and superstition hinted that any man who could live untouched through Samosierra, the battle for the University, Guadalajara and Brunete must be blessed, if not by God, then by the Kremlin.

Aragón was a desert of worn rock and restless dust that sifted beneath the pitiless sun. The local peasants were right: *Seis meses de invierno y seis meses de infierno . . .* six months of winter and six months of hell. And Brigade did nothing. The garrisons neither drilled for assault nor maintained an alert defense. Everyone knew the Republic would attempt to destroy the Teruel salient in order to take pressure off the north. Even Connie knew it, a girl not yet eighteen.

I have been looking at father's maps, the topographical ones he bought years ago for some reason. Where you are now must seem like the surface of the moon. A crater here, an outcropping

there, a river surely dry at this season. And in between? Nothing.
Nothing at all.

Exactly. There *was* no defense line on the Aragón front, just a
series of fortified positions the enemy could easily bypass. Solid stuff
and then a great hole, just like the local cheese. And brigade staff
referred to this invitation to disaster as a "citadel defense system." The
enemy dared not strike. Space was strength. A scatter of small cement
forts made Pilarmadre impregnable, a little bastion specially protected
by the Virgin in Zaragoza's cathedral. Wasn't the Virgen del Pilar officially named commander-in-chief of the whole province?

The soldiers did not mix; even the sun could not melt them together.
The few Moors kept apart, the Falangists had stopped recruiting, his
own Navarrese suffered so from the dry heat that they did not so much
despise the new conscripts as fail to notice them. It must have been
much the same when Iberia was a colony of Rome. A mongrel garrison,
demoralized by the dust storms, the paralyzing heat of the sun, and
their own boredom slouching in the shade while the Visigoth chieftains
gathered on the far banks of a river, too distant to cause alarm.

Pedro rose and turned back toward the town. He heard a horse
whicker and stamp again and wondered if it was his own. Up in Navarre,
the stables were empty and the dung dried on the barn floors. The
family horses had once been valued at more than a quarter of a million
pesetas. Two left and one team of burros for all the estate. A death,
a drought, his duty—and now something worse.

> *I have prayed, Pedro, and I have melted the keys to certain*
> *cupboards and chests. I have put a lock on the kitchen door to*
> *keep her away from the knives. I have foreclosed two mortgages*
> *for the few céntimos they are worth and was turned away from*
> *the transport office in Pamplona empty-handed. Spies may go*
> *to France. Party members may take the waters in Vichy. The*
> *wives of senior officers pass through Switzerland on their way to*
> *Hitler's Germany. My mother, Condesa de Gualvidal "does not*
> *qualify" for "prioritied transportation" out of Spain! If I could*
> *have done it, I would have taken her, shown them her face,*
> *her eyes . . . like the marbles children roll on the streets. I have*
> *paid the chaplain—Father was right, he is a pious brigand—*
> *for the rites of exorcism.*

She was mad. His *mother* was mad. Not raving, not a Lucia of the
Lammermoors with loose hair and a white gown. Proper, dressed in
black silk, spraying roses in her ruined garden and licking the arsenic
powder from her lacquered fingernails. A widow, trimming the fringe
from a curtain with a straight razor of honed Swedish steel. In a muslin

walking dress with a Chinese parasol, stopped by a tenant on the precipice that crumbled down onto the railroad track. A woman who knelt all night in vigil, praying for pneumonia.

His boot heels tocked on the stones as he walked slowly back into the town where too many officers did nothing with too few men, and the moonlight lay like spilled milk on the stiff, crusted plates of the German-designed fortifications, knobs of artificial stone protecting a mutilated half battalion of radio-listeners.

Above the dark slopes of sagging tile rooftops, the shaft of the church loomed still and stiff, the crenelated tower like a sleeve, the square-frilled cuff of a Christian knight, the stout forearm of a *hidalgo* pledged to ruin his patrimony to recover the Holy Land.

Pedro shrugged the fancy off. The church was an ugly, utilitarian stone carton of God, the granite walls two meters thick. The windows were set high and narrow, God's sunlight and stars tolerated to the width of a crossbow. The great doors yawned on the dull, hot, dusty August night. Inside, more than a hundred men, volunteers for Our Lady of Montserrat, sprawled and muttered on heaps of straw. The nave was crimson, wet with the blood of a hundred votive candles weeping in red sockets. Inside the heavy walls of the church, the local commander had raised scaffolds of raw, splintery wood, steep ladders and limber planks. At each broad window sill a machine gun spraddled on steel legs. The starlight touched and glittered on the cartridge belts. Not the words drooled over them all from a radio, not the harsh mechanics of concrete fortifications, not the arid, gritty space of Aragón, but here, within the walls of Holy Mother Church—here was the true citadel.

Pedro walked softly down the aisle, stepping like a hunter in a stone forest, and knelt to pray before the crimson-washed altar. His knee skidded on a sheet of paper. He saw the stone floor littered, as though a bundle of printed stuff had burst at the holy-water font and had been blown down the aisle by the dusty breath of August. Fuddled and annoyed, he plucked the piece of paper out from beneath his knee. He tilted it up to the starlight that slid down into the nave through the sandbagged windows. It was not a pamphlet, just a reproduction of three faces: Jesus of Nazareth, General Mola of Navarre, and Francisco Franco, Generalísimo of the Nationalist State. The soldiers tore out the face of Christ when they took the sheets to the latrines.

He crumpled the sheet of paper and flung it away, turned and walked back to the open door. His fingers felt slick with excrement. He snatched his hand away from the font and wiped his fingers on his pants.

He could sense it before he felt it, the stroke of the night wind like sandpaper on his face. The grit, fine as talcum, blew into his eyes, seethed gently between his parted lips. His teeth grated, and he sneezed. The stars were gone now, lost beyond the high, soft clouds of dust that blew on an east wind over the sleeping plains of Aragón. He unbuttoned his tunic, buried his face in the sweaty cloth and stumbled out into the square. He groped through the fine, stinging swirls that sucked and gushed through the blackness of the night. He walked like a blind man, his thumb and fingertips clamped on his nose.

The sentries on duty outside his quarters were hiding in the lee of the building. They saluted guiltily but did not move. Pedro ignored them. He climbed to his room and washed the dust from his face and throat. The dust hissed against the glass panes. The room was hot and stuffy. He pulled off his boots, hung his tunic and pants over the back of a chair and stretched out on his hard bed. He lay listening to the flying grit scour the walls and window. He felt alone and unwanted and despised. A kind of helpless grief filled him.

How long would it be his duty to stay in this place, waiting and watching, praying but paralyzed? How long would it be his duty to serve as a warder in this forgotten prison? Why had he been condemned here, forbidden to act, prevented from leaving, sentenced to do nothing, nothing at all?

His disguise, his faded blue coveralls, hung on a nail, the empty legs touching a pair of worn sandals. Dressed like a worker or peasant, he had crossed the lines to reconnoiter the Red positions. The same garments could, with luck, conceal his identity all the way to Navarre. He could use the dust storm. No one would see him leave.

He played with the idea, imagining the route he would take, the other disguises, the lies, the bribes. He would hang his uniform on the nail, his decoration for loyal service and leadership pinned to the tunic. He would go home, take up the estates and by hard work and with the grace of God restore everything while the war, like millstones, ground on, pulverizing devotion and duty to the dust of death.

He lay listening in the dark to the flying sand rustling at the windows. He was tempted. The thing might be done. Surely it was right, more right than remaining here, used but useless. His duty was to his father, was it not? Rebuilding the estates would be an act of recreation, rehabilitation. Something better might be worked out for the peasants and tenants on the estates. By going home, he would actually be making a sacrifice, deliberately destroying his reputation by asserting his inheritance. Wasn't that what he was fighting for, the traditions of Spain?

He was very tempted. He began to perspire, the sweat bursting from him. He strained to see the garments hanging on the walls, persuaded that the overalls and sandals might serve as the symbolic dress of the disciples of the new Spain. Others of his class would learn of him, imitate him. While the lower orders grappled and gnawed at each other, a kind of brotherhood of Christian landowners would rise up, spontaneously, creating by their own energies and selflessness—why, what a triumphant irony—they would build the mansion and plant the crop, raise the chapel, water the land and the animals *before* the war was over! The ends thus accomplished, the means could be forgotten! A new golden age would thrust above the dust and the shouting. When the sounds of war stilled, the weary faces would turn to stare, gape, amazed. He saw himself mounted on a fine horse riding through deep green fields toward a road clogged with women and children and men in faded uniforms. It was spring and the blue winds tattered the almond blossoms and the wheat was already sprung and the sheep browsed in the meadows of thyme and clover. The people rushed to him, smiling and weeping with gratitude. A faceless messenger arrived, somehow carrying his uniform and a document proclaiming the gratitude of the Spanish people.

The window sucked open with a single smash of wood and glass. He jolted awake, shouting, and heard the brittle music of the panes falling on the dark, swirled stones. Tepid billows of dust blew around him as he wrestled the window shut again. Four panes were gone, and the latch smashed. He tore the *mono* off the nail and stuffed the worn cloth into the gaps, then tied the sash down with the laces of the sandals, stumbling over his boots, knocking over the chair and cursing in an even monotone until he fell back again on his bed, wide-awake, his damp body plastered with dust, his heart thudding slower and slower.

Somehow the window and the wadded clothing was funny. He laughed at them, then at himself. So it was his sacred duty to desert, was it? The boredom of garrison duty could turn a bad attack of homesickness into a noble plan of Christian action?

Not all the windmills were in Estremadura. Some, it seemed, were here in dusty Aragón.

He had the duty at reveille. Stable inspection. He closed his eyes and grinned in the darkness. Not Quixote of La Mancha, after all, but Augeas of Navarre.

White lay in the big tub, the water up to his chin, the tub so full that when he moved for the bar of soap dissolving near the drain, the water spilled over onto the tile floor. It was very quiet, so quiet that it didn't seem that he was in a city at all. There was almost no traffic in the streets of Madrid, and the hotel room was up too high for him to hear the sound of voices.

He rolled, buoyed and easy onto his haunch and stared down through the soap-milky water at the scars on his leg. It had stopped aching. It was a mystery. The leg held him up fine until he started to climb the stairs at Pasteur Hospital. When he reached the door of the ward, the nerves in his thigh jumped like frogs, the muscles seemed to quail and slacken, to go all loose like taffy candy. By the time he made it to the chair beside the bed where Schwartz lay, he was limping, drag-footed and sweaty. Every day he dropped into that chair and had to pretend he had a stone in his boot, had to bend down his head until the faint feeling went away.

He slid down under the water and blew bubbles, feeling the sweat trickle on his scalp. The three of them had just about worn the bathtub out. It was a big one, long enough even for Rosenbaum's legs. They took turns just soaking in the hot water. The first night, Mahoney hadn't been able to sleep in the bed. Too soft. He had rolled up in a blanket on the floor.

For three days they had been on leave together, really a kind of come-and-go rotation, one of them on duty out at Fuencarral every day.

Maybe it was being wounded, helpless, that had made Schwartz take the reorganization of the battalion so hard. He still thought of Rosenbaum as a new recruit. Schwartz had been hit at Mosquito Ridge, when the Republic was winning the Brunete offensive. He hadn't seen Rosenbaum take over a section during the shambles that followed. With so many killed, and the walking wounded sent home to help raise money and more volunteers, it was just a natural thing that Rosenbaum had been promoted to company commissar. Just like Mahoney had been bumped up to adjutant.

Mahoney-Baloney had been okay about it, so far. After all, it wasn't the first time a colored guy had command. Oliver Law had led the George Washingtons. Maybe it had been a Party stunt. Not everybody had liked him. There were funny stories about the way he had died during Brunete. But there was Walt Garland, a real fine comrade, wounded twice, and going to be invalided home now with a wrecked hand. It seemed to White that his promotion to company commander had been really just taking Walter's place.

After lying back for a while, the Party was showing its strength and abilities. Steve Nelson was now commissar for the whole 15th Brigade, with a new guy, Dave Doran, as his adjutant. Now that had made Schwartz kind of happy. He'd met Doran a few times and knew he was big, a member of the National Executive Committee of the Young Communist League, a college boy from up North, Harvard or Dartmouth or somewhere. He came on like real working class, but he and Rosenbaum argued for hours about poetry and such. It would all work out. The Party would hold everything together, would have to, since maybe half the battalion weren't Communists. Hell, there was even a couple Wobblies, older white guys.

White sighed, rolled in the water until it slopped, and then heaved up, sending the water plunging off him and grabbed a big, soft towel. It was a pleasure just to let the water run off, knowing that there was more, gallons and gallons of it. He looked at his image in the mirror on the wall. That was funny, too. You forgot about mirrors, forgot what you looked like. He grinned at himself, amazed at the big white teeth that flashed back at him.

"Like them Chiclets," he said aloud. "Mmmm, Grammaw! And this Spanish sun, don't it give a nice, all-over *tan*, though . . ."

He pulled on his pants, quartermaster-issue riding breeches that laced beneath the knees and fit into high leather puttees that were really too small but had begun to stretch what with wear and the hot weather. He buttoned his tunic. The shoulder-straps were blank, and he missed not having the insignia there. What was the point of being company commander with Mahoney and Rosenbaum to help him? Rosey had an officer's cap, too, even though it fitted him like a loose stove lid. Mahoney refused to give up the Spanish army forage cap with the tassle, the "cunt-cap" he called it and said every time he took it off it reminded him of his girl back home, same size and all, seven and a half.

White set his new officer's cap on his head and touched the brim with his clenched fist. He looked all right. The uniform was old and worn in spots, but clean and pressed good, not a wrinkle. He hung up the towels and walked into the bedroom.

The table between the beds was stacked with candy bars, cartons of smokes from the States—some kind of CP organization had sent them—scented heaps of soap bars, cans of corned beef and sardines, a dozen oranges and a paper sack of peanuts. On the floor, set back where nobody could kick them over, were jugs, three liters of red wine, a bottle of vermouth that tasted like hair oil and some pig-wash in a Johnnie Walker bottle that Mahoney had won shooting dice. When Rosenbaum dropped his toothbrush in the stuff, the bristles had melted.

He opened a carton and took out a pack of Luckies. Not much in Madrid you couldn't get for a pack of smokes. Everything but food. He lit a cigarette and stood at the open window. He could see a line of Spanish women outside a market, like a thick dribble of tar on the gray stone street. He wondered what Mahoney and Rosenbaum would bring in from Fuencarral. Only the army ate good in Madrid, if you meant by good *enough* rather than really *good*. The first night, the three of them had tried a restaurant, two spoonfuls of watery soup, one sardine each for the fish course, then a sliver of horse meat and a dab of boiled turnip. Oranges and hazelnuts for dessert. No bread, no coffee, not even the burned malt kind. And the wine had been cut with water, sour red ink.

White rinsed his mouth with the bad vermouth, mixed some with the red wine and tasted it. He lay on the big, broad, soft bed and groaned, rolling his shoulders and rear on the springy mattress. He stuffed pillows under his head, lit another cigarette and refilled his glass. He tried to read the new brigade newspaper, *Volunteer for Liberty*, but gave it up.

He pushed the fresh pages away. Through the open windows he could hear the faint metallic slither of a submachine gun firing in the trenches down near the dry river. Like a snake married to a woodpecker. He didn't want to think about it, but his mind slid back into the hours of the morning, the hospital, and Schwartz.

Pasteur Hospital was a big place and plenty well-staffed, not just with Spaniards, but all kinds. Schwartz said he had met a colored girl from the States at a dressing station, Salaria somebody, Lou? Lee? Most of the Internationals were at Pasteur, the *inútiles*, bad belly wounds, burn cases, and amputees, all waiting to be moved to Valencia or Alicante, somewhere on the east coast far from the fighting. The Americans and the English could be got out and shipped home.

The ward had them all, all white guys, but from everywhere, with names on the fever charts: Dorczy, Herrera, Giamoni, Heggstrom, Lluiki, Komrov, Vallencz, Kupperschmitt, Blawenburg, Jones. The ward had that smell no wind through the open windows could blow away, always the same, anywhere, antiseptic, stale bandages, sweaty pillows, uneaten food, medicine, and bedpans, the heavy, sweet, sad stench of any hospital. And the men lying on the beds were bad. They just lay there, still and pale, most needing a shave, if their faces showed. And Schwartz, trussed up with steel cables, a pulley and a cluster of sash-weights like a bunch of iron bananas, all skinny arms, shaggy dark hair and his sad, white face with marks under the big, weary eyes like bruises. The bit of paper clipped on the fever chart said INÚTIL, ALICANTE, 8/?/37.

White smoked and drank some wine and decided that he'd have to go back every day, just to get the spook out of his leg. Rosey said it was "mental," and it was true enough. He had the dreads from that ward. It smelled of pus. No wonder Normy was full of crazy, kid notions about learning how to swim at Alicante, building himself up good and getting back to the battalion.

Schwartz would be lucky if he could walk, much less march with a blanket-roll, munition belts, canteen, and helmet. He had the idea that they'd take him on the staff of the newspaper or in the Transport section. Somehow, he was dead set, Jew-stubborn about not going back home. Anybody with sense and a few pesetas would be figuring boat-time back so he could hear the World Series on the radio, but not Schwartz.

They hadn't been able to figure it at first, but what he had seen made White know. It was a woman, the ward-nurse, a little Spanish girl with big, dark tilted eyes, pretty mouth, and short curly hair. Her name was Carmen Libro, and she was married to a fighter-pilot in the Gloriosa. Schwartz had fallen in love with her. He talked about the train ride to Valencia like they were eloping on a honeymoon. The broken hip was nothing. Schwartz was in love. The others didn't believe it, but White was sure. Schwartz had it in his head that they would ride the train to

Valencia and then "something would happen." He didn't seem to know what that "something" would be, but he was sure of it. Schwartz was the kind that believed in "somethings."

Madrid was full of women, from girls just out of pigtails to old grandmothers dressed in black. At least three or four women for every man. They were everywhere the men on leave went, the movies, the bars, standing outside the shops and hotels. Dyed hair was a big thing, a lot of conked blondes and redheads at Gaylord's and Chicote's. Not real whores, just women without a regular man, tired of empty beds and the bad food and nothing to laugh about. It was funny about the dyed hair. Most of the Spanish girls had pretty hair, long and dark and shiny. They walked on the Gran Vía and around Puerta de Sol in groups of two or three, singing sometimes and easy pick-ups. They seemed to like the Internationals best, except for the French. The word was out that the French were all clapped-up.

He had written three letters home. He didn't bother to answer mail-call. She wasn't the kind to make up a letter. What she couldn't see or touch kind of fell away from her, he knew that. When he got back to Chicago, she'd be waiting, most likely. If not, she'd have taken the boys back down to Tennessee. He could write there and tell her that he needed her back. She would come to him, he was certain.

> *En el frente de Jarama,*
> *No tenemos aviones,*
> *Ni tanques, ni camiones . . . Ay, Manuela!*

A hound-dog duet in the corridor, Mahoney and Rosenbaum. There wasn't two guys in the battalion who sang worse and who liked to sing more.

"Hey, Manuela, open the friggin do-ah!"

"Hold your hosses," White said, rolling off the bed. He stepped across the room, slid the bolt and jumped back. Mahoney and Rosenbaum, carrying packages and bottles, blew past him in a tangle and fell, whooping and kicking, on the bed. White looked at them and shut the door.

"Well, well," he said. "Looks like fiesta time's started early. What happened? We just win the war?"

"Nah, the red-dog game at the motor pool," Mahoney said, sitting up. "Mother Luck loves little Jimmy. *Loves* me! I won enough funny-money to stuff a fart-sack. Right, Rosey?"

"Right, right," Rosenbaum said, kicking off his boots. "I must bathe. I must bathe. Did you ever read Hemingway's *The Sun Also Rises*, Comrade Company Commander White, sir?"

"No," White said. "How many times have you asked me that? I'm a Steinbeck and Norris man. Little Upton Sinclair."

"Steinbecker, steinpecker," Mahoney said. "This town is runnin over with gash and you guys just sit here talkin *books!* Mahoney is organized for a fiesta. With babes!"

"Don't say fiesta," Rosenbaum said, peeling a sock off his foot. "Every time they give us a decent meal, we get shipped back into the lines."

"Some commissar," White said. "You look kinda looped, Rosey."

"Soitenly," Rosenbaum said and peeled his other foot. "Anyway, there's this character, a very sad, tragic female character in this book who keeps saying 'I must bathe.' It takes place in Pamplona, mostly. I appeal to you, Comrade White, not to this bet-a-million bog-trotter here . . ."

"Watch dat shit," Mahoney said, twisting a cork from a bottle. "Here, palsy, some real stuff. French cock-nack. Which reminds me!"

Rosenbaum groaned and drew his legs up. Mahoney poured the liquor in two glasses, handed one to White and clinked his own against it.

"Here's looking up yer old relatives," he said. "Taste it!"

White drank off half the glass. It slid down, smooth and easy, like a glass of hot gold. Rosenbaum watched them, tugging at his hair.

"Have you ever *seen* a game of red-dog?" he said. "I mean have you ever *seen* Mahoney . . . *play . . . that . . . game?*"

"Soitenly," White said. "Jimmy, you got the real stuff here."

"Betcher ahss," Mahoney said. "WHICH REMINDS ME!"

"You promised you wouldn't tell!" Rosenbaum said, whimpering and grinning at the same time. "You *promised!* You swore a holy Irish oath!"

"This kid here," Mahoney said, stalking across the room at Rosenbaum, "This kid here! *Is! CHERRY!*"

"You're kiddin," White said.

"CHERRY!" Mahoney shouted, pouncing on Rosenbaum and shaking him, "He's cherry-cherry-cherry-cherrycherrycherry! NEVER! BEEN! LAID!"

"I had a sheltered childhood," Rosenbaum said. "Don't, you're strangling me!"

"'You're stran-glin-guh, me,'" Mahoney said, releasing Rosenbaum. "You don't even speak *English*, you cherry-Yid, much less Spanish! What are you gonna say to the queen I fix you up with tonight, huh?"

"I'll say . . . uh, 'I must bathe,'" Rosenbaum said.

"Don't stran-glin-guh, though," Mahoney said. "Not only did I win us two days' chow and two crocks of Frenchy hootch, but I got the name of a real high-class cathouse. How 'bout that? I mean a ritzy place. I mean a lace curtain, carpets-on-the-floor and champagne knuckle-joint. Gents, yer admission tickets!"

Mahoney opened the pocket of his tunic and scattered packages of prophylactics over Rosenbaum. He emptied his glass, filled it and waved the bottle of cognac at the packages on the table.

"With this loot, we're in for an all-night stand! Yer comin aincha, Andy?"

"He must bathe," Rosenbaum said softly. "We all must bathe."

"I just did," White said. "Company adjutant, your commanding officer has an empty glass. Ah, I thank you."

"How can you *do* this thing?" Rosenbaum said. "My, I have white, furry toes! You *can't*, Andrew. You're *married*."

"I ain't *that* married," White said and picked up two of the packages from the bed. "Go take a cold bath, Commissar. You gotta be an inspiration to the troops, remember? What's it say in the book? 'The commissar is an educator in the broadest sense of the word.' Right?"

"Broads is right," Mahoney said. "Spanish gash."

"And somethin-somethin 'uses every opportunity to clarify all political issues that arise,'" White said, leaning over Rosenbaum.

"Don't make a mockery," Rosenbaum said. "How's Schwartz?"

"In love with that nurse," White said. "I told you last night. Your political issue rised yet, Rosey?"

"Soitenly," Rosenbaum said.

He clenched his fist and brought it to his forehead, knocking the glass from White's hand.

"Ooops, sorry," Rosenbaum said. He closed his eyes and recited, "'The commissar never forgets that the interests of the soldiers and the civilians are the same; he strives to develop the most fraternal relationship between the troops and the population.'"

"And how's he gonna do that?" Mahoney said, dragging Rosenbaum off the bed in a wild smash of bare feet, long legs, blankets, bottles, and newspapers.

"How's he gonna do that?" Mahoney roared. "If he's a goddamned *cherry*-commissar? Huh? Huh? He's gonna go *in* there! Head high. Back straight. *AND! GET! LAID!*"

The bathroom door slammed shut, and White could hear the sound of water running. Mahoney came out after a minute and crawled on the floor collecting the glasses. He sat cross-legged on the carpet, grinning, and lit a cigarette.

"Lady Bret'll be right out," he said.

"What do you know about any Bret?" White said.

"I kin read any dirty book you guys kin," Mahoney said. "If you get a chance to see Schwartzie tomorra, tell him we're gonna get to Valencia before he does."

"Who says?" White asked. He could hear Rosenbaum giggling in the bathroom.

"Me. *I* say."

"Another shithouse rumor."

"I seen the train. I seen the trucks. I seen the ammo dump."

"Yeh. Well, where we goin?"

"Take a guess."

"Teruel."

"That's it."

"Jeez," White said. "Gimme a drink. We'll need it. I talked to some Spanish comrades at a barbershop this mornin. Cataláns. That Teruel place is a big, bare, sandy bitch of a place, with mountains and no water, like Brunete. *No tenemos aviones, ni tanques, ni camiones.* You better have a good night, Jimmy, cause the next piece of ass you get your hand on's likely to be your very own."

"Why are you always such a cheerful bastid?" Mahoney said. "Why ain't you dumb and happy, like Rosey and me?"

"I am. I am," White said, grinning. "Deep down inside. It's just I got this habit."

"What habit?"

"I like to call a spade a spade," White said. "Toss me a smoke, comrade."

Mahoney flipped the cigarettes and the matches to him, drank and shook his head.

"Yer a funny mud-duck, awright, I'll say that. Drink up."

Rosenbaum wanted to go to the Hotel Florida first, to see if Hemingway was there. They walked to Chicote's and had a drink. It was too early, and the place was nearly empty, and there was no ice for the bad vermouth. Mahoney kept pulling out a piece of paper, checking the address of the place and looking at a map someone had given him. Rosenbaum was lit up some, but pretending to be half gassed and not responsible, at the same time trying to be very easy and nice. White watched him, thinking that it might be easy to pull him back from the door of this place. Mahoney ordered another round of drinks and stared at Rosenbaum.

"What the hella you up to, huh? A coupla belts and you start goin all loppy-sided smile and Shucks-Maw. Who you playin at now, Henry-Fuckin-Fonda?"

"Shucks-Maw is an ancient Hebrew practice," Rosenbaum said, nodding so hard that the leather brim of his cap dropped down and touched his nose. "The first recorded instance involves David and Bathsheba. She said . . ."

"I must bathe," White offered. Rosenbaum smacked his lips.

"Exactly. And Dave . . ."

"Doran," Mahoney said. "Adjutant comic-star."

"The King of the Hebrews!" Rosenbaum said, saluting with the clenched fist. "He looked on her and he thought that she was fair. So he sent her husband off to Jarama. And he knew her. He knew her shoe size and her telephone number and he knew her Aunt Sophy who was organizing in the garment industry. And later, when his mother came around and said, 'David, what will the neighbors think?' David said, 'Shucks-Maw.' End of parable."

"Let's go," Mahoney said.

It was a long walk, or seemed so. The sidewalks were crowded, and they tipped their hats back and sang some, off key and bad, and the people smiled at them.

"You know," White said. "I could live in this country for good. This is a all-right city. Not a bad place for a working man and a lover. Looka them girls. I think they like our style."

"How do you say 'I've got a wart on the end of it' in Spanish?" Mahoney asked. "Saloo, honey!"

"*Tengo un* wart on the end of it," White said.

They were early, but the *sereno*, a shifty-looking kid with a bad eye let them in for a pack of smokes. Rosenbaum was as skittish as a girl. White pulled him aside.

"Look, Rosey," he said, almost whispering, "just because Mahoney found this place, that don't mean it's gonna be any good. We can just look it over, check the girls."

"Sure, sure," Rosenbaum said. He was very nervous. White felt sorry for him and suddenly contemptuous, all at the same time.

"We check out the girls. See what kind of issue this outfit has. If we don't see anything good, there's other places I know."

"You do? Other places? But we're here already."

Mahoney was in the dim hall, talking to the bad-eyed Spanish kid about the *muchachas* and showing him the food and candy and cigarettes. The kid kept trying to swipe stuff from the paper bags.

"Hey, come on, comrades! We're wastin time!"

"Really look em over good," White said. "Then, if he wants to stay, okay, let him. We can go somewhere else, get it?"

"Soitenly," Rosenbaum said and plunged toward the elevator. White followed him. The Spanish kid clashed the door shut in his face.

"*Tres. Tres. El ascensor no puede tomar más que tres . . .*"

"What's the big idea, *chico?*" Mahoney said.

"He says it only holds three at a time," White said. "That's okay. You scout on ahead. I'll be right up."

The Spanish kid pulled down on a cable. The elevator was an old dumbwaiter thing that worked on a counterweight. It slid up into the darkness. White could hear their voices.

"*Ingleses? Ingleses?*"

"Naw. *Americanos. Quince Brigada.*"

"Ohhh. *Quince Brigada! Muy famoso, muy valiente!*"

"Betcher ahss!"

The cable clicked and slithered, and the voices faded. White lit a cigarette and leaned against the iron cage. He heard the gate clash. A woman spoke in Spanish, very fast. She sounded surprised. It was pretty early for clients. Footsteps sounded, and the cable squirmed. The kid was running down the stairs. The elevator only worked up. That was Spanish elevators for you. Half the stuff in Spain only worked one way.

The kid appeared, gray and skinny. He gazed up the shaft and turned and stared at White.

"Gimmee Lookies," he said.

"*Tienes dos paquetes, chico,*" White said. "*No somos millionarios.*"

The elevator dropped down and jerked to a stop. The Spanish kid pulled feebly at the door and shrugged.

"*No marcha,*" he said. "*No funciona, el ascensor.*"

"It don't march, huh?" White said. "You bullshit little bandit."

"Gimmee Lookies," the boy said.

"Yeah."

White walked to the stairs and started up. The kid was beside him, pulling at his arm, scrambling up the stairs. He ran up and stood there, his arms out, trying to block the way.

"*No puede usar la escalera! Prohibido usarla! Solamente el ascensor!*"

"So," White said. "The elevator only goes up and the stairs only goes down, huh? *Vaya, cabroncito!*"

He reached up to grab the kid. The boy ran up to the landing and pulled a knife from under his ragged jacket. White laughed.

"*Cuidado, chico* . . . careful, kid."

The kid rolled his bad eye and jerked his head, throwing the greasy hair away from his eyes, trying to look tough. White slouched up the stairs. Spaniards were crazy about knives, but they held them wrong. The kid looked like he was going to clean his fingernails. White stepped up on the landing and faked a move, shifting quick in the darkness. The kid yelled and broke on up the stairs. The knife clattered and spun slowly at White's feet. He grinned and picked it up.

"Better stay away from the South Side, *chico,*" he said. "That's razor-country."

The kid wasn't really scared, just sore that he didn't get his *propina*. He was a three-pack pimp, or thought he was, and figured he'd been cheated out of his cut. Maybe he used the smokes to buy a piece for himself, after the clients had all gone.

White climbed the stairs, stopping at the entresuelo, which was quiet, all the doors shut. The place was higher up, maybe the third *piso*. The girls had better be worth the climb.

They were waiting for him, the kid and the madame, the kid hiding behind her, jabbering like a Tommy gun. The woman was old, with a wrinkled face powdered white and two red spots the size of quarters on her skinny, flat cheeks. She glared out into the hall and clawed at a wig of kinky dyed blond hair that tottered high and trembly on her head.

"*Muy buenas*," White said. "*Creo que mis camaradas están aquí.*"

"*No hay nadie*," the woman said. "*Un apartamento privado. Silencio, Pablo!*"

"*Dos camaradas*," White said evenly, "*de la Quince Brigada.*"

"There are no soldiers here," the woman said. "This is a private house. No one here but my son and myself. You are mistaken."

"What passes?" White said, beginning to grow angry. "My comrades came up in that cage of an elevator with this cigarette-thief."

The woman set a chain on the inside of the door.

"If you don't like the elevator, take your filthiness to another place. You are drunk! Go away before I call the militia!"

"The militia are all my friends," White said. "Here is Pablo's knife."

He showed it. The woman started to say something. The kid kept on yelling, and the madame turned on him and hit him across the face, an absent-minded, backhand swat of bony fingers and loose dime-store diamond rings, a single spat across the mouth that broke blood from the kid's flinching mouth. He clapped his hands to his nose and howled. White pitched the knife through the open slot. It hit the chain and spun into the hall. He stuck his boot in the slot and leaned against the door, waiting calmly until they both stopped yelling. The woman glared at him with black, hating eyes. Her wig had slipped over her left ear.

"Hey, Mahoney! Rosey! Get this old bag outta the way, comrades!"

"Drunk! Drunk! Get out of here with your knife! You can't come in!" the madame screamed. The bad-eyed kid, whimper-faced and drooling blood scrambled on the tiles for his knife. The woman kneed him expertly in the ribs and sent him sprawling. A big whore in a red dressing gown appeared. White waved his fingertips to her.

"Hiya, honey. Just me, your lover-man. Tell your mama to open the door, huh? Hey, Mahoney-Baloney! Any Lincolns in there? We need reinforcements! Got a Fascist road block out here!"

The big whore stared over the madame's tottery yellow wig, clutched at her tits, and screamed.

"*Un moro! Los moros están aquí! Madre mía, los moros, los moros!*"

"*Qué va*, a Moor!" White said, furiously, "I'll moor your washtub pussy, bigmouth! Mahoney, for Crissakes! I'm gonna *break* this door *in*, you old bitch!"

The whore and the madame began to hammer and tear at him, trying to rip his face and slam the door on his arm. The kid had the knife again and was yelling and making little stabs in the air. Mahoney appeared, bare to the waist already, white-bellied, with a tuft of red hair at each nipple. His arms and face were burned so raw that it looked like he wore a mask and long red gloves. Everyone was shouting and screaming. Mahoney shoved and grabbed, half-drunk, grinning and mean-eyed. White was glad to see him.

"This old lady don't wanna let me in, comrade. Magine that? Take the chain off. See the chain there? Just . . . Where's Rosey?"

"Gettin laid. Gettin blowed. Hey, señora! *Qué pasa*, huh?"

The kid swooped the knife back under his jacket, slicked a dirty grin on his face and started to pat Mahoney gingerly on the freckled, milk-white hump of shoulder.

"Good *camarada*," he said, wiping his bloody lips. "Good *inglés*. No fight here. Okay, okay."

"*No moros!*" the whore shouted and tied a vicious knot in the belt of her scarlet robe. She set her fists on her pillowy hips and bit her thumb at White.

"I'll give you more than that to bite, you big-assed pig!" White said. He lunged against the door. The whore screamed. The bad-eyed kid stroked Mahoney's shoulder.

"Kill him," he said, nodding at White. "For you, free suck-suck."

"Whatthefuckisalldisshit?" Mahoney said, balling his fists and sidling around the hall.

"Come on, comrade adjutant," White said. "Open the goddamn door and lemme in."

"This is a private house, Colonel Inglés," the madame said, her white-dusted face rigid with a smile. "My girls are good girls. Only white men."

"*No moros!*" the big whore yelled.

"I'll belt your ass," White said. "That's a promise! I'll belt your big white ass blue, you fat cow!"

"Just a gahdamn minute," Mahoney said. "What's up?"

"Christ, that big fat whore thinks I'm a Moor!" White shouted. "I'm your goddamned comrade-captain, Mahoney! Open the fuckin door!"

Mahoney poised, on the balls of his feet, middle-weight eliminations at Boston Garden. He snuffed his busted nose on his red knuckles and threw out a short left. White leaned against the door and groaned.

"Come on, huh?"

The madame knew a furniture-buster when she saw one. Mahoney aimed another left at the whore and brayed with laughter as the girl dodged back and slammed against the wall. A cheap gilt mirror slid loose and splashed on the tile floor. The whore screamed, the kid went for his knife again, and the madame smiled and brought Mahoney's fist to her crimson, sneering mouth.

"You are good, a strong *caballero*. For you, all our girls. Tonight, free! Not a peseta."

"Bullshit," White said. "They never give it away. House rules. Don't listen to her, Baloney!"

He was furious now, raging that he was forced to plead. Mahoney moved around, shadow-boxing, trying to throw his left with the madame hanging on his arm, stroking the milky bulge of his bicep. Mahoney dragged her away.

"We never have black men in here," the madame said sweetly. "What would people think? The girls don't want them. No Moors, never."

Mahoney brayed with laughter, shook the woman loose and cuffed at the loose pile of her curly wig. The madame ducked and weaved, her long skirt swishing. She looked set to throw a short left to Mahoney's white gut. Mahoney grinned, his raw face stiff with liquor and malice, loving all this.

"He ain't a Moor, you old twot," he said. "He's a nigger! Can't you see nothin?"

"*Negro, sí,*" the woman said, ducking. "We never have had them in here. The girls refuse. This is a house of dignity, pride and respect . . ."

"Open the door, Mahoney," White said. "That's an *order*, here?"

"This ain't good," Mahoney said. "These cunts are all riled, see? We'll meetcha back at Chicote's, huh? I mean, it's too goddamn *noisy* in here, see, Andy?"

"I'll bust you, you Irish bastard! I'll call a cell-meetin on you for this! The Party'll read you out!"

He slammed against the solid dark door. They all laughed at him. Mahoney cuddled the madame. She went stiff in his freckled arms, clutching her wig. The whore bit her thumb. The kid jabbed with the knife. Mahoney roared with laughter and shrugged.

"Tell it to the comic-star! Maybe there's a boogie-joint in town, huh? No *pasarán.*"

The hot lump in White's belly shot up through his throat. He drew back, his boot sliding from the doorslot.

"Mahoney!" he begged in a bellow.

"No *pa-sa-rán!* No *pa-sa-rán!*"

The three, the four of them were chanting it at him. The chain drooped, the links tinkling together. The heavy door swung a few inches and clicked, shut.

"I'll kill you, you white sonofabitch!" he muttered, throttle-voiced and shuddering. He slammed his fist against the heavy panels. His hand bounded back in an ache to the elbow. He spun around in the dark hall, scalded with rage. The shrill chorus chanted against him.

"No *pa-sa-rán!* No *pa-sa-rán!* No *pa-sa-rán!*"

He backed off across the hall and set himself to rush the door. He threw himself forward, the cry boiling up out of his dark chest like a bubble of bile.

"Rosenbaum!"

He bounded back, stunned by the solid panels, lost his balance and sat down, hard, humiliated, his hat slugged over his eyes, ache-assed in shower of cigarettes jolted loose from the pack in his breast pocket.

The flying cigarettes pattered down on his stiff, leather-sheathed calves and into his heaving lap. The little white cylinders rolled gaily over the dirty hall floor. He picked them up with shaking fingers, whispering with loose, frothy lips. He stood up, weak-legged and stared at the door. It was silent in there now. The Spanish kid would have his good eye pressed up tight to the Judas-hole, watching. White raised his big fist to his mouth, set the nail between his teeth and snapped it at the door. A titter leaked back at him. He turned and stumped down the dark stairs. He was soaked with sweat, dripping, crawly with sweat from his clipped, harsh scalp down his hairless torso. His balls were soaked; his scrotum a slick sack. His boots slipped on his feet. He clung to the bannister, afraid he might skid on himself and plunge down into the darkness.

He went from bar to bar, drinking *chatos* of white wine. People stared at him, asked what brigade he served with or what battalion. They called him *camarada* and sometimes paid for the wine. The bartenders offered him little dishes of hazelnuts, all there was for *tapas*. He gave away a few cigarettes, then realized he'd run out and stopped. The Spaniards left him alone. He drank his wine standing in a little clear space at each bar. When he left, they shouted slogans and wished him luck. He walked another block, found a bar and walked in. The same thing happened.

He worked through the streets. He had a good head for booze, and the wine wasn't very strong. He was somewhere near the Puerta del Sol. Almost every doorway was a bar. He looked inside and if he saw uniforms, he kept going. There were a few women standing in dark doorways or waiting outside the bars. He walked on and saw the reflection of his face in a window. No wonder they gave him room at the bars, left him alone. A stiff, sullen dark mask glowered back at him.

Light came from a doorway and the sound of a guitar. He walked in and stopped, blinking slowly, surprised. It was Moorish-style with tiles all over, on the floor and the walls and the arches, glittering peacock colors, gold and green and blue. The bar was small, but there were a dozen wooden tables, half of them empty. He took off his cap and scaled it onto a table, sat down, his arms folded across his chest and looked around. Curious faces stared at him. A smile. A clenched fist. A man on a stool playing the guitar stopped and began to play "Los Quatro Generales." One of the verses was about the Moors. White looked across the room at the man.

"Hey!"

"*Le gusta, camarada?*"

"*No me gusta. Toca un bolero.*"

The man grinned and stopped. His fingers slid on the strings. He snapped his fingers at one of the waiters. He was the owner, then.

"You like *flamenco* music, comrade?"

"Yes. Very much. No war songs."

"*Muy bien.* No war songs. What will you drink?"

"White wine."

"A bottle of white," the man said.

"And two glasses," White said.

The man with the guitar bowed, sitting down. A waiter brought the wine and two glasses, filled both and carried one to the *patrón.* White lifted his.

"*Salud,*" he said. "Health."

"*Amor y pesetas,*" the *patrón* said. "Love and money."

They drank the wine, and then the *patrón* started to play. White lit a cigarette and listened. The *patrón* was pretty good, maybe even very good. It was odd, hard music that sprang from his fingers and filled the gaudy room, a line of melody, then variations as he improvised around it, nervous, pinging lunges and long, intricate runs broken with butting, off-beat stuff he did with his fingertips and hand heel on the guitar like a drum. All the fingers on both his hands moved. Sometimes he seemed to slash and whip the shivering strings with stiff fingers, striking angry, tight sounds with his fingernails. White grunted and filled his glass. This was a place to stay.

The men at the tables sat and listened. The waiters leaned against the walls with their eyes half closed. Smoke drifted under the tiled arches. The guitar sent stinging needles through the smoke, music like a cry, a pang in the chest, the stutter of a heartbeat, a pounding strum, five notes picked hard and clean, a throat-tightening pause, a final plunge and then blue silence on a hot night.

"*Ole,*" White said, softly. "*Ole!*"

The *patrón* nodded gravely. Dark men at other tables murmured their *oles.* White sat still, tense, moved almost to tears. The *patrón* set down his guitar and gazed at his fingertips, absently. The waiters stirred and moved through the smoke. White looked at the *patrón.*

"Do you smoke, artist?"

"When there is tobacco."

"I have cigarettes."

The *patrón* sat with him for a polite glass and a cigarette. White gave him four more cigarettes. The *patrón* thanked him. He was a small, wiry man with an Andalusian mushy lisp and dignity. White liked him.

"No one in my country plays the guitar like you," he said, and stopped, sensing that compliments were not necessary. The Spaniard inclined his head.

"No one in *my* country plays the guitar like *me*," he said. Irony flitted the corner of his mouth. White tried again.

"You have a good place."

"One can drink the wine here," the man said.

"And listen to the guitar."

"Given ears, yes," the *patrón* admitted. "You are not French-African, I think."

"American."

"Are there many like you in America?" the *patrón* asked.

"Too many. And not enough," White said.

"The same can be said of gypsies."

White nodded. He had come to like the solemn humor of the Spaniards. It was special, like their music. The *patrón* pointed at the officer's hat, the tunic.

"You are an officer. In the 15th Brigade?"

"Yes."

"A Communist, then?"

"Yes."

"There are too many Communists," the *patrón* said. "And not enough."

"The same can be said of men with guitars," White said.

The whole room rumbled with laughter. The *patrón* puffed his cigarette. He did not turn around or raise his voice.

"Another glass," the *patrón* said, looking over White's shoulder. White did not move until the waiter had left the table. He looked around. A woman was standing there behind him. A Spanish woman in a black dress and blond, disheveled hair.

"*Buenas*," the *patrón* said and waved at a chair. The woman sat down. She was thin, with a sad-tough face and drinker's eyes. White poured her a glass of wine and set it before her. She glanced at him.

"*Gracias*," she said and looked at the *patrón*. "You play well tonight, Vincente."

"I have played worse," the *patrón* said.

White shook a cigarette loose and held it out to the woman. She glanced at the nearly empty pack and hesitated, her long fingers plucking at the air.

"I have more," White said. "At the hotel."

The woman nodded and took the cigarette and bent over the *patrón's* match. She inhaled.

"Tremendous," she said. "Thanks."

The *patrón* looked at White and at the woman. He emptied his glass in a single gulp. He stood up.

"I will play for you," he said. "*Un momento*."

When Vincente set down his guitar and walked off, disappearing beyond the last, smoke-hung, gaudy arch, she finished her drink and stood up.

"I suppose you have more wine there, too."

"Where?" he said.

"At your hotel."

She sat on the edge of the bed eating sardines from the can with her fingers. She crammed the little silvery fish into her mouth and chewed greedily, making pleasure noises, licking her fingers. White sat on the floor, smoking and sipping the last of the French cognac, looking up at her.

"Have an orange," White said.

"I will."

She began tearing the peel off, dropping the pieces on the floor.

"You don't have this big place all alone," she muttered, gnawing and spitting the seeds into her cupped hand. "Where are your comrades?"

"At a house."

"Oh. Well, this is better, no?"

"Vamos a ver," he said.

"Claro . . ."

"How much?"

She shrugged and went on eating the orange.

"Maybe you'll think I'm worth more than two cans of sardines and one orange. Maybe not."

"Have another orange."

"No, a cigarette. And a drink. If you wish. If not . . ."

He gave her a Lucky Strike and a good belt of the cognac. He wanted her now, but there was no hurry.

"What did you do before the war?"

"I was a nurse. Before the war. During the war."

"The People's Army needs nurses. Why did you quit?"

"I couldn't stand it any longer," she said. "I am a coward. Too many wounded. Too many burned. Too many killed. I ran away from it all. Now I'm with the living. I do what I do. I make money. I live. I eat. Drink."

She began to unbutton her dress.

"Leave the lights on," White said. "I want to look at you. I want to see you. What's your name? I don't know your name."

"Oh," she said. "My name is Teresa."

BOOK NINE

The Battle Is Bloody
October 1937–February 1938

Comrades, the battle is bloody and the war is long;
Still let us climb the gray hill and charge the guns,
Pressing with lean bayonets toward the slope beyond.
Soon those who are living will see green grass,
A free bright country shining with a star;
And those who charge the guns will be remembered,
And from red blood white pinnacles will tower.

Sam Levinger

Killed at Belchité, August 1937

The hot air rushing over Mahoney felt like big, invisible pillows swung against his face. He fondled his rifle, patting it with his red, nervous hands. The truck plunged on into the dust, the bad Russian tires flailing on the burro-track road. White and Rosie were one truck ahead, the rest of the company in another THC behind. The driver shifted gears cautiously, nudging the floor lever toward the dusty dashboard and dancing his foot on the clutch. The whole truck shivered and floundered on. The guys riding in the back had stopped singing and horsing around. The kilometer stones came at them through the sandy dust like tomb-markers. PILARMADRE 10 K. BELCHITÉ 10 K. Somewhere ahead, there was a fork. White had showed him the map, a peek, like showing a down card in a seven-card stud game. The truck jounced slowly down a curve cut between two vineyards. Sweat prickled down in the damp fur on Mahoney's bare, burned arms.

"What if we miss the friggin turn?" he shouted.

The driver, a kid from North Dakota, shrugged, hypnotized by the heat, the dust and motion. The tires were flogging themselves to bits. Maybe they would never make it to the fork in the road.

"I dint get no leave in Madrid," the driver said. "I dint get no sleep last night. Loading gas. I dint get no sleep the night before. Driving this heap to meet you comrades, see? I never been to this place, any- way. Oh-oh. Oh-oh . . . and we got no more spares . . ."

A soft, flubbery sound came from the right front wheel. The driver wrestled with the steering wheel, pumping the brake. The Russian truck slowed and drifted off the dirt road out into a parched field. The next two trucks passed, honking. Mahoney wrenched open the door and fell out into the hot, sandy air. Faces looked over the wooden sides at him. Mahoney scowled and slung his rifle over his shoulder. He butted the door shut. The driver had fallen forward over the steering wheel. His lips puffed. He was asleep. Another truck, a dusty hulk packed with men heaved through the hot morning; the horn squawked, voices jeered. Mahoney spat on the ground.

"This is the most frigged-up brigade in this friggin army!" he said. "First they tell us we got trucks to ride in, then the trucks aint no good. *Viva la fuckin Quince Brigada!*"

"We broke down again, Jimmy?"

"Yer ahss," Mahoney said. "From here on, we walk."

There were twenty men in the truck, no machine guns, five of the twenty were Spanish kids. They stood around the truck, dustyfaced and scared. Mahoney formed them in a column and swung off. Someone shouted at him.

"What about the driver and the truck? Huh?"

"Screw em," Mahoney said. "We don't owe em money. Come *ahn . . .*"

It was dry, dusty, rocky land. They marched and halted, marched again and found Rosenbaum's group trying to fix their own truck. Mahoney eased the strap biting into his shoulder.

"Come *ahn*," he said. "Shake a leg, you guys."

"Did you just abandon your vehicle in hostile territory?" Rosenbaum said.

"Soitenly," Mahoney said. "Piss or get offa the pot."

A flight of Moscas came over, four of them, low with small bombs slung under the stubby wings. The marching column waved clenched fists and plodded on. They came over the crest of a dry hill and found another truck, abandoned. The Moscas were over Pilarmadre, strafing the streets and bombing. Rosenbaum folded up his long legs and squatted by the side of the road. Mahoney fanned out a squad and sent them on ahead. The men walked slowly, as though the dry earth was a sheet of glass. Mahoney snorted in disgust. Rosenbaum fingered a damp piece of paper. Mahoney scanned north, using Rosenbaum's binoculars.

"Them ain't our guys," he said. "Them is Dimitrovs. What the hell are they doin here? Where's White? Where the hell is anybody?"

"This is very confusing," Rosenbaum said. "We're supposed to bypass this place. What's it called? *Pilar*-something, or something *madre*. Go *around* it, see?"

"I see about twenny Dimitrovs and they got an anti-tank gun," Mahoney said. "Come ahnn, huh?"

"The orders are to *go around this place!*" Rosenbaum said, his voice edgy. "I countersigned these orders."

"The spade ain't here," Mahoney said. "I'm adjutant. Let's go in and bust a few faces. Hey, *cabo!* Rosey, start being a comic-star and get these kids to load up their *fusiles* and move on up."

"We'd better close the gap on the flank," Rosenbaum said. He looked ready to drop off asleep. The bill of his officer's cap touched his nose. The Moscas came back, the bomb-racks empty. They wagged their wings, but didn't stunt around. Saving gas. Rosenbaum hesitated, sent a runner to talk with the Dimitrovs, another to look for White. Mahoney mashed a *chorizo* and smoked a cigarette to kill the soapy taste of the sausage. He waved a hunk under Rosenbaum's nose.

"You know somepin?" he said. "This stuff tastes red. Not like food. It tastes like a friggin color. Red soap, it tastes like."

"Not so loud," Rosenbaum said. "You'll demoralize the comrades."

"Frig you," Mahoney said. "You got any wine or any water left?"

"We distributed all we had communally when we had the last flat," Rosenbaum said.

"Yer a dumb shit, Rosey," Mahoney said. "Come ahn."

Support came up, THC trucks hauling cannons and after the trucks some light tanks, eight of them. One hammered and clanked over near the column and stopped, the whole big, riveted, shimmering thing. Mahoney stood up and cracked his knuckles.

"I'm gonna ride into this burg," he said. "Ta hell with dust-eatin. Less go."

The tank bucked back, the steel treads creaking as the turret gun fired. The sound bunted against Mahoney's face. He felt light and easy now, "high-cocked," he called it. He could hear the shell-case rattle inside the tank, as the Spanish gunner dropped it. The motor roared and the tank heaved forward twenty meters. A plume of dirt went up, the sound walloped out, and everybody bellied on the ground. Mahoney looked across four feet of red dust at Rosenbaum.

"Sh-e-e-e-e-e-t! They got cannons in there!"

"It would seem so," Rosenbaum agreed politely.

White showed up later in the afternoon, big and sweaty and sour and giving orders he had brought down from Brigade. The tank had moved off north, still trading shells with the single piece buried somewhere in the gray smear of houses on the dry horizon. Every time the tank fired, a round came back, a flat, smacking sound with a plume of dirt and stones, like a big feather. Mahoney had changed his mind about riding into this place. He stuffed his greasy pull-through and the length of string into his pocket and waited. The company had sort of fumbled up a couple of hundred meters. A machine gun hammered and stopped, fired again. *Shave-and-a-haircut-two-bits.*

"That wall up there's a cemetery," White said. "We're gonna take it. Get the guys ready, huh. We pissed away mosta this day. It'll be dark soon. Mahoney, move this company up into assault position."

"Right."

Mahoney looked straight ahead. It confused him to look around. Everyone just seemed to be running through the dust and the sound of the machine guns and the gritty, pounding racket of the tanks, the exhaust-stink and the wow and hiss of shells and bullets in the hot, dusty air.

The company reached the low wall in a loose bunch, the Spanish kids huddled too close together. White slapped a big brown hand on the wall and vaulted over it, big and slow in the dust like a dream. Rosenbaum just stepped over it, the stone top snagging the crotch of his pants. For a second or two he stood there, mild-faced and picking at his fly. Then he dropped down safe behind a thick gravestone. Mahoney prodded one of the Spanish kids. The boy ran forward holding his rifle in both hands. A bullet struck him in the face, a *whuck* that blew blood out in a soft, hot mist. Mahoney dove over head-first, as the kid sagged away, one dark eye staring out of drooling pulp. Mahoney landed hard, cursed and scuttled. Bullets hissed and struck around him. A Fascist anti-tank shell flicked a tilted stone cross, dissolving it to a sleet of flying pellets. A burst of machine gun slugs ripped a foot in front of Mahoney. He winced back and lunged forward.

"Jesus! *Jesus!* My leg . . ."

Mahoney didn't turn around to look. The voice shouted and then stopped. Some other men were hit, too, off to his right. Mahoney lay behind a slab of granite as thick as his chest and a meter high and wide, a solid plate of stone. He grinned and patted it, blew it a kiss. Slugs struck the gravestone and flattened harmlessly or gnawed and nibbled at the edges and spanged off into the hot dust. Mahoney sneered and gave the Fascists the finger. He was safe, wonderfully safe. He looked around.

Everybody had a stone or a cross or crouched behind low, broken tombs. The dead and the wounded lay exposed. Little spurts of dust danced everywhere, and some light cannons were firing but pretty far away. The company settled, "making house," Mahoney called it. The men used their helmets to scrape up little heaps of dirt, were fussy about where canteens and cartridge packets were placed, each one building a nest behind the sheltering stones. White bawled for them to start shooting. The men began to bang away at the church. Three times they silenced the machine guns firing from the church windows. Three times they got up reluctantly and darted forward to the next stone ahead. They lay there, looking back for a minute or so. The new stone wasn't as good as the old one. They were mournful about it, homesick. Then they made new nests. White bellowed again, and the company rifles slammed and rattled again in the hot afternoon.

Mahoney wondered if they were going to dig in or pull back? If they stayed, they'd be like fish in a barrel for a night grenade attack. One good mortar crew could pound the crap out of them, dropping rounds between the stones that were so safe now, such good protection from small-arms fire. If they pulled back, they'd give up what they gained and have to take this place all over again. Fuck it. It wasn't his decision. White had been dodging from stone to stone all afternoon.

White had it in for him, riding him, giving him extra duty all the time, trying to split up him and Rosey with a lot of Party crap, making him look after the Spanish kids all the time with the excuse that he should learn to speak Spik. Andy had it in for him, but Mahoney didn't know why, except that he was a nigger—a colored comrade.

One of the guys from Headquarters had found them in the house and dragged them out into the dawn to a truck for Fuencarral, then to a troop train. The leave in Madrid was over, just like that, with no real warning. Mahoney had a dim memory of being in the cathouse with Rosey and White. But there had been some mix-up, and White had wandered off or they woke him up later or something. They had been on the bottle pretty good for a couple of days. Give a guy command, and right away he started to hand out the shit, comrade or no.

The rifles made little spatting flames, bluish, like a gas stove, when the guys fired. Mahoney rolled on his side, snuggled comfortable and safe behind his stone and yelled across at Rosenbaum.

"Hey, stud! How's da back of it?"

Rosenbaum grinned feebly, his teeth a dirty crescent in the dusk. The kid had given the girls a real workout. He had a cock like a horse and had put the boots to three of them, plus getting blowed. He was so heavy-hung one of the *muchachas* took him from room to room, leading him by his big pecker, to show to the other girls and talking about *leche, leche*. Rosey let himself be towed around by his foot-long cock, red-faced and grinning like a sap. Then all the way to Valencia he had worried about getting a dose and kept sneaking off to look at his dick. The other guys kidded the pants off him about it. Mahoney was certain White had been there to see Rosey led around by his whang. He was just being biggity and carrying himself good in front of the company. Setting an example, he called it. Typical Party bullshit. Sometimes the Party comrades behaved like a bunch of parish priests.

They came through the slow-settling dust cloud like dream-walkers. First he saw single figures, then groups creeping, hunched over, carrying wooden chests or crates. The whole drab gang came sidling toward him, their faces hidden behind kerchiefs. White pointed his rifle at them, his heart jerking in his chest. Some of the gray figures saw him and raised their fists. White worked the bolt on his rifle, and clawed the kerchief from his face. It was a trick. The Fascists had come out under the dust cloud, circled around and were on them from behind! He raised his rifle and snugged the butt against his shoulder. He was sweating like a pig. Now he could hear the soft scuffle of their rope sandals on the ground. Stone-colored bodies hunched like pallbearers. They stopped and lowered the chests or crates, slowly, very slowly, a few centimeters at a time until they settled, soft-crushing the loose, gravelly soil. Then they straightened up and seemed to wait. White felt a cold shock slide up his spine. The rifle wavered in his hands. Somehow, he could not shout or squeeze the trigger.

A slender figure slipped between the waiting gangs of crate-carriers. The man walked quickly, easily. White saw the holster bound on the man's hip. An officer. He stared down the sights at the man and listened to his boots crunch the pebbles. The man grew bigger. He was bareheaded, a young, tough-looking Spaniard. He, too, saluted with the clenched fist. White aimed directly at his chest. The officer stopped and, astonishingly, smiled.

"Will you lead us to the commander of your company?"

He spoke clearly and slowly, unlike most Spaniards.

"What group are you?" White said.

"Guardia Roja," the officer said. "We are to pass through that section of the lines held by 4th Company. You are Comrade White, no?"

"Yes. This is 4th Company sector. I am company commander. Who are you? Why are you here?"

"I am El Asturiano."

White lowered his rifle and stood up. His thigh ached, and he felt sweaty and foolish.

"Your pardon, Colonel Larra. It is the dust."

The Spanish officer nodded and gestured to his men to pick up the crates and chests. The stone-colored figures bent and lifted, very slowly. They crept forward.

"The dust," El Asturiano said. "Exactly. We must be in position before this clears. Go back and warn your men to spread, please, comrade. We will pass through them."

"No one told me," White said.

He was much younger than White was ready to accept. A thin face, burned leather-brown and taut with lank, dirty hair falling over his tired eyes, jerking with every stride, no more beard on the bony cheeks than grew on his own. Dark, darting eyes and lips cracked and frilled with tiny, pale curls of dry tissue. He walked steadily, hissing and clicking his fingers to move his men up and deploy them.

Clyde Beatty, White thought, *in a dust storm I meet Clyde Beatty.*

"What do your men carry with such care, Colonel Larra?" he said. "Nitroglycerin."

"That's the truth?"

"For the hedgehogs," the Spaniard said. "In small bottles. Like hand grenades. We'll wait here. Go move your men. You are to follow us. After the artillery. We get the fortifications. You carry the attack."

He spoke with such assurance that White saluted and trotted forward through the dry, shifting clouds. He followed the useless telephone line and found Rosenbaum and Mahoney.

"Get these guys spread out!" he said. "Twenny-thirty feet apart. We got the Red Guards coming through with nitro to blow up the stuff out there! Jimmy, take half the company and stay the hell away from these guys. Rosey, we'll circle off up through the olive grove with the rest. Let this bunch go right on through the cemetery. What's up?"

"A runner come in," Mahoney said. "The Dimitrovs gonna hit on the other side. There's a cement factory there. Two companies. We're supposed to bust into the main drag, Calle Mayor, up a side street. Dimitrovs took some prisoners. There's a barricade up beyond a hotel, and the church is all walled off on the other side. They run men and ammo up and down that street, see?"

"Look," Rosenbaum said, scribbling in the dust. "It looks like this, see? Here's the hotel and here's the church. Nitroglycerin? Listen, tell 'em not to *drop* that stuff, Andy!"

"Thirty feet apart and on your bellies," White said. "Here they come!"

The dust clouds glowed golden from the hot sun. The Red Guards appeared, bearing their chests and crates. The young officer snapped his fingers. The Spanish troops formed lines; each man took a half-liter bottle, cuddled it and slid forward to the broken wall of the cemetery. Rosenbaum watched, his mouth open.

The Oerlikon guns began to fire, an even *bong-bong-bong*. The golden, gritty air hissed as the shells passed overhead. The young, lank-haired Spaniard snapped his fingers again and pointed at the dim shaft of the steeple. His men slid over the wall like cats. At once, a white flash bulbed, and a section of the wall sagged out in a clutter of stones. Mahoney crossed himself. White shoved him forward. The shells hit in the town, bright points of light, a lag of time, then a flat smack. The telephone chittered wildly. White snatched up the receiver. It was Bob Merriman from Brigade staff, ordering the attack. The company was to follow the nitro-bombers, stay well clear and break into Pilarmadre from the terraced olive grove. White shouted above the slam of the guns at Rosenbaum. The squad leaders were up. The machine-gun company began firing over the heads of the Red Guards. White grabbed Rosenbaum and dragged him back to the telephone. Two Spanish boys, their runners, had appeared.

"Stay here!" White shouted. "Get some *municiones* up! Get ammunition!"

Rosenbaum nodded.

The sandy air blotched white, and the concussions from the exploding nitroglycerin butted White's ears ringing-deaf. He lunged forward, roaring.

They were all up and moving forward, the company splitting around the cemetery, the men in small groups, but not bunched up. White ran and fell down and got up again, shouting. Blood pounded in his face, and his chest and belly boiled with rage. His lips flattened tight against his teeth. He sucked in the sandy air and blew it out in a long, happy groan. He shouted and rushed forward, pulling the knots of stammering men with him. Tears burned his eyes. He tore cartridges free and fired again and again at the dim shapes and gnarled trees that swam through the golden dust. He bellowed and could not hear himself. He yanked the ring loose from a Mills grenade and flung the hand bomb at a blue light that fluttered above a line of sandbags.

The sandy air hissed with flying bullets. His men scrambled clumsily over the stone walls, crying out in Spanish and English, their dust-plastered faces stiff and smiling. They staggered and danced like drunkards through loose coils of wire and flung themselves over the sandbags, ramming bayonets down at the squirming blue bodies.

White trampled and tore, long shuddering cries beating between his clenched teeth. He felt flesh wince and cloth go slippery. He swung his rifle, slashing and prodding with the bayonet. A jolting blow struck his hands empty. He swarmed forward, clawing and punching. Sand and olive leaves sprayed down into the shallow trench. All around him, dim forms grappled in a oozing haze, a roaring ecstasy, a huge, squeezing lust that drove them over the trench and on up the slope, bashing blindly at the trees, shooting and falling.

Machine guns hammered, and the company faltered and shrank. The men dropped, giggling and weeping, behind a low wall and lay there, panting and stupefied, satisfied to sickness, watching with dull eyes as steel slugs chipped and spanged at the brittle crest of the wall. They lay in the dusty, crashing sunlight, forty meters from the first house on the southeast side of Pilarmadre.

The first mortar-round, fired from the garden of the hotel, fell on them from the hazy sky. The dry earth shook. Pebbles, searing scraps of metal and slender leaves of silver-green showered down upon them.

Mahoney saw the cork, the slender neck, the bottle held in two dark hands above the barricade. He sat up and reached for it. The Spaniard moved his lips, saying something Mahoney could not hear. A bullet bit

into the loose bricks. A rusty cloud washed in his face, stinging his lips
and eyes.

"*Cuidado, camarada!*" the Spaniard said. "Careful!"

He held the bottle tenderly. The colorless liquid danced and shivered.
Sweat rutted his dusty face.

"Gimme the fuckin stuff, *camarada!*" Mahoney shouted. "Gimme it!"

He rose to his knees and felt a bullet tug in the loose, damp cloth
of his shirt. He leaned over the rubble barricade and grabbed. The
Spaniard screamed and moved his hands away. Mahoney's fingers brushed
the warm, smooth glass. He wanted the bottle more than he had ever
wanted anything. His face contorted as he lunged again.

"Gimme it, you bastid!"

"No, no, no! *Cuidado! Cuidado, coño!*"

Mahoney leaned against the barricade, cursing. For three hours he
had begged in broken Spanish by this long heap of broken stones.
Two platoons scraped and sweated behind him, pinned down by sniper
fire from the church steeple and the house directly ahead of him. Now,
when the Guardias had agreed, this one wouldn't give him the bottle. It
was just one half-liter bottle. They had plenty, boxes and crates of bottles.

One of the old Maxim machine guns fired, a slow, heavy churning
and jammed. The crew shouted and swore. The Spaniard beyond the
barricade shook his head sadly.

"*La máquina no marcha,*" he whispered.

"Fuck the *máquina,*" Mahoney said. "Gimme that. Be a pal."

"*Sí,*" the Spaniard said. "*Cuidado, eh?*"

"Yeah, yeah! Awright."

Somewhere back in the billowing dust, a tank chattered and squeaked,
then the turret gun slammed, and the shell went over Mahoney's
head with a sound like someone ripping cloth. The Spaniard screamed
again, and reached out at Mahoney but Mahoney didn't hear him. His
right hand closed around the bottle, pinning the Guardia's fingers underneath his own.

"Leggo, you shit!"

The air snarled and rang around them. The Spanish soldier moved
his lips, cursing in a soft, steady monotone, as he guided Mahoney's
other hand to the base of the bottle. They faced each other, both
kneeling, the bottle of colorless liquid held in the tangled web of their
fingers. The Guardia's dark eyes were fixed on Mahoney's face; trapped
by the bottle and the American's fingers, he could only curse and stare.

"Hand it over, you yellow bastard!"

"*Y tu abuela!*"

Mahoney opened his fingers. If the Spaniard snatched the bottle away,
he would kill him. The Guardia's trapped hand slid free. The bottle

tilted sideways. They both squealed. Mahoney caught it, hugged it to his chest and dropped down behind the shelter of rubble.

"*Muchas gracias!*" he shouted.

"*De nada!*" the Guardia bellowed furiously.

Mahoney heard him slide back down into the gully. Mahoney lay on his back, the bottle on his chest, and looked at the low stone house. It was the last building on the street, a squat, square two-story place with steel shutters fitted with gunports. There were at least three submachine guns in there. The street was empty but probably mined. The company could not advance until the house was destroyed, and could not retreat because of the snipers in the church steeple.

The tank had punched two holes in the house before pulling back into the swirling clouds of dust.

"Cover me, you bastids!" Mahoney shouted. He rolled over on his belly and began to squirm toward the house. Every time he moved, the liquid jiggled and danced. The rifles opened up. He could hear the slugs clang against the steel shutters. The tank cannon fired again. A third hole, up on the second story. Mahoney crawled to the broken sandbag and hid there.

Three times he told himself to get up. He could not. He counted to ten and did not move. He looked at the house. Smoke was coming out of the shutters. The last tank shell had set something on fire. The hole in the wall he wanted to use was the size of a washtub. Even with his good arm, he'd have to be no more than twenty feet away to heave the bottle inside. He couldn't keep his hands dry. What if he got set to throw, reared back and it slipped from his hand? The Guardias had lost four men knocking out the "hedgehog." A silvery burst, like a flashbulb, and a soft wallop of sound. Then a hole blown in the earth with dust settling down.

He lay clutching the bottle, working himself into a rage. The guys stopped firing cover for him, and he cursed them. A sniper spotted him and hit the sandbag twice. Mahoney shouted and prayed and bolted up and began to run, directly at the house. He did not feel himself running. He held the bottle like a football. Bullets ripped around him. He saw the cracked stones very clearly, the little dark gaps where the tank shells had jarred the mortar loose. He raised the bottle and in midstride slung it like a forward pass. As soon as he could see it in the air in front of him, he dove on his face, hit, and rolled.

Holy Mary, Mother of God, blessed . . .

Air sucked around him and the hard ground quivered like a mule shaking flies. For an instant he was blinded by the white flash and then big chunks of stone began sailing out, very slowly and dropped all around him. The earth trembled as they hit. Mahoney blinked and breathed. The whole side of the house had been blown open. Loose timbers and plaster from the second floor crashed and tumbled. A second explosion, inside somewhere, bulged up a section of the roof, and broken tiles shattered in the street. Mahoney crawled over to the house and fell inside. He lay there, patting and fondling himself. He sat up and looked out. It was dark and charred-smelling where he was, very bright and dusty outside. He could see faces, rifle barrels, someone waving to him. He waved back. He could see the tank, a clumsy shape like a box churning up more dust. Debris sprinkled down on him, and he jumped up, snarling and jerked his pistol from the holster on his hip.

Three small rooms on the first floor had been wrecked by the nitroglycerin, the plaster blown off and the white powder hanging in the air. Mahoney stumbled around. The house was his now. The stairs had been smashed to kindling. Mahoney gazed up, puzzled, then slowly fired his revolver at the remaining planks. The cylinder rolled and the firing pin snapped. Mahoney reloaded the pistol and decided that anybody there was dead.

One of the rooms was the kitchen. Mahoney pushed over the iron stove and smashed a pottery bowl. He found two tin cups and a canteen and pounded them flat with his pistol butt. There was no more stuff to ruin. He went back to the hole torn in the wall and looked out. Nothing had changed. They waved to him. He waved back.

He pissed in the plaster-dust, trying to write his name. The urine puddled around an iron ring. He stared at it, looked around and scuffed at two hinges until he could see the shape and size of the trap door. He bent and lifted the ring, heaved up and pulled the trap open.

A faint light glowed down in a dim pit that smelled of earth. A clumsy, thick-runged ladder led down into the dark. Mahoney grinned and wiped his hand on his shirt. They were down there hiding. He cocked the pistol and went down the ladder to kill them.

The pit was small and low. The explosions had knocked part of one wall into a loose heap. The other walls were smooth and cool, dry to his touch. Across the pit was a wall of wooden planks. Yellow light leaked through the cracks. There was a door. Mahoney scraped away the loose dirt with his boot. He held his breath and listened. The door opened out. Mahoney eased up the latch and pulled, springing back, using the door as a shield. He pointed the pistol in at the light and waited for the first shot to smash at him. He counted to three and flung himself around the door and into the room. He landed on his knees. His arm flailed a stool aside. He jumped up, shouting.

Three old men sat around a small, square table covered with playing cards. A candle stuck in a lump of clay lit their sad, still faces. Their bristled cheeks and chins sagged. The three old men sat with bowed heads, and the blood still dripped from their ears and patted softly, slowly on the playing cards. One of them wore a beret and held two cards in one slack hand. Mahoney watched as his mouth brimmed with blood and spilled down his lip. The three old men were dead.

For a long time, Mahoney stood and stared at them, half expecting them to mutter, stir, and go on with their game. Their dark eyes still glittered in the candle flame. Mahoney put his pistol on the table very gently and touched a card, turned it over. The queen of coins. He pressed his finger against one of the dead hands. The flesh was warm and rough. Mahoney snorted and shook his head. He brought the stool over to the table and sat down. He looked into each face. Three silent, seamed Spanish faces. They looked the same to Mahoney. They were brothers, he decided. They had come down to hide in the cellar while the fighting went on. They played cards to make the time pass. There was no money on the table. Somehow, the concussion that had killed them had not snuffed the candle flame. Mahoney gathered the cards and wiped the blood on his shirt. He shuffled the sticky deck. He wanted to do something, but could not think what it was. He counted the cards. Fifty. And two more in the brown hands curled on the table.

"Dealer's choice," Mahoney said. "Stud. Five card. Deuces wild. Jacks or better to open."

His voice sounded strange, and he knew that he was whispering. His hands moved slowly, dealing out the cards. The dead man to his left slumped with blood in his ears.

"Openers, pal?"

Mahoney dropped the deck and picked up his pistol. He pointed it at each man and tried to think of something funny to say or something tough, like Bogart in the movies, maybe George Raft. He wanted to put the pistol in their dead faces and pull the trigger. He wanted some of the other guys to come down and see this, get a few laughs. He stood up and backed out of the room. The three slumped corpses sat with the candle flame reflected in little points of gold in their open eyes. Mahoney kicked the door shut and listened. He climbed the ladder and dropped the trap door back into place. He gazed around for something else to do.

Outside, in the sun and dust, a heavy Maxim gun lashed. *Shave-and-a-haircut-two-bits*.

They lay behind a wall. The sun was still hot. Only three men were firing. The wall was broken in seven places. The men crawled from one place to another, squeezing off a shot and ducking back. The others just lay there, holding their rifles. It was a dangerous time, White knew. The men were bored, now, and getting restless. They talked about the dead men. A whole platoon wiped out. That had never happened before. Mahoney and the rest of the company were off somewhere on the other side of El Asturiano's Red Guards. No one was moving. The whole attack was stalled. They envied the Dimitrovs, safe in their captured cement factory.

White ordered the dead and wounded dragged back to the shattered olive trees. Hidden by the dust, the men along the wall were gripped in survivor-frenzy. They cursed and rammed their rifle bolts and sent a battering fire at the dim, stiff shapes of houses. Some of them began to sing.

They held on for twenty minutes, a half hour. They ran back and stripped ammunition from the bodies beneath the trees. Rifle barrels overheated and the bolts jammed. The Fascists returned a puzzled, probing fire, concentrating their machine guns at one section of the wall at a time, as though they expected an attack.

A Spaniard from the Red Guards came sprinting through the smashed olive trees and flung himself down beside White. He gasped out his message. El Asturiano was pulling back to the cart track and the stables at the base of the slope. The rest of the American comrades had taken at least one house, but they had no tools to break through to the next cellars by tunneling. The nitroglycerin was all gone. White nodded, comprehending slowly. The Red Guards were not directly under the command of the Lincoln battalion officers like the Dimitrovs. They were a special shock force responsible temporarily to Brigade. They could be pulled back whenever Colonel Larra felt like it. When they did, two hundred meters of the line would be open. White cursed helplessly. The runner didn't know if reserves were coming in or not, but the other Americans with El Rubio were too far forward, flanked on both sides. Perhaps, when it grew dark . . .

White passed the order for a general withdrawal, two squads to form a thin line as a rear guard, the rest of the men to pass through them. He explained this to the runner, who nodded, satisfied. At one quarter past the hour, El Asturiano's Guards were abandoning the barricade and the gully.

The Fascists dropped some mortar rounds on the wall, and two more men were hit, but not badly. White stumbled back with the rear guard, firing somebody's rifle that he had picked up. They backed into a platoon of English reserves digging rifle pits. The company reformed by squads along the cart track with the Red Guards on their flank. White sat cross-legged, the rifle in his lap, and waited for somebody to come up from Brigade and place him under arrest. The anti-aircraft cannons were still firing at the church. His knees were ripped and bleeding, but he couldn't feel anything. The men lay like lost bundles. The church steeple floated against the sky.

A big, dirty truck with loudspeaker horns on it jounced and groaned up the cart track. Long legs with unraveled puttees thrashed wildly, and Rosenbaum fell out on the ground, pulling his helmet down onto his head. He sat there, folded awkwardly, rubbing his brow and staring at nothing. The truck backed down the cart road. Rosenbaum pointed at the stone barn and said something. White wondered where the military police were. He fumbled his papers out of his tunic, ready to hand them over. Rosenbaum stalked over to him and stood there, swaying. White looked at his commissar's legs. The puttees looked like mummy-wrappings.

"I pulled the company out," White said. "Without orders from battalion or Brigade. See, when the Red Guards . . ."

"I know, I know," Rosenbaum said impatiently. "I just spoke at length with Colonel Larra. The runner that saw you went right to headquarters. No problem. You did the right thing. Everyone says so. Now then . . ."

White flopped back against the bank and closed his eyes. So. El Asturiano had covered for him. He wasn't going to get arrested for desertion under fire or disobeying orders after all!"

"There's a horse in that barn over there," Rosenbaum said.

"Yeah? Alive?"

"Last time I looked he was."

"Tell the kitchen crew to come fetch him. You're the comic-star, right? Feed up your men."

"We found Mahoney," Rosenbaum said.

"Everybody found Mahoney," White said wearily. "Get him his ass back here with the rest."

"That's what I'm going to use that horse for. To get the orders to Mahoney. Brigade approved the withdrawal."

"Can you ride a horse, Rosey?"

White looked up. Rosenbaum brooded, scratching his nose. A shell whomped down at the cemetery. The dirt-plume hung in the air and then drifted down.

"I don't know," Rosenbaum said. "I never really *tried* to ride a horse. He's a rather big one. I could make it to Mahoney quicker, see? I think they usually have something up front. To steer with, don't they?"

It seemed perfectly sensible for Rosenbaum to ride over to wherever Mahoney was. They could eat the horse later. White nodded.

"Let's go find him," he said.

The barn was dim and cool and smelled of manure. Somehow, it hadn't been touched. One room was filled with saddles, bridles, and other bits of equipment, all neatly stacked and hung on pegs, oiled and soaped. A dozen stalls were empty, but at the back, a bony-looking bay whickered and stamped. White and Rosenbaum looked at the animal.

"Does that stuff back there come in different sizes?" Rosenbaum said. "Like thirty-eight regular or size twelve, like shoes?"

"Beats me," White said. "I'm a city boy. He looks all right, but for them rolly eyes. Got no hay. He's hungry. We gotta requisition this place, Rosey. Get the guys in here and a phone-line and we're set, you know?"

"Help me get some of this stuff."

It took them an hour of nervous wrestling and ducking to tie the horse still, cinch a saddle on and cram a bit behind the animal's foamy teeth.

"I wonder if his ears supposed to be flat like that under them straps?" White said. "He bite you bad, Rosey?"

"Got me in the belt, mostly. Open the gate."

They led the horse out into the dusk. It lunged for a water-trough, dragging White like a doll. They both held the reins and watched the animal suck down a couple of gallons of water.

"Well," Rosenbaum said. "Here goes!"

He made a running dive up, clutched the saddle and hung there, his thin legs flailing. The horse shuddered and sidled off, snorting. Rosenbaum levered himself up on the saddle and crammed his floppy feet into the stirrups. His knees, higher than his hips, stuck out at an angle. He looked like an unraveled grasshopper.

"Boy. Boy-oh-*boy*, it's high up here! Think I need a whip, Andy?"

"Uh-*uh!*" White said, grinning but uneasy. "He's got a real fine shag-step to him now. Take these to steer him with . . . hold on, Rosey!"

The horse, drifting sideways, jolted into a full, sailing gallop out through the open gate. Rosenbaum went up and forward and from side to side. He grabbed a fistful of flying mane with one hand, the back of the saddle with the other. His legs stiffened and shot him high, collapsed, and he bounded. The horse bolted down the cart track, scattering the Lincolns, heading west with Rosenbaum leaping around, all knees and elbows, but still up there. The men cheered as the horse thundered past, blotted out suddenly by a dirty gust of wind.

"Things like that make me sure wish I'd brought a camera," White said.

A telephone crew rode in on the kitchen truck bringing wine, water, mule stew, and boiled potatoes. White set up his command post and sat down to study the new map sent him from Brigade. The firing quieted to sporadic sniping up and down the line. His company came back by squads to eat and drink. A dark wind sluiced dust up into the sky. As he looked at the map, a sour mush of dread filled White's belly. There was a solid hunk of fortified trench between the stone barn and the captured house where Mahoney was supposed to be holed up. Despite a tank and El Asturiano's nitro-bombers, the section of trench was still held by Fascists. Rosey would have to ride between that outpost and a long string of houses. White ran outside and looked at the sky.

"Come on," he begged. "Get dark, will yuh? So they just think it's some horse got loose."

A motorcycle popped and skidded into the barnyard.

"White?"

"Here. What's up?"

"We just found a sewer-culvert and a warehouse with a hole knocked in it! Get your company up and moving. We're inside this goddamned town!"

"Mahoney's still out there. We're half strength."

"Battalion will send him on up when they get back. Get a move on, comrades! We're gonna break this burg wide open!"

The motorcycle sputtered away down the line. The men seated around the food pots groaned. White set his fists on his hips. Now his scraped knees were stinging.

"That, comrades, is a young fella from Brigade. He's cheery like that cause he's *from* Brigade. And he talks like that cause he's *young*. He's a map-boy. He's a motorcycle-boy."

"He's a Trotskyite," a voice said. A bottle gurgled.

"Lay off that *vino*," White said. "Pass the word and form up on the road. One squad and the runners stay here with the phone. Rest of us comrades gonna stroll up and give old Steve a hand. Shake a leg, you guys."

"They refuse to move up to their positions?" Paco demanded. "And they give this children's story as an excuse? You told them you were coming to speak with me of this, as a matter of discipline?"

The young lieutenant nodded, miserable with humiliation. He tried to smile.

"I said I would shoot them, but they are all older than I am."

Paco nodded. He pushed aside the list of casualties and the bits of paper on which he had been counting ammunition.

"Never say anything you would not do within the next moment," he said. "Remember that."

"Yes, Colonel Larra. I know discipline is . . ."

"For animals and servants," Paco said. "In the People's Army, discipline is made by reason. We are comrades here. Never talk of shooting comrades because they refuse an order. That is the way of the Fascists. We cannot defeat Fascism by becoming Red Fascists ourselves. You have not been with us from the first days. You would know what I mean. Now you must watch and listen. Come with me."

He buckled on his revolver and left the dugout. He followed the lieutenant up to the lines. The black sky was thick with stars and held a moon big as a *duro* coin. They worked up the slope, stopping twice to watch tracer bullets streak into Pilarmadre. A pause, then the sound of a machine gun. They found the squad packed into a shell hole like rabbits.

"El Asturiano!" the lieutenant said dramatically and sat down on the lip of the crater to watch and listen. Paco dropped down into the hole. The men shrank from him. He clucked his tongue.

"What am I? The priest who catches you in the choir loft showing each other your long ones?"

"Without disrespect for the Republic, we could use a priest," one of the soldiers said.

"In the beginning of this war, a priest was my friend," Paco said. So much for that. The lieutenant nodded and cleared his throat.

"Well, am I then your auntie who catches you playing milkmen, a peseta for the first who delivers into the bucket?"

"It's . . . you say it, Curro. You saw it first."

The soldier called Curro had been waiting for the invitation. He set his clenched fist over his heart and stood up, one gesture for sincerity, the other to show his scorn of the consequences.

"Comrades, did we all see what the American called El Rubio found in the cellar or not?" he began.

"We saw it," they agreed. "With our own eyes. The dead ones."

"Dead, true," the soldier called Curro agreed. "Seated at a table. The candle still lighted. With a deck of cards out so . . . for each man. Some game not one of us knows. But we can imagine such a game. We are not ignorant men. We have lived. We have heard from others how men have died in this place."

"I have heard stories, too," Paco said. "Men flung against a ceiling until their skulls burst. And of how the leader of the Anarchists died. Run over by a truck. Like a toad. I have no fear from stories. We in Guardia Roja have *made* stories, too. Only children are afraid of stories."

"Only a fool fears nothing," Curro said. "It is not cowardice in a man to fear death."

"It is courage to overcome fear," Paco said. "Tell me. What did you see? Besides the three men in the cellar."

"Dead. Without a mark on them," Curro said. "But . . ."

He paused, making a drama of it.

"Where was the *fourth* man?" he whispered. "He who held the deck? He who plays such a game that makes blood come from the ears of old men? His stool . . . his very stool was there at the table! We saw it! And the cards, just as he dropped them, before he hurried away. And why was the candle left burning?"

"Why?" said Paco. "A freak. An accident."

"No, El Asturiano, no, no. Because the game . . . was . . . not *over!*"

The lieutenant perched on the lip of the crater coughed appreciatively, intrigued by the story. Paco bit his lip.

"And so you saw the fourth player. Who was he, Quiepo del Llano? Mola? Franco? What did he look like?"

Curro waved his arm at the battlefield, the dry, dark earth crusted with ruined fortifications, pitted with craters, a plain of blood now dried and flesh already putrid.

"Out of a dark cloud of dust. Tall and thin and ugly. A thing seen in a bad dream. Riding on his horse."

The other men in the shell hole murmured and stirred, nervous as cats, remembering. The soldier called Curro nodded repeatedly, for all of them.

"The fourth player in the game. The victor. It was Death we saw, comrades. And where Death has been on his horse, no plant grows and no man may walk or even breathe."

"You believe that?" Paco said. "Yes, you do."

"We know what we saw. He came riding to finish the game. Go to that house now. You will find no one, and the candle has been put out."

"And the cards?" Paco asked quietly.

"Gone."

"You touched the cards, though," Paco said. "In order to learn of the game, as you call it. Yet, you are all well, no?"

They froze, their eyes rolling. They had not thought of this. Curro kicked a clod. Everyone waited for him.

"Well, the night's not over yet. We hope for luck."

"You shot at this rider from the clouds?"

"*In* a cloud," Curro corrected patiently. "Yes, we fired. Of course, we fired. Fascist cavalry, we thought first. Our bullets passed right through him."

"You believe that, too?" Paco said.

"We know what we know," Curro said stubbornly.

"Well, I do not know," Paco said. "So I must go look. Come, *teniente*."

Paco climbed out of the crater. The lieutenant followed him fifty meters. He laughed bitterly.

"What tales a coward can invent!"

"Death or the Devil," Paco said.

"Or God. All stories, even one."

"Never laugh in the face of a superstitious man," Paco said. "When you turn your back, he may drive a knife in it."

"You wish me to apologize to them, Colonel Larra?"

"I wish they had not seen what they think they saw."

"Ah."

"I wish, too, that we may find something to prove they saw something else. And quickly. I have no third wish to get killed by a sniper out here."

They found nothing. The dust clouds had blown away any hoofprint, covered any trail of blood. No dead horse bulked in the moonlight. They drew fire three times and went back to the crater. Paco dropped down among the men.

"We have been, both of us, to the place you showed me. Beyond it and behind it, too. We are both untouched, as you see."

"As *we* see, El Asturiano," Curro said. "What did *you* see?"

"Out there?" Paco said. "Nothing. Stay here if you wish. The headquarters squad can take your positions. You will lead them out, *teniente*."

The men in the shell hole murmured approvingly for an instant, then fell silent. The headquarters squad consisted of those too badly wounded for action, the one-arms and broken-legs who would be taken away in trucks before dawn. Now the men turned on Curro. Paco waited until the whispered debate faded to growls, shrugs, and the snap of a bayonet fixed on a rifle.

"Let them rest, El Asturiano," Curro said casually. "We will follow the *teniente*. We know our duty. After all, every day a man looks at Death. The game is no doubt over, anyway."

"*Claro*," Paco said. He saluted them and walked back to the dugout.

"Colonel," one of his aides said. "One of the Americans was here. From the Lincoln battalion. Looking for a company commissar."

"There are no Americans in our lines now," Paco said. "Their wounded went back on the tank, and the dead are buried."

"I told him that. He wanted to check down the line. He was an officer, his runner said. Company adjutant. The one with red hair. El Rubio."

"El Rubio," Paco said. "And El Blanco, who is as black as a Moor."

"We let him go on."

Paco shrugged and finished his casualty list and ammunition count. He lay down on his blanket and slept. A hand shook him awake. "What is it?"

"The American is back again. He has found no one. Neither . . ."

"Have we. It is a night for not finding people," Paco said and rolled over. "Neither what?"

"Neither horse nor rider."

Paco sat up.

"Where is he?"

"Gone again."

"Go after him. Tell him . . . tell him that a horse and rider . . . one of our squads fired a volley. At fifty meters range. They thought it was . . . enemy cavalry. They couldn't have missed. We searched for the body but found nothing. Surely in the morning. Say that the commissar is dead."

"*Muy bien*."

Paco lay awake until the aide returned.

"Well. What does the American with red hair want now?"

"Nothing. *Está llorando* . . . He is weeping for his comrade."

"Eh? Americans are sentimental. What was the man's name?"

"Rosaboom," the aide said. "Americans have funny names, no?"

Pilarmadre burned. Pale, pointed tongues of flame seethed up into the black shroud of smoke overhead. The foul stench of the dead was mixed with the rich smell of roasting flesh. The air, heated like an oven, rang with screams and curses. Grenades and shells crashed in the streets. The stones of Pilarmadre gnashed and groaned. Men in uniform and scuttling civilians darted down the rubbled alleys, hysterical with panic. The Reds were everywhere, burning, bombing and shooting prisoners. Pilarmadre was surrounded, the garrison trapped. Annihilation inched down the side streets, crushing every pocket of defense with anti-tank shells, nitro-bombs, bayonets and rifle butts.

The only radio, fitful above the surf of static, brayed feebly from the broken choir stall of the church.

"*Remain steadfast to the Cause . . . Belchité has been recaptured . . . Quinto has been recaptured . . . Relief . . . column . . . approaching from the north and east . . . aircraft will drop supplies and ammunition . . . defend every house . . . sacred . . . heroic . . . faithful to the death . . . prepare counterattack . . . we will remain in contact . . . decisive movement . . . breakthrough . . . counteroffensive . . . destruction . . . Bolshevik murderers . . . General Ponte . . . Franco . . . Cristo Rey! . . . Quinto has been recaptured . . . Repeat . . . relief column approaching you . . .*"

The interior of the church was filled with smashed scaffolding, the stone floor frosted with shattered glass. Bodies were sprawled in puddles of red paste. The altar was heaped with ruined machine guns, jammed rifles, food tins and punctured helmets, all flung beneath the splinter-slashed ciborium. Long streamers of torn brocade twisted down and brushed over the piled offerings. The base of each of the four columns rose from a dull, foul drift of discarded cartridge cases. Hot air and ashes spewed into the center aisle from the gaping windows. A heap of wounded chanted in hopeless agony. The living squatted, waiting for them to die, so they could be carried and stacked on the barricades of bodies that rose behind each of the three oak doors. A black knot of women wailed on their knees before a niche sacred to the saint. The riddled wooden statue of Pilar held out arms stumped at the wrists.

Pedro bulled his way through the crowd jammed in the choir stall. He struck aside gray, red-eyed faces and drove his shoulder between bodies that tottered feebly in the spluttering gloom. The dim dials glowed and faded like the glare of an animal surprised at night. He raised his rifle butt, lunged forward, tripped and fell heavily against the hot, crackling carcass. Voices around him rose, lamenting, as he heaved back and drove the steel butt into the face of the bleating radio.

"Lies! Lies!" he shouted, his voice cracking into a scream of rage. "The Reds still have Quinto and Belchité! There is no relief column!

No counterattack! They are telling you lies! No escape! No relief! Lies, all lies!"

He rushed down into the side aisle. Fingers plucked at his ruined uniform, hands tangled his legs. He staggered through a mad maze of crushed timbers snaked with empty ammunition belts. Sparks and ashes belched down into his face. At the font, a figure in parade dress dabbled the still-damp bowl, made the sign of the cross, and bit the muzzle of a revolver. The pistol popped like a toy balloon. The sodden cap, filled with blood and scraps, sailed into the aisle. The suicide dropped sideways, the pistol skidding in a rainbow spray of glass.

He tore open the small door inset in the great oak portal and darted down the pinging steps. Dark herds roamed behind the last barricades and milled across the Plaza Mayor toward the hotel. The cobbles were littered with discarded rifles. The mobs shuffled, open-mouthed, as a metallic voice beat through the smoke with stunning power, a Red loud-speaker truck.

"*The Fascists are the enemies of the people! When you are on their side you fight against your own brothers, against the people of Spain! Our side fights for the people of Spain! Our side is the people of Spain!*"

The voice brayed and echoed off the groaning stones of Pilarmadre. Men fell to their knees, crying out and praying. The voice battered the length of the street, amplified and inhuman.

"*If you remain on the Fascist side, you will be killed. If you keep fighting, you are condemned to death. All of you! Every single one of you. We are your brothers, and we want you to live. Come over to the people's side, where you will have freedom and a new life awaits you!*"

The sweltering air streamed ashes and echoes. Pedro climbed on the hood of a burned-out truck and beat his rifle butt on the cab roof, a toneless cymbal sounding above the hiss of flames licking the doom-tinted sky.

"Lies! *Lies!*" he shouted. "Don't listen! Hear me! We have recaptured Quinto and Belchité. General Ponte has launched a relief column from Zaragoza! We are counterattacking all along the front. They are telling you lies!"

Hundreds of sweating faces turned up to him, slack with fear, hunger, and sleeplessness.

"In the name of our Cause and Christ the King we must fight on until they reach us! Our true brothers are coming! A relief column! Prepare to counterattack when the order is given!"

A cold, cackling crash, like the fall of a lightning stroke ripped over the top of the barricade, slammed off the pocked façades of the buildings and rumbled away. The voice struck after it. Hundreds of faces turned to it, slack with sleeplessness, hunger, and fear.

"*Take your choice! Further resistance means death for every one of*

*you. Come over to us and live. All who come over to us will live. Drop
your arms and come over the barricades one by one. Take your choice!"*

There was a silence deep as death. The truck hood buckled and
bonged under Pedro's boots as he climbed down. The machine guns
ceased their chatter. Rifle fire stopped. A great hush smoldered in the
single broad street that led from the church to the hotel headquarters.
Pedro walked slowly away from the truck. His boots seemed to beat
with his heart. All around him he saw brother officers and men, moving
their lips, but not speaking, as though tasting two substances, savoring
the choice, the bread of life or the cup of blood. They sat and stood
and knelt under the hot wash of ashes, tasting, tasting.

The entrance to the Hotel Pilarmadre was unguarded. A gang of
drunkards sprawled and pissed in the lobby, dreamed in pools of purple
vomit on the stairs. Officers and aides in Falangist and Carlist uniforms
milled about, shouting like asylum inmates, threatening each other with
pistols and ceremonial daggers. A priest knelt in the cloakroom, hearing
confessions. Pedro hesitated, bit his lip, and dragged himself on up the
stairs.

The main ballroom was a ruin of tumbled, broken chairs, ripped maps,
shattered dishes and empty bottles, laced together with useless telephone
wires. A cigarette stub in a splintered cup sent up a slender thread of
blue. A huge photograph of Generalísimo Franco gazed down from above
the dais, stern and serene. The main ballroom was empty, abandoned.
Garrison headquarters had ceased to exist. Pedro's chest broke, a single
deep sob from the heart.

He walked to the big windows where fangs of glass swayed and
chinked together, held by strips of translucent tape. Some Falangists
were heaving files of documents onto a blazing heap of wooden crates.
A dismantled mortar was knocked apart in a heat-buffeted clump of
brown weeds. It looked like so much pipe dropped by a drunken plumber.
The garden gate, leading to the narrow street that paralleled the Calle
Mayor all the way to the church, was open.

Pedro lowered himself down the rusty fire escape. He sat down on the
gravel walk and watched the files burn. He knew he was nearly spent.
He could not remember when he had slept or eaten. Two days, three
days? The flames jittered before his eyes. The wood popped softly. Bits
of burning paper rose and ballooned away. The nerves shivered along
his legs when he stood. He walked slowly through the gate, using his
rifle as a cane. Far ahead, he could see a ragged blue column marching
toward the church and the final, useless sacrifice.

He limped between the silent houses. It was like a dream. In the center
of the block, a command car stood at the curb, directly in front of a
café. The awning had been rolled down and a half-dozen officers were
seated at the small metal tables, drinking and laughing. A waiter in a

spotless coat brought more wine and poured it. The officers were eating, too. They all sat facing the command car. Pedro moved toward them, certain that if he blinked, the scene would vanish, the figures melt beneath his lids.

"It's Alemany! . . . Hey, Navarrese!"

They called him, beckoned him, smiled and held up a glass. He picked his way through the rubble. He recognized their faces. Junior officers, comrades of the same mess. How happy they seemed, how glad to see him! He smiled, pained to think he would rush to them, only to find the tables empty, the car an empty ration carton, the waiter a towel snagged on the twisted door.

"*Purísimo!* We thought you had been killed yesterday or the day before!"

"No," he said. He could taste the wine, almost. His tongue curled, yearning for one of the crusts they scattered. He sniffed the pungent odor of a cigar. They had cigars, *real* cigars! One of them got up and kicked the door of the command car shut.

"Hurry *up!*" he said.

Pedro reached them. They swarmed around him and dragged him to the table. They were real, solid. They touched him. He could feel them, smell the wine on every breath. The waiter was Julio, a commander of a machine-gun company. He was drunk. They were all drunk, Pedro realized. They gave him a chipped glass of wine and pelted him with bits of bread. Julio sat down heavily, smirking.

"Welcome, you . . . you," he stammered. "We are having some fun, eh? How quiet it is! The others have gone on to the church. To pray and die. We're having a party . . ."

Pedro crammed a bit of dried bread into his mouth and chewed like an animal. His hands trembled so that he spilled the wine down his tunic. The others, inexplicably, roared with laughter. Pedro blinked and chewed, dazed. He held out his glass. Wine poured over his knuckles. He drank, mixing the wine with his tongue to soften the bread. Their faces bobbed around him like carnival masks.

"Party? It's the Last Supper! Swallow it down! It's consecrated! We stole it from the chaplain!"

Pedro's throat constricted. His belly heaved, and he spewed lilac pulp into their faces and flung his glass at Julio. He tottered to his feet, gasping with horror.

"You *swine!* . . . You filthy pigs . . . I nearly drank it!"

They swarmed him down on the table and wrenched his arm, pressing his wrist up between his shoulder blades. He gasped and struck at them feebly.

"Confess! Confess!"

"God forgive you . . . you will be damned for this!" he said, his face pulled stiff with pain. "Let me go!"

"He has nothing to confess, this one!" they shouted. "It's the Virgin of Navarre! *Santo Sin-cojones!* Show him! *Show* him!"

They dragged him across the sidewalk. He sucked his cheeks and spat over and over, blowing out the last pasty bits, the sour saliva. They held him, opened the door of the command car, and thrust him forward.

A man in the blue tunic of an officer was on top of a woman. His naked white buttocks pumped. She lay tangled in her ruined clothes. Her eyes were shut. She moaned. Her legs were locked around the man. He shut out the sight and struggled, but he could smell them, hear them, the liquid rhythm, the beat of their breathing.

"You're next, Alemany, next! Push his face down into it! Make him lick it up!"

He groaned and opened his eyes. He stared, fascinated, watching the woman knead her fingers in the blue tunic. A ruined stocking was gartered up her slick, black-downed thigh. Pale mounded muscles plumped and pushed in a frenzy. The woman rolled her head on the leather seat, whimpering. Pedro groaned, feeling his own flesh swell.

"The colonel's wife!" the voices said. "We're all having her! She's like a jar of hot honey! You're next! Open up and get on her while you've got a chance, man!"

Pedro pulled an arm free, struck, and kicked. He fell into the gutter against the rear fender, lunged up and scattered them. He reeled out into the street, puke gushing sour in his throat below his tongue. He shook his fists at them, and they raised their arms in the stiff salute of the Fascists.

"I have your names!" he croaked. "I—I shall report you!"

Their jeering laughter spun him around and prodded him into a feeble trot. At the end of the block, he hesitated and looked back. The one who had been in the command car was now stumbling on the sidewalk, his blue breeches snarled down over his boots. Another pushed him aside and disappeared into the sedan like a diver entering a shallow pool. Pedro swallowed down his nausea, crossed himself, and turned away.

It really was the colonel's wife! Julio had once written an obscene poem about her that had circulated through the junior officer's mess. Now they were taking turns with her in the rear seat of her husband's command car. He gagged again, remembering the bread and the wine.

The barricades that plugged the side streets were undefended. Fine falls of ash powdered the clumsy bulwarks of pulverized furniture, wadded mattresses and cobble heaps topped with spiky wire. Beyond them, out in the seething dark, the enemy scraped and murmured, a long gathering before the final heavy surge that would drown everything to blood and blackness beneath its roaring plunge. The village waited in silence for this to happen.

Pedro limped through the chipped, echoing arcades, then up the agonizing spiral of steps to his room. The window had been blown in by concussion, and his narrow cot was covered with broken bits of glass. He gathered up his *mono*, a cloth cap and his sandals, stuffed everything into a musette bag. On the stairs again, giddy temptation tugged him, urging him to one long plunge down the dark well. He rubbed down the far wall.

When he reached the street, the first shabby figures swayed on the barricades, picked at the wire, dropped over into Calle Mayor, spreading out in stealthy bands, gliding against the house fronts, all the enemy faces turned toward the granite fortress of the church. Pedro fled from them, terror sucking at his brain.

He fought and floundered a passage into the church and over the parapet of bodies. Around him, hordes of men made a crazy crooning in the dim broken cave. The sacristy was locked. He pried the door open with a bayonet. His trembling hands found the hinged panel in the west wall. The wormy oak slab yawned over a flight of stone steps hacked down into darkness. He had discovered this, looking for a place to store company medical supplies.

He wrestled off his tunic. His boots seemed glued to his calves. He pushed his pale, stinking feet into the sandals and forced himself to knot the laces neatly. The blue *mono* was loose enough to draw on over his pants. He tugged on the cap and slipped through the broken door out into the church. He demanded the risk of escape at the last possible instant.

There were three doors, one at the end of each arm of the cross and the huge double portal at the base. Each was machine gunned at point-blank range, then pounded to spinning planks and shards by anti-tank shells. Fragments whined and cackled in the side aisles. Ladders scraped along the outside walls. Flaming blocks of hay bales whished down and jounced between the columns, scattering burning bits and licking at the stones with long tongues of dun, acrid smoke. Pedro crouched, thumb and forefinger in a cross to kiss. The south door was levered open by the orange jolt of an enemy grenade.

Waffled-iron eggs bounded over the worn stone slabs and burst, driving the bleeding congregation toward the main portal. Doomed, shrill shouting in the center aisle called up a final loose bristle of Fascist bayonets. Footsteps pelted away in the groaning darkness. There was a long, choking silence. Then the enemy was in the church.

The Reds came like weary wraiths, bowed and tottering, like thieves and beggars gliding to sanctuary. Horror flowed before them in a wave. Where it touched, the trapped defenders churned and whispered curses.

Pedro watched the Reds steal forward, their stiff weapons slung and snouty at knee-level. He was amazed.

They are as weary with death and dying as we are!

Three of them hunched like apes, their backs to him. Blue bubbles squirted from their submachine-gun muzzles. They sprayed the stinging gloom, their guns making a weird, sluicing chatter. The incense of cordite burned Pedro's nose. The tearing slugs drove the congregation out through the great, ruined door. There they postured and sprawled down the stone stope blooming with grenades, spiked with the long leaves of waiting steel.

How can they continue when we have abandoned hope?

He went through the panel and slipped it shut. He had no light and groped down, down, until the steps ended and the rough floor of the tunnel ran away into the chill dark. Pedro could see nothing, hear nothing but his own breathing and the scuff of his sandals. The tunnel shrank, and he began to crawl, his hands and knees shredded by the tunnel floor. The darkness smelled of cold stone. He dragged himself, with every meter more certain that the iron gate hidden in the shallow, dry cistern would be blocked by stones and shell-thrown earth. The far end of the tunnel was too narrow to turn around in. He was using his last strength. Claustrophobia would clamp on him. He pitied his own certain death, trapped like a mole, and prayed steadily for the strength to reach a confessional.

His body ached. Little flickers of pain licked up the inside of his thighs and arms. He went faint with the long pleasure of his penitential grovel in this pipe of wounding stone. He nearly shrieked from the nervous, thrilling certainty that someone was crawling *toward* him. He scrambled forward, eager to be torn, to suffer and to die.

When the dim coin of light swung before his streaming eyes, he stammered and gibbered in shame and gratitude. The secret cistern was untouched, the iron door still open!

He squeezed out through the narrow, rended lips and fell into a basin of dry softness. He lay there, gasping slowly, released but condemned to life, overjoyed and dismayed to feel the dull slugging of his pulse. He sank to exhausted sleep, a thick whirl of delirium, while the blood of his new preservation dried on his face like a mask.

He woke into a gray time of either dawn or dusk. He lay curled, stiffened like a cripple, seeing minute objects, dirt flecks and bits of dry leaves with the magnified clarity of suffering and fast. He pushed through and up into air tepid and thick as wool-waste. He clung to the lip of the cistern, his legs trembling like shafts of gelatin. He dared to grasp up a palm of sandy soil and he kissed it. He was afraid to kneel, certain that he would be unable to rise again, and swayed there while his mind fumbled over a promise of some single act of gratitude. His dry lips formed a vow that rang inside his skull. He begged permission to wear his cowardice and corruption like a leper's sores. One day, somehow, he would do the thing that would bring him before the throne of grace. His brain bumped and sidled among the possibles. At last the thought bloomed, perfect in its simplicity. Granted this shame of life, he must pay with a perfect death.

Prepared, poised and pure he must place himself to take a single stroke, the smiting pulse of pure gold that would blow him like a spinning mote of dust. His death would shake him onto the hem of the Virgin's robe; he would be flicked away to touch the mild blue down of heaven.

He was not greatly surprised, then, to see the horse, saddled and bridled, grazing on sweet weeds beneath the twisted branches of the olive trees. Pedro climbed out of the cistern and walked slowly, unsteadily, toward the animal. The horse saw him, whinnied softly and came to meet him. The velvet nose nuzzled at Pedro's uplifted palm. The heavy, drooping head had been so clumsily bridled, so cruelly bitted that the animal's mouth was torn.

"*Pobrecito,*" Pedro muttered. "Poor fellow."

His hands were gentle, freeing the straps and buckles. He clucked and patted the horse reassuringly. The animal was a token, a portion of the patrimony that awaited him, the present promise of a greater gift to be freely given. The horse gave a great-chested, shuddering sigh.

The left stirrup and leather was tangled with a filthy cotton wrapping, a bandage or a puttee. Pedro plucked it free and cast it over the stone lip into the dry cistern, then led the horse there and mounted.

He rode at a walk through the dry, pewter-tinted air, letting the horse breath and blow, scenting water. They came to a shallow stone basin where a single pipe dropped a crystal arc that tinkled in a pure pool. Pedro knelt and cupped up the water. Three times he poured it over his head, almost fainting at the cool run of it through his scalp, down his forehead and face. He rinsed his hands and chin and cheeks, knelt and drank cautiously, rationing himself. The water was delicious, so chill it made his teeth ache. He untethered the horse and brought it to the water to drink, then tethered it again and carried water in his cap and washed away some dead man's blood that had slopped and crusted on the animal's flanks.

On the dry heap of the third hill, a half-smothered little cry of joy burst from his throat. The roads before and below him lay in the shape of a cross. Sign followed sign, sweet wonder after balm! The signs and kilometer stones would have been removed, of course. He rode down the slope, slack-reined, prepared to allow the horse to choose the road that he must follow. As they drew closer, he recognized the place. On some off-duty time, to use up the hours, he had come this way before. Then,

it had meant nothing more than a place to halt a lathered horse, turn
and walk back to the barracks.

The road to the left led nowhere, a peasant's track that ended in dry
ruts on a wind-eroded hillside. The road straight ahead ran on to meet
the rail line to Zaragoza, headquarters for his brigade, his division. In
Zaragoza, General Ponte and his staff sent messages of hope and relief
to garrisons abandoned to their doom, lies about Nationalist counterattacks and relief columns from towns already taken by the enemy. The
dust-deep track gouged straight to the horizon lost itself in the pale
mounds of northern hills. Followed long enough, cleverly enough, it
might lead him home to his lands, his mother and his forsaken sisters,
home to the estates that death had pushed into his hands, the fir forests
on the granite mountain-slopes, the narrow, rich fields licked by moist
tongues of resin-scented wind, home to sweet Navarre.

Which road would the horse choose? Death in desolation, duty under
the heartless piety of Fascist generals, or desertion in the face of fire,
escape to the north? Carefully, he slipped his sandals from the stirrups
and cast the reins before the pommel. He must not exert the slightest
pressure of his will. Let God show him the way that he must ride!

The horse, unchecked, unguided, moved into a soft, hesitant trot, the
long, slab-muscled neck swinging left, then right. The animal's ears
lifted, listening on the faint breeze. The nostrils soft as plush tested
this moving air.

God chose for him the straight road, hoof-cut, crimped by tank-
treads, waffled by tires, packed by the feet of marching men, the strait
road to headquarters, the road to Zaragoza. Pedro slipped his feet into
the stirrups and gathered up the reins. He posted on at a steady trot.

Just before dark (for the time of his wakening had been twilight,
and he knew finally that he had slept away all the night and the day)
he came upon another traveler.

The mule cart seemed to stand still, although Pedro could hear the
slow clutter of hoofbeats in the dust and the creak of the axles. It
seemed as though the earth rolled toward the old man holding the reins
on the seat, as though they slid together. The old man reined back and
stopped. The mule wheezed and blinked sleepily, pushing a white-
plastered tongue against the bit. Pedro rode a few paces until he and
the old man were face to face, nearly on the same level.

"Ola, viejo."

"Muy buenas, señorito."

"I am that obvious?" Pedro said.

The old man looked at him. His dark eyes were set in wrinkled lids
like a lizard's. He smiled and shook his head.

"You are not of this place. Not with such a horse and such a way
of riding."

Pedro bowed in the saddle.

"I am the *Conde de Gualvidal*," he said, surprising himself. It was the first time he had spoken aloud the title that had passed to him from his father.

"We all have some excuse," the old man muttered, his mouth quirked maliciously. He stared down the road.

"Is there a place where you have passed for food and water?" Pedro demanded, abruptly recalling his father's favorite remark that the insolence of the very young is exceeded only by that of the very old. He straightened to see what the old man carried in the cart, but noticed only a shovel and a pick.

"There is a station of Civil Guards," the old man said. "No doubt they will welcome Your Excellency. If they look long enough, perhaps they will see, too, that you are not of this place."

The old man was warning him. Pedro bowed again.

"Perhaps there is another road to Zaragoza? Through the hills?"

"They say that if you turn into the sheep track near the next kilometer stone certain difficulties may be avoided, although the way is somewhat longer. You are in no hurry, Excellency?"

"No. Not now."

"Then the battle is over," the old man said, and nodded.

"Which one?" Pedro said. "Belchité? Quinto? Pilarmadre?"

"It makes no difference to me."

"Then you do not search for a relative, to see if he is alive?"

"No," the old man said. "I only go to see who is dead."

"Too many," Pedro said, and crossed himself.

"But not enough," the old man said, grinning. "Not yet."

Pedro said nothing. The old man ignored him and finally stirred.

"Well, Excellency, with your permission. I am expected. Or needed, at any rate. If you enter the city from the east, you will find a squadron of cavalry, men from your province. You need a uniform, Excellency. The Civil Guards can see a uniform, always."

"Many thanks for your advice. I will enter from the east then. Go with God, old man."

The old man made a sound something like laughter and cracked the worn reins over the bony rump of the mule. The cart creaked away into the darkness.

"Is this the place?" the driver asked. Carmen pushed the blanket away from her face and looked ahead.

"Yes," she said happily. "Go straight ahead, Pavito."

The sedan jolted over the frozen ruts, throwing her against Frank's shoulder.

"What is it, a monastery?"

"A farm," Carmen said. "A place where El Asturiano sends the *inútiles* from the Red Guards."

"And they come here to die of boredom," Pavito said. "Or the cold. Madre, what weather!"

"It doesn't look the same," Frank said. "Of course, it was spring then. All the almond trees had flowers."

"I don't care," Carmen said. "We have two whole weeks. Imagine it! Fourteen days."

"Fourteen nights," he said. "Are you still cold?"

"*Claro*, I'm cold! And I don't see any smoke, either. Not even from the kitchen."

Pavito stopped the car before the big stone farmhouse and switched off the engine. He turned around and stared at them, his face gloomy.

"You really want to come to this place, *jefe?*" he said. "It's not far to Madrid. Fine hotels there. Where the foreign comrades stay. The Florida. Gaylord's. I forget the others."

"We will stay in this place. Take the automobile back to the motor pool at Cuenca and thank the comrades there. There is a telephone in this place. If it marches, I will call you. If not, I'll send a message."

"*Muy bien*," Pavito said and shrugged. "*Mire* . . . Look, the reception committee."

An old woman dressed all in black stood outside the door, hugging a shawl around her thin, bent body.

"A witch," Pavito said.

"The cook," Frank said. "Talk to her, Carmen. Pavito and I will get the luggage."

Carmen walked up the rough stone path, the blanket trailing behind her.

"*Hola, señora*," she said. "You were told that we were coming?"

"I was told," the woman said. "We have only rations for four. One Leg, El Loco, No Hands and the one with the silver plate in his head. *No hay carbón* . . ."

"We have food and fuel, a bag of charcoal," Carmen said. The two men came up the path with the suitcases and burlap sacks. They leaned against the wind that droned through the olive grove. Dark clouds spilled across the sky. Frank tugged the blanket up around her neck and hugged her. She smiled up at him, too happy to speak. Pavito looked at the old woman, the house and up at the sky.

"The rest of the comrades from the squadron must be in Madrid by now," he said. "Drinking Fundador at Chicote's and telling lies."

"Bring those bags inside," Frank said. "Then you can go, Pavito."

He swung his arm against the backs of Carmen's knees, caught her, and swung her up. He carried her to the door and kicked it open.

"Is she sick?" Pavito said.

"An American custom, *camarada*," Frank said. "Remember, Carmen?"

"Oh yes," she said, almost crying. "I remember. But I'm not a bride. Not now, Francisco!"

"*Mi mujer*," he said. "This is our real *luna de miel* . . . honeymoon."

"I don't believe it," she said. "You look so different with your beard. Are you the same man I married?"

He carried her into the hall and set her down, grinning like a boy.

"Pavito doesn't approve," he said. "He thinks we should be at the Gaylord with the Russians. Pavito says the Russians have more dignity even than Spaniards. Remember when Dorlov . . ."

He stopped and looked away, swinging his fist against the palm of his left hand. Carmen watched him.

"*Qué va*, the Gaylord," she said. "*Aquí, señorito, estás en tu casa!*"

"*Mi casa*," he said, frowned, and scrubbed his beard.

"Oh, look," she said. "Francisco, *look!*"

The walls were lined with bare branches. Dark, dry arms reached up out of pots and vases. The floor was littered with tiny brown bits, the dried almond blossoms. The wind from the open door blew them across the worn planks. She bent to touch the branches. Brittle curls fell away from her fingers.

"How sad it looks," she said. "Remember when . . ."

She followed him to the big room. The tables were as they had been left, pushed against the walls to make room for the dancing. The sound of her boot heels echoed, and the maw of the fireplace was clogged with dead leaves. Their breathing smoked. Frank picked up a wineglass and shook out a ruby crystal that fell on the dusty cloth.

"Why didn't someone clean it up?" he said. "Where's that old señora? Who takes care of this place? They've had six months."

"So long?" she said. "It seems longer . . . and only a few days ago. Remember how they sang for us, the Guardias?"

In the hall, Pavito sat on the luggage, smoking and staring at the old woman.

"At night they put on their overcoats and listen to the radio," Pavito said, "In Madrid . . ."

"They put on their overcoats and listen to two radios," Frank said. "Take the *coche* back to Cuenca."

Pavito nodded and went out the door. Frank followed him, and they stood near the sedan for several minutes talking about spare parts for the aircraft. Pavito took a list, a letter and a packet of tobacco. He did not want to leave, and stared reproachfully at Carmen.

"This is not a very good place, señora," he said.

"*Basta*," she said. "It's a fine place for us. Drink all the wine in Cuenca."

"How long would that take? Ten minutes," Pavito said.

He climbed in the sedan, started the motor and drove slowly away. "Let's go inside and get warm," Frank said.

"Please, Francisco, could we walk across the field to the chapel?"

The wind pulled and fluttered the blanket. He put his arm around her, and they walked slowly over the frozen field.

"He is very fond of you, Pavito," she said. "You can see it in his face."

"Pavito allows me to fly one of his airplanes," Frank said. "With reluctance. He's a good comrade. The parts worry him. If anything goes wrong, we have an *avión* on the ground, useless."

"And things go wrong?"

"Always," he said. "I want to forget how bad it is. That's what a leave is for. So you can forget."

The door of the chapel sawed in the wind. Inside it was cold and dusty, the floor littered with animal droppings. The door banged like a gunshot.

"Let's go back," he said.

"I wonder what happened to the priest?" Carmen said. She felt cold, dull, and unhappy. He was right, Francisco. It was a mistake to bring back memories.

Frank shook his head.

"Perhaps we should have brought some people from the squadron," he said. "Maybe Pavito was right. Too many spirits . . . ghosts."

"We can heat some water," Carmen said. "A real bath for you."

"I had one last month," he said. "I could shave."

He was silent on the way back to the house. In the front hall he bent over the baggage and straightened up, cursing in English.

"Where is that señora? Bring her here, Carmen!"

"What's the matter?"

"They have stolen the food! Some of it. Some of the wine and tobacco!"

He was very angry. Carmen got out of his way as he marched down the hall to the kitchen and flung open the door. They were there. Four of the Red Guards, one swaying on a crutch, his left trouser leg pinned up below the knee, another wiping wine from his lips with the back of his hand. His left eye was covered with a circle of green blotting-paper threaded on a headband of twine. His right lid dropped and opened. The woman stood by the stove, her jaw moving, a bit of potato bread in her hand. The two others crouched on stools before the stove. Charcoal chinked and rustled, and thin smoke seeped from the oven door.

They said nothing. The men at the stove did not turn around. Carmen leaned against the door-jamb. Frank walked to the table and leaned on his fists.

"Is this the discipline of the Guardias? Of citizens of the Republic? We brought bread and wine and *chorizo*, some tobacco and a type of coffee. For all. To share equally. You have stolen most of it. Bring it out! So that we may share it."

The others said nothing. They ignored him. The charcoal made little musical sounds.

"There are seven of us. I will divide what we have. One half for us, the rest for you. Of everything. Then we will be comrades and friends. I will wait in the big room. Put it back in the sacks. I will not look to see you. Come, Carmen."

He took her arm and pulled her down the hall into the front room. They sat down at one of the big, dusty tables. He drew something in the dust.

"Tomorrow, they will clean this whole place," he said.

"But you see how they are, Francisco."

"We will help them. We must have some kind of system to live here. Some kind of order. Even if they are *inútiles*, they need an officer. I'll make the one with the eye a commissar of this place. We'll collect wood. The wine will be rationed."

"Half for us, half for them?" Carmen asked.

"We brought it," he said. "We brought everything. That's fair."

"But it's not *equal*."

"Yes, it is."

She watched him. He was not so angry now. He was being reasonable. He smiled at her stiffly and pulled at his beard.

She sighed and shivered. They sat for a few minutes, listening to footsteps and the bump of a crutch in the hall. He nodded at her and smiled.

"You'll see," he said.

"Rich Americans must be different from rich Spaniards," Carmen said. "Are the poor Americans different, too?"

He looked at her, blank-eyed.

"Yes. I don't know. I think so."

Carmen shrugged. She didn't really care. The whole business was foolish. She wanted him to hold her. She wanted to kiss him. He made her feel young and stupid. He got up and walked out into the hall. She waited, bored. Her feet were cold. He came back, angry again, and slammed his chair against the table.

"Well?"

"Now the bastards stole the cognac and the blankets!"

"Come," Carmen said, getting up. "We don't need extra blankets and cognac. Let's take a bottle of *tinto* and go to bed. We'll keep warm that way."

He nodded, and they walked out into the hall. She helped him carry the suitcases and sacks up the stairs.

"We'll lock it inside and take the key," she said. "What's inside is *ours*, what's outside is *theirs*."

"Fair enough," he said. "I was going to shave, though."

"Later," she said. "You have fourteen days."

"And fourteen nights," he said.

She lay between the cold, musty sheets, shivering and watching her breath smoke. He drew the cork from the wine bottle, kicked off his boots and trousers and climbed into the bed, still wearing his leather flying jacket.

"*Hola, Carmencita*," he said and kissed her.

"*Hola, Francisquito*," she said, catching his rough beard between her teeth. "*Por Dios*, what cold hands you have!"

For two days and nights they stayed in the bed. Frank's watch stopped, and they ate and drank, talked and slept. He burned a hole in the top sheet with a cigarette, and Carmen spilled a tumbler of wine. The floor was littered with dry bread crusts, cigarette stubs, empty bottles, and the pale, dried shapes of used prophylactics. Rain and sleet drove against the windows like bird shot. He lay with her, warmed and drugged, in a deep, lumpy nest of mattress, stale sheets and clothing. He got up only to use or empty the big enameled chamber pot and to rummage in the burlap bags for food and more wine. In the dim room, her curly hair that smelled now of cheap, black tobacco made a dark shape on the wrinkled pillow, and her hip mounded the blankets and overcoats.

"Francisco."

"*Qué quieres?*"

"Come back to bed. I want you."

"I'm getting something."

"There's a packet under the pillow here."

He burrowed close to her. She drew his hands to her breasts. He kissed the bruises he had already bitten into the back of her neck. He reached under the pillow while she fondled him.

"There's my *gordito* . . . my little fat one," she said.

He dozed and dreamed. He was flying and the plane was hit. Gasoline burst in streams from the bullet-punctured instrument panel. When he tried to bail out, he discovered that he was chained inside the aircraft, fettered like a convict, while streams of gasoline gushed out, soaking him. He lurched and fought to be free. Just at the terrible, hissing instant of explosion he broke awake, bellowing and drenched with sweat and sat up in the cold darkness while her soft lips brushed his forehead again and again.

They talked in the darkness.

"Francisco, do you believe in dreams?"

"Yes. No."

"That they come true?"

"Dreams are like prayers. They don't come true."

"But you dream in English and Spanish and sometimes French. You said so. You're lucky. I only dream in Spanish. Do you understand what they're saying to you, the people in your dreams?"

"I understand what they're saying. I just don't know what it is I want."

"Maybe you want to go away from Spain. To leave us here. Don't you want to go home?"

He slid his hand down her soft, warm belly.

"Here is my home."

"You want to again? One of the girls in the convent told me she did it with the family chauffeur until instead of *leche,* he gave blood and fainted. He went to the hospital, and her family locked her up. She said after that he could never do anything again and one night hanged himself in the garage."

"Some convent," he said.

"It was terrible. Turn over, I want to get my back warm."

"Tomorrow we get up and take a bath," he said.

"Together?"

"Yes. And I'll shave. We'll get what is left back from those people downstairs. There'll be no more lying and cheating. We'll have some new rules."

"How exciting!"

"Rules only seem to work in Spain if someone has a gun."

"*Claro, querido!* What's important is the rules you can break, not the ones you have to obey."

"Don't talk so fast, Carmen. You know I can't understand you, when you go . . . *brrrrrrt* . . . like that."

"I'm sorry."

"Aren't there rules that you want to obey?"

"At the hospital there are as many rules as in a convent. I have to obey *them.* Most of them make sense. Some of them."

"Not have to. *Want* to," he said.

"Of course . . ."

She trailed her fingers down his spine and stroked his hip. He rolled over on his back, a cigarette between his lips.

"Name three."

"Three rules. Why three?"

"I don't want you to get tired from thinking."

"That's not what makes me tired. It's *gordito.*"

"Three rules."

"Okay," she said. "Cigarette?"

"*Hokay,* yourself. Don't set us on fire."

She sat up and smoked, wrapped in a blanket, with his leather jacket around her shoulders.

"Rule One: Don't get caught."

He pulled the blankets and sheet up under his chin. Cold air rushed down his side.

"*Magnífico*," he said. "Wouldn't it be better to have as the first rule, the rule that you don't break rules? That way you don't have to worry about being caught."

"I don't worry about being caught. I worry about what they'll *do* to me. In the convent, you know. And now in the hospital. No, your way is impossible."

"Rule One," he said, "is a rule that there are no rules that should not be broken. Rule Two is: don't get caught. What's Rule Three?"

"I love you."

He felt his heart swell with happiness. He took the cigarette from her.

"The seventh commandment. Is that a rule?"

"*Claro*, that's a rule! In Spain? That's the big rule for women. But of course it doesn't count for men. Not even in your America, I'll bet!"

"Jesus God," he muttered. "What the hell, you know?"

"I love you most of all when you try to teach me something, Francisco! Is tomorrow Wednesday?"

"I don't know," he said. "I think so. If today is Tuesday. If we don't get up soon, we won't be able to walk. Rule number one: there is a limit to everything."

"That's a bad rule."

"Maybe. But it's true."

"Everything?"

"Everything . . . Now for God's sake, don't start to cry. Lie still. Go to sleep."

"What time is it?"

"I don't know. Early morning. Late afternoon."

"I'm not sleepy. I want to . . ."

"You always want to. I'll be finished, like that chauffeur."

"Ask you a question. You are a rich man. Back in America, I mean."

"I was born lucky."

"But you say there is a limit to everything. Luck, too?"

"Yes."

"I see. And love? There is a limit to love, then?"

"Well, you get old."

"I don't mean that. I mean love."

"No."

"Then your rule number one is not absolute?"

"No. Not absolute."

He fell asleep with his next breath. She stubbed out her cigarette and lay staring into the darkness. She did not believe him and began to weep quietly so as not to awaken him.

Carmen sat in a big wooden tub, soapy water up to her chin. Frank crouched beside her, muttering and scraping his chin with a straight razor. The kitchen was warm. It had taken three hours to heat the water. Carmen sighed and patted suds on her knees.

"This is delicious. You know, in the convent we had to bathe in cold water and wearing a robe? From the neck to the feet. You had to wash underneath it."

The razor in his hand hung for an instant, glinting in the candlelight. He scooped his hand in the water and smeared soap on his upper lip.

"You're joking. You make up all these stories," he said.

"It's the truth! The nuns said it was a sin against modesty to look at yourself. There's that sound again."

He listened and shrugged.

"A train whistle. A train from Valencia to Madrid."

"Is the charcoal all gone?"

"Yes. We'll collect wood. Get out of there. Or move over and let me get in."

She glanced over the edge of the tub.

"Look at you," she said. "*That* is surely a sin against modesty."

"That is the official salute of the Republican Air Force," he said. "It is for such salutes that we are called La Gloriosa. Move over."

"Turn the radio on first," she said. "The others are listening. If to-night is Wednesday, we can listen to Quiepo del Llano talk about what he had for dinner."

He stood and walked across the room. How white and strong he looked, with heavy muscles across the shoulders, his back very straight and his plump, hard behind! He switched on the radio and stood there, absently scratching the auburn hair at the base of his belly.

"I thought only Jews had the end of it cut off," she said.

"*What?*"

"Nothing," she said humbly. Perhaps he *was* a Jew. She had never asked him.

Dance music came on, fuzzed with static. He walked back to the tub.

"That's Radio Seville, isn't it?"

"It sounds like it."

She slid forward until her knees touched the wall of the tub, making room for him behind her. He scooped water against the nape of her neck.

"You have blue marks," he said, and put one foot into the tub. He started, his legs stiffening. The tub skidded a few centimeters and water slopped onto the floor.

"There's someone outside!" he said.

"One of the people. It's all right. They can't see us."

"I hear voices! Someone is giving orders."

"Turn off the radio! Get me my blanket!"

She tried to get up and fell back into the water. He was across the room, snapping off the radio, a pistol in his hand as he flung the blanket at her. Voices shouted out in the darkness. A sudden terror seized her. She stood up and steadied herself, one hand on the edge of the tub.

"The door . . ."

He ran for it. The door smashed open. Carmen screamed and saw Frank fumbling with the safety catch on his pistol. A man in uniform stood in the doorway, a submachine gun cradled in his arm. He walked into the kitchen and stared at them, amazed.

"*Paco!*" Carmen cried.

He dropped back and down, swinging to the right, and the snout of his submachine gun pointed at Frank.

"Paco, *no!* It's *us!*"

His thin face snapped around to stare at her. She scrambled out of the tub, trying to cover herself, and crouched on the floor.

"Don't shoot!"

She snagged her toes into the blanket, dragged it to her and around her. Paco stared at her, blinking, then looked at Frank.

"Of course," he said. "I had forgotten. Forgive me."

He stood up, slung the submachine gun over his shoulder, pushed the door shut, and dropped the bar into place. Carmen laughed unsteadily.

"We were having a bath. I mean, *I* was having a bath."

"Yes," he said, staring at the door. He stood there motionless. Carmen gestured frantically for her clothes. Frank hopped on one leg, trying to put on his pants, the pistol still in his hand. He turned on the radio. They dressed in frantic haste, both talking at once, their voices drowned by the music that roared into the room. The sound stopped and Carmen heard herself scream.

"My pants! My God, I forgot to put on my pants!"

Frank looked at her, open-mouthed. He was dressed, with bits of lather around his ears, his leather jacket buttoned and the pistol shoved into the belt. His pale face, suddenly strange to her, grinned and he made his snorting laugh. She felt herself blush, and snatched her hands from inside her khaki trousers. Paco cleared his throat, a long, disapproving shatter of sound. Carmen sank down on a stool near the still-warm stove and rubbed the damp blanket over her hair. She peeked out. Frank touched Paco on the shoulder; he turned and they shook hands, neither of them smiling.

"*Bienvenido,* Colonel Larra."

"*Muy buenas, Capitán Libro. Señora.* A thousand pardons. I had not expected . . . in the kitchen . . . Some other room, perhaps. Where are the people?"

"Stealing," Frank said. "Upstairs, probably."

"Stealing?" Paco said. "No one steals. It is forbidden."

It was as though he no longer saw them or was aware of them. He walked out of the kitchen. His boots pounded away, and he shouted, once, in a dark, urgent rip of sound that made Carmen's belly quail.

"Oh, my God, you never should have told him!"

"They're his people," Frank said.

"Turn off the radio, quick!"

They sat on two stools near the stove, not looking at each other, like two guilty children. Paco's voice rapped and stuttered. The house shook with hurried footsteps. They sat and waited. Paco came back into the kitchen and stood there.

"We will go into my office until the big room is cleaned up and a fire made. The mess crew will be in here. I have two companies to feed. We have some rations."

"There's no charcoal or wood, Paco," Carmen said feebly. "We used it all."

"We have wood," he said. "We cleaned out a church yesterday. Plenty of wood. We have no feed for the horses. That's why we brought them here."

"You came by train?" Frank said, as though he had never spoken Spanish before. "We heard a train."

"Yes," Paco said. He stood waiting for them. They looked at each other and got up. Carmen hesitated, looking at the stove.

"Let me stay here and help," she said. "I can make soup, remember? We used to call it 'machine-gun soup' up in the Sierras."

She saw her underpants on the floor and moved her boot to cover them. Paco glanced at the floor, saw what she tried to conceal and looked away at Frank.

"That will not be necessary. We have three excellent cooks."

Carmen nodded, blushing and miserable.

"I'll be with you in a minute, then," she said weakly.

"We saw Moscas in the air over Belchité and Pilarmadre, *capitán,*" Paco said. "Your squadron?"

"What's left of it. We started out with fourteen. Now we have seven."

"Appoint a new commissar. Report the old one. This cannot be tolerated! Come, we will talk of this over a bottle of wine. With your permission, señora?"

"Oh, Paco," she said, feeling ruined.

They were gone. She bent and picked her underpants from the floor.

Paco sat across the table from Carmen. He ate and drank slowly, deliberately. Carmen was very gay and feminine in a wool skirt and sweater. Her eyes shone, and her cheeks were flushed from the wine. She and Paco talked constantly, too fast for Frank to follow. He felt he was eavesdropping, lit a cigarette and poured more wine.

"Then it's true? La Pasionaria's lover, what *is* his name? Antón! That's it! Was transferred to the front? I heard she was living with the Italian. Togliatti."

"They were both living with her."

"*Both* of them? What a scandal! With her husband and son at the front."

"That's where Antón was sent. As a commissar, believe it or not."

Frank emptied his glass and filled it again. He ate a piece of hard Manchego cheese and looked at the young Spaniard. Paco ignored him deliberately, only speaking to him from time to time and then in slow, measured sentences as though to a child or someone slow-witted. Yet he did not flirt with Carmen. They seemed like brother and sister. But they shut him out. He drank his wine. He was tired of being called *capitán*. That's what happened when you made some kid a colonel and gave him a gun to play with.

"There is some bad news from International Brigade headquarters, *capitán*."

"Oh? Tell me."

"It is said that much money has been taken from the treasury there. Also difficulties between the French and German comrades."

"And Marty?"

"Marty the spy hunter. He has been sent to Russia. Not all of his talk of spies is suspicion. But it is the missing money he must explain."

"Well, money is . . ."

Paco nodded, dismissing him, then smiled as he leaned forward to listen to Carmen. She was chattering like a telegraph-key, smiling, too, clapping her palm over her lips, giggles bursting through her fingers. Her hand flicked through the candlelight like a quick bird. Paco fingered the stem of his wineglass and laughed, a short bark of amusement that tilted him forward until their heads nearly touched. They looked very young, like high school kids telling family secrets. They rattled on and on. A dismal loneliness filled Frank. He let the stiff smile fixed on his face fall away. Why should he pretend he could understand them? They had forgotten him completely. His mind picked at resentment like a scab, but when she suddenly thrust her fingers into her short, curly hair and smiled with delight, her small teeth shining, he felt his heart bound and skid. She fumbled with a cigarette, and he tipped the candle for her. Her fingertips brushed his knuckles, and she winked at him, a secret, long-lashed, bold wink, dark-eyed and impudent. He winked back, but she had already glanced away.

Money. His letters of credit had been drawn on the banks of the Republic. There were rumors everywhere that all the gold had been shipped out to guarantee the arms and munitions from Russia. The Republican peseta was worthless outside the shrinking borders of the state, and inside there was nothing of value to buy. He had drawn his flight pay and bonuses due him in dirty bits of paper that nearly filled a small suitcase. He had tried to send two letters to England, arranging for a conversion of what he had into pounds sterling. The letters had been opened by the censor and returned to him. He had no dollars left and no French francs. The only real hope was to convert Republican money into Nationalist pesetas, then change those into pounds or francs. But that could be done only by a spy, someone who crossed regularly into Nationalist territory. Pavito had told him that it would take months to change that amount. And the commission was fifty per cent.

"Oh, that reminds me of the joke about Prieto and Negrín," Carmen said.

They were off again. Frank looked away. The big room hung dark around them, as though they sat within a protecting globe of golden light. Drafts licked at the flames, and long shadows twisted on the cloth. The room smelled faintly of soap and carbolic. The scattered tables were ranked like a military mess, and a log fire burned on the big hearth. The meal of soup, potato bread, sausage, and tortilla had been served by the old woman and the one-eyed soldier. While they ate, figures slipped up and down the stairs with buckets, brooms and fresh bedding. Two of Paco's Guards stood at every door that led outside, and night patrols walked the fields and olive grove. The big stone house had become a barracks, headquarters for this thin-faced, calm young man in the clean uniform called El Asturiano.

Paco held up his palm to check the rapid words and laughter that bubbled up out of Carmen. Frank watched the pulse beat in her neck. She smiled at him, breathless and shining-eyed. A man appeared at once.

"Is there coffee, comrade?"

The figure nodded.

"Take a cup with some wild honey in it," Paco said. "Bring us what is left, comrade. Oh, and the cognac for La Gloriosa. They are short of fuel, so we must take good care of them, no?"

The figure nodded and slid away out into the hall. The coffee was served in demitasse, black and very strong and very sweet. Carmen drank it and swore that it was like before the war.

"Italian," Paco said. "When we captured the train, we found three bags of it. Also in the train, the horses. You can ride a horse, *capitán?*"

"A little," Frank said.

"These are something! From the estates of the Conde de Gualvidal, no less! Arabians. As big as in very big. Seventeen hands, at least. A present from 'The Hero of Pilarmadre.' Did you see the Fascist papers? No? He must have been the only officer we didn't kill in that place. He is to be awarded some important decoration. A piece of tin and a ribbon. A picture of Franco. For what? Surviving, that's all. They are getting as bad as the Italians on the other side. I suppose it is because his father, the old count, was one of the leading Carlists, right from the beginning."

"I know," Carmen said evenly. "He came to Madrid to bring a message to my father. His cousin was an organizer for the Falange. Killed near Luis Candelas."

"I know," Paco said. "I was the one who shot him."

Frank pushed back his chair and walked to the fireplace. Carmen picked up her coffee.

"Let's talk of something nice. Tomorrow we'll go riding, then. Oh, I got a letter from Anita! She's dancing in Argentina and Mexico. Giving nearly every céntimo to The Cause! Isn't that wonderful?"

"If it's true," Paco said. "Do you need clothing?"

Carmen suddenly blushed and looked across the room at Frank.

"No," she said. "Nothing."

"Some of the *chicos* got into a store or two in Belchité. I have about fifty meters of light blue flannel. Take some for a dress."

"Cloth. Horses. Coffee. The Guardias are a *batallón de lujo!*"

Frank stared at them as he warmed his legs and rear at the fire. One minute they talked about shooting each other in the streets, the next about dresses. And dancing in Argentina. He shook his head. No question about it. The Spaniards were basically an unstable people.

He was not pleased when Carmen darted away to bring in the most recent newspapers from the kitchen and Paco rose and came to the fire, carrying a brandy glass.

"I heard you got two planes last month."

"Three," Frank said. "*Gracias. Salud!*"

"*Salud.*"

They touched glasses and drank. Paco kicked a log with his boot, jerked his head and looked around approvingly.

"We never had such fires in my home. The entire house of my father would have fitted into this room."

"I think this is more your size," Frank said. "Colonel."

"I do, too," Paco said, grinning suddenly.

Frank slapped him on the arm. It was difficult to dislike him. Every once in a while, he dropped his guard and you saw, with a little jolt along the nerves that he was . . . what . . . twenty? In Philly's south side, he'd be stealing hubcaps off Packards and bragging about the time he got to the ball park early and saw Connie Mack in the dugout.

"I fought with your countrymen. The Lincolns. They were ahead of us at Quinto and Belchité. They suffered much. I think there cannot be more than half the battalion left. Not two hundred men. Well, less than three hundred. It seems we may lose them."

"What?"

"You have not heard?" Paco said.

"Our field is small in Aragón. We have only a telephone and get few newspapers."

"Well, this is not official," Paco said. "But the English have proposed a system to withdraw all volunteers. On both sides. Franco has accepted. He wants to get rid of the Italians. As long as they leave all their airplanes and artillery. The Italians are always going west when Franco is going east, north when he's pushing south. It is a joke that the Fiat tanks have only one speed forward, but four in reverse. Anyway, some three thousand are going back to receive the blessings of His Holiness. If Negrín agrees, the Republic will release the same number. That might be the Eastern Europeans, the Slavs. Maybe the French. Not the Germans or Italians, of course."

"Why not?" Frank said, puzzled.

"They have no countries to go to."

"I had forgotten. It's hard to imagine it. No country to go to. Men like Kopa."

"Why do you speak of him?" Paco demanded, setting his glass on the mantel. "Why do you speak of Kopa?"

"I don't know. We talked of him a day or so ago. He is hard to forget. He was a good soldier, a good comrade, wasn't he?"

"He was the best soldier in Spain. On either side!" Paco said loudly. He gazed around the room and wiped his forehead.

"We would have lost the University and Madrid, too, last year. But there was Beimler and Kopa and the rest of the Thaelmann column!" he said.

"A pity he died in Barcelona like that," Frank said.

"¿Cómo?" Paco said. "Like what? Died like what?"

"An accident," Frank said. "We got a truck full of gasoline from some tankists a couple of months ago. Their commander knew him. Old comrades. A Pole, fat, with teeth."

"Comrade Kolodny," Paco muttered. "Yes, a fatal accident."

"He might have had a splendid military career," Frank said. "In the States . . . I guess not. You have to go to West Point and not be a Communist."

"He should have commanded a division," Paco said.

"Oh, at least," Frank said. "Too bad. I remember his eyes. We got talking once. In Madrid. I forget what he said, but it was true, whatever it was. Three thousand to go, that might mean all the British and the Americans. Right?"

"What?" Paco said. "Yes, perhaps."

"Well, there's a limit to everything," Frank said, and finished his drink. He lit a cigarette and wondered where Carmen was. He could hear voices from the back of the house. Paco's chair scraped. His arm moved and brought the glass up and set it down again, empty.

"But that wouldn't affect you, *capitán*," he said. "Would it?"

"Why not?" Frank said.

"Look in your pocket, *capitán*," Paco said. "At the little book you carry there."

"You mean my passport?" Frank said.

"*Claro*, your passport! You are a citizen of the Republic of Spain! No?"

"Well, in a sense . . ."

"Your American passport is not valid for Spain, now. Is it?"

"No, but what about the others? In the Lincoln Brigade."

"Battalion," Paco corrected. "They are all Americans. Here illegally, most of them. But Americans."

"Hell," Frank said in English. "So am I!"

"No, *camarada*," Paco said from across the dark, cool room. "You are Captain Francisco Libro, pilot in the air force of the Republic of Spain. If your countrymen go home, they go home. But *you* stay here."

Frank opened his mouth to shout. He heard the sound of steps in the hall and saw the faint golden drift of a candle carried in the darkness. Carmen came into the room, a wad of newspapers under her arm. She set the papers down before Paco and placed her hand on his shoulder. His shoulder quivered as though her touch had stirred him to silent laughter. They stood together in the honey-bath of light, their young Spanish faces staring across the room at him.

"Here," Paco repeated. "With *us!*"

Frank stared, stunned. His hand moved up to touch the stiff pad of the passport in the breast pocket of his tunic. Inside was his photograph, his fingerprints, his printed name, accepted and approved by his own signature: FRANCISCO LIBRO.

"Why, of course he is," Carmen said. "My husband is fond of coffee. And Spanish cognac. Aren't you, *querido?*"

He leaned back against the mantel, took out a cigarette and struck a match.

"Sure," he said.

Some time later, Frank left them, took a candle and a glass and climbed the dark, creaking stairs. Their voices fell away to meaningless dribbles of sound. He set the candle on the table beside the bed. The floor had been swept. There were clean sheets and two of the blankets had been given back. He pulled off his boots and got into bed and lay propped on the pillow. He smoked bad black tobacco until his fingers grew too cold to roll the cigarette papers. He drank wine chilled to tastelessness and stared at the candle. A cold wind rattled the windows. His mind moved sluggishly.

I should send a telegram. No, they wouldn't send it. I'll go into Madrid and see Louis Fischer or Hemingway. I'll send a telegram to Paris. To Malraux. He'd remember me. Would he? I don't even remember the names of all the fellows in the squadron. There was that Italian. Viriato? And that German. I forget. When was it that the volunteers were brought into the regular air force? When was the last time my real name was put down on a piece of paper somewhere? When did I sign my name? The Russians would have the records, somewhere. How many of the fellows were using their real names, though? Not very many. I'll go to the Ministry of the Interior. Explain everything. I let Carmen arrange for the passport, but she didn't really do it. Some friend of hers, a clerk, a girl. Bookkeeping error. Happens all the time. If they refuse, I'll claim it's a forgery. I never should have turned in my passport. There's no American embassy or consulate. Over the bridge in France now. I'll fly out. Sure! How will I get a two-seater? Where? Alcalá. The Russians have security everywhere. Too slow. Some goddamned Kraut in a Messerschmitt. Get a boat from Barcelona. To hell with the Wop submarines. But how would we get out? You have to have papers, a permiso. Double-signed by the ranking officer and his commissar. Never do it. He's right . . .

Can't run away. People count on you. Wouldn't be square-shooting. Everybody must feel this way. Every now and again. Be responsible. Hell, I took the military oath! Never told any non-affiliate the Psi U password or showed the grip. Like being baptized. Can't break the faith. What did I come here for? Don't join the team to quit in midseason. I can't do that. Just wouldn't be right. If you run away, you betray them. Peter and Harry didn't try to get out. Tom Coltringham. Brian I almost had a fight with, dead at Bobadilla and they never found him. When Jean was hit over Brunete, he climbed and rammed that German plane. What the hell's the matter with me? Either go by the rules or don't play the game! Not a game. No, no. Look what happened to Dorlov. Those dirty bastards . . .

I was going to help them. But they got killed. Every one. Lose all your friends and all you've got left is comrades.

What the hell good is anything? I'm just tired of everything, this country full of broken towns where everyone hates everyone else. These people hate God and God hates them. Beautiful Republic that was going to win the war and already stinks like a dead burro buried under a bombed building. What kind of a country is this where we're all beaten back into some cold, dirty corner like a bunch of rats? Maybe all this mattered once, but now? What the hell! There's a limit to everything.

Is there? With her? Just say this girl, those people, why we came here, this belief, that hope, just nothing? Nothing at all? My sweet love with your name that nobody at home will ever be able to say without smiling inside them and your curly hair and tilted dark eyes and the way you walk with your back so straight as though you didn't know your little rear was sending signals. How many nights have we even been together? My pretty Spanish girl, my wife. And this is Mrs. Buckminster. Oh no. Señora Libro. It's all ridiculous. Straighten it with a phone call or two, a telegram. Get a damn good team of lawyers cracking on this, take it all the way to The Hague court!

It's only worth being alive when you think you've got a way to change things. Can't even change pesetas to francs. Buckminster the banker? Don't know him. No record. Nothing on the books. The account closed out. Sorry. The firm regrets that the enterprise seems to have collapsed because of internal mismanagement. The Desmond branch went first. All this baloney about the People's Republic. They should turn Spain over to a Swiss bank, hire some German engineers, some French chefs and get an American sales force on. These people have no business sense! Foreclose! Go into bankruptcy and start all over. Constitution written up by grad students from the Wharton School. These people can't even keep names straight!

What the hell good is there in having a sun tomorrow if we're all going to die in the darkness? What good is there is getting hurt for the truth when everyone has lied so much already? What kind of crusade is this, when two gangs of strangers hide in ditches and blow each other to bloody pulp?

All I really want is a whole skin and her with me. I was born lucky. Rich and lucky. I never had to really want anything before. Just reach out my hand. Sign a check for it. Now, I'm overdrawn. Doesn't do any good to make a little noise, say it was a mistake. I just want my pretty little girl with me. Listen, for God's sake, I have a right. She's my wife! She's mine, not yours! We don't belong to you. Leave us alone! Or help us. One goddamned thing or the other. That's the trouble with socialism. Nobody owns anything, but all the people belong to the state. Telegram to FDR when we get back. Write a letter to Eleanor. Something for her to get those big buck teeth into . . . Either that or send in the Marine Corps!

The candle guttered, and the bottle was empty. He could feel cold tear around his heart and in his belly, like slush. He had done something he could not undo, made promises he could not break. When the leave was up, he would go back to Aragón, the cow-barn hangars, the frozen landing strip, bad food and no spare parts. Seven aircraft, fourteen pilots and ten ground crew. All Spanish now. No one to talk to. Old Tom Coltringham dead, too, like the others. He never married that girl with the braids. What was her name? Naomi.

The others had been killed by accident. Harry, Peter, Saulnier. Even Dorlov. Accident. Mistake. Bad luck. But not Kopa. There was something fishy there. Kopa lived . . . deliberately, that was it, protected by some kind of secret plan hidden behind his blue faraway eyes. How much it must have hurt him to live that way! He must have died so. Deliberately. Let himself be killed. Jesus God . . .

All of Spain, its mad people and its bad gods, lay groaning in an icy midnight, trembled to the low thunder of crude gears and iron wheels. The dark winds blew the blossoms into brown, ruined bits and the dry blades of olive leaves whirled away. Blood and wine daggered frozen down the broken, smoke-struck walls.

Come to bed, Carmen, come to bed . . .

All day long they reminded Carmen of two dogs in a village square. They stalked around each other slowly, quill-necked and gurgling, eyes narrowed and tongues sliding over long teeth, all waiting muscles, ready to pounce.

They washed and shaved at dawn, tried to out-fast each other at breakfast. The beet-sugar bowl and jam pot slid back and forth across the table like counters in a backgammon game, and they exchanged politenesses as though arranging for a duel. When one of them walked into a room, the other walked out, not merely leaving, but *making an exit*. The exchange of a newspaper involved the formality of negotiations with the Vatican. They made her so nervous she wanted to scream at them, and instead drank too much wine at lunch and came to her senses only when she heard herself suggesting that Frank give Paco lessons in English so they could learn to be even better friends. She thought she could hear their molars grate as they smiled, and so decided that it would be necessary to go riding.

She nearly fell asleep on the bed when she went up to change into riding pants and boots. The candle on the table had melted into a white puddle. What that reminded her of added the sweet itch of desire to the sleepy melancholy of a wine hangover. She wandered downstairs dull-headed and distracted. They had gone out to the stables, and she dove after them into the hard winter sunlight. The wind, cold and shocking, slipped beneath her sheepskin jacket and pinched her nipples thick. She huddled in a sunny patch of shelter behind a shed and watched the soldiers bring out the horses.

The stallion slammed the stall door to splintered slabs of rusty kindling and churned out of the barn like a dancing dragon, a great, shiny, big-rumped body with a neck and head like muscled velvet, a streaming mane, eyes brilliant with excited malice and nostrils flared and pulsing stiff with blood. He reared and showed his huge, crimson, pointed thing flailing like a torpedo glistening up from a foamy sheath and double-bulbed scrotum. She turned away and closed her eyes, her legs weak. Whistling hoofs cut into the hard turf like hatchets, and when she dared to look again, Frank slipped aside as the long, beautiful head snaked out and down at him and white teeth bit the air like blades. Frank's hand moved so fast she could not see him catch the bridle and clash the glittering bit and chains into the soft, frothy lips. The stallion reared and struck again where Frank had just been. He slipped around the stallion like a stocky wraith while the soldiers shouted *ole, ole!* The horse snatched once at the double reins that tethered him, shivered violently, and bent to crop softly at the brittle threads of frosted grass. Frank snapped his fingers.

"Will a comrade bring the blanket and the saddle?"

They sidled off, watching, wide-eyed, as Frank stroked the stallion's nose. Paco nodded and ordered out the two geldings. They were nervous from the train, the unloading and the strange barn, but quieted in the few minutes it took for Frank to saddle the stallion. Then the soldiers came to help Carmen mount.

They were hard-faced and stubbled up to their hot, dark eyes, lean and bony in worn-out uniforms and torn boots. Their quick, frantic hands were everywhere on her hips, her thighs and between, before her boots were in the stirrups and Paco shouted them away, pale with fury. He rode the other gelding at them, scattering them along the wall. They vaulted over it, laughing wildly and running out to the gate. She rode out slowly through gusts of whispered obscenities and lecherous groans. Paco followed behind, and she heard a whip hiss before the gate boomed shut on the wind.

The day was hard, pure Spanish winter, rich and punishing, the earth like fettled iron, the sun small, tantalizing, and cruel. The wind punched and ruffled, pouring around her face and wrists like liquid sapphire. Every breath ached in over her burning lips and smoked out in soft frost conjured off to nothing. They could not hold the horses back to a trot and let them run in a wild, blasting gallop beneath the long rows of twisted olive trees.

They slowed to a soft canter through the winter-flattened fields of uncut hay, an easy heaving stride, powerful and disturbing, down the wind with the long Arabian manes flying like banners of shredded silk. The golden matted and tussocked earth sprang with wild hares and rocketing spill-tailed pheasants.

The huge stallion swung around them, every white gush of breath streaming above the supple leg-pistons stroking the sun-licked earth, the bright crescents of steel ringing on the rimed pebbles, the long tail pennoning in rhythm to the surge and creak of stiff leather and the froth-smeared clushing of bit and ring and chain. The earth tilted as they swung away and back. Frank dropped the reins and set his hands on his hips, kneeing the stallion in a soft-lunging canter, weaving down a stand of young fruit trees like a skier down a slope, around in a long circle and back again through the trees so close his shoulders brushed sparkling tubes of ice from the sagging boughs, trailing a comet's-path of sailing, shattered diamond bits. The stallion and rider boomed directly at her, surging bigger, swelling like a dream. She snatched at her reins and closed her eyes as the bulk of them thrust the wind aside and spilled a breath of scummy-lather sweat, a tepid buffet of slick flesh, a shocking instant before the wind struck it away from her greedy lips.

She turned, twisting her hips to watch, and felt the saddle ridge between her thighs. She tilted her hips forward and down, pressing. The reined-in gelding walked her off at an angle. She clamped her knees tight, still looking back. The stallion thundered around. The gelding beneath her walked steadily, and she slid and squirmed, her boots lifting from the stirrups, the saddle ridge humped and delicious.

The high stone wall ran across the west and melted, a golden gap beneath the burning sun. The stallion floated, trying to break free of the frost-locked earth, spinning back a bronze ribbon of shadow across the ragged field. Every silent stride stroked her like a tongue. The blood burned in her face, and the breath hissed in little clouds between her clenched teeth. It was beginning to happen, as the dark streaming form neared the wall. The rider crumpled forward as the vaulting shoulders and taut neck came up in a black pushing arch and slid across the sky, sailing free, falling in a dazy little torment of sliding time held between fluttering, sun-struck lids, sinking dark and strong and molten, long, sweet, space-dwindled, diminishing giddy surges, and slowly it was gone.

Carmen leaned forward, crying aloud, until her teeth clenched in the long, harsh hair of the gelding's streaming, wind-chilled mane. She, too, had melted in that instant across the sun. She was a sweet syrup from the nipples to the knees. She started to slide off and pushed herself up, laughing and shuddering and fumbling with the reins and swinging stirrups.

"Sweet God," she whispered, a giggle breaking past the single strand of mane hair caught in her teeth, "Now I know why Papa said a lady never rides any way but sidesaddle!"

She brought the gelding back beneath the orchard trees, stripped dripping necklaces of ice from the branches and crushed them to her hot cheeks and brow. Her heat faded to languor, and her boots now felt like lead.

"Are you all right?" a voice shouted clubbing at her sleepy joy. She looked up, shielding her eyes. It was Paco, looking worried.

"Lost your irons for a minute there, eh?"

"Yes," she said, "I did."

She rode away from him, slightly shocked at her own smugness. How she hugged the secret moment and how she longed to blurt into his proud, so-sure face what she had helped happen. How stupid men were, so selfish and so *vulnerable!* I could do it again right in front of him and he'd just think I had a muscle-cramp. The thought delighted her, and she cantered away to meet Frank, to twitch the same furtive easy little lust under his blue, blind eyes. Paco shouted after her.

"Hey, he's some *caballero*, your man, eh?"

She let a laugh of pure and wicked joy peal into the rushing, pure blue wind. She had never felt so weak, so free, so empty and so filled. She could not bear it, and began to sing at the top of her lungs.

She found the stallion and the rider in the field beyond the wall, the horse stamping and sidling away from its own sworled shadow. Francisco's face was bright pink, and sweat drops frosted in his pale brows. The stallion breathed like a forge bellows, great nostril-tearing houghs of steam that washed around the heaving chest where the farthingale strap rubbed away drops of thick, white lather.

"What an animal!" Francisco shouted. "Did you see him take that wall? I thought he'd never come back to the ground!"

She nodded. It was hard to tell who was happier, Francisco or the horse. A hot lump was in her throat.

"Did you have fun, *querida?*"

She had to turn her face away from them.

"Yes," she manged to say. "A little . . ."

They rode ten kilometers and came back to the *finca* at twilight. The soldiers were waiting for them.

"Get the mess crew," Paco ordered, "and keep the rest of the men out of the stables. Have you collected the wood?"

"Yes, the fire is already burning."

Paco nodded, turned, and walked stiffly into the barn. His legs were not used to riding. In the barn it was dim, and the breathing of the horses shot clouds of steam over the high doors of the stalls. Carmen and the American were waiting near a pile of burlap sacks.

"We should rub them down and put blankets on them," Carmen said.

"In a minute," Paco said, and took his pistol from the holster on his thigh. They both stood watching him. The horses stamped and steamed. Paco held the Luger by the barrel out to Frank.

He took the pistol and stood with it in his hand.

"Which one will you shoot?" Paco said. "The men are waiting."

"Shoot?" Frank said. "What for?"

"To eat," Paco said. "We did not bring them here for amusement."

Carmen turned away. Paco caught her by the arm and held her.

"Don't go," he said. "Not yet."

Frank hesitated, as though he did not quite understand.

"Pick one of the horses and shoot it," Paco said. "We must feed our-selves. The men cannot live on potato bread and wine in this weather."

The American looked at him, then at Carmen, then at the horses. Paco leaned against the wall, his fingers ready to take the pistol back. He was certain the American would refuse. Any man who rode so well would not kill a horse. Americans were sentimental.

The sound of the shot was deafening, and the dim air stank for an instant. In one of the stalls, a horse staggered. The walls and uprights creaked and shivered from the great, slow crumple to the floor. Dry bits of old straw floated up in the gloom. Carmen had both hands to her ears, her eyes shut. The American walked back, his face without ex-pression and held out the pistol.

"*Finito*," he said. "Now we eat."

Paco took the pistol.

"Which one?" he said.

"The stallion."

"Ah," Paco said, putting the pistol in the holster. "So no one *else* can ride him, eh?"

"No," Frank said in a flat voice. "A stallion suffers if he has no mare to serve."

Carmen dropped her hands to her sides. Her mouth opened and she wailed and shook her head.

"But he was so beautiful! He was magnificent!"

She looked at Paco, then at Frank.

"What dirty brutes you are!" she said, her voice shaking with anger. "*Both* of you! I *hate* you! You didn't have to do that. The fields are filled with hay! We saw the rabbits and the pheasants!"

"*Qué va*, rabbits," Paco said. He did not understand why she was angry.

"You have the habit now!" she shouted at them. "You *like* to do it! Does it make you happy? Yes, yes, it *does!*"

"Listen, Carmen," Frank said, reaching out to touch her.

"Leave me alone!" she said furiously. "Go ahead with your game! Shoot the other two! Then you can start on the people!"

She ran out of the stable. Frank glanced at the stall and put his fists in his pockets. He looked guilty for a moment, then kicked the moldy straw and shrugged. He walked away.

The men had gathered in, because of the sound of the shot. They pushed into the stables, but against the walls, making a path for the American.

"*Coño*, do you see? With a pistol he killed the big one!"

"*Por qué no?* He dominates to the end! It is his *right!*"

"*Qué hombre!* Rides like a *rejoneador!*"

"*Qué caballero,* eh? What he does, he does! *Pam!*"

They jostled around the stall, peering over the door at the dead horse, talking and gesturing. Others out in the yard brought their fists to salute as the American walked between them. The last rays of the sun made long dark shadows on the earth.

"Get rope and some knives," Paco said. "Let us eat tonight, not tomorrow."

The men murmured and shifted around. Some of them trailed after the American. Others stood in little groups talking, pointing their fingers and saying *Pam!*

"Are you all deaf?" Paco shouted. "Butcher this beast and talk about it later!"

Paco left the stable, slammed the door, and stalked across the frozen earth. The American had cheated. Americans should behave as Americans, always. Not to do so was dishonest. Paco swore in the dusk. He knew that if the American had handed back the pistol that he himself would have shot one of the geldings. He could never have killed such a magnificent horse as the stallion of the Conde de Gualvidal.

"*Cabo!*"

"Right here."

"Get out the automobile. Pack my clothing. At once. I am going to Madrid!"

Four days later, three Matford trucks arrived, loaded with snow-crusted crates and boxes. Paul Voget rode in the cab of the first truck. He stood in the wind, his shoulders hunched under a heavy greatcoat, a dead cigarette plastered to his lower lip, watching the Guardias unload the boxes.

"Equipment for the ski," he said. "The French border is open. How long, no one knows. I told them I was planning to open a lodge in the Sierra Gredos."

"What's really inside?" Frank said.

"Equipment for the ski," Voget said. "Paco requisitioned jackets with hoods, waterproof pants, gloves, and boots. Even goggles. For the ski. I had to go to Stockholm and Oslo. Too many spies in Switzerland. Where is Paco?"

"In Madrid."

"Ah. And you are in command here?"

"*Comme çi comme ça.*"

"Your wife? Carmen?"

"Inside."

"She is not well? This weather. I have a chill on the liver, I am certain."

"Where is Paco going to ski?"

"I imagine that is being decided in Madrid. I have gifts for Réveillon. Christmas, no? Coffee, chocolate, tobacco, *foie gras*, Camembert."

"You are an *entrepreneur*, comrade. Better be careful!"

"It's not that so much," Voget said. "There has been an embarrassment at Albacete. Let us be candid. A large sum of money was embezzled. A scandal. The SIM is investigating."

"SIM?"

"Servicio de Investigación Militar."

"Oh-oh."

"Exactly. *Oh-oh*. They investigate everything. Everyone. Me. You."

"Why me?"

"The Republic has agreed to the proposal to withdraw volunteer troops," Voget said.

"We heard that. I suppose it's my passport. Again."

"Let us go inside. Out of the wind. Voices carry. Some of these men may understand French. One or two may be with the SIM. Who knows?"

They sat on chairs before the fire in the big front room.

"The tobacco is welcome," Frank said. "We have been smoking the leaves of hazelnut trees. Why is the SIM investigating me?"

Voget looked at the fire and wriggled his toes. He spoke without turning his head.

"Let us say that a certain officer, not a Spaniard, has made certain inquiries, before any announcements had been made about the withdrawal of volunteers, certain inquiries about money. About changing money of the Republic for Nationalist pesetas. And word of this reached the SIM. Suppose, too, that the SIM had this officer under scrutiny, because of his background, his lack of proletarian political convictions. Discount his admirable military record, his decoration, his promotions to positions of responsibility. Suppose that very recently this officer has submitted pay vouchers for others who no longer were living. Pay for dead men, in short. Suppose finally, that this officer is married to a Spanish woman regarded by the government as a heroine, an example for Spanish youth. Suppose this officer is a citizen of the Republic. Don't you think that officials at SIM would be wondering exactly what this officer planned to do?"

"Look, Voget . . ."

"No," Voget said. "I don't look. That's not my job, my responsibility. But I am entrusted by Madrid and the Party to carry orders."

He reached under his greatcoat and drew out an envelope. He passed it to Frank and sighed.

"You are to report back to your squadron in Aragón. Your wife is transferred to the International's hospital at Valencia."

"When?"

"You know how transport is. The sooner you leave, the sooner you'll get where you should be. The pay vouchers will be honored. You will need the money to bribe those in charge of spare parts in Barcelona. That is understood. But I would not play at being the Banco España, if I were you."

"Are you going back to France, Voget?"

"If the border is open still, and I am so ordered."

"Take her with you. Take Carmen to France."

Voget straightened and shook his gray head. He touched the envelope. "She has her orders. Someone from SIM is already in the hospital in Valencia, waiting to make sure she gets there. Besides, I do not take people *out* of Spain. No, my friend. I bring people *in*. I bring in equipment for the ski. Perhaps if it were a delicacy of health, but that would require all sorts of *permisos*, doctor's examinations and all that. Well, I must go to Madrid. Tonight we will celebrate our Réveillon, eh? I have some champagne!"

Despite the *pâté* and the wine, the cheese and tobacco and dance music playing over the radio, Réveillon was not a fête, but a failure. Paco had promised to return from Madrid in time, but his empty plate glared at them throughout the slow progress of the meal. Frank, the American pilot, spoke good French, better than Voget remembered and they talked of the war and Non-Intervention and Paris, forgetting that they excluded Carmen. Before the soup plates were removed by a one-legged waiter, she had given up pretending to understand. She smoked the dark Algerian *tabac* and fiddled with the radio knobs. Voget tried to be polite and festive, but the effort exhausted him. When the roast meat was served, Carmen pushed her dish away. They drank champagne, but made no toasts, and the wine gave them very little pleasure.

They had cheese and quince-paste and coffee. Frank took the wheel of cheese, the soft fibrous orange block of sweet paste and a knife. He left the room, muttering about sharing the treat with the Guardias. Voget sighed and lit a cigarette. Carmen waited until the sound of boots on the bare floor faded.

"You did see him today?" she asked in Spanish.

"Paco? At the Ministry of War. He promised he would be here, but . . ."

"I know. Things happen."

"Exactly," Voget said, rousing himself with an effort. "And what has happened here? Perhaps you would tell me? The Guardias behave as though your husband were their commandant. Ever since I arrived I have noticed that they follow him around, wait for his orders, as though he had been elected commissar. Now he takes them cheese and quince-paste."

"A foolishness about a horse," Carmen said vaguely. "Nothing, really."

"Nothing? Enough to make Paco stay away. I knew when he told me, that he would not be here. He has never lied to me, even for the sake of politeness. I don't like it. It's bad for . . ."

"Discipline," she said, shrugging. "I said it was foolishness."

"I don't want anything to happen to Paco," Voget said coldly.

"And you have sent us both away. Francisco and me."

"He showed you the orders?" Voget said. "Then you know they were written *before* I came here, not afterward. You have importance, *señora*. And responsible work to do. Your husband the same. You are both needed by the Republic."

"I know, I know," she answered, blowing smoke at the candle flames. Her long dark lashes fluttered as she squinted and stubbed out her cigarette. She waved her hand, picked up her glass and drank. She seemed a little tipsy to Voget.

"It was so nice here . . . for a little while," she said.

"Eh bien," Voget agreed, yawning. "That is how we measure time. A little while."

"When do you go back to France?"

"As you say. In a little while. Perhaps. Never, perhaps. Who knows?"

"If you go," she said, hesitated, shook a cigarette out and lit it. "When you go . . ."

"Yes?" Voget said, anticipating the rest of her sentence.

"Could you take someone with you?"

"Who? Negrín? *La Pasionaria?* A truckload of orphans?"

"My husband."

"Impossible," Voget said. He watched the girl across the table from him closely. She had marvelous, absolutely murderous dark eyes, slanted so that every glance was suggestive. She raised her glass, and her soft pink lips formed a kiss at the brim. She glanced at him. She wants something, Voget decided, and so she is acting now. This is not sincere.

"I found out something," she said darkly. "Proof that he is not well. Abnormal."

"He's an American," Voget said. "They all seem abnormal. Perhaps they are. I have never known many."

"He told me that he has submitted the pay vouchers of pilots in his squadron. Dead men."

"Oh," Voget said, relaxing now. "Everyone does that. An old Army trick."

"But that's not *like* him. It's not legal. You say everyone does it. Perhaps. But not Francisco. He would never do anything dishonest. You should hear him, how he talks about obeying rules."

"It is hard to live long in Spain without becoming a little bit Spanish," Voget said. "When in Rome, you know. He has learned how to live in this war."

"But he would never break the rules!"

"All is fair in war . . . and love," Voget said. He waited. Several minutes passed. She looked at him, a slow tilted stare.

"Take him with you," she said. "Please. As a favor to me."

Voget shrugged and looked away. It took courage on the American's part to marry a girl with eyes like that. He felt suddenly old and flustered and weary. She changed stations on the radio.

"Do you dance?"

"No."

"Will you take some cognac?"

"No, *gracias*. It will just make me drunk."

She lifted her shoulders in a quick, pretty shrug, smiled slyly and unfastened the top button of her sweater.

"It's rather warm in here, no?"

"I feel quite cool," Voget said. Her finger traced down the dusky, glowing skin and slid another button free. Voget looked away.

"You could hear the radio more clearly if you came over here," she said.

"I'm not really listening."

"Do you like me, Voget?"

"Yes. Of course. You are a good comrade."

"I don't mean that way. Your room is at the end of the hall, no?"

"True."

"I . . . I could come to you, Voget," she said, her voice trembling. "Tonight. Would you like that? Later tonight?"

"I did not hear you say that, Carmen," he said.

"Then I will repeat it. Would you like me to come to you tonight?"

"Look," Voget said, more angrily than he intended. "Listen to me. I am very fond of you. You are young and very pretty and I have always adored Spanish women. You are also the age of my daughter. If I had a daughter. Thank God, I don't. If you try anything tonight I'll kick your behind, understand?"

"You . . ."

"Listen. Your Francisco loves you. Don't you know that?"

"Yes . . ."

"When he sits so . . . and you sit there . . . Why, to walk between you is like swimming through soup. The very air is thick. I can feel it. Everyone can. And you love him, too, no?"

"Oh yes! Yes!" she said. "All right. You won't tell him, Voget? Please . . ."

"I will say nothing. Forget it. That's that."

"But I want him out of Spain," she said doggedly. "You could take him to France. You *know* you could. He could get back to America. Then, after the war . . ."

"You see?" Voget said. "It makes you cry. Here. My handkerchief. Stop that, for the love of God! You won't get what you want by crying."

"You won't help me?" she said, and suddenly snorted into his handkerchief.

"What you suggest would not help. I have no wish to be shot by your husband or beaten with fists or whatever it is jealous American husbands do. Besides, I have already spoken with him of this."

She froze, staring at him over the crushed handkerchief. A tear trembled on the long lashes of her left eye.

"He wants to leave Spain. I knew it. I said so."

"No, Carmen," Voget said. "He asked me to take *you* out."

"He did? *Me?* To France?"

"Of course I refused!" Voget said. "What do you people take me for? The chief conductor on the Sud Expreso?"

She nodded and gave him back his handkerchief, then scrubbed her nose with her knuckles like a street waif. Voget grinned at her and shook his head.

"Ah!" she said triumphantly. "You refused because you are a man of principles and a good Communist!"

"I have spent the last months concealing the fact that I am neither," Voget said gloomily. "It is impossible, that's all!"

"You don't have to shout," she said primly. "And you said you didn't want me, that's good enough. Perhaps it would not be healthy anyway. A man of your age, I mean . . ."

"*Aaaaarh!*"

Voget got up and limped over to the fireplace. His left leg had gone to sleep, and his flesh prickled to a thousand, tiny, hot needles. He humped his shoulders, insulted. The cigarette stuck to his lip bobbed down and spilled ashes on his jacket.

"Another thing that's not reasonable and that's this foolishness of horses. From Paco, too. Of all people! It just goes to show. You can never tell."

"About *what?*"

"I am not *that old*," Voget said. "Ask the girls at Chicote's. Paco is certain it was Kopa. Absolutely positive. It is dogma. A matter of faith. You can never tell."

"Kopa?" Carmen said. "The German? But he is *dead*."

"Of course he's dead!" Voget snapped. "That's the whole point!"

"I don't understand," Carmen said, and buttoned up her sweater.

"I don't either," Voget admitted. "It happened some time back. In the summer. August, I think he said. At a place called Pilarmadre. Have you heard him speak of it?"

"Of Pilarmadre? Yes. A village near . . . oh, Belchité and Quinto, no? The offensive was there. But the foolishness about the horse was . . ."

"Real?" Voget said and shrugged. "I refuse to accept superstitions as the truth."

"Every good Communist is an atheist," Carmen said. "Go on."

"This horse appeared. At the end of a battle for three days or so. The Guardias saw it. Some of them. Or claim to have seen it. You look puzzled."

"Well, of course they saw it. We *all* saw it."

"Eh? Well, Paco admits that *he* did not see this horse. Nor the rider. The men, the Guardias believe that the rider was . . . was Death. Now, you're laughing. Why?"

"Such foolishness," she said, and laughed again. "Men . . . you are such babies."

"Perhaps," Voget said. "Anyway, Paco says he thought nothing of it at the time. However, now that he knows what happened in Barcelona, he has convinced himself that the man on the horse was . . ."

"Kopa."

"You are clairvoyant! Exactly! Kopa, on a horse, was looking for him. For Paco. A spirit. Or demon. Something. The men shot it. Then it went away."

"Oh no," Carmen said. "No. Francisco shot it. Out in the barn."

"What?"

"That's what really happened," she went on. "We had it for dinner tonight. It was the *way* it happened. I couldn't eat it. That's what really happened."

"My God," Voget said. "Who cares what happened or didn't *happen?* It's all crazy anyway. I want to know what it all *means!*"

"I don't know," Carmen said. "I don't know *anything* any more! I know what I want, and you say it's impossible. So, to hell with it! Have a drink, comrade. You look like . . . I don't know what either. We'll stay here in Spain, Voget. We'll report where they want us to. What else can we do?"

"He is seeing things that are not really there," Voget said.

"So is everyone. Everyone. Me. You. Blum. Mussolini. Hitler. Even Franco."

Voget placed his hand on his belly and bowed formally.

"That's very true. I take back all I ever said about women and politics. You should be a government adviser. That's it, advise Paco."

"No one has been able to tell Paco anything since the night he saw them shoot his father. You think you gained a good recruit for the Party when you took him off to Russia. He has told me. He gives you no more than he feels like. He *takes,* Voget."

"I know it," Voget said. "I am not a child. I don't understand this. I ask you to help me, no . . . to help him. You *must* help him, Carmen."

"How can I?" she said, shaking her head. "He doesn't even like me."

"Like you?" Voget shouted. "My God, Carmen, Paco is in *love* with you!"

Carmen shook her head.

"I . . . I want to go away from this place . . . It was a mistake to come here . . . Pavito was right . . . He was right . . . A leave is to forget . . . We should have gone to Madrid . . . We could have been . . . dignified and normal . . . We should have gone to Madrid . . ."

"That's everybody's solution for everything!" Voget said furiously. "How do I know who I am? *I go to Madrid.* How do I know what I think? *I go to Madrid.* How do I get away from what I don't like? *I go to Madrid.* How do I run away from Madrid? I go there *first!* How will I know when this thing of a war is over? Either I can go to Madrid or I cannot go to Madrid. *Madrid, Madrid, Madrid!* . . . They never should have written that damned song! Madrid, the New Jerusalem . . ."

"You enjoy being cynical," Carmen said accusingly. "It's just because we're young and you're old and . . ."

Voget lunged away from the fireplace and crashed his fist on the table. The knives and forks sprang off the plates, and the wine jumped. Carmen gave a little cry and caught the glasses.

"I do my job!" Voget said, his voice thick with excitement. "I don't *enjoy* anything. Not any more. It's true . . . I *am* getting old. But I do what I must. And I say this war will not be decided in Madrid. Madrid was the beginning, not the end. Franco will let Madrid alone because if he wins, he must have the city to govern from. If he loses, then Madrid is nothing to him. Don't you people see? You're right here and you see nothing! Madrid was grand, fine, splendid. Madrid was everything. But that was *last* year! That is past. Now Madrid is unimportant. Really. It is to the east that this will be decided. In Aragón. In Catalonia. In Valencia. Barcelona. Everything moves now. East. *East!* That's why you two must go there. To stop them. Not out of Spain. Not to Madrid. No, no. Not now. If the war is to be won, the resistance must be made *there!*"

"*Resistir es vencer!*" Carmen quoted. "If we resist . . . but we're not going to win, are we? You *know*, Voget. Tell me the truth."

"Carmen . . ."

"We are *lost!* We, us, you and I and Paco and him and the men out in the barns and everywhere else in Spain! That's the truth, isn't it? The Republic is a nice dream. For a little while, as you said. That's really why you say things are impossible. That's why you agree that everyone is seeing things that aren't there. Because you know that it doesn't make any *difference!* That's the truth, isn't it, Voget? Nothing makes any difference, because it's *all over!* We lost everything back on the first days in July, so long, long ago. That's the truth. I *know* it!"

She glared across the table at him, angry but unafraid, challenging him, daring him to lie. She did not look like his daughter, the daughter he never had, not now. If he lied to her, she would spit in his face.

He leaned there, his weight supported on his knuckles, musing, listening to the echoes and seeing the phantoms of memory, a guitar pounding and crying, these empty tables ranked like a mess hall crowded with laughing, singing men in uniform, the dim walls screened with an orchard of almond blossoms, the smell of wine and happiness and perfume. Lost, long, long ago. A bride in a dress white as the blossoms. With a slight, painful jolt Voget realized that her wedding was the only one he had ever attended. There would be no more.

She was waiting, one hand flung forward on the cloth, her fingers loose around the stem of a wineglass. She breathed evenly, her nostrils flaring slightly, her dark eyes watching him. He opened his mouth and closed it. He shrugged. She nodded once, satisfied.

Footsteps sounded in the hall. Voget pushed himself erect and walked back to the fireplace. *Too bad*, he thought, over and over, *too bad, too bad* . . .

The American walked through the open door into the candlelight, spinning a bottle of champagne by the neck like an Indian club.

"I'm back, honey," he said in English and bent and kissed her dark curls. She closed her eyes. He tore the foil off the wired cork and scattered the tinsel like petals across the table. He thumbed the cork and it powed away and capered on the dark floor. Bubbles burst up and foamed down the neck of the bottle. He filled three glasses.

"*Camaradas*," he said in a strong voice that tried to push happiness into them. "It is Réveillon! Christmas Eve! *Noche Buena!* When we wake up in the morning it will be . . ."

"Tomorrow," Carmen said.

"Christmas. Papa Presents will have come and gone. *Père Noël.* Sandy Paws. Drink up. Give us a *bon mot*, Voget. Here, honey . . . Paul. Get your glasses. Ready? Go ahead."

Voget walked to the table and picked up his glass. The wine bubbled and hissed softly. He looked across the table. How *young* they were! The American had his hand on his wife's shoulder. They looked as if they were posing for a photograph. Voget felt feeble and useless. He had nothing to give them but words.

"*Salud*," he said gently, "*Salud, amor . . . y pesetas.* Health, love, and money."

BOOK TEN

Breakthrough to the Sea
March–April 1938

My dearest sister,

Your last letter finally reached me here in Seville. Now that the official ceremonies are over, I have the time to respond, before reporting to my new command on the Aragón front. Since this will reach you, if it does, by private messenger, I can say such things. How hard it is to write, knowing that every line will be scanned by a frowning censor with an ink-brush!

Instead of selling the remaining Asturian mine-shares and taking a considerable loss, post them as security for Mother's expenses at the sanatorium and hope for the best. What you have heard is true; Franco has promised the Germans the bulk of the mined ore as repayment for the military supplies they have given us. But, after the war (a short time, God willing) the shares now almost worthless will have value again. If they object at the sanatorium, look down your pretty nose at them and beg them to remember that a pledge in honor by the house of Gualvidal, unlike stock-shares and currency, has never been known to fluctuate in value.

About refugees. That they seek you out is God's will. That you take them in is God's work to be done with joy. But joy need not be folly, and God's will is the preservation of all who trust in His holy name. A paupered house can help no man seeking charity. Have our advocate, Don Asilio, draw up five-year indentures, and have him date them prior to the Rising of last July. I mean July of 1936, of course. Take in no family who will not sign an indenture, and then be cautious, prudent. Take those who have a mule, a cow, a few sheep, a crate of chickens. Without domestic animals, you will continue to suffer every deprivation, simply dividing less food among more mouths. Close the tenant-cottages. Practicality before pride, my girl! Move all the people into the main house. You will save on light and heat, and all your refugees will submit more readily to your gracious control.

You say that you have seen the papers and find me handsome in the photographs. Remember that even you, my sister, see only the costume and cosmetics, the outside alone. I find it my burden (which I bear, if not in joy, then with a sense of duty) to be something of an actor, too. It has become revealed as part of my quest, my pilgrimage, to endure in stubborn silence (which others, not knowing, must interpret as pride) that which, if it had fallen on another would strike me, I know, as comic.

When I arrived at Zaragoza, I reported to staff headquarters and wrote a brief statement that "Pilarmadre suffered martyrdom again." I just dashed it down on the paper, intending no poeticism. I meant that the town had been taken and destroyed by the Reds. I never thought of the double meaning, a second martyrdom of *Santa* Pilar. A hasty line becomes a slogan.

Four days later, in the course of an interrogation at Intelligence, I discovered that I alone had escaped. I felt like one of the messengers come to Job, I assure you. Simply stated, the Reds, mostly Americans, had massacred every officer in the garrison. They took only some 300 prisoners, all enlisted men, out of more than two thousand. Nearly half of the village was burned. As the sole survivor of rank, I was prepared to suffer every indignity while never ceasing to thank the Blessed Virgin for preserving me. I expected, at the very least, to be stripped of my rank, demoted to a common soldier, denounced as a coward and all the rest. Instead, astonishingly, I am declared a hero! I can only believe this is God's will, part of the destiny He has chosen for me. I read that my *nemesis*, El Asturiano, with his band of butchers is hiding like a wolf in the mountains before Teruel. I will find him one day! My new command may make this possible.

The ceremony took place at Seville airport. A bright, clear day with very little wind. A large crowd, not merely of the military, but Falangist youth and their female auxiliary, and many civilians from the city.

I received my decoration for valor in company with a young . . . well, a little older than I am . . . a pilot of the German Luftwaffe. That's German for air force. He received what they call the Iron Cross. The highest award they give, I was told. His name is Schmidt. Kurt Schmidt.

Very handsome, and Luftwaffe uniforms are elegant. Dark green, with boots that glitter, a great deal of gold braid and swastika arm bands. The swastika is a gammadion or sort of Greek cross with extended arms clockwise, an old Christian symbol, of course, that struck me as very ugly. I was nervous.

I did not notice that Herr Schmidt seemed disturbed, by so much as a hair. Modesty is not a Luftwaffe virtue, it would seem. He behaved, throughout, like a man receiving a parcel from the post office, mysteriously delayed and long overdue. I tried to imitate his composure, but with no success.

There were two military bands, and that was amusing. Ours and theirs. Our band looked as you might expect, bull-ring musicians in uniforms that fit them poorly and suffering from too much wine and too small a repertoire.

The Luftwaffe band was a real military orchestra, twice as many members, instrumental virtuosi and a leader with a great tasseled baton nearly as tall as himself. Whenever our band began to tootle, the Luftwaffe symphony struck up the Horst Wessel song (some petty criminal the Nazis consider a saint). What a din, a cacophony!

The ceremony itself was, mercifully, quite brief. I was called forward from the ranks, the citation read, pinned, embraced and let go to creep back and hide as best I could. Franco was supposed to be present, but the Generalísimo was taken up with more serious matters on the Aragón front. I am glad he was absent. I can imagine how foolish we would have looked, since he is nearly two heads shorter than I am. He would have needed a ladder.

Schmidt followed me. Great concern here. Diplomatic conferences. The order of our presentation was decided, I believe, by the toss of a coin. The Germans were furious that their man lost and so prolonged the presentation with a display of massed banners, more music, motorcycles, and staff cars. The citation was read in German, mystifying everyone in our ranks. Stiff-armed salutes and "Deutschland, Deutschland, über alles." (Their state anthem. "Germany, Germany, over everybody." Pleasant thought, eh?) Then we all went in to lunch.

The decoration, as you obviously know now, I am forwarding to you. It should go in the glass case in the chapel, Concepción, with the others graciously bestowed upon our ancestors. If I am unworthy of the honor, it was the will of my superiors and God Almighty and so must be accepted in the spirit given, even if merit is lacking. Perhaps another case might be constructed to hold it alone. All the others were granted by royalty. Mine is, let us say, a secular gift, and of lesser value. Certainly Father would have been pleased by the award, but displeased by the donor. This is a real difference, a Christian difference, between a decoration conferred by a monarch and by a confederation of army officers.

The final irony, it seems, is my new command. Herr Schmidt was transferred from bombing aircraft to interceptors. He has the second highest number of "kills" and quite correctly hopes to help the Cause by destroying what remains of the Red air force. I have been transferred from infantry to . . . guess. You can't. The tanks. Some of the herd of Italians we have been plagued with have gone home, leaving their Fiat machines behind them. Our gratitude is twofold, therefore, but we are short of commanders. My superiors, after carefully noting my service with volunteer cavalry, retraining with light field pieces and infantry command posted me to command a squadron of these mechanical monsters.

Inside it is very cramped, deafeningly noisy and stinks of oil, gasoline and human bodies. I find it degrading and quite sympathize with the men of my squadron who despise the machines as being inhuman. Any Spaniard prefers to stand and fight, exposing his body with grace and courage to his enemies, rather than huddling inside a groaning beast that shields him with a steel skin. The tank removes the possibility of heroism. Also, they are by their size, much too good a target. The morale is very low at present, and since my superiors are convinced that the presence of the Conde de Gualvidal will somehow make service in the armored columns more acceptable, I have agreed to serve. From horses to horsepower. There is the modern world for you.

So. You must think of me rattling across Aragón toward the sea in my rolling sardine tin! I will think of you, far away in sweet Navarre, faithful to your inheritance, your people and your God. Let us pray for each other every day, my sister, sustained through our devotions to accept every task and blessing bestowed by a God Whose benevolence we cannot think to question. So long as Spain and Spaniards love The Father,

The Son and The Holy Spirit and pray to the Blessed Virgin and the Sacred Heart of Jesus the Christ, we shall be certain that our nation will be reunited at last and peace will descend on our bodies, minds and spirits. I kiss your little hands and send my love.

Your brother,
Pedro

The locomotive, far ahead, *wheep-wheeped,* and the long train slowed again. The couplings gnashed and ground, and the wheels shrieked, steel on steel. Schwartz braced himself, gripping the worn-smooth stretcher pole. The carriage jounced and lunged on through a series of switches. Schwartz could hear the heavy thuds behind him as the bulky casts were flung against the carriage sides. The men cursed in Spanish and English. Carmen and the other two nurses staggered toward the far end of the carriage, calling out to the men, telling them to hold on. The train slowed to a rackety crawl, the brakes gasping.

Schwartz was feverish and lightheaded. They had eaten only twice in three days, broth with barley and rice in it. He craned his neck forward like a turtle and breathed on the dirty pane of glass. All morning he had been building a patch of thick white frost with his breath. For three days now, he had been breathing and making frost in the mornings, then scraping it with his fingernails in the afternoons. The first day he had scratched his initials, some Party slogans and a heart pierced with an arrow. The second day, he had made a head of Mickey Mouse and a crude American flag with only fifteen stars. He had joked with the nurses about inventing a new form of proletarian art. He was planning his first major work, a commissioned portrait of The Patriot, who had promised him two pieces of Hershey bar if it came out well. He breathed, and watched the crystals fog white and crawl stiffly on the glass. The position was awkward, and he sagged back, shrunken, raw and chilled inside the rough shell of grimy plaster from his armpits to the hips. The cast extended in a hard tube down his left leg to the knee. Freezing air licked at his legs.

"Hey, Patriot," he said. "Fix the blanket, huh?"

The Spaniard on the next stretcher reached over and dragged the blanket back into place. He moved awkwardly, weak and top-heavy in gray plaster armor that shielded and supported his broken neck, collarbone and shoulder. His right arm was raised, frozen in permanent salute. With his good hand, he rammed the blanket down inside Schwartz's cast.

"*Camarada,*" he said wearily, "you steenk."

"Yeah," Schwartz said. "*Lo sé.* You steenk, too, *amigo.*"

"*Lo sé* . . . I know it," The Patriot said politely. He sat back on his stretcher and groaned.

The Spaniard stared at the little, useless iron stove in the corner. They had run out of wood and coal the first day from Madrid. A down-draft blew ashes out on the dirty wooden floor. The Patriot, his head thrust up and back by the plaster collar that rubbed his chin raw, gazed back down the car at the other men Schwartz could only hear.

Schwartz grunted cautiously. His bowels gurgled. He needed the bed-pan, but didn't want to ask for it. The train stopped, like a toy that had run down. One of the nurses came back. The Patriot said something to her. She shrugged, chafed her hands together, sat down, leaned against the cold stove and fell asleep, snoring, her mouth open. Her face disappeared behind puffs of vapor. She was old and fat, and no one liked her well enough to remember her name.

Schwartz lifted his sweater and pushed his hand down inside his cast. Cold air leaked in, and he shivered. On the ribs below his left nipple, the skin was peeling again, big, soft, rotten flakes that clotted beneath his long, ragged nails. He dug at himself, whimpering with pleasure. He was covered with sores that seeped and scabbed and itched. As long as it was light, he lay on his side and endured the torment of a dozen spots between his shoulder and along his spine that he could not reach. At night, he lay on his back and squirmed, grinding himself raw. When he fell asleep at last, he was pasted by blood and lymph to rotten gauze and soft plaster. When The Patriot heaved him awake on his side, all the places on his back tore open again and oozed, tickling dribbles that tormented him until he gibbered and tears twitched down his face.

"Hey, Schwartzie, where the hell are we?"

The voice startled him. It was Frankie Norton, a longshoreman from the Coast.

"Wait a sec."

Schwartz heaved himself forward again and frowned. His frost-patch was good-sized, a three-hour spread, big enough for The Patriot's picture, too big now for him to see over or around it. If he melted a big hole, it would take a long time to breathe it up again to the same thickness.

"Where the hell *are* we?" Norton bellowed. His whole face was covered with blotched mummy-wrappings, except for the dark, wet hole of his mouth. He was always asking where they were, what time it was, what the weather was like.

Schwartz pressed the heel of his hand against the gritty frost and held it there until the cold ached up to his wrist. He rubbed and looked out. He could see parallel steel tracks and snow swirled over some dark ties by the wind. He melted another spot as the first one glazed over.

He could see two uprights, wooden posts, and a narrow roof of rusty corrugated iron.

"I dunno," he said. "Somewhere. A railroad station. East Bronx? Jersey City, maybe."

It was a game they had played since leaving Madrid. The others took it up.

"Jackson Heights."

"Bullshit! Kansas City. Good old K.C."

"Only pimps and rotten old hoors come from K.C. We're in Omaha. I can smell the stockyards."

"That ain't the stockyards. It's Whitney. He crapped his pants again."

"Up yours, comrade . . ."

"It don't make any difference," Norton's voice said. "We ain't never gonna get there."

"Sure we will," Schwartz called, thinking about morale. "We'll be in Valencia at eleven-oh-five tomorra. Right on time."

Norton's voice was funny-sounding, muffled and guttural. His mouth had been torn by a mortar fragment and he'd lost some teeth.

"They're gonna unhitch the cars," Norton's voice said slowly. "That's what. They're gonna unhitch the cars. Right here."

There was a long, gray silence. Schwartz shivered from a chill. The Patriot sat there, blinking into the silence, his chin rammed up, holding his breath. Norton had said what they all feared.

Why not just unhitch them at a siding? They had all heard that such a thing had happened. Not by accident. They were all prisoned in heavy casts. Only The Patriot could move, could walk. Every time one of the nurses left the car, they were all frightened until she came back. Schwartz saw the sweat gleam in cold drops on The Patriot's thin, sallow face. He couldn't shake his head, but swung himself, ponderously, from side to side.

"No, no," he breathed. *No puede ser* . . . It can't be."

"No pway-day my asshole," Norton's voice gurgled. "Why'd we stop, if we ain't *got* anyplace? Huh? Huh?"

A chilled panic rustled from stretcher to stretcher.

"Look again, Normy, 'at's a kid!"

"Whadda ya see out there, Schwartzie?"

"Tell us what's *out* there, huh?"

"See somethin, *will* yuh? *See* somethin, fer Crissakes!"

He melted a third spot, as far to the right as he could reach. He looked. They waited, breathing heavily, plumes of vapor shooting up over the mounded blankets.

"Not really a station," Schwartz said slowly, loudly enough for them all to hear. "Posts up, you know, like usual, like a trolley stop back home. With an iron roof. It's snowing out."

"See any *people*, Norm? Anybody out there?"

"Nope," Schwartz said, falling back. "Nobody."

Schwartz lay still, cold and exhausted. His side was numb. He moved his foot, then his leg. The blood prickled and tingled. His leg had gone to sleep. The leap of panic in his chest died away. He was afraid of frostbite. They all were. Someone back in the center of the car coughed, a hard, wet, racking sound. Saliva sputted on the floor.

"Cut it out, you bastid!"

"I'm sorry, comrade. I was chokin."

"Swallow yer own goddam Fascist germs, pal!"

"Don't blow no lungers on our side, see?"

They all understood about pneumonia. Almost no one died of a wound. It was pneumonia that killed you, not Fascist bombs and bullets.

They did not move. The men plucked at their blankets and cursed the bitter, sulphurous air that leaked in beneath the loose windows. They strained to hear the slow pant and sniff of the locomotive and the waterfall roaring rattle of coal plunging down the chute into the tender. They lay, cased in stained plaster, wired and strutted, staring up at the ceiling, watching every breath smoke up and vanish. No one spoke.

Then Schwartz sensed it, a deep, distant vibration. The frosted pane shivered. He opened his eyes and held his breath. The carriage began to tremble.

"Normy!"

"Hey, what's up, Schwartz?"

"*Por Dios, camarada!*"

"Have another look-see, Yank! There's a chap!"

"Yeah, yeah," he said, and flung himself at the window, lapping his palms and pressing them against the frost. The spots slicked over as soon as he snatched his chilled hands away. There was no mistaking the slow, slugging beat that set the whole car quaking, but he had to see it for them all.

He wet his aching fingertips and rubbed. A black snout, a big, single, bitter-yellow lens, a rusty cow-catcher, shaped like a plow, then the bare, brilliant slick steel rod easing in and out of the drip and whiff cylinder and the dream-slow turning of the slabbed drive-wheels.

"A train! Another train going the other way. Back to Madrid!"

"No *shit!*"

The whole car stirred and murmured, awed and relieved. Nothing was going to happen to them with another train alongside. The news went from stretcher to stretcher. There were, then, other trains, different destinations. It took them a few minutes to comprehend it. The skeptics asked Carmen.

"*Claro*, it's a train!" she said, poking her curly hair back under her crumpled nurse's cap with small, deft, chapped fingers. She smiled around hopefully. The Patriot raised his good arm and clicked his tongue, pretending to take her picture. She shook her fist at him.

"Well, what did you expect," she demanded. "A submarine? Stay under the blankets, all of you. You will freeze. *Qué chicos!* What a bunch of kids. Lie still!"

She ran up the car, pushed The Patriot gently aside and leaned over Schwartz. His heart lurched as she knelt on the edge of his stretcher and her body, small and solid and healthy, brushed his.

"A locomotive," she called. "And many, many carriages. That's nice."

Schwartz had a hard-on. He tried to touch her.

"Don't go away," he begged.

She glanced down at him and pushed his hand away, sniffed and wrinkled her nose.

"You need a bath, comrade," she said. "When we get to Valencia, we'll throw you in the ocean."

"I can't swim," Schwartz said. He could. But she was still kneeling on his stretcher. The Patriot moved up behind her. She slid away from him and wiped her hands on her sheepskin jacket.

"The water isn't very deep," she said absently. "At least it wasn't before the war."

"Oh," Schwartz said, nodding until his neck ached. He loved her. She walked suddenly to the door at the end of the car and yanked it open. Snow whirled in on a blast of bitter wind, and the men shouted and cursed and whistled.

"You lucky bastid, Schwartz," someone said.

"Come sit with me, honey, and sharpen my bayonet," someone else said. Norton laughed, a deep, damp sound.

"You dirty guys!" Schwartz said, furious. "Shut up. Shut up."

"She's got the prettiest little can, that one."

"Cut it out. That ain't no way to talk. Be decent. Tell us about the train, Norman."

"Well," he said, scrubbing at the window, "Once upon a time there was a Little Engine That Could . . ."

"Named Carmen. She could, but *will* she?"

"And," Schwartz said, feeling his erection subside, "hey, whadda you know! It's a troop train. It's fulla soldiers!"

"For Madrid?"

The voices steamed up from the dirty plaster lumps, swirled and vanished above the blankets slung over wires and weights, a group howl:

"You'll . . . be . . . *sorr-eeeeee!*"

Schwartz listened to them laugh as he scraped and licked and rubbed until he had opened a smeared rectangle. He lay and looked, greedy and shivering and puzzled. The cars of the other train were sliding.

Or was their own train in motion again? He tried to sense movement, to feel it. Nothing. It was the other train, then. He heard Spanish voices, men shouting. He saw cars, another, another, then another. Figures in winter uniforms with caps and overcoats had lowered the windows and were leaning out, yelling. Schwartz watched them, weak with envy. They could stand up and move around, bend and straighten, pummel and shove each other. All of them! Lucky guys, lucky guys . . .

They were doing something queer. They held their left hands out, making loose fists and slipped their stiff middle fingers on their right hands in and out, quickly, grinning and shouting. Schwartz grunted, deciding that it was some sort of railroad signal. The door of the car smacked open and snow blew over him. Carmen shoved the door closed with her rear, snatched off her crumpled cap and dashed the snow from her hair.

"What pigs you men are!" she said angrily. "I can't even get down to ask for food and drink without . . . that's all you ever think of . . ."

"Hey!" Schwartz said, suddenly inspired. "*Camarada!* Open the window!"

The Patriot had to lift him up. Carmen watched, open-mouthed, then began to slap at both of them, talking so fast that Schwartz had no idea what she was saying. They clawed the catches loose, and The Patriot heaved Schwartz up until his arms hooked out over the top of the window, now halfway down. Fine snow sugared around him, and he stuck out his tongue to taste it. He sucked in air so cold and acrid that his throat and chest ached. The Patriot stumbled down between the stretchers like Boris Karloff in the movies, yanking down more windows. The other nurses ran after him, screaming.

"Stop that!"

"Opening the windows is forbidden!"

"You'll all die of pneumonia!"

The men yelled and whooped, urging The Patriot on in his clumsy, one-armed wrenchings with the warped window frames. Vapor shot out of his puckered lips.

"Who cares?"

"Atta baby, open em up!"

"It's springtime in the Rockies!"

Schwartz felt thin and weak, as though he were cold jelly, loose inside the heavy plaster shell that supported him. He waved his right fist and yelled at the faces he could see through the smoke and snow.

"*Viva la República!*"

They noticed him right away. They stared at him, nudged each other and pointed. They looked like Spaniards, all of them, some old, but mostly young and happy-looking. They shouted back to him. The wind tore through his thin woolen sweater and poured like ice water down his slick, scabby spine.

"Eh! Cuál brigada? ¿Cuál es tu brigada?"

"The fifteenth!" Schwartz shouted. "I mean . . . Quince Brigada!"

"Los Quinces? Verdad?"

"No puede ser," one with a beard said solemnly. "It can't be. The fifteenth is up at Teruel with our boys. He's been wounded. He must be crazy. Or kidding us."

"No estoy bromeando, ni loco!" Schwartz bellowed back. "Somos los inútiles de la Quince Brigada!"

The one with the beard looked dumfounded. Schwartz laughed, delighted at his own Spanish. He waved his clenched fist. The windows of the coaches in the troop train were now open as far as Schwartz could see, clotted with men in dark uniforms and tasseled forage caps, all waving, saluting, shouting, grinning and sliding their middle fingers in and out of their fists.

"Hey, did you hear that? They're all wounded over there. From the Fifteenth!"

"Salud, comrades! You want some tobacco?"

"Which battalion, chico?"

"The Lincoln battalion!" Schwartz said. "Hiya, buddies. Go get 'em for us! Viva Madrid!"

"Cómo?"

"Los Lincolns!"

"No puede ser," the one with the beard said thoughtfully. "The Lincolns are part of the Fifteenth, no? The Fifteenth is fighting with our boys at Teruel, no? Therefore, they are there and not here. He is a great liar, that one. Or a spy."

"Your mother! They are wounded, you donkey! Can't you see the cast on him? What do you think, he's a snow-man? Ole! Ole! Inglés!"

The other nurses had most of the windows back up. The men in the carriage were still shouting like lunatics, and the wind spewed loose sheets of snow onto the blankets and faces. Schwartz hung at the window. The weight of his cast dragged down, pulling his arms on the top of the window. He couldn't feel his arms and hands at all.

"It is absolutely against all the regulations," Carmen said, her face very close to Schwartz, her eyes wide with anger. She threw her arms around him and tugged.

"What will the doctors say? Have you all gone crazy? Stop it, at once!"

The sudden snug warmth of her was delicious. Every time she tugged, she fell back against him. Schwartz whooped, and when she came in again, cursing and half-laughing, he puckered up and tried to kiss her. The soldiers howled and whistled. Fingers rubbed frantically in fists. Schwartz was drunk on cold air and happiness.

"Oh, baby, you make my pecker stand!" he shouted. "Lookit!"

The wounded men shouted with laughter. Carmen shook him, puzzled.

"*Cómo?*"

She glanced down, *oh*ed and jumped away. Inside the carriage and across the tracks in the other train, men roared and shouted. Schwartz grinned at her, proud and delighted, watching the blood mount in her face as she blushed.

"*Qué espectáculo, tú!*" she stuttered, "Well . . . freeze, then! A gang of dirty . . . Pigs, that's what! Here, you crazy, put the blanket around you, at least! What a circus!"

"Hey, *inglés!* When you're through, send her over, eh?"

"*Ole! Ole!*"

"You dirty guys," Schwartz said, waving and grinning and trying to make his fingers close in a fist to salute.

"*Somos Americanos!*" he yelled.

"Hokay, *inglés!*"

"Good. Good *camarada, inglés!*"

"*Viva la Quince Brigada!*"

The windows of the troop train thrashed with dark arms raised in the clenched-fist salute. A jumbled roar of noise beat back and forth. The train crew and some officers dropped down in the snow and looked across. Schwartz saluted them. Now he saw that some of the men in the other train were crying and blowing kisses and saluting all at the same time. He hung there, panting and cold and dazed and deafened by the voices. He saw that big red stars had been painted on the sides of the troop-train cars. He tried to find out the brigade and battalion numbers of the men in the other train, but the Spaniards were making too much noise.

"*Están llorando,*" The Patriot said and turned to pantomime tears to the wounded on the stretchers. The laughter was shocked down to mutters.

"Yeah," Norton's guttural voice said. "Them yellow bastids is crying cause they're so goddamned scared to go up to the line!"

The car echoed with angry, smothered-sounding voices. Puffs of vapor hung over the ragged hole of Norton's swaddled face.

"Get up there and *fight*, you yellow pricks!" his voice croaked.

Schwartz turned half-around, balanced precariously, outraged. Carmen and The Patriot rushed to support him, both of them jabbering at him, trying to get him back down flat on the stretcher.

"They're not crying for their own tough luck, you dumb dope!" Schwartz said. "They're crying for *us* . . . for you and me because we're wounded. They feel sorry for *us*, for God's sake!"

The Patriot grunted and heaved him back into the open window. It felt as though he was standing under a cold shower. Snow blew down inside the heavy plaster shell. Suddenly, all at once, the Spanish troops in the other train started to sing. Maybe one of their officers had given them an order, maybe they just started. Hundreds of voices roared the song through the coal-stench and bitter wind that tore the steam from their moving lips.

> Los moros quieren pasar;
> Los moros quieren pasar;
> Los moros quieren pasar, Mamita mía,
> No pasa nadie!
> No pasa nadie!

Then, Carmen and The Patriot began to sing, and Schwartz joined them singing that the Moors wanted to pass, but, baby, nobody's going to pass! His throat felt hot and choked with emotion. The men in the packed troop train began to wave their clenched fists to the slow, swelling thunder of their song. Schwartz swung his arm, too, and tried to sing, but his voice kept choking and faltering. He moved his lips, whispering the words.

> Madrid, oh, bien resistes!
> Madrid, oh, bien resistes!
> Madrid, oh, bien resistes—
> Los bombardeos, los bombardeos!

"You hear that?" Schwartz shouted. "You hear those guys? Come on, you sons-a-bitches! Sing, sing! Viva la Quince Brigada!"

The men on the stretchers, caked in plaster, splints and struts, propped up on bed-sored elbows, ragged and bearded, began to sing, feebly at first, embarrassed, the voices little puffs of vapor, then stronger.

> Viva la Quince Brigada,
> Yum-buh-buh-bum-buh-buh-bum-bum-bum!

Across the snowy space, the Spaniards heard it, faltered into rhythm, and joined them.

> En el frente de Jarama . . .

Fists pounded a booming, stuttering chorus on the walls of carriages. Boots beat on the floor and clenched fists tossed and sank behind the whistling sweeps of snow.

> No tenemos camiones,
> Ni tanques, ni aviones!

The cry sounded back and forth between the two trains, shivering the windows.

Aiiii, Manuela!

The locomotives *wheep-wheep-wheeped,* and the hospital train, with a rippling clash of couplings, jerked ahead a dozen feet. Schwartz slid sideways, singing and saluting, and crashed against the window frame. A soft, pulpy snap like rotten wood happened deep down inside his cast. His head struck the window frame in the next instant, and his left arm went suddenly numb from the shoulder all the way to the hand. The carriage jolted, and he slid heavily the other way. A pink mist jigged and squirted across his vision as he lurched, stunned and helpless.

He caught the window and hung there for a second, while the snow-bits stung his hands and arm like wasps. The train was rolling now. So was the Spanish troop train. Carmen and The Patriot caught him. He fought them, and something pulped again, a spongy crumbling of his pelvis. Ten meters apart, the two trains slid past each other, the engine whistles wailing. Words and bits of sentences swirled at Schwartz through the sour smoke and stinging snow. Ice crinkled on his lids. Every breath burned his chest. He struggled like a drowning swimmer, caught in the thunderous surf of sound and motion.

"*Viva . . . Brigada . . . Proletarios del mundo . . . Resistir! . . . Luchamos . . . Salud, ingleses! . . . Muerte al Fascismo! . . . Victoria . . . Viva, Viva!*"

He let them pry his hand from the window. The pane crashed up and locked, and the icy wind stopped. He lay beneath their cuffing, caressing hands. He was chilled through, blue-lipped and chattering. Something was leaking softly, secretly, inside him. He smiled and shook his head. The whole car was filled with racket, a steady uproar, everyone talking, shouting, singing and crying. Carmen was scolding him and scuffing the sleeve of her sheepskin jacket across her eyes.

Something clicked in Schwartz like a spark at the base of his spine. He could feel nothing at all from the waist down. Carmen bent over him. Her hands snugged the blanket roughly around his shoulders. She held his head up and gave him something to drink from a tin cup. Cognac.

"*Qué loco, tú!*" she scolded calmly. "The idea. What got into you? The whole train is crazy. You are wounded. You can't do this sort of thing, yelling and singing. Lie down and go to sleep."

"I love you," he said. "Really. I don't even have a girl back home, either."

"Sure, baby," she said in English. "I love you, too. *Calma, chico, eh? Silencio . . .*"

"You hear that, Norton!" Schwartz howled. Suddenly, he was sweating, a clammy gush inside the chafing crust of plaster.

"You buncha stiffs," he said happily. "You old-time, sour-gut-rank-and-filers. You union goons and working-stiffs . . . 'bout time . . . you showed a little . . . solidarity . . ."

He could not sense his voice slurring off to a sloppy whisper. He saw Carmen's face. She was biting her lower lip.

The snow ticked against the window. Schwartz shivered and squirmed his shoulders inside the dank shell of his cast. The cognac glowed down in his empty belly and buzzed in his head. He felt numb and drowsy and completely happy.

He shivered and sweated, muttering and rocking to the sway and plunge of the carriage and the steady, light, even beat of the tripping, spinning wheels.

The troop train chuffed and skidded up the long, steep grades to the west where the wind bit between tumbled scarps of granite. The hospital train spilled down across the snowy plains to the seacoast where the waves rolled in on the soft, coarse sand. The engine whistles shrilled through the sooty dusk, and the yellow headlights probed the swirling snow. The driver-wheels thundered down the long, groaning rails cleated to the frozen earth.

Schwartz dozed and dreamed. He felt numb and weak, melting in the darkness. Fingers lifted his left eyelid and a bright point of light jigged before his dilated pupil.

By the time the hospital train reached Valencia, and the American doctors swarmed on board, Schwartz was unconscious, his lips shrunken, his tongue white and dry. His heart was fibrillating. The thread of mercury in the thermometer crept up to 105.2 degrees on the Fahrenheit scale. Two orderlies carried his stretcher behind a shuttered newspaper kiosk and set it down there. The orderlies went back to the crowded cars that smelled of pus and urine, and helped to carry the other stretchers to the waiting ambulances. They came back to the newspaper kiosk and squatted down by the stretcher and shared a cigarette. One of them stripped the paper and saved the dry bits of tobacco. The other flipped the blanket over the thin, cold face. The orderlies carried the stretcher through the crowded waiting room and ticket hall, down the steps to a THC truck waiting at the freight platform. There were three other stretchers, removed from other cars, already in the back of the truck. They dropped the stretcher and lifted the tailgate up and locked it. The last ambulance, loaded now, was waiting for them. The two orderlies strolled toward it, their hands in their pockets against the morning chill.

"What do they die of, those Americans?" the first orderly said.

"Enthusiasm," the other orderly said. "The French die of syphilis, the Americans of enthusiasm."

"What do Spaniards die of then?" the first orderly said.

"Hunger. Spaniards die of hunger."

They walked on. Behind them, the driver of the truck started the motors, shifted gears and let in the clutch. The truck rolled away from the freight platform. The ambulance pulled out in front of the truck. At the first intersection, the ambulance honked twice and turned right, into the street that ran to the hospital. The truck honked once and turned left, into the street that ran to the municipal cemetery.

Cold. Cold beyond jokes or curses. It was cold beyond experience or escape. The sky above them was a brutal plate of rotten ice slush-patched with clouds. Cold froze their feet and fingers, ear lobes and nostrils. Black, bitter nights denied sleep. By day, the men were numb-brained drunkards, chattering, wisp-breathed and swaying. A spare boot turned stiff like greasy zinc, and no bare hand could touch anything metal. The north wind whetted on the rough surface of the big, shallow valley and slashed through the scrub-growth and flailing weeds from the first gray of dawn to the exhausted, whimpering darkness. Then the food details risked the bright shock of flare shells, light artillery, and the whip and crackle of sniper fire. They brought up tin buckets of frozen malt-coffee and clumsy pails of mule stew, icy mush the men prodded apart with trench knives. They sucked ravenously on the chilly bits that stuck to their blue lips. The Lincoln battalion huddled, cramped and shivering, in rifle pits gouged by grenades. They squinted and winced at firing slots, narrow, wind-worn gaps in the rough parapets they heaped of crystallized, hunky earth. The temperature was zero all day, every day, and dropped to twenty below zero at night. The Spanish volunteers called the place Altas de Celades. The Americans called it "The North Pole."

For the first time the enemy was not an armed body of men, directed by a state of mind, but a force, a condition. They themselves had no shelter, just a loose string of pits blown in the frozen dirt, a scatter of shell craters without a system of connecting trenches. They had no wood, no paper, no matches, no weapons against this force that dulled and dumbed them. They had no way to resist the thing. The pits and holes were too shallow and too crowded to move around in. There was no way to make anything better or even bigger. Earth was brown ice that bent entrenching shovels and struck the picks from their stiff, feeble hands. And it was dangerous to dig.

Exercise made you sweat inside your two shirts, sweater, and over-coat. When you stopped, the soaked cloth froze solid. You got tired, saw faces, things that weren't really there. A sick, sad, delicious stupor filled you. You skidded slowly down the honeyed slide of sleep. Then, you finally stopped shivering. You were numb all over. You were happy at last. You were freezing to death.

They were shelled from dawn to darkness, a steady, senseless fall of artillery and mortars that chewed the sloping hills to pocky ridges of coffee-colored rubbish.

They had issue boots of leather. Their toes became white, cold crushy lumps of dead flesh. Every darkness, when the food details crawled down the dark slopes like swaddled dolls, two or three of the company staggered away with them down the rutted snow-packed road to the ruined village of Cuevas Labardes, a huddle of blackened, blasted buildings. There was an *auto-chir* there, the battalion mobile-hospital unit. There was an American nurse with an ether cone and an American doctor with a scalpel, who cut off toes to save a foot, part of an ear to save a face.

They had blankets shredded by the prongs of lumpy earth, woolen mittens and leather gloves stiff on their aching hands. They were swaddled to the eyes with scarves and knitted helmets, and their breathing frosted the raveled threads. They had plump, gray lice sucking in the armpits and crotch hair. Their eyelids leaked and froze, and they rubbed and picked off bits of skin. They crouched and squatted, huddled together like dirty parcels.

And then suddenly, they were ordered to move. East, closer to Teruel. After months of build-up, the Fascists were on the move, and there was trouble all along the line. The new positions were rocky hills overlooking narrow valleys. The best hills were manned by the British machine gunners and the Canadians. The Canadians fascinated Mahoney. They were a mixed bunch, with only one Canadian officer, and a couple of Spanish lieutenants. The rest of the officers were American, some of the men were, too, mixed with the "Canucks," Spanish volunteers, and a few members of the old Dimitrov battalion who had somehow managed to stay on with the brigade when the rest of the Slavs had been transferred. They called themselves the "Mac-Paps," from Mackenzie and Papineau, and had been trained, longer than any other group, long enough to hate Albacete and the Base Police. When they marched or built rifle positions they sang to the tune of "Popeye the Sailor Man."

> *My muscles all ripple,*
> *When I hit a cripple.*
> *I'm B.P. the fighting man.*

Whenever he could steal some cognac, Mahoney clambered over the stones to the "Mac-Pap" positions to join in their "turkey-shoots," long, risky sniping sessions at the Fascist lookouts. A Moor counted two points, a Legionario three, a Requeté five, because there weren't so many of them. They drank Mahoney's cognac and beat him at "turkey-shoots" and told him stories about hunting in Saskatchewan and Manitoba.

The "Mac-Paps" had been shot to pieces in their first action, an assault on a place called Fuentes. Before them, the George Washingtons had been wrecked, and before that there had been Jarama. But the Canadians seemed to forget Fuentes. They joked and horsed around and sang songs, their voices echoing off the cold tumbled masses of stone.

> "We are the fighting anti-Fascists
> Our rifles, bayonets, gleaming in the sun!
> We are the fighting anti-Fascists,
> And when we get back home once more,
> We'll do, we'll do the same thing there!"

The first line was boomed out by a lead singer, then the men sang the next line in response, the same for the next pair of lines, and they all sang the last one. The tune was Spanish, and Mahoney liked it nearly as well as the one about the Base Police. He sighted at the Fascist position, while one of the Canadians watched through field glasses. He squeezed the trigger, and the rifle butt slugged against his shoulder.

"That's a stupid fuckin song," he said. "That's a Eskimo song. Only blubber-eaters sing that kinda song. It don't even rhyme. I got him."

"Two points for Mahoney."

"Luck."

"The luck a the Irish," Mahoney said. "Pass the canteen."

When they were shifted in closer to Teruel, Mahoney helped evacuate the nuns, novices, and inmates of an insane asylum. The "Mac-Paps" accused him of feeling up the nuns. Mahoney sang the song about muscles that ripple.

The food was better, at least hot, but getting it to the lines was still dangerous. For every hilltop the brigade held, the Fascists had one like it. Mahoney used the trenches and kept his head down. He was twenty feet away when Phil Detro, the Lincoln's commander, refused to crawl through a trench cut across a road. Detro laughed and said something about trenches seven feet deep. He was nearly six-five. A sniper got him in the thigh halfway across. He died in the hospital.

Mahoney was "turkey-shooting" when the air battle started. He lay in the "Mac-Pap" trench, counting the planes. Less than thirty fighters up with red wings against a couple of hundred Fascist ships. After the bombing and strafing, the artillery opened up. Mahoney slid down the line from position to position. The Fascists came at them, not in skirmish teams, but in columns, marching with battle banners snapping in the cold, cloudy wind. Mahoney ran out of ammunition, and crouched,

open-mouthed as the columns flowed up the stony slopes. The British
Maxim guns opened up, slow, thrashing bursts with the belts jumping in
the breeches. The columns melted into dark, tumbled shapes. Mahoney
carried the story back to his company. The Limeys were the best gunners
in the brigade. The rumor went around that three of their headquarters
company had cut a full-scale cavalry charge to pieces. Three British
clerks with Maxim guns had stopped three or four squadrons of Moors.

That night, the dark sky burst and oozed scarlet and gold. Long silent
banners of blue and green flowed between the clouds. Rumors went
around that a Fascist ammo dump had been hit, that the Germans were
trying out their secret weapons, that Zaragoza was burning. The night sky
flamed and quivered, sank to black and flared up again. The Spanish
kids crossed themselves. The Americans huddled in the cold and stared
at the weird sky, awe-struck. Mahoney went off to talk to the "Mac-Paps."

"Gloriola Borrey-asses," he said. "That's Latin for Northern Lights.
Happens alla time up where them Canucks come from. You kin let
yer balls down outta yer bellies now, comrades. It ain't gonna hurt you."

"Ain't we lucky," they said. "Man alive, we're lucky! We got us a
comic-star from Bahstin, Mass. He goes to Harvard College. Din't you
know? Sure. He's gotta a degree from Harvard College. B.S., they call it."

White was in the little cold, cramped dugout they shared, big, dark
face scowling at some papers. His pink tongue licked his cracked lips.

"You get them guys up to reinforce next to the big rock, Jimmy?"

"Yeah. We got pinned down by mortars."

"Anybody hit?"

"Naw. Seen the Gloriola Borrey-asses?"

"Yeah. I don't go for that stuff. Makes me feel crawly."

"Go dance around under that Russian shower-truck. You was a sight
to see last week."

"I'd rather have bugs," White said. "Better bugs than one frozen
black ass, comrade. If I didn't know you were fightin', I'd turn you in,
I swear to God."

"I'm buildin solidarity," Mahoney said. "Whadda you sore about now?
You been talkin to Doran again?"

"He's been talkin at me," White said, writing something. "Bout you."

"Again?"

"Again. He don't like you, Baloney."

"He's a snotty shit. Some commissar. All this crap about political
lectures. Indoctrination. Steve never bothered with that."

"Steve was different. Doran's an intellectual."

"He's a phony. He ain't a workin'-man. I kin tell. An intellectual-phony.
He's gotta lousy memory, too. So busy givin lectures he forgets stuff."

"Like what?" White said.

"Like food and blankets and leave when it's due. The boys got a right to go into Teruel."

"They got a right to steal an ambulance? Try to desert?"

"Listen," Mahoney said. "We voted on that. No punishment. Give them guys another chance, right? Democratic. That Doran woulda had them guys shot! That's . . . that's . . . proto-Fascism!"

White dropped his pencil and looked at Mahoney, shielding his eyes against the candle-light. A faint smile lifted the corners of his wide mouth. "That's *what?*"

"You heard me. I know what it means, too!" Mahoney said sullenly, bending forward to light a cigarette at the candle. He blew the smoke in White's face. White grabbed the pack from Mahoney's pocket.

"Mahoney," he said. "You gotta make up your mind. Either join the Party and do your talkin on our side or shut up."

"The Mac-Paps don't have all this political bushwa stuff. Not since Joe Dallet got his. Him and Doran musta been intellectuals together. Nice and easy over there now."

"You maybe oughta ask Doran for a transfer, seein's you like the Canucks so much."

"Aw, shut up. I finally got them guys to teach me how come they shoot so good. Goat-huntin'."

"They hunt goats? Good for the Canucks."

"In the Rockies. Maybe it's sheep. Anyway, you gotta figure the wind."

"In this company it's the hot air you gotta figure. The Gloriola Borrey-asses."

"It's windage, you gahddamned dummy! Like it's blowing *so,* see? You shoot *into* the wind."

"Figures."

"I won the turkey-shoot today. Before it all started. I'll show the guys about windage tomorra."

"You do that. I'll put in the report that you been TDYed to the Mac-Paps today for sniping instruction. Just today. Not tomorra, get it?"

"Yeah. Awright. Them Canucks is awright. Treat you like a white man."

"You want me to bust your face, Jimmy?"

"Shit. I'm sorry. I fergit."

They stared at each other across the candle. A fire fight started down the line. They both listened. Some mortar rounds came in, but too far back. They smoked, listening. The shooting stopped. White sighed.

"Jesus, I'm tired. Just *tired,* you know?"

"We held em. All day we held em," Mahoney said. He nodded sleepily.

"That's what I'm sayin to Brigade. Today, yeah. What about tomorrow?"

"We'll hold em," Mahoney mumbled. "Turkey-shoot."

"Yeah."

"Who got killed?"

White looked at his sheets of paper, the casualty reports from all the companies in the battalion.

"Larry Kleidman. Pablo Carbonel, the Cuban fella from the MG Company. Carl Keller. Charley Ashley. Nels Fishelson. Matti Haukale."

"That Finn from Minney-soda?"

"Yep. Him and Johnny Field. Walt Swiderski . . . couple others."

"I heard a colored guy, comrade, I mean, got it, too. I thought it was you."

"You *never* gonna be that lucky, Mahoney. It was Lisberg."

"The skinny kid used to hang around here?"

"Yeah. He's dead, too. It's kids like that make me wish . . ."

"Wish what?" Mahoney said. "You stayed at home?"

"Maybe. Somethin like that. From time to time."

"Not me," Mahoney said.

"No?"

"I never had so much fun in alla my life."

"Some fun," White said and signed his name on the bottom of a sheet of paper. "Freeze your ass in sunny Spain."

"Tell it to Earl Browder. He's here now."

"Don't bull with me, Jimmy."

"He's here. Some guys in the Party with the Mac-Paps told me."

White rubbed his face and nodded. He smiled.

"Say! That's all right! You sure? Positive?"

"Soitenly," Mahoney said. "Earl Browder is in Spain. Now I suppose you're gonna go ga-ga like you did over Paul Robinson."

"Robeson. I didn't go ga-ga."

"Anybody who'd walk ten kilometers to listen to some guy sing on the radio is ga-ga and you done it!"

"Din't you tag along? Din't you stroll around a bit that night?"

"I was stewed. I was afraid you'd get lost by yerself."

"Drunk commissar. I'm gonna turn you in."

"Tell it to Browder."

"I'll tell him never to sign you up for the Party, that's what!"

"You know him real good, huh?" Mahoney sneered. "Gimme my butts."

"Here. Piker. I have met up with Comrade Browder many, many times. Formally and informally, you might say," White began. "In Chicago. Dee-troit. New York, of course. Official Party business. I've heard him speak on numerous occasions and . . ."

"And he don't know you from Amos and Andy," Mahoney said.

White opened his mouth and closed it, frowning. Mahoney stared at him, sleepy-eyed, but spoiling for an argument, as usual.

"I know Comrade Browder and he knows me. We're Party, that's all. You'll never understand that, Mahoney. You ain't smart enough. What's dumber than a dumb Irishman? I ask you."

Mahoney grinned.

"What's dumber than a dumb Irishman? A smart nigger."

"Shut your face. There's a blanket over there. Roll up a caterpillar and come out a butterfly."

"Soitenly. I bet you yer gonna run them papers alla way down to Doran, huh? Well, you can kiss his ass, cause I won't. Tell that to yer buddy Browder!"

"The runners are all tired out," White said feebly. He did intend to talk with the brigade commissar about replacements and clothing. He knew he'd have to listen to a lecture about morale first. He started to get up.

"In the old days, Rosie woulda gone down there," Mahoney said. "That skinny bastid woulda gone down there and talked Doran's ears offa his gahddamned *head!* He could out-Marxist-dialectic anybody. Anybody! Remember?"

"Yeah," White said. "I remember. Rosie was a fine kid."

"I bought him his first piece of ahss," Mahoney said. "In Madrid. Remember?"

"Yeah," White said. "I remember that real good. Real good."

Mahoney was rolled in the blanket, breathing heavily. White picked his revolver up off the table. One squeeze of the trigger. An accident. Another name on the casualty list.

He stood up until his helmet bumped the roof of the dugout. The pistol hung heavy in his hand. He looked down at Mahoney.

"Be careful," Mahoney said.

His voice startled White.

"Huh?"

"Be careful, Andy. There's a moon. Watch out for snipers. There's a bad place near where the British are. You gotta crawl. Keep yer ahss down, buddy."

"Okay," White said. He pushed the revolver into his holster, drew on his gloves and picked up the papers.

"Don't forget."

"I won't forget," White said. "Go to sleep, you dumb Mick."

"Watch dat shit," Mahoney muttered and fell asleep.

The shelling of the Red positions began at dawn, when the first cold fresh winds of March shredded the ground mists. Tiger and the remnants of his company of Legionarios marched to the ordnance depot. As they were counting off into loading teams, the planes of the Kondor Legion, Messerschmitts, Heinkels, Dorniers and the Junkers trimotors hammered across the sky in measured black formations. The earth shook and the sky quivered. The offensive had begun.

By sunrise, the first trucks arrived for ammunition, dozens of them, driven by Italians who were cheerful and smoked cigars near the gasoline dump and honked their truck horns incessantly. The trucks came in the west gate empty and rolled out the east gate, crawling to the artillery positions. By midmorning, the rumor was around that the Red lines had been broken. The Legionarios, exhausted from heaving crates of 88-millimeter shells, sat down on the rust-colored earth and wiped the sweat from their faces. The German guns were firing slowly, steadily, a continuous barrage. The eastern horizon was a single, long cloud of dust and smoke, spotted with the red spurts of exploding shells. Squadrons of bombers beat through the soft spring clouds. The Italian drivers honked their horns furiously. Tiger waited until the first fight started. An Italian kicked one of the Legionarios in the rump. By the time Tiger got to the crowd that gathered, the Italian had been beaten half-dead. The other drivers stood near their trucks, at a safe distance, cursing and shaking their fists. A flight of nine Messerschmitts snarled overhead, very low. Tiger looked down at the unconscious Italian driver and shrugged.

"What is all this?" he said. "Get back to work or you'll look like this one here."

The Legionarios muttered, but did not move.

"Let them load their own trucks!"

"We're Legionarios, not pack-burros!"

"Right! We were ordered here as a shock-force! You said so yourself, Sergeant."

"*Hombre*, we're fighters. The lines have been broken! We should be killing Reds, not loading trucks for these macaronis!"

Tiger set his hands on his hips and stared at them. The soldiers closest to him stepped back, out of reach.

"Fighters?" Tiger said. "You? No, *chicos*. You are turds. You are the bottom of every latrine. Fight? Look at this one here. Why didn't you kill him, finish him off? Now he's only got one eye. No good as a truck driver. Get back to work. Load the trucks."

"We don't work for Mussolini's *mariconcitos!*"

"Shut up," Tiger said. "You work for me. Until the tanks get here."

"The Black Arrows? *Mierda!*"

"From the Fourth Navarrese Division," Tiger said.

"Just as bad. What the hell are we doing assigned to the children of Christ? They spend half their time on their knees, those little Jesuits!"

"You spend half your time on your knees, *chico*," Tiger said. "Sucking. Load the trucks. Load this one here, the General Motors. Throw this lump of Italian garbage on top when you're done."

That seemed to please them. They laughed and went back to work. They threw the Italian driver up on the heaped ammunition crates. His comrades took him down and drove the truck away. Tiger stopped it at the east gate.

"When you come back bring a skin of wine and a bottle of cognac, understand?"

"*No tengo dinero* . . . I don't have any money," the Italian said.

"Bring wine and the cognac or there will be no more loading of the trucks."

"You can't do that! You have no authority!"

Tiger pointed his revolver into the cab. The driver flinched away, raising his hands. Tiger laughed.

"Good! Good! That's how you salute in your army! Both hands in the air! Good Fascists, all of you. Bring the wine and the cognac or you'll end up like your comrade. Get out of here, pretty-face. Come back in a half hour!"

The loading went on. The Legionarios drank the wine and sweated in the spring sunshine, heaving the heavy crates up onto the trucks. The thunder of the cannons and the roar of the truck and aircraft motors drowned their curses. Tiger drove them, a bottle in one fist, a length of wood in the other. He drove them until they collapsed, let them rest a few minutes, and then kicked them back to their places. The great piles of ammunition melted. The depot stank with exhaust fumes.

Two mules appeared with food. The Legionarios were all drunk. They staggered around the mules, tearing at the bread sacks and yelling. The last of the loaded trucks went away. Some bombers came back. Tiger waved his bottle at them.

"You see them? You haven't worked! This is *nothing!* This afternoon, it will be bombs and gasoline and machine-gun ammunition, too. Three, four times as much. Four or five times as fast! You'll be puking purple all afternoon, all of you."

They looked at him, stupefied. They knew he was right. They pried the tops off the stew buckets and dipped in their mess kits. They sniffed and tried to swallow the stuff, then spewed it on the ground, trampled the bread to muddy paste.

"Hey! For Christ's sake! It stinks! It's rotten, this stew! The bread is moldy!"

Tiger drank some cognac and wiped his mouth.

"Eat and be poisoned or don't eat and starve!" he said. He lit a cigar and sat down on a case of hand grenades. The German cannons kept on firing. The land to the east erupted as the shells hit. The earth shuddered constantly.

"Smell this!"

Tiger sniffed the mess kit. The stew was sour, putrid. He shrugged.

"Good enough for you."

"Are they trying to kill us?"

"Why not?" Tiger said. "What else are you good for? I told you that you are all turds. That's what they give you to eat. Turd soup."

The bread was green and crawling with small, white worms. Tiger threw it away.

"Write a letter to Franco," he said. "Tell him you want to eat with the officers of the general staff. Work begins in thirty minutes!"

"We want food!"

"You *have* food," Tiger said. "Eat it and choke!"

He sat and drank and smoked his cigar, his pale green eyes gazing from face to face. They muttered and walked away from him, back to the stew cans. They squatted on the ground, watching him.

Before Tiger had finished his cigar, the tanks arrived, twenty medium Fiats, with mud splattered over fresh-painted insignia Tiger had never seen before. The treads chattered and churned the ground, and blue exhaust drifted on the wind. The turret hatch on the lead tank opened. A slender young man with an oil-smeared face and dirty officer's field dress climbed out, dropped to the ground and shouted, in Spanish. The tank engines were shut off. It seemed very quiet suddenly. The officer walked through the gate, showed his papers, and strode up to Tiger.

Tiger slipped his bottle of cognac behind the case of grenades and stood up, palming the cigar. The officer was young. They were all young these days, kids, still wet behind the ears. This one wore a scarlet heart sewn on his breast, big leather gauntlets and a tank helmet.

"You are Sergeant González?"

"That's me, *capitán*," Tiger said, grinning cheerfully.

The officer sniffed once and frowned.

"You are drunk on duty, Sergeant."

"I am been drinking, but I am not drunk. I'm not on duty. We're loading trucks. While we waited for you to bring your tin cans here. We're supposed to ride on those things?"

"You have been assigned to the first shock-team of the Fourth Navarr-ese. I am Captain Alemany, tank squadron commander. How many men have you? Can you remember?"

"Forty-three."

"Where are the rest?"

"Dead," Tiger said, surprised. "In the ground somewhere. From Cádiz to here."

"Where is your lieutenant?"

"Dead," Tiger said, puffing his cigar. "We've had four, I think. Maybe five. Some the Reds got. The rest had . . . accidents."

The young captain swung his gloved hand and struck the cigar from Tiger's mouth. The blow tipped Tiger off balance, and he sprawled back over the grenade case. The officer reached down calmly, picked up the cognac bottle and broke it on the corner of the case.

"The days of accidents are over," he said. "Get up. Bring your men to the gasoline pumps. The tanks must be filled at once. We need shells for the cannons and sixty boxes of machine-gun ammunition. *Get up.*"

Tiger stood. He stared at the officer.

"The Hero of Pilarmadre," he said. "We've heard about you, *capitán.*"

"Assemble your men," the officer said, turned, and walked away. Tiger's hand dropped on the holster on his hip. He shrugged and walked to where the men were squatting.

"Right on his fat ass," one of the Legionarios said. Tiger kicked him. The soldier didn't move.

"Get up, pigs. We're going to gas those tanks. They want ammunition, too."

"Your mother."

"Get up."

"Your mother."

Tiger caught up with the officer near the gate. He saluted, as the captain turned around.

"The men refuse to work, *capitán,*" he said. "I gave them your orders, too."

The officer walked back to the men. They sat on the ground or squatted, ignoring him.

"Work detail to fuel the tanks and load ammunition," he said. "When the squadron is ready, you will be issued two days' rations, grenades and bayonets. You will ride on the tanks to the assault point. In two days, we will retake Belchité, Quinto, and Pilarmadre. *Vámanos.*"

"Rations, is it?" one of the soldiers said. "We're men, not pigs! Smell this stew. It's rotten. Eat your own rations, little Navarrese!"

The officer's face turned pale. He clasped his hands behind his back.

"Stand to attention!"

The soldier stood. He held his mess kit in one hand.

"Your name?"

"Hyena. Private first class, and I won't eat this shit!"

"He's drunk, Captain," Tiger said. "I'll take care of him. He's yellow as piss except when he's drunk."

"Your mother," the soldier said.

"You will be issued rations from our supplies when the tanks are fueled and armed," the officer said.

"We're Legionarios," the soldier called Hyena said. "We don't eat wafers and drink wine with a bunch of priest lovers."

The soldier swung his hand forward and poured the contents of the mess kit on the young officer's boots. The men laughed.

"That's the stuff, Hyena!"

"That's showing him!"

"Screw the Navarrese!"

Tiger rubbed his chin thoughtfully. When the young officer turned around, the men would jump him. Already, some of them had their hands in their pockets for their clasp-knives. There was going to be another "accident." Tiger grinned, waiting.

The officer took off his right glove. Hyena glared at him, red-eyed and swaying. The officer held out his hand.

"Give me your pistol, Sergeant," he said evenly. Tiger drew out his revolver and hesitated. The men were all watching him. The officer snapped his fingers. Tiger handed him the revolver.

"Turn around, Private," the officer said. Hyena stared at him.

"Fuck you."

The officer's face was white as wax. He pushed the safety catch off. His hand trembled as he raised the revolver. Tiger watched, interested.

"Three to one he doesn't," he said, throwing a *duro* coin to the ground. There were no takers. Tiger shrugged. The officer raised the revolver until the front sight pointed at Hyena's chest. He wasn't going to do it. Tiger sighed and bent down.

Just as Tiger's fingers brushed the coin, the smash and ring of the shot struck him deaf. A pair of muddy boots, a dim, flailing body half-floated across his vision. Hyena fell back. The thud of his shoulders on the earth struck the drooling mess kit into the air. The black pistol slid forward and down, jerked with a second shot that punched a hole in Hyena's forehead. The mess kit bounded away, clattering. Tiger straightened slowly.

The Legionarios were silent, hunched or crouching, their mouths open, teeth clenched. The officer flipped the pistol, caught it neatly by the barrel and thrust it back to Tiger.

"Man the gas pumps," he said. "Double-time them over there, Sergeant."

He turned, dark and slender, and stalked away, his heavy gauntlets clasped together behind his back. The Legionarios stirred and murmured, like dreamers awakening. Tiger bounced the revolver on the palm of his hand, shrugged and slipped it into his holster. The men were already slitting the dead man's pockets, tearing the stained tunic from his chest. They tumbled the broken-headed body around and left it face down. Then they divided up the tobacco and coins from Hyena's money belt. Tiger waited until they had finished. He prodded the dead man with his boot.

"An accident, understand?" he said. He jerked his head at the figure of the officer. The Legionarios said nothing.

"He has *cojones*, our new little Christer," Tiger said. "I like that, see?

Maybe he knows how to kill Reds, too. You want to fight? *Bueno!* Me, too. Double-time to the gas pumps. Our *capitán* is waiting."

A work-gang of Moors was requisitioned from a discipline compound by the new Navarrese officer. They loaded the tanks with ammunition, while Tiger distributed grenades and bayonets to his own men. The bayonets were new ones, glittering and greasy. Tiger seized a handful and flung them at the Legionarios.

"*Armas blancas!*" he bellowed. "We'll rip the stinking guts out of those Reds!"

The Legionarios swarmed up onto the steel gratings welded to the tank bodies and crouched there, arms through pipe brackets. Grenades were pinned to their tunics like giant lice. They began to sing their "My-bride-is-death" song. Tiger scrambled up to the turret top, carrying a Navarrese battle flag and a new Fiat submachine gun. He set the steel staff deep in the socket and hammered the gun butt on the hatch.

"*Viva!* Long live Death!"

The hatch cover clashed open. The captain rose up out of the dark interior of the tank, looked back down the column and nodded, once. He raised his right hand. The great steel bulk beneath Tiger shivered for a few seconds, then the heavy motor caught and thundered. The tank trembled and spewed blue fumes.

"*Coño!*" Tiger said, clinging to the turret, "Is it all right?"

The young captain swung his arm forward.

"*Adelante!*" he shouted. "*Hasta Pilarmadre! Y por Dios!*"

The cool, windy afternoon exploded with the sound of engines. The hatch clanged shut, and the heavy treads began to churn, chattering and creaking. The column of tanks lurched down onto the highway. They rolled for three kilometers, while the Legionarios shouted and sang. Military police halted the column at a checkpoint. A compass reading was shouted through the driver's window slit. The tanks jolted down off the highway and rolled across a sandy plain green with new-sprung gorse and bitter weeds.

The motors roared, thunderous, vibrating the steel plates. The raw earth flung up in spattering clods from the whirling tread-cleats. They plunged at the Red positions. All the eastern horizon was a leaping, flame-shot sea of explosions. German 88 shells screamed overhead and higher, dark stiff birds wheeled and darted down, soared up again. Tiger howled with joy, crammed a clip into his gun, and let it off in a single pounding burst. The tanks went faster, the motors bellowing. They plunged into a cloud of smoke and choking dust. The artillery barrage lifted and swept forward. The hills vanished beneath the fall of high explosives, and shrapnel cracked over the shallow valleys.

A stone wall appeared. The bow of the tank butted it to fragments. Gears squealed and churned in the deep steel guts, and the tank hurtled across a ruined vineyard, crushing the bud-tipped vines, banging and tilting over shell holes. Full speed, wide open, with twin tails of gravel torn up and flung away in a sound like falling water. Tiger grinned and looked back. The squadron was fanned out in a big V; he was riding the point of a steel spear plunged at the enemy. The whole world was roaring motion, under him, behind him, above. He beat his fists on the warty steel armor and sucked in the stink of cordite and scorched rock.

Qué va, the infantry that ate dirt all day! *Qué va*, the cavalry with farting horses that broke their legs in rabbit-holes! *Qué va*, artillerists stuffing shells up a howitzer's ass! Tanks! Tanks! This was something! Wonderful! *Fantástico!* You could blow the Reds to bits with the cannons, cut them down like scuttling chickens with the machine guns, smash and crush and grind them to bloody messes beneath the treads! The *capitán* was *loco*, mad, magnificent! *Cuidado* Cataláns! *Tanques! Tanques!* They didn't go around things. They went right over them, full speed. Rusty frills of barbed wire snapped and flickered away like twigs. Whole sections of abandoned, body-strewn trenches collapsed, the sandbags popping like lice eggs beneath the great, clanking belts that chewed and clawed across the earth, stamping long, gridded scars across the dry face of Aragón. *Los tanques! Los tanques! Vivan los tanques!*

They crashed and churned through the booming, dusty afternoon. The whole squat, stinking, solid bulk of the tank bucked like a burro every time the turret cannon wheeled and fired. Perfect smoke rings sailed out from the muzzle into the ringing mist and vanished in an instant. They drove across fields, between broken, burning houses, heaved over highways and went slewing down the gravelly slopes of foothills, the machine guns battering at the dark, fleeing bands that swirled up out of the dust, went rigid with terror and dove for cover. An enemy plane, a Mosca, hung before them an instant, blue flames dancing at the gun muzzles, then swept over like a saw ripping a wet log. There were armored cars, little whippet tanks beetling crazily back and forth while high-explosive shells cascaded down from the cool spring sky. The sun glowed, a gray disc in the sandy clouds. The enemy was scattered, broken, here, there, nowhere. They took on fuel and water at a crossroads marked PILARMADRE 8 K.

The captain caught a convoy of Red trucks in a shallow valley. The turret gun slammed, and the lead *camión* exploded and turned over. The jolt of the recoil shook loose one of the Legionarios. He slid, clawing and screaming, off the rear deck and sprawled directly in front of the port tread of the tank behind. The tank covered him, and the tread rolled up again, a band of bloody paste. Tiger laughed until the tears ran down his face. Then they were on the convoy, butting the jammed trucks, lobbing grenades. The submachine gun stuttered and slugged at Tiger's shoulder. The Legionarios dropped on the wrecked convoy like a swarm of flies, their bayonets plunging. A Messerschmitt screamed down the road and strafed them all, the bullets gonging off the tank sides, and touching off a whole truck loaded with gasoline. Rivers of flame poured across the shattered pavement, and the tanks bucked away.

Every village and outpost was broken and burning. Bands of Moorish and Italian infantry were shooting prisoners and civilians. The roadsides were clotted with bodies. Shells slithered across the sky. The clouds were filled with hissing snakes. Steel fangs punctured horses, men, women, and machines. The smoky air reeked of roasting rubber and flesh. The tanks thundered on, always at full speed, right into an Anarchist road block, three kids, a ruined truck, two bedsteads, a woman with a red arm band and six bottles filled with kerosene. Tiger sprayed them with his submachine gun, until it heated and jammed. A signpost in the wreckage said PILARMADRE 3 K. And only midafternoon.

The captain stood in the open hatch, his chest and shoulders exposed. He seemed to be swimming in the heat-quivering pit of oily air that lifted, supported him. His face was dark and glistening. He smoked a cigarette in a small, ivory holder. He looked down at Tiger slumped on the hot broad bow and smiled tightly, his teeth showing very white. Tiger saluted. The Navarrese captain nodded, once. Tiger felt insulted, envious, and honored.

"You go like hell, Captain Alemany!" he shouted. "Always so fast?"

"*Por qué no?* We'll get there sooner."

Tiger waved at the tanks parked behind them.

"Some outfit! We thought you'd be the CTV. Those Mussolinis."

"All Spaniards," the officer said. "From Navarre. This is the first time the squadron has been in combat. We have trained for two months for this day."

"Not bad. We'll take Pilarmadre, easy."

The captain nodded once and turned around. The land behind them was covered with columns of moving vehicles, the hills crusted with the spitting snouts of mobile artillery. Hundreds of tanks snorted and nosed as far south as Montalban.

"How big is the breakthrough?" Tiger asked.

"Maybe fifty kilometers north-south."

A flight of trimotors rumbled slowly across the sky. Tiger shook his fists.

"Blow them out of their kennels, the Red sons-of-bitches! So we can run them down. Hey, *capitán*. Where will we go after Pilarmadre? To the river? To the Ebro?"

"There first," the captain said. "Then all the way to the sea."

"*Bueno! Cojudo!* Killing Reds all the way! That's for me!"

The captain crushed out his cigarette on the hatch cover, dropped the ivory holder into his tunic pocket, and wiped his face on his shoulder.

"We will kill them all," he said. "It is our mission. God will forgive us."

"Sure. Sure he will," Tiger said. "Why should he give a damn?"

Fuel trucks groaned out of the dust, headlights glowing. Ammunition vans jounced across the fields. Tiger tallied his men. Thirty-eight. Not bad. The captain wanted to see their trophies, weapons, and insignia patches pulled from the enemy soldiers they had killed. Mostly Anarchists. He seemed disappointed when he flung the prizes back down on them from his steel pulpit. The Legionarios gaped and shrugged.

"*Qué diablo, ese!*"

"What does he want? Negrín's head?"

"Now he's reading. A little book. What's he reading, Tiger?"

Tiger looked up.

"The Bible, *hombre*. He's Navarrese, isn't he? What do you think he reads, Franco's memoirs?"

"All tanks are fueled, *capitán!* Fueled and armed!"

"*Muy bien*," the captain said, clapping his little book closed. "Get your men aboard, Sergeant. Start engines!"

The motors stammered and coughed. The turrets turned slowly, like elephants' heads. The cannon snouts were black. The treads creaked and chattered. Gears groaned as the throttles were pulled open. The squadron clanked up a long, switchback dirt road. The captain rode in the open turret. At the top of the rocky hill, some Germans were unlimbering an 88 cannon. Down in the broad open valley was a town shaped like a warship sailing a sour-green sea. The spire of a church rose like a broken funnel, midships. The stone ship was battered, burning, sinking into the shell-dimpled bay. Tiny dark bits struggled and floundered toward the east; the crew and passengers had abandoned her.

"Pilarmadre," the captain shouted above the sputtering engines. "Ours again! *Gracias a Dios!*"

"Thanks to God?" Tiger said. "What about Hitler and Mussolini?"

The German gunners snapped the lanyard. The long, slender barrel spurted and sank back into hydraulic recoil-dampers. The shell shrieked out over the valley. Tiger counted, watching. A plume of earth bounded above a match flare, in the center of a dark, drifting mass. Tiger chuckled.

"Got 'em!"

The hatch cover clanged shut. The motor roared. The tank trembled, as though it tried to fling off the riders clinging to its sides. The German gunners waved, as the column plunged down the slope. Tiger bit his thumbnail at them.

"Go back to Germany, you white-headed shits!" he shouted. "Spain for the Spaniards!"

Pilarmadre was undefended. The tanks circled the town, the Legionarios riding exposed, to draw fire. Not even a sniper from the church. The

main streets running west to east were all barricaded, plugged solid
with cobblestones and rubble. The burnt-out concrete "hedgehogs" had
not been repaired. Some slogans had been daubed on the cracked concrete. There were three big, new cemeteries, the mass graves sunken by
the weight of winter snows that still glistened and seeped in wind-
wedged drifts beneath the battered walls of the railroad station and the
cement factory. Four tanks drew up abreast and fired point-blank at the
remains of one abandoned barricade, opening a hole into the silent,
smoldering bark of stone. There was no return fire, not a shot.

The captain sent two men back to the German artillery position on
motorcycles off-loaded from the last two tanks in the column. Another
tank carried a crew of *radioperadores* and a huge spool of telephone
wire. The men calmly strapped spikes to their legs and walked up the
wooden poles. The Legionarios wanted to shoot the glass insulators off
the crossbars, but Tiger had a better idea.

"A whole town," he said, swatting his hands together. "Until the piss-
pants Italians and the moros get here, it's all ours. All of it! The
captain won't take his tin cans inside. The streets are narrow in old
towns like this. I know. I'm a Spaniard, no? I was born in a town like
this. Maybe right here, who knows? Not me."

"On a garbage heap. Your mother had a curly tail!"

"On a garbage heap," Tiger agreed, staring at the silent walls, his
pale green eyes glittering. "Inside, *chicos*, there is more wine than we
can drink! Food, left behind by the Anars. All kinds of stuff to steal.
Money! Jewels! The captain thinks we saved this place for God. Then
he can't mind if we collect the rent, eh? Down in the cellars, there's
something else."

"Gold! Cognac!"

Tiger shook his head, and slid a clip into his gun.

"Women," he said. "They always stay behind. The old ones who can't
run away. And the young ones with new babies. Girls with big juicy
tits. We'll suck *leche* out of one end while we squirt it in the other!
Come on!"

The *Legionarios* roared and ran toward the broken walls, their bayonets
shining in the late afternoon sun. The captain shouted for them to halt.
Tiger laughed and threw a grenade back at the tank. It exploded, and
fragments panged off the armor. The Legionarios scrambled up and
over the broken barricade and ran down the silent, shadowed streets.

Calle Mayor was where the best shops were, the expensive wine cellars
and restaurants. The other pigs broke into the first place they came to.
Tiger slid along, alone at first, keeping close to the house fronts, listening.
The others followed him in small groups, laughing and singing, shooting
up at the shuttered windows.

He turned a corner and shouted in surprise. He nearly squeezed the trigger. A woman, young and good-looking, with thick, shining hair, dressed in a bright, torn dress stood in a doorway, staring at him with dazed, dark eyes. Her legs were slender and golden-shiny. She was wearing silk stockings. It was too good to be true!

"*Muy . . . buenas,*" he stammered, slinging the weapon in his shoulder.

"*Nacionalistas?*"

"Sure," he said. "We've recaptured this place. Surrounded it. The Red are all gone, eh?"

The woman looked up at the sky. A tic near her right eye twitched. Tiger crossed himself.

"After the *aviones* and the bombing," she said. "They all went away. Maybe that was the other time, though . . . You are from my husband's command?"

"Eh? Oh, *sí, sí.*"

He didn't really trust her. If she turned around, he'd let her have one in the back of the head. She might be a Red with a grenade between her tits.

"He was in command of the defense garrison," she said. "They kept trying to tell me he had been killed. But, of course, that's impossible. We had more than one car . . . They lied to me. They said they would drive me to him. Instead, they . . ."

"I'll take you to your husband," Tiger said. "Come with me, señora."

"Where is he?" she demanded, narrowing her eyes.

Tiger looked around. He was inspired, he told the others later. It just came to him. The perfect place.

"In the church," he said. "There is to be a solemn Mass said here. In honor of the victory."

"Then we will be married again," she said happily. "It will all be just as it was before . . . before . . ."

"Sure," Tiger said.

He could hardly keep his hands off her. He wanted to knock her to the ground right there and tear the dress off her. She was crazy, out of her head. The church would be dark. They always were.

"We'll be married again," he said. "Come along with me."

They walked up the street. She had good breasts and meaty hips, a sweet, swaying ass. Their steps, his heavy boots, her light, rapping heels echoed off the still stone house fronts. He was nearly sick with lust.

The church was a big, empty, gutted shell that smelled of damp ashes still. The sunlight fell in a big patch through the broken door. The woman turned to him. Her face twitched again, and he crossed himself to keep off the evil eye.

"You are devout, too," she said. "Like my husband, the colonel . . . He's here? I don't see him . . ."

"Stand by this pillar," Tiger said. "I'll get him for you."

She moved where he gestured. He backed away, watching her, ready to spring if she tried to run. She stood there, her lips moving, talking to herself. Crazy in the head. The colonel's wife! Somebody's sweet piece, sure enough. A prize for the Tercio.

He tore his blanket roll off his back and kicked it open on the stones. He set the submachine gun beside the blanket, within reach. He looked up. He had spread the blanket before a niche dedicated to the Virgin. A sweet face smiled down at him from behind bent iron bars. The body of the statue was pitted and chipped with bullet holes. Tiger winked and tore open the flies of his pants.

"Keep your eyes open, sister, and you'll see what you missed!"

He was shaking all over, when he walked back to the woman.

"He's waiting?" she said, smiling up at him as her face spasmed.

"Right over here," he muttered, seizing her arm. She didn't resist, not even when they reached the blanket. She was staring up at the Virgin, whispering, when he clamped his hand over her mouth, butted his knee against her legs and bore her down to the ground. He champed his teeth in her scented, glossy hair, pounded her face once against the stones, ripped up her skirt, rammed her thighs apart and was on her, groaning and thrusting.

When he had finished with her the second time, he cut away her soaked, sticky underclothing. She lay with her eyes shut, blood still trickling from her nose. He tied her left ankle to the snout of the submachine gun, her right ankle to the trigger-guard.

"Now," he said, "we're in business, *querida*. A sample, for advertising, though . . ."

He rubbed his hand, thrusting his fingers into her, buttoned his pants and walked out the door. He found the first bunch, half-drunk already, looting a co-operative store.

"A *duro* each," he said. "In cash or watches, rings, whatever you've got. You don't believe me? Take a sniff, *chicos!*"

He sat outside on the church steps, collecting the money, refusing most of the rubbish they brought him. She screamed for a while. The Legionarios went for that. They brought him a canvas sack to keep the money in. He went in again himself when he heard the first convoy of trucks pull up beneath the walls of the town. One of the Legionarios was on her, another one, who had paid for twice, was watching and playing with himself. Tiger looked down at the woman.

"You shits!" he said. "You've gone and killed her. She's dead, you bastards!"

"So what? I paid for twice didn't I?"

"Hurry up, then," Tiger said. "The Moors are here."

He freed his submachine gun and when the soldiers were finished, jerked the blanket over the pale, sprawled form and trussed it tight. He pulled out his revolver.

"All right," he said. "You've had your fun. Now pick her up."

They carried the bundle down the steps of the church, Tiger following with his canvas sack slung over his shoulder. The captain was at the bottom of the steps with some Navarrese officers and men from the tanks. The rest of the Legionarios had disappeared.

"You! Sergeant! What have you got there?"

"A suicide," Tiger said. "Some old woman killed herself in the church. We knew it was a wrong thing to leave her there, so we're taking her down to the cemetery . . . I mean, a shell crater somewhere. My *chicos* have gone to get some shovels."

The captain said nothing. Then he pointed to the sack.

"What's in that?"

"Small arms confiscated from Anar headquarters," Tiger said. "We don't need old junk like this, but we have to turn it over to the military police, right, *capitán?*"

"You are lying," the officer said. "But I have no time for you now. Get out of here. Get back to the tanks before I have you all arrested!"

They tottered away down a smoldering side street. They were unable to stop laughing, and dropped the bundle two or three times.

"A suicide! Christ, that was perfect, Tiger!"

"Small arms, he said, you heard him say it. Small arms!"

"Come on," Tiger said. "We still have business to do."

"With this? Where? Who with?"

"The Moors," Tiger said. "We'll sell it to the Moors."

"Shit, you're kidding!"

"We split three ways or it's no go."

"All right," Tiger said. "Come on! The moros will buy it dead or alive. As long as it's got white skin and two mouths to squirt off in. Maybe we'll get a hundred pesetas."

"I want another turn first!"

"Move, pig," Tiger said, cocking his pistol. "There will be other towns, other women. Leave it to me. Me and the captain will give you everything you want. Piss, shit, blood, and *leche!* This is just the beginning *chicos*, just the first course!"

Indignation of a High-Minded Spaniard

We can endure that He should waste our lands,
Despoil our temples, and by sword and flame
Return us to the dust from which we came;
Such food a Tyrant's appetite demands:
And we can brook the thought that by his hands
Spain may be overpowered, and he possess,
For his delight, a solemn wilderness
Where all the brave lie dead. But, when of bands
Which he will break for us he dares to speak,
Of benefits, and of a future day
When our enlightened minds shall bless his sway;
Then, the trained heart of fortitude proves weak;
Our groans, our blushes, our pale cheeks declare
That he has power to inflict what we lack strength to bear.

Wordsworth

"One has faith in the Royal Navy," Jacques said, nodding at the skinny Englishman.

"But none whatever in Chamberlain," the Englishman shot back at once in surprisingly well-accented French. "The Prime Minister of my country is an absolute idiot."

"Jacques," the woman called Beatrice said, laying her pale, ink-stained fingers on her companion's arm. "Mr. Lockridge is on the *News-Chronicle*."

"Ah," Jacques said, and poured himself more *café con leche*.

"Four hundred civilians killed yesterday!" the Englishman said bitterly. "The British Prime Minister will not be able to comprehend what that means until the four hundred dead are British citizens. But by then it will be too late. We shall be at war. First Austria, then the Czechs. Then us. You cannot appease the Fascists."

"Not appease, *contain!*" Jacques cried, upsetting his cup. "That is the great thing, an alliance of democratic and socialist republics around the Fascist states! A ring of steel, *comme ça!* The Czechs are said to have a first-class army. Naturally, there will be talk of concessions to German territorial demands. But to think that a brother republic would be dismembered, piecemeal, to placate Hitler . . . no, no, please, you will make me laugh. That, that would be too absurd! The French Republic will stand fast with Czechoslovakia!"

"Do you agree, Monsieur Voget?" the Englishman asked politely.

"Has the French Republic stood fast with Spain?" Voget said.

"But the border is open!" Jacques said triumphantly. "The fact of your presence here at this table indicates . . ."

"Monsieur Voget is a Communist, darling," Beatrice said, patting his sleeve again.

"*Dommage,*" Jacques muttered and began to mop up his coffee, wringing the serviette out into his cup.

"I came in with a convoy of trucks," Voget said. "North of Perpignan, they are cutting trees."

"Whatever for?" the woman called Beatrice asked, in English. "Road blocks for tanks?"

"The wings of the Russian aircraft are too wide," Voget said. "They were delivered through the Balkan states partially assembled."

"How many planes?"

"What kinds?"

"Did you see any tanks at all?"

They all talked at once. Voget shrugged.

"I didn't count them," he lied. "Quite a few."

There were three hundred, mostly interceptor aircraft of the Mosca make, part of a total shipment of twenty-five thousand English tons of war matériel. He had delivered the bill of lading from his convoy to an under-secretary of the Ministry of Defense, a careful copy to the chief officer of the SIM, a bald Russian with a Spanish name and an excellent interpreter.

"There," Jacques said. "You see? One has only to trust the heads of states. It will all work out. We Socialists have complete faith in Indalecio Prieto!"

"Isn't that a bit like trusting the treasurer of your club?" the cadaverous Englishman asked. "You trust him because he is a member of the club and because he is the treasurer."

"I give you Prieto, Minister of Defense," Jacques said, waving his scum-lipped coffee cup. "*Le seul grand homme de la République!*"

The others murmured and raised their cups. The Englishman coughed dryly. Voget looked out over the burning city. There was a rumor, more than a rumor, a confirmed story that there was to be a demonstration later in the morning, headed by the U.G.T. A demonstration against Indalecio Prieto, "the only great man of the Republic."

"And the price for these Russian aircraft?" someone asked.

Voget raised one shoulder.

"They have been paid for."

"In money, yes," Jacques said, winking slyly. "But we are . . . men of the world . . . women, too, of course. We are aware that there is a *political* price on all aid from the Soviet Union. No answer? How typical. You Communists are so voluble on all other subjects, but the infiltration of Negrín's government . . . not a word."

The others laughed. Voget shrugged.

"Oh, there are no secrets in Spain these days," Jacques said, patting his lips daintily. "For Comrade Voget the border is a tennis net. *Pom,* he goes over! *Pim,* he is returned! *Pif,* over! The only real secret is the progress of the peace negotiations, the correspondence between Negrín and some relative of Suñer on the other side."

"Why should Franco accept a negotiated peace?" the Englishman said. "The new gains in Aragón, fresh supplies every day. My government does nothing. The French . . ."

"We were asking the political price of Russian aircraft," Jacques said rudely. "Our Communist is silent."

"Hidalgo Cisneros has been chief of the Republican air forces for many, many months," Voget said. "He is a member of the Party. His assistant, Nuñez Maza, is also a member of the Party . . ."

"And Cordon is to be named Under-Secretary for War, Prados has been confirmed for the Navy, Cuevas as Director General of Security," the Canadian woman said, ticking the names off on her pale, stained fingers. "Right, darling?"

Jacques nodded.

"Most of the corps commanders. Most of the brigade commanders. Most of the battalion commanders, even. All Reds, all of them!"

"Perhaps they have earned promotion by their abilities in the field," Voget said quietly. "There is always talk that the Communist units get all the new weapons from the Soviet Union. If they are the best troops and have proved themselves so a hundred times, why not? Would you have Negrín deliver a fortune in weapons to incompetents? There is no conspiracy except in the minds of foreign journalists much like yourselves. Ask the men at the front."

"Most of the British volunteers have been CP," the Englishman remarked. "Hardly most of your countrymen, Beatrice, I should think."

"I should hope *not!*" the woman said. "Oh, look, the fire down there is out. What quarter is that, anyone know?"

"A worker's quarter," Voget said. "The men are at the front, the young women in the munitions factories, and the old ones and the kids have been bombed for two days running. Curious, is it not that the Luftwaffe and Mussolini's 'White Eagles' cannot seem to hit the dock installations, but cannot seem to miss the tenements of the working class?"

There was a moment's uncomfortable silence. They all looked out over the city with the strained attention of a group before a famous painting in a museum. One of the journalists pushed away his cup and sighed.

"How are we expected to file copy these days?" he demanded sourly. "Franco will drive all the way to the Ebro. Perhaps to the sea. It's suicide to try to fly to Valencia, and who can get permission to board the mail submarine?"

"Retreats are so . . . *boring*," Jacques agreed. "Thank God we've been granted the interview with the Minister this morning at the palace. I can always write about Prieto with a full heart!"

"Perhaps some arrangement can be made so that Monsieur Voget can accompany us all?" the Englishman suggested. He tilted his long, bony face into the shocked silence like a horse thrusting its head into a church. Voget grinned, suddenly liking the Englishman's nerve. He drew his wallet from his jacket pocket and flipped his press cards on the table.

"That won't be necessary," he said quietly. "As you see, I have credentials as a journalist. This one is good for the Republic. This other for the Nationalist side."

He picked up the cards, fanned them like a table-tennis paddle and batted an imaginary ball.

"*Pom!* . . . *Pim!* . . . *Pif!* . . . And if I get caught . . ."

The Englishman pointed a long finger at him and cocked his thumb.

"*Pam*," he said quietly. "The game is over."

The steel chair legs scraped on the concrete floor of the balcony. Cups rattled. Jacques pocketed the paper sack of coarse beet sugar. Beatrice snatched up her packet of cigarettes. There were murmurs of the time, the difficulty of transportation, the possibility of another air raid. Voget folded his arms on the balcony railing and ignored them.

"Cigarette?"

The Englishman, Lockridge, had remained. He pushed some papers and tobacco to Voget.

"I have some," Voget said. "I only took hers to be polite."

"There is nothing more tedious than an Anglo-Saxon woman who has become the mistress of a Frenchman," Lockridge said. "They insist that you *know*, don't they? If you don't *know* . . ."

"*Le jeu est fini*," Voget suggested. "True, but think how tedious it is for the Frenchman!"

"I find this to be the relationship between our two countries," Lockridge said, "on the Spanish issue. England is a rather skittish old maid, while France is . . . afraid of losing her love, perhaps? They had a passionate affair during the Great War, of course. Neither can forget it. Both have grown older. Neither can forget that, either."

"But not at the same rate of speed," Voget said. "France is the oldest country in the world. Only a nation that is senile can tolerate government by imbeciles and charlatans. France has had no other rulers."

"I have an automobile," Lockridge said. "Don't ask how. Will you . . . I mean if you're not busy . . ."

"I shall be pleased to ride with you," Voget said. "I think you are a damned good chap."

"Well . . ." Lockridge said, and blushed.

The roads were blocked by militia and rescue teams. Water sprayed from fat hoses into the broken-fronted houses. Bodies lay under canvas sheets. Lockridge drove slowly, stopping to offer the Cataláns a ride. The men and women refused, their faces blank with shock. At last they reached the Diagonal. On one side, Voget noticed the banners and placards of the demonstrators already gathered. He was surprised to see a delegation of C.N.T. workers with their red and black Anarchist banners and arm bands.

"I'm afraid that female missed the point on her question to you," Lockridge said. "Barcelona *has* changed. At one point, the C.N.T. ran this whole city, or appeared to."

"I was not here during the P.O.U.M.-sponsored uprising against the government," Voget said. "I know nothing of it."

"I didn't mean that. But this was an extremely proletarian city in the early days, wasn't it?"

"It was very fashionable to wear the workers' blue *mono*, the coverall," Voget said. "Men and women, too. Now suits again, smart dresses, silk stockings. Nothing lasts so short a time as *voluntary* social equality. A quick change, like at the Follies."

"Yet the feeling for the Republic is as strong as ever."

"The war has come home," Voget said. "That changes everyone. Now the Catalans know what the Madrileños have suffered."

They rolled on. The streets were crowded with sullen-faced men and women. Armed patrols stood on the corners. Loudspeakers were being wired to light poles. Voget saw a slogan daubed on the wall of a bombed office building.

AVENGE THE RAPE OF AUSTRIA IN SPAIN!

"You see that?" he asked.

"What about that one," the Englishman said, pointing.

ABAJO-PRIETO-ABAJO-PRIETO-ABAJO-PRIETO.

"I imagine," Lockridge said conversationally, "that you fellows in the Comintern have long ago decided the same thing. *Le seul grand homme de la République* must go, eh?"

"I am afraid there has been some mistake," Voget said. "I have no knowledge of the Party line on Prieto. My position is that of purchasing agent and *fonctionaire du transport*. I aid in the obtaining of arms and men for the Republic and assure the deliveries whenever the bourgeois states permit it or are willing for their own reasons to look the other way. You see? I am a rather small gear in a very large machine. If I move others, it is because I am moved myself."

"I should like very much to interview you, if it can be approved by your superiors," Lockridge said. "I think you might make better copy than the illustrious Minister of Defense."

"That is impossible," Voget said. "I am a very dull fellow and really know nothing at all. I am a glorified truck driver. Interview Dolores Ibarruri, La Pasionaria. She will make you good copy. That is her greatest talent, making good copy for journalists."

The Englishman smiled and flexed his long, skeletal fingers around the steering wheel.

"You do not greatly admire the lady spokesman for the Communist Party in Spain? You disapprove of women in politics?"

"I am a Frenchman," Voget said.

"I don't follow you."

"Women belong on their knees in church, seated across the table in a café, bending over a stove or a cradle or dancing on a stage wearing a handful of paste jewels."

Lockridge laughed, a high, happy whinnying. Voget lit a cigarette and looked out at the streets of Barcelona. There was something in the air. His nerves could sense it, the dull, dangerous hush before the spring storm. When the car stopped at a cross street, he rolled down the window and listened.

"My father keeps bees at his little place in the country," the Englishman said. "From time to time, naughty boys throw stones over the wall at the hives. It sounds like that, doesn't it? The buzz. They want to sting."

"You are acute," Voget said. "No, to the right here. We must part in front of the palace. Also modest and prudent."

"Why do you say that? A journalist like myself . . ."

"If you were only a journalist, Mr. Lockridge, you would not enjoy the privilege of driving around the capital of the Republic of Spain in a private automobile."

"Oh, I shouldn't say that," the Englishman said. "The American chap, Hemingway, has his own auto."

"Hemingway is not a journalist. He is a literary celebrity who has raised fifty thousand dollars to supply mobile hospitals for the 15th Brigade. He is an official friend of Spain and everyone knows him. I have never heard of you and neither has anyone else. Including the editors of the News-Chronicle, I am certain. Your press credentials are a cover, Lockridge, just as mine are."

"Dear me, you make me sound somewhat sinister," the Englishman said lightly. "That's the palace just there, isn't it?"

"There is nothing sinister about the British Foreign Office," Voget said bluntly.

"Nothing so official as that," Lockridge said. "A certain M.P. has a very wealthy first cousin in the City. A banker, I mean. Named Desmond. This banker's two sons came to Spain as volunteers. This banker received one letter from an American nephew, saying that both boys had been killed. Since then, not a word. I am here to discover the bodies, if there are bodies . . ."

"That may be quite difficult."

"The American, a pilot who came over with André Malraux's group, has also disappeared."

"Indeed?" Voget said. "Well, that happens in Spain. Ask Hidalgo Cisneros. He's the chief of air forces, as you know."

"I have," Lockridge said. "There is no record of Franklin Pierce Buckminster anywhere . . . or at least in any of the group rosters I have been allowed to examine. The Desmond boys are listed as missing."

"Then you have been to International Brigade headquarters. You are thorough, I see."

"Not so thorough as the SIM," Lockridge said. "This American Buckminster was an ace pilot . . . or is . . . or has been. Ten or twelve kills, I believe. He was decorated in Madrid. I have several newspaper articles, photographs of him. This certain M.P. could arrange for a very substantial sum in return for precise information. Accurate information. The banker, Desmond, is determined to discover what happened to his sons. Money is no object. Franklin Pierce Buckminster. With a name like that, no man simply disappears. It's not possible."

Voget climbed out of the car, stretched and threw away his cigarette.

"In Spain, anything is possible," he said. "It is even possible for the Republic to win the war."

Lockridge unfolded himself out of the automobile and locked the door, staring at Voget over the roof.

"You supply aircraft, Voget."

"Sometimes."

"You must have heard of this man. He was a companion of a rather well-known test pilot, himself related to a manufacturer of aircraft in France. Jean Saulnier. Unfortunately, he died at Brunete."

"Unfortunately, a great many men died at Brunete. From all nations."

"Perhaps your memory . . ."

"My memory is excellent," Voget said. "And I tell you I do not know of any pilot in the Gloriosa named . . . whatever you say."

"Franklin Pierce Buckminster."

"There are no foreign volunteers in the Republican Air Force," Voget said, walking toward the security shack. "Of course you know that."

"Just as I know there are no Russians in the Servicio de Investigación Militar," Lockridge said. "I have spoken with any number of Gonzálezes and Sánchezes and Gómezes. All with shaved skulls, a passion for tea and long cigarettes and fully equipped with interpreters."

"Papeles, señores-camaradas?" the security guard demanded.

Voget and Lockridge handed over their press credentials. Voget smiled inwardly. Somehow it pleased him that the British Government should be still so confident that it could employ an agent like this great, gaunt, conspicuous water bird who called himself Lockridge. He was precisely so out of the ordinary as to allay the suspicion even, apparently, of the officials of SIM. No doubt he really did have a father in Sussex somewhere who kept bees. British agents, in Voget's experience, were stupefyingly authentic. It would not have surprised him if the Englishman had suddenly offered him a pot of honey. Real honey, of course.

The papers were examined, their names inscribed with many carbon copies, the papers returned. They were waved forward into a group gathered outside the massive iron gates of Pedralbes Palace. Lockridge waved to their breakfast companions he had spotted in the crowd.

"Halloh, Beatrice . . . Jacques . . . Jolly fine turnout, eh?"

The gates swung in, and the journalists flocked forward, gabbling in a half-dozen languages.

"The advance of the Trojan forces," Lockridge said gaily. "Homer compares them to a flock of geese. In *The Iliad*, you know."

"Never heard of it," Voget said. "I only read *Frente Rojo*."

They proceeded through reception halls like vast marble railroad waiting rooms, up a frozen waterfall of white stone stairs, down long corridors hushed with thick carpets. Pencils were out, and notebooks flapped. They crept forward between statues on pedestals, uniformed attendants with dim, well-fed faces. Certain personages in claw-hammer coats and striped trousers, clutching wax-sealed dossiers, slid along the walls, accompanied by officers from all the services in immaculate uniforms, medals and mustaches. Everything smelled of perfume and dust.

The gathering of literary pilgrims clustered at a respectful distance from double doors of pastel wood beautifully worked with baroque scrolling in faded gilt. Everyone stared at these important portals, smoothed hair, adjusted cravats, guiltily concealed pads and pencils.

The right door opened first, and a very old, grave, pale creature bent stiffly and undid the floor catch, stretched and released the ceiling stop and pushed the left door open, then stood there, one of those ancient puppets, dusty, mute and dignified, who had opened doors for ministers beyond anyone's recollection but his own, who remembered past dictators and monarchs when they were children in velvet suits and lace collars. The old creature bowed, very slowly, very stiffly, creating an instant's panicked certainty that he would topple gravely forward on his face and burst apart in a shower of faded rose petals, desiccated moth eggs, and a silent swirl of dust.

A brisk, plump under-secretary or under-under-secretary in a stickpinned cravat and oiled hair bustled forward.

"Gentlemen of the press . . . and ladies, too, a million pardons! . . . request the opportunity to be admitted to the company of the Minister of Defense for the People's Republic of Spain. Señor Indalecio Prieto y Tuero!"

It was a very large, very empty room, with a featureless carpet framed by a glossy parquet floor. On one wall, the façade of the palace, were a number of windows, tall, many-paned, rounded at the top, and draped with rigid plunges of velvet. A vast crystal chandelier, illuminated with feeble bulbs, hung from a ceiling of cherubimed and rosetted plaster. There were no chairs. The journalists stood in a shallow crescent before the dark, empty, and therefore efficient desk. On the desk stood a single object, a polished brass telephone. From the base of this instrument ran a single wire, a direct connection, without doubt, to all of Republican Spain.

The under-under-secretary received a question in French, revolved it beneath his glossy cap of hair and directed it, predigested, in lisping, liquid Castilian Spanish to the Minister of Defense. Someone had asked about the military future of the People's Republic of Spain. There was a very short, very expectant silence. Voget stooped and looked between Lockridge and the woman named Beatrice, who was scribbling furiously.

"We are lost!" a tenor voice cried in merry despair. "I assure you, we are lost!"

Voget's belly muscles tightened as though he had been punched. He stared, fascinated and repelled, at Indalecio Prieto y Tuero, Minister of Defense for the People's Republic of Spain.

He was small, short, and fat, roly-poly, like an overgrown baby, with pudgy pinkish cheeks smooth with powder. Like an infant, too, his small, round skull was nearly hairless, and downy, dainty brows licked above slitted dark eyes lazy with insolent authority. The tyrant of the nursery, preened to receive doting relatives. Someone had dressed him in an astonishing adult dark double-breasted suit, soft white shirt, and dark necktie. He waved his hands, little, dimpled miniatures with perfect, manicured nails like bits of mother-of-pearl.

"Write whatever you wish," the Minister cried. "Please yourselves! But at this stage in our affairs, any continuation of the conflict would be contrary to the best wishes of the people. I assure you, we are lost, quite lost! There is nothing to do now but to negotiate a just peace equitable to all parties. I beg you as intelligent and objective visitors to our unhappy, tormented nation to see this as the only practicable, indeed humane, solution."

He sat back, his little rosy lips curled in a smile, fingertips pressed together, as complacent in his self-proclaimed ruin as a rich man refusing a loan because his "affairs" have reduced him to penury. Nothing could, of course, give him greater happiness, had he been able to respond to a wish that wrung his heart. If there were only time, he would have the chief accountant bring in the ledgers of the corporation and the latest, disastrous report to the board of directors. Not a pound, not a franc, not so much as a single peseta! In the face of such obvious ruin, the question of a loan—why, one could only see the humor in it!

"*Salaud!*" Voget said furiously.

This beautifully tailored, smirking little globule, this hairless brat snatched up aircraft, cannons, tanks and played with them awhile as toys, until he became fretful, bored with the game. Thousands suffered, the city that nourished him had been blasted by bombs and now smoldered, Aragón was being ripped with shells, a shrunken, tormented nation of battling refugees believed that this self-adoring little swine would somehow save them and he waved his pink patties and shrieked with glee, "*Estamos perdidos! . . . We are lost!*"

The reception proceeded. Question, translation, pause, poison. Inquiry, translation, hesitation, defeatist drivel. Astonishment, translation, amusement, laughing despair. Incredulity, translation, hysteria, despair. Voget looked down at his shoes, longed for a cigarette or a pistol. Minister of Defense . . . the only great man of the Republic. Workers in the Leningrad arsenals sweated overtime to aid their proletarian brothers in a Spain they knew only from maps hung on the canteen walls. Volunteers against Fascism had bled and died at University City, Guadalajara, Brunete. Orphaned children with famine-bloated bellies whimpered in dry ditches. When the sirens moaned, the pavements trembled as the people rushed to cellars and subways. The people who made up the Republic of Spain were bleeding to death, ripped by the fangs of Fascist steel. A slender tube across Europe transfused the Soviet Union into Spain while nervous French fingers plucked at this tube, pinching off the life-giving trickle. And this people had such a petty, fretting suckling as . . . Minister of Defense.

Voget was the first to hear the voices in the outer court. It *was* like the swarming of bees, then the wash of surf on a stony shore, a sustained, threatening boom and crush that rose and rose, swelling until the tall windows shook and dust-motes jittered down long slanting shafts of sunlight. Voget stepped away to the closest window, just as the under-undersecretary's voice increased in volume to a gurgling shout.

Voget looked down. The broad avenue was a solid mass of humans, moving, marching, singing, shouting, waving placards and banners.

No Peace Negotiations!

Down with Traitors!

¡Viva Negrín!

¡Abajo Prieto!

The red flags jerked wildly. There were the black banners of the Anarchists, also, trade union placards, posters and pictures brandished by youth groups, delegations from the munitions plants, the docks, the workers' quarters. Wounded men in white, muffling bandages and stiff, bulky casts rode in open trucks. Whistles, the jeering, Spanish whistles of shrill contempt and blatting trumpets, the cadenced croaking of truck and taxi horns to the rhythm of the chanting crowd-roar.

"*A-ba-jo Prie-to! A-ba-jo Prie-to!*"

The under-under-secretary faltered, shouted something and stopped, mopping his brow. All at once, the journalists rushed to join Voget at the windows.

The crowd, one solid force of flesh, pressed the security forces back against the tall, spiked, iron fence and plucked open the gate as easily as one might drop a velvet rope away from the threshold of a theatre or a restaurant. Hundreds of heads and shoulders, fists and banners flowed through the open gate into the interior court, right up to the walls. A truck nosed forward, a sound-truck with four clumsy horns on the roof and a red star on each steel side.

The journalists all talked at once. Voget watched, smiling grimly. A voice like one of the Furies ripped through the sunny spring air.

"*Comrades! Men and women of Catalonia! True proletarian patriots!*"

"I believe that is La Pasionaria, isn't it?" Lockridge murmured.

"Of course," Voget said.

"Would you rather she were home scrubbing the kitchen floor?"

"Let us say that I am grateful not to be her poor husband," Voget said absently, listening to the excited voices of the others at the tall windows.

"What a scandal! Why don't the police *do* something?"

"Of course, it's all the work of the Communists. This week Prieto, next month it will be Negrín."

"That hideous female! Listen to her scream!"

"This sort of thing could happen only in Spain . . ."

"Just a lot of noise whipped up by the Reds. A few shots fired over the crowd and . . ."

Voget turned around. The under-under-secretary was mopping his face, glaring at the journalists and shifting from foot to foot. The Minister of Defense rose from his chair, swung his short arms behind his back and clasped his hands there. He gazed at the journalists and listened to the crowd.

"*A-ba-jo Prie-to! A-ba-jo Prie-to!*"

The Minister of Defense smiled slightly, and his fat smooth cheeks pushed up and creased his lids to proud slits. He stared across the room, his face a pudgy pink mask of lazy-eyed contempt. His moist little lips moved. He turned and walked from behind the desk, his hands still clasped across his back. A panel in the wall opened, and he disappeared through it.

"Ladies and gentlemen, the reception of the press by señor Indalecio

Prieto y Tuero is now terminated. The reception of the press is now terminated. The reception . . ."

A half hour of labored, polite Spanish muddle followed.

Voget and the others trotted up and down stairs, through reception halls, along back corridors. Messengers darted past them and vanished into anterooms, only to appear moments later from the opposite direction. Everyone milled along, jostling and apologizing, pretending it was all rather amusing in order to conceal their annoyance and anxiety. Finally, they entered a short, dark hall, some sort of service entrance. Voget counted six men in leather overcoats, waiting for them. The journalists escaped into a rear court filled with security guards and military officers.

"You observed, I hope, the absolute, unshakable calm!" Jacques said for the fortieth time. "Let us emulate the Minister and . . ."

"Don't shout, darling," Beatrice said, stroking his sleeve. "I believe these people will provide transportation. It's perfectly safe, I'm sure."

Beyond the wall stood a rank of black sedans, the motors purring. Two men came up beside Voget. He sighed and waved to Lockridge.

"You are Comrade Voget?" one of the men asked. "This way, please."

They drove for some time, turning finally through the gate of the convent of San Juan, headquarters of the Servicio de Investigación Militar. The two men escorted him down dark stone passageways and opened an iron door.

A man sat at a table beneath a single bare light bulb. He was dressed in an officer's tunic but without any insignia. Large-lensed dark glasses concealed his eyes. The door clanged shut.

"Sit down, comrade," the man said, pointing at a wooden chair.

"May I smoke?"

"Of course," the other said, opening a thick manila file folder. "Your papers, please. The ones in your wallet. The others from your hotel will be returned."

They would keep his tobacco, Voget thought, annoyed. Every time they went through his hotel room, they always confiscated his cigarettes. He passed his wallet across the table and sat smoking. The other bent over the folder, riffling carbon flimsies with short, blunt fingers. Voget saw copies of his requisitions, reports, duplicated rosters of volunteers, photograph negatives neatly pinned to cardboard sheets, what appeared, upside down, to be copies of official correspondence from Madrid, Marseilles, Paris, Antwerp, Albacete, and Moscow.

"Very good. All in order."

The man across the table spoke French with an accent, middle-European, not Spanish. The bright bulb washed out the color of his hair and turned the skin of his face and hands the shade of parchment.

"You have saved me a telephone call," Voget said. "But perhaps you know that the Englishman who calls himself Lockridge is certainly an agent of the British Government."

"He drove you to the palace."

"Correct," Voget said. "He has a convincing cover . . . he is merely attempting to discover the whereabout of two British volunteers. Both are dead, of course. But I think it's the American pilot who might cause us the most trouble. You see, Lockridge has expertly forged press credentials. It will be quite easy for him to simply follow one delivery of the new aircraft at a time. Perhaps it is the aircraft he's really interested in."

"There are no American pilots with the Republican Air Force."

"It will not take him too long to find a pilot named Francisco Libro. Lockridge speaks good Spanish. If he buys a few cognacs in the right cafés, one of the Spanish pilots is sure to say something. I don't believe Lockridge's story about the two dead Englishmen, but certainly he has been carefully prepared. No doubt he, too, has photographs, copies of letters. He is very disarming. He will open Buckminster up like a cheese packet. How long will it be before the Royal Air Force knows the standard performance, range, and armaments of Soviet aircraft?"

The man in the smoked glasses grunted, took out a notebook and fat fountain pen, wrote something and raised his head slightly.

"How do you spell the name?"

Voget told him. The sound of the page being ripped from the notebook was very loud in the empty room. The other reached beneath the table, pressed a concealed bell-button and waited. The iron door opened, and a Spanish guard entered, took the slip of paper and placed another manila file folder on the table. When the door closed again, a sheet of paper skidded against Voget's fingers.

"Read it. I have a copy in French, if that is too difficult."

Voget looked over the sheet. His own name and Party registration number had been typed in at the bottom. The page accused Felix Kolodny, battalion tank commander, of various crimes against the Spanish people and acts of treason against the People's Republic.

"I did not realize that Kolodny was a Russian," he said, looking up. "I believed him to be a Pole."

The man in the smoked glasses grunted noncommittally. Voget stared at him.

"It is a masquerade these days," Voget said. "Everyone is really someone else. It gets so that the perfect cover will be the truth."

"Will you sign now, please?" the other said.

"Kolodny has been arrested?"

"We have him in custody. You were responsible for bringing him to Spain."

"I provided money, papers, transportation. I did not provide Kolodny. Obviously."

"As you say."

"How do you know you have the right man?"

"I believe we have a reputation for thoroughness," the other said, tapping the second file. It was thicker, Voget noted, than his own.

"But not for perfection," Voget said. "No one is perfect. For example . . . Hans Kopa."

"What of Kopa?" the man in smoked glasses said.

"He was shot. That was a mistake."

"Was it?" the man in smoked glasses said. "In your opinion, apparently."

"There are other opinions, I know," Voget said.

"Exactly."

"Forget it then," Voget said.

"I have. We have. It is you who persist, Comrade Voget. Let me explain something to you. Very short. Very simple. It has been reported back to Communist Party underground leaders in Germany that Hans Kopa was captured alive, turned over to the Gestapo by the Falange, interrogated, and executed. This is very useful. To us, Comrade Voget. To you."

"I understand that the German Communist Party has been supplied with another martyr. I do not believe they need another martyr. The Spanish people have lost an expert battalion commander. Their loss is greater than the German's gain."

"You allow yourself to wallow in bourgeois sentimentality. You are clever, resourceful, and co-operative. Fundamentally, you are weak. You are given to personal likings and prejudices. I believe you have tried to eradicate these trivial class whims. Basically, you have not succeeded. You need re-education, Comrade Voget."

"I would be grateful for that," Voget said.

"You have a habit of making such statements, Comrade Voget, that may indicate a propensity toward irony."

"I accuse myself of possessing a sense of humor, if that's what you mean," Voget said.

"After this in Spain, you may well be called to Moscow. I would be inclined to recommend it. Have you ever been to China? No, I see not. China will cure you, Comrade Voget. Humanism has nearly been eliminated there. In a few years, such sentiments will be unknown, like bacteria at the North Pole. Sign the paper, please. I am quite busy today."

"Where is Kolodny? Here, in this place?"

"I think it would be quite correct if you identified him. Come."

They walked together into the Convent of San Juan.

"This place is ideally suited," the other said. "The nuns' cells, of course, required no alteration. This row down here, the records say, were used to exorcize demons from the young novices. Several are constructed in such a fashion that it is not possible to sit, stand straight or lie down. The demons, being uncomfortable, were grateful to escape through special ventilating shafts leading outside the walls. Some demons were not so co-operative. . . . We use these places for black-marketeers, thieves, criminals involved in incorrect distribution of food. Now, down this corridor . . ."

Voget saw stone cells, stale, cold, spattered boxes. He saw batteries of electric lights, loudspeakers powerful enough to break the thin membranes trembling inside human ears, a stone trough filled with blue chunks of ice, a small blacksmith's forge with iron implements, tweezers, hooks, plates, and branding instruments.

In another cell there was a tub of rubber truncheons, leather straps, and clotted strands of barbed wire.

"Who goes . . . in that . . . place?"

They moved under an overhead bulb. The man turned and faced Voget. A dark shadow flung down from the bulb hid his entire face, as though a hood had been dropped to his shoulders. He spoke in a flat, impersonal voice.

"Those who believe."

"In what?"

"Up and down. Right and wrong. That they know the truth. That others have been guilty of mistakes. That they themselves are innocent."

"*Je comprends*," Voget said.

"No, you do not comprehend," the other said. "You have received a powerful suggestion. Now you will see Kolodny."

Voget was led to another iron door. The flap over the Judas hole was lifted for him.

"Look."

The small stone cell was brightly lighted. A pale, naked man sat on a plank bunk facing the door. The eyes stared at nothing, the jaw drooped, a vacant, imbecile's face.

"What is he doing?" the other said.

"Masturbating," Voget answered, turning away.

"You have just seen fundamental man. Mankind."

Voget reached out one hand for the wall. Hands steered him to a wooden seat and pressed his head down between his knees. Cold shock played in Voget's spine. His stomach heaved and subsided. He gazed down at the stone floor. The voice prodded him.

"He has been like that for twenty-four hours. He has been . . . reduced. He can be developed now in many directions. He could be a guard at a labor camp, perhaps. Or a schoolteacher. At this period in his re-education, he has withdrawn from all other human beings. He is no longer capable of either fear or hatred. Would you believe that?"

"Yes," Voget said. "I believe that."

"Gradually, with proper stimuli, he could be trained so as not merely to forgive his instructors, but to feel for them very strong affection. He will love them. He will be grateful to them. And why not? He has had experiences previously limited only to saints. You have just seen a saint, Comrade Voget. A modern saint. Spain is famous for its saints, Germany for its martyrs, France for its humanists. Feeling better?"

"Quite well," Voget said, and stood up.

They walked together back to the first room. The other sat down across from Voget.

"Would you say that we had been kind to Hans Kopa? He really suffered very little pain."

"You have been very kind—I mean you were very kind."

"No, comrade," the other corrected. "*We. We* were very kind to Kopa."

"We were very kind to Kopa," Voget repeated.

"Good. Now, we are prepared to show similar mercy to Kolodny, let us call him. That depends on you."

"On me?"

"Of course," the other said. "Who else? This sheet of paper, unsigned, means we shall keep him here until a decision has been made as to what he shall become, what his future services shall be. We may utilize him as a demonstration, a specimen, a living report of our methods."

"I see."

The man in the smoked glasses took out his fat fountain pen and unscrewed the top. He set the pen down near Voget's right hand.

"Uh-eh! No. Think about it a moment. If you do not sign, he will live . . . until natural causes. If you sign, his life will end in two weeks' time. Either way, he will be completely happy, I assure you. But think. Pretend you are Kolodny, and he is now seated where you are. Reverse the roles. Just for a minute. Now think again. You are Kolodny. You have just seen Paul Voget. What will you do? Sign or not sign?"

Voget picked up the fountain pen without hesitation and wrote his name in bold, flowing letters above the under-typing.

"So. You have only done what is your duty, comrade. It may please you to believe that you have acted on the best humanist principles. But understand, all this means nothing, nothing at all. If it had not been you who signed this, it would have been another member of the Party. This paper will affect you more than Kolodny. The moment he was arrested, he was disposed of. All that has been determined here is the manner and purpose."

Voget nodded. He did not doubt the other's words. The flat middle-European voice echoed dully off the walls of the stone cell.

". . . *manner and purpose.*"

"Any questions, comrade?"

Voget thought an instant. It was no longer important, and he did not plan to do anything, but he simply wanted to know. He glanced across the table.

"You must be the one they call Jiménez," he said.

The man across the table reached up and touched his smoked glasses. Voget thought he was going to bare his face, but the fingers merely brushed the frame in a little, preening gesture, then sprang away to touch the bell-button concealed beneath the table. The gesture chilled Voget. He sat very still, his hands loosely clasped together, half expecting the iron door to crash open and guards to fall on him and drag him away.

The other picked up the two folders and tapped the stiff edges with his fingers. He did not look up.

"You will return to your duties, Comrade Voget," he said flatly.

Voget stood up as the guard entered the room. He followed the Spaniard down the long, cool corridor, holding his breath, struggling toward the far patch of light like a man swimming under water.

Two silent men in leather overcoats rode with Voget in the black sedan back to Barcelona. The clear, warm spring day quivered and pulsed. Sirens moaned, and aircraft circled in the skies. The city was under attack again.

The SIM officers in leather coats left Voget at the doorway of Communist Party headquarters. A long, faded banner filled and flattened in the smoky air.

¡No ceder un solo palmo de terreno al enemigo!

Do not yield a single hand's-breadth of ground to the enemy.

The all-clear sirens sobbed and fluttered over the city. The black sedan rushed away on squealing tires. The guard at the desk checked Voget's papers and waved him on. Three or four soldiers sprawled on wooden chairs, cursing in soft, sullen English, obviously but discreetly guarded by a very young Spanish boy smoking a cigarette.

"Don't tell em nothin," one of the soldiers said in English. "Just say we got separated from the friggin outfit and thought it was gonna get reorganized here in the city, get it."

"They gonna ream our ass-holes," one of the others said. "They know we fucked off. They gonna turn us over to the Party. Jail, maybe."

"Bullshit," the first soldier said. "Did you ever see a Lincoln officer that wasn't no snot-nosed bastard? We just didn't have the breaks, that's all. They ain't gonna do nothin but send us back."

"Mahoney's gonna ream our ass-holes," the other soldier said. "Him and his nigger buddy. Them two will have us shot!"

"Frig em. Frig everybody. Frig everythin. Next time, we'll make it to France. Just trust old Al."

"We done that. They gonna ream . . ."

"Don't tell em nothin. We just got separated from the outfit. It happens all the time."

"How we gonna get outta this fuckin country? The Party's got our passports."

"Trust old Al. In two weeks, you'll be making speeches at Madison Square Garden and Earl Browder will shake your hand."

Voget walked slowly between them and on to the *cantina*. Despite the rain, lunch was being served. Voget took a tin bowl and spoon and stood in line for the midday ration of watery lentil soup.

There were about a hundred of them left. It was hard to keep count. New stragglers appeared, so accepted as dead or captured that their faces and voices were a shock. They dropped down beneath the trees, ragged and filthy, and fell asleep, the tears of happiness drying on their bearded faces. Others, feeble with dysentery, minor wounds, sprained ankles, and fever drifted off. The machine guns had been lost or abandoned. Only a few men in each company had rifles, and each company had shrunk to a section of shuffling, surly lice-pickers waiting for the next food ration. They lay or crouched under the trees. There were no tents, no lean-to shelters, no blankets, no mules, no transport. No one gave orders; no one listened. They lay under the trees on a hillside overlooking the two towns of Gandesa and Batea and waited for something else to happen to them.

There was nothing to talk about. What was left of the battalion was under the command of Milt Wolff, with Johnny Gates as commissar. Wolff had a mustache and a long black cape. Gates was the only one with much of a uniform. They spent most of their time at Brigade.

Mahoney blamed Brigade for the disaster. Now that the officers, Colonel Čopic and Bob Merriman were back, they were at fault for being on leave when the Lincolns were hit by the surprise attack. Doran, the Brigade commissar, had been in command, for how long Mahoney didn't remember. He thought it was longer than White said it was, but they had given up arguing about it. Doran had ordered the counter-attack. Then Merriman had showed up. Most of the British officers had been killed, too, and the Mac-Paps were down to a handful. Mahoney stayed away from them. The Canadians blamed the Americans for losing them somewhere back in the hills west of Gandesa.

The men blamed White for lost comrades and blamed him, too. They scattered around under the trees, mixed with the men from other companies. The Spaniards stuck to themselves. Everyone gave the outfit another day, maybe two, before it busted up. But no one had the strength now to get up and walk away. It was useless. There was nowhere to go, nothing to do. There had been more than five hundred. Now there were one hundred.

He lay under his tree in a listless stupor, indifferent even to being alive. He watched the clouds break against the mountain tops and spill down the slopes. He listened to the far rumble of artillery dropping on Lister's troops off to the south. He could feel the liquid squirm of his belly and bowels and the ruin of his feet, like rocks loose under the skin.

A bulky shadow fell over him.

"Get the company together, Jimmy."

It was White, half his face hidden in a dirty bandage nearly as dark as his skin. His voice was too tired-sounding to be an order, and Mahoney looked away, plucking at his flimsy map-overlay.

"Get em yer ownself," he said.

"We got replacements," White said, sitting down.

"Bobby Merriman," Mahoney said. "He's gotta great idea. We're gonna counterattack again. Go ahead, you dumb fucks. I ain't movin. I *can't!* You know that. I got these fallen feet. I need some supports. Did you tell the *practicante* that, huh? You did like hell, you bastid . . . You don't give a goddamned now more'n the next sucker."

"I didn't see nobody who even looked like a *practicante*," White said. "They're down at Brigade, I guess. Anyway, this Spaniard came up."

"Give him the whole friggin country," Mahoney said. "Let em have it. Just get my ahss back to Southy."

"There's new replacements come up from Corbera. Spanish and Americans, too."

"No shit," Mahoney said.

"Lissen to me," White said.

"Bullshit."

"There's over a hundred Americans," White said. "Guys from home. Been trained for a couple of weeks, I guess. Every company gets some."

"What for?"

"Lay off that, huh?" White said wearily. "They'll be along in a little. We're supposed to get fed tonight, too."

"Yeah," Mahoney said, and closed his eyes. White sprawled back under the next tree. He sighed.

"We coulda used these guys comin in, huh? Last week. I look around now and see who's lost, and you know, I can't even *remember?* Somebody shows up and all his buddies start bawlin. Like kids, babies. We aint got nothin left, Jimmy, and they went and sent us some more. I got the roster right here."

A Spanish runner woke them up. The runners could always find Capitán Blanco. He pointed off at the trees, said something, White grunted, and then the new replacements appeared. Joe Bianca limped by, one end of his handlebar mustache sucked down into the corner of his mouth. Mahoney squinted at him.

"How's the end of it, Joe?" he said.

The big Italian machine gunner glanced down.

"Up yours, Baloney," he said, and fell down under a tree and began digging at his armpits.

The new recruits were dusty and sweaty-faced and carried blanket rolls. They tiptoed down between the trees, apologetic and nervous-looking. They all had clean, shaved faces. One of them tried to salute and looked at White.

"Scuse me, comrade. Is this sector held by Company Five?"

White looked at him and laughed, a tight, dark, menacing bark and turned away. The new kid sat down, after looking around at the five or six others who seemed to be with him.

"We've been looking around for our company," the kid said.

"Me, too," White muttered. "You just keep on lookin. Holla if you find anybody."

"This is Company Five?" the kid persisted.

"Yeah."

The others sat down, murmuring to each other. Mahoney ignored them.

There was a long silence. The replacements whispered together, wondering if there was any water or food. One of them had a pack of cigarettes.

"You comrades care for a smoke?"

Mahoney took the pack. White glared at him.

"Gimme one, now. You can't keep alla them!"

"Yer ahss," Mahoney said, but made no effort to keep White from snatching up the pack. They lit up, sitting close together, not looking at the replacements now ranged before them in a loose ring.

"Is there . . . When is chow?"

"We ain't been fed since the day before yestiddy," he said. "There *ain't* no chow."

"Can't you bring this to the attention of the company commissar, comrade?" the kid said.

"*I'm* the company comic-star," Mahoney said, grinning. "Now ain't that just piss in yer eyes, huh?"

"But . . ."

"Go complain to Dave or Johnny Gates," Mahoney said. "Run off and cry to them smart fucks at Brigade that got all our ahsses into this mess! If you don't like it, fuck off like the other heroes we got!"

White lolled out his pink tongue and spat on the dirt. The new replacements looked at him. He stared back with big, bloodshot eyes.

"You're Comrade White, then, sir?"

"Yeah," White said.

"We're your replacements, comrade."

"That's your tough ass, kid," White said. Mahoney laughed at their shocked faces. He pulled the roster from his pocket.

"Which sucker are you?" he said.

The replacement muttered his name. Mahoney found it on the list and nodded.

"I'll write and tell yer mamma when you get yer balls shot off," he said.

The trouble with White was he couldn't help being a good guy. Just because they'd given him a few tailor-mades, he felt obliged to them and sat up, answering their stupid questions.

"What happened after that, comrade?"

"We got out again over the hills," White said. "Marched most of that night. No water, no food. Soon as it got light, we saw right off we was outflanked again. They got there before us."

"No foolin!"

"Did you attack the Fascists there, comrade?"

Mahoney looked up at the new spring leaves on the branches over his head. The sun came through in patches, hot and blinding.

"Naw," he said. "We fucked off."

The space around them was very quiet. Someone scraped a match. Far away, artillery boomed. The replacements whispered together.

"What did he say—*run?*"

"Jeez, the morale in this outfit. . . . You *sure* this is the Lincoln battalion?"

"He *can't* be the commissar . . . my Christ . . ."

"Oh yeah," Mahoney snarled, sitting up again. "That's what you fuck-faces think, huh? Lookit this!"

He snatched his map from his breast pocket and spread it over his thigh.

"We'd been whip-assed for three-four days and nights runnin," he said. "*Avión* on our necks, artillery all around. We din't even know where the other guys was *at*, see? About that time, we were . . . uh, about here, huh, Andy?"

White bent over the flimsy sheet.

"Little to the east," he said, poking the paper. "Arty Kindall went off his rocker there and we left him, remember?"

"That's right," Mahoney said, recalling only the sound of splintered bits of boulders howling and whining around them, the sudden flash of orange that had knocked him down, and the rifleman named Kindall running down the slope, back toward the enemy they couldn't see.

"You *abandoned* a member of the company, Comrade Mahoney?"

"He was off his nut! Sure, we left him. Then we run like hell, huh, Andy?"

White nodded slowly, wiping his face. He looked at the new kids.

"All that day. Hidin from *avión* and duckin shells and run when they let up."

The replacements stared at him, disgusted.

"When do you expect to be relieved of command, comrade?" one of them, red-faced and trembling, demanded.

"Anybody wants it, all he's gotta do is live long enough," White said. "Promotion's easy in this outfit."

"You *ran?* And nothing has been done?" the red-faced kid said, very excited. "Comrades, I can't believe it!"

White looked at Mahoney and lifted one heavy shoulder.

"Some replacements they sent us," he said dully. "They don't believe it."

"Let's have this very clear," a new spokesman said, older, heavier in the face, with steel-rimmed glasses he kept taking off and polishing on his shirt. "Speaking frankly, I can't really believe that you two comrades are company commander and commissar of 5th Company. If this is some kind of joke, it strikes me as pretty damned bad taste . . ."

He paused and let the others murmur and nod before leaning forward to tap Mahoney's ruined boot.

"Don't get me wrong," he continued, shaking his head mournfully. "We don't intend to get either of you in trouble with Captain White and Lieutenant Mulvaney—"

"Mahoney," Mahoney said.

"—the company commissar. I think we can even accept the fact of morale in a complete, well, nearly complete state of total disintegration due to fatigue and short rations . . ."

"Uh-*huh!*" White said.

"But for you two men, comrades in the anti-Fascist struggle to—well, practically *boast*, for God's sake, of running away—You *don't* have rifles do you?"

White and Mahoney shook their heads. The recruit polished his glasses and glared at them nearsightedly. Mahoney belched.

"Where I come from, comrades," the replacement said, snapping the steel bows down over his ears, "that's cowardice and, worse, sabotage of the people's efforts! Do you two fellas have any real idea of how hard it is for the government to obtain weapons for us? I see you don't have much to say on that. And retreating—why, look here, fellas, you've been on the line longer than we have, sure, but have you been here so long that you've forgotten the very nature of the Fascist foe? Huh?"

Mahoney made a farting noise with his lips. White lit another cigarette. The spokesman rushed on, sure of support from the other replacements.

"It's not possible to retreat from Fascism," he said. "It's everywhere. You've got to stand and fight it wherever you come upon it and . . ."

White puffed on his cigarette and fingered his bandaged face.

"Awright," he said finally. "I guess you've had your say, fella. When you been through a week like we've had—and you come out alive—you come back lookin for Andy White and you can set down and tell me all about it—*all* about it, huh? But right now, lemme tell you that you keep on with this rear-rank bullshit, I'm gonna reach out and knock the teeth outta your head. You got no right to call coward at these boys. So haul ass away over there, see? Me and Mahoney'll let you know what you can do some little time from now. So—*git!*"

"Look, comrade," one of the other kids said. "Maybe there's been some kind of mistake . . ."

Mahoney took the last cigarette, crumpled the pack and flipped it at them.

"Just you stick around," he said. "Just stick around."

The replacements crept off and huddled around a tree, eying White and Mahoney, trying to strike up small talk with other survivors of the retreats. The Lincoln veterans shrugged, grunted noncommittally or turned away. Mahoney watched them until White woke up in the late afternoon. Then he pulled his broken boots on his feet.

"Where you off to on them bad feet? You'll never make it further'n the next tree, Jimmy."

"I'm gonna see Dave," Mahoney said. "I'm gonna see the Brigade comic-star, college-boy hero who saved our asses so somebody else could get em blown off us."

"What the hell for?" White said.

"I'm comic-star, ain't I?" Mahoney snarled. "No gahdamned buncha punk kids kin knock my company. I ain't gonna be back until I got chow, candy bars, cigarettes, every man a foo-seel and three grenades!"

There were no orders, no food, no weapons, but Division had found them a truck and a hot meal was promised. The drinking water was gone, and he did not think he could walk down into the valley, fill canteens and make it back up the hillside. He flipped coins with a Spanish runner, and won a liter of lukewarm stuff purified with iodine. The truck came at last, and when the new replacements lined up for the meal, Mahoney stood at the tailgate, handing out tin cans and pieces of wood to those who had no mess kits. He hovered over each meager portion of cold rice, brown lettuce drenched in olive oil and hard bread, as though he had cooked and hauled the food himself.

Mahoney scuffed down the line of twigs and stones he had placed on the sloping earth. The replacements sat like a school class, bored but intimidated, the younger ones reluctantly awed.

"This here is Alcañiz," he said. "Where these here rocks are, see? Lister, I guess you heard of him, his corps holds this section. They're getting the shit dumped on them every day from Fascist artillery you can hear. There's a crap-house rumor goin around that Mussolini is gonna land forty thousand more men down at Málaga or somewhere. Don't believe it and don't repeat it. Political information is relayed through the company commissar to the rank and file. Pretend I'm a shop steward, like in the union back home, see? Besides, we got Italians on our side. The Twelfth, that's the Garibaldis, and some big brain got them guys strung out for twelve kilometers along here. Now, the Thirteenth, them guys is Hunkies, Czechs, and Polack comrades, they went here to support Lister. And here we are, sitting on our asses with empty bellies and no guns and that's the political situation. Health report. You new guys ain't been swimmin, yet. That's an order. The truck leaves in thirty minutes. Pick up a bar of soap for each section, one pair of socks per man and . . . Yeah, you there?"

"Comrade, what about enemy aircraft?"

"Lots of em, ain't there?" Mahoney said, and spat on the ground.

Mahoney marched alongside the column. It was dusk and raining again. The men moved in a slow, hunched strung-out herd, sneezing, shivering, and snorting mucus out their knuckled nostrils.

"Oop-au-ay-arro! Oop-au-ay-arro!" Mahoney chanted doggedly. "Pick em up and lay em down, you monkeys! You ain't no Boy Sprouts. This here's Comp'ny Five, so pick em up and look alive!"

The column groaned and squelched on down the dirt road. Mahoney trotted ahead to check the time with White, then drifted back, the rain beating in his face, pattering on his helmet.

"Whatsa matter, *chicos*, you got homesick for that crummy *chavola*? This mornin it was, hey, comic-star, how come we gotta sleep in these friggin lean-tos? Now you don't wanna walk five miles to these here millionaire-capitalist mansions yer old buddy Mahoney organized. Some outfit! I'm gonna tell Milt tonight the next time he gets replacements to get us some Spanish Girl Scouts. Come *ahnnn*, move it!"

"Like this, see? Keep down. Head low. Keep lookin. Then, *hit it!*"

Mahoney flung himself forward. The replacements nodded, nervous and impressed. The company commissar was quick, certain. They were still watching him fall, and there he was, snug as a lizard behind a sheltering boulder, the rifle ready, cocked and aimed. He rolled over and shot upright, his shoulder dipping into the rope sling.

"This here's yer first patrol, like Andy White said. He's got one section, you birds is with me. You better keep yer traps shut and yer eyes open. You ain't gonna get no next time. This friggin outfit only got seventeen rifles for the whole battalion, right? That's one foo-seel for every twenny a you heroes. Lose the one you got, jam the breech with mud, and I turn you over to Doran at Brigade and you get shot, see? What's the order, you with the runny nose?"

"I got a cold, comrade."

"Who don't? You don't get no Purple Hearts in this outfit unless you got a cold *and* a fever and room-a-tizz. You know what yer gonna get from chomping on them cold *garbanzos* and hoss-piss cawfee? The Purple Farts. What's the order?"

"All personnel on patrol are to shoot on sight any non-civilian that don't answer a challenge and take cover."

"Whadda you do you see some Spanish skirt pickin wild onions like yesterday?"

"In the case of non-civilians, notify the section leader at once or the comic-st—I mean commissar, if available."

"Smart guy," Mahoney said, grinning. "College boy. Okay, grab yer foo-seels and let's go. Follow me, you bums."

Mahoney danced with one of the Spanish girls up from Barcelona, doing a clumsy shag, the light from the bonfire turning his face bright red. The girl in her modest Unified Socialist Youth outfit frowned, trying to match Mahoney's steps. He winked lewdly at the replacements sipping the warm champagne and sucking on hazelnuts. Somebody cut in on him, and he shagged back to the group, snapping his fingers, stole a tin cup, and drained it. A voice shouted for attention. The men gathered around the bonfire stopped singing.

"Here comes da bullshit," Mahoney said loudly. "Every fiesta it's the same. Some Frog moonshine, a few skirts to get yer pecker up, and then they start the speeches."

He glared around at the replacements and demanded a cigarette. Someone handed him one and a match. He struck it on the seat of his pants and swaggered off a few paces.

"You dumb bastids think this is just fer a good time, huh?" he sneered. "You know what a fiesta means? Naw. It means we're going into the lines, see? Inna action. It's sucker-stuff. Lap up the booze and make like you love speeches."

"But we don't have any weapons, Jimmy."

"That Frog in the truck din't just bring this bubbly," Mahoney said. "He come in from France with plenty a trucks filled up with foo-seels from Russia. We get our issue tomorra at five o'clock."

"Where's the rifle range, Jimmy?"

Mahoney grinned, the cigarette in the corner of his lips, one eye squinted against the smoke. One of the girls from Barcelona was speaking. Mahoney pointed west, into the darkness.

"Right out there, comrade. Right out there."

They all turned to look.

"April Fool, you jerks! April Fool."

Fifth Company lay along a humped hill, digging in, loosening the red dirt with their long "pig-sticker" bayonets and watching the woods, the roads and the sky. Mahoney dodged from section to section passing the order to hold what ammo there was left. White squeezed the blisters on his palms and watched the crossroads, the Gandesa-Batea fork. Enemy armor and motorized infantry shifted and rumbled beneath the heavy dry clouds that hung over the valley like rust, hiding them. Artillery flashed off to the right and left.

White leaned forward, straining to see. A shell hit west of the fork, then another and a third, big spouts of earth leaping up, then the sound. Running figures seemed to spring up out of the ground, scrambling back across the road, halting there for a ragged volley, and ducking away again. Someone shouted in what sounded like German to White. Maybe it was what was left of the Thaelmanns, being driven back by the Navarrese, plenty of infantry with tanks supporting their push.

"Jimmy!" he shouted. "Send a runner after Billy Carroll. Confirm enemy at the crossroads! Tell him not to bother with battalion . . . too late! Get his ass to Brigade and tell Čopic!"

He lay, cursing softly, grinding the new sage leaves between his blistered palms until the pink, taut bubbles raised by his hot rifle smelled of the pungent herb. They always had tanks, and there was never any ammo left for the small Czech cannons that could pierce the warty-looking armor or blow the broad, creeping tracks off them. There was a crate or two of nitro bottles back at the dump near Gandesa. Too late. The flank was turned. In a half hour, the Fascists would come up behind them.

"*A tierra!*"

A flight of planes hammered over, strafing, and roared very low toward Gandesa and spilled fragmentation bombs into the fields and terraced vineyards. The little valley filled with hot flashes.

It had all gone wrong, from the very first. Lister had been hit so hard, so long, that he broke and pulled out about the time the bonfire burned at the fiesta. The few British that got away said they walked right into tanks twenty kilometers *inside* the lines. The Mac-Paps were lost. So was the Spanish 59th. It had all busted to pieces everywhere, and they hadn't known it for nearly a full day. Now it was too late. All that was left was the narrow dirt road, and the tank shells hit again, only fifty meters short.

He saw an armored car, weaving slow and heavy down the road with mortar rounds hitting and a Fiat machine gun sputtering up rusty spouts all around it before the car roared on under the shelter of 5th Company's hill, turning away toward the command post. It was from Brigade, either Merriman or Dunbar. White slid down the slope, his feet suddenly tangled in the bipod of the jammed Dikterov light machine gun. He kicked out frantically.

"*Secciones!*" he shouted. "Get ready to pull! Jimmy, soon's you see that runner, get this bunch back!"

He was playing a hunch, but when the runner came up, he was right. It had been Merriman in the armored car, and the new order was for all units of the division to evacuate the pocket, Quince Brigada back first, with 11th holding the line till dusk, if they could. White led the company away, hurrying them by instinct, even though he didn't know which direction led to safety. They hit the ditch twice as planes swept over.

By late afternoon, the space around the big stone house, patchy with flaking whitewash, the Brigade first-aid station was jammed. Everyone shouted and milled around, collecting ammunition, stepping on each other, stragglers coming in looking for their units. The crews from the machine-gun company began dismantling the heavy Maxims, dividing the loads. The heavy metal boxes between their scuffling feet cast shadows like grave-markers. Some scouts went out. Artillery fire hammered, and a motorcycle rider appeared. The rumor swept around that the Gandesa fork had been captured by Italians, not Navarrese, and enemy patrols were in Batea! White looked at Mahoney and shook his head.

"Don't tell the guys, Jimmy."

"Sonofabitchin Doran wants to make a stand for it like at Caspé," Mahoney said bitterly.

"Cut it out," White said. "Quit the jokes. That ain't funny."

"Him and Milt and Bob are chewing the fat on it."

During a lull, some tanks came in. Fifth Company spilled back into the field, out of the way. Infantry rode on the tanks, part of the 11th Brigade pulling back.

"*Capitán Blanco?*"

"Yeah, yeah," White said, and got up. "Let's find out the bad news."

Mahoney was squating in a circle of men, sucking on a tiny cigarette butt talking about food, that place in Boston he liked. The men listened automatically, their empty bellies aching, hollow, dust-ringed eyes scanning the clouds for enemy planes. It was not possible now to tell the old-timers from the replacements. They all had the bitter, beaten look of men forced to retreat again and again and again.

"Listen," White said. "It's gettin on to dark. We're gonna try and slip around Batea and get up into the hills. That means everybody's got to keep contact. If you lose the guys in front of you in the dark, sing out contact, real loud, understand? Command's going out right after the scouts . . ."

"They would," somebody said. White looked, but saw bent-down heads and here and there a wavering trickle of cigarette smoke.

"Supply's got ammunition and grenades," White went on. "Pick up all you can carry. I been hunchy today, right? Well, we're gonna need some stuff. Maybe tonight. Maybe first thing tomorra. Don't go empty-handed. But keep contact, that's the big thing."

"*Batallón a formar!*"

It was Milt Wolff, his tall form draped to the knees in his long black cape, a beret crammed on his head, Frenchy-style. He waved his long arms, and the Lincoln battalion stood up, groaning and cursing. It was about eight o'clock. The march to the rear began.

White took two grenades and three cartridge packs and stepped out of the line of march. His company shuffled up, shying away from the guys handing out grenades and ammo. The battalion commissar stood watching, too. No one said anything. White stepped in beside Mahoney.

"Pick up some stuff," he said. "Set an example, *huh?* For a change?"

Mahoney took a grenade and two packets of rifle cartridges. The column moved on. The 11th was getting it close now, mortars, machine guns, rifle fire. The column rushed on half a kilometer, then slowed again. White could see Mahoney's hands. Empty.

"Them things don't fit my foo-seel," Mahoney said blandly. "What's the use a truckin stuff that don't fit?"

"Keep contact," White said, and swung forward to head the company. He repeated it over and over, *Keep contact, Keep contact.* It wasn't an order. He was begging now, pleading with them.

A dump of abandoned ammunition went off, lighting up the sky with a long, spurting, stuttering roar. The column hurried forward again. The cartridge packs flogged against his thighs. The grenades felt like sash weights. White tossed the Mills bombs away, into the ditch, coughing loudly as each one hit.

The units shifted forward; the dim forms stood up, stiff-muscled, and hobbled on again. They were getting near Batea. Artillery whistled and thumped up ahead, then the sky-splitting sound of shrapnel. The scouts nosed and fumbled in the hills and came back in. White moved up to the head of the long column to confer with Doran, Merriman, Wolff, and the other officers. There was no map. They were going to skirt Batea and head for the high hills over Gandesa.

They tripped over equipment flung away by the men who stumbled on ahead of them, blankets, ammunition, the flat heavy cans for the Dikterovs, the new rifles sent from Russia. White groaned and moved on, lifting his leg, throwing it forward, flatfooted, then the other, counting a hundred paces, then stopping to rest. He counted seventy paces and rested, then took fifty steps and stopped, gasping and wiping his face.

They were in some sort of broken little valley, cut by two or three rough tracks. He could hear someone moving, feeling his way forward. White followed the sound, and the rest of the company followed him. Now he stopped after every twenty-five separate efforts to lift his legs.

"Who's at?" he whispered.

"Dunning," the man said, as though he had to stop and think about it. White knew him, a seaman from the NMU, a thin blond guy with a broken nose.

"Where's Blackie Maprahlian?" White rasped. "Fourth Company's at the head of the column, ain't it?"

"I dunno. Andy?"

"Yeah. We been keepin contact on you."

"You *have?*"

Dunning panted slowly, considering this amazing fact.

"Jeez, I been just walking in front of you guys."

"You mean Maprahlian and the rest *ain't* in front a you?"

"I dunno where the fuck they are. See, I figgered you knew where we was goin, so I just walked on ahead."

"But we been followin you!" White said.

He wanted to kill Dunning, but didn't have the strength left to do it. They had broken contact. They were lost.

His mind moved very slowly, fumbling with the alternatives of pushing on and staying where they were. He knew the company was strung out. If they went on, it would break up slowly but surely into sections, each bunch losing contact. Then the sections would bust up. Every mother's son would be lost all by himself then. This way they were at least all lost together.

"Awright," he said into the darkness. "Halt and sleep. That's the order."

He sat down and stretched out his legs. It was so good just to sit there. He felt fuzzy-headed and sensed he was weaving, his body swaying from the hips up. He was falling asleep and waking up between breaths. He heard the column collapse in the darkness, a slow, sighing, rattling settle, then the soft sound, *huh-huh-huh*, of every man panting like a worn-out dog. He should put scouts out on the point and flanks, go back and check with Mahoney, send someone back to make contact with the 11th. He should never have thrown away the grenades. He should . . .

He fell back, propped on one elbow. His head was so heavy. It pulled him down toward the ground, making the muscles in his throat hurt. He listened, the sounds of the night on the cliff edge of consciousness. Trucks, tanks, motorcycles and ambulances, wheels and motors, all grinding in on them from the west, from the south. His lids fluttered. Some of the sound was spilled out of the Big Dipper. The North. They were lost. They were surrounded, almost.

"Yeah," he said, letting his elbow slide. His shoulders and head touched the still-warm earth. He seemed to keep on sinking, sinking, dropping away from everything.

The sound was the furtive click of a rifle bolt somewhere above and outside him. He went up to it, driving, pressing, like swimming under water, straining for the surface, breaking up and out, a gulping gasp awake in the cool, dew-gray dawn, his eyes open and his heart ramming in his chest.

There were three of them on a gully lip rising above the white mist. The middle one was frozen in the instant of pushing the bolt lever down, cocking the rifle pointed down at him. White slitted his eyes, and felt the flesh crawl on the back of his neck. He could not make out the color of their uniforms; their faces were dim, dark blurs.

He muttered and flopped over, flinching against the bullets he expected to tear him, his hand dropping on the cool, greasy barrel of his own rifle.

"No estás durmiendo, tú!" one of them said.

White snatched his hand away.

"No," he said. "No estoy durmiendo."

He rolled his head a little, so that he could see them better. They looked at each other.

"Número de Brigada?"

"Quince Brigada," he said. "Y tú?"

"No puede ser. Es un moro, éste!" one of the other ones said. "That can't be. He's a Moor."

"Inglés? Spik inglés?"

If he made the wrong move, they'd shoot. He had to make them believe he was an inglés.

"You betcha, pal," he said slowly. "I'm not English, though. I'm an American. We're part of the Lincoln battalion and we're just mighty glad to see you comrades."

"Inglés. Charlando en inglés. I spik inglés, too. Muy poco. Okay?"

"Y tu brigada?"

"Brigada número once," two of them said at the same instant. White sat up, very slowly, rubbing his eyes and stretching cautiously. Eleventh Brigade had walked up on them during the night. These chicos were lost, too.

The middle one smiled, a tight-lipped little grin that lifted away from his white teeth. He nodded and worked his rifle bolt, catching the cartridge as it fell out of the breech. White released a long, shuddering sigh and stood up. The three Spanish boys came down into the gully to shake hands.

The land was crumpled, stiff folds of parallel hills, like the spines of gigantic animals sleeping in the stony soil. There was cover, wind-twisted oaks and stunted pines and beneath the trees thick sage, darker than grass, pungent beneath the soles of their sandals and boots. They found the old man and the burro cart shortly after noon. He was watering the animal from a tiny stream.

'Hola, viejo," White said.

That was the signal for the flankers to stand up. They surrounded the old man completely. The maneuver had taken better than a half hour. The old man set down his leather bucket and wheeled around, looking, before he faced White again.

"*Fantástico*," he murmured, his dark eyes glittering in leathery, deep-wrinkled lids. "*Un Negro con su tropa de elefantes . . .*"

"You like my troop of elephants?" White asked. "We move with great quietness and secrecy, no?"

The old man tilted his head this way and that. In the quiet gully with the sun coming down hot and no trees moving, White could hear the far sound of motors, trucks, tanks, motorcycles and ambulances.

"Which way to Corbera, old man?" he said.

The burro twitched an ear, shaking a fly. The old man patted the animal absently, staring at White.

"If I say that way, you will believe me," he said. "Also, if I say that way. Only, in truth, the village of Mora lies in that direction."

"Then Corbera lies *so*," White said, pointing. The old man nodded. He reminded White of a huge tortoise he had once seen in a zoo, slow, old, miserable, and safe. It was quite possible that the old man would direct them right into a trap. Old men and old women in Spain hated the Anarchists, hated the war.

"And you, *viejo*," he said. "For which are you? The Republic or the Fascists?"

"Plug him," Mahoney said.

The old man slowly raised his arm, and pointed a finger dark as an oak twig at Mahoney.

"*Rubio*," he said triumphantly. "*Un irlandés!*"

A couple of the Spanish boys in first section grinned. El Rubio, The Redhead, was what they all called Mahoney. Somehow the old man knew he was an Irishman. He cackled softly, his shoulders humping.

"Who holds the nearest village?" White asked.

"*Nadie*," the old man said. "No one."

"Civilians there?"

The old man shook his head and bent for the leather bucket.

"Only the dead," he answered.

"Is there food in this place?"

"*Mucha*," the old man answered. "Also a *camión*."

"A truck!" Mahoney said. "Let's go, fer Crissakes!"

"Easy. Maybe it's a trap."

The old man's dark eyes glittered, and he laughed softly.

"We'll take a chance," White decided. "*Cola! Cola!* Let's get outta here. He gives me the creeps. *Adiós, viejo*."

"*Hasta la vista, jovencito*," the old man muttered. "Until the next time we see each other, young man."

Since there was no map, the fact that White had forgot to ask the name of the place was unimportant. It lay on the east slope of a long hill picked clean. They climbed down a slope of boulders and bare dirt to reach it, a cluster of stone houses with roofs of faded, cracked orange tile. There was no smoke, no sound. It was shaded, cool and quiet, absolutely quiet.

When White gave the order to spread out and encircle the place, no one obeyed. They fell down the stone-strewn slope on the village, buckle-legged and bracing themselves with their rifles. The blind, weak rush stopped a few paces from the first house. They looked at each other, tensed for the smash of sniper's rifles. Nothing. Nobody.

The truck had been abandoned in the middle of the slot of packed dirt that ran as a road between seven stone houses. It was a THC with a red star on the driver's door. All four tires had been shot flat. Some Remington rifles and cartridge belts were scattered in the back, thrown down on top of big wooden crates labeled with Russian words no one could read. The rifles and belts were swept aside, and the men used bayonets to pry open the crates.

"Food!" Mahoney shouted, lurching up, a chunky can of corned beef in each hand. "We eat!"

Mahoney began pitching the cans out of the truck to the men. White felt hot saliva gush in his mouth. His tongue curled, quivering. He took a lunging step forward and caught himself.

"Line up!" he ordered. "Fall in by sections. Let's get scouts out and—"

His voice was drowned out. The men swarmed around the tailgate, shouting, pushing and cursing. They dropped their rifles and fought over cans of corned beef, sardines, and stew, packets of hard brown biscuit.

"Coffee! Real coffee. Start a fire, you bums!"

Mahoney found a ten-kilo sack of beet sugar and a dozen big jars of George Washington.

"No fires!" White shouted. "You crazy? No fires!"

Mahoney dropped down to the ground and stared at the houses. All around him, men were hacking open the cans, cramming their mouths with red, fibrous lumps of corned beef, wet and slick with warm, runny gold jelly, gnawing the hard Russian bread, plastering their lips with shiny bits of sardines. Two men stomped a packing crate to kindling.

"They got stoves here," Mahoney said. "Find a pan."

They sat in the shade, looking at the truck, and eating. White pawed up the bits and sucked his fingers, ground the hard, sweet bread between his teeth.

"Take it easy," he muttered. "Don't eat too much. Save some. Eat too much you'll get sick . . ."

The men swapped what they had extras of for what they wanted. In a few minutes, the price of corned beef rose from one can of sardines to three, then four or three sardines and two rounds of the bread. A blue feather of smoke twisted up out of a tile stove pipe and quivered the cool air. White groaned and ate and ate.

A barrel rolled across toward the truck from an open doorway and stopped. The men stared, their jaws still, listening to the deep slush and gurgle. Mahoney leaned in the doorway, a wooden cup in his hand.

"It's on me, you bastids! *Vino tinto* from Casa Mahoney!"

He drank from the cup and poured the rest of the wine over his head, laughing. The wine soaked his hair and ran down in red streams into his eyes, into the corners of his mouth. The men without cups drank from their hands or lay on the ground, snatching at the thick stream pouring into their faces. A Spanish boy brought White wine in a ragged beef can. Bits of meat floated in little golden circles.

"*Salud!*" White said and drank the can empty, groaning over the harsh, nutty flavor of cool red wine. Never had wine tasted so good. He leaned back against the stone house front, moaning and grinning, feeling it plunge in his blood.

The final miracle to go with the scalding sweet coffee was tobacco, flat cans of Russian cigarettes Mahoney discovered under the seat of the truck. The talk was low and easy. They smiled and yawned, sharing the sugar and the cigarettes with lazy generosity, redivided the extra food section by section, insisting that the Spanish boys take whatever was left over. There was a lot of gentle punching of shoulders, shoving and soft jokes. They were all comrades, and life was good. They were all safe, all together and sleepy now in this nameless place of cool stones and shadows.

Mahoney and two other men were tinkering with the truck. White watched them, indifferent but pleased in a vague, satisfied, paternal easiness. He stood up and sauntered over, dipped up some more coffee, and looked at Mahoney's rump and legs dangling over the front fender.

"How long you figger, Mister Henry Ford?" he said. "About four days to get that heap runnin? Another time, why we'd wait, but we're gettin on soon."

"Bullshit we are," Mahoney said. "They just pulled the coil and a few wires, see? Drained the radiator. Won't take long. There's a kit and a pump for patchin them tires. Couple hours and—"

"We'll be ten kilometers away," White said. "Come on outta there and run up the guys. Get em up and movin. We're pushin on."

Mahoney squirmed backward and dropped to the ground. His red face was running with sweat and smeared with grease. He scowled, half drunk and angry.

"Who says?"

"I says!" White barked. "Forget this heap a junk, Mahoney!"

"It's mine," Mahoney said flatly. "I found it and I'm gonna fix it up. We're gonna ride home nice and easy. Safe and sound."

"You crazy? Ride where? Where's safe and sound, huh? Looka that big red star. You think somebody up in one a them ugly-birds can't spot that? He'll come down and shoot us all up."

"Who's us? You don't like it, shove off, comrade! Dis ain't no Fresh Air Taxi, Amos. You wanna walk, walk. We'll catch up to yuh."

"Yer comin *with* us! Git away from that truck now, hear?"

Everybody still awake had come up to the truck. There were twenty of them, maybe, half-drunk happy, standing around with their arms on each other's shoulders.

"You get yer ahss away from *my truck!*" Mahoney squawled, the sweat spraying as he jerked away. He straightened, holding a long, straight-shanked steel wrench. He smashed at White's hand and the wrench rebounded from the fender leaving a deep dent where White's fingers had printed in the red dust. The men around murmured and shifted.

"We can't stay here for two hours, Jimmy, they'll catch us!" White said. "Now come on, cut it, see? Call the guys."

"You call em!" Mahoney shouted. "Tell em yer gonna walk all day, all night, all day till they can't do it no more and couldn't fight if they had to! We're tired of walkin, see? Tired of no maps and no food! Tired of all these fucked-up orders from Brigade! Tired of all dis shit! Now we got chow, we got gas, we got dis-here truck, and, by Christ, I'm gonna fix it and drive any guys that wants to stay and help me, so *fuck off* and leave us da hell *alone!*"

Mahoney swayed on his feet, his red face twisted, panting. He hefted the long wrench, his furious blue eyes measuring the distance, as his head jerked, snapping the lank hair that hung over his sweating face. A thick, taut vein pumped in his raw, sunburned neck.

The crowd of men milled and muttered, beginning to take sides.

White felt himself shaking with rage. He balled his fists and jammed them on his hips. His heart thudded.

"You been at the *vino* too much, Jimmy," he said thickly. "Let's you and me get inside somewheres and talk this over."

Mahoney sidled closer to the truck. White edged after him. They were two paces apart.

"Fuck you!" Mahoney said.

"You big-mouthed sonofabitch!" White shouted. "Get this company formed in a column to march! Right now! That's an *order!*"

Mahoney's face contorted. An incoherent scream wrenched violet flecks from his spewing lips. He slung himself back against the truck fender and came at White like a welterweight bounced off the ropes. He drove forward, slashing the wrench down at White's head.

White slipped in and off to the right. His left fist snapped into Mahoney's belly with a solid smack, stopping him, buckled over. White saw the black blur of his own cocked right arm. He hit Mahoney for every time he hadn't before, black-blind with the rage to kill, a single, massive smash that drove Mahoney sideways and down, skidding on his face in the dirt, his legs kicking like a rabbit.

The men in the circle made a single, pained groan and shrank away as White whirled on them. The blood-mist lifted and the air tore in and out of his chest. He unclenched his fists and let his arms fall. He was suddenly exhausted. If they jumped him . . .

"Form up!" he said. "This company is gonna march out. *Now!*"

White halted the march after what he thought was an hour. He looked back. The column had broken in two. Most of the men who had seen the fight and all of the Spanish boys were together close behind him. Then there was a gap of fifty paces. The ones who hadn't seen the fight, old-timers and replacements alike, walked in a ragged formation around Mahoney. The younger boys, their dark eyes anxious and sorrowful, trotted back and forth, trying to make peace.

"*No vale la pena,*" they repeated in their eager, nervous soft voices. "*No vale la pena* . . . It's not worth it, not worth it . . ."

Every hill was a menace. From the eastern, shadowed slope they had to cross a cramped valley, then climb up the sun-scorched western slope of the next hill, pushing up over boulders, through the tangled growth of oak and pine saplings. The crest of every hill was bare, stony, with tough, scattered sage plants. Every man stood exposed on the sky line. They were strafed, two slow runs by an Italian bomber. No one fired a shot. The plane slid away, leaving three men dead, two wounded.

The shadows grew longer; the pace slowed; the gap between the two groups widened. White's section reached the hollow of the valley, before Mahoney's advanced scouts crested the hill. White rested the column, but the stragglers did not close up. They were just barely in contact.

They were near Corbera, creeping through flimsy pines at dusk. One hill over was a dirt road filled with enemy trucks and tanks. Back another fold of the land beyond Mahoney's rear guard, a parallel road was clogged with fuel trucks and flatbeds carrying artillery ammunition. Fifth Company was hemmed in on both sides. The hill that concealed them on its slope crumbled into a broad field strewn with boulders. White sent a runner back to Mahoney, requesting that the company commissar come forward to confer on tactics to be used for a breakout to the east after dark. The runner came back saying the commissar of the company regretted being unable to come forward for the conference. Some unknown unit had closed to less than five hundred meters directly behind. The commissar was investigating. If a breakout was planned, the commissar would support it and follow.

The end of the day echoed with motors, the dull chatter of tank treads, shouts in German, Italian, and Spanish, the trample of cavalry units coming in to bivouac. They could look down into the road to the right from the crest of the hill. Ansaldo medium tanks rolled past, a whole squadron. White could see the commander at the open turret hatch, smoking a cigarette. Two platoons of Navarrese infantry broke ranks to rest directly below them.

The end of their hill was suddenly overrun by a noisy company of the Tercio and a big banner floated languidly in the jerky sweep of head-lights. Military police were everywhere, shouting, directing traffic with headlights, cruising on slow-puttering motorcycles.

Fires were lighted and a company of *transmisiones* plodded down the road, the wire wheel squeaking as the glossy line dribbled down into the near ditch. One of the Spanish boys whispered to White that he still had some wire cutters. They lay, still and cramped, flutter-nerved, every rifle cocked, watching the road, listening and waiting. White ordered the column to close up. Mahoney sent word that it was too dangerous to move that many men.

The road would never clear completely, White knew. The Fascists always moved their supplies by night, with the headlights on. But the convoys were spaced out, five minutes, ten minutes, perhaps. The cavalry had watered their horses, and the animals stamped restlessly, settling down. The cooking fires faded. The moon sailed cool and serene above the ragged, restless hills. White stood up. Down the line, in a gap between two trees, a dozen paces forward down the slope. Mahoney was standing, a Dikterov gun with the round cartridge can in place cradled in his arms. White could see the lank spill of his hair, and the silver moonlight on the muzzle-cone and bipod legs of the light machine gun.

White stepped forward, feeling the ground slope away from him. The others followed him, as quietly as they could. They passed through the last trees, and the little seedlings whipped against their legs. A stone bumbled a few feet and stopped. The Spanish boy ghosted down into the ditch. White heard the sharp, single nip of the cutters. Faint voices came from the left, the military police at the crossroads. The road to the right was a long, flat dark tunnel. A truck started.

White jumped the ditch and fell forward on his hands and knees in the road. The night rustled and clinked as the men spilled down out of the dusty bushes, running, leaping the ditch, out onto the tank-rutted surface, across into the other ditch. It seemed to take forever. Where was Mahoney?

White counted to ten. Mahoney's group crossed the road in a single, scuttling rush. White turned and moved on, across a narrow belt of weeds into an uncultivated vineyard, terraced at the far end where the moonlight touched the stone wall. Vines snagged at his ankles. He crept forward, stopped, moved on. There was no one at the wall. Beyond lay another terrace, then the field strewn with stones and finally the wooded slope of the next hill.

But there were no stones in the field. There were men. They lay everywhere, rolled in blankets. White waved his arm. They started forward across the moonlit plain mined with sleeping soldiers. They covered twenty meters. The shape nearest White stirred and muttered. He waited, crouching. The man rolled over.

The shape of a tank hulked ahead. A match spurted, tiny and terrifying. Someone behind White bolted, tripped, and fell.

"Hey, coño, cuidado . . ."

White stood up, just as he heard the clumsy blow of the rifle butt.

"Cabo! Cabo de la guardia!"

A swaddled shape lurched up in front of White. He sprang away to the left and nearly stepped on another man.

"Cabo de la guardia! Rojos! Rojos!"

The night exploded with shots, the sudden, dazzling wallop of a grenade, bullets snapping in the darkness and shouting, cursing men. A flashlight beam whipped wildly, and he dodged away from it, whimpering. The night in front of him tore open in little hot pockets. He had an instant's rippled vision of the low wall and dark woods beyond. He slowed to a halt, flung up his rifle and fired, the butt jolting him.

"Rojos! Rojos!"

"Fuego!"

He worked the bolt, dropped to a crouch, and fired again. A bullet powed near his ear.

"Mahoney!" he yelled. "Jimmy! Jimmy, for Crissakes!"

He shrank down, waiting for the slithering blast from the Dikterov as Mahoney emptied the pan at the low stone wall, tearing a path for them.

"Jimmy!"

The hard bulk of a body smashed into him from the side, even as he turned. He felt the rifle torn from his hands and the body lurch back off.

"Manos arriba! Manos arriba, Rojo!"

White slowly raised his empty hands. The Dikterov had never fired.

"Levántate! Manos arriba!"

White scrambled to his feet clumsily, his hands high above his head. He swayed in the darkness, panting, sensing two or three men around him. The night echoed to hysterical shouts and the ragged crackle of rifle and pistol fire back near the road. He strained to hear the stutter of Mahoney's Dikterov, holding his breath. Boots crunched behind him and stopped. A match hissed and flared before his eyes. He blinked at a whiskered face.

"Coño," the face said, stupefied. "Un moro . . ."

The tip of a bayonet wavered at his chest. He could smell garlic and wine and sweat. He blew out his held breath at the match, ducked and struck at the bayonet. The match went out, and the rifle at his back flashed, deafening him, a lick of pain searing the top of his skull. He lunged toward the wall, swinging both fists.

A flashlight. A yellow dazzle. A new voice.

"*Alto el fuego!*"

Boots behind him. He hunched against the bayonet or the rifle butt, his clenched fists sliding up level with his shoulders.

"*Manos arriba!*"

He squinted and saw a squad of Legionarios in their berets and long capes, an officer with goggles on the visor of his hat. Light lay like honey on the barrel of a Luger pistol. The light was too bright, the glare burning red on his twitching lids. He closed his eyes and felt the blood slug in his ears. They came up to him from all sides, closing him in their ring. His arms felt like lead.

"Sergeant González," the new voice said evenly. "This man is no Moor."

"Look at his face, *capitán!*"

"I see his face. I also see the red star on his cap. Bring him over to the tank."

White felt something press into the heavy muscles in the small of his back, like a nail shoved slowly into the flesh. The tip of a bayonet. He stepped forward away from the pain, his eyelids slitted against the dazzling light.

"*Un Rojo negro,*" the first voice said. "A black Red. What does he bleed, this one, coffee?"

"Later, Sergeant," the officer said mildly. "First, I want to ask him a few questions."

White clenched his teeth and kept walking. There was no yelling in the night now, no more running. He walked directly at the hot golden blossom burning his eyes. The dark air was cool on his face. His palms wept and the raw flesh was stung with grit. The blisters on his hands had broken. He could feel little drops trickle down over the veins leaping in his wrists.

April 22, 1938

My Dearest Sister,

Yes, it's sand! From the beaches near Viñaroz! You remember how Papa refused to use blotting paper and always kept his box of sand on his writing table? I brought a handful back to sprinkle on these sheets. Not sacred soil exactly, although I took care to catch up these grains from the spot where our group confessor celebrated Mass the very day we drove our tanks over the dunes and saw the Mediterranean before us, a deep, placid blue.

The honor of serving under our celebrated Alonso Vega came as a complete surprise. We had been in heavy action on the Aragón front for two weeks, then a sudden order shifting us down here. Do not believe what the newspapers claim to be the complete destruction of the enemy. It is true that we smashed several of the so-called "International Brigades," but Lister and his fanatical band slipped out of the pocket as has happened before. We captured a good amount of equipment, mostly small arms, some cannons, all Russian stuff, of course, and took some prisoners. We dealt with them in a manner fitting for international criminals.

The shift from the Gandesa salient to Vega's command looks but a short distance on a map, a hundred kilometers or so, but it was a nightmare of loading and unloading our tanks onto railroad flatcars for a few hours, then off onto bad roads, back on the cars. Day and night. Our spaghetti-twirling allies attempted to deny us gasoline, water, and food, despite our written orders and a copy from their General Berti pledging "complete co-operation." We were halted several times while their planes bombed undefended towns well behind their own lines!

Two bits of news from the Other Side. You know that Prieto has resigned from Negrín's Red government. He was kicked out, of course, everyone knows that. He was, somewhere, in his soul, a Spaniard first, a confused Socialist second, but Spaniard enough to strive for peace and to defy the Bolsheviks. *Frente Rojo* printed some photographs in a recent issue, the usual propaganda stuff, a Basque, two gypsies from Andalusia, some fugitive madrileños all grinning at the camera to illustrate the "solidarity" of criminals and fools for their Republic. He was there, embraced by the others. El Asturiano, posed with a loop of dynamite fuse around his neck, instead of the noose I dream of setting there with my own hands. Paco Larra. What a name! Like the yapping of a mad dog. He is much changed. I have imprinted that face in my memory, I assure you. I will find him yet. Before this is over, he will pay for Emilio's murder with his own blood. I swear it. I carry the photograph with me always.

At last we reached Vega's command, fueled our tanks and drove east, right for the coast. We left it to the infantry to take Viñaroz, after a bombardment, and rolled north of the town to cut the road. There was very little resistance. Long before we reached the sea, we could smell it, the salt air sweeping over us. It smells *blue*, I swear it does! We drove in high gear, right across the dunes, kicking the sand up like a herd of bulls, then across the highway, more low dunes and the beach. My gunner saluted the sight by sending a shell spinning out to splash like a dolphin in the sparkling waves. We were like schoolboys on vacation. I drove our stinking, clattering tortoise right into the water. How the steam hissed from its belly when the low waves sparkled and foamed between the treads! I managed to come to my senses finally, with us wallowing like a barge, and get us back on solid sand before we stalled and flooded. I sat on the turret and took pictures of our *chicos* swimming and splashing in the surf in their tank-dress, helmets and all. What a scene! We were so crazy with joy, that the delay now that keeps final victory beyond our outstretched fingers has become a torment. High hopes unfulfilled poisons pure hearts, as Father used to say. At any rate, we played like children until the priests arrived in full vestments, walking on the sands. I heard that General Vega himself drew a cross as he knelt by the water's edge, but I did not see him do this. The Mass was celebrated in this strange place with the greatest solemnity, if you can believe that possible, with hundreds of soaking men kneeling on the beach beneath the bright sun surrounded by the black monsters that had carried us safely so far.

Since then, inaction, the newspapers, indifferent food, good swimming and much boredom. We are all longing for action across the Ebro and selecting the blossoms we shall purchase for our sweethearts, our sisters and mothers on the day we roll down the Rambla de las Flores.

May the Holy Virgin protect you until we meet again.

Your brother,

Pedro, Conde de Gualvidal

NATIONALIST

REPUBLICANS

DIVISION OF SPAIN
SUMMER 1938

BOOK ELEVEN

Resistir Es Vencer—To Resist Is to Win
May–November 1938

The blue air poured past the open canopy like a torrent of water, a steady roaring thrust. The Mosca bounced on an updraft like a stubby speedboat hitting a wave, then nosed down into the invisible trough. The sun shot up, a great golden balloon in the eastern sky.

The engine clattered as the interceptor dropped into another air pocket. The headgasket on cylinder number five had blown again. Frank looked ahead and down. Clouds, soft and silent, flowed against the ragged crest of Mont Blanc, shredding to patches on the steep, dark rocks.

Gunfire stuttered to starboard. He looked, startled, and saw pale flames spurt from the muzzles, then the dark green wing lift up like a drawbridge, showing the red under-tip as Manuel barrel-rolled. The Spanish boy hung upside down, held by his seat belt, his plane motionless in midair as the earth rippled beneath him, a vast dirty fabric snatched away by huge fingers. Manuel grinned, a weird upside-down crescent of white, and saluted with his clenched fist. Frank signaled angrily. The Mosca twenty meters away rolled upright. Pantón, the other pilot, came in close on the port wing. Pantón was *serio*. He did not smile or wave. He did not fly like Manuel, either. Manuel was a natural.

The patrol was over. They had knocked down an Italian Savoia bomber about ten kilometers northeast of Falset. Manuel had never seen a kill, much less made one. He followed the bomber down until it struck the earth, then circled the spot in a puzzled, stunned way before the joy seized him. Then he came snarling up to patrol altitude and began stunting all over the cool morning sky.

Frank grunted as he cranked down the landing gear. The Mosca mushed and fishtailed as the crank pushed the stubby struts and plump wheels into the stiff blue air. Frank began to sweat inside his fleece-lined suit and the air spilling around his face scrubbed his jaws, a brief shocking-cold pummel that made him blink and gasp. The air-speed needle sank, and the bull-hide colored earth of plowed fields floated up to take them. They were home safe.

The telephone poles and wires along the east-west road grew from pins and a single thread to string between pencils, then to a dark, darting line that scooped down and up, down and up, with astonishing speed, lunging from blur to flicking blur as the Mosca flattened and settled, three diminishing jolts, on the smooth packed dirt road. Dew-heavy dust blasted back along the fuselage. The smeary patter of it always released the clenched muscles in Frank's belly and sent a pang into his bladder. He kicked the rudder against the churning dust and taxied through the open lumber gate, across the weed-splotched corral and killed the motor outside the stone shed used as a hangar. The propeller slowed like a switched-off fan, flickered, and stopped.

Frank unfastened his seat belt, stood up, and climbed out on the wing as the *animales*, the ground crew, came running to push the plane into hiding. Back beyond the breeding pens, Manuel's plane disappeared into the gulping gloom of the hay barn.

Frank's skull still pulsed to the dull, rough vibration of the motor, a sensation that took him a half hour to shake off. His ears ached from the sudden change in pressure. He yawned, an acidy feeling at the base of his jaw joints.

"*Hola, jefe!* Any luck?"

"An Italian. Trimotor bomber. Tell Triana to take the salvage truck."

"Yours without doubt, *jefe*, no?"

"Manuel got it," Frank said, dropping gingerly down on cramped legs. "Beautiful. Once across, like so, wingtip to wingtip, then like a diver down and up, so. From underneath. *Brrrt-brrrt!* Beautiful."

"*Ay, Manuela!*"

Like schoolboys waiting for the bus to bring the team back from an away game, they shouted and scattered, streaming away across the corral to tell everybody else. They shouted and waved their arms.

"*Manolo! Manuelito, hijo mío, matador de Fascistas! Ole! Ole!*"

"*Venga!*" Frank shouted.

His voice was like a wire snapping at their blue-overalled legs. He jerked off his flying helmet and felt the sun pour over his head like honey.

"Put the Mosca in its cage."

"Ohhh, *jefe* . . ."

They kicked at the weeds, clung on the fences, pleading with their groans. He did not look at them. They followed an order better when it was given and they were left to either do it or not. Triana seemed unable to understand that. The squadron commissar had a way of hovering, waiting to pounce, that the *animales* hated. They came trooping back to the Russian fighter plane, slinging the tow ropes at each other as they rigged. Some pulled, others pushed on the trailing edges of the short, broad wings. They rolled the plane toward the shed, singing at the top of their voices.

"*Las chicas de Barcelona . . . ona!*"

Their favorite song, with its vulgar last line. They loved it and sang it constantly, despite his attempts to discourage them, now that the girls of the Socialist Youth group had come out to the ranch.

"*Marchan por las calles . . . calles!*"

It was a full Spanish summer morning. The hot Catalán earth steamed as the sun cooked it, and sharp weeds lunged up at the sapphire sky. Larks called and fluttered in the empty corrals. The tool shed he dodged behind smelled of sweet mustiness, old boards, dry leather and hot wood, unpainted. He tore open his flying suit, the bulky parachute butting the backs of his knees. The puddle of his urine frothed and sparkled, sank into a pungent spot filmed with tiny collapsing bubbles. He zipped up and slung his parachute over his shoulder, carrying it like a pack, and hiked up the road to the main house. The day was going to be hot, and the warm air smelled of earth and growing. A cicada stitched madly from a dusty ilex tree drooping over a lush, uncropped pasture.

Manuel and Pantón were on the broad veranda, already out of their chute harnesses and stripping off their flying suits. The star broken-field runner and his blocking back in the locker room. Frank scowled automatically at the cigarette bobbing in Pantón's mouth. Breaking training. The other pilots were still asleep. There were not many, with only six Moscas left and the two Chato biplanes used only for training hops and map flights down to Valls, where the big base was located. Manuel waved, a shy little flip of his fingers. Pantón was bawling the song, a few beats behind the ground-crew chorus floating across the fields and fences.

"*Marchan por las calles . . . calles!*"

Manuel nudged him and Pantón whirled and snatched away his cigarette, a guilty flush in his smooth cheeks. Frank walked up the steps, his boots booming on the planks.

"*Venden carne con pollo!*" he said. "No?"

The two boys grinned sheepishly as he walked by, then began to punch each other and wrestle while Frank hung his flight suit on the wooden peg in the hall labeled LIBRO, F. He watched them in the dim, mottled mirror. Shoot down a bomber before breakfast, then spend the rest of the morning in the shade of a hay barn kicking a soccer ball, sleep for three hours, fly again, then serenade the Socialist Youth girls outside their dormitory windows until midnight when Triana chased them to their own narrow, empty beds. They had no nerves at all, these new *chicos.*

"*Manolo,*" he said curtly. "*Venga.*"

The boy bounded through the doorway into the hall and stood there on one leg, breathless and grinning shyly. He blinked, his long lashes falling on his olive cheeks, as demure as a girl.

"Yes, *jefe?*"

"I will write in the report that Manuel Chávez of this squadron should be credited with an enemy aircraft of the bombing made on the . . ."

"Third of July, Don Francisco!" the boy said. "Tomorrow is Independence Day in your country, I know. But today is my birthday! Really, it is!"

"And how many years have you?" Frank said thoughtfully. "Eight? No, ten, I think."

"Ohhh, *jefe*, no . . . I'm nineteen!"

"*Qué viejo!*" Frank said. "Listen to me, antiquity. Apply to Triana for a *salvoconducto.* Since you seem to like to sing of the girls of Barcelona . . ."

"We're sorry, *jefe*," the boy said, trying to look sincere. "Really we are. We forgot, that's all . . . See, when the animals on the ropes started it, Pantón and I just joined in without thinking . . ."

He was breathless and squirmy with excitement. He looked as though he wanted to jump up and down. Frank turned away and smoothed the straps on his chute harness.

"And since I will need a *chofer* to drive the car into the spare-parts warehouse today—"

"We were just . . . excited, Don Francisco."

"You will have forty and eight hours in which to shame your family forever," Frank said, turning back to him. The boy made him nervous, and he frowned to conceal it. Manuel gulped, his big dark eyes brimming and anxious.

"Did you hear what I said, Manuel?" he demanded.

"Yes, *jefe*. A *salvoconducto.* A thousand thanks, Don Francisco!"

"A present for your birthday. You and Pantón got in the *camión* with the commissar. Ask Pavito what he needs. Get to the enemy plane before the *chicos* from the base at Valls. Now get out of here with your music and give me some peace."

They went off the veranda like kids leaping into a swimming hole, all legs and whoops.

Frank wrote the combat report in triplicate and filled out the flight log, seated at the big mahogany desk in the office off the hall. He heard Pavito shouting down near the blacksmith's shop.

The truck motor drowned out the chief mechanic's voice. Frank pushed the extra copies into the morning mail pouch and left the soft leather bag on the top of the desk. The walls of the room were covered with photographs in cheap lacquered frames. Black-hided bulls, with steep muscle humps, broad square muzzles, big almond-shaped eyes, and wide, curved, wicked horns. Each photo had a name, a date, and a plaza written in where the bull had died. There was an autographed picture of a matador, an ugly, wolf-jawed man with cunning eyes. Juan Belmonte.

He walked past the dining room on the left and the big, dim vault of the formal salon where chairs of mahogany slabs and slick, tormenting horsehair cushions stood in rigid groups, all facing a portrait of Spain's last king, Alfonso the Thirteenth. Heavy drapes kept out the summer sun, and the air in that room was stale, left over from the previous regime, as the boys said. It was used only for formal gatherings of the squadron.

The woman frying *churros* in a black oil pot wiped her face, lubricating her cheeks. She smiled and showed her missing teeth.

"*Hola, jefe!*" she said. "Nice ones, just for you. You had luck today?"

"If three go out and three come back, that's luck," Frank said.

"Shoot them all down," the woman said. "The murderers."

Frank took a cup of steaming malt-coffee sweet with wild honey, hooked two greasy *churros* and wandered out the door to the porch that overlooked the big drinking pond where the fighting bulls had once stamped in the soft red earth. Now the pond lay like a still sheet of glass, reflecting the sky, fringed with tall, sweet weeds. Frank sat down in a sagging wicker chair. He drank the hot malt-coffee slowly, pulling bits of *churro* with his teeth and chewing carefully. The fried dough was indigestible. His feet were loose and cool in straw slippers Carmen had found for him in the city. He propped his ankles on what he had learned was a gout-stool. He had a new pack of Chesterfields and a box of matches. He sighed and gazed out over the blue water pond, the broad pastures and green fields that rolled, linked by heavy, high fences, to the small stream where the *chicos* caught crayfish and went swimming. This place was another bit of Buckminster's luck.

The *ganadería* now used as the squadron base had been a famous ranch used for raising the fighting bulls. The animals had all been shot for meat. The owner and both his sons had been shot, too. There were three graves behind the family chapel now used as a weather-station and control tower. The ranch was a big one, more than a thousand acres, with three huge hay barns and a dozen stone sheds, breeding and branding pens, grain bins of solid concrete, a big, empty horse barn filled with dusty saddles and tack, sturdy corrals, and two loading chutes that ended at a battered platform overlooking a rusty spur line that came in from the main railroad.

The main house was a bulky, shapeless stone pile with a terra-cotta tile roof, electricity on the ground floor and a telephone, a looted wine cellar used for storing ammunition and twenty-kilo bombs, eleven bedrooms and no toilet.

Two broad roads of rolled and tamped dirt running east-west and north-south crossed in the exact center of the ranch, a perfect double runway system between the plowed fields. The local agricultural syndicate provided seed and commercial fertilizer from Chile. District P.S.U.C. headquarters had sent youth groups with huge appetites and no food rations out to plant and cultivate the fields and their own social awareness. The *ganadería* was an inefficient potato farm supervised by a middle-aged Catalán Anarchist named Carlos, husband by mutual consent to the squadron cook. From the sky, there was no sign whatever that the place was used as a landing field for Russian-built interceptors. They had never been strafed or bombed.

Frank finished his coffee and the second *churro*. He lit a cigarette and calculated for the hundredth time the potential income that could be realized from a horse-breeding enterprise. He installed a vet from Upper Bucks County and scattered thoroughbred mares across the empty pastures, Morgans, maybe Palominos. He heard the high whinny of colts, the clink of iron on iron down at the forge . . . after the war . . .

The motorcycle from Valls arrived and puttered away. No one had signed for the mail pouch. Triana would complain in his cold, sullen way. The commissar was a Communist from Ciudad Real, a humorless Puritan with a passion for files and paper work. The young pilots had given him his nickname, after the gypsy city.

"*Muy buenas, comandante.*"

A packet of mail tied with twine flopped into his lap. Frank lurched out of his revery of thoroughbred bloodlines. He burned the twine with his cigarette and leafed through the mail, looking for the fat lilac envelope.

"*Hola*, Comrade Carlos," he said. "Sit down. How goes the struggle on the potato front, the offensive against bad herbs?"

The Catalán crouched warily on the porch rail, fanning himself with a folded copy of *Frente Rojo*. He was swarthy and slope-shouldered, a tough, powerful ex-railroad worker who knew nothing whatever about farming. He blamed mysterious "high personages" for sending him to the *ganadería* and wrangled ferociously with the squadron commissar.

"These kids, they know nothing of work, Comrade-Commander," he said bitterly. "For them, speeches and songs are politics. They do not comprehend that work is political. I try to show them, but . . ."

The Catalán looked away hopelessly at the blacksmith's shop. He and Pavito were close comrades. They "understood." Occasionally, they disappeared on Sundays. Frank had discovered that Pavito was trying to improve the Catalan's ability to read. He had found them, two grown men, hunched in a ditch over a newspaper, sounding out words. It had been oddly touching to see.

"Someone will hear of it," Carlos sighed gloomily.

"High personages?" Frank suggested.

"Ah, they are like fat cats now," the Catalán said. "They play with us. Like mice. It's politics, of course. The Communists draft all the decent workers and send them off to get killed, then ship us children to play in the fields. If the crop is bad, who is blamed?"

"Have a cigarette," Frank said.

"I heard Manolo got a bomber."

"Yes. He's a good *chico*."

"He pays those Italians back for Granollers. Five hundred women and kids killed in a rotten little *pueblo*. Remember Guernica?"

"I remember," Frank said. "Very well. I remember Madrid, too."

"Exactly," Carlos said quietly. "Don't worry about us, Comrade-Commander. You harvest the skies, and we will harvest the fields."

A voice interrupted. "Go then and do it! Leave Don Francisco to read his letter from his lady!"

Carlos banged the door shut and went in to argue with his woman, both of them speaking Catalán in short, cruel-sounding spurts that ended in a peal of female laughter and the solid smack of a hard palm on the woman's rump. Frank snapped his cigarette over the railing into the weeds. He talked to himself.

"Carlos, what you need is about four families of Amish from Lancaster County, buggies and black hats and bare feet and all. We'd be up to our chins in potato bugs every time we knelt down to give thanks to the Almighty. Well, now, Carmencita, what's new? *Dígame. Qué pasa?*"

Carmen wrote to him twice a week, sometimes more often, rambling notes in her sprawly, little-girl handwriting wrapped around headlines and articles that she shredded from newspapers, everything from recipes for soybean meatless meatloaf to a full reprint of Premier Negrín's most recent speech, little curled snapshots of squinting nurses standing with their arms around sad-faced, gaunt men in striped bathrobes and usually an extra sheet of note paper covered with X kiss-marks.

Frank's Spanish had become good enough for him to notice that the good sisters in that convent she had been jailed in before the war had never quite succeeded in teaching Carmen to spell. She scribbled on, cheerful, incoherent and incorrect. It was all a little like receiving a "pash-note" from a high-school cheerleader whose father edited the home-town newspaper. He could never decide whether to keep all the letters she wrote him or throw them all away.

Once, he had culled through the squadron wastebaskets, gathered old weather reports, Triana's sick-lists, the ammunition count and fuel totals, a page from a brochure on manure, stuffed it all in an envelope, scribbled some political slogans on a sheet writing left-handed, signed it PHRANSISKO and dropped it in the mail pouch. An hour later, he was stricken with guilt, a lump in his chest. For six days, twelve mail de-liveries, she wrote nothing. He tried frantically to call her at the hospital without success. He felt as wrong as if he had struck her face turned to his for a kiss. He had two terrible nightmares, the old ones, about his plane catching fire. He got drunk with Carlos and reported himself too sick to fly the next day. On the sixth day, he wrote a long, formal, cringing letter that left him exhausted and furious, since Triana, as squadron censor, was required to read it. The next morning, the motor-cycle courier brought a bulging lilac envelope bandaged shut with surgi-cal tape. She had been on temporary duty to Tarragona. Her room in the nurse's dormitory had been changed and all her mail thrown out by accident. He had been grateful nearly to tears.

He turned the pages, the sun pleasantly warm on his slippered feet. She was alive, very busy, very tired, but would try to get some sleep BEFORE. Rita had fallen in love again with a Bulgarian, making Ri-cardo Somebody very jealous. Her father had stayed at the Hotel Ma-jestic once and said it was very nice. She could get a ride out in a truck to OUR café. Was he well? Scotch whiskey was 600 pesetas a bottle and no one had any but Americans who worked for newspapers, so he should ask them. A Norwegian with a head wound had jumped from a window into the rear courtyard during lunch. [He had morphia-sickness.] She missed him constantly and thought about him every time there was an air attack. There was a story that some Russian in *Pravda* had called the Falange "Spanish patriots!!!!" Wasn't General Menéndez a magnificent hero of the People's Republic? Had he seen the splendid photo of Paco in the newspaper? She had GREAT NEWS. Until THEN!!!

He looked at the picture, a propaganda shot from *Frente Rojo*, Paco draped with a coil of dynamite fuse, glaring at the camera.

"By day, wealthy Lamont Cranston, by night . . . What evil lurks in the minds of the Kremlin? The Asturian knows! . . . heh-heh-heh . . . Jesus God. What the hell, you know?"

Today, there was another page. He opened it and felt his heart burst like a yolk and run down inside the flesh of his arms, into his fingers. In the exact center of the sheet, in a nappy little canyon of erasures gouged there, she had printed in big penciled capitalized English:

I LOVE YOU O.K.¿

He sat for a long time, looking at the piece of paper. His nose watered, and, as he stood up, the letter folded carefully and tucked in his shirt, he blew his nose into his fingers, wiped his hand on the porch railing and walked slowly down the weed-sprigged path to the blacksmith's shop to see The Magic Carpet.

Pavito was waiting for him in a litter of worn-looking metal parts, a serpent pit of ruptured rubber hosing. The shop smelled of cheap tobacco, crank-case drippings, and scorched steel. The rest of the mechanics had disappeared. Pavito thrust a small brass sheet of mesh under his nose. It smelled like the thick soft plate of paraffin found on jars of home-made jam.

"Look at this, *jefe!* They call this a strainer in Leningrad, see? I took stones, big ones, out of that fuel pump! Lucky Manuel was right over the field when it happened or he wouldn't have got that bomber today. That's right, smell it? Eh? Wax! Wax, that's what. The last two hundred liter drums we got. It's sabotage, that's what!"

Frank studied the strainer. Wax in the gas was not new. The brass mesh had been perforated, as though jabbed by a pencil or screwdriver.

"Show this to Triana," he said. "They got a whole tank truck of gas with wax in it at Valls yesterday. Fifth columnists in the city, I guess."

"*Qué canallas!*" the mechanic said. "Sons-of-bitches! How did the motor go today?"

"The cylinder blew. About halfway around. It shakes. I can feel it."

"You can feel it?" Pavito said. "Don't you think *I* can, Don Francisco? But what do you expect? Here we make gaskets from leather boots and old drain pipes, fuel lines from tubing your señora steals from her hospital, rivets from roofing nails . . . Thank her for me when you see her, please, eh? And tools because a thick-headed Russian forgot to send them. You know what? One of those little Socialist cunts comes in here this morning and wants me to fix her bicycle. Her *bicycle!*"

The mechanic laughed abruptly and wiped his hands on a rag, as though polishing himself. His heavy forearms and thick-fingered hands were black with grease from the elbows to the nails. All the hair had fallen out and the skin peeled off now in soft sheets like carbon paper. He refused to go to the base hospital at Valls.

"Don't tell Triana, but I made Carlos a cultivator for his fields. From some pipes I found out back and wheels from a burro cart. Never made one before, but it does three rows at a time, neat as you like."

"Pavito, you can make anything."

The mechanic ducked his head and flung away the rag. He nodded once.

"I guess we both know that, huh? Want to take a look? Safe enough.

The *chicos* will be out with those girls. Why are girls in the Socialist Youth so ugly. *Qué feas!* Not like that sweet one on the posters they stick up."

"That's Carmen," Frank said. *"Mi mujer."*

"It *is?* You're not joking? The girl on that poster is your señora? Oh well, then. Good thing I didn't say what I was going to!"

Frank laughed and followed the mechanic to the rear of the shop and out into a trash-strewn dump. Beyond the charred heaps of oil cans was a low wooden shed with a padlocked door. Pavito fumbled out a key, squinting against the bright sun.

"Our gypsy is suspicious, *jefe*," he said. "I told him we keep the machine-gun parts and the bomb releases out here so they don't get mixed up. But he smells something. He knows I'm here at night, I think. So that's your wife, eh? *Jefe*, you are a lucky man."

"I was born lucky," Frank said.

"There we are," Pavito said, pushing open the door. "The Magic Carpet. I'm thinking of applying for the patent rights. Instead of going to Russia, I'll make them for your company, eh? Well, maybe we won't need it. Who can say, with this bitch of a war."

"The Magic Carpet," he said. *"El avión más feo del mundo!"*

It was pretty ugly, all right. Pavito had assembled the engine and fuselage from a burned-out Fiat, a Heinkel landing gear with aluminum spats, the wings from a wrecked Chato and fabric peeled from an old British Avro Airspeed someone had smashed up coming back from Guadalajara in a snowstorm. The engine was exposed, and wires and cooling system pipes drooled down into a stack of worn-out tires. The shed stank explosively of fabric dope.

"The cable you stole didn't fit through the pullies," the mechanic said apologetically, "so I used some telephone wire. It seems strong enough."

"And the extra fuel tanks? That's the important thing, Pavito. Did they fit?"

"No. I used wineskins. Hundred liters in all. Two fifty-liter skins."

"They'll leak," Frank said. "What about the shift in weight?"

"Ah!" Pavito said. "Let's both believe that this magical rug will actually lift two people. So. When the fuel pump—if it works—empties the wineskins they collapse. Like—like the breasts of a nursing mother. Then the passenger slides forward on top of the collapsing skins to keep the trim, nose to tail. Maybe."

"Maybe," Frank said. "We'll never know until the day we need it. A magic carpet. How many hours more must you work?"

"A day, perhaps. If you are the pilot, it will fly, *jefe*."

"Trust me, Pavito."

"I do, Don Francisco, and to hell with Karl Marx. If I did not trust you I would never have built this—monument to defeatism. But in truth, I believe we are going to win the war. So, there are two republics. An offensive that recaptured Aragón would be—"

"A miracle," Frank said. "Therefore, this."

"Therefore this," Pavito agreed. "Across the border to France! Paris? No. Marseilles . . . with a strong tail wind, yes."

"Finish it," Frank ordered, and ducked out the shed door.

He walked back up to the main house. In the pouch on his desk lay the flight orders for the week, subject, as always, to last-minute telephone calls. As the Republic was split in two, so was the air force. Any day, a single sheet of paper or the jingle of a bell could send them from this familiar, almost perfect base to some muddy field near Valencia, a wrecked orange grove, or a dried-out rice paddy, or anywhere else along what the Spanish called "the Levante sector." He might be too far away. If the front there collapsed as quickly as it had in Aragón . . .

He didn't believe that could happen. The fighting seemed to have slowed to a stalemate, artillery bombardments and assaults on fortified positions the Republic forces were able to stop cold or contain without yielding precious ground. Every day there were new rumors that the Non-Intervention Committee had finally approved a plan to withdraw foreign volunteers from Spain. So what if the Italians had a special agreement with the British that allowed them to stay? Lately, the Kondor Legion flew patrols; only occasionally did they experiment with their new Stuka dive bombers. Every night, the new equipment sent from Russia moved from the Barcelona warehouses and storage dumps to the Ebro. The French had closed the border again. Their new Premier, Daladier, was afraid of the Germans. But no one was more confident than the Spaniards themselves.

"Franco?" they said, shrugging. "He's had his chance and he missed it. Soon the Germans will force him to bring back General Yagüe. Now Yagüe is a true Spaniard, not a Gallego and a Jew like Franco. Franco was too slow. But Yagüe is impulsive. He will move too quickly. He will stick out his neck and . . . Pam! We will cut it off. Then the Germans will go back home . . . Look at this business with Czechoslo-vakia . . . Then we will counterattack and kill all the Italians. The Falange will make peace, and then we will build a new Spain on the thirteen *puntos de Negrín!*"

It sounded more than plausible when it was explained that way. It was necessary to believe it could be done, despite the losses, despite the retreats, despite the closed border. The Republic was taking The Long Count, like the Dempsey-Tunney heavyweight fight.

The scrap-heap creation that Pavito had secretly patched together was like an overdraft allowed by British banking concerns, a margin for unintentional error. A sudden thrust of tanks against a weak sector, a new salient pushed up from Tarragona—nothing was certain, after all, and passports and papers or not, the Nationalists usually shot any foreign officer they captured. The Quince Brigada had been cut off and torn to pieces across the Ebro. The Lincoln battalion had lost the commanders and commissars for their first three companies and the story had been going around for weeks that the Brigade chief-of-staff, Bob Merriman, and the Brigade commissar, Doran, had been captured and then killed.

Frank dressed, turned the squadron over to Triana, and filled his wallet with the dirty scraps of paper the Republic used for money. The cook brought him a liter of wine, a loaf of bread, and a bit of hard Manchego cheese.

Manuel, in his best uniform and smelling strongly of perfume, drove the command car, his *salvoconducto* displayed like a decoration in the breast pocket of his tunic. They drove out through the main gate of the *ganadería* as the Socialist Youth, in a double column, girls on the right, boys on the left, marched in from the potato fields for lunch. Carlo, leading them, saluted as the car rolled by, and Frank touched the brim of his cap with his clenched fist.

It was a slow drive on bad roads with many detours [despite the fact that they headed for the base at Valls and not for the city]. Every clump of ilex trees substantial enough to cast a solid shadow had a few dusty trucks, loaded high, parked in the shade. Every farm and little *pueblo* was a rest area for some unit of infantry or a gun crew slumped around a Czech field piece hitched to four bony, lathered horses. They saw tanks hidden inside what Manuel said was a storehouse for wine. A blond Russian was dancing in a squat to the wheezy melody of an accordion. A machine-gun company lay in a vineyard surrounded by women and children. Everywhere military police waved and shouted at barricades.

The landing field at Valls was quiet. Most of the hangars were empty and the camouflage nets hung dusty over two "Katyushka" bombers.

The security guard waved them on past the fuel-storage area to the base *intendencia*. The supply depot, a concrete structure with a rusted roof, smelled of hot dust, oranges, and motor oil. An area nearby bigger than a football field was stacked with welded steel structures, long beams braced with short pieces, the welded joints so new that they were still burned blue, not yet rusted. Planks cut the same length, hundreds of them, were neatly piled under the big, sagging nets that shielded what seemed a giant's Meccano set from enemy observation planes.

"What is this, Manolo? They have a circus in this place? This is the stadium, no?"

The Spanish boy shook his head and kicked one of the girder-structures.

"*Pasarelas*," he said, doubtfully.

"What is a *pasarela*, Manuel?"

"A kind of bridge. These are pieces for two or three bridges, maybe more. There are boats back there. Big enough for eight or ten men. I counted twenty groups of four each. Eighty boats, eight hundred men. A battalion, more or less."

The Cuban quartermaster was effusively polite and officially helpless. The requisitions for food he would honor, temporarily, although the district officials were supposed to provide rations for all Socialist Youth working the farms. The gasoline with wax in it could be turned over to the local anti-tank company for Molotov bombs, but since it was not flight fuel, the comrade-commander understood that it could not be credited as such.

"Going fishing?" Frank said, jerking his head at the stack of welded steel beams. The Cuban smiled.

"What kinds of fish can be caught in Aragón? With luck, of course."

"Oh," the Cuban said, "sardines."

"Really?"

"Of the Italian type. Perhaps German herrings. And the local sort of Falangistas."

"And news when the fishing will begin?" Frank said.

"Soon after the boats are in the water, I would think, no?"

"And when might that be?"

"Oh," the Cuban said. "Soon after they are taken to the river."

"Which is the best road to Barcelona?" Frank asked.

"There are two ways. *Muy lento y cerrado.* Very Slowly and Closed. They are turning back the refugees. The refugees get in the way of the fishing parties. I will explain to your *chofer,* okay?"

The Cuban supply officer had not been joking. The roadsides were dark with civilians, old men, black-shawled women, and hundreds of children. Some walked slowly, burdened with bedding, cooking pots and clothing. Others sat in the dusty weeds, staring at nothing, the women brushing flies away from the white, exhausted faces of their children. Whenever the sedan slowed, the women rushed on it, hands extended, begging silently.

"*Vámanos,*" Frank would say.

They drove slowly on. Hands, empty hands, stretched out to them all the way to the crossroads. They turned right, were stopped again and showed their papers.

"There was an air raid," the soldier said in the mushy, hot-potato accent of Andalusia, pointing at the sky to the north. "They usually send over another flight to drop leaflets and take pictures. Be careful, comrades."

They drove on. Manuel rapped his fist on the steering wheel.

"A raid, and we missed it. What a shame! We would have shot them all down. I wonder if we were called?"

"They come in from Mallorca," Frank said. "It takes them only twenty minutes to get over the city. They've always dropped their stuff before we get there. It's happened fifty times."

"But with luck . . ."

"Stop at the olive grove there, see it? We'll have lunch."

They sat in the shade, drinking red wine and eating hazelnuts that Manuel cracked between two stones, offering them with exaggerated politeness. He was very shy and pleased, very responsible and went twice to check the air in the tires and the water in the radiator of the sedan. Frank cut the bread and sausage, unbuttoned his tunic, and lay looking at the sky, the wine bottle on his belly, a cool, solid weight. He could see into the next valley. The road was black with men filling in bomb-craters. There was no hurry.

Manuel ate slowly, apologetically and drank little of the wine.

"I must drive the *coche*, Don Francisco. You have it."

Manuel was from Gerona in the north. His father was a pharmacist, not very political, but a Republican all the same. He had wanted Manuel to study medicine, but he had been good at football and clever with his hands. Apparently, on that, he had been offered the chance to fly. Frank nodded.

"You need good co-ordination to be a combat pilot," he said. "You didn't really think at all when you went for that Italian bomber this morning, did you? I mean, consciously?"

"No," the boy said. "My hands and feet just seemed to know what to do. It all happened very fast. I could see the rear gunner's face. He looked so surprised! It was comical, really. I was trying to kill him, and he just looked—like so, with his mouth open."

"He fired at you," Frank said. "Were you frightened, Manolo?"

"No. Yes. I don't remember. I must have been . . ."

He paused and looked at Frank, the long lashes dropping over his dark eyes. He hung his glossy head, ashamed.

"It's not . . . death. It's being hurt. I am afraid of pain, Don Francisco, isn't that stupid?"

"No," Frank said. "That's what everyone is afraid of. If we knew that death was something that just happened, like going to sleep . . ."

"That would be all right. Yes, it's not the black bull, but the sharp horns. This is all terrible, I think. All those people, the old women, kids with their bellies all puffed. But today. How pleasant it is! Do you like Spain, Don Francisco?"

"Very much," Frank said. "After the war I will come back to visit very often. It was not so good at first. I didn't know the language. It was hard to understand what was going on."

"They say you lost many comrades, many friends . . ."

"Yes," Frank said, lifting the bottle. Manuel blinked and broke a twig.

"It was very enchanting to meet your . . . Doña Libro," he said. "At the fiesta of the First of May. We recognized her. From pictures."

"Yes, the pictures. From the early days," Frank said.

"She is very enchanting," the boy repeated. "A real Socialist heroine."

Frank nodded and tried not to smile. He felt very pleasant. He liked Manuel and told himself that he should have private talks with all the young Spanish pilots. They had been entrusted to him. He was to train them and at the same time protect them. He smoked and drank the wine and was interested and philosophical, unconsciously adopting the mannerisms of a headmaster at a boarding school he had attended, the only blend of masculine affection and control he had ever experienced. The senior boarders had all been a little bit in love with the headmaster's wife. It did not displease him to remember that Carmen had been quite subdued, a "lady-wife," as the cook insisted on calling her, half mother, something of a "pal," gay but not silly, remembering everyone's name and willing to dance with them all, and just slightly flirtatious.

"She was good enough to think I should study medicine after the war," Manuel said hesitantly. "Of course, Doña Libro knows many doctors. I much admire—his name is hard to say—Berthune. He is famous for his bottled blood. It is very odd to think of. Blood in bottles, like *salsa de tomate*, but he has saved many lives. That, to me, is inspiring. I like to fly, but I would like to be a surgeon."

"Tell me about your family, Manolo," he said.

The boy talked and he listened, without hearing.

It was not good to think back. He had to live on the ground floor of memory. Upstairs there were doors, all of them shut. It did no good to stand in the dim hallway, looking up at those doors. Behind every one there was a face, some very dim already, others brighter, the echo of their voices like music heard from far away, broken melodies on a piano. He kept their pictures in the locked drawer of his desk and never took them out. It was too soon to look at them. Perhaps in five years or ten he would be able to see them without the squeeze around the heart that even their names caused now.

No loss in his life before the war had been more than a trivial absence, usually of something like a favorite sweater he had suddenly outgrown, something taken away but immediately replaced by something better (his Shetland pony "put to sleep" and the Morgan gelding delivered the next weekend, fraternity-house friends who graduated, but came back on homecoming weekends). He had never learned to lose people. The real power of money was how it could be used to replace things. But Spain was somewhere different, a landscape of losses, of shocking, final disappearance, a rutted field pitted with fresh graves like traps, holes to fall into with a sickening jolt every time. He had never been educated for Spain. He had never been poor. Spain was a place where things were snatched away and smashed and you could never get them back.

He had been married over a year. On his anniversary, Carmen had been clearing the soft, bloody, human rubbish from a hospital train that had been bombed and strafed, the big red crosses on the car roofs riddled with machine-gun bullets. He had been working all day and night with Pavito, taking an engine down and rebuilding it. There were times when he became so used to her absence, the lack of her, that it seemed she was not his wife and never had been anyone more important than a girl from Bryn Mawr willing to go off with him for a weekend in New York.

She was one on the ground floor of his memory, but in a distant room, often locked to him. She was not snapshots and the echo of old music, but rolls of badly processed film he toted about, jerky, amateur from-out-last-vacation-home movies, each roll imperfectly complete, beginnings and blinding overexposures, sudden darks and too soon over with the lights back on and a head and heart full of *remember-whens*. It was infuriating not to have her whole, constantly present, yet he had no clear idea at all of how or where he would live with her, what they would talk about or do, day by day, for years on end. He felt sorry for her and pity for himself that the room in his memory-house where she was kept was, so obviously, a bedroom. Worse, a bedroom with bottles and condoms on the floor and ashtrays filled with butts and the sheets damp or stiff in little pale places. He wanted her in a tweed skirt and a sweater and a single strand of pearls, waving to him from the stone terrace as the Irish setters tumbled down the steps to meet him after a long day at the office. He wanted her in a red velvet gown beside him at the symphony, slightly but politely bored, her program tapped against her firmed lips as her dainty nostrils winged out pale with a yawn. He wanted her in jodhpurs and a checked jacket riding down an autumn trail toward casual cocktails somewhere while a cool September breeze tore antique coins from the birch trees and poured a treasure over her smooth twilled thighs.

Instead, he had rolls of bad film, a small, tired girl in a filthy sheepskin jacket and stained blue pants crushed into muddy boots, or a dim naked form sitting in tangled blankets, driving her fingers through her short, curly hair, a face on the pillow, her pale mouth open, her lashes fluttering, the tip of her tongue pressed against her upper lip and the tight, hurt-sounding moans fading into the slow, steady push of breath as she slept hours without moving, her face hidden from him, exhausted. It was all, somehow, debasing and improper, all their greedy lust, a sad weariness that made being torn apart again a relief. It was wrong and dirty to see her jaunty, unmistakable swagger through a street-corner crowd, the soldiers turning around to smile after her, the wide, kid's grin and wave she flung at him, the sudden, starchy, hard hug and wet, smacking kisses scandalizing the sober Catalán *funcionarios* and their prim wives. It was wrong because he watched her with a kind of sick glee. She was his, and when he used her, his selfish flesh stirred her very easily. Then, afterward, he would catch her looking at him with her tilted dark eyes, appraisingly, cynically, as though he were nothing more to her than a long nub of useful muscle.

He knew her, really, in only a casual, sexy way. She was thirteen years younger than he was. She didn't seem to care anything about his money, but maybe that was only because he had been unable, here in the Republic, to show to her what Philadelphia money meant. He found himself, from time to time, forcing himself to be "fascinated by her," because she chattered like a schoolgirl and wanted to make love all the time and he was disturbed to think that she might find him, really, rather boring.

"What do you think, Don Francisco?"

The voice, intruding, unwanted and familiarly expecting a sensible answer startled him. There was a finger of wine still left in the bottle. He tipped it up and let the warmish stuff run into his throat.

"I don't know," he said slowly. "I just don't know."

The boy nodded, apparently satisfied that there were some things in the world for which even another man twice his age, more or less, and a foreigner would understand no more than himself.

Frank looked at him. Hell of a nice kid. Maybe something could be rigged through the Dean's office at Penn, special dispensation to get him into the med school. Wasn't the library at the Wharton School supported by the Buckminster Fund?

"The road is fixed, Don Francisco," Manuel said. "We can go on now."

"*Claro*," Frank said, getting up. He felt the wine and was large and secure. Somehow, everything was going to be all right.

"We go on," he continued grandly, "because we can't go back. And that's the truth. Thinking doesn't change the way you live. It's changing your way of living that changes how you think."

He surveyed the twisted highway ahead, his hands on his hips, aware that Manuel was watching him, an admiring, luminous, shy glance. The boy murmured, repeating the words that had poured out so easily. Somehow glibness and clichés achieved a new dignity in Spanish, a nice compensation for the gutter-monotony everyone spewed. Frank sighed. The friendly man-to-man with the headmaster was over, the boy turned adroitly out of the office door in time for compulsory chapel, his restlessness lulled by a pronouncement on life that would do him little good and less harm. Frank shook himself, displeased, and buttoned his tunic.

"Let's go," he said and flung himself into the car.

They drove to Communist Party headquarters and nearly had an accident with a big *camión*. The work day was over and the streets were swarming with girls in light, short dresses, high heels, and Jean Harlow peroxide-blond permanents. Manuel looked everywhere but at the road before him and whipped a comb repeatedly through his hair.

"Stop here. *Careful,* man!"

"Sorry . . ."

"You have your papers, Manuel? Take the car to the motor pool and leave it. Where will you stay?"

"Stay?" the boy said. "Well, Don Francisco, I hope to encounter friends, and—"

"I see," Frank said. "How much money have you, Manolo?"

"Enough, I think. I hope that these friends I encounter—"

Frank pushed some bank notes into the boy's pockets and slid out of the car.

"Call the Hotel Majestic," he said. "Tonight. Leave your address and telephone number, if there is one. That's regulations. You'll get in trouble if you forget, both with the police here and with Triana back at the base. And with *me*. Understand?"

"Yes, Don Francisco," the boy said and grinned, the kid brother out to paint the town red. He shot away from the curb out into the traffic.

"Watch out, *chicas*," Frank muttered, "here comes Manolo!"

He walked into the building.

"Voget?" the clerk said. "Fourteenth Brigade, then. Which battalion and company, comrade? Perhaps we have some information."

"No," Frank said. "He's not with the 14th Brigade. He's not with any Brigade. He's—Paul Voget. Everyone knows him."

"Oh! *Paul* Voget. Yes, well, next office on your left, comrade."

And to the office on the next floor above, and three doors down the corridor to the left and finally someone who was guarded or at least accompanied by a pair of Barcelona toughs and spoke with an Italian accent.

"Comrade Voget? Who wants him?"

"A comrade."

"We are all comrades here."

"A friend," Frank said.

"Name?"

"Libro. Pilot in the Gloriosa."

"You're not Spanish."

"American."

"Ah. Party member?"

"No." Frank said. "Where is Voget?"

"In Madrid."

"Madrid?"

"That's correct. Good day."

It occurred to Frank on his way down the stairs that he might possibly have spoken to Togliatti himself. It was hard to think of Italians as anything but cobblers and landscape gardeners. The idea of them being Communist officials was somehow both funny and unpleasant. He did not like to think of Voget as somehow an underling to Togliatti. It was like discovering that a college friend had underwritten life insurance for Al Capone.

"Gotta match, bud?"

Frank turned from the bulletin board covered with newspaper clippings in a dozen languages, including Chinese. He saw a young, tired Irish face, blue eyes and raw, peeling skin, vaguely, shockingly familiar.

"You was at Alcalá," the soldier said. "I never forget a face."

Frank thought. "You . . . sang a song," he said. "About Jarama."

"Put er there, pal," the soldier said. "Lincoln battalion."

"I'm afraid I'm bad about names," Frank said. "I remember the song, though."

"Mahoney," the soldier said. "Call me Jimmy. Gotta match?"

"Sure, sure," Frank said. "Let's have a drink."

"Awright," the young soldier said. "I know a place."

"I'm meeting someone. It's not far."

"They got cognac?"

"They'll find some for me, I think."

They walked out onto the sidewalk. Mahoney glared over his shoulder at the big banner flapping over the door and shouldered a Spaniard aside rudely, the cigarette jammed into the corner of his mouth.

"Let's get outta here," he said. "I'm t'rough with them bastids."

"I didn't have much luck in there myself. Looking for a friend, but he's in Madrid. At least that's what they told me."

"They told me to git lost," the soldier said. "I come here to join up, see. Take out a Party card, plunk down the bucks or pataters or whatever they wanted. They said no dice. Beat that, will yuh?"

"They wouldn't let you join? Why not? I thought they were always recruiting?"

"Ah, sure, the spiks," the soldier said. "If you ain't a dago, you gotta have a sponsor. A sponsor, no less! They don't want no sponsors at Hibernian Hall. I come all the way in here to take his place, like, see? And they turned me down. Like I ain't good enough for em."

"That's funny," Frank said. "Let's have a drink. Here's the place."

The waiter in the café recognized him and swept a *reservado* sign off a table in the front.

"I'll drink anyt'ing," the soldier said. He looked at the girls on the sidewalk and flicked his cigarette.

"Great town for cunt," he said. "I wrote a letter to his wife. Took me all day yesterday. I give to them. Maybe she'll get it."

"A buddy?" Frank said.

"Yeah," the soldier said. "He got it. I was fouah days on the otheh side a the friggin Ebro. No chow, no fooseel, no shoes, even. Me and five guys, see? Hide all day and walk at night. Goin crazy. I could heah him shoutin to me at night, just like it was. Big nigger shout, you know? And laff. How that sonofabitch could laff! I never knew no colored guys before. Hell, you don't see any dinges in Southy, except maybe on an ice wagon. *Saloo!*"

The soldier emptied his glass and caught the waiter's sleeve.

"Just stick the *botella* right down here, mac, huh? Tell him, pal."

The waiter's eyebrows rose and stayed there. Frank nodded, and the bottle was placed beside the soldier's empty glass. Frank picked up his *vino* and sniffed it. The waiter hovered. Frank tasted the sherry.

"*Muy bien!*"

"*Ah, gracias, gracias . . .*"

"What's that you got? Sherry?"

"Yes."

"Gimme this stuff any day. Franco's Revenge. *Saloo.*"

"*Salud,*" Frank said. "So you got caught over there and lost your buddy, huh? It happens."

"Not my buddy. That's what I tried to tell them bastids. My comrade, I says. *Comrade,* just like that. They look at me like I'm some freak. See, he was company commander. I was his comic-star."

"Oh. And you got along?"

"Like a friggin house afire. He'd been in the National Guard or maybe the army, I fergit. He was our group leader. We come over on the boat together. Now . . ."

"Have another drink," Frank said. "Cheer up. You'll get home, commissar. Back home to . . ."

"Bahstin," the soldier said. "Good ol' Bean-town. *Saloo!* I quit."

"I don't follow you. You quit what? The Lincolns?"

"Shit, no! The Lincolns is the best. The *best!* I'll never quit the battalion. I quit as comic-star. You know that Milt Wolff was behind the lines for *nine days!* We thought they got him, like the others. But he showed up. El Lobo, the kids call him. He's some guy, awright. Looks like Abe Lincoln hisself, with a big, droopy lip-brush up here. From Brooklyn. He's the new battalion commander. Čopic's gone from brigade."

"Is that good or bad?" Frank said.

"I dunno. I don't give a shit no more. The new guy's called Valledor. Čopic was a showboat. Valledor's just . . . there, you know. The thing that bites my ahss was I come in here—this is a great town for cunt—

to join up with the friggin Communist Pahdy and they *turn* me down! *Fuck* 'em."

The young soldier got drunk very quickly and finally spilled his glass. He shook his head apologetically as the waiter mopped the table dry.

"See? I got no self-discipline. You gotta have that or you can't be no officer or no comic-star. Well, that's me. Why kid myself? I'm a rank-and-filer, just a workin stiff. Now you, you're a gent. No, I can tell, I can tell. You been buyin all this stuff and I needed a drink, lemme tell yeh. Maybe it's just the wrong time. I guess yer really waitin for some other gents, huh? It's awright . . ."

"My wife," Frank said.

"I think I remember you was with a babe—I mean a girl. Little one with dark hair. I hear Spanish babes get fat when they get old."

"This one won't," Frank said. "Don't go."

"Mahoney never horns in. That's what I told em. I never horn in. It's the wrong time, see? Maybe when I get back home, settle down a little, see, get responsible and some self-discipline, I'll try again. I really wanna join the Communist Pahdy. I'll take his place like. You wanna join the Communist Pahdy, pal?"

"Not especially."

"I think maybe they take gents."

"I think maybe gents don't take them," Frank said. "Have a drink, Mulvaney."

"Gimme the jug. It's a long ride back to the outfit. Take me all day tomorra."

"Take it. Keep the smokes. *Suerte*, fella."

The soldier held out his hand and crushed Frank's fingers. He squeezed back until their knuckles whitened.

"Yer aw-right, pal," the soldier said. "Yer awwww-*right!*"

"So are you, fella," Frank said. "Look up some day when we fly over."

"I will," the young Irishman said.

He stood and kicked in the chair. He held the bottle in his left fist and saluted with his right.

She wore a cotton dress of lilac, snugged at the waist with a blue sash. She had little white gloves on her hands and new white, high-heeled shoes. Her hair had been clipped and was poodle-curly in the muggy summer air. She smiled when the traffic policeman held up his white baton. She came across the street in her tremendous, straight-back hip-swinging strut straight into the sidewalk crowd that parted before her like the Red Sea. She saw him, and her wicked dark eyes shone.

Frank stood up and opened his arms. She slid around his grasp, brushed his cheek with her soft lips and settled down on her chair with a soft, rustling wash of petticoats and skirt. The waiter glanced at Frank, rolled his eyes, and shrugged. Frank cleared his throat. She bounded up and flung herself against him, a fierce hug, pulled his head down and kissed his face, his eyes and his mouth.

"Oh, Francisco!"

"*Ole!*" the waiter murmured.

They stood, hugging each other and laughing. The people seated in the café began to applaud. Carmen peeked around at them, her head pressed against his chest. She stood on tiptoe to whisper in his ear.

"Take me to the hotel!"

"Hold the bill," Frank said to the waiter. "We'll be back . . . later."

"Our pleasure," the waiter said, deftly gathering the glasses onto his tray.

The big, broad-bladed fan turned lazily on the ceiling, stirring the air over them. She rolled against him and kissed his cheek. He felt like he was settling down to earth in a balloon.

"Carmen?"

"What, *mi amor?*"

"Don't you think you could take off your gloves now?"

"Ay, what a stylist you've become, my husband . . ."

She lay on her back, her ankles crossed, and pulled off her left glove, loosening each finger, one at a time.

"What a splendid fan! It looks like an *avión* up there, stuck in the ceiling."

"The last time I saw one like that was in an A&P in Easton," he said. "Want a cigarette?"

"Ladies with gloves on do not smoke cigarettes. In your country, possibly, but not here in Spain, my husband. What's the A&P, some political party?"

"A market," he said. "Now is it time for the great news?"

She dropped one glove on his left nipple, the other on the right.

"There. No, this would be better."

She squirmed around and dropped her head on his chest.

"What are you doing, *loca?*"

"There. They are shaking hands with you."

"Funny place to shake hands," he said sliding his fingers into her curly hair.

"You should see what's going on down there . . ."

"What's the great news? Tell me," he said.

"This is more important, no?"

"Yes."

The dining room was a huge room with a vaulted glass ceiling. Tuxedoed waiters crept about. The tables were filled with government officials and men in uniforms. Conversation was muted, as though everyone feared to bring the fragile ceiling crashing down. How it had survived the air raids was a wonder. The waiter set down the soup, a few spoonfuls of watery *gazpacho*.

"Who was your friend?" she said.

"Friend?"

"The one with the red hair. *El Rubio*. An American, obviously."

"Are we so obvious?"

"*Querido*, I can tell them in the operating room when they are covered with a sheet from head to feet."

"A soldier," he said. "From the 15th. Remember when we went to Alcalá? On May Day?"

"With—yes I remember. There were lots of Americans and English there, drinking, after the parade. Singing songs."

"He was one of the singers."

"Oh."

The waiter took away the soup plates and brought the fish, a square bit of herring placed in the exact center of the dish, topped with a dribble of tomato sauce. He bowed and creaked away.

"I guess they're saving the roast burro," Frank said. "*Especialidad de la casa.*"

"Isn't it splendid, though, the way they keep up the standards, despite the war."

"I thought you were a daughter of the people, an example to Socialist Youth," Frank said. "We should be eating lentil soup in a *cantina*."

"That's all I do eat these days," she said. "And salad, now the lettuce is in. We get a chocolate ration every other day. You know what? The girls, the other nurses, all saved their chocolate and gave it to me this afternoon. In a little box with a ribbon."

"What for?" Frank said, swallowing his bit of fish in one bite.

"Energy," Carmen said demurely.

Dessert was an apricot each, presented in little silver baskets and accompanied by fresh napkins and finger bowls.

"*No hay café,*" the waiter whispered. "*Lo siento.*"

They ate the apricots and finished the carafe of wine. The glass ceiling was dark, but there were no stars. Carmen looked up and shivered.

"Let's not go out," she said. "I don't like it with no lights anywhere. It's like being in the land of the blind."

"All right," he said. "There is hot water here. For the bath tub."

"Really? You're not joking, Francisco?"

"Of course not. This is the Hotel Majestic, remember?"

"I will take a hot bath then. How wonderful!"

He lit a cigarette and stared across the dining room, trying to locate the voices speaking English. A half-dozen men, dressed it seemed, to go hunting or fishing, were drinking wine together. He listened. They were Americans.

"Excuse me, Carmen," he said. "Wait here for a minute. I want to see some people over there."

"More friends?"

"No. Journalists."

"Aren't newspaper reporters friends?"

"Not where I come from."

He walked across the dining room to the table. There were five men and one empty chair. The men looked up at him. One of them was very drunk.

"Well, well, look who's here!"

"Hiyuh," Frank said. "I thought you guys must be from the States."

"Where do you call down-home, comrade?"

"K.C.," Frank said, sitting down and taking the glass of wine the drunk one gave him.

"*Qué si?*"

"Kansas City," one of the others said. "Ernie worked for the *Star* out there. You remember."

"Oh sure. When are he and Herb coming back?"

"They went out to see what's left of the Lincolns. You with the 15th Brigade, comrade?"

"Yup," Frank said. "With the Zapadores. *Saloo!*"

"You fix shoes?" the drunk demanded.

"No, for Crissakes, he's an engineer. Well, what's your name, bud? Maybe we can shoot something back to reassure the folks at home."

"Mulvaney," Frank said. "James X. Mulvaney of the engineers with the 15th Brigade and boy-oh-boy are we busy!"

"You are, huh? That's interesting. Doing what?"

"Fixin shoes," the drunk said. "He fixes shoes."

"Can it, will you? Go on, Mulvaney . . . That's with an e and a y, right?"

"Yup," Frank said. "Well, I really can't say. I mean I'm not sposedta."

"Have some *vino*, comrade."

"This stuff sours my gut," Frank said. "I'm a whiskey drinker. Back in good ol' K.C., that is."

"Yeah," one of them said, noncommittally.

"How come you engineers are so busy, Mulvaney? Fortifications? 'The heroic pioneer-battalions of the People's Republic blah-blah-blah, determined to stem the tide of Fascist aggression blah-blah-blah . . .' Well, maybe we could monkey somethin up around Mulvaney and the Maginot Line."

"Oh, it ain't fortifications we're busy at," Frank said. "No, siree! Oh gee. I guess I shouldn't have said that. It's just so great to talk to somebody from back home that . . ."

"Ernie took that big silver flask with him, didn't he?" one of them asked across the table.

"Ever see him without it? Mother's milk. You think . . ."

"Yeah."

"Yeah!"

"Mulvaney, how would you like a good slug of real scotch whiskey from the private stock of Mr. Ernest Hemingway, huh? On us."

"Gee," Frank said doubtfully. "I wouldn't be very democratic to just hog it all myself. I mean, that's what we're fightin against, right? You see, we fellas in the outfit share everything. Why just today, while we were stacking the *pasarelas* . . . Jeez, there I go again! I *gotta* watch myself!"

"What's a *pasa*-whatever, comrade?"

"*Pasodoble*," the drunk one said. "It's a dance. After blondie here fixes the shoes, they all go dancin."

"Will you shut up and let him talk?"

"A *pasarelas* is a—well, I guess I did just come right out and say it," Frank said, sticking out his lower lip. "It's a secret. Plenty important. Jeez, this old *vino* sure sours my gut."

"This—whatever—It's like a secret weapon, Mulvaney? Where's it at?"

"Don't be such suckers," the drunk said. "If he's from Kansas City, I'm Mussolini."

"Jeez, I couldn't tell you fellas that," Frank said. "Why, you might—"

"Remember the guy Ernie got ahold of? About blowin up that bridge?"

"Yeah."

"Yeah!"

"Just between us, comrade. Like a confessional, Mulvaney."

"I couldn't," Frank said. "It's really a secret, see? I just couldn't."

"Irving? Matt? Whadda you think? A jug of Ernie's Red Label? He won't mind. For a good cause?"

"Keep him here. I'll run up and get it."

"He's a con artist," the drunk said. "What part a Kansas City, pal?"

"Fourteen thirty-two South Water Street," Frank said. "Across from the beanery down near the gasworks. Where you fellas from? New York?"

While they waited, Frank invented a family, membership in the CIO and a flesh wound at Brunete. One of them came back carrying a paper bag. He set it down under Frank's chair.

"Never been opened. Okay. Let's have it. Shoot, Mulvaney."

"Boy," Frank said. "The boys in the outfit will sure appreciate this, what with tomorrow bein the Fourth of Joooly."

"Never mind the patriotic bushwa. What's the scoop, comrade?"

"Well, back home we'd call a *pasarela* a footbridge, I reckon," Frank said. "Only these ones are about three hundred feet long."

"*Yeah?*"

"Only one bridge, pal?"

"Oh no," Frank said. "We been workin on five or six."

"Five or six? Go on. Go *on*, Mulvaney!"

"And there's boats, too. Big rowboats, like."

"Sonofa*bitch!* Go on, kid!"

The door opened, and Carmen came out of the bathroom wrapped in a huge white towel like a toga. Frank grinned at her and lifted his glass.

"Look at you," he said. "The Last Days of Pompeii."

"Look at you," she said. "Don't you think about anything else?"

"Have a drink of Mr. Ernest Hemingway's Red Label scotch whiskey," he said. "You will notice on the table a bottle of soda water, and this curious stuff here is called ice. Ice is frozen water and a great rarity. I will prepare a *bebida* for you."

"Do American women drink scotch whiskey?"

"Some do. When they are young," Frank said. "When they get old they drink sherry out of teacups."

"I never know when to believe you, Francisco," she said taking the glass. "Mmmm. It tastes like—like smoke, no? It's—splendid."

"You'll get used to it," he said.

"Oh, yes. If that's what American women drink, I'll get used to it. But sherry from a teacup, never."

"Okay," he said. "*Salud y victoria.* We can drink sherry at the café tomorrow."

"*Salud.* Wasn't it splendid for your friends to give you this whole bottle as a present?"

"They are splendid friends," Frank said. "Journalists always have whiskey. For them, it's mother's milk."

"What did you say?"

"Mother's milk. Why such a funny look?"

"You guessed!" she said accusingly and looked away at the black-out curtains.

"Guessed what?"

"The news."

"What? Oh yes, your great news. Well, go ahead. You've put it off all night."

"But you know," she said. "It was to be a surprise. Are you angry? Yes, you are furious, I can tell."

"About what, for God's sake?"

"You see? Furious."

"I am *not* furious! What are you talking about?"

"I am going to have a baby," she said, not looking at him. "But you knew it. You are always *so* clever. I forget, not seeing you, except as we do—"

He sat up.

"A baby? You? Jesus God!"

"Ay! You spilled the drink, Francisco!"

"A baby? A *baby!* Are you sure, Carmen?"

"I can count to twenty-eight," she said, and burst into tears.

He fell back on the bed and stared up at the ceiling fan slowly spilling the air down on them. Of course, the last few times they had been together, he hadn't . . . But he thought *she* . . . She must have wanted one.

"A baby," he said. "What the hell, you know?"

Maybe that was what she had been trying to tell him with her special I LOVE YOU OK in the letter. He reached out and touched her shoulder, sat up and slid over next to her. She was trying not to cry.

"Carmen," he said. "Don't cry. There's nothing to cry about. Please? It's—"

"There are places to go," she said tightly. "There's a clinic in the hospital. They must take care of forty women a day in there."

He was appalled. A little shock reeled through him, memories of fraternity brothers and girls, "townies," and trips to special doctors in New York.

"Are you *crazy?*" he said. "You can't do that!"

"Oh yes. It's perfectly legal. And I will, if you wish it, Francisco. It was very stupid and careless of me—"

"Oh, Carmen," he said. "Come here. Come here to me."

She turned her face. When he kissed her, he could taste her tears. She held him tightly. He set his glass down on the carpet, set hers beside it and settled back on the bed. The fan in the ceiling churned slowly, around and around, spilling the air down on them.

They lay side by side, under the big towel. Carmen snuggled up to him with a soft, comfortable grunt.

"That was splendid," she said. "How gentle you can be! Now we are positive, of course."

"When will he be born?"

"Oh, not for a long time. I don't show yet, do I? No, you see? In April, Francisco. The spring is nice, a good time, so they say. You get used to him, you see, before the weather gets too hot. Then they get rashes and cry all the time. So I'm told. Naturally, *he* will not be so naughty."

"Maybe it's twins," Frank said. "It's bad to be an only child. I know."

"God forbid," Carmen said, taking her glass from his fingers. "Every April, if you like. For ten years. But one at a time, eh?"

"One at a time," he said lazily. "Penn Charter or maybe Exeter."

"What are they? Markets, like the P and A? He won't need food for a while. You see, that's why when you said about mother's milk, I thought you knew. I wonder if I'll be big enough to feed him. Do you think so, Francisco. Look at me."

"You're fine," he said. "Mmmm, yes. Just fine."

"For you to play with, fine, but what about him?"

"That's some news all right," he said.

"Thank you, *querido*. Look, I'm crying again. It makes me so happy. I think I'm very tired or maybe just drunk on this stuff . . ."

The fan swirled like a propeller on the ceiling. Pavito was a Spaniard. He said one day's work to finish The Magic Carpet. That meant three days, maybe four or five. It would not be possible to test fly it. They were too close to Valls. She would have to come out, not to the *ganadería*, but close, maybe down near the main gate. He could taxi down. He would tell Pavito he was just ground-testing. She would get in the back seat. Then they would turn, back up the runway and take off. This changed everything. He had to get her out. Get *them* out. Land in France. Maybe Marseilles. Once she was safe, he could come back. He wasn't going to betray anybody. It wasn't quitting. It wouldn't be like stealing something. He might even fly back in. That way there wouldn't be any hitch at the border and Pavito would still be . . . Of course, they might not *want* him back. Probably not. Technically, he'd be deserting. Well, if they felt that way about it, let them. He'd done his share. Hadn't the other volunteer pilots all gone back to their own countries? It was a perfectly normal, sane thing to do. If some idiot Communist in the Ministry of Air wanted to arrest him . . . Voget could find that out. But he was in Madrid. A telegram to Party headquarters. Explain everything. Voget would understand. He was the only one who would . . . How long would it take? Two hours. Three hours. Pavito would have to put a radio in. The French would send up interceptors. Unidentified aircraft crossing the border. Take off just before daylight and . . ."

"What are you thinking about? Are you asleep, too?"

"No, no," Frank said. "I was—ah—thinking about names. The name is very important. He has to have a good name, don't you think?"

"Yes. Oh yes, the same."

He propped himself on one elbow and put ice and whiskey in their glasses. The stuff was getting to him. It was crazy. Sure, Pavito was a first-class mechanic, but the plane itself was made out of junk and spare parts. A hundred things could go wrong. There was a field between Gerona and Figueras where they assembled the planes brought across the border and tested them. The Pyrenees were too high, too cloudy. Anti-aircraft. Jumped by a Messerschmitt. Never have a chance. There was no other way, though. The only one who could help was Voget. And he'd said no dice. Goddamned Reds had everything tied up. Must be some way to get her across the border with a refugee group. Orphans, that was it. Orphans and pregnant women. Couldn't refuse. Sure.

"My God," he said. "How the Biddles worry over names. The Rittenhouses! And the Whitneys!"

"Are they—"

"They are families in America. One of the Vanderbilt girls was named Consuelo."

"How lovely," Carmen said. "Consuelo!"

But they were turning them back at the border. Concentration camps. Like prison. Might get shipped back into Nationalist territory. Look at this stupid business of changing his name. She might get confused, sign the wrong papers. Better to take the chance. Why had he talked Pavito into making the plane, if he hadn't planned on using it? Take a chance. Born lucky. [The Jenny he soloed in was in worse shape than The Magic Carpet.] She might not want to go. Might refuse. Tell her—tell her she *had* to go. Because of the baby. After the war, they'd come back. If the Republic won.

"I always wanted a lovely name like that. Consuelo. Don't think it's amusing to go to a girl's school in a convent with the name of Carmen. How many times have I been asked about my Don José. And the sisters! They spied on me all the time. Just because my mother insisted that I be called Carmen. Bah! If it's a girl, we drown it. Like a cat."

"Don't talk like that," he said, disturbed. "I forbid it."

"Oh. It is forbidden. Okay."

He was her husband and the father, for God's sake, and she'd do what she was *told* to do. The whole business of the Republic and the revolution and all that, why, that was swell when she was a kid. But now. It would only take them two hours, maybe three. Was there a landing field at Perpignan? Must be, for Air France mail service to Algeria. An emergency field. That was it! That explained everything. Why hadn't he thought of it! Of course. It was an emergency. If they didn't think so, the hell with them. *Sin camaradas fuertes . . .*

"What are you talking to yourself about?"

"I was just thinking . . . about what you were thinking of for a name."

"Why . . . well, I thought that it would be nice . . . What do you think of Paco?"

"He got across the river, didn't he? You sent me his photo. In the letter."

"No, *querido*, I mean as a name."

"Paco? *Paco?*"

"Paco Libro y Bravo. That's an elegant name. *Muy fuerte!* Very Republican, don't you think?"

"Paco? Paco Pierce Buckminster? Jesus *God*, Carmen!"

"What's the matter?"

"Matter? *Paco?* They'll laugh at him in Bala Cynwyd!"

She sat up suddenly and snatched the towel off him.

"Well they won't laugh at him in Madrid!" she said hotly, covering herself.

"Uh-*uh!*"

"What is this *uh-uh*, Francisco? Tell me at once!"

"No."

"No what?"

"No Paco. That's what."

"Who says?"

"*I* say it."

"You!" she said, lunging off the bed. "*Celos!* Yes, that's it."

The towel only covered the front of her. She stumbled across the room, stepping on the hem, her naked back very straight. He laughed softly.

"*Qué gordita*," he said. "What a nice, fat, little rear end you have . . ."

She switched the towel up around her and glared at him.

"You are jealous!" she said.

"Jesus God . . ."

"You *are!* You never liked him, *never!* I have told you that we were like brother and sister. There was *nothing* between us! Not even up in the Sierras at the beginning. Why, he even protected me against the others that wanted to . . . wanted to . . . And I haven't seen him since we took our leave together in Cuenca at his *finca*. That was months and months and *months* ago! My God, Francisco, he presented me at the wedding, remember?"

"Of course I remember! It is *he* who is jealous! Not me."

"Well, naturally he's jealous! He has a *right* to be!"

"I don't? I am only your husband—"

"You admit it, then! *Ah!*"

"I admit nothing! Ah, yourself. You are hysterical. Stop that, or you'll put the curtains down on your head and the police will come."

"Let them come! I have a right to be hysterical. You are insulting my honor! *Bruto!*"

"Oh, Lord . . ." he said.

Carmen emptied her glass and looked at him, measuring the distance. When she raised her arm, the towel fell away. Frank applauded. She dropped the glass to the carpet and burst into tears again.

She stood, clinging to her towel and to the heavy drapes, one foot raised off the floor, her face turned away from him. He felt the slow air slide over his naked shoulders with weak gusts. She was being silly and childish, but he didn't dare to laugh at her. Not now.

"I am sorry, Carmen," he said formally. "I did not mean to insult your honor. I agree that I have been jealous of Paco, but that this was foolish of me. I did not mean to insult your honor."

"I should hope not," she said, her voice muffled in the curtains. She sobbed more slowly.

"Or anybody else's honor," he said. "In all of Spain!"

"Now you are making fun of me," she said bitterly. "I can't help it if I'm Spanish. Why did you marry me? Why didn't you marry some American girl. I wouldn't have cared. I don't. I'll be your—your *chica* in Barcelona—"

"Oh, Carmen . . ."

"Stay right there. Leave me alone. Don't touch me."

"I love you," he said helplessly. "Okay?"

It seemed to him that it was a very long time before she stopped crying. She stood across the room, very small and sad, as though he had punished her. He felt guilty, and angry that he felt guilty, and guilty again about being angry. It was all so silly.

"Okay?" he said.

Her shoulders lifted and fell. She raised her face from the curtains, wiping her eyes with the back of her hand. She looked young, terribly young, and he knew he had done something very wrong to her. It was not fair that she was pregnant. It all should have happened later, not so accidentally. It was all his fault. He was oversexed.

"Okay," she said.

"Want a drink?"

"If you like. A very small one. I feel tired and dizzy."

"Come sit down. Over here," he said, patting the other side of the big bed. "It is settled then. We will call him Paco. Paco Buchanan Buckminster. After my great-grandfather."

She bent and picked up the glass. He went to help her. She shouldn't be doing a lot of work, lifting heavy things. She brushed him aside and marched back to the bed, sniffing, and flounced down, kicking her feet.

"Don't be silly, *querido*," she said in a shaky voice, not looking at him. He made drinks in mad haste, afraid to break the mood of truce, and slipped gingerly onto the mattress, his legs down beside her. She took the glass he gave her. He winked experimentally. She sighed and sipped, coughed and patted her chest.

"You are his father," she said. "Naturally, it is your right to choose his name. I was only making a very little suggestion."

"It is all settled."

She patted his ankle in an infuriating, absent-minded way that made his toes flex. He swallowed a huge gulp of whiskey and soda and nearly choked.

"I refuse to consider Paco as a name," she said calmly.

"*Huh?*"

"Paco Libro y Bravo? No, no. He can't go through life sounding to everyone like a political slogan. I have known perfectly nice girls of good family, the kind that should have married and have had dozens of children who took the veil just because they had such *Catholic* names. No other reason at all. They felt an obligation."

He lay there listening. It was very odd. Sometimes he was certain that he knew exactly what she was saying or what she meant, even though he could not really say that he understood every word. He lay there, understanding her without any effort at all. It was like a very precious gift she had given him.

"I mean, names are not without significance," she was saying, or so he understood her. "Paco is a perfectly good name. For a worker. Of course, we are all workers, but still . . . It would have a certain *political* significance, at least for a while. We don't want him to feel like those poor girls at the convent, do we?"

"Of course not," he said, delighted, flinging a little chip into the swirl of her words.

"He might decide to be a Communist for the wrong reasons," she finished and, suddenly, wonderfully, smiled at him.

"Are there any *right* reasons for being a Communist?" he said.

It was really something very special. She really was his wife, not just some girl, even a steady girl. She really was pregnant. And when they got back they could always speak together, like kids talking pig-Latin, even though she would have to learn English. I LOVE YOU OK¿

"Now you are not being serious at all, Francisco. I don't think you are even listening to me."

"*Al contrario*," he said. "Please do not pull all the fur off my legs."

"He will have blond hair, just like you," she said, dreamily. "As fine as silk. That's very rare in this country, you know. Only Gallegos have red hair or blond . . . I mean, naturally, of course. His nickname will be Rubio. Now don't frown, so. You can't prevent people from calling him that."

"I can on Broad Street and Market."

"Just think," she said, kissing his left knee. "There have been three of you already, no? I think that is very, *very* elegant. Like a dynasty of kings."

"That's the general idea," he said. "You know the Main Line."

"Mmm-hmmm," she said.

She did understand, too, he was certain. He had explained about the Main Line at some time or other. At first she had thought it was a new form of Fascism, but then had accepted it as a make-believe, American aristocracy, all the more important, for being obviously, not legitimate.

"You know what you look like?" she said. "A big, soft white snail. *Pobrecito*, how tired he must be!"

"That is no way to talk," he said, covering himself. "You never learned that at the convent."

"*Al contrario*," she said. "We seldom talked about anything else. I never had a brother, you see. But there were girls there who did have brothers. They drew the most interesting pictures and passed them around. One year we had modeling clay—"

"Oh-oh."

"Exactly. For about two weeks. Then the sisters caught some of the girls—well, you can imagine what they were making. Great, great big ones! It was awful. There was a terrible scandal."

"I never thought that girls were interested—"

"*Interested!* My God, Francisco, what do you think we *prayed* for?"

He laughed. She giggled and suddenly flung herself on him, kissing his chin and nose, her eyes very wide, important-wide. He had kissed off all her lipstick. He watched, fascinated, as her pale mouth slowly formed the awkward syllables, sensing as he listened that she would always speak English with a low-comedy accent.

"Franklin Pierce Buck—that's right, isn't it?—um—Buckminster the Fourth! What a splendid name!"

"Well done!" he said. "When did you learn 'the fourth'?"

"Yesterday. Tomorrow is some holiday. I have a book of English."

"Throw it away."

"And tomorrow is, *el cuatro de julio*, let me try it . . . ummm. Fourth of Yew-lie. There!"

"*Bravo!*"

"I can't practice when you are kissing me, my husband . . ."

"Well, when he's at home, this *chico*, we can call him by his nick-name."

"Rubio. Yes, I suppose it will be natural."

"No," Frank said. "At home we will call him Paco. What the hell, you know? . . ."

There was an air-raid warning, and the lights shut off. Carmen went to sleep. A few bombs dropped, deep, soft, sledging sounds, far away. The sirens sobbed the all-clear. The lights stayed off. The city was short of power. Frank held her loosely. The thought that bothered him was the realization that she and the boy, Manuel, were both the same age, and he was no longer able to remember what it felt like to be that young.

A chinkling drilled at him, stopped, again, stopped, again. He opened his eyes. The fan was still. The room was pitch black, stuffy. He closed his eyes, groaning. His mouth felt thick and mucky, too many cigarettes, too much to drink. The chinkle whirred again, pressing in through the thick, sleepy blur of his mind. He lay listening, balancing himself. He was in Barcelona. The girl with the face on his arm was—where was his wristwatch, the matches?

He knew what it was now, and slipped his arm out from underneath her. She stirred a little, muttering comfortably, and rolled over. He tried to cram his eyelids open wider. He could see nothing at all. Everything was black. A terror of blindness lunged in him, as though he had touched an open fuse socket. He sat up, gasping, and seized the telephone as it rang again.

He cursed softly as he picked up the receiver, a lightweight thing, old-fashioned, like an infant's rattle. A thought stirred in the hung-over blankness, as though the thought, too, had been suspended in sleep. It was Manuel. He had found some girl and taken her to bed, then left her to go boast of what he had done over too many glasses of cheap wine. The air raid had sobered him up. He had found a place to sleep and had just now remembered to telephone at some ungodly hour.

"*Manolo?*" he said thickly.

"*Dígame?*"

The flimsy receiver let out some more sounds that seemed to bite at him. He flinched away, feeling miserable, disoriented. Any telephone that rang in the middle of the night should speak in English, a courtesy, at least. He fumbled for his cigarettes and matches, while a little voice ranted at him in the darkness. He thought dully about the old saying of go to bed smart and wake up stupid. He dropped the matches to the carpet. His head ached when he bent for them. The tin voice blittered from his hand. He clapped the receiver to his ear.

"*Oiga! Oiga!*"

It yelped now, like a puppy.

"What the hell does somebody want?" he said in English. "*Dígame!*"

"*Dígame?*"

"I said it first. Monolo? *Dónde estás?*"

"Capitán Libro?"

"*Hablando,*" he said cautiously. "Who is speaking?"

"Teniente Triangara, comrade. From the base."

The connection was very clear as it sometimes was late at night. He recognized his commissar's dull, unpleasant voice.

"What's the matter?" he said.

"Orders from the Ministry of Air, Captain. You must return to the base. At once!"

"*No puede ser,*" he said. "I am on leave until tomorrow night."

"*Lo siento mucho,*" the voice said.

Like hell he's very sorry.

"*Capitán?*"

"*Sí, sí.*"

"*Ordenes del Ministerio . . .*"

"I understand. What about?"

"A special flight."

"What?"

"A special flight, Captain. Three aircraft."

"What for?"

"I cannot say, Captain. Not on the telephone."

He could hear Triangara breathing. It was true that the telephone system served both sides and the lines were frequently tapped. The commissar would not tell him more.

"Have Pantón and . . ."

"Your name is on the flight plan, comrade. Pantón, too. And one other."

"Manuel Chávez?"

"No. Another. But your name is."

"I understand. What hour? My *coche* is in the motor park."

"The Air Ministry is sending a motorcycle with a sidecar to the hotel."

"*Cojudo,*" Frank said. "Now?"

"Right at this moment, yes. You must leave immediately!"

Then the flight would be at dawn or a little later. Probably an escort hop to Valencia. A transport with government officials or high-ranking officers. Was the squadron to be transferred to the Levante?

"Will there be other flights? Later?"

"We have no information. Just this order."

"*Muy bien,*" Frank said.

"I will confirm with the Ministry."

It would be too much to call and confirm himself. Apparently, it was just this single flight. What was a commissar for?

"Please confirm with them, *teniente,*" he said. "I will be back as soon as it is possible."

"*Muy bien.*"

The receiver clicked like claws snapping in the darkness. Frank felt with his feet, located the matches and hung up. There was a candle on the table. He groped and found it, struck a match. The point of light hurt his eyes. He stared unhappily at the soda bottle, the bowl half filled with tepid water, the ashtray, the half-empty fifth of scotch. His clothes were slung over a chair, just at the dull rim of light. He stood up and tottered to the chair, running his tongue over his fuzzy-feeling teeth. He dressed and found some aspirin in his musette-bag. He squirted out a glass of water from the siphon-bottle and swallowed the pills. He felt cheated, lost and unhappy.

She was sound asleep. He didn't know whether to wake her or not.

Either way it would be bad. He found her letter and a pencil stub. He heard the motorcycle stuttering out in the street. He spread the sheet of paper out on the table and wrote a few words, signed his name and made a row of X marks. He picked up his boots, blew out the candle and opened the door. The hall was dark and still. Somehow, he had remembered his watch. Or he had never taken it off. He closed the door very gently, until the lock clicked.

Lieutenant Triangara took his fingers away from the telephone quickly and gently, as though he had placed an explosive on the table. He glanced across at the man in the unmarked uniform with the dark glasses.

"I do not think he guessed that I am in the city. The connection was very clear. Almost as though he were in the next room."

"The whole ring," the other said, without any evident satisfaction. "The entire gang. It was difficult. They have been so clever in their discretion that it almost looks coincidental. To someone outside our organization, I mean. You have done your part well, Triangara. With distinction."

"A very small part," Triangara said.

He was certain that somewhere in the convent of San Juan there was a manila folder with his own name printed on it in neat black letters.

"But crucial," the other said. "This aircraft. In itself, nothing. Not in and of itself. A mechanic with extra hours. He makes a shower-bath, a cultivator for potatoes, the Republic is short of planes and he has access to this and that. So, he makes an aircraft."

"For the escape," Triangara said. "It was that, I sensed, at once."

"It was the letter you intercepted," the other said. "Conclusive evidence. The squadron reports. Disguised handwriting. The signature. Madrid has a cryptographer, too. In a week, we will have our local interpretation and Madrid's deciphering. There is no code that cannot be cracked. That is the easy part. That and interrogations . . ."

"It was an honor to play even a small role in unmasking this group of criminals," Triangara said, hoping that he would be dismissed.

"Spies are criminals only if they are caught," the other said. "Unlike sin, there is no internal sense of guilt. That is what we teach them here. In the cells."

"Will they all . . . learn?" Triangara said. He did not like to think about the girl. She was a pretty little thing.

"Let us consider them and the circumstances of all this," the other said, stacking the manila folders and laying them down as he spoke, like a player at Patience.

"One must learn to comprehend spaces. Yes, the spaces between things, people, events. It is the space that makes the logic. There is more air than steel to the links of a chain, no? We begin with Larra. Son of a leader of Asturian miners in the 1934 rising. The father is shot, with all other male relatives. The boy is seized, his escape is made possible by certain people locally. He leaves Spain . . ."

The second folder felt huge beside the first. It was very thick, almost like a book.

"Who takes him? Paul Voget. To Russia. For two years he studies in Moscow, Leningrad, and other places. There are other Spaniards, too, all older. But he is extraordinary, everyone agrees. There are certain signs of genius, even. He returns to Spain. Madrid this time. His mother has died, also. He is alone. Perfect. He conceals himself, but is widely known. The infiltration of the Socialist Youth goes off without a hitch. Provocations are planned and executed to perfection. The revolution begins when the army officers rise against the Republic. There is street fighting of a confused sort near a convent. Enter, the girl."

The third folder fell. Triangara wet his lips.

"This was very daring of them," the other said. "Her father was a second- and third-level conspirator, an enemy of the Republic back to 1931. But the propaganda value of her is enormous!"

The tinted glasses turned. What did the eyes see through those dark lenses?

"They go to the Sierras. Fight there. Again with great efficiency. He has learned everything, this Asturian boy. His group is formed into the Red Guards and he returns in triumph to the city. The priest . . . but we understand the part played by the priest, don't we? And the German, too. Perfect screen, using Kopa, with his provable and quite legitimate anti-Nazi activities, the escape from the Gestapo, and so on. Voget brings *him* to Spain. He and Larra meet—where else?"

"In Madrid," Triangara said.

"Kopa, too, is a hero. *Bona fide.* The German anti-Fascists are magnificent at University City and later at Guadalajara. No one else would have seen the friendship as more than comradely affection bred in resistance. But—the *spaces,* eh?"

Triangara nodded. Another folder.

"The American. As much a legitimate capitalist as Kopa was anti-Nazi. He has hobbies. Polo-playing and racing airplanes. Suddenly, he appears in Spain. Why? What is his motive? He is wealthy beyond payment, even by the grasping hyenas of Wall Street who dominate what Americans call a government. Call it idealism? Impossible. He is a *banker!*"

"Impossible," Triangara agreed.

"He meets the girl. Dorlov—I have explained about Dorlov's trial in the Soviet Union, have I not, his abject confessions, the part he played in this affair?—Eh?"

"Quite so."

"Now the new aircraft are delivered. Now our American sportsman flies the new models no one in the West has ever seen. Voget we may consider French. Kopa is German. The pilot is American. All those countries want to know the strength of the Soviet Air Force. So far so good. The priest appears—*hooplah!* Like magic. The marriage ceremony —what a *natural* gathering, no?"

"It is possible to believe that the girl knew nothing," Triangara said. "I mean, at this time."

"At this time, probably so. Voget crosses into Nationalist territory, as directed by Moscow, returns to France. The American pilot officially disappears. He is now Francisco Libro, a naturalized Spaniard."

"It was the marriage that you suspected, wasn't it?"

"It was the telephone call from Larra. To me. About Kopa, on my part. About the American on his. There was *the space!* The meaningful nothingness. The first step was to remove Dorlov, of course. The American and the girl had become too well known, but at least we could separate Larra from them and hold Voget away. That way we could keep information from getting out of Spain, although we obviously could not prevent them from gathering whatever came to them. It was important not to alert them. Now, the little reunion at Cuenca."

"It was at the Cuenca reunion, as you call it, that I was ordered to become squadron commissar when the group was shifted," Triangara said.

"You have performed well, in both roles," the other said. "But tell me. Do you not perhaps feel some particles of—oh, masculine sympathy, let's say? For her?"

"None whatever!" Triangara said quickly.

"Of course, no one in the military knew a thing. Hence, we made no interference with the reorganization and equipping of the Red Guards as a shock group, deployed as the army high command wished. Kopa had been settled with, so the Luftwaffe was out of it. All mail had been stopped, months earlier. The American was cut off. He could communicate what he knew to no one."

"But why . . . ?"

"The Royal Air Force must have demanded information. If nothing could be gotten *out*, except through Voget, and *that* had to come through the Quai D'Orsay with a change in government after Blum fell from power . . . Well, they had to risk sending *in* a new agent."

"Oh."

"They sent a man with excellent qualifications. He called himself Lockridge. Voget seems to have sensed at once that he was both too good to be true and too true to be good. Do you follow me?"

"And that is why he reported Lockridge here?"

"Of course, we showed him Kolodny, also. He was . . . impressed."

"But the building of the aircraft began several months ago," Triangara said.

"About the time the American sent his so-called wife—for they are not really married, of course—his so-called comical letter that you intercepted and that is now in the hands of our cryptographers. Somehow, the British role was suspected or not trusted. They betray each other constantly, these capitalist countries; therefore, their agents do the same. It is their nature—yes, a question?"

"But the priest? The ceremony?"

"Padre Ortega was not aware of the fact, but he had been relieved of his priestly duties. A letter was found in the effects of his bishop, prior to that bloodsucker's execution. A priest who is no priest can hardly be said to perform a religious ceremony, can he? I ask you as a Spanish national!"

"I am an atheist, of course," Triangara said. "But I think no. Of course, the church was banned then. Marriage could only be performed by civil action."

"Which our American was careful *not* to undertake."

"He's a clever swine," Triangara said. "He has deceived her, then."

"Ah. That slight touch of compassion. You see why your transfer has been ordered? You might not be able to help yourself."

"She is an enemy of the people! I would spit in her face!"

"Would you?" the other said, so carelessly that Triangara's blood chilled along his spine. He stared down at the floor, his heart thumping. It had been insane for him to say anything.

"You understand, then, why he was so willing to become Spanish."

"Because she would have become an American by marriage?"

"Quite so. That might have proved an embarrassment all around. His usefulness as an agent would have become sharply limited. The government of the United States, while no doubt willing to pay blood-money to receive military secrets was certainly unprepared to pay twice, once for him, once for her. They are so thrifty and indirect, the Americans, that you would hardly think they employed intelligence agents in Spain at all! At least of that type. Their military has placed some people within the Lincoln battalion, of course. They have always attempted to infiltrate the Party. No, it was all very neat. Mutual gratification, no doubt. Odd how the sense of danger sharpens the sexual drive. I suppose that is why I am so placid. It is so very calm here."

Triangara looked up, startled.

"Well, it's all exposed for what it is," he said slowly. What would they do to her?

"But what does all this *mean*? Eh? Eh?"

"I suppose I have wondered that," Triangara admitted.

"You? The Kremlin—I tell you the Kremlin *has demanded to know!*"

"Ah."

"Now I can tell them. They are all *his* agents."

"Whose?"

"Trotsky. They are all agents of *Trotsky!*"

"Incredible!" Triangara said. "Even Voget?"

"Ah," the other said. "Only the NKVD knows that. I am inclined to believe that Voget is a double agent, employed by the Party at a rather high level to smoke out these Trotskyites in Belgium and France. He speaks good Spanish due to his Party work in Central America. He was . . . available, perhaps. I do not know . . . everything."

"What will happen? I mean, if Voget is *not* . . ."

"Then who is left? The girl? Hardly. Kopa is dead. The priest, also."

"Larra? El Asturiano? You mean you believe that *he* is a Trotskyite? An agent of?—No! No!"

"And now you understand why I have delayed you," the other said smoothly. "You who know what you know, now have been told what I know. We see the reaction. Disbelief. Partial or total?"

"Total. Yes, complete disbelief! It is incredible! Paco Larra is—El Asturiano! It's like saving that Juan Modesto—or, or Lister, or—or, no, it's not so! I can't believe it! The others, yes."

"You see how clever they are?" the other said. "Like devils. Even in Mexico, Trotsky is a menace. His evil influence corrupts everywhere! The Red Army was riddled. Like a disease! The purge has been absolutely necessary for the health of Socialism on an international level!"

"I don't understand," Triangara said. "I am merely a local member of the Party. Perhaps it's true. It's true if you say it is, I'm sure. But it's incredible! Then all the while Larra was in the Soviet Union . . ."

"He was being contaminated. Every one of his instructors has confessed to monstrous crimes of spying, conspiracy, direct supply of information to the capitalist countries. Larra was poisoned in Russia. Drop by drop. Into his bloodstream. He is sick. But he can be cured. It will take time. You—"

"I cannot bring myself to comprehend this," Triangara said. "Not yet. What will be done?"

"With the American?" the other said. "Since he is an American, nothing. Sooner or later, he will leave Spain. Either under orders or because he suspects us finally. His motivation is mysterious to me, I admit."

Triangara listened, afraid to interrupt. The manila folders were picked up, one by one.

"The girl? She will find another man. A flesh and blood lover who will beat her, perhaps. After all this, she must have some artificial anxiety, don't you see?"

"How monstrous it all seems," Triangara muttered. "How terrible!"

"How predictable, you mean. How *dull*."

"Larra, then. You will arrest him? Charge him with his crimes?"

"El Asturiano? The pure one. The unsuspected. Product of his class and rising above it by a genius at destruction that could, with proper conditioning become a great force for construction. The ideal young revolutionary. There are hundreds of them in the world. Thousands! Like termites in the beams of capitalism. When it all comes crashing down, a new era of Marxist heroism will begin! Do you understand me?"

"Not really," Triangara said. "You accused him of being a traitor. A Trotskyite. Now, you praise him."

"He *is* a Trotskyite," the other said. "By inclination, by training, by will! By nature! But—it is not safe to destroy him. No, no. That is not the way. It is not necessary to lift a finger. We will simply watch."

"Watch what?" Triangara said. "If he is an enemy of the international movement and a traitor to the spirit of socialism, he should be shot at once! That's only logical."

"It was logical to shoot Buenaventura Durrutti. The Anarchist leader."

"Of course."

"Ask Larra. He did it."

"*He* did?"

"Of course. He will do absolutely anything."

"And—" Triangara said, and stopped.

"True. Jiménez will do absolutely anything, too. If the Kremlin orders it, I will have him assassinated in such a way as to discredit the Anarchists in Barcelona, perhaps. That would be simple enough. If the Republic might benefit from another martyr, he will be killed in battle. That, too, would be simple. But, until I am given orders, I have a certain discretionary authority. And so, I will watch."

"Watch what?"

"I will watch Paco Larra destroy the mythological creature you Spaniards called El Asturiano. He will break away from his moral course—through frustration. Like his master, Trotsky."

"I understand," Triangara said.

"That is a conventional phrase that means very little. You mean it is getting late. You mean you have heard a great deal. You mean you wish to leave this place."

"I don't know why you tell me all this."

"You cannot believe that Larra is what I tell you he is because you— you *admire* him! And that's the truth! You are going to help me, yes. We will watch together. You will be close. I will be far away. You will tell me everything!"

"What . . ."

"Your transfer, Triangara, is written out. You will become the new commissar for El Asturiano's Red Guards."

"No—No!"

"Yes. Surely you don't think of refusing? After Kolodny? What are you thinking, eh?"

"I . . ."

"I will tell you. Right now, just a second ago, you thought of killing me, didn't you? But you have no weapon. Too bad! And you decided in the next second that you did not dare to attempt it with your bare hands—see? You cannot help yourself! You turn and look at the door to see if the guard is watching. Now what you think . . . is this. Just this. You think, you have begun, completed, resolved it. You think I am mad, don't you? You *know* it. I am *mad*. Eh?"

"Let me go!"

"Of course! You will stand on the runway when the sun comes up. You will salute as the planes take off for the Levante. Then you will arrest that mechanic, Pavito, on crimes against the people and the Republic, specifically for—here is the warrant, read it, if you wish—for appropriating property belonging to the people for his own personal benefit and gain. This second document is all the proof the tribunal will need. Your accusation. Sign it, please. Not now—in a minute. Your hands are trembling uncontrollably. Now—oh, there you go. Thinking again. Now you are thinking, what will happen to me if I refuse to sign anything? I will be a noble fellow. I will not become commissar. I will get away from here by appearing to agree with everything, and then I will go to Larra and tell him everything! You didn't think I'd let you out of here alone, did you? You will go back to the base with two special officers. You will do everything as I say. You will return here. Or shall I give orders to have you go through what Kolodny has endured?"

"No—no!"

"Very good. You will be transferred, as I say. Understood?"

"I understand."

Mahoney sat by the side of the road with the Spanish boys of his *pelotón* smoking a stale Chesterfield, a dead man's smoke, doled out daily by the new company commissar. The British swung through the white, dusty afternoon singing.

> *"Marching, marching, marching,*
> *Always fuckin-well marching,*
> *God send the day when*
> *We'll fuckin-well march no more!"*

He took the canteen and sipped the lukewarm water, sour with chloride of lime. The British marched past, too tired from the day's maneuvers to kid around. Their light trousers had been ripped by the undergrowth they had scrambled through. The whole brigade had been out, a mock-attack across the steep, rocky hills, infiltrating the rain-washed clefts and ravines. Many of the men limped, their feet bruised and bleeding. There were no boots.

The Mac-Paps had been down closer to the river and came up a path worn through the light woods and weeds. There were not many true Canadians left. More than half of every battalion was Spanish; some companies counted three out of four. He watched them and scraped at the scabies on his legs. He handed the canteen back.

"*Gracias.*"

"*Nada . . . de nada . . .*"

His own section was all Spanish, and he was their sergeant, even though he had said he didn't want it and had requested the Machine Gun Company. The Mac-Paps scrambled up the path, sweat-soaked and exhausted, the sun beating down through the trees on them. They scattered small, whipping lizards off the hot rocks and coughed in the dust.

The food was bad and there wasn't much of it. His *chicos* were young and soft. They got tired easily and their legs cramped. It was hard for him to talk to them. He used sign language most of the time. He didn't believe they would hold together across the river. They were all homesick and none of them had to shave. The rest of Number Five Company called them "Baloney's Boy Scouts." He didn't care.

They said that Spain had finally gotten to him. They said he was punchy. They kept an eye on him in a kind, clumsy way he could not respond to, not even in anger. They gave up kidding around and wandered away, leaving him a few smokes or a copy of *Our Fight,* the daily news sheet that he never bothered to read, even when they drew pencil lines under his name. There were a few "intellectuals," college boys with books who were serious about morale and self-awareness and the struggle against Fascism. They thought he was some bum and was just hanging around until the volunteers were all sent home. He had been ordered to special lectures and had not listened, not even to Johnny Gates. He applied for the scouts, but they told him the Spanish kids needed him, as a veteran. There were others who had been at Jarama and Brunete, the "North Pole" at Celades, Quinto, and Belchité. There were even some second-timers who had been back to the States or who had been wounded bad enough to go home, but had returned to the battalion. He marched with them, ate with them, dug *chavolas,* even stood in line at mail call for the letters and packages that never came. They shook their heads and muttered about "shell-shock."

He was not used to thinking, and the effort made him nervous and sleepless. He wandered down to the bank of the river and sat there in the muddy, rank weeds, listening to the pull of the broad current against the banks, looking at the stars swimming in the dark, swirling water. They thought he was going crazy or was already off his nut, but he wasn't.

It was the first time for him that he had pushed anyone into a grave. All the others had just happened, a bullet, a shell, something. It was as if he had been marching and suddenly there was a hole in the smooth ground. It took all he had to keep from falling in it. It had happened across the river. It had been a dark night with stars and the moon. It had happened, and he had dropped the Dikterov. He had run away.

He kept the grave-marker hidden in his worn knapsack with his blanket, his tin spoon and the can he used as a mess kit. It was two pieces of wood, painted white, with black paint dribbled carefully into the rutted letters he had gouged with the tip of his bayonet. Just the name, company number and Lincoln battalion, 15th Brigade. Others had made markers. He had seen them at Jarama and Brunete, especially. But it was not the same. The other guys knew where to set their markers, and he didn't.

He had never in his life been guilty, not in his own mind. He had knelt before the wooden confessional-screen and had confessed to stealing, lying, fighting, and getting a girl in the family way. But he had never felt that he deserved to be punished.

He was haunted. Every voice that shouted now was an echo of the call he had not answered. A nothingness lay across the river and he had to go there.

So he moved in the battalion like a dreamer, his blue eyes fixed and far away, listening, yet always inattentive, apparently indifferent to the details of outfitting and training for the assault across the Ebro, but helpful in a silent, eager, penitential way, an unnaturalness that the other men shied from. Spain had, in fact, got to Mahoney at last.

The Ebro Valley was hot with occasional brief, pelting rainstorms that brought swarms of stubborn, biting flies. Every day was a busy, brainless monotony of waiting, marching, target practice, company and battalion exercises over the miserable, rocky, sun-smitten hills, advance, retreat, infiltrate, scout, signal, march, wait, wait. The narrow dirt roads boiled up clouds of dust that sifted through the treetops and powdered the ilex leaves. Section, company, battalion, brigade, sunburned and stripped to the waist, swatting the flies and swigging the warm water doused with iodine, falling down at last into the *chavolas*, the flimsy lean-tos over pits scraped between the nut bushes, huddled under dirty blankets, sharing drags on cigarettes while the big moon spilled over the foot-worn earth and the low-voiced anxious conversations turned the same two subjects over and over: If we're going into action, what the hell are we sitting on our asses here for? If we're going to be repatriated, what the hell are we sitting on our asses here for?

The two questions, over and over; there was nothing else to talk about.

Everything was bad, worse than bad, some final, fumbling fuck-up that had trapped them all, just at the time that release from duty in the international brigades was certain, and not soon, either, but long overdue. The question became one of *when. When* were they going home?

And then the Brigade marched, beginning one midnight, cold and moist, to an olive field near Falset and rested all that day. At night, they marched again, up and down long winding roads through silent, stone villages into the deep trough of a canyon near a town called Mora la Nueva. The sides of the canyon were so steep that a flight of enemy bombers could have buried them all. It was a dangerous place and a dangerous time and the two questions were baked out of them. Herded together, armed and equipped, the aches eased and the stone-bruised feet got better and the sense of being so close to something very big tipped a kind of belligerent, dazy toughness into them.

The commander of the Lincoln battalion wore Spanish overalls that ended halfway between his knees and his ankles. His officer's stripes were pinned to his shirt, not sewed. He had a pistol slung from his shoulder. He stood on a terrace, so they could all see and hear him. He began speaking, in English, Brooklyn-tinged. They sat or squatted or sprawled and listened.

They were going to cross the Ebro, the entire Army of the East, eighty thousand men. The offensive was to take the pressure off Valencia, divert Fascist men and equipment from the Levante front. The maneuvers had been a rehearsal for the big effort they were going to make. They would hit hard, travel fast and light, penetrate deep and then dig in, holding positions while other units came across on the bridges. There would be no air cover at first, and it would be some time before food and supplies, ambulances, trucks, and tanks could cross. The ammunition would come first.

This action had been planned long in advance. There was plenty of information. The lines across the river were thinly held by the Fascist Battalion of Burgos, of the Mérida Regiment, mostly new recruits who had seen no action and were untrained. The exact location of Nationalist troops, even the names of company commanders were known. Their ammunition dumps had been located, and there were big *intendencias* filled with supplies in Corbera and Gandesa. Chocolate, food, clothing, tobacco, and even beer at Corbera. There were exactly fourteen machine guns in the sector where they would cross, posted behind excellent fortifications. These positions were to be infiltrated, not attacked. The target was Gandesa which the American comrades would remember. There would be vengeance for the comrades who fell there back in April.

Maintain discipline and contact. At Gandesa before, companies had separated and lost contact. It must not happen again. If everyone kept together, it would be successful, a major blow delivered to Franco, much

more important than taking back a few towns. They could drive the
enemy out of the spots were Merriman and Doran and all the others
were lost. The whole complexion of the war could change. Stick together.
Attack and dig in, fortify positions. Every man to stand by, prepared to
move at a moment's notice.

"*Viva el ejército popular! Viva la República!*"

"*Viva*," they shouted back. "*Viva!*"

"*Vivan las Brigadas Internacionales!*"

"*Viva!*"

"*Viva La Quince Brigada!*"

"*Viva!*"

The big double blast of sound echoed away. A man stood up, his
fist clenched.

"*Viva la victoria final!*"

"*Viva!*"

A young Spanish boy stood, his rifle slung, his fist raised. He looked
up at Milton Wolff, commander of the Lincoln battalion.

"*Viva El Lobo!*"

"*Viva!*"

After such shouting, the men were feverish, restless, dreading the
anticlimax that settled down on them at once. They demanded the
right to questions, answers. Wolff nodded agreement and went into greater
detail as to what each group was to do, what any man might do.

A question floated up from the packed, sweating mass. There is always
someone who dares to ask this question, and it is impossible to say
whether he is stupid or brave to do so.

"Comrade, how are we going to get back across the river in case this
offensive fails?"

There was a brief, surly, threatening mutter against him, and a feeling
of relief that he had the nerve. Wolff dropped his hands on his hips and
stared down into the crowd.

"We aren't coming back," he said.

The Spanish boys in Mahoney's *pelotón* looked at him. He was looking
westward, in the direction of the Ebro. He had not seemed to be
listening at all, but now his dirty red hair fell over his peeled forehead
as he slowly nodded his head.

On a topographical plan of the Pandols Mountains region of Aragón,
it was three concentric circles, part of a chain of foothills called El Puig
de Aliga that sloped down into a valley southeast of Gandesa. It was
marked on the maps of military concentricity, at the heights of army
corps, division, and brigade, as Hill ※481. The British, the first to assault
it, called it "The Pimple." The Canadians, positioned south of the
Corbera-Gandesa road, their extreme right flank touching the first houses

on the outskirts of Gandesa, could reach the first gentle rise of flinty soil dark-bushed with wild sage by means of a dry, eroded *barranca* they soon had reason to name "The Valley of Death."

Hill ※481, heavily fortified on all the slopes and the rocky crest and manned by a mixed force of Moors and Legionarios, was the single geographical strong point that dominated the valley, a natural obstacle and observation post that prevented a flanking movement by either of two Republican divisions. With Hill ※481 bypassed, and the town of Gandesa completely invested, the Nationalist lines, even stiffened with three new reserve divisions, could have been broken, permitting the offensive thrust to spill back into the rolling plains of Aragón, open country, ideal for maneuver, difficult to defend. But the momentum of the Republican assault that had carried thirty kilometers in two days, without artillery, tank, or air support, dwindled to feeble, scraping lunges up the slopes of Hill ※481.

On the first day of August 1938, Mahoney was killed. A burst of machine-gun fire, four bullets, struck him in the skull, the chest and the abdomen, caught him in midstride, punched the last breath from him in a burst of blood and flung him back. He was dead before his body slumped loosely into the tramped sage. The dark leaves, pungent and broken, were spattered with sweet, sticky blood. A mortar shell, a few seconds later, blew a crater in the rocky earth and scattered dry soil and fine bits of powdered rock over his body, dusting the stiff leather of new Italian-made boots. A Remington model rifle with bayonet fixed lay just beyond the outstretched left hand. The body was struck once more, later in the day, as the assault was checked and driven back before dusk. A rifle bullet tore through the already stiffened muscles of the left thigh, a single, smacking impact that drove the two legs closer together. The body lay at attention, the face turned up to the sky.

The weather was very hot, hour after hour of dry, bright harsh light. The ground quivered and leaped as bombs fell, mortar rounds burst and shells slammed into the stones. It was cooler at night, although the earth held the day's heat for hours. Sniper fire crackled like kindling and glowing balls buoyed by the darkness, sailed through the night, the tracer-bullets from heavy machine guns. The day's dust and fine-blown stone grit settled, a gentle cosmetic powdering dead cheeks and brows.

The ants came. Singly at first, scurrying, tapping, climbing in swift little rushes over high folds of dusted cloth and spraddling creased sun-heated skin, they picked away dark bits of stale bread from the bottom of a torn pocket and pincered up minute flakes of chocolate and dirt from beneath the fingernails. Dozens of ants, in frail, frantic caravans shredded tiny sheets of tissued skin from the forehead and stiff lips and portered off crystals of dried blood mined from the clotted dent in the temple, just at the hairline. Hundreds of ants streamed into the labyrinths of dirty cotton, scrambling and clinging. They plucked and gnawed the waxy, tangled armpits and rooted in the succulent caverns of the nostrils.

The sun shimmered in the pale summer sky that rustled like silk with the passage of shells and roiled with clouds of rising dust. The morning dews evaporated in a little time, a brief steaming of the battered, strewn earth. The all-purpose German 88-millimeter cannons, hauled by diesel-powered tractors to sandbagged positions fired beneath net canopies, sage-sprigged tabernacles that heaved softly with every blast and recoil. A two-hour barrage, broken by shocking strips of silence while the long barrels cooled, fell from bomb-blown Gandesa to the outskirts of Villalba. Heinkel bombers soared up heavy from the west, flight after flight, the bay doors cranked open. The bomb-fins vibrated and the hot air screamed as the heavy projectiles plummeted down to strike the quaking stones.

The first fly settled and preened in the crusted corner of the open right eye. It buzzed and walked, then plunged its radula again and again, rasping loose the dried crinkled gelatin of the eyeball, wearing a tiny flap, a trench deep enough to hold a spew of minute white eggs. By scorching noon, swarms of flies fizzed and crawled; the frenzy of their wings drafted off the film of dust, and the flesh thus exposed cooked and bubbled as juices oozed. The flies probed and darted at the thick wad of the blackened tongue that swelled and wedged the mouth open on the stiff hinge of the jaws. The ants rushed into the tender maw, tore away scraps and scrambled on the dry, cusped teeth.

The next night, a man came alone, his mouth and nose swaddled in a rag. He crawled beneath the faint, blurred stars in the dim hour before the summer moon makes a silver rind in the blue-black sky. He was swift, furtive, and alert. He crawled in brief scrambles, always positioned so that he faced up the slope of Hill ⚔481. He moved, lay, and listened, then moved again.

It is difficult to take new boots from a dead man's feet, even when the tendons have begun to soften in the muscle sheaths corrupting beneath the punctured, egg-shielding skin. Locked in dry leather, the feet pointed up, toes at the dim stars. The man tugged, first with one hand, then with both. He moved a canvas sack up and pouched the mouth of it, as if he needed to trap the boot so stubborn on the still leg. He loosened the right boot, the inner sole rapping softly against the dry, calloused heel, the open throat stirring the dusty trousers at every careful tug. It loosened, but it could not be made to slide free. The left boot was the same. The tugging scraped small, smooth fans in the still-warm earth.

The man breathed heavily, a smothered, panting respiration beneath his mask. He watched the slope and listened. One half of his hour was gone. The moon would rise and reveal him. A rifle spat far off to the right, and the bullet screed off a boulder like the cry of an insect.

The man rose to his hands and knees, then sat and thrust his legs forward, slowly, until one sandaled foot touched the foul, crusted crotch of the body sprawled before him. He pressed his sandal, once, twice, until he felt the inner lump of the pelvis bones. Thus braced, he flung his other leg wide and seized the nearest boot in both hands. He pulled, a single hard jerk. Something parted with a soft pop inside the dead leg, but the boot was wedged. He tugged repeatedly, but it was pressed fast or caught somehow on the foot.

He slid his left hand down and forward, easing his fingers above the boot top. His palm touched lukewarm, swollen flesh and soft springy tendrils of hair. He snatched his hand away, then grunted at his own foolishness. The body still held the sun-heat that had cooked it. He tugged the torn, dusty trouser leg down before clamping his fingers on the shin. A glutted fly buzzed sleepily. The man pressed down with his left hand and pulled up and away with his right. The boot came off so suddenly that the man fell back on his canvas sack. He lay there, clutching the boot, looking up at the stars.

He sat up and floundered cautiously, heaving his buttocks over, lifting his right leg and settling the left sandal in the dead man's crotch. The effort of movement, constrained and furtive, made him gasp. A little damp pocket on his rag face mask valved in and out, in and out. He wiped his brow on his sleeve and cursed, a short, glottal grunt. Wet substances seeped through the canvas covering his left foot.

Suddenly, up on the stony hilltop, the Moors on sentry duty began a weird, wailing song. He hunched himself small and froze, listening to the high floating notes, like a loon-call across a northern lake. The song went on and on, a shrill bubbling beneath the stars. What good is a single boot?

He sat up again and levered, pulled and pried, wearing a saucer in the dirt with his rump. He saw the bluish spurt of the rifle and the bullet hissed overhead, not very close, then the crack of the shot. The boot would not come free. He clamped it under his right armpit, straightened his left leg and leaned back, flinging himself away from the lumpy sack of stenches he had wrestled with for ten precious minutes. Sweat dribbled down into his brows and twitching lids, salty and maddening. He stamped with his sandal and felt some things burst and sigh. With a soft, clotted, peeling sensation, like the separation of bacon slices, the other boot came off the foot. The dead leg seemed to lower him back upon the earth. He lay gasping for a minute, then rolled over, found his canvas bag and stuffed the boots inside. The Moors on the hilltop stopped their song.

The feet stuck up stiffly, not together now at attention, but in the position of parade rest. The man clawed off his face mask and gasped for air, gagged at the first deep breath, and smothered his lips and nose again, cursing the dead man for his stiff, stubborn feet and his stink. He hated the dark hulk before him and sprang on it, enraged, seizing the cool bony ankles. He staggered up, heaving the body, and began to walk recklessly, his back to the Moorish rifle pits, his heels butting down into the flinty soil. The body scraped a crazy track through the whispering sage bushes. The man backed, sawing the dead legs from side to side, when the clothing or the knapsack under the shoulders snagged on a stone. He dragged the corpse fifty meters up the slope, the wet splotch on his face mask pumping in and out, in and out. A bullet powed very close.

He dropped to the ground and dragged himself away, his fingers creeping forward until he found the track like the rutted passage of a tortoise. He slithered into it and felt small dribbled spots, globules of dust and liquid. He hunched up over them, his breath held with loathing and looked back only once. He could just make out the body.

"They killed him," he muttered into his mask, "let them bury him."

Bacteria swarmed in the flimsy caldron of the belly. Acid and gall gurgled in a sack of rotting matter. Gases puffed, inflating the body, stretching the thin fabric until the buttons slit the cloth and seams spluttered open. The sun, heavy and relentless, burned and cooked the flesh. Liquids seethed and tissues softened and skidded beneath the taut, dry skin. Stench farted rotten-sweet through the pouting wound-holes and hissed up between the yellow teeth. The exposed skin split like sausage casings and pale froth spouted and dried along the fissure-lips. The cartilages of the knees floated in hot juice and white bits sagged from the soles of the feet and the loosening knuckles. The skull bubbled. The lungs churned into granular jelly.

Crank-winged Stukas, slow and laden, wheeled in flights above the Sierra Pandols. Between the stiff, spatted landing gear, sleek and dandified on an aircraft engineered to ugliness, sirens screamed. The clumsy craft rolled one by one and plummeted. Gridded air brakes shimmied from the pressure of the dive. The German pilots were pressed by inertia into their seats, their legs dangling like dolls. They watched, squeezed weak, as the air-speed needles climbed and elastic earth rushed wide and trench lines squiggled beyond the bomb sights. The whole airplane shuddered in its plunge. The scarlet bomb-release button pressed, and the steel yoke snapped forward between the wheels, flinging the 200-kilo bomb down and away. The stick back. The wing roots groaned, as though the struts and stringers would wrench loose and the wings whirl off. The deep, gut-sucking, jaw-pulling drag, down, down at the earth. Rivets strained and squealed. The miracle of the upward swoop, the roller-coaster lunge up into the blue sky, the joyous shout of all the nerves. The soft, plump concussive nudge of the explosion, beyond and behind.

By late summer, the wild sage plants blossom in the plains of Aragón, and the scented leaves are rich and oily. On every plant, the lower leaves are withered and dry and trail on the hard, stony soil.

The bombs bloomed on the dark green slopes, vast petals of flame and dust snatched up through the blasted air. The sage plants writhed, attacked at the earth line by thrashing golden worms of fire. Pungent smoke leaked off in spiraled tendrils. Whole bushes smacked fatly and pale flames fanged the next clump. A skirmish line of fire scurried to the crest of a rocky rise, fluttered a line of banners and crackled on down toward the dark lumps of the dead. The smoke dulled the flies. They circled stupidly on shriveled wings and tumbled down among the stems, just as the flames had eaten all.

The touch of a falling insect jars the perfect balance of light ash still glowing on the heated air. In an instant's shock, all the leaves dissolve at once, and the blackened twigs nod and waver like bits of wire jabbed into a blackened slope of broken stones and light, swirling powder.

The rotten corpse-flesh stewed in a field of flaming sage. Charred garments flaked and sloughed off like loose black scabs. The skull-hair crinkled and smoldered and the waxy ears puffed and spatted. The dry lips shrank and the nostrils melted. The scorched torso steamed like a pudding for Saturn. When it cooled, thousands of midges whined in dense clouds, and the ants and the flies returned to feast, pillage, and plant.

Both the defenders on the hilltop and the attacking troops huddled at the base were issued small muslin sacks to be worn around the neck, outside the shirt or tunic. Each sack contained a lump of camphor, and the fumes bit, clean and astringent, through the hot, rotten layer of stench smeared across the broken slope.

Sergeant González of the Tercio never wore a camphor bag and always scraped his anus with his thumb. He went out through the barbed wire every night. He alone had noticed that one of the bodies had been moved, before the bombers had burned the fields, not after. He wondered about it both times he had been able to steal enough wine to make him drunk.

"That's my stiff out there," he warned the others. "Hands off it, see?"

It lay face up, and that was good. Foreigners carried folding wallets in their back pockets. For nearly a week, he had kept such a wallet. When they had shot all the Red prisoners, Captain Alemany had taken the papers and identification cards away with him to headquarters, but had let them keep the wallets and whatever money the Reds had been issued. There were reserve troops pouring in, more every day, whole new brigades camped back by the German cannons. New troops were always eager to trade tobacco or wine for real battlefield souvenirs.

Tiger crawled down the slope, a pistol in one hand, his knife loose in the scabbard on his hip. The body was the closest one to the defense-wire, not far from the gutted hulk of a tank canted into the hole blown by the shell that had wrecked it. A slight breeze was blowing. He found the corpse easily.

He scraped the top of it with his knife, feeling the flesh mush off the ribs. Then he probed in the dirt, looking for a trip-wire. The Reds were dirty shits and foreigners and you couldn't trust them. They would mine their own mothers. The tip of his knife snagged on the shoulder of the thing. Not all the uniform had been burned away. Maybe a strap for a holster or binocular case. He crawled closer.

After about a week, some of the stink went out of them, because the sun started to dry the meat faster than the maggots could swim in their pools of pus. Tiger moved down until he came to the legs, like two charred logs, and the feet. He sat for a moment and batted a few of the toes off with his heavy knife. There was no sound from the Reds.

It lay on top of some kind of pack or knapsack. In order to get close enough to tell, he had to lean into the smell of it. It seemed to sleep inside a glass casket of stink. Tiger patted down the thing until his knife rapped on the pulpy crest of a hipbone. He started to dig.

He had seen a lot of dead ones at Madrid, Badajoz, Cádiz and in Africa, too, more Moors than anyone could count. At this stage, the body was open and the flies got inside and the ants made nests underneath. Turn one over, and the spinal column was half picked clean, covered with wriggling things. He still was not sure about a buried grenade. He dug slowly with his knife, picked out the stones and cleaned a tunnel with his hand. He stopped and leaned away to breathe. It was only half cooked, this one. He reached into the tunnel and punched up, awkwardly, until the roof collapsed over his knuckles and he could feel the tickle of ants. His fingers touched something. He tugged and cloth ripped. The remains of the trousers, greasy with melted fat.

He had to crawl off a few meters. The stink got to him, filling his chest and head. They made you puke sometimes, the Moors especially, but everyone was a bag of shit, blood, and worms. He breathed slowly, feeling the sweat cool along his arms. The sweet whores of Tetuán would smell the same, four days dead. One day he would make his own stink in the sun.

He went back and reached into his tunnel. He had disturbed some of the worms and wiped them to mucus smears on the dirt ceiling. He groped again, found the back pocket and pulled down. No wallet. No nothing. Maybe he was on the wrong side? Maybe kick it over, hold his breath, duck in and grab? No. The Red bastard who had moved it the first time got the wallet.

He took it by the legs, above the bones and rubbery scraps around the ankles and began towing it down the slope. It wasn't heavy, just smelly. It nearly made him laugh out loud when the skull knocked on the stones. Hello? Anybody home? The arms kept working out, too, dragging and catching in the stumps of charred sage. He kicked the arms in and began dragging it again. The arms came out. It wanted to fly and was flapping its wings. He dragged it a hundred and twenty-three paces, counting every one, some fifty meters east of the burned-out Russian tank, not too close, but a decent pistol shot. He flung down the legs and wiped his hands, considered for a few seconds, then opened his fly.

"*Vino blanco*," he whispered as the urine splattered on the carcass, "Lap it up, it's *vino blanco*."

He arranged the fingers around the handle of the knife. They felt like pebbles inside an old glove. He was careful about touching the fingernails, though. They grew on the dead, long, like wolf claws. That was how you got leprosy, from touching a dead man's fingernails or a dead woman's hair. The knife kept falling over, and he had to scoop a little pile of stones to brace it. It took a long time, and he was glad to crawl away from it. But the trap was baited. He went up to the tank and lay there to watch.

"It's one of theirs," he said, easing the safety catch of his pistol. "Let them come out and bury it. They'll see the knife and then . . ."

He waited as long as he dared, until the sky began to lighten. There was no movement from the Red trenches, not so much as a whisper. He cursed them all for *maricones* and cowards, but he couldn't stay. He had no food and no water, and the tank was in easy range of their machine guns. He crawled away, straight up the hill, keeping the bulk of the tank between himself and the Red machine guns.

He was back in his own trench before he remembered the strap on the shoulder. He had forgotten about the knapsack. Now the thing was too far down the slope. He couldn't tell the skull from the blackened stones, not even with field glasses. He cursed. There he had went and lost a perfectly good knife, just for a joke, and got nothing for it, not even a damned Italian cigar!

The crow, despite its size, is a politic scavenger, selfish and cowardly. The crow flies heavily and cannot soar. It swims through the gray dawn mists and drops with a stiff-feathered flop, a short, strutting run and then cautiously, rustling and tentative, moves closer. The crow does not strike and carry, like the hawk, but walks in tattered apprehension to rend, peck, and gorge. Easily frightened off, the crow is persistent, returning again and again, until finally it is tolerated or ignored. Even in flocks, each keeps its somber gluttony apart, eating until it cannot fly, its pasted plumage cannot lift the plump belly. Then it stalks away to sleep and squirt excreta. The crows came one at a time to harvest the slopes of Hill #481.

The barrage never ceased, and the daylight skies were filled with aircraft, flights of a hundred, two hundred, three hundred. Villages already wrecked disappeared. Roads vanished, and hills were brought low. The steady rumble of the guns could be heard in Barcelona, one hundred and fifty kilometers away, and every dusk saw a double sunset smolder on the rim of the west. Smooth plains became cratered like lunar surfaces. Every shell or bomb that struck rechurned a soil already crusted with the shards of broken bomb casings and rusted shrapnel bits. The air itself became a weapon, buffeted and sucked by explosives so that its very touch caused deafness, bleeding at the nose, derangement of perspective and balance, final stupefaction.

The sector chosen for the experiment was called "The Verdun of Spain" by foreign journalists. The Spaniards called the Red-held hummocks and battered trenches *"las cotas de las viudas, huérfanos y novias,"* the hills of widows, orphans, and sweethearts. Now it was the Nationalist assaults that were smashed back, again and again by men who had been officially, statistically and scientifically eliminated by a new system of assault. Every meter of territory taken by Yagüe's Moors and the *banderas* of the Tercio was snatched back by Lister. The Loyalist 35th Division broke companies of Italians and Spaniards on its wire and sandbags. A rock crest changed hands four times in a single day. The battle flags of ruined regiments were shredded beneath the steel cleats of the tanks.

"Don't run over it!" Pedro shouted. "To the right, *a la derecha!*"

The driver could not hear him above the roar of the motor and the slick, greasy chatter of the turret gears. The interior of the tank was a jolting, cramped, stifling-hot steel pit with spilled oil, urine, and broken wine bottles slopping beneath the floorboards, a foul bilge washing the loose debris at every tilt and pound as the Ansaldo crept down the slope.

Pedro braced himself and peered out through the narrow slit. Something dark and burned lay there, half hidden by dirt and smashed rock. Bullets spanged against the bow plates, and Pedro jerked away. There were Reds still in the trench, although it had been reported as collapsed, completely abandoned. The legend of dragon's teeth again. He could tell by the sound, a light machine gun. The driver looked at him and shrugged. Since the Reds had no anti-tank cannons left, they scraped holes in the ground, fired at the driver-slits and hand-bombed with gasoline bottles or bundled grenades. Pedro had seen two drivers die at the controls from bullets fired through the slit.

The dials glowed and the dim bulbs near the ammunition racks winked. The motor roared, a stupid bellow of noise. If they closed the slit, there was only the periscope, almost useless for this sort of business. Even pulled low, there was a blind zone straight ahead for ten meters. The Reds knew it. When the driver-slits were shut, they came slipping in, planted their charges and were gone. The next thing you knew was the lift of the explosion and the tank belly ripping you to bits as it blew in.

Pedro shook his head and mouthed that it was better to see what killed you. He glanced again. It was there, something. He did not trust it any more than he trusted bridges. The Reds mined everything.

"To the right!"

The driver pulled back the shift and let in the clutch. The left tread rumbled and caught. The tank lurched around, then rolled forward. It was dangerous to stop, dangerous to go slow, and if you went too fast a shell hole would snap the treads. This whole area was supposed to be empty, and it was crawling with Reds!

He looked again. The thing was closer, but at an angle. The sun dazzled on metal. It was a dead man, a body, with a knife still clutched in the right fist. So close to the Red trenches, it had once been a decent Spanish boy, killed in an earlier assault, a new recruit. Only the kids carried knives and bragged what they'd do, hand-to-hand, in the trenches. The tank bucked on, flinging Pedro against a stanchion, and the thing slid away, out of view. He looked at his watch. Twenty-one minutes until the infantry swept forward, dropping down from the trucks. For every dead boy, Navarre had a dozen to take his place. That was the latest propaganda. A good thing, too, since eleven of them were going to get it, just like that one back there on the hill.

He leaned back and slammed his fist against the gunner's boots.

"Fire! Fire, you idiot!"

"At what, sir?"

"Straight ahead. What difference does it make? Two hundred meters' range. Fire!"

When the cannon slammed, it was as if the tank had hit a stone wall. The recoil lifted the bow and the spent shell case came clashing down to roll crazily underfoot as they lumbered forward, deafened, nearly blind, bullets stinging off the plates. The cannon slammed again. Pedro crossed himself and kissed his thumb.

Holy Mary, Mother of Our Saviour, let none of us who love You die this day by steel or flames. Preserve us so that we may spend each one of us a lifetime in Thy service and adoration. Help us, Mother of God, now in our hour of need . . . Let us, please, please, pass beyond these hills . . . Just beyond these hills!

The sun begins it and the sun ends it. The crows flap away first. There is little left for the maggots to feed upon, and the sun dries them now before they can grow to flies. The ants, orderly and intent, their storehouses filled, scout and forage out of habit, instinct. The sudden pelting rains make a slight settling of what burdens the stony soil, but that is all. It is the sun that begins the rot and dries what rotted. A dead man, finally, smells no worse than the dry scraps of fur and feathers flattened on a highway or lodged in a chimney.

The old man worked slowly, patiently, putting them underground one by one. In the town of Gandesa there was nothing to do but pour liquid lime down through the broken masonry. Underneath were women, children, a few deserters caught beneath a collapsing wall. The trenches provided a convenience. He buried men and burros, slashing the abandoned sandbags with his spade and letting the sand spill over them. Often, the bodies had been buried once, exhumed by later shell fire. He tumbled the pieces off his cart while the burro blinked in the autumn wind.

He had long ago ceased to be curious about the ruined machines, the twisted aluminum plumage of an interceptor smashed on a rutted field, the scalded carcass of a burned truck, the heavy rusted plumbing of a cannon. He ignored the wrecked tanks. They could be carried off, perhaps, somehow, or left forever. It was somebody else's affair, *los tanques*. When God made a shovel big enough, perhaps, but until then, no. *Un día, una peseta . . .*

Since the body lay near the trenches, but closer to a mortar crater, the old man was puzzled what to do with it. It was whole, or nearly so, part of one foot gone. The knife was a curiosity, worthless, a cheap thing, orange and soft with rust, but he took it, anyway, and put it in his belt. The knife distinguished it, though, and the old man decided on a private crater.

It was eyeless and grinning, bleached and picked, with tanned strips of skin and tendons like old twine. A few threads of hair, reddish-colored, were plastered to the crown over the broken bone there, the dainty fretted joint. It wore burned and withered straps, arching out where muscles had once fit. The fibrous, tufted ribs lay on a rotten sack of some sort. When the old man dragged it to the crater, the pack burst on the stones and two pieces of wood dragged free. The old man dropped the dry carcass into the crater and kicked in the shreds of burned and rotted cloth, the remains of the shoulder straps.

The two pieces of wood had been painted white, then carved, perhaps with the very same rusted knife. Black paint had been put into the letters. The two pieces were not equal in length. The long one was pointed, to enter the earth. The two pieces were notched and fit together to make a cross. The old man could not read what had been carved and had no curiosity beyond solving the problem of which way the horizontal bar should be placed so that the letters in some foreign tongue would be correct. He paused, leaning on his shovel, and examined the effect first one way, then the other. Perhaps it was Russian and correct thus? No. The other way.

He covered the body with more than usual care, piling earth up in a long, narrow mound. The rains and winds would flatten, level it. Then, as the dirt settled, the place would be a very shallow depression on the slope. He set the cross upright, pressing the pointed tip in the ground. He had never buried one with the foresight to provide his own marker. A philosopher, no doubt.

The old man drove the stake deep and stepped back. He was tired, and the day was nearly done. The cannons rumbled like thunder and bombers crawled across the sky. It had pleased him to make it to this place. He stared thoughtfully at the black letters on the white horizontal bar:

ANDREW J. WHITE, Co. 5, 15th BRIGADE

long, narrow mound. The rains and winds would flatten, level it. Then as the dirt settled, the place would be a very shallow depression on the slope. He set the cross upright, pressing the pointed tip in the ground. He had never buried one with the foresight to provide his own marker. A philosophizing, no doubt.

The old man drove the stake deep, and stepped back. He was tired, and the day was nearly done. The cannons rumbled like thunder and bombers crawled across the sky. It had pleased him to make it to this place. He stared thoughtfully at the black letters on the white horizontal bars.

Andrew J. White, Co. 5, 11th Engineer

BOOK TWELVE

The Mountains and the Valley
December 1938–April 1939

VERY HEAVY FIGHTING ALL ALONG THE FRONT. COMMANDERS AT
BATTALION LEVEL OR LOWER WHO ARE DRIVEN BACK ARE GIVEN THE
CHOICE EITHER OF A FIRING SQUAD OR LEADING A SUICIDE ASSAULT
TO RECAPTURE THE LOST GROUND. EXHAUSTION IS THE COMMON
STATE. EFFECT OF THE AGREEMENT AT MUNICH HAS CREATED DE-
SPAIR AT ALL LEVELS BUT FEW DESERTIONS. A PERIOD OF CALM
IS EXPECTED BEFORE THE NEXT OFFENSIVE BY THE ENEMY. CAT-
ALONIA IS DOOMED.

HE HAS TAKEN TO WEARING A GRENADE AROUND HIS NECK LIKE
A HOLY MEDAL IN CASE OF CAPTURE. IT HAS RUBBED A SHEET OF
SCAR TISSUE ON HIS CHEST. BEFORE THIS HE WAS LOVED. NOW
HE INSPIRES FEAR. DESPITE ORDERS HE FIGHTS IN THE TRENCHES
WITH HIS RED GUARDS.

TRIANGARA

He adjusted his smoked glasses and read the sheet sent to him by the
cryptographer twice through before dropping the original into one manila
folder labeled LARRA. The carbon flimsy slipped into Triangara's file.
There had been eleven earlier messages.

"Quite as expected," he said. "But this business of the hand grenade
as a holy medal—a treasure, a real treasure!"

The uniformed clerk said nothing, but stood with his empty hands
curled at his side as though he had just dropped an ax.

"Nothing from Madrid? You telephoned?"

"They say that they can make nothing of it. Nothing whatever. Perhaps it is not a code message, but some sort of nonsense. They explain that they have no examples of love notes written by foreigners to use as a model and therefore . . ."

He touched his smoked glasses with his fingertips and smiled slightly, shaking his head.

"Madrid believes that it is *not* a code message because it is difficult to decipher. Look here, we have more than a dozen members of the P.O.U.M. right here in the cells, no? It has been difficult for us to extract confessions from them, despite ingenious and repeated interrogations. Does the lack of confessions make these persons innocent?"

"Not if you say they are guilty."

"Of course they must say that they are guilty! Just as that silly scribble must state unequivocally the transmission of military secrets to Trotsky's headquarters in Mexico! They must redouble their efforts to discover useful facts! Have they picked up Voget yet?"

"He is gone."

"Gone? *Gone?* That's impossible! His arrest has been ordered. All the papers have been prepared!"

"Cryptography got a message that read VOGET HA SALIDO DE ESPAÑA. They are confirming with Valencia."

"What blundering! What carelessness! Do you people think this sort of thing happens in Kiev? Leningrad? Odessa?"

"I don't know."

"Moscow will not tolerate this! You fools! Such carelessness seems—"

"Yes?"

"Seems almost deliberate!"

The clerk stepped from the room and closed the door, then looked in through the Judas-hole. He sat at his desk, shuffling the manila folders and laying them out upon the table, always in the same pattern, as though playing at solitaire.

The orders were to hold, hold at all costs. Tanks appeared before the trenches, but halted beyond machine-gun range to shell the low ridges held by the British. The Spanish 59th held off the first infantry assault, but the positions held by the Lincoln battalion were abandoned. The tanks came on. Two were hit on the road, but three broke in behind the Mac-Paps. Artillery fire and mortars pounded the whole sector held by the 15th Brigade. Three flights of bombers came over. The Poles were driven back, then the Americans again. The Canadians gave five hundred meters to their second line of trenches, but they had lost all their machine guns. Reinforcements sent out to help the British were caught by artillery and strafing planes. The British retreated.

The conscripts were volunteers from prisoner-of-war camps. They huddled in the trenches. When the third attack wave came forward, they stood up, their arms raised in surrender. The whole Brigade staggered back, retreating. It was their last day of commitment to battle. All the international volunteers were being withdrawn.

Just before midnight, September 23, 1938, the first companies of the Spanish 46th Division arrived to relieve the survivors of the Quince Brigada. The Slavs, the Canadians, the British and the Americans slung their rifles and formed into sections and companies. There was little talk, no singing. The men were jittery, impatient, anxious to get away. And they *could* get away from the shells and the bombs. It was hard to understand it. They marched to an olive grove and rested beneath the trees, waiting for the trucks to come for them.

To get beyond the range of the German guns was one thing, but the enemy *avión* was another. The morning sky was filled with planes at five, ten, fifteen thousand meters, the fighters snarling, diving and circling, protecting the sluggish bombers.

Beyond Mora de Ebro, one truck roared east, the men in it clinging to the slatted sides, watching the skies. They cringed down away from the dark shapes that flashed up straight ahead of them, flying low. The driver braked and the truck skidded. His foot stamped on the gas pedal and the truck lunged forward. The flight of planes swept over them, the motors hammering, three green Moscas with stubby, red-tipped wings.

"*Nuestros,*" the Spanish boys said. "Ours . . ."

The blue sky was filled with diving, twisting dark shapes. The machine guns sputtered. The soldiers in the truck looked up, spectators now. The planes disappeared into thin clouds and came out again. Bombs were falling. Then there were two, diving down out of the battle in the skies, a terrific straining noise, as though they skidded down on steel rails. A Mosca with a Messerschmitt on its tail.

The red-tipped wings of the Russian-built fighter flashed as the pilot pulled out of the dive and turned toward the truck. The Messerschmitt seemed to make a final lunge. The men in the truck shouted. The Mosca had fooled him! The German had overshot and was going to power-dive right into the earth. They counted one-two-three and waited for the bright bulb and then the sound of the fighter plane hitting. The Mosca made an Immelmann turn up, around, and back, but the Messerschmitt screamed over the fields only twenty feet above the ground and passed just behind the speeding truck. The men gaped at the instant's vision of a helmeted man inside the canopy and then the propeller-blast struck them and he was up, climbing, stiff and slender against the sky, powerful and easy. The Mosca tried to shake him, but the German was faster. The shark-snouted fighter lunged and turned, always outside the more maneuverable Russian ship with the red wingtips. The German could climb more steeply. He jockeyed cautiously, and butted the throttle wide open. The Mosca hesitated, rolled, and dropped, trying to lure the German into another dive or to shake him off for good.

The truck rattled and swayed down the road. Men were out in the fields, rifles and light machine guns raised. Bullets splashed and sang around the truck. The men were deafened as the Mosca went over them, and the men in the fields opened up at the Messerschmitt. The German sprayed machine-gun bullets and fired the nose-cannon, a deeper *crong-crong-crong*. The planes shot up in a billow of dust, twisting, looping, too close and too fast for the men in the truck to tell one from the other. They howled and cheered, watching the dark shapes churn and slide through the morning sky.

The pilot in the Mosca dove a third time, the old trick, desperate and dangerous, trying to lure the German plane down. The green interceptor pulled up, shuddering in a near-stall over the fields. But the pilot of the Messerschmitt had not been fooled; he was waiting, hanging there, throttled back at one thousand meters in a slow, stiff, banking turn, as deliberate and crisp as the leg of a compass swinging across the pale parchment of the sky. The Mosca climbed slowly, seemed to thrash up dust. The truck darted around a banked curve. The men were flung to one side.

They watched now with dulled, impotent fascination. The Mosca pilot made a final, doomed dash for a gap in the hills. The stubby-winged fighter bellowed, a last burst of speed, and a fat shadow raced across the earth. Lean, angular, unhurried, the Messerschmitt dropped down to kill. He caught the Mosca only a hundred feet above the highway. The men in the truck could see the brief twinkle of flames on the stiff, lop-tipped wings, then hear the harsh rattle of the machine guns. The Mosca slewed sidewise and lunged, once, up at the sky.

It exploded, blooming out in a poppy-tinted gush of flame and metal. The wings, blown free, scaled like shingles flung from a barnroof. Dark bits sprayed out and away. The big radial engine held for a miraculous second while the rind of the aluminum cowling peeled away and flaming gasoline squirted in streams and spinning globs. The propeller blades screwed furiously in the smoky, fragment-ripped sky. The image of the fire-flower seared and jigged on the dulled eyes of the men below as the engine began to plummet slowly, the propeller still flickering. A single, thick hissing concussion walloped the moving truck. The severed engine, with a veil of smoke spilling, fell to the field, and the men hunched down against the crackle and pinking jangle of metal and hissing bits of wood and wire, a shower of rubbish pouring down from the gas-reeking sky.

A heavy cloud of earth and stones chuffed up as the engine slammed into the ground. The propeller blades churned and slewed, bending in the instant of striking. The sharp steel drove, wheeting and grinding, levering up a second shower of clods and dust. The engine buried itself in a final, gigantic thud.

The truck raced on. The dust flowed down and spread away, a smudge behind them. The other plane was gone. Some light bits of stuff tumbled down and blew across the road. The men swaying in the truck looked back. They blinked and bumbled together, elbows and useless rifles, twisting their heads to see until the road dropped and there was nothing but the fields streaming back behind them and the far thunder of the guns.

"Jesus!" one of the Americans said. "Which one was it anyhow?" A Spanish boy shook his head and shrugged.

"*Uno de los nuestros,*" he shouted above the racket of the truck motor. "One of ours!"

Carmen placed the letter and the telegram on the counter. The uniformed man glanced at each, then at her and looked away, fingering his little mustache.

"There's been a mistake," Carmen said. "You see. The letter came after the—this thing here. It's a mistake."

The man cleared his throat and pretended to look at them again. Carmen placed her hands, palms down, on the worn counter.

"The mail is often delayed," he said slowly. "You know how it is. Now I have showed you our copy of the telegram, señorita. I am very sorry. Terribly sorry. But there is no mistake."

"But the letter came the next day! The letter is three weeks old! Look at it! See the date on the envelope. There's been a mistake!"

"I have seen it," the man said. "And you have seen the copy. See? Right here. Yes, the letter is three weeks old. Yes, it seems to have been mailed the day after—the day after. But the mail is normally submitted to the censor, as you know. No doubt at division or somewhere. The letter was simply examined and postmarked the day after. Who can say when it was written?"

"You have made a mistake! I demand to speak with your superior!"

"I am sorry, señorita. The office is about to close and he is . . ."

"I have waited all morning! All afternoon!"

"I know that. I regret very much. Look, we only send the telegrams when we are instructed to do so by the ministries responsible. In this case, the Ministerio del Aire. Obviously they would not have given us the list without checking at division and squadron, eh?"

"I have told you that the squadron has been disbanded, moved somewhere. No one will tell me!"

"I am very sorry. Truly. But what can I do? We receive lists, names, addresses. We send the telegrams. Later there will be an official letter."

"No! No!"

"Please, señorita . . . I beg you . . . I can do nothing . . . the office is closing now. Try the Ministry. It's four o'clock. Special closing. Because of the parade."

"I will come back tomorrow. I insist on seeing your superior!"

"As you wish, señorita. But it will do no good. I am sorry. But there has been no mistake. Please, forgive me. Please, go away. . . ."

He closed the shutter. Carmen hammered on the wooden panel. She heard him walk quickly away, the door of the office close. The lights fluttered and went off.

"You won't admit it," she said, gathering the letter and the telegram, "your type never admits anything! You . . . you coward!"

She walked slowly out of the musty, tired-smelling post office down the worn stairs to the street. Her legs were tired, and a dull ache had settled in the small of her back like a big bruise. There was a bench, empty, and she sat down and stared at nothing. An old woman came up to her.

"*Una pesetita.* One peseta, señorita . . . for the rent."

Carmen dropped the envelopes into her lap and searched in her pocket for a coin. The old woman sighed and shook her head, looking at the blue telegram.

"Forget it. Sit there and rest, *hija mía.*"

"I have money," Carmen said. "Right here somewhere."

"Buy flowers," the old woman said. "Buy them some flowers . . ."

She went away. Carmen closed her eyes and breathed deeply. She felt very faint. It seemed as though a cord was twisted around her head, a band of pressure and pain, cruel and familiar. It was hunger.

The rations in Barcelona had dropped to two ounces of beans or lentils per person each day, with a spoonful of beet sugar and a few grams of dried salt cod on Fridays. The nurses were on the heavy-labor supplement, two dried apricots every morning and two ounces of brown rice at noon. But no wine. The patients got wine, even the children. It made them sleepy.

A telegram, the blue envelope meant only one thing. No one had wanted to be the one who handed it to her. For a day and a night, it lay on the ward clerk's desk. Finally, she had noticed it, her name neatly typed.

THE GOVERNMENT OF THE PEOPLE'S REPUBLIC REGRETS WITH EVERY
EXPRESSION OF SORROW TO INFORM YOU THAT . . .

She had fainted in the middle of the corridor. Then she had been hysterical. One of the doctors had given her an injection. When she woke, she had found herself in the children's ward, tied down with restraining straps. The ward was nearly empty. The evacuations had been going on for a week, one train every day for the French border. She remembered only being thirsty, terribly thirsty, and swallowing glass after glass of water until she felt bloated and ill.

The next day, the letter arrived, very dirty, as though it had been dropped in the mud. She had held the letter in her hands, unable to open it, weeping, staring up at the ceiling. A doctor came to see her during the night. He had a quarter-liter of goat's milk and two English biscuits. He made her sit up. She had been trying to swallow the dry bits when she had noticed the postmark on the letter: 26 Sept. But on the telegram?

. . . ON THE 24 SEPTEMBER . . .

She drank off the goat's milk, demanded that they bring her uniform, and reported for duty at the air-raid ward. The other nurses smiled shyly, but no one spoke to her. She worked through until the dawn, then rode in an ambulance to the railroad station. They were loading children for France. There was no food for them, none whatever. Two thousand children. The Quakers, three Englishwomen, had a carton of powdered milk. The train pulled out. She went back to the ambulance.

In her off-duty hours, she wrote letters. The doctors she worked with, the other nurses, the clerical staff mailed them or hand-carried them. The answers came back slowly.

Manuel Chávez joined our group on July 4. He flew at Ciudad Real, Valencia, for a brief time at Barajas field in Madrid, then returned to duty with us. Unhappily, he was killed in action, August 9, in the Campesinos sector, while on a routine scouting mission . . . a brave pilot and a good comrade. He spoke in the warmest terms of your late . . .

The days and nights spilled together. She worked until someone came and made her stop, ordered her to sleep. She carried the letter and the telegram in the pocket of her uniform.

Personnel Division has no record of any member of the P.S.U.C. named Triangara, Teodoro in any branch of the armed services. Suggest you contact the medical service, Barcelona district.

She ate what there was to eat and drank water, glass after glass, until they sent her to the dispensary or the receiving room where it was quiet and busy.

Files contain duplicate order from Ministry of Air ordering closing of interceptor strip #6 and immediate transfer of all flight and ground personnel into central replacement pool, Barcelona. That order dated Sept. 20, 1938. No other information. All personnel rosters restricted.

When the train with the paraplegics left for Figueras, she hid in the basement of the hospital so they could not send her with them. A delegation of nurses spoke in her behalf before the hospital board of directors. She was censured and forgiven, "due to circumstances and private distress."

Central Replacement Bureau, Catalonia Sector, Northern Division, Air Forces, Ground and Repair Services, Personnel and Parts, Office #3, Desk A. Unable to locate Mechanic of Aircraft, Chief, Interceptor type M, Non-Approved for Multi-Engined Equipment Pérez, Eduardo. No record July 20 or after. No persons surnamed Pavito, Pavoto, Padito or Perdito listed.

She was quite fine, capable and sure for many hours together, but some little thing, the sound of a horse passing outside in the night, a voice speaking French, the tinny cascade of notes from a barrel organ on a windy corner of the courtyards, anything colored blue. Someone always came to her. The others looked away and let her weep. After a while, she washed her face and took up her work again. It went on and on.

Guardia Costa Station #132 confirms recovery of aircraft, type M interceptor, motor serial number 3019–03410 by two sardine boats, Alicante harbor, Oct. 14, 1938. Pilot identified as Pantón y Oyarzabel, Julio. Death caused by gun-shot wounds. No further information available.

She had difficulty sleeping and lay for hours folding and opening the letter and the telegram, reading neither. The *practicantes* gave her the radio from their recreation room. She listened to music and gave up smoking.

Military Police Barracks, District 12, Battalion 7, Records Office Reply to request negative. All information classified and restricted to authorized persons only.

They allowed her to keep her uniform. She had no other clothes that fit except her old blue *mono*. She was registered as pre-obstetrical with calcium supplement diet, one capsule per day. She sterilized instruments and washed bandages, working half-shifts. She was not allowed in the out-patient clinic where the refugee children were treated.

5th Army Corps, 11th Division, 9th Brigade. All information re Battalion 101, Guardia Roja, Lt. Col. Larra commanding, restricted information to authorized personnel only.

It seemed to rain quite often, and the fog rolled in from the sea. She was allowed to walk in the courtyard fronting the nurses' dormitory. They took her blood pressure every day.

Servicio de Investigación Militar, San Juan, Barcelona. Negative.

The reply from the SIM and the posters that appeared announcing the parade convinced her utterly. There had been a mistake. She put the letter and the telegram away in her bureau and returned the radio to the *practicantes*. They might attempt to conceal the mistake, but they could not hide him. He would march in the parade with the others. It was all very simple and very clear. He had been born lucky, after all.

The hospital psychiatrist was an Austrian, a bony, sad-faced Jew, slow-talking and gentle, persuasive. He was leaving Spain for Paris. At the request of the hospital board of directors, especially the chief of pediatrics, he came to offer her a place in his automobile, approved transportation to the frontier. There was absolutely no question of anything. Grief was perfectly normal, in fact, often the source of deep, future strength. It was barely possible that some sort of clerical error had indeed been made. Such things happened, and the mail service of the Republic was notorious, one might say. But to make of this an obsession was *nichts gesundlich*, unhealthy, both for herself and the unborn child. Coupled with the loss of weight due to inadequate diet, the strain from overwork . . . No, he had never stayed at the Hotel Majestic. Yes, he would attempt to contact Ernst Toller, the journalist. Was she aware of the preconditions that so often produced tuberculosis? It was common in Spain before the war. Now the incident of disease was much, much higher. She must consider the future. Which seemed more desirable to her? A fine clinic for expectant mothers in southern France or a tuberculosis sanatorium? There were steps that might have to be taken. For commitment. He would give her a night and a day to think it over. There was the child to consider. She was not alone.

She told them on the ward that she wanted to see the parade. The news of it was everywhere, wall posters, in the newspapers. She simply mentioned that she had seen them arrive in Madrid and now she wanted to see them leave Spain. They looked at her, each other, shrugged, and let her go. She could be considered a delegate, representing the staff and patients of the hospital. They took up a collection. She was to buy flowers—and anything else that she saw and wanted.

She had come into the city on a truck, a mud-bellied THC with a whitewashed dumping body, the kind used to collect the dead for burial. The driver was a boy, reckless and conceited. They had a flat tire and then broke down, something in the motor. The trucks always seemed to break down. She had walked the rest of the way, stood in line for hours at the post office. Then that coward had slammed the window in her face.

It was a dim, dull day, brightened every few minutes by a timid wash of weak sunshine. It was autumn in Catalonia, but not the crisp, dry days and cold nights she remembered in Madrid. Even October here was cowardly, a sullen tilt of time into winter. Muggy days and fog-shrouded moonless nights. She stood up, put away her letter and telegram, turned up the collar of her jacket and began walking to the parade.

Barcelona was very dirty, all the sidewalks and narrow streets cluttered with filth, old scraps of paper. A few leaves, too damp to scrape and rustle, were pasted in the gutters. Most of the shops were closed, boarded up long ago. NO HAY CAFÉ. NO HAY HARINA. NO HAY CARNE. NO HAY LEGUMBRES. But there were people everywhere, old men, women in black dresses, children. They stood in weak clusters on the sidewalks, milled in feeble herds between the battered, smoke-stained buildings. The heavy air carried the flat reek of excrement. They sat and sprawled against heaps of rubble. There were long lines of people, dark, silent strings that led nowhere. Around the corner was a gutted market place, picked clean, empty railroad tracks, a closed door lettered NO HAY NADA. Every face bore the dark bruises of hunger and dirt. The men and women moved with dreamy slowness, drained of energy and hope. Little children tottered, balancing their swollen bellies on legs like sticks. They had forgotten how to play. Everywhere, hands reached out, thin palms and withered fingers, silent hands, empty hands begging for a scrap to eat. Here and there was a body, always barefooted, ignored.

The city muttered all around her. Only a few months ago, before the Ebro offensive, Barcelona had roared back at the bombers that came every day, every night. Now whole quarters were abandoned, mute, with ruined walls against the damp, sullen sky. The bright posters had begun to peel, bubble and fade. Already the Fascist symbols, the yoke and arrows and the German swastika, were daubed on the pavements, black cancellations over the hammer and the sickle.

She walked steadily, brushing past the outstretched hands. The children horrified her. Before the war she had seen gypsies with their scrawny, flea-bitten children, but these were some new race of little, white-lipped helpless animals whining and poking in the sewage-clotted gutters. It was impossible to look at them for more than a single guilty glance. They were too weak to pursue her. Beneath the loose overalls, her own belly had started to swell. She had been so happy, so proud. Now she felt shame, as though she had been caught. She was guilty of a crime. It would serve her right when she brought forth some white, hairless creature that would squirm a few hours before it . . .

The central sections of the city, the middle-class quarters they had once been called, were cleaner, the streets had been washed down and swept for the parade. There were bright flags hanging from the balconies and fastened to the street lamps. The broken pavement had been patched, the craters filled in. There were people, mostly women and children, too, but a bright skirt or kerchief flashed in the weak sunshine and the voices were louder, clearer, even cheerful. There were delegations of workers in clean, neat clothes, with raw, shaved faces and banners and arm bands, gangs of girls dressed in native Catalán costumes flirting with boys in Socialist Youth shirts and sashes.

There were wooden barricades, too, manned by military police, middle-aged men, stern-faced and important. There were Civil Guards in their long green capes and black leather hats, for the Guards in Barcelona had come out for the Republic long, long ago in that half-forgotten July. They demanded papers, identification, work-permits, travel-passes. They turned back the silent beggars and exhausted refugees and ignored the well-fed men in loose fall overcoats. Beyond the barricades, behind the backs of the police, these men took up their positions, ready for business. They whispered to Carmen as she pushed by them, shaking her head.

"Chocolate bars, señorita? Swiss chocolate? Oranges, oranges?"

"Real bread from white flour. I take gold and jewelry . . ."

"Potatoes . . . sugar . . . Algerian tobacco . . ."

"Canned beef, *muy rico*. From the Argentine. No paper money . . ."

"I know a rich man, *guapita*, who will give you a wool blanket and a pail of charcoal. Half an hour with him . . . Close your eyes and pretend it's your *novio*, eh?"

"*Garbanzos* and sausage. I take works of art, paintings, ivory . . ."

There were flowers everywhere, all the blossoms of the autumn season in the Costa Brava, bunches, wreaths, big, loose bouquets and old women chattering happily at flower stalls holding up masses of fresh bloom. But there was no *fiesta* spirit in the air, no gayety, not even with the flags and placards, the banners and uniforms. Everyone pressed slowly in one direction. Every face was touched solemn by a sense of duty, obligation. It was to be a ritual without joy. Carmen had never seen so many people in the streets, not even in the early days in Madrid.

She felt a dogged, secret certainty. It would be different for her. She was positive that he would be marching in the parade. The time: 1630 hours. The place: The Diagonal. The reviewing stand would be occupied by Premier Juan Negrín and the members of his cabinet. There would be music and speeches, but in the middle of it all, in an instant, the mistake would be swept away.

The crowds flowed slowly, and she let the pressure of bodies carry her along. At the edge of the pavement, she hesitated, confused. She could see the raw lumber of the reviewing stand. Some men were already there in dark morning coats and tall hats. They looked very un-Republican, and that seemed a bad sign. The Diagonal was very wide. What if she were on the wrong side? The barricades stretched as far as she could see. Would the police let her cross?

She took out the telegram and held it in her fist. Somehow, she was certain, it would be a permit for her. She would show it to the police if they tried to stop her. They would let her cross to the other side.

It was like all parades, little flurries of anticipation, people leaning forward to see better, children darting out and being driven back behind the barricades. A sedan arrived and two more men got out and waved their hats to applause. Carmen edged, pushing between people, right

to the barricade. Someone had dropped a bouquet of white chrysanthemums. She picked up the flowers. That was a good sign, canceling the
morning coats and the tall hats. She felt very lightheaded, but very certain.

"La Pasionaria! She's here!"

Carmen could see her, the secretary of the Communist Party, a
stocky woman with straight dark hair in a severe bun, a dour Asturian
face, large, long nose, thin, pale lips and big, burning eyes. Carmen
applauded awkwardly, knocking petals from the flowers. La Pasionaria
was her special favorite, a real woman of the new Spain. A microphone
squealed as someone adjusted it. The woman on the reviewing stand
saluted with the clenched fist and stared out on the crowds, brooding,
unsmiling. She wore black. La Pasionaria was in mourning for those
who had . . . who had . . .

"Ah, now we'll hear something!" a voice in the crowd said. "When
Dolores opens her mouth, all Spain speaks!"

Carmen nodded. She had been presented to La Pasionaria twice,
both times in Madrid. Certainly she would be remembered. How many
times had La Pasionaria intervened to help another woman of the new
Spain? A little thrill stirred in Carmen. La Pasionaria was a comrade, a
friend, a good force. She applauded again. Premier Negrín had arrived.
Now the waiting was painful, infuriating.

Then, a drum. A drum, bunting in the distance, soft and far, but
steady as a heartbeat, insistent. The crowd sighed and pressed forward.
Faces and forms swam suddenly before Carmen's eyes. She rubbed her
knuckles against her lids, hurting herself. She blinked up at a grinning
policeman.

"It's all right, *guapita*. We don't need them any more. Give them a
smile and blow a kiss, eh?"

She swallowed, staring straight ahead. The policeman tried to flirt with
her. She ignored him, concentrating, holding herself in. She must be
able to see them, look carefully into every face. No doubt he would
be changed, thinner. But somewhere, with them, he would come
swinging down the street in his short jacket and riding pants and high,
polished boots. He would be at the head of a column, with the other
officers. It would be easy to see him, really, even if he marched on the
far side of the column.

An agony of happiness seized her. She remembered how he walked,
with an air of ownership, like a señorito, but more gentle, too, like a
tourist, impressed and unwilling to let it show too much, a half-smile
curving his mouth. He had an elegance made all the better by some
little boy's carelessness, his officer's hat set firmly, the visor glossy and
fine, but a sprig of blond hair escaping over his forehead. He would be
looking around, pleased with the crowds and the flowers, as if somehow,

he had arranged it all for the entertainment of his friends at a moment's notice. He would be talking in his own way, rapid and incorrect, his own mixture of elegant phrases and appalling slang. He owned the language, too, and so used it as he saw fit, proud and careless, an American. She clutched the restraining rope, the tears in her eyes again. She felt clumsy and helpless. If he did not hold her, she would fall on the street and disgrace both of them.

Trombones blurted and trumpets smeared. The crowds along the Diagonal rustled as though a great wind poured through them. The cymbals smashed and shivered above the chest-squeezing thud of the deep drum and the rattle of the snares. Above the crowd she saw the tilting banners of red and purple and gold, lifting and sliding toward her with every cadenced step. Behind them, spaced irregularly, the battalion flags hung limp in the cool, damp air. The band crashed down upon them suddenly, bold, dull-gleaming horns and then the air was filled with flowers, hundreds, thousands of blossoms flung up and out into the street, a shower of color pouring down from the balconies, raining from the tattered palm trees, hurled from a hundred arms that rose around her.

"Here they come!"

"Mira! Mira! Los Internacionales!"

"Viva! Vivan los voluntarios!"

They wore old boots and new white canvas sandals, faded and patched khaki pants and shirts. Some had short jackets, here and there an olive-drab overcoat. Each man carried a single blanket, neatly rolled, over his right shoulder and fastened at the left hip. They marched very well, but in a curious quiet, no slam of boot heels on the pavement, no stiff, military strut. The music smashed around them, bright and glittering inside the great torrent of noise the crowd poured upon them. Flowers cascaded over them, striking them on the shoulders, falling against their thin, sun-darkened faces. But there were no rifles slung from broad shoulders. They had no helmets, no canteens, no long bayonets. Their arms swung to the music or reached out to catch the pelting sprays of bright bloom. But their hands were empty.

They were straight and tall with set, sad faces. Here and there a smile flashed for an instant as a girl rushed upon the ranks with a big wreath. They swung down the broad avenue beneath a storm of falling flowers, the internationals, the Czechs and the Poles, the Italians, the French, the Scandinavians, the British, the Canadians and the Americans, the Belgians and the Germans. The mass of men and women and children cheered and covered their faces and wept. Carmen smeared her eyes and flung her white chrysanthemums.

The dim, drab sky rattled and burst apart. A flight of aircraft roared over the city, Chato fighters and "Katyushka" bombers, dipping their red-tipped wings, low and reckless over the rooftops. The sound of the crowds was steady like the crash of surf, washing and rebounding off the buildings. Handkerchiefs fluttered, a storm of white whirling flecks. Carmen waved her clenched fist and clung to the restraining rope as the colors and sounds swirled and boomed around her.

How few they were! A whole brigade, ankle-deep in flowers, shabby in their uniforms, numbered less than a battalion. The wounded marched, too, with short, cautious strides. A battalion counted only the strength of a company, every company a few dozen men. They kicked through the blossoms. Suddenly, there were no more.

The loudspeakers on the street lamps crackled. The band blared a final measure and stopped. The crowd seethed and sighed down to listen. The voice burst over the heads of the crowd. It was *La Pasionaria*.

"It is hard to say a few words in farewell to the heroes of the International Brigades, both because of what they are and what they represent."

The meager columns were facing the reviewing stand, the men at parade rest, standing in flowers, some wearing wreaths around their necks.

Some of them were tall, some stocky, some had mustaches, others were clean-shaven. They blinked slowly, staring at the platform, listening.

"You came to us from all peoples, from all races. You came like our brothers, like sons of undying Spain, and in the hardest days of the war, when the capital of the Spanish Republic was threatened, it was you, gallant comrades of the International Brigades, who helped to save the city with your fighting enthusiasm, your heroism, and your spirit of sacrifice!"

All around her people were clapping and crying. A roar flooded the Diagonal, and the handkerchiefs burst into another storm. Carmen edged sideways, stood on her toes, balanced precariously, studying one face at a time. The banner hung limp on the worn wooden staff. Was this group the Slavs or the French?

"For the first time in the history of the peoples' struggles, there has been the spectacle, breathtaking in its grandeur, of the formation of the International Brigades to help to save the freedom and independence of a threatened country, the freedom and independence of our Spanish land."

One of them was blond, but he wore the peaked cap of an enlisted man. He turned his face and said something to a comrade. He looked German, with a square jaw and a broken nose. These were the survivors of the 12th Brigade, then.

"Communists, Socialists, Republicans . . . men of different views and different religions, yet all of them fired with a deep love for liberty and justice . . . And they came and offered themselves to us . . ."

The people in the crowd were rigid, like statues, a frieze of grief and gratitude, hands clamped over their down-wrenched mouths. Carmen pushed and slipped between them. Which was the 15th Brigade, the Americans and the English?

The voice wowed and spluttered from a loose-wired loudspeaker far above her head. She ducked under the restraining rope.

"Banners of Spain! Salute these many heroes! . . ."

The blare of the trumpets startled her. A policeman half turned, as she ducked and picked up a tattered handful of petals. Scarlet and gold flag peaks nodded into the strident brass call of the trumpets. She ran a few steps and ducked back under the rope. Surely these men were of the Quince Brigada? The trumpets ceased and the banners straightened. The voice crackled down on her. She froze, chilled by La Pasionaria's call.

"Mothers! Women! When the years pass by . . . when the memory of the sorrowful, bloody days returns in a present of freedom, peace and well-being . . ."

Carmen's hands dropped to her sides. She straightened and stared at the speaker on the platform, a solid, dark shape on the blurred rim of vision.

". . . then speak to your children. Tell them of these men of the International Brigades!"

She nodded automatically. Yes, yes, later. But now . . . Were these the *ingleses?* Their faces seemed reddish beneath their caps and some of them had blue eyes. But they were all looking the other way now, listening.

"Tell them how, coming over seas and mountains . . . these men reached our country as crusaders for freedom, to fight and die for Spain's liberty and independence threatened by German and Italian Fascism. They gave up everything: . . . their countries, home and fortune, fathers, mothers, brothers, sisters, wives and children and they came and told us: 'We are here. Your cause, the cause of Spain, is ours—it is the cause of all advanced and progressive mankind!'"

Carmen grimaced and craned, twisting and waving her fist while the crowd roared and applauded. She flung her flowers. The movement caught the glance of one of them. He grinned at her. She smiled and nodded. He nodded back, but did not bend down to pick up the flowers.

"Pssssst!" she said. "Eh!"

"Quiet, will you?" someone snapped. "Ah, these *chicas!*"

He turned around, but his head came back again, slowly, then forward, then toward her again. She opened her mouth, waved to him frantically.

"Comrade, do you know. . . ."

The voice slower, flatter now, echoed off the stone buildings and settled on the crowd. Carmen chewed her fingers, biting hard.

"Today they are going away. Many of them, thousands of them, are staying here with the Spanish earth for their shroud, and all Spaniards remember them with the deepest feeling . . ."

"*Pssst!*" Carmen said.

The soldier turned and looked at her. He had a very ordinary face, neither ugly nor handsome, neither dark nor light. He was thin and tired around the eyes, but looked calm, if not happy. The words seemed to clot in her throat. She blinked away tears, trying to see him more clearly. What could she say? Why had she not learned more English?

"Okay?" she said.

"Okay," the soldier said, his voice very faint, but his lips making the word she knew. She smiled and beckoned to him. He smiled back and shook his head slightly, helplessly. He was still in the ranks. When the voice called, he turned automatically, commanded.

"Comrades of the International Brigades! Political reasons, reasons of state, the welfare of that same cause for which you offered your blood are sending you back, some of you to your own countries and others to forced exile. You can go proudly. You are history. You are legend! . . ."

Carmen began to slide forward. A uniformed arm pushed her back. She struck out, furious, and dodged away. Now two or three of them in the same rank were looking at her. The first one said something, cocking his head toward her. Another waved his fingers. She ran out under the restraining rope.

"Okay?" she said.

What else? The gray bulk of a police uniform loomed up. She dodged back to the crowd, stopped and called to the soldier, to his comrades.

"I love you!" she said. "Okay? Okay."

They grinned and elbowed each other. The first one nodded cheerfully.

"Okay, baby," he said. "I love you, too."

A hard hand closed on her shoulder. Another hand turned her around and shoved her against the rope. She whirled around, ready to spit, and checked herself. The policeman glared at her and turned around, blocking her view. She began to cry. The voice crashed off the stones of Barcelona and fell on the huge mass of people who had come to bid two thousand men farewell.

"We shall not forget you! And when the olive tree of peace puts forth its leaves again, entwined with the laurels of the victory of the Spanish Republic—come back!"

It was a cry from a huge heart. Carmen stretched out her hands, begging while the tears flowed down her cheeks.

"Come back to us! With us, those of you who have no country will find one! Those of you who have to live deprived of friendship will find friends! All of you will find the love and gratitude of the whole Spanish people who, now and in the future, will cry out with all their hearts:

Long live the heroes of the International Brigades!"

The band played and there were cheers and more flowers and everywhere the people waving handkerchiefs and weeping as they marched away. They swung past Carmen, rank after rank, moving slowly, treading on an avenue of flowers. She leaned against a street lamp, exhausted, watching them.

Neither soldiers of the Republic nor citizens anywhere, many of them, they marched in slow, careful cadence while the band crashed away and the people of Catalonia sang them out of the city.

> Serenos y alegres,
> Valientes y osados,
> Cantemos, soldados,
> El himno de la lid!

Their feet fell steadily into a vast field of flowers. Their shoulders rose and fell. The skirts of overcoats swung to the slow rhythm and they wore petals in their hair and sprinkled on their faded berets. The red and gold and purple banners rolled softly in the dusk. They passed by her and away and she could not tell the Poles from the Germans, the Italians from the British, the Americans from the Slavs. They all looked the same, a moving body, empty hands, a dark face and weary eyes, comrades who had come to fight and now were going away from Spain.

The last rank passed and the police gave way and the crowd spilled into the street, following them. Carmen huddled at a post, bumped and buffeted, elbowed and ignored. The flags tilted into the twilight and the echoes faded and were gone and the autumn twilight, soft and moist, settled on the vast emptiness of the long, silent avenue.

She caught up a wreath to take as a souvenir, shredded the flowers and scattered them, turned and began to walk more swiftly, kicking the blossoms away. She turned away from the center of the city, heading for the nearest motor pool. With luck, there would be a truck going out somewhere near the hospital. She did not want to go there. The place had become a prison not a refuge. But there was no place else for her to go.

The door of the schoolhouse crashed open on a surge of black, bitter wind. The door sucked shut again with a smash that shivered the whole small building.

Paco stepped into the disc of light and stripped off his sodden jacket. "It's snowing," he said. "It will snow all night."

Triangara grunted and bent over his notebook. Beneath his hands neat columns of figures spread across the page, estimated needs of the battalion under separate headings: food, ammunition, clothing, transportation. He often left his notebook lying about, the pages open to show the wishful thinking of a conscientious commissar. The columns of figures made a message in complicated cipher, each number standing for another number which in turn converted into a letter of the alphabet. He had been carefully instructed by the cipher-clerk at the convent of San Juan.

Paco hung his sheepskin on a low chair near the iron stove and watched the water drip from the sleeves. Snowflakes beat wildly against the dark windows.

"Any word from division?" he asked. Triangara shook his head.

"Good enough," Paco said. "What can they tell us? The lines have broken again. Here. Over there. We are flanked. We must pull back, but make resistance. If possible, counterattack. It's all stupid. We'll stay here tonight. Tomorrow, too, if those Navarrese bastards will let us. The men must sleep, dry their boots and clothes. How much can we feed them tomorrow?"

Triangara turned back two pages, to the real figures that indicated their supplies.

"We can't," he said. "The last of the wine and the Russian iron rations went tonight. There's nothing left now but a little rice and a few liters of oil—less what I used to fill the lamp here."

"That's all?"

"Comrade, we fed three hundred civilians yesterday," Triangara said. "Three hundred and four, to be exact. Three days' rations! *Pouf!*"

"They were starving," Paco said. He sat down at one of the small desks and folded his hands like a child.

"Retreat," he said bitterly. "Since the day before Christmas. Even the Pope himself could not hold Franco back. I hate to retreat. It is shameful!"

"You should not confuse tactics with *pundonor*," Triangara said. "Granted it is dishonorable to run away. But will it do any good to stay here? In two days at the most we will be surrounded. Is that what we should do?"

"No," Paco said and slammed his folded hands on the desk. "We should attack!"

He leaned forward, and the thing he wore around his neck swung out and bulged the damp, dirty cloth of his shirt. Triangara turned the pages of his notebook again.

"We have less than two hundred men, counting the new conscripts. We have fourteen Dikterov machine guns with two cans of ammunition for each gun. For the rest we have rifles and an average allotment of nineteen rounds per man. We could hold these buildings against a well-mounted attack for twenty minutes."

"Call it a half hour, if it's the Italians who find us," Paco said. "But what if that Navarrese tank group gets here first, eh? Well, the snow will slow them. It covers our tracks. But they are like a pack of wolves in old Russia. I remember hearing stories how they used to take the children of serfs out in the sleighs. When the wolves closed in, they threw a kid out into the snow to be torn to pieces. The people in the sleigh got away, you see."

"An exploiting class is always inhumane," Triangara said.

"Only exploiters?" Paco said. "I have just thrown three hundred people to that Navarrese. I gave them food so that they would have the strength to walk directly into his line of advance. In the darkness and the snow, the enemy will think it's us, attacking. There will be shooting and hand grenades. Some of those people will be killed before the Fascists discover the truth. Then they will feel sorry for their mistake and try to help the survivors. If I have fed them, then the blue shirts will give them transport, medical care. While all this takes place, we gain a good night's sleep. That is how El Asturiano defends the Republic."

"That's very shrewd," Triangara said.

"It takes a rotten heart," Paco said. He stood up abruptly, walked to the desk and picked up a bottle.

"Retreat destroys us," he said. "Inside. We think only of escape for another few hours, another day. Anything we do is justified. From now on we will commit crime after crime. And think nothing of it."

His jacket steamed and stank by the glowing stove. He waved the bottle at it.

"That's what they want, now," he said. "The animal's hide. A trophy to nail on a wall."

"You need to sleep," Triangara said. "This is a good place. Warm and dry. A model village, you said?"

"Built by the Anars. Never finished. That's typical. The intention is everything, the accomplishment unimportant. A schoolhouse where no one ever learned anything. For us Communists it's the reverse. The accomplishment and to hell with the intention, no?"

"How long were you in Russia, comrade?" Triangara asked.

Paco tipped up the bottle and drank wine, his throat jerking. The bottle was nearly empty when he set it on the desk. He slouched back to his desk and tore off his boots, slung them on the floor near the stove.

"Nineteen months. It seemed much longer. Like being in prison. I remember the snow. I thought I had seen snow in my Asturias! But the spring is like a miracle, really. Both summers, we went on maneuvers. Very secret. Russians and Germans together, near the Polish border."

"Germans? Oh, German Party members, you mean."

"That's what I thought at first. No. They were regular officers of the Wehrmacht. Studying tank warfare."

"But that's . . . incredible!"

"That's Russia," Paco said calmly. "It's a big country. Things happen and no one knows it. Not like Spain. I lived in a barracks all the time and learned to drink tea with lemon and sugar from a glass."

"You were alone?"

"No. We were a group. Sometimes small, sometimes bigger. Juan Modesto was there. Lister, too. Funny, the three of us from Asturias. Lister was crazy about the women. It was like a zoo. A time to eat and to study and to sleep. Every so often, a vodka party. Then they would bring in a few women. I refused them. Not for me."

"They weren't pretty?"

"Some were quite all right," Paco said, shrugging, "Of course, I was much younger then . . ."

Triangara smiled. Age what—twenty?—condemns the child he was at eighteen. He had been shocked to discover how young the man known in the Republic as El Asturiano really was.

"They thought that because we were foreigners, we would do anything."

The snow ticked against the windows and wind rattled the loose sashes. Triangara adjusted the wick of the lamp, touched the telephone, his notebook, glanced at the stove.

"Your mother died when you were in Russia, no?"

Paco pointed at the map and swung his arm to circle all of it.

"My mother is dying now," he said.

"The Republic?"

"Spain."

"How did your mother die? May I ask?"

"Little by little. Then all at once," Paco said. "How does anyone die? Any thing? When my time comes, I pull this ring here and wait five seconds. Once the ring is pulled, I deny myself the luxury of being able to change my mind. I pull the ring and choose death. *I* do it. Me. They will never have my skin to display. I will never crouch before some tribunal, begging for my life."

He pulled open the throat of his khaki shirt. The hand grenade hung on a leather thong. Triangara could see the waffled iron, the handle and the steel ring. Larra tapped the bruised and chafed skin.

"It is very ugly," Triangara said and pretended to write something in his notebook. "You are an absolutist, as everyone says."

"No compromise is possible," Paco said. "Not here in Spain."

"You believe the war is lost?"

"*Claro*," Paco said, spreading his hands. "Look at us, man! They are across the Ebro, everywhere. Borjas Blancas has fallen. Artena was taken, and Yagüe has surrounded Tarragona. Catalonia is doomed. We threw everything we had at them. We're used up. They will crush us. We're not fighting now. We're retreating."

"But there will be a stand before Barcelona!"

Triangara was stunned when Larra shook his head slowly. It was impossible that the capital of the Catalán state should not become another Madrid.

"No," Paco said. "That's not a choice we can make. We have what? Thirty thousand rifles? Our bare hands. That was good enough in the early days. But not now. We throw bodies into the machinery. The machine grinds them up. More bodies, but the gears are too big and the engine is too strong. We can slow it a little, but not stop it. Barcelona will be surrendered without a shot."

"And us?"

"We will go into the mountains. I know mountains."

"You—we—will not surrender?"

"Never," Paco said. "Not to Captain Alemany."

"But if victory is not possible?"

"That does not make surrender an obligation. Now, I am tired. Tired of talking. The stove and the wine make me sleepy. You will sit up and write. You like to write, eh, comrade?"

"It is my duty as commissar of this battalion," Triangara said easily. "The daily report, you know."

"To brigade headquarters?"

"Of course. Sick list. Rations. Ammunition."

"I know how to write, too," Paco said. "But the story that I learned how in Russia is not true. The priest in our village taught me."

He made a rough barricade of small chairs, a kind of roofless little hut and hid himself within it. One side was kept open, so as not to block the heat from the stove. He seemed to do it unconsciously, as part of the process of sleeping itself.

The telephone rang. Triangara started and knocked his notebook to the floor. Paco's head appeared over the barricade of chairs.

Triangara lifted the receiver.

"*Dígame? Guardia Roja. Estado mayor. Triangara.*"

The voice seemed to be at a great distance, calling across a huge, dark gulf. Triangara plugged his other ear, listened and scribbled.

"Map thirty-seven? Yes. Position K. Very good. What about transportation? *Mierda*, they broke off. I'll get the map case. We can put it on the wall here."

"Position K on Map thirty-seven is eighteen kilometers northwest of Barcelona," Paco said.

"Oh?"

Triangara did not doubt it. Larra studied maps constantly, the way a priest read his daily Office.

"I told you there would be no defense," Larra said. "What reason did they give for the change?"

"General Yagüe has accepted the surrender of Tarragona. Unconditionally."

"There, you see?" Paco said. "*Finito.* It's over. We have neither food nor transport and no way to get either. I'm going to sleep."

"What shall I tell the company commanders?"

"Nothing," Paco said. "Let them sleep."

"But they will want to know when we plan to move. What routes."

"*Mañana,*" Paco said. He took his sheepskin jacket from where it hung, wadded it into a pillow and lay back down. He looked up at the ceiling.

"And who will feed us?"

"The people," Larra said. "Yesterday we fed them. Tomorrow it's their turn. Don't worry. Go to sleep."

He closed his eyes. The snow ticked against the window panes and the cold wind blew, roaring in the stove pipe. Triangara could see the dark lump of Larra's chest rise and fall, rise and fall.

"You will continue to fight?"

"Yes," Paco said. "I will fight until he comes for me. I dream of it nearly every night."

His voice trailed off. His hands slid down to the floor. He woke for an instant and spoke quite loudly, as though he had just remembered something important.

"On a horse, naturally."

He was asleep again, at once. Triangara frowned and picked up his notebook, smoothed the pages and bent over, frowning.

"Naturally," he muttered and began writing numbers.

RETREAT EVERYWHERE. SOME DESERTIONS REPORTED BUT NONE WITH US. MORALE STILL GOOD. NO FOOD. NO TRANSPORT. ESTIMATE ARRIVAL K-37 JANUARY 25/39. THEN TO THE MOUNTAINS. EXPECTS OR ANTICIPATES RESCUE BY VOGET. SUGGEST ALERT BORDER PATROLS.

Triangara stood up and walked to the stove, carrying the sheet of paper. The snow lashed against the windows and the glass panes shivered. It was a real storm. What a temptation just to stay here. But they would move on. There was no choice. Not for him. For anyone? Was not the pursuer trapped by the hunt, the priest by the sin, the politician by the vote?

It was impossible that Larra did not know he wrote to SIM headquarters. If he didn't know it, he sensed it. It was the same. It was Larra who spied on him, not vice versa. There was no choice, just a solution.

He bent over and gazed down. The hand grenade made a disfiguring bulge on Larra's chest, like a single breast on a woman. The light from the stove glinted on the steel ring. Five seconds. It was a Mills bomb, a bulky pineapple of iron packed with powder. Five seconds. Long enough to pull the ring, run to the door and throw himself down in the snow. Suicide. He could say he went out to piss. It would be easy.

He would report what he had done to the man in the smoked glasses at the Convent of San Juan. The manila folder would be closed. *Finito.* He would be free.

No. His own folder would still be open. There was only one way it could be closed. He was trapped. The solution was no choice at all.

Triangara took up the stove lid with the lifter. He dropped the sheet of paper down into the hot glow. It curled and burst into flame, all at once, consumed by the quick kiss of the fire. One, two, three, four, five. It was a sloppy, shrunken leaf of ash and swirled and broke into a thousand pieces. *Finito.* He knew he would never write another.

"What are you doing there?"

Triangara stood very still. He did not think that Larra had been sleeping. He had been watching him, or sensing him. He dropped the lid with a single, steady clank.

"I came to look at the fire. Stir it a bit. I thought it was burning low. It won't last until morning. There's a chest of wooden blocks over against the wall. I thought I'd add them one by one."

"If you are cold break up a chair or a desk," Larra said. "I saw those blocks. They are alphabet blocks. For children. Leave them alone."

He walked back to the desk, turned down the wick and huffed once into the hot glass chimney. The room went black. He crossed his arms on the desk and rested his head there. He could hear the easy sweep of the wind spraying snowflakes against the fragile panes of glass.

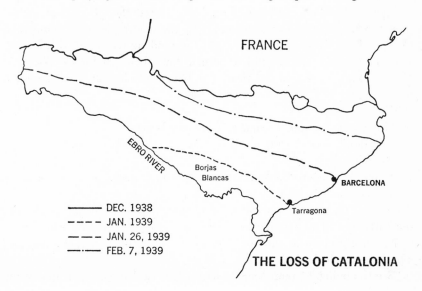

THE LOSS OF CATALONIA

A command car appeared, horn blatting, a blue streamer flailing from the radio antenna, the signal to start. The Ansaldo whined and erupted, jetting blue smoke from the exhaust stack.

Pedro dropped down into the open hatch and braced himself, leaning comfortably on the top of the turret.

"First gear," he shouted. "Forward."

The column of tanks and armored cars rolled down the broad Diagonal, the motors echoing off the blank-windowed buildings. The cold wind tumbled heaps of rubbish. The air smelled dirty, charred, the reek of a smoldering rubbish dump. Pedro stared, furious and appalled. Not a man, not a woman, not even a child. He could feel the blood beat in his face. The city of Barcelona was a huge, humiliating sprawl of empty stones.

They clanked and chattered past block after block of silent, gray buildings. Not a flag, not a face. The Diagonal was an empty, speckled slab of pavement stretching away and narrowing, until it vanished in the raw, smoky air. Paseo de Gracia opened into the vast, blank plate of the Plaza de Cataluña. They rattled down the dull, double canyon of the Ramblas. No one stood and gaped beneath the trees in the center island. The porticoes of the hotels were grilled and padlocked. The walls battered back the roar of engines. They reached Paseo de Colón and the waterfront. An oil tank rolled soft black clouds up into the sky. The command car halted, and two men snatched down the red and gold banner. The triumphal parade of the Nationalist forces into the capital of Catalonia was over.

Tiger sat on the ground and cursed. He cursed the city and people of the city who had run away. He cursed all the officers he could remember. He cursed the stones and the sky and the God he had never believed in. Then he smoked a cigar until it burned down between his knuckles and blistered him. He cursed the cigar. The pain made him angry. He wanted to do something. He kicked the boy awake.

"Get up, you."

"No—songs. *No puedo cantar.* Give me bread."

"We don't need bread. To hell with food. We need wine."

"No wine."

"Wake up. Listen. Look. Now I teach you a game. You play a game with Tiger."

He took his pistol from the holster, opened the barrel and shook out the cartridges. The action was stiff from the cold, and his hands were clumsy. He grinned at the boy. He was drunk again and that was good. The boy watched him.

"See the bullets? Count them. I have killed twelve men with this pistol.

Moors and Reds. White men and a big black one, too. I put one bullet back. I close it. So. Now I spin, see?"

The barrel whirled sluggishly and stopped. Tiger thrust the pistol at the boy, butt first.

"Take it. You have seen all the pretty things I have. They get you food. Maybe. Even some pants. Maybe. Take it. You can hold it. Come on! Play the game with me."

The boy stared at him. His fingers moved slightly, closed around the wooden handle of the pistol and trigger guard. Tiger laughed and slapped the boy's cheek.

"Wake up, *chico.* So. I put this end, the muzzle between my teeth. You pull the trigger. Pam! You get my uniform, my knife, the pistol and all the pretty things. Maybe. It's a bet, see? A game?"

He dragged the boy to his knees, raised the broomstick arms until the cold snout of the pistol prodded against his face. He clamped his teeth on the muzzle. His breath fogged and frosted the steel.

"So. Pull. Pull the trigger!"

He laughed, staring at the boy's face. The boy was still stupid from the wine. It took him a minute or so to understand. Then his little bloody lips crimped and new drops oozed. His eyes squeezed shut. He looked like an old man. His fingers worked slowly, stiffly, tightening. The hammer reared back and out. The barrel turned. The boy gasped.

"I can't . . . my hands . . . I can't feel my hands . . ."

The hammer eased forward again. Tiger pushed him away.

"Weakling. I show you."

Tiger closed his hand around the pistol and squeezed the trigger. The hammer reared back and out and the barrel turned. The boy watched him, his dark eyes wide open. The hammer snapped, a dry click. Tiger roared with laughter.

"Too bad, *chico!* Too bad. No luck for you today. You lose. Come. Get up!"

Tiger pushed the pistol back into the holster and stood up. He grabbed the boy by the hair and leaned on him to keep from falling.

"Now you take me to your sister."

"But I don't have a sister."

"We find her. You take me."

They staggered through the broken rubble and climbed out of the bombed cellar. A cold wind struck them. Tiger drew the boy inside his long cloak. They stumbled together along the walls. Tiger sang "The Bride of Death." The wine was in his blood now. He wanted more. At the first corner, he tightened his fingers in the boy's hair. The heavy cloak bellowed and pounded around them. They went faster, staggering across the empty, littered street. It was either early morning or late afternoon, bleak and shadowless. Broken glass crunched beneath Tiger's boots.

Splintered doors flailed in the suck of the raw harbor wind. All the windows were shuttered. Tiger glared around, furious and baffled.

"Where are they? Where is everyone? They should be out here!"

"Gone. To the frontier."

"May they freeze and die!"

Beneath the bar of a wrecked café, the boy found a half-liter of cognac. Tiger swallowed some and put the bottle inside his tunic.

"Good. I will stay drunk all day. And tonight, too!"

They turned another corner. The boy stopped walking, his flimsy body suddenly rigid. Tiger blundered against him, and they both fell sideways against a building.

"*Qué pasa, chico?*"

"*Policia!*"

Tiger closed one eye and squinted until he no longer saw everything double. There were dark shapes at the end of the street. Four with both eyes open, but two when he squinted. Two police. Another dark shape vanished between the buildings, walked into the walls, and was gone.

"What was that?"

"*Una mujer.* A woman—hiding."

Tiger crammed his knee into the boy's back.

"We go there, too. Quick!"

Between two gray silent building, there was an alley. The boy led Tiger down it to a stack of boxes, a barrel and a recessed door. The boy pulled aside the cloak and groped with his bound hands.

"Psst! Carmen, is that you?"

"*Chico!* Where have you—"

Tiger pushed the boy into the doorway and wedged himself out of sight.

"Shut up, *chico!*"

The woman, her face hidden by a big, black shawl, sidled away. The boy snatched his hands back under the cloak when Tiger twisted his hair.

"Shut your mouth!"

They stood together, waiting and listening. The boy suddenly hiccuped. Tiger cursed and ran his hand down over the boy's face to his mouth. The boy spasmed again, silently. Tiger tried to squint at the woman, but her face was hidden from him. Tiger leaned forward, one eye squeezed shut, until he could see the mouth of the alley. Two dark shapes sprang sharp and black as iron. Visorless bicorn hats, long cloaks, short carbines slung at the shoulders.

"*Mierda . . . Guardias Civiles . . .*"

He tightened his hand over the boy's mouth. The boy stood still, shivering and jerking when his belly spasmed. Tiger leaned back and glanced at the woman. She was shivering, too, despite the old sheepskin jacket she clutched around her. They waited and listened, breathing softly.

The police hesitated, taking in low voices. One of them kicked a bottle and broke it. The boy jerked and shivered. Tiger leaned forward, one eye closed again. The police had seen them. If they were in the alley, he could push the boy out first, to draw their fire. Then, then, he would do something. His mind could think of nothing. He looked. The mouth of the alley was empty. He tilted back. They waited, standing there, a long time. Tiger grunted at last.

"They're gone."

He relaxed and took a breath. He wanted a drink and reached for the bottle inside his tunic. The boy squirmed free, blundered out from beneath the cloak and tottered up the alley on his rag-wrapped feet, twenty paces, before Tiger sensed what had happened.

"Run, Carmen!"

The boy stood there, his hands raised before his face. Tiger cursed. His hand dropped to his holster. The boy whirled and staggered up the alley. His head whipped right and left, and he was gone. Tiger lunged out into the alley and turned, his cloak flaring. He had the woman trapped.

"Come here, *coño*. Let's see you."

He crouched, pointing his knife at her. The woman pressed back against the door. He shuffled closer, hooked the tip of the knife into her shawl and pulled, as the woman ducked away.

"Ah."

She was young, pretty, with ragged, curly hair. He shook the knife free of the shawl.

"*Hola, guapita!*"

She moved awkwardly, slapping and catching at the stone wall of the alley. Tiger closed one eye and squinted at her.

"Bread in the oven, huh?"

"Let me go."

"Shut up. The boy goes, but now I have you. Good, good."

"I'll scream. The police will come."

Tiger chuckled and shuffled forward. She backed away from him and tried to dodge. He blocked her, and she backed away toward the end of the alley.

"You're hiding from them, too. You won't scream."

She raised her hands to guard her big belly. He flicked the knife at her. She stepped back.

"Now I'm going to stir that bread in your oven."

He unfastened his cloak and slung it on the stones between them.

"Get down on that and open your legs."

She tried to dodge him, to slide her clumsy body between his shoulder and the dark, dripping wall. He toppled against her and clutched his fingers at the throat of her jacket. His knife was tangled in the heavy folds of his cloak. He could only shake her slowly, bumping her against the wall. His feeble clumsiness infuriated him. He shoved her away and fumbled his knife free. She backed away. He shuffled after her, one eye squinted shut. He pulled open his tunic.

"See what it says here and here? Sweet on this side. Sour on the other. For women to suck. For you. Then you go *abajo*. Come here and begin."

"No."

"Then I stick your belly."

He jabbed the knife at her. Her shoulders brushed against the wall. She doubled over, her arms folded in front of her.

"All right. I will. Don't kill me."

He dragged her back to the cape and pushed her down. She knelt clumsily, her face turned away. He opened the front of his pants and groped for her. He felt her hand hook behind his knee. He saw the blur of her fist too late.

The pain punched in a single shock from his groin to his chest. He swayed back, clutching at himself, and fell. A breath-stopped bubble of agony drifted up his spine and powed at the base of his skull.

He woke into blackness, curled like a fetus. A soft and terrible pain flowed in him like melted wax. Whenever he tried to move his legs, he fainted. He lay on the cold stones, panting, gibbering, too feeble to curse. The pain stopped only when he fainted and began again when he recovered consciousness. Sweat burst from his skin and froze in his beard. Snow began to fall on him, cold wet bits pecking at his brow, his eyes, his torn lips. He tried to call, but his voice was a feeble, clucking groan with every shallow breath.

The pain dribbled and slid in his body. He could not get himself away from it. Bright shapes panged in his brain, and his ears roared. His hand at last knew the shape of the bottle inside his tunic and worked it up beneath his chin. He worked off the top and drank. The liquid had no taste. He spilled most of it, choking as he groaned. The molten pain leaked and burned. There was another shape his hands knew. He fainted again as his thumb caught and pushed it up before his face. It lay before his blind eyes and he paddled it with his blunt fingers until he could catch the steel muzzle between his teeth, snapping and champing at it.

His heart bobbled and hot juices seeped like acids in his flesh. His hand writhed and settled, his thumb dropping down inside the chill ring of the trigger-guard. Breath gargled in his throat, and the cold snow bits pelted as he jammed his thumb tight. The firing pin snicked, far away, a tiny, trivial sound. He clutched and bit until his front teeth broke and the fragments floated in salty blood. He squeezed his thumb again. The firing pin snapped.

A convulsion of agony seethed in his body. He screamed and thrashed, both hands clamping wildly, stuffing the cold muzzle of the revolver deep into his mouth until he choked. He felt the barrel slide against his battered mouth as it turned, as the hammer reared back against the pressure of the spring and snapped forward.

The bullet shattered his neck and blew the base of his skull against the dark stones of the alley wall.

At map position K-37, northwest of Barcelona, El Asturiano unfastened his troops from Lister's 11th Division, without a word of warning or explanation. The Red Guards went to sleep as the 101st battalion and woke as a nameless band of outlaws. All they possessed in common was their plight and their commander. It did not seem to Triangara, at first, to be enough. Some instinct impelled him to step aside, to abolish by default the position of battalion commissar, to make his own declaration of freedom, to surrender to a condition for which he had no name.

The sudden looseness seemed to be collapse, not a source of strength. El Asturiano not merely tolerated arson and looting, he encouraged it, participated, excelled. Triangara himself could not resist the temptation. They plunged and swerved across the snowy hills of Catalonia, leaving behind them burning villages, wailing women, and wreckage strewn and trampled in the drifts. It was not until the fifth or sixth day that any pattern emerged from the anarchic indulgence, that a picture could be seen made of snow, blood, and ashes. The rumor of pursuit reached them. Tanks could be seen on the dull horizon. El Asturiano raised his head and gave orders. The Red Guards formed and swung off toward the mountains. It was then that Triangara discovered that not one man had deserted. He watched, listened and approved. He was not a commissar now, he was an apostle.

There were subtle strong changes. Without being told to, the men threw away what they had never needed. Triangara saw that they had equipped themselves well with stolen blankets, better boots, pails of sheep tallow for waterproofing, dried fruits, beans and rice, even coffee beans. Without his assistance or advice, the men were ready to march and fight in the mountains.

As a battalion in a defeated army, they had been too weak, too demoralized to counterattack, even to survive. As a smashing, burning, band of plunderers preying on the Catalán civilians, they came to feel themselves conquerors. It was a dangerous, canny game that Larra played. The men were flushed and truculent, like small gangs of armed drunkards spoiling for a fight. Every hour was risky; orders were given by actions to be imitated. No one considered rebellion against what seemed an invitation. El Asturiano did not lead or drive them to the mountains, he guided them, discreet and good-humored.

Much depended on maintaining contact with their pursuers. License was half their new strength, threat the remainder. With both maintained in perfect balance by Larra, they would survive, every man and as a unit capable of future fighting. They would be tough, loyal and disciplined enough to yield to discipline far and long beyond the French frontier. A clumsy word, a compulsive twitch of arrogance at the wrong moment and the Red Guards would succumb to themselves, become a wrangling, drunken herd, wallowing aimlessly until they were butchered. The day that contact with their pursuers *was* lost, Triangara endured an agony of apprehension. El Asturiano watched the horizon with a fatal, unnerving calm. He gave another order as though the thought had simply occurred to him. He gestured vaguely at the mountains. Perhaps it was now time for them to climb. There was no mutiny, not a desertion.

Triangara was aware that he had witnessed a kind of rebirth. Larra had played the first two moves of the game without error, so effortlessly that their individual and collective survival appeared not only desirable, but natural. They had brutalized and butchered themselves to unspoken, tribal brotherhood. Some few of the men seemed to sense the significance of the gift El Asturiano had contrived for them out of their time, their place, and his silent, sure will. They loved him in their regained strength and yearned to prove themselves to him. Only Triangara comprehended the depth and strength of the conversion they had experienced together, but even he was not able to estimate the third and final move in the game. Now that Larra had created a missionary brotherhood, how did he plan to use them? Now that they had become what they were, what would they be?

When Triangara raised his eyes to the mountains he saw teeth. He stared up at great tilted incisors, canine peaks, cusped, and twisted molars set in splintered, crude bones of basalt and granite, the maw of a gigantic fossil beast. Larra looked into the hills that had no names or numbers and he smiled. His fingers twirled the lanyard that bound the gridded bulb of the hand grenade around his neck. He nodded, apparently satisfied.

"*Vámonos!*" he said, and the men sprang forward up into the snow and mist and stones.

Feb. 1939

My dearest sister,

It is very cold here, with snow as deep as the drifts at home. We were forced to abandon the tanks. The radiators froze, and the fuel trucks could not get to us. All that we gained with them has been lost, but still we follow his path.

He is up there in the snow-covered mountains, watching. Every road-sign broken to splinters and burned, kilometer stones stumped in dynamite craters. We have no maps, of course, and every day we must choose a dozen times which trail to take. Even when we come upon his campsites, ashes and ice in a narrow, trampled plain, we know that he has swerved away. The bitter wind sings with his voice, taunting me. It is maddening.

At dawn and at sunset, we kneel together, pray and make our pledge anew. He forgets that we are of Navarre and have lived with mountains, snow and freezing winds. He is driving slaves with a whip of wire, and we rise and follow, inspired, strengthened by faith. True, every step he takes draws the frontier nearer, but for every step, we take two, the second a gift from the Virgin Mary. Every choice he makes simplifies our task. He consumes mountains, squanders valleys and high ridges. It is a matter of hours, now, not days. We must reach him before our horses collapse. We have no food for them. Soon his rear guard will stagger to his tent and cry out that we are closer to him than he is to the French border. He will know then that he cannot make it, that it is denied him. When he turns to fight, we have a mortar. He will choose a high place, but death will drop down. Against these slopes, white and cold, every man is a perfect target.

Every blackened heap of stones, every looted hut, every body that sleeps in a white bed of death proclaims that all his hopes and all his actions were and are, nothing but sin. His name will be a curse on the lips of Spanish children, cried again by their children's children. His total vileness makes him worthy of my quest. He seeks to destroy what was, what is and what might have been. Dusty books and logical priests are nothing. It is here, in these mountains, that I have come to understand, to approve and to emulate the holy Inquisitors! I go forward, my lips singing, my heart light as a shimmering bubble, a whirled flake, my soul floating up to brush and melt on the hem of Her holy blue robe! He is my brother, for who but a brother would press such a marvel into my outstretched, eager palms!

Pray for me, my sister. When this is accomplished, I will return to you. You shall hear my voice again. I have made my pilgrimage from Pilarmadre to this place, and here I shall tip a goblet of blood into a vast, mild blue sea. Then I will kneel and bathe my hands. I know that you will understand and forgive me, as does our Holy Mother, as will our Gracious Lord!

The voices of my good Navarrese echo in the valley. My horse stamps and mumbles the snow, poor hungry beast. I fold these sheets and place them between the pages of my little Bible and slip the Word of God beneath the Sacred Heart you embroidered for me so long ago, in my Navarre, so far away! Some day, as your tears of joy fall to spot these pages, remember that it is often Satan who draws us to Christ. Remember, too, that we both know how God loves Spain. No sacrifice is worthy unless the gift is absolute. Try to be as grateful as I shall be, when at last I meet him face to face!

Your brother,
Pedro

In the valley, the snow had been trampled, melted, and mashed with the earth, refrozen in wrinkled waves and choppy shoals the color of rust and hard as iron. Higher, beneath and between the wind-pruned and tormented trees, the snow lay deeper, unmarked, heavy and wet, topped by a treacherous frozen crust that shattered beneath the paw and pressure of a hoof or human foot, that broke in thick plates, crunching, and let the body down in a short terror of plunge through the deep, wet and clinging cold to spine-jolting painful relief as the foot struck upon a hidden boulder or a rotting tree trunk. Beneath the treacherous crust were pine branches, sharp and brittle beneath sloughing scales of frozen bark. When a leg plunged down, there was the sudden snatch of nightmare hands, a witch-grip beneath the stiff serene spread of white. Above the timber, the snow was light, fine, each minute particle hard and pure as a tiny gem. When the wind blew, the granules slithered and hissed over the rocks, swirled and streamed away on the cold pure air in stinging veils. A footprint pressed one instant, vanished in the next, a single horizontal skid that bared a tilted slab of whining granite.

Far above, silhouetted against the numb blue sky, perched on high fissures, crouched on ledges and in deep fractures, a hundred shapes loomed and shifted with every step. A deep, sluggish, powerful wind buffeted away soft frills and clinging scarves of snow and showed to every upturned face the brooding sentinels of stone, scoured and shaped by the crystal chisels of ice and the slow careless chafe of a million winds.

On the steep, silent slopes, long, dream-blue shadows flowed down into the ravines and hollows, numb, enchanting pools, sweet and merciful plunges of indigo spilled down the pitiless pure drapery of icy whiteness.

Over an unplumbable gap, a solid-seeming bridge, a vast span poised on sparkling abutments sighed away, a tremendous gentle diffusion into the blue wind and then the whoofing boom as its soft tons smashed and thundered down upon a valley far below.

The sun melted them, astonishing, sensual and stupefying. They worshiped its noon warmth, a benign pressure upon them. They struggled on and sweated their clothing to sodden, clinging wraps of leaden stench. A single grateful step into one of the blue pools of shadow, and their tunics and trousers stiffened to mushy breastplates and chilling, crumpled greaves; their gasping frilled midget icicles in the matted fleece of their jacket throats. Frost-locked useless rifles became canes and crutches. They strapped bayonets to their legs and stamped the points down to prong and scrape upon the stones.

The sun burned them, seared every centimeter of exposed flesh to juicy blisters that broke or froze, bubbles of torment. The sun poisoned the pure blue air with reflected glitter; a billion needles jabbed their aching eyes until they wept and cursed and clung together and stumbled on, blinded in puffy pain, up into the next long shadow. There, a chill like a vault settled on them like a terror, a tomb-breath. They prodded and pushed on, up and up, while their burning lungs dragged the thin oxygen into their heaving chests and the great golden shimmer in the sky flayed their salty, whiskered faces.

Every dusk came too soon, a silent tide of dim, numbing cold. They huddled beneath stiff blankets, drugged with exhaustion, smoking, shivering heaps. Every hour they lurched and tottered, changing positions, the ones on the outside herded into the pack, the snug ones in the center driven out into the bitter black night. Big brilliant stars, a hoard of cold glory, glittered above them. The cold crept into them, sinister and sweet, gentle and dreadful. Groans and curses sank to murmurous lamentations and shallow-breathing silence, slow as heart-tick, slow, slower.

Angry shouts cracked and powed like exploding stones in the dark. Fists beat on their numb bodies, scrubbed snow they could not feel against their faces. Blood beat like daggers thrust into their half-frozen flesh. The black agony lasted until the gray, misty horror of the mountain dawn.

The march and the sun thawed the living to new frenzies of ambition and fear, giddy hungers and hallucinations. They sang and shouted, cursed and prayed, a long, sun-smitten dance across the ice and stones and gleaming plains of snow. Pursued and pursuers, they floundered on, as the sun rolled across the depthless ocean of cold blue. Prey and hunters, they toiled, their hearts tearing in their chests, every groaned breath smoking like a chant above their bowed, blind heads. They were two colonies of gnats struggling up the cold bosom of an angel.

The last of the horses, snow-blind and starved, pawed and lurched down into the shallow, boot-packed path worn in the shallow valley. Pedro lifted the sodden visor of his cap and broke the sheet of flimsy ice that had formed across his forehead, down to his eyebrows. The horse heaved forward another step, the snow squeaking beneath its trembling stride. Pedro turned in the saddle to look back at the column. The horse could not last another hour. The men watched the staggering beast with red, famished eyes. When it fell at last, they would swarm over it, hacking and tearing bleeding hunks of hide and muscle from the kicking carcass. Pedro turned back and looked ahead. He was certain, somehow, that they were close, very close to the border. There seemed a humming in the air, rising up from the white valley below them. He had seen what might be columns of refugees.

The mountains lay around, not above them, huge spurred shafts, clumsy boxes of granite, pillars and hammers, gigantic cogs and couplings, all frozen and hurled together, the gear works of some titanic engine cast aside by God or not yet assembled, the entire process motionless, inert, for want of a single, awful bolt.

The blue air crackled and an invisible palm clapped against the horse's neck, just where the muscles slabbed into the heaving chest. The animal staggered and dropped, snorting a cloud of steaming blood into the snow. Pedro slid forward into the deep, cold drift as the echo of the single rifle shot slammed off the wall of stone, echoed and re-echoed. The horse kicked once, gave a great, bubbling groan and lay still.

Pedro floundered and swam in the cold white sea. He found his binoculars and struggled to the shelter of the dead horse. The body-heat melted the snow beneath, and the steaming carcass shifted and settled as he propped his elbows on the saddle. He flung the lens-caps away and in a single, wild glance saw that the column had bellied down into the snow trench, wrenching at their rifle bolts. He raised the field glasses.

The brightness of the single, magnified disc made him cry out. He swept the binoculars to the north, along a snow-swathed rampart of granite. At first he thought it a smear of blood from the horse, but when his stiffened fingers brought the focus sharp he saw it was a flag, a red banner flailing and snapping in the wind, the pole bending with every gust.

They had won! He had turned to fight! *María, Santísima ayúdanos!* "*Mortero!*" he shouted. "Mortar! Three hundred meters! Fire!"

Triangara worked the rifle bolt. The spent cartridge spun away through a little cloud of scorched, gassy stink. The echo cracked back. Boots crunched and blundered over stones. Triangara scrambled to his feet and crouched, holding the rifle, Larra stood at a gap between two boulders, staring down into the valley.

"The horse is dead!" Triangara gasped. "It's not Voget and it's not that German! It's that damned Navarrese! My hands are stiff. With luck I would have got him!"

"It's not important, the horse," Larra said. "In twenty minutes they would have climbed to this place. He is not for you. It's me he wants. I know him. It's Alemany, the count."

The column was strung along the rampart, the men fumbling the rifle bolts out from beneath their clothing. Larra shrugged.

"That's why I raised the banner. To tell him I am here."

Triangara snatched the bolt from the rifle. His voice cracked with astonishment, outrage.

"But—but the frontier is right *there!* You can *see* it, man!"

"You see it. The men see it. Good. I see *him.*"

The rampart of boulders ended like a ruined wall. The mountain slope was smeared with a broad steep field of runneled slush, spotted with stones like cannon balls. The slush field turned to mud, there was a belt of dry gravel then a stone bridge, a barricade and wire. Triangara could see the tricolor, the flag of France. Beyond the barricade and the wire, the earth was covered with people. Safety was a kilometer away, downhill. The rampart, crumbled at the northern end, could be flanked. One machine gun there, and the Navarrese could kill them all!

Triangara did a little dance of dismay, waving the rifle bolt. It could not be that they were to stand and be sacrificed here, within sight and stumble of their goal, slaughtered before an audience of refugees and French border guards! Triangara's legs collapsed and he fell into the wet snow, his mouth making a high, broken *ah-ah-ah* sound. He hit himself with the rifle bolt and stared at the thing, wondering if it were heavy enough to knock Larra unconscious.

The air whistled and a rock vanished in the slam and flash. Triangara jumped up and fell again.

"*Mortero! Mortero!*"

He heard the echo, the odd clanky cuff of a mortar firing, as the snow hissed down and the stone bits pelted and pinged. Larra straightened and nodded. No one seemed to be hit or hurt.

"Get them into squads," he said. "Down to that field of slush. They will throw the mortar up there soon. To hold us all here while they flank. When a shell hits, send one squad down. When they reach the gravel—*cuidado!*"

The second round hit close by, but down the slope, beneath the rampart. The explosion snapped up a plume of snow, and several big stones groaned and shifted, grinding and shuddering.

"When they reach the gravel, they will be safe enough, I think. He won't dare fire on them. Too close to the border. He might overshoot and drop one in France. When they get on the gravel, they should form a column. They are to march into France, Triangara, understand? By cadence count, with their rifles slung. They must *march*. Like soldiers, like men. Go on! Get them started!"

Triangara got to his feet, dazed, shaking his head. Larra's voice drawled and stopped. Triangara reached out, still clutching the rifle bolt. Larra stared at him.

"Don't touch me. Get out of here. That's an order."

A third mortar round smashed. Snow and stone bits seethed up and blew against the red flag that thundered and flailed in the wind. Triangara crammed the rifle bolt beneath his jacket, gasping as the icy metal struck his skin. He ran down the rampart, skidded to a stop, trotted back a few steps, whirled and stumbled on, shouting and pointing at the frontier.

"*Secciones! Secciones!*"

The high wall of rocks crumpled away at the north end. The trail stamped through the soft snow snaked across the floor of the little valley and up into the boulders at the south. It was very tempting. The men could crawl in the track, completely hidden, then, when they were close enough, kneel and fire, destroying the rear guard. It would take twenty minutes, long enough for him to escape down the slushy slope.

They had very few mortar shells and they were firing blindly. The whole force up there might have pulled away to the west. A few rounds dropped in the slush might check them long enough to get a light machine gun up close enough to . . .

Pedro stood up, his arm windmilling.

"First squad! Straight on! This way, this way! Mortar! Two rounds due north, maximum range. Fire! Fire!"

The men waded cautiously out into the slush. It was knee deep, water-rotten, trickling, soft, translucent and slippery. Triangara could look down into the valley. The mortar pipe was a dark twig, angled up from the slot of the snow track. When it fired, the concussion twitched up a small cloud of snow, as much as a small child might fling with both happy hands. He snapped his head back, squinting at the sky. He was positive he could *see* it, the finned projectile sailing, a dirty little smudge hanging there at the top of its flight. He blinked, and a geyser of blue lunged up. The mortar round bared a hollow of hard, dry dirt for a single, smoking second before the slush poured in, drowning it.

The men slipped, fell down, sprawled on their hands and knees, groped and fetched up dripping rifles and waded on. It was the steep slope that did it. Two or three sliding steps and they splashed down on their rumps. Some of them were trying to paddle like dogs in the stuff.

"Next section!"

The men were packed in tight against the loose wall of stones. They came away, rifles held at the ready position, their burned faces rapt as they skidded down to flounder from the cold shadows into the sun-warmed slush field. The third section lunged up and took the shelters just abandoned. No one looked back or out into the valley. Triangara crouched, waiting for the next round to fall. He moved to the man with the Dikterov gun.

"Give me that! You take my rifle."

He turned and plodded back into the dark, cold shadows. At the first gap he paused and flung himself against the stones as the mortar shell smashed, a single ringing wallop that made the earth leap. He cuddled the Dikterov gun against his chest.

The Navarrese waded in the snow, very slowly, leaning forward. There were four of them carrying the barrel, the tripod and the ammunition. They stood straight, balancing, thrust out a leg and flung it forward, plunged after it, dragging the other leg. They were dressed in dark blue uniforms and blanket-capes that trailed behind them. Triangara set the bipod on top of the boulder and snapped the ammunition pan into place. The safety lever was stiff. He hammered it with the heel of his mitten until the leather punctured. He snugged the butt against his shoulder, aimed at the moving men down in the valley and pulled off his mitten. His finger closed over the trigger. The Dikterov erupted, a loud, slugging chatter. Triangara fired half the can, swinging the muzzle back and forth, up and down. The snow swallowed the flying slugs. He could not see where they hit.

The first man fell forward on his face. Triangara shifted the Dikterov and pressed the trigger. The gun pounded his shoulder. The other two went down. The fourth man just stood there. He dropped the ammunition box and tried to turn, to flounder back in the deep track they had rutted. Triangara pressed the trigger. The ammunition pan rotated slowly and stopped. The last man was down in the snow. The gun was empty.

Bullets panged and hissed all around him. Triangara ducked and stumbled back to the flag staff, crushing his hand back into his sodden mitten. He heard the section leader shout, as the third group headed out into the slush field. A mortar shell hit.

Pedro saw the four men fall as the bullets from a light machine gun positioned in the rocks sprayed wildly down into the valley. The echo of the gun's rattle drowned his shout for them to take cover in the drifts. They died standing thigh-deep in what could have hidden them. Their stupidity infuriated him. Now none of the others would take their own machine gun forward or even crawl out to find the pieces dropped in the deep, wet snow. They tried to conceal their cowardice by firing rifles at the sheltering bulwark of boulders that concealed the enemy.

"Cease firing!"

The echoes died away. Pedro looked through his field glasses. He saw the flag again, then, very distinctly, two heads, both wearing officer's caps. The mortar round clanked down into the tube, and the weapon fired, a single concussive cuff. The finned missile burst among the boulders.

He was certain from the snow and the stones that the entire valley broke down steeply at the broader, northern end. The untracked plain beyond the four dark shapes simply ended, as though the snow touched and dissolved into the blue sky. Beyond a thin layer of mist more mountains rose, but far away. They were the French Pyrenees. The frontier lay north and down. They had reached a ravine or a valley running roughly east-west. Tears glittered and blurred in his eyes. He could sprawl in the snow, helpless, while French frontier guards waved encouragement to an enemy he could not strike, capture, or even see!

He stood up. The soldier nearest him had a broken branch for a walking-stick to poke and probe the drifts.

"Give me that!"

"Get down, Capitán. Stay down and they can't see you!"

"Give me that stick!"

The soldier shrugged and pushed the stick at him, then rolled over on his back and began frantically working the bolt of his rifle. Pedro stepped over him, fumbling in his overcoat pocket until he found the square of soiled cotton cloth he had used to strain gasoline, the last time they had refueled the tanks. The men in the snow trench gaped at him. He stood with his back to the enemy, carefully knotting the cloth at the top of the stick.

"*Jesús y María!* Now he's going to surrender us to the Reds!"

"This is a flag of truce, you idiot," Pedro said. "Listen carefully. I will walk up the path they made. When you can no longer hear the sound of my boots in the snow, crawl along in the track after me. Not too close. I will ask to speak with their commander. When he comes down, I will demand his unconditional surrender."

"An officer. With a truce flag," Triangara said. "It's a trick. They must be crawling behind him, down in the track there."

"The mortar has stopped firing," Larra said. "Look to see if the men have gone down into that wet stuff. There was only one section left, eh?"

"One company," Triangara said. "The size of a section. They broke trail yesterday. Then last night, the cold . . ."

"Are they moving out?"

"Yes. If we go now, we can catch up and cross with them."

"Go ahead," Larra said.

"We. Both of us."

"No. Go away now. That's an order. You must head the column as they march into France. You have no weapon. You can do nothing if you stay."

"I have no weapon? Neither have you!"

Larra tapped his chest, once.

"I have all I need."

"No! You can . . . you will . . ."

"I have done all that I know. If it had been different . . . if the Republic . . ."

"You can still fight! Somewhere else!"

"But that's all I can do, don't you see? That's all I'm good for."

Triangara did not dare to touch him. He was afraid. Larra looked at him and smiled ironically.

"In five, ten years, you would have shot me," he said. "I have been to Russia. I know what happened to the men who fought and won their civil war."

"Never! We are comrades. Comrades!"

"Ask your friend, if I am not correct. Ask Jiménez."

"Paco. Paquito, forgive me!"

"For what? You were the best commissar we ever had. The only one I ever trusted. Therefore, it is you who must go to France. I must stay here. I shall not be alone. No. You see? He's coming for me. *Qué paciencia! Cómo Dios y diablo?* With his white flag and his soldiers crawling in the snow. Look, you can see their blue rumps . . ."

"I will stay. We will go down there together."

"I have given you an order to lead the men into France! Will you disobey?"

"No. I will obey. Not your own order. But the Cause."

"Screw the Cause. Save your ass, marry well, and live a hundred years, comrade," Larra said.

Triangara stepped away. He tried not to look north, but could not help himself. He spread his hands and tried to speak. Larra was not looking at him. He was watching the Navarrese officer climb up the trail to the rampart of rocks. Triangara shook his clenched fist.

"Kill him! Kill him!" he shouted wildly.

"*No pasarán,*" Larra said, and slipped out through a snow-covered cleft between two great boulders, striking the drift to sparkling pieces like an actor sweeping aside a curtain to play the last scene.

Triangara rushed for the cleft and knelt there, his face pressed against the opening, watching.

Pedro was out of breath. He leaned on the pilgrim's staff and wiped his face on the white banner, gasping. A puff of snow broke out between two hulking lumps of stone. Before it settled, a slender, shabby figure stepped down into the path to meet him.

The snow steps were steep, slippery, like the path a shepherd wears down for his flock, or the short cut battered by miners down the hillside from the shaft to the village street. He dropped down from step to step carefully. The Navarrese officer was a slender, shabby figure toiling up the path to meet him. He wore the red Sacred Heart on the breast of his blue tunic.

Paco slipped his hand beneath his sheepskin jacket. His fingers touched the leather thong, the ring, the solid gridded lump of the grenade.

Triangara watched. They were a hundred meters apart. As one climbed, the other stepped down. As the bulk of Larra's body diminished, the blue form of the Navarrese grew. They were fifty paces apart. The Navarrese shifted his staff to his left hand. His right hand hung straight down, the inside of his palm touching the leather holster. Larra's arm was bent hidden beneath his jacket. Larra moved down. The Navarrese climbed up. They moved very slowly. The Navarrese paused to catch his breath. They stepped again, closer. The snow track was nearly level. The Navarrese moved his hand, pulled his pistol free and pointed it. He pushed himself up another step and cast the bannered staff away. Triangara lunged into the opening, his warning shout locked, frozen in his chest. He could see the Navarrese move his lips.

"Manos arriba!"

Larra took another step, another, and slowly raised his left, then both hands in the air. *Both* hands! There were soldiers with rifles kneeling in the snow. *One.* Larra took another step. *Two. Three.*

Larra lunged and caught the Navarrese officer, clasping him, breast to breast in an embrace. *Four.*

Larra shouted something into the other's face. The pistol fired, a single, stinging report. Triangara leapt up with the flash and detonation of the grenade, a shout of pain and triumph bursting from his own chest.

A blue shaft of splendor shot into the air, blown and balanced on the blast. The shock of the sound struck off the stones, and the pillar collapsed, a pink flush plunging, deeper drenched, a heavy sigh of crimson crystals, a spattering shower of bloody slush that made a single, perfect circle in the cratered snow.

Carmen sat and leaned against the kilometer stone. She peeled the gritty skins from the lank, feeble stalks of the wild onions she had found in the field and ate them, chewing slowly and spitting the hairy roots out into her palm. Her broken boots were caked with the thick, gluey mud from the unplanted field. The sun was warm, but the breeze was cool, the odd, exhilarating balance of thaw that is neither winter still nor yet quite spring.

She had passed a family the day before and since then had seen no one. The sky above and the road beneath were empty. She did not know how far it was to the next village or if there was a food distribution center there for refugees. The kilometer stone said BARCELONA 18 K. She closed her eyes, feeling the sun and the wind on her cheeks and brow. The heavy fetus kicked suddenly, and she gasped. The woman in the family had told her she had three weeks, perhaps more, since first babies were often late, but every time it swam and kicked, she was afraid. Perhaps she should walk back to the family and stay with them.

She heard the dry squeal of ungreased axles and opened her eyes. The wagon was at the crest of the hill, directly east. It seemed to float in the glare of the morning sun. She could not look directly at it, but shielded her eyes and watched the strange shadows of the burro and the driver lengthen on the earth. They moved slowly, down the slope, the sleepy-eyed burro leaning back into the harness of frayed rope, lifting and dropping its small, hard hoofs with jerky reluctance. The old man on the seat held the reins and stared over the burro's back-slanted ears. He, too, seemed asleep, a deep, wrinkled, reptile-doze. The wheels turned, biting through the skim of thawed, red mud to the hard, crystaled earth beneath. Carmen watched plastered, patchy bits break from the wheel rims and fall to strike the spokes before dropping back to the mud again.

She did not move when the cart drew near. Perhaps the burro smelled the raw, wild onions. The right lid opened wide, and the big, glossy eye stared at her.

"*Hola,*" Carmen said.

The burro twitched its ears at the sound of her voice and minced on past, the wagon shifting, the wheels creaking, turning and dropping bits of mud. The old man did not look at her. In the back of the wagon was a coffin of raw pine planks, a worn, shining shovel, and a blunt pick. Carmen looked away and touched her brow, her breast and each shoulder. The wagon rolled a dozen slow steps. Carmen ate a wild onion, chewing frantically, roots and all. Onions were a protection against typhoid germs; everyone picked the unplowed fields for them.

The wagon stopped. She heard the dry wheet of the axles cease, and the stamp of the burro's hoof. She looked up, shrugging. There were no more onions. What could the old man have stopped for?

"*Venga,*" the old man said, not even turning around.

Carmen stood up, her hands pressed against the small of her back and walked slowly out into the road.

"*Qué quieres, viejo?*" she asked. "What do you want?"

"*Yo? Nada,*" he said. "Nothing."

Carmen walked to the cart, looking at the ground so as not to see the coffin. The old man stared straight ahead, as she struggled up onto the narrow plank seat, her belly making her heavy, awkward. The burro minced on, twitching its ears. The wheels whined and the mud bits pattered onto the road. The old man was not asleep. His wrinkled lids flinched and he spat suddenly down into the mud.

"*Me llamo Carmen,*" she said.

The old man grunted softly. The sun lay warm against Carmen's neck, but the breeze was cool. She tugged her jacket. It had been months since she had been able to button it. She sighed and folded her hands primly around her big belly, her fingers locked loosely.

"Is it far you go?" she asked after a bit.

"Today, no. To the cemetery. A few kilometers. To bury him. The German."

"A German? Oh."

"He floated down into a field beneath a flower of white silk," the old man said. "Out of the clouds. It was a bad place to fall. An empty field like that. No one around."

"Was he injured?"

"In the process of dying, yes," the old man said.

"Then he was killed?"

"Yes."

"By soldiers? But this is Nationalist territory."

"There were no soldiers in the field."

"Then who killed him?"

"I did," the old man said calmly.

He spoke no more until late afternoon, when they had finished at the cemetery, eaten bread, tinned octopus, and wine. The burro stopped at a fork in the road. The old man looked at her for the first time.

"The road to the left leads to Pilarmadre," he said. "Much damaged, but there is food there, if one works."

"I can work."

"In a few weeks, you will work indeed," he said.

"Yes."

"To Pilarmadre, then," he said. "Though you are not of Aragón, no more than I."

"Castile. Madrid."

"*Yo,*" the old man said, touching his chest. "*Asturiano.*"

"A long way," Carmen said.

"Several weeks, if there is food, no snow and the police are willing. I do not travel by way of Madrid, though."

"Nor do I," Carmen said. "I have no family there."

"Ah," the old man said.

The day grew quickly cool, and long shadows ran ahead of them. At the top of a hill, the old man pointed to a dim shape far ahead.

"Pilarmadre," he said.

"Is there a priest at the church? I can see the tower."

"A priest? Yes."

"I would confess," Carmen said. "This is my first, and I am afraid."

"The priest will hear you, no doubt."

"I am married," Carmen said. "It's not that. I was married by a priest, too. In Cuenca."

"Ah," the old man said.

They stopped before dark and Carmen gathered some wild onions to add to the thin stew bubbling in the iron pot. She knelt and held her hands out to the warmth of the fire.

"Does the war still go on? Somewhere I mean?"

"In Madrid," the old man said. "But now one bunch of Reds fights another. Franco waits. They know how to wait, the Gallegos. It will be over soon. There is a blanket for you. You sleep in the wagon."

"*Muy bien,*" Carmen said.

Triangara was allowed to stand outside the barricade at the frontier post as the soldiers of the Republic crossed into French territory. Two members of the Garde Mobile were with him at all times. Two other uniformed Frenchmen and a representative of the Red Cross met the civilians and took them away in buses. With the soldiers, it was more difficult, since not all of them were Spanish nationals. Triangara translated, since he could speak some French and a few dozen words each of Italian and German.

The weather was odd, changeable, a few hours of sunshine, then a low blanket of heavy clouds and more snow. The border was closed from sunset to dawn, and the soldiers and civilians huddled together at night in a sort of free zone beyond the bridge. Almost no one had any sort of papers, passports, or travel visas. It was easier to admit the soldiers by units, the civilians by the busload. Transportation was short; the roads were bad; there was very little food, and no medical assistance whatever. Local French officials came out once a day, checked the number of those who had crossed, and grumbled and shrugged over the expense. To hear them talk, it cost thousands of francs a day to herd fugitives inside the wire compounds and forget them. The border guards, too, managed to combine a kind of rough decency with indifference. For two days Triangara had argued patiently for entrenching tools.

"Almost everyone has dysentery," he said. "We need shovels to dig latrines. Even though the soil is sandy, you can't expect every one, even children, to scrape up a little spot. It's unsanitary. People are dying in there now. Unless there are proper latrines there will be an epidemic!"

"Seen from the air, a big latrine looks like a trench," they said. "We don't want an incident because somebody on your side passes the word to Franco that fortifications are being constructed by refugees. Just mark out a special area and have them scrap up a spot, as you say. Look, now you want shovels and entrenching tools. Tomorrow you will ask permission for bayonets to carve meat and cut bread . . ."

"There is no meat. No bread."

"Well, the idea is the same. No, it can't be done. Sorry, but we have our orders. All weapons are to be surrendered in Spanish territory."

A Red Cross official complained, and the order was rewritten. Shovels and entrenching tools would be permitted in both military and civilian camps. The trouble was that none of the refugees brought such useful items with them. They brought sodden, infested bedding that had to be collected and burned, cooking pots and family portraits, broken sewing machines, all their children and hunger and hopelessness. Triangara stood for hours in all sorts of weather. They came forward in endless shivering lines, civilians on the left, soldiers on the right. The soldiers did not stack their rusty rifles, but simply dropped them on the heap, handed over whatever ammunition they had, usually very little, and stood shivering beneath their blankets.

Several of the men, the remnants of two units, bent down and scraped up a handful of dirt. One of the guards with Triangara stopped the soldiers at the bridge. Without saying a word, he forced open their hands and shook the dirt back onto the ground. Some newspaper correspondents were there, saw it, and shook their heads. Triangara noticed that one of the soldiers, wearing a blue beret, slipped the earth into his pockets, showed his empty hands and was allowed to pass. Triangara spoke to the French guard, checking his anger. They often shared their coffee and tobacco with him.

"Why did you do that? It's not a weapon, a handful of dirt. It's just Spanish earth."

"Maybe, maybe not," the guard said, embarrassed and touchy. "But if it's Spanish earth, as you say, then I guess it belongs to Franco now. Anyway, what do they want to go and do that for? They won't need dirt where they're going. Plenty of sand behind the wire. Any luck with shovels today?"

"No," Triangara said, stepping out to meet the next group. "No luck. All right, comrades, what's your unit? Who was your commander?"

"The best. Juan Modesto. But he left us in the lurch."

"Over there. Keep your men together. Unless you have enough to fill a bus right away, you have to wait. The big groups go first, see?"

"How long do we wait?"

"Until the last bus leaves, comrade. A truck comes then with the Garde Mobile who take night duty. You may have to walk. We'll go with you."

"Go where?"

"To a camp," Triangara said.

"A prison camp?"

"A concentration camp."

"*Mierda*. It's all the same."

"You can go back if you like," Triangara said angrily. "It's not *my* fault. I was told to help out."

"A concentration camp," the man said bitterly. "*Viva la República!*"

Triangara found the soldier with the blue beret standing by himself, looking at the civilians.

"What unit?"

"Eleventh Division, I guess you'd say. Anyway, we were supposed to be under Lister. Our *tenien'* got on a truck two weeks ago and we haven't seen him since. He was a Catalán, so maybe he's got a place to hide. Until someone turns him in."

"All these from the Eleventh?"

"I guess so," the man said. "Does it make any difference? Christ, it's cold! Look at those people. Funny, I was standing here looking at them. Do you know I was looking for my wife? I haven't seen her since thirty-six. In Toledo, would you believe it? We never got on well, anyway. Is it true there's food and tobacco here?"

"No," Triangara said. "Look . . ."

"That's what I thought. Lies, lies, right up to the end. Lister made it, though, right?"

"So they say," Triangara said. "Listen, I saw what you put in your pockets, even if the French didn't. Give me some."

The man shrugged and put his hands deep in his pockets.

"Go get your own."

"I'll give you a cigarette."

The man shrugged and looked away. Triangara touched his shoulder.

"Be a comrade, eh?"

"I never want to hear that word again," the man said. "I had a decent life, no matter what you might say about my old lady. Now look at me. Look at all of us."

"You have two handfuls," Triangara said. "Give me just a bit."

"Oh, what the hell. Here."

He thrust out his fist, furtively, and dribbled a handful of soil into Triangara's palm. He shrugged off thanks.

"Don't let these French blue shirts catch you,' he said. "They think it's dangerous stuff, a handful of Spanish dirt."

"Maybe it is," Triangara said.

"Only when you're standing on it," the man said. "I'll take that cigarette."

Triangara handed him a Gauloises and walked back to the bridge.

Pilarmadre was three days and three nights behind them and they had eaten all the bread they had been given. It was a wonder, the bread, made of white flour with a thick, crunchy crust. The old man shrugged. Behind the Nationalist lines there had been white bread all through the war. Carmen played with the cheap rosary the young priest, a chaplain, had given her. The beads slipped through her fingers. She tucked the rosary into her jacket.

"Let me walk now, *viejo*," she said. "It makes me feel sick to ride."

They took turns now, walking and riding, while the burro paced daintily down the roads.

"*Muy bien*," the old man said. "It makes me feel sick to walk." It was their joke, the first joke between them, so new that they must say it a dozen times a day. He came to the wagon and held his hard dry hand up to her.

"Be careful," he said gruffly, "The road is uneven and I am no doctor of medicine. I left you a thing on the seat. You can read, I suppose."

It was a thin paybook with a canvas cover, printed and written in German. A photograph of a young man looked out at her. He had short hair and a serious face. The tears came to her eyes. She closed the paybook.

"I took it from him," the old man said. "I use the pages for starting fires, you know. I should burn it. What would I say if they found it on me? You keep it."

"Why me?"

"It might help you. Who knows?"

It was not until she looked at the paybook the next day that she discovered it contained nearly three thousand pesetas, the dead man's money. His name had been Schmidt, Kapitan Kurt Schmidt of the Luftwaffe.

"I don't need money," the old man said, waving it away. "You know how I earn my bread and wine. There's always that sort of work, war or peace. Keep it for your *niño*."

"But you could use it. Nearly three thousand. Why, you could buy another burro," Carmen said.

The old man straightened and stared at her. He turned his face from her and did not speak for two days, so great was the insult to the burro he owned and therefore to himself. Carmen kept the paybook in the same pocket with her rosary and took it out from time to time to look at the photograph of the German.

They moved across Aragón into Castile, always moving north and west. The weather held, sunny days and cool, drying winds, no rain. Food was difficult to find, since they avoided the main roads when possible, but it could be obtained. It had been the coldest winter Spain had known for more than twenty years, and every village had work for the old man, for there were many of all ages who had fallen to sickness. Carmen waited for him and saw that the burro had water and whatever forage could be found. When he was done, he came with his pick and his shovel and a bag of food slung over his shoulder. Carmen hitched the mule and they went on, the old man up on the narrow plank seat, watching the sky and resting.

"If we continue, we'll be in Navarre soon, no?" Carmen said, turning to look at him.

"Yes, though there may be three of us by then, not two."

Carmen laughed and shaded her eyes to see him. He was smiling, actually smiling, showing his few, stumpy teeth.

"Oh, not for a while yet," she said. "I feel very strong now."

"You will need it, the strength," he said, and Carmen crossed herself.

"If we go on, we will come to Santiago de Compostela," she said.

"Pamplona," the old man said. "Some soldiers gave a letter to me. They were Navarrese. From a dead comrade."

"Oh," Carmen said.

"I will walk now."

"It makes you sick to walk," Carmen said and patted the burro.

"No, it makes me sick to watch you walk. Like a *vaca*, a cow."

"*Qué bruto, tú!*" Carmen said. "'Adios, Pamplona!' Remember the song?"

"I have heard all the songs," the old man said. "And I remember none of them. It is bad to remember anything."

"Is it? But it is hard to forget. They say you never forget."

"They are wrong, whoever they are. It is lies. All memories are lies. You are too young to know that yet. There, you see? You've gone crying again."

"It's the wind," Carmen said.

The burro stepped daintily down a slope. The wagon grated and squeaked over the spring ruts. Carmen's legs ached. The old man dropped down, and they walked together, holding the burro's head.

"This Navarrese," the old man said slowly, "is said by others to have been rich, a señorito, an aristocrat. He has some family, sisters, others have said."

"Do you think they will welcome us? With that letter you have? What good is a letter? You have said as much yourself. Isn't that letter all lies, too?"

The old man sucked his cheek and walked a moment, thinking.

"Not when it was written," he said finally. "The truth is what happens. But as soon as it is done, then it is not the truth. It is something else."

"Perhaps you are right," Carmen said. "I think you are old enough to know everything and respect nothing."

"Better that than the other way around."

"Like me?" Carmen said.

"There, you've gone crying again. What do you want to do that for? It won't do you any good. No, nor anyone else, either."

"It's the sun," Carmen said. "The sun gets in my eyes . . ."

They walked on, the wagon creaking, the cold wind blowing in their faces. Carmen wore the old man's blanket draped around her like a cape. The ends trailed on the muddy ground. After they stopped and ate together, she rode on the narrow hard seat and the old man walked beside the turning wheel just below her.

"What was it like for you?" she asked, after a long silence. "The war, I mean?"

"It was bad," the old man said. "*Mala. Muy mala.* Not without interest, but bad."

"Do you suppose Madrid has surrendered yet? Maybe they're still fighting there."

"Each other," the old man said. "It always comes to that at the end. The best time is always at the beginning. After the beginning, it just gets worse. *La vida no es sueño . . .*"

"*No pasarán,*" Carmen said.

"Well, they'll pass some fine day," the old man said. "Then the jails will fill up. I will be busy. They will have work for me."

"Then it will get worse, you think?"

"I think nothing. You should do the same. I don't think they'll do much to the women. Why bother? Enough had been done to them already, if I may say so."

"You are an old cynic," Carmen said.

"I don't know the word," the old man answered, "but I know what's what. That's more than you do, or you wouldn't have that shape."

Since the road was long and the burro slow, because she was young, alone, and afraid and he was old and asked no questions whatever, she told him everything.

It took Triangara so many days to find him that he lost count. There were several camps, and he found him at last in the one at Argeles. He was dressed in a wrinkled civilian suit and a short leather overcoat. Triangara found him pissing on the base of a stunted pine near the barbed wire. When he turned around, even at some distance, Triangara was certain. There was no mistaking the dark glasses.

"That's Jiménez," he said to the others. "Go back to the place and stay out of sight. I'll bring him. We'll use our belts."

They nodded and went away, back through the small, stinking village of sand holes and packing-box shelters. The wind blew sand against Triangara's boots. He strolled down the slope. The man in the dark glasses loitered by the pine tree as though he had been appointed curator for it. Everyone in the camps had some special corner or spot. There was privilege and privacy, even in misery.

"Well!" the other said. "Imagine it! What a coincidence!"

Although he seemed genuinely pleased to see Triangara, he did not offer his hand. He stood near the pine tree fingering a brown needle, rolling it between his thumb and fingers.

"They have to put us someplace," Triangara said.

"I have brought up the whole matter with the camp commandant," the other said. "But the Russians have refused to accept refugees! Incredible. Naturally, I gave my name."

"Which one?" Triangara said, forcing a smile.

"Oh, a useful one. If it gets to the right hands. There is always confusion in these situations. A matter of documents, but it will all be straightened out."

"Speaking of that, I saw him die," Triangara said.

"Who?"

"El Asturiano. Larra."

"Of course! Do you know, I had forgotten completely. You are . . ."

"Triangara."

"Right. Perfectly right. Well, we'll have to forget all that. How quickly you people gave up! Frankly, I am not alone in my disappointment."

"What makes you think we've given up?" Triangara said.

"Pouf, a government-in-exile is a debating circle. Soon they will begin to publish memoirs. After they have checked to make sure the records have been destroyed. We were careful enough in our section, believe me. One doesn't want to leave a lot of paper lying about."

"Care to walk a bit?" Triangara said.

"Nothing else to do, is there? Miserable place. We were quite comfortable at the convent there. All conveniences. Here, it's impossible. The very first day my suitcase was stolen. I have suffered since, let me tell you."

They walked toward the south wire, avoiding the refugee camp.

"I came across with the army," Triangara said, "but how did you get here?"

"We had some prisoners," the other said, pressing his smoked glasses carefully against his temples with both thumbs. "The P.O.U.M. Remember the P.O.U.M.? Incredible types. Neither fish nor fowl as the saying is. Well, they came up for trial. Did you hear about it?"

"I heard they were acquitted for lack of evidence that they had conspired against the Republic," Triangara said.

"The evidence was good enough," the other said firmly. "I should know, I think. It was simply not admitted. Negrín and his crew were determined to play the farce of Popular Front right to the end, you see. Well, anyway, we had planned to leave these P.O.U.M. types for Franco to finish off. I don't remember why, but I decided to take them along. Something told me we might need them somehow. For something. It was all such chaos."

"Like peasant children to toss from the sleigh to the wolves in old Russia?"

"Very good! Yes, something like that. Only more comical. You'll never believe this, but . . . up this path here?"

"I suppose so. It's private here. We can talk."

"Good, good. I've never been down at this end. Quite a little forest here. I suppose it is forbidden to cut the trees."

"They put a guard and a searchlight in the tower at night. During the day there is no one."

"A chance to get out of the damned wind. The sand stings the skin, have you noticed?"

"No," Triangara said. "I am in charge of latrines."

"How comical."

"Isn't it? You were saying . . ."

"Yes," the other said. "Well, as we move closer to the French border, let us say that the political situation became . . . um, a state of flux. Party members were few. It was every man for himself, you might say. Quite disgusting."

"No doubt."

"Moreover, we quickly learned that our prisoners had been personages of some local reputation. Even in their panic, the civilian populace had not quite forgotten. Amazing loyalty."

"Amazing," Triangara said.

"I have always believed in expedience. In that way, the Party is like the Church. The important thing, after all, is the perpetuation of . . . of . . . well, things, you know. You take my meaning, I'm sure."

"Of course."

"Well, then, we surrendered ourselves to our prisoners! A very neat thing, if I say so myself. In return for a *salvoconducto* to the border, we renounced our judicial and political authority! Our prisoners became our captors and marched us right into France! The fools think they have some authority or something here over us. That holds up the documents, you see. But it will all blow over."

"Exactly," Triangara said. "It will all blow over."

He began to giggle. It was too appropriate, and his nerves would not take the strain. He saw the entrenching tool against the tree, just as had been planned.

"One of your new . . . um, constructions of public convenience?" the other said.

"Not public," Triangara said evenly, stepping away to get the entrenching tool, "this is private."

The other gazed down at the deep pit hacked in the damp sandy soil. He turned and smiled, as Triangara picked up the tool.

"Generously proportioned," he said. "Either you and your friends suffer astonishing distress or you are planning a long stay."

"A long stay," Triangara said.

The others came out from behind the trees. Picking up the entrenching tool had been the signal. They had their belts in their hands. The other did not see them for a few seconds.

"Ah," he said, "members of the club, no doubt. You must present me . . . um . . . uh."

"Triangara."

The others closed in quickly, a tight ring. Triangara swung the entrenching tool twice, striking Jiménez on the right shoulder and knocking him down, then beating him once in the ribs. The others had him strapped up with the belts before he regained consciousness.

"There's only this," Triangara said. "We'll take turns shoveling."

"Let him come to, first."

"Right," Triangara said, and bent down to remove the dark glasses.

They stopped at the edge of the trees to brush the damp sand and pine needles off each other's clothing. It was ridiculous, this clumsy dusting and nervous picking. Who would notice, in this place? The grimness was gone from them now; they were satisfied and domestic and avoided looking in each other's faces.

"*Justicia*," Triangara said at last. "Not vengeance, comrades. Justice. Now look, we've decided not to come together again. About this. Or anything else. At least not here in the camp."

"There will be a time and a place," one of them said.

"This was a perfect spot," another said. "The wind was right. Every scream blew right out through the wire."

Triangara bounced the smoked glasses on the palm of his hand. He longed to try them on, to see how the world looked through those dark lenses. Just once, a quick peek. But they looked too small. He kept the others waiting until he rummaged out a bit of string, tied some knots and a loop. He passed the loop over his head. The smoked glasses, folded and furtive like a hiding crab, scuttled down the throat of his tunic and lay on his bare, sweating chest.

"I always wondered what color his eyes were," he said. "But I forgot to look. I know, anyway. The color of fear. Just like everybody else's."

No one replied. They began to walk toward the sprawling camp of collapsing holes and flimsy shacks. They separated silently, moving away from each other, until they formed a long, ragged idle line across the sand. Triangara walked alone, his right hand in his pocket crushing and kneading a fistful of gritty soil. He began to tremble violently, like a man suddenly taken with a fever. Only the greatest mental effort kept him from tearing the loop of string up over his head and flinging the smoked glasses away into the sand. When he became used to the weight and shape hung around his neck, brushing his chest, he would be strengthened. He might even be known by them. One day, with luck, he would take them from a cigar box kept in a bureau drawer and display the warped frame and faded lens to a polite, bored grandchild. He wondered why his mind created a cigar box. He had never smoked cigars.

The road, worn in deep double ruts, led up through a forest of huge pine trees thick as cathedral columns and spaced so, too, supporting a roof of solid deep green through which the wind sighed. Snow still lay in white crusted patches scattered across the brown, needle-strewn naves. The air was chill and astringent with the scent of resin. Spring came late to the mountains of Navarre.

The entrance was marked by two pillars of mellow stone, the flat flanks grown glossy with moss, the fissures pasted over with pale stiff lichens. An arch of rusty iron leapt through sunlight and shadow. In the center of the arch was a family crest, a dove and a wolf, and a motto.

"What does it say, Carmencita?" the old man said, gazing up.

"*Dios y Patria*," she said. "God and Fatherland."

"This is the place then."

"*Claro*," she said and reached down to touch the bundled blanket on the seat beside her.

"How do you feel?"

"Well enough," she said.

The old man shrugged and clucked to the burro. The wagon creaked beneath the rusted arch and rolled down a long, gravel drive just sprigged with new weeds. The old man turned and looked back at her.

"You heard them say in the village, that this young woman runs a hospital for orphaned children."

"I heard them," Carmen said.

"And you are a nurse."

"I was a nurse. Also a cook. Also a machine gunner. Also . . ."

"Well, then," the old man said. "It's settled, eh? You can earn your keep."

"If it is allowed," she said and shrugged. "What do you care, *viejo*? You mean to dump me off here. You are glad to be finished with this. You and your burro."

"It's not that," the old man said. "I have work to do."

"Give the girl the letter. The famous letter."

"*Qué va*, the letter," he said. "You will do as I said, eh? It will be better that way. You might get something. Otherwise . . ."

He shook his head and turned back to stroke the burro's head. Carmen closed her eyes. She was too exhausted to argue. She wanted to rest, to sleep, to be somewhere safe until the wound healed. The wagon creaked and jolted slowly forward.

"*Mira*," the old man said.

She put her hand down to the swaddled blanket automatically, a quick, guilty movement. Surely her eyes had been closed for just an instant. She saw a huge stone house with great, steep tiled roofs and blackened chimneys, a heavy, durable pile, half farm dwelling, half fortress. The burro minced down the gravel. A dog barked somewhere. The door of the house, a high studded oak portal swung open. A young woman with blond hair, dressed in a white blouse, red kerchief, and blue skirt strode out onto the terrace, a skinny fawn-colored hound bounding beside her, stiff-legged and foolish. The young woman, a girl, really, wore dark riding boots that struck heavily upon the worn stone steps.

"Well, that's her, I guess," the old man said, sweeping off his cap. "The Countess of what is it, now that her mother died, too, according to the village?"

"La Condesa de Gualvidal," Carmen said, reaching for the bundle. "My father knew the family, father and son. I had a ride once, on one of their horses."

"You see?" the old man said, stopping the cart. "You're friends, you might say. Just speak right up to her, see? Need some help?"

"No," Carmen said. "I can manage everything."

The old man fumbled in his jacket. The dog stopped a dozen paces away and barked furiously. The burro lifted its tail and squeezed droppings that plopped and steamed on the gravel.

"Here. You give her the letter, eh? She's about your age, it looks. Woman to woman, you know. I'll get along. The sun goes down early in Navarre, and I've got a long way to go yet."

Carmen stood holding the bundle. The old man gave her some sheets of stained paper closed in a shell of twisted and scorched steel plates.

"Tell her . . . tell her . . . make something up, eh? It'll be easier that way. For everyone."

The young girl clapped her hands and called the dog away. It crouched, lolling its red tongue and panting furiously.

"I will," Carmen said. "A thousand thank, *viejo. Adiós.*"

"*Adiós*, Carmen," the old man said, climbing stiffly up to the seat. "*Y suerte. Mucha suerte* . . . Much luck."

Carmen turned, holding the bundle and the packet he had given her.

She walked cautiously toward the young woman with blond hair. The burro snuffled and the wagon wheels creaked. The dog bolted down the drive, all legs and tremendous barking. The young woman waited, her hands set lightly on her hips. Carmen pawed at her tangled, dirty hair and tried to smile.

"I have something for you, señorita," she said cautiously.

"So I see," the young woman said. "So I see."

The room was high-ceilinged and smelled of dust and seeds. The air had the color of an old painting, a drab luster. It was the office of the estate, Carmen thought. She could hear the sound of voices somewhere in the house.

She sat on a straight wooden chair, dressed in loose flannel pajamas and a worn robe, her feet in stiff, straw slippers. She felt clean and strange and defenseless. The young woman sat behind the big, dark desk, filling out a form and smoking cigarettes.

"The doctor will see you early tomorrow morning," the young woman said. "He is a Swiss and very good, very devout. He will examine you thoroughly. Although the head nurse, that's Concha, says you are fine. But that's the outside, eh? The doctor will tell us about the rest."

Carmen nodded and swallowed.

"Well. The baby was born six days ago? March 25. Very good. You want him baptized at once of course. Say, day after tomorrow. You can meet the chaplain later. He must have his siesta. He's not young, and the children tire him out, I'm afraid. But that's children. Have you picked a name?"

"Francisco," Carmen said.

The young woman across the desk smiled briefly and lit a cigarette from the stub of the one she had just finished.

"That's a very popular name these days, for obvious reasons," she said. "That and José Antonio. We've had a lot of baptisms. You couldn't imagine the barbarous names some of our mothers chose. One little girl was named Cooperativa. It took a little persuasion, but she is now called María Dolores. Do you find your room pleasant?"

"Very pleasant," Carmen said.

"You'll like your companion, I'm sure. We try to put the new mothers together whenever possible. It's easier with the feedings and special diets and all the rest . . ."

Carmen nodded.

"Did you get the papers?" she asked.

The young woman wrote something and patted a stack of loose sheets on the desk.

"Oh yes. Don't worry. They'll be returned. But we must register you. Both of you. Not only our records but with the new government. It will take time; everything's in such a turmoil at Burgos. You just fainted, that's all. Not surprising, is it? I mean, everything . . . everything . . . considered."

"I never fainted before," Carmen said.

"The first child is always the most exhausting," the young woman said. "That's why you must rest. Regain your strength."

"All the papers? The letter, too?"

The young woman dashed a slim hand through her hair and puffed her cigarette.

"The letter. Yes. Well, I will read it tonight. I haven't the time now. It was a great pity. It is, I mean."

"Yes, of course," Carmen said.

"About your husband, I mean. He was a pilot, it seems. The little boy favors him. Such blond hair. I looked while the nurse bathed him. He's underweight, but seems fine. The doctor will tell us. I will forward the documents as soon as I know where they should go. When were you married, please?"

"In Cuenca."

"No, *when*, not where. Can you remember? I'll bet you can if you try."

"Yes," Carmen said and gave the date.

"Ecclesiastical ceremony? Are you *sure* it was in Cuenca? That was on . . . the other side, you know. Think again. Perhaps . . . well, lots of people are confused. Toledo? Sevilla?"

"Yes, it was Sevilla. Now I remember."

"Ah, good. I'll just put down Sevilla, then. There was a big base there. I remember reading about it. In the papers."

Carmen nodded.

"I want to see him. He's all right?"

"He's *fine*. The nursery is just at the head of the main stairs. Then you'll continue to keep your husband's name? It will make it easier for everybody. You may be entitled to a pension, don't you see? For you and the child. I'll check with their consulate. You can't be the only girl this happened to. Keep that in mind. You will find our evening devotional services a great source of strength, too, I'm sure. I'll write it down here. Tomorrow you'll be issued clothing. For the baby, too, of course. Used, but clean, very clean. We have our own laundry. Perhaps you could lend a hand. When you're well and strong, I mean. It was—let me see—I have the papers right here . . . the last name was . . ."

"Schmidt," Carmen said, and covered her face with her hands.

Madrid was occupied on the first day of April, 1939. The walls of the broken buildings were covered with freshly painted slogans. HAN PASADO! They have passed. The official communiqué was issued from Supreme Headquarters of Generalísimo Francisco Franco:

THIS DAY, WITH THE RED ARMY CAPTURED AND DISARMED, THE NA-
TIONAL TROOPS HAVE ACHIEVED THEIR FINAL MILITARY OBJECTIVES.
THE WAR HAS ENDED.

Lifting up our hearts to the Lord, we give sincere thanks
with Your Excellency for Spain's desired Catholic victory. We
express our vow that your most beloved country, with peace
attained, may undertake with new vigor the ancient Christian
traditions which made her great. With affectionate sentiments,
we send Your Excellency and the most noble Spanish people
Our Apostolic blessing.

                                              PIUS XII

The Valley of the Fallen

The Valley of the Fallen, northwest of Madrid near the Cuelgamuros crossroads, was personally selected as the site of a monument commemorating the Civil War by Generalísimo Francisco Franco, Caudillo de España during the winter of 1941–42. Totaling 46,000 acres, much of the area was farm lands, once the estate of the Count of Villapadierba. Before actual construction could be begun under the supervision of architect Diego Méndez, a special road connecting the site to the Madrid highway was constructed and an estimated 800,000 tons of rock blasted from the mountain sides. Despite official disclaim and denial, a certain amount of this preliminary labor was done by political prisoners who were allowed or forced to work off their terms of sentence at the monument site. An unknown number were Asturian miners, ex-Anarchists and Communists, experienced dynamiters and stonemasons. The early stages of site-clearing proceeded very slowly as a result of the deliberate inefficiency of the laborers. From 1949 on, an annual average of 700 men were employed, although at one time the number of masons, carpenters, glaziers, electricians, and specialists reached a yearly figure of 2000 men. These workers lived in a village constructed within the valley for prolonged periods of time with little or no contact with persons not directly associated with the project. Although no official figures are available, it is widely believed that such laborers were paid twice the officially approved rate for labor of this sort.

The Valley of the Fallen is easily reached from Madrid by a well-maintained macadam highway. There is more than ample parking for private and chauffeur-driven automobiles and hundreds of tour buses. No vehicles are allowed beyond the main entrance, formed of four pillars, each thirty-eight feet high, cut in the sixteenth century to support an aqueduct to bring water from the Tagus River to the city of Toledo.

The Way of the Cross, an open courtyard surrounded by multistoried stone buildings, is a half mile in length from the entrance gate to the doorway of the Basilica of the Holy Cross. The courtyard could hold, standing, 250,000 adult human beings. The buildings that flank the Way of the Cross are smaller in scale than the ponderous symmetry of El Escorial, the stone softer in hue, the decorative elements less severely geometrical. These structures were designated as dwellings for a group of the Franciscan order, but the luxuriousness of the appointments and facilities (electric dishwashers, automatic laundry equipment, private bathrooms and soft carpeting) caused the Franciscans to refuse politely. The present guardians are a group of Benedictine monks, led by Fray Justo Pérez de Urbel. He, too, felt the quarters too sumptuous for a monastery, and a more austere home has been completed. Since the original bathroom fixtures included bidets, the buildings are now used as a state-run hotel for tourists and pilgrims, presumably as was originally intended. Other buildings located around the Way of the Cross include a choir school for fifty boys chosen for their talent and piety and a school of social studies built as a place where students from all over the world can come for reflection, study and to give and hear lectures by ecclesiastical philosophers and lay teachers.

The entrance to the Basilica of the Holy Cross, beneath a giant statue of the Pietà, is a granite semicircle cut with twenty niches, each 73 feet high holding sculptured works in bas-relief. Massive doors guarded by the angel Raphael and the angel Michael open onto a marble-paved corridor running more than 700 feet to the crypt proper. The walls of this corridor are cut with niches spaced at regular intervals holding more bas-relief works. A huge, intricate, and massive bronze grille rises from the marble floor. The walls are hung with richly worked tapestries, woven in Segovia, depicting scenes of the Civil War. Tall organ pipes in gleaming clusters stand between the tapestries, but these pipes are for ornamental purposes only. The Basilica of the Holy Cross has no organ. Music is supplied electrically, through concealed loudspeakers.

Beyond the bronze screen is the crypt and above the crypt a dome 138 feet high, 134 feet in diameter. The dome is covered with a gilded mosaic that took fifteen artisans more than eight months to install. Against a background of muted, glowing gold, Nationalist soldiers and civilian martyrs rise from postures of twisted suffering as though materializing from the blended banners of the Nationalist army, the

Carlists and the Falange. They soar past figures of angels and the Virgin Mary to judgment before Christ.

A simple altar lies beneath an alabaster statue of Christ crucified.

All the crypt space has been designed to hold a hundred tons of human bones, twelve tons behind the chapels and sacristy, forty-four tons each in twin vaults beneath the floor.

Generalísimo Francisco Franco has periodically expressed his hope that the Basilica of the Holy Cross will be nominated by the Vatican as a cathedral within his lifetime. Tens of thousands have entered the gates, proceeded the Way of the Cross and entered the vast, cool corridor of marble to gaze at the great bronze grille and the glowing, golden dome. No visitor has left unimpressed with the size and grandeur of the Basilica, and commentary in magazines and journals has reflected the feelings of adoration and awe: "It has to be recognized as one of the wonders of European civilization."—*Die Welt*, 1958. "An almost unbelievably magnificent new Spanish shrine . . . a breath-taking monument . . ." *America*, 1959.

The Basilica is open to the public during the late spring and summer months. One architectural problem has so far denied solution. The Basilica of the Holy Cross has no central heating system whatever, despite the fact that it is quarried into a granite mountain side and is completely underground.

In his dedication speech of April 1, 1959, Generalísimo Franco declared: "Our victory was not a partial victory, but a total victory for everybody. It was not achieved in favor of one group or one class, but for the whole nation. It was a victory for the Spanish people."

In its initial announcement, the Spanish government declared that the dead were to be reinterred within the burial vaults of the Basilica of the Holy Cross *"sin distinción ninguna"* (without any distinction whatever). It was immediately pointed out by Spanish editorial comment and numerous private letters that this would, perforce, include Protestants, Mohammedans, Jews, and atheists. The statement was promptly clarified in the form of an invitation to the surviving families whose relatives were killed during the Civil War as soldiers or civilians on either side— provided proof could be shown that the deceased had been baptized Roman Catholics.

While rumor and hearsay insist that no applications whatever for such reinterment were filed by families of the war dead, it is more probable that the number of applicants were embarrassingly low. A second pronouncement followed, dealing with the mass graves where the dead sleep unnamed. Careful study of historical records and maps roughly establish where the Republican mass graves are located and where the Nationalist dead lie. The official statement flatly announced: "In the near future, the remains of those who fell gloriously or were sacrificed during the Crusade for Liberation will be excavated from all common graves, makeshift cemeteries or provisional cemeteries."

The wording of this statement clearly reinforced the earlier announcement limiting reinterment to Roman Catholics in its preamble but the general sense seemed to be all-embracing. How could the enemies of the Church be identified? Certain territories and towns changed hands several times during the course of fighting. Was there some system by which the skeletal remains of a Moor might be singled out from a trench of uncovered bones? Confusion, hopefully silenced, deepened into mistrust, even among the most devout, the most loyal.

A third decree served only to worsen the situation further. This statement decreed that relations of "identifiable dead" whose relatives lay in single, clearly marked parochial graves could either apply for reburial at the Valley of the Fallen or not, as they chose. No appeal was to be permitted, despite the fact that only a very small percentage of the war dead, military or civilian, had been buried in such a fashion. More commonly, the living members of families know only in which cemetery of several or in which mass grave among many their dead relatives lie.

In Madrid, the Association of Martyrs formed a committee representing those families who had dead relatives at the great Paracuellos de Jarama graveyard. An estimated 12,000 corpses were interred there in the years 1936–39, the victims of Republican firing squads, civilian air-raid casualties, and an uncounted number removed from hospitals and gathered from the trenches and fortifications surrounding the city. Some of the trenches were identified soon after the war as the resting places of supporters of the Nationalist cause, members of the Falange Party, priests and nuns, those guilty of acts against the Republic, those presumed guilty, their husbands, wives, fathers, mothers and children. This subcommittee protested to the bishops of the Madrid-Alcalá dioceses that they did not wish the remains disturbed by anyone. The ecclesiastical authorities replied that it should be considered an honor to lie in the Valley of the Fallen. The committee then appealed to Rear Admiral Luis Carrero Blanco, assistant to the Spanish Chief-of-State. Admiral Blanco did not receive the members of the committee. Some short time later, the government let it be known through the auspices of parish priests that the bodies at Paracuellos would not be moved.

On the mountaintop at the end of the valley is a cross of reinforced concrete and stone towering 492 feet above the base. On a clear day, some claim to be able to see it from the taller buildings of Madrid without binoculars. The arms of the cross are sixty feet long from the central shaft to each tip. The arms are hollow and are twenty-one feet high and thick. Elevator cars rise from the base to observation windows. The total weight of the cross, including the elevator equipment, cables, and counter-weights is 141,000 tons.

The estimated cost of construction for the entire monument, highway and parking lots, entrance, buildings, The Way of the Cross, the Basilica of the Holy Cross, the interior decorations and art-work, and the tallest free-standing reinforced concrete cross in the world ranges from a low of six million American dollars to a high of seventy-five million dollars. There is some general agreement however that the complex should be calculated as costing twelve million dollars. Officially, the money for the Valley of the Fallen was donated, the free gift of the Spanish people. Unofficially, whatever the cost, the money for labor and materials was diverted from tax and license revenues by the Franco government.

It is generally believed that the body of José Antonio de Rivera, son of the dictator Primo de Rivera and founder of the Falanage or Spanish Fascist Party will some day be removed from his present tomb in front of the altar in the Church of Felipe III in El Escorial. By tradition, only the legitimate sovereigns of Spain are buried in El Escorial. It is expected, therefore, that José Antonio's body will be placed on one side, before the Altar of the Basilica of the Holy Cross.

In his turn, upon his death, the body of Generalísimo Francisco Franco y Bahamonde, Caudillo de España by the grace of God, will be placed on the other side of the altar, or perhaps between the sarcophagus of José Antonio de Rivera and the altar. Under those circumstances, it is not considered likely that the Vatican will ever designate the Basilica as a cathedral.

The bodies of all those who died in the Spanish Civil War will continue to lie untouched in the graves, marked and forgotten, where they fell, and the great vaults beneath the polished marble floor will remain forever empty, forever hollow.